THE LONG ROLL

THE LONG ROLL

BY MARY JOHNSTON

THE JOHNS HOPKINS UNIVERSITY PRESS
BALTIMORE AND LONDON

𝕿𝖔 𝖙𝖍𝖊 𝕸𝖊𝖒𝖔𝖗𝖞 𝖔𝖋

JOHN WILLIAM JOHNSTON

MAJOR OF ARTILLERY, C. S. A.

AND OF

JOSEPH EGGLESTON JOHNSTON

GENERAL, C. S. A.

Originally published in a hardcover edition by Houghton Mifflin Company,
Boston and New York, 1911
Johns Hopkins Paperbacks edition, 1996
05 04 03 02 01 00 99 98 97 96   5 4 3 2 1

The Johns Hopkins University Press
2715 North Charles Street
Baltimore, Maryland 21218-4319
The Johns Hopkins Press Ltd., London

Library of Congress Cataloging-in-Publication data will be found at the end
of this book.

A catalog record for this book is available from the British Library.

ISBN 0-8018-5524-1 (pbk.)

FOREWORD

PUBLISHED in 1911 by the Boston firm Houghton Mifflin Company and graced by handsome illustrations by N. C. Wyeth, Mary Johnston's *The Long Roll* was the fourth novel in a professional writing career that had begun before the turn of the century and was to include twenty-three novels, as well as other works (*Pioneers of the Old South,* 1918; and a verse play, *The Goddess of Reason,* 1907), before the author's death in 1936. *The Long Roll* received mixed notices when it appeared, after having first been serialized in the *Atlantic Monthly.* On several occasions, the novel was criticized for its failure to follow, and exploit, the tried and true resources of its perceived genre—the historical romance. Johnston had already earned an enviable reputation in that popular form with the extraordinary success of her second novel, *To Have and to Hold* (1900), an old-fashioned swashbuckler, if not a premature bodice-ripper, set mainly in and around the Jamestown settlement. The book sold in excess of 500,000 copies in hardcover and made her name in the literary scene. For a time thereafter she commanded advances of $10,000 on her books, extraordinary at that time.

There was much more to Mary Johnston's art and craft than the conventions of the historical romance allowed; and even while working comfortably within that genre, she took chances and displayed other interests. Her sense of place, real and imaginary, was always vividly realized and gritty, with firmly evoked detail. And beginning even with her first novel, *Prisoners of Hope* (1898), about pioneers in southwest Virginia, she seldom settled for conventional happy endings. Romance or not, real life took its toll in her work. Even lucky survivors were scarred and bruised. Mary Johnston was simply and boldly imaginative, able to write about distant times, and able, also, to create credible characters of all kinds. For example, *To Have and to Hold,* set in 1621–1622, is a first-person story told by a thirty-six-year-old man. Then and now, no critic has complained that the point of view is in any way inadequately realized. She also earned critical praise for her handling of the first-person narrative by a fictional Spaniard, Jayme de Marchena, also known as Juan Lepe, who sails on the first voyage of Columbus in *1492* (1922).

One cannot escape the language, assumptions, and conventions of one's own times. Shakespeare did not; Chaucer could not; even a contemporary escape artist and literary Houdini like Kathy Acker cannot. Why and how should we expect a very successful professional writer like Mary Johnston to break out of the form she had been given and had mastered? But it is clearer now, looking both backward and forward from her two novels about the Civil War, *The Long Roll* and its companion, *Cease Firing* (1912), that she regularly dared to take great risks and seldom, if ever, settled for easy ways and means. It looks as if with each new novel she was working to reinvent and redesign the established form.

Even though some of the critics and reviewers of *The Long Roll* complained that her use of the conventions of the historical romance was at best cursory, others saw what Johnston was up to and praised her for it. The influential *North American Review* (August 11, 1911) was unequivocal: "'The long roll' is the best fictional study of the civil war that has yet been done in America, and it achieves the impossible; it fairly makes that worn and hackneyed subject throbbingly alive." A day later the *Saturday Review* announced: "Since Zola wrote 'La Debacle' there has been no more vivid story of war than this 'The long roll.'"

The reality in the scenes of war and combat, perhaps surprising in their accuracy and authenticity, came from several sources. First of all, Johnston had the benefit of memories and voices from two family members, to whose memory the books are dedicated—her father, John Williams Johnston, an artillery major, and her cousin, General Joseph E. Johnston. In the note "To the Reader" the author acknowledges her debts to "the historians, biographers, memoir and narrative writers, diarists, and contributors of but a vivid page or two to the magazines of the Historical Societies," adding "that many incidents which she [the author] has used were actual happenings, recorded by men and women writing of that through which they lived. She has changed the manner but not the substance, and she has used them because they were 'true stories' and she wished that breath of life within the book." *That breath of life.* She wanted a story beyond mere fiction, rooted in hard fact and real experience. We know from her papers that Mary Johnston mastered all the primary and secondary sources available at the time, and she walked the roads and explored the terrain of the battlefields herself to make her story as factually accurate as it could be. By the time the second volume, *Cease Firing* (1912), was published, these books had been recognized for what they were, and H. W. Mabie could write of *Cease Firing* in the *New York Times* (November 17, 1912): "It takes its place beside 'The long roll'; the two are our greatest stories of war."

What was this author's own life experience? Mary Johnston was born in 1870 in Buchanan, Virginia, in Boutetort County (locally pronounced Botuhtot) County in the Shenandoah Valley, nestled among the Blue Ridge Mountains and close to the James River. She was privately tutored and self-educated, and very well and widely read. She was nineteen when her mother died and she assumed parental responsibility for her five younger brothers and sisters, in addition to serving her father as hostess and housekeeper until his death in 1905. Afterward she looked after herself and the rest of the family, earning her living as a novelist. While her father was still living, the family lived in New York City, Birmingham, and Richmond; and she traveled with her father to England, Scotland, Ireland, France, Italy, and Egypt. Beginning in 1912, after the publication of *Cease Firing,* she built and lived in a large house, "Three Hills," beautifully situated on a hilltop in Bath County close to Warm Springs. She was a leader in the Equal Suffrage movement and was involved in the formation of the Equal Suffrage League of Virginia. During the First World War, Johnston was an outspoken pacifist. She studied socialism and attended some meetings of the Socialist Party, though she never actually joined that party. A fascinated student of science as well as psychic phenomena and forms of mysticism, she was profoundly concerned with, as she put it, "adventures in consciousness."

In the literary world, Johnston knew from her travels Thomas Hardy and J. M. Barrie. She was both friend and correspondent to

Ellen Glasgow and Evelyn Thomson, and, through conferences, she came to know some of the younger generation of moderns. She was one of some thirty-three southern writers who were invited by Ellen Glasgow and Professor James Southall Wilson in the fall of 1931 to a gathering at the University of Virginia. Among those also present were DuBose Heyward, Paul Green, Allen Tate, Carolyn Gordon, Donald Davidson, James Boyd, William Faulkner, Struthers Burt, Josephine Pinckney, and Alice Hegan Rice, author of the immensely popular *Mrs. Wiggs of the Cabbage Patch.*

On the whole, however, Johnston lived a quiet life in a quiet place; in Warm Springs to this day, the loudest noise is the splash and trickle of the steamy creeks, fed by the springs that give the hamlet its name. But as a voracious reader and a disciplined professional writer, she lived an adventurous imaginative life. Fifteen of her novels concern the life and times of Virginia. In others, she moved freely and easily in time and place: Elizabethan England and the high seas in *Sir Mortimer* (1904) and *Lewis Rand* (1908); seventeenth-century England in *The Witch* (1914); twelfth-century France in *The Fortunes of Garin* (1915); eighteenth-century Scotland in *Foes* (1918); Tudor England during the reign of Henry VII in *Silver Cross* (1922) and fifteenth-century Spain (and the ocean sea) in *1492* (1922). One of her later books, *Exile* (1927), is a utopian novel set in the future on the imaginary island of Eldorado. She is credited with two early feminist novels— *Hagar* (1913) and *The Wanderers* (1917). In all of these works Johnston proves herself able to create large casts of credible characters with widely diverse points of view and with an appropriate and acceptable language for a wide variety of social classes and types, high and low.

All these gifts are strongly evident in *The Long Roll.* The book begins before the war and then divides itself between the early Valley campaigns and the large battles fought in the east in and around the Richmond area, ending with Chancellorsville and the death of Stonewall Jackson, with a scene of Jackson lying in state in the Virginia Hall of Delegates in the Capitol of the Confederacy. This, then, is a narrative of the war up to what she sees as the high tide of the Confederacy and the turning point. N. C. Wyeth's frontispiece for the original edition was, appropriately, a picture of

Jackson with his horse, Little Sorrel, standing on a high place, heroic, very stern and also somehow ungainly, an awkward, heroic, and enigmatic man brooding, as it were, over the whole story that follows. From beginning to end, *The Long Roll* is a blend of real and fictional characters. Among the characters who appear and receive more than mere expository mention are Robert E. Lee, Jeb Stuart, Jefferson Davis, "Fighting Joe" Hooker, A. P. Hill, and a good many others in cameo roles.

Meanwhile, the cast of fictional characters is caught up in various personal plots and subplots that could, in another context, turn this story into a more conventional historical romance. There could be little or no suspense for the reader about the outcome of battles and the ordained end of things. But the shape of the story and the way in which it is told surprise the reader just as the characters are surprised by events. Moreover, the narrative is an implicit critique of the world of the historical romance, a world we witness being broken to pieces against the edges of hard facts. Among the fictional characters—each one with a personal story and with problems to be resolved—there is a romantic triangle: Richard Cleave, Judith Cary, and Maury Stafford, all upper-class people, each with the usual extended network of family, kinfolk, friends, and enemies. There are other important, central characters—for example, Billy Maydew, the mountain man, and Allan Gold, the schoolmaster. And there is a splendidly realized cowardly low-life, Steve Dagg, a *miles gloriosus* right out of Plautus or Shakespeare, talking with a Southern accent and a mountain dialect. He goes to great trouble to keep skin and bones, body and soul, intact during all situations. There are also a variety of women and there are the slaves. All these characters have different points of view. Only the slaves speak in a phonetic dialect, as was the literary custom of the time.

Various kinds of language, rhetoric, and voices are summoned up to tell the tale. There are the voices of the different social classes and individual points of view, expressed in narration as well as in dialogue. There is also a diversity of narrative rhetoric, ranging from a public, historical narrative voice, a kind of chorus or collective vision, to the texts of real and imaginary documents; there are even song lyrics and, in one case (p. 274) the musical notation for a bugle call. Gradually, we sense the way that the collective vision begins to overwhelm and often replace the individual (and often innocent) points of view. The problems that come from particularities of character and complexities of plot become an expendable pattern of desires and events no longer of much significance when measured against the enormity of the war. The Civil War slowly becomes an inhuman character with a life and will and death of its own. Never completely—though it will be more complete in *Cease Firing*—the war takes over from its managers, the generals and statesmen of both sides, and even from its victims. The movement of the language of both books is from small to large, from particular to general, from the concrete toward the abstract.

Some of the language, both literary and vernacular, is dated. We are still too near in time to allow language to fade into a generalized historical past, so the language seems to be, at this stage, more like a slightly awkward version of our own. In *The Long Roll* and *Cease Firing* we are witness to the end of the literary language of the late nineteenth century and the beginning of our own. In that sense, Johnston's work in *The Long Roll* and *Cease Firing* can be taken as transitional—certainly a precursor to the habits of modernity which derived from the shocking experience (real and imaginary) of the First World War, an experience that, with its imagery and memory, still haunts the contemporary consciousness. We tend to forget that Mary Johnston grew up among old soldiers, in a defeated society in which one out of four men between the ages of eighteen and sixty-five had been killed or permanently disabled—a society with one-armed and one-legged men everywhere. Mary Johnston knew the history of the war at first hand. She knew that to tell the truth of it, she could not discard the conventions of historical narrative; but she must also simultaneously engage the imagination of her reader. The conventions of fiction could serve this purpose. And so she helped invent a form for our time: the novel that blends fact and fiction in subtle and shifting proportions, one whose chief aim is to seek and to share the truth, outward and visible, inward and spiritual, of an experience. The whole idea of what constitutes fiction about war, and the full range of its possibilities, has been changing constantly in response to the events and complexities of this bloody and terrible century. Near its beginning, Mary Johnston, seeking to honor her father's memory and to do justice to one of the most traumatic experiences in American history, was forced to recreate and redefine the novel. In creating *The Long Roll* and *Cease Firing,* she served all of us who have come after her.

George Garrett

CONTENTS

I. THE BOTETOURT RESOLUTIONS 1

II. THE HILLTOP 7

III. THREE OAKS 19

IV. GREENWOOD 28

V. THUNDER RUN 45

VI. BY ASHBY'S GAP 60

VII. THE DOGS OF WAR 72

VIII. A CHRISTENING 83

IX. WINCHESTER 100

X. LIEUTENANT MCNEIL 112

XI. "AS JOSEPH WAS A–WALKING" 121

XII. "THE BATH AND ROMNEY TRIP". . . . 135

XIII. FOOL TOM JACKSON 150

XIV. THE IRON-CLADS 172

XV. KERNSTOWN 193

XVI. RUDE'S HILL 207

XVII. CLEAVE AND JUDITH 217

XVIII. MCDOWELL 229

XIX. THE FLOWERING WOOD 247

XX. FRONT ROYAL 263

XXI. STEVEN DAGG 277

XXII. THE VALLEY PIKE 296

XXIII. MOTHER AND SON 312

XXIV. THE FOOT CAVALRY 331

XXV. ASHBY 343

XXVI. THE BRIDGE AT PORT REPUBLIC . . . 354

XXVII. JUDITH AND STAFFORD 371

XXVIII. THE LONGEST WAY ROUND 382

XXIX. THE NINE-MILE ROAD 399

XXX. AT THE PRESIDENT'S 412

XXXI. THE FIRST OF THE SEVEN DAYS . . . 434

XXXII. GAINES'S MILL 446

XXXIII. THE HEEL OF ACHILLES 465

XXXIV. THE RAILROAD GUN 481

XXXV. WHITE OAK SWAMP 498

XXXVI. MALVERN HILL 516

XXXVII. A WOMAN 530

XXXVIII. CEDAR RUN 545

XXXIX. THE FIELD OF MANASSAS 557

XL. A GUNNER OF PELHAM'S 572

XLI. THE TOLLGATE 580

XLII. SPECIAL ORDERS, NO. 191 589

XLIII. SHARPSBURG 602

XLIV. BY THE OPEQUON 616

XLV. THE LONE TREE HILL 629

XLVI. FREDERICKSBURG 639

XLVII. THE WILDERNESS 655

XLVIII. THE RIVER 670

TO THE READER

To name the historians, biographers, memoir and narrative writers, diarists, and contributors of but a vivid page or two to the magazines of Historical Societies, to whom the writer of a story dealing with this period is indebted, would be to place below a very long list. In lieu of doing so, the author of this book will say here that many incidents which she has used were actual happenings, recorded by men and women writing of that through which they lived. She has changéd the manner but not the substance, and she has used them because they were "true stories" and she wished that breath of life within the book. To all recorders of these things that verily happened, she here acknowledges her indebtedness and gives her thanks.

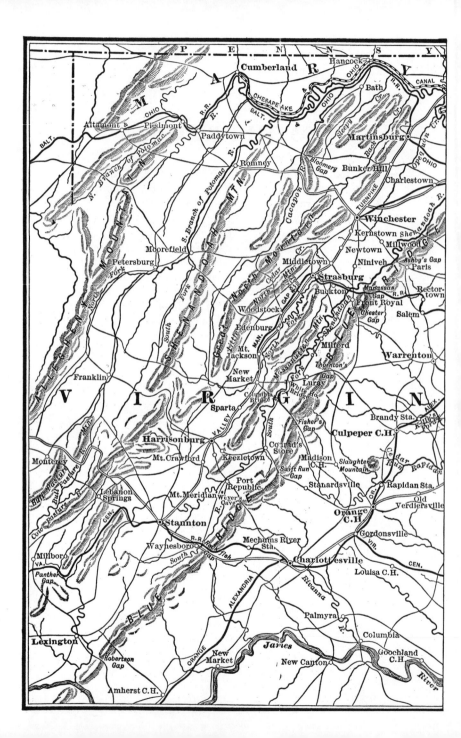

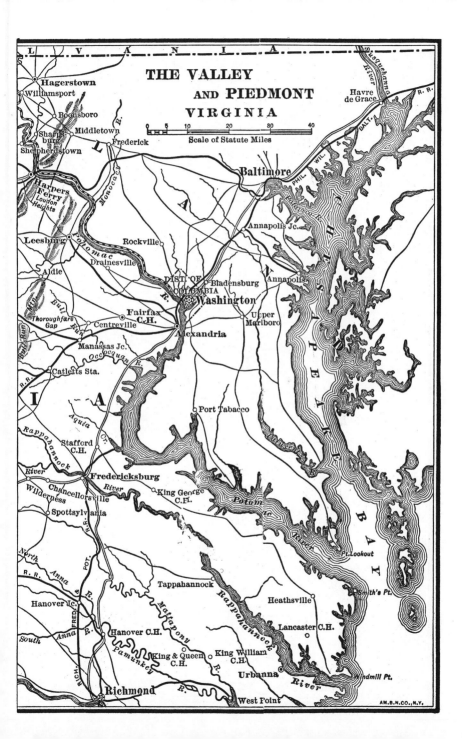

THE VALLEY
AND **PIEDMONT**
VIRGINIA

Scale of Statute Miles

0 5 10 20 30 40

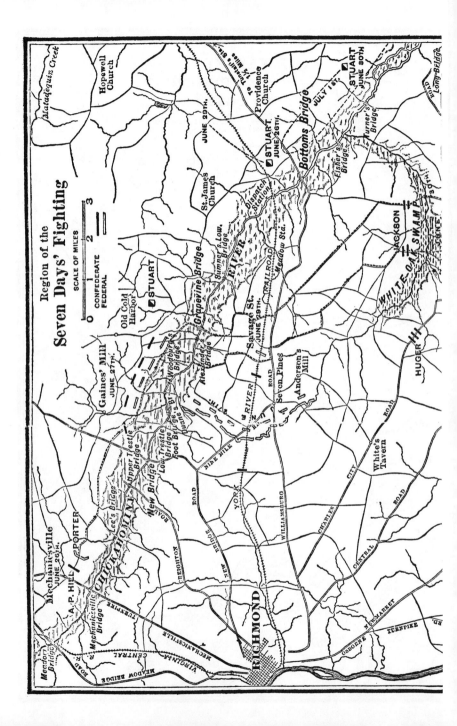

Region of the
Seven Days' Fighting

SCALE OF MILES

0   1   2   3

CONFEDERATE
FEDERAL

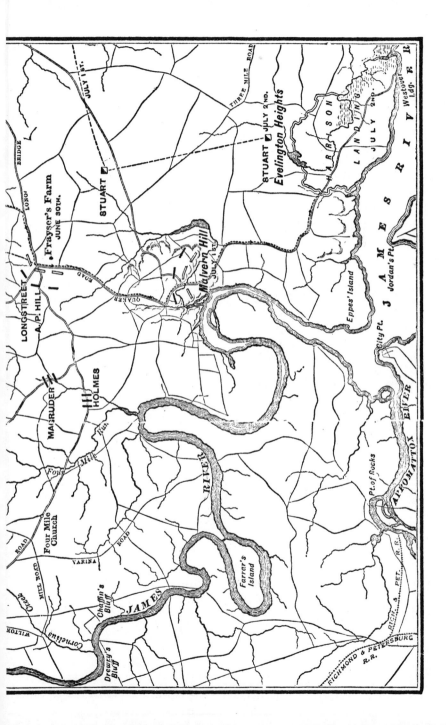

THE LONG ROLL

CHAPTER I

THE BOTETOURT RESOLUTIONS

O N this wintry day, cold and sunny, the small town breathed hard in its excitement. It might have climbed rapidly from a lower land, so heightened now were its pulses, so light and rare the air it drank, so raised its mood, so wide, so very wide the opening prospect. Old red-brick houses, old box-planted gardens, old high, leafless trees, out it looked from its place between the mountain ranges. Its point of view, its position in space, had each its value — whether a lesser value or a greater value than other points and positions only the Judge of all can determine. The little town tried to see clearly and to act rightly. If, in this time so troubled, so obscured by mounting clouds, so tossed by winds of passion and of prejudice, it felt the proudest assurance that it was doing both, at least that self-infatuation was shared all around the compass.

The town was the county-seat. Red brick and white pillars, set on rising ground and encircled by trees, the court house rose like a guidon, planted there by English stock. Around it gathered a great crowd, breathlessly listening. It listened to the reading of the Botetourt Resolutions, offered by the President of the Supreme Court of Virginia, and now delivered in a solemn and a ringing voice. The season was December and the year, 1860.

The people of Botetourt County, in general meeting assembled, believe it to be the duty of all the citizens of the Commonwealth, in the present alarming condition of our country, to give some expression of their opinion upon the threatening aspect of public affairs. . . .
In the controversies with the mother country, growing out of the effort

of the latter to tax the Colonies without their consent, it was Virginia who, by the resolution against the Stamp Act, gave the example of the first authoritative resistance by a legislative body to the British Government, and so imparted the first impulse to the Revolution.

Virginia declared her Independence before any of the Colonies, and gave the first written Constitution to mankind.

By her instructions her representatives in the General Congress introduced a resolution to declare the Colonies independent States, and the Declaration itself was written by one of her sons.

She furnished to the Confederate States the father of his country, under whose guidance Independence was achieved, and the rights and liberties of each State, it was hoped, perpetually established.

She stood undismayed through the long night of the Revolution, breasting the storm of war and pouring out the blood of her sons like water on every battlefield, from the ramparts of Quebec to the sands of Georgia.

A cheer broke from the throng. "That she did — that she did! 'Old Virginia never tire.' "

By her unaided efforts the Northwestern Territory was conquered, whereby the Mississippi, instead of the Ohio River, was recognized as the boundary of the United States by the treaty of peace.

To secure harmony, and as an evidence of her estimate of the value of the Union of the States, she ceded to all for their common benefit this magnificent region — an empire in itself.

When the Articles of Confederation were shown to be inadequate to secure peace and tranquillity at home and respect abroad, Virginia first moved to bring about a more perfect Union.

At her instance the first assemblage of commissioners took place at Annapolis, which ultimately led to a meeting of the Convention which formed the present Constitution.

The instrument itself was in a great measure the production of one of her sons, who has been justly styled the Father of the Constitution.

The government created by it was put into operation, with her Washington, the father of his country, at its head; her Jefferson, the author of the Declaration of Independence, in his cabinet; her Madison, the great advocate of the Constitution, in the legislative hall.

"And each of the three," cried a voice, "left on record his judgment as to the integral rights of the federating States."

Under the leading of Virginia statesmen the Revolution of 1798 was brought about, Louisiana was acquired, and the second war of independence was waged.

Throughout the whole progress of the Republic she has never infringed on the rights of any State, or asked or received an exclusive benefit.

On the contrary, she has been the first to vindicate the equality of all the States, the smallest as well as the greatest.

But, claiming no exclusive benefit for her efforts and sacrifices in the common cause, she had a right to look for feelings of fraternity and kindness for her citizens from the citizens of other States. . . . And that the common government, to the promotion of which she contributed so largely, for the purpose of establishing justice and ensuring domestic tranquillity, would not, whilst the forms of the Constitution were observed, be so perverted in spirit as to inflict wrong and injustice and produce universal insecurity.

These reasonable expectations have been grievously disappointed —

There arose a roar of assent. "That's the truth! — that's the plain truth! North and South, we're leagues asunder! — We don't think alike, we don't feel alike, and we don't interpret the Constitution alike! I'll tell you how the North interprets it! — Government by the North, for the North, and over the South! Go on, Judge Allen, go on!"

In view of this state of things, we are not inclined to rebuke or censure the people of any of our sister States in the South, suffering from injury, goaded by insults, and threatened with such outrages and wrongs, for their bold determination to relieve themselves from such injustice and oppression by resorting to their ultimate and sovereign right to dissolve the compact which they had formed and to provide new guards for their future security.

"South Carolina! — Georgia, too, will be out in January. — Alabama as well, Mississippi and Louisiana. — Go on!"

Nor have we any doubt of the right of any State, there being no common umpire between coequal sovereign States, to judge for itself on its own responsibility, as to the mode and manner of redress.

The States, each for itself, exercised this sovereign power when they dissolved their connection with the British Empire.

They exercised the same power when nine of the States seceded from the Confederation and adopted the present Constitution, though two States at first rejected it.

The Articles of Confederation stipulated that those articles should be inviolably observed by every State, and that the Union should be perpetual, and that no alteration should be made unless agreed to by Congress and confirmed by every State.

Notwithstanding this solemn compact, a portion of the States did, without the consent of the others, form a new compact; and there is nothing to show, or by which it can be shown, that this right has been, or can be, diminished so long as the States continue sovereign.

"The right's the right of self-government — and it's inherent and inalienable! — We fought for it — when did n't we fight for it? When we cease to fight for it, then chaos and night! — Go on, go on!"

The Confederation was assented to by the Legislature for each State; the Constitution by the people of each State, for such State alone. One is as binding as the other, and no more so.

The Constitution, it is true, established a government, and it operates directly on the individual; the Confederation was a league operating primarily on the States. But each was adopted by the State for itself; in the one case by the Legislature acting for the State; in the other by the people, not as individuals composing one nation, but as composing the distinct and independent States to which they respectively belong.

The foundation, therefore, on which it was established, was FEDERAL, *and the State, in the exercise of the same sovereign authority by which she ratified for herself, may for herself abrogate and annul.*

The operation of its powers, whilst the State remains in the Confederacy, is NATIONAL; *and consequently a State remaining in the Confederacy and enjoying its benefits cannot, by any mode of procedure, withdraw its citizens from the obligation to obey the Constitution and the laws passed in pursuance thereof.*

But when a State does secede, the Constitution and laws of the United States cease to operate therein. No power is conferred on Congress to enforce them. Such authority was denied to the Congress in the convention which framed the Constitution, because it would be an act of war of nation against nation — not the exercise of the legitimate power of a government to enforce its laws on those subject to its jurisdiction.

The assumption of such a power would be the assertion of a prerogative claimed by the British Government to legislate for the Colonies in all cases whatever; it would constitute of itself a dangerous attack on the rights of the States, and should be promptly repelled.

There was a great thunder of assent. "That is our doctrine — bred in the bone — dyed in the weaving! Jefferson, Madison, Marshall, Washington, Henry — further back yet, further back — back to Magna Charta!"

These principles, resulting from the nature of our system of confederate States, cannot admit of question in Virginia.

In 1788 our people in convention, by their act of ratification, declared and made known that the powers granted under the Constitution, being derived from the people of the United States, may be resumed by them whenever they shall be perverted to their injury and oppression.

From what people were these powers derived? Confessedly from the people of each State, acting for themselves. By whom were they to be resumed or taken back? By the people of the State who were then granting them away. Who were to determine whether the powers granted had been perverted to their injury or oppression? Not the whole people of the United States, for there could be no oppression of the whole with their own consent; and it could not have entered into the conception of the Convention that the powers granted could not be resumed until the oppressor himself united in such resumption.

They asserted the right to resume in order to guard the people of Virginia, for whom alone the Convention could act, against the oppression of an irresponsible and sectional majority, the worst form of oppression with which an angry Providence has ever afflicted humanity.

Whilst therefore we regret that any State should, in a matter of common grievance, have determined to act for herself without consulting with her sister States equally aggrieved, we are nevertheless con-

*strained to say that the occasion justifies and loudly calls for action
of some kind. . . .*

*In view therefore of the present condition of our country, and the
causes of it, we declare almost in the words of our fathers, contained in
an address of the freeholders of Botetourt, in February, 1775, to the
delegates from Virginia to the Continental Congress, "That we desire
no change in our government whilst left to the free enjoyment of our
equal privileges secured by the* CONSTITUTION; *but that should a tyran-
nical* SECTIONAL MAJORITY, *under the sanction of the forms of the*
CONSTITUTION, *persist in acts of injustice and violence toward us, they
only must be answerable for the consequences."*

*That liberty is so strongly impressed upon our hearts that we cannot
think of parting with it but with our lives; that our duty to God, our
country, ourselves and our posterity forbid it; we stand, therefore,
prepared for every contingency.*

RESOLVED THEREFORE, *That in view of the facts set out in the fore-
going preamble, it is the opinion of this meeting that a convention of
the people should be called forthwith; that the State in its sovereign
character should consult with the other Southern States, and agree upon
such guarantees as in their opinion will secure their equality, tranquillity and rights* WITHIN THE UNION.

The applause shook the air. "Yes, yes! within the Union!
They're not quite mad — not even the black Republicans! We'll
save the Union! — We made it, and we'll save it! — Unless the
North takes leave of its senses. — Go on!"

*And in the event of a failure to obtain such guarantees, to adopt in
concert with the other Southern States,* OR ALONE, *such measures as
may seem most expedient to protect the rights and ensure the safety of
the people of Virginia.*

The reader made an end, and stood with dignity. Silence, then a
beginning of sound, like the beginning of wind in the forest. It grew,
it became deep and surrounding as the atmosphere, it increased into
the general voice of the county, and the voice passed the Botetourt
Resolutions.

CHAPTER II

THE HILLTOP

ON the court house portico sat the prominent men of the county, lawyers and planters, men of name and place, moulders of thought and leaders in action. Out of these came the speakers. One by one, they stepped into the clear space between the pillars. Such a man was cool and weighty, such a man was impassioned and persuasive. Now the tense crowd listened, hardly breathing, now it broke into wild applause. The speakers dealt with an approaching tempest, and with a gesture they checked off the storm clouds. *"Protection for the manufacturing North at the expense of the agricultural South* — an old storm centre! *Territorial Rights* — once a speck in the west, not so large as a man's hand, and now beneath it, the wrangling and darkened land! *The Bondage of the African Race* — a heavy cloud! Our English fathers raised it; our northern brethren dwelled with it; the currents of the air fixed it in the South. At no far day we will pass from under it. In the mean time we would not have it *burst.* In that case underneath it would lie ruined fields and wrecked homes, and out of its elements would come a fearful pestilence! *The Triumph of the Republican Party* — no slight darkening of the air is that, no drifting mist of the morning! It is the triumph of that party which proclaims the Constitution a covenant with death and an agreement with hell! — of that party which tolled the bells, and fired the minute guns, and draped its churches with black, and all-hailed as saint and martyr the instigator of a bloody and servile insurrection in a sister State, the felon and murderer, John Brown! The Radical, the Black Republican, faction, sectional rule, fanaticism, violation of the Constitution, aggression, tyranny, and wrong — all these are in the bosom of that cloud! — *The Sovereignty of the State.* Where is the tempest which threatens here? *Not* here, Virginians! but in the pleasing assertion of the North, 'There is no sovereignty of the State!' 'A State is merely to the Union what a county is to a State.' O shades of John

Randolph of Roanoke, of Patrick Henry, of Mason and Madison, of Washington and Jefferson! O shade of John Marshall even,whom we used to think too Federal! The Union! We thought of the Union as a golden thread — at the most we thought of it as a strong servant we had made between us, we thirteen artificers — a beautiful Talus to walk our coasts and cry 'All's well!' We thought so — by the gods, we think so yet! That *is* our Union — the golden thread, the faithful servant; not the monster that Frankenstein made, not this Minotaur swallowing States! *The Sovereignty of the State!* Virginia fought seven years for the sovereignty of Virginia, wrung it, eighty years ago, from Great Britain, and has not since resigned it! Being different in most things, possibly the North is different also in this. It may be that those States have renounced the liberty they fought for. Possibly Massachusetts — the years 1803, 1811, and 1844 to the contrary — does regard herself as a county. Possibly Connecticut — for all that there was a Hartford Convention! — sees herself in the same light. Possibly. 'Brutus saith 't is so, and Brutus is an honourable man!' But Virginia has not renounced! Eighty years ago she wrote a certain motto on her shield. To-day the letters burn bright! Unterrified then she entered this league from which we hoped so much. Unterrified to-morrow, should a slurring hand be laid upon that shield, will she leave it!"

Allan Gold, from the schoolhouse on Thunder Run, listened with a swelling heart, then, amid the applause which followed the last speaker, edged his way along the crowded old brick pavement to where, not far from the portico, he made out the broad shoulders, the waving dark hair, and the slouch hat of a young man with whom he was used to discuss these questions. Hairston Breckinridge glanced down at the pressure upon his arm, recognized the hand, and pursued, half aloud, the current of his thought. "I don't believe I'll go back to the university. I don't believe any of us will go back to the university. — Hello, Allan!"

"I'm for the preservation of the Union," said Allan. "I can't help it. We made it, and we've loved it."

"I'm for it, too," answered the other, "in reason. I'm not for it out of reason. In these affairs out of reason is out of honour. There's nothing sacred in the word *Union* that men should bow down and worship it! It's the thing behind the word that counts — and who-

ever says that Massachusetts and Virginia, and Illinois and Texas
are united just now is a fool or a liar! — Who's this Colonel Anderson is bringing forward? Ah, we'll have the Union now!"
"Who is it?"
"Albemarle man, staying at Lauderdale. — Major in the army,
home on furlough. — Old-line Whig. I've been at his brother's
place, near Charlottesville —"
From the portico came a voice. "I am sure that few in Botetourt
need an introduction here. We, no more than others, are free from
vanity, and we think we know a hero by intuition. Men of Botetourt, we have the honour to listen to Major Fauquier Cary, who
carried the flag up Chapultepec!"
Amid applause a man of perhaps forty years, spare, bronzed, and
soldierly, entered the clear space between the pillars, threw out his
arm with an authoritative gesture, and began to speak in an odd,
dry, attractive voice. "You are too good!" he said clearly. "I'm
afraid you don't know Fauquier Cary very well, after all. He's no
hero — worse luck! He's only a Virginian, trying to do the right
as he sees it, out yonder on the plains with the Apaches and the
Comanches and the sage brush and the desert —"
There was an interruption. " How about Chapultepec?" — " And
the Rio Grande ?" — " Did n't we hear something about a fight in
Texas?"
The speaker laughed. "A fight in Texas? Folk, folk, if you
knew how many fights there are in Texas — and how meritorious
it is to keep out of them! No; I'm only a Virginian out there."
He regarded the throng with his magnetic smile, his slight and
fine air of gaiety in storm. "As you know, I am by no means the
only Virginian, and they are heroes, the others, if you like! —
real, old-line heroes, brave as the warriors in Homer, and a long
sight better men! I am happy to report to his kinsmen here that
General Joseph E. Johnston is in health — still loving astronomy,
still reading du Guesclin, still studying the Art of War. He's a
soldier's soldier, and that, in its way, is as fine a thing as a poet's
poet! I see men before me who are of the blood of the Lees. Out
there by the Rio Grande is a Colonel Robert E. Lee, of whom
Virginia may well be proud! There are few heights in those western deserts, but he carries his height with him. He's marked for

greatness. And there are 'Beauty' Stuart, and Dabney Maury, the best of fellows, and Edward Dillon, and Walker and George Thomas, and many another good man and true. First and last, there's a deal of old Virginia following Mars, out yonder! We've got Hardee, too, from Georgia, and Van Dorn from Mississippi, and Albert Sidney Johnston from Kentucky — no better men in Homer, no better men! And there are others as soldierly — McClellan with whom I graduated at West Point, Fitz-John Porter, Hancock, Sedgwick, Sykes, and Averell. McClellan and Hancock are from Pennsylvania, Fitz-John Porter is from New Hampshire, Sedgwick from Connecticut, Sykes from Delaware, and Averell from New York. And away, away out yonder, in the midst of sage brush and Apaches, when any of us chance to meet around a camp-fire, there we sit, while coyotes are yelling off in the dark, there we sit and tell stories of home, of Virginia and Pennsylvania, of Georgia and New Hampshire!"

He paused, drew himself up, looked out over the throng to the mountains, studied for a moment their long, clean line, then dropped his glance and spoke in a changed tone, with a fiery suddenness, a lunge as of a tried rapier, quick and startling.

"Men of Botetourt! I speak for my fellow soldiers of the Army of the United States when I say that, out yonder, we are blithe to fight with marauding Comanches, with wolves and with grizzlies, but that we are not — oh, we are not — ready to fight with each other! Brother against brother — comrade against comrade — friend against friend — to quarrel in the same tongue and to slay the man with whom you've faced a thousand dangers — no, we are not ready for that!

"Virginians! I will not believe that the permanent dissolution of this great Union is come! I will not believe that we stand to-day in danger of internecine war! Men of Botetourt, go slow — go slow! The Right of the State — I grant it! I was bred in that doctrine, as were you all. Albemarle no whit behind Botetourt in that! The Botetourt Resolutions — amen to much, to very much in the Botetourt Resolutions! South Carolina! Let South Carolina go in peace! It is her right! Remembering old comradeship, old battle-fields, old defeats, old victories, we shall still be friends. If the Gulf States go, still it is their right, immemorial, incontrovertible! —

The right of self-government. We are of one blood and the country is wide. God-speed both to Lot and to Abraham! On some sunny future day may their children draw together and take hands again! So much for the seceding States. But Virginia, — but Virginia made possible the Union, — let her stand fast in it in this day of storm! in this Convention let her voice be heard — as I know it will be heard — for wisdom, for moderation, for patience! So, or soon or late, she will mediate between the States, she will once again make the ring complete, she will be the saviour of this great historic Confederation which our fathers made!"

A minute or two more and he ended his speech. As he moved from between the pillars, there was loud applause. The county was largely Whig, honestly longing — having put on record what it thought of the present mischief and the makers of it — for a peaceful solution of all troubles. As for the army, county and State were proud of the army, and proud of the Virginians within it. It was amid cheering that Fauquier Cary left the portico. At the head of the steps, however, there came a question. "One moment, Major Cary! What if the North declines to evacuate Fort Sumter? What if she attempts to reinforce it? What if she declares for a *compulsory* Union?"

Cary paused a moment. "She will not, she will not! There are politicians in the North whom I'll not defend! But the people — the people — the people are neither fools nor knaves! They were born North and we were born South, and that is the chief difference between us! A *Compulsory* Union! That is a contradiction in terms. Individuals and States, harmoniously minded, unite for the sweetness of Union and for the furtherance of common interests. When the minds are discordant, and the interests opposed, one may be bound to another by Conquest — not otherwise! What said Hamilton? *To coerce a State would be one of the maddest projects ever devised!*" He descended the court house steps to the grassy, crowded yard. Here acquaintances claimed him, and here, at last, the surge of the crowd brought him within a yard of Allan Gold and his companion. The latter spoke. "Major Cary, you don't remember me. I'm Hairston Breckinridge, sir, and I've been once or twice to Greenwood with Edward. I was there Christmas before last, when you came home wounded —"

The older man put out a ready hand. "Yes, yes, I do remember! We had a merry Christmas! I am glad to meet you again, Mr. Breckinridge. Is this your brother?"

"No, sir. It's Allan Gold, from Thunder Run."

"I am pleased to meet you, sir," said Allan. "You have been saying what I should like to have been able to say myself."

"I am pleased that you are pleased. Are you, too, from the university?"

"No, sir. I could n't go. I teach the school on Thunder Run."

"Allan knows more," said Hairston Breckinridge, "than many of us who are at the university. But we must n't keep you, sir."

In effect they could do so no longer. Major Cary was swept away by acquaintances and connections. The day was declining, the final speaker drawing to an end, the throng beginning to shiver in the deepening cold. The speaker gave his final sentence; the town band crashed in determinedly with " Home, Sweet Home." To its closing strains the county people, afoot, on horseback, in old, roomy, high-swung carriages, took this road and that. The townsfolk, still excited, still discussing, lingered awhile round the court house or on the verandah of the old hotel, but at last these groups dissolved also. The units betook themselves home to fireside and supper, and the sun set behind the Alleghenies.

Allan Gold, striding over the hills toward Thunder Run, caught up with the miller from Mill Creek, and the two walked side by side until their roads diverged. The miller was a slow man, but to-day there was a red in his cheek and a light in his eye. "Just so," he said shortly. "They must keep out of my mill race or they'll get caught in the wheel."

"Mr. Green," said Allan, "how much of all this trouble do you suppose is really about the negro? I was brought up to wish that Virginia had never held a slave."

"So were most of us. You don't hold any."

"No."

"No more I don't. No more does Tom Watts. Nor Anderson West. Nor the Taylors. Nor five sixths of the farming folk about here. Nor seven eighths of the townspeople. We don't own a negro, and I don't know that we ever did own one. Not long ago I asked Colonel Anderson a lot of questions about the matter. He says the census this year gives Virginia one million and fifty thousand white people, and of these the fifty thousand hold slaves and the one million don't. The fifty thousand's mostly in the tide-water counties, too, — mighty little of it on this side the Blue Ridge! Ain't anybody ever accused Virginians of not being good to servants! and it don't take more'n half an eye to see that the servants love their white people. For slavery itself, I ain't quarrelling for it, and neither was Colonel Anderson. He said it was abhorrent in the sight of God and man. He said the old House of Burgesses used to try to stop the bringing in of negroes, and that the Colony was always appealing to the king against the traffic. He said that in 1778, two years after Virginia declared her Independence, she passed the statute prohibiting the slave trade. He said that she was the first country in the civilized world to stop the trade — passed her statute thirty years before England! He said that all our great Revolutionary men hated slavery and worked for the emancipation of the negroes who were here ; that men worked openly and hard for it until 1832. Then came the Nat Turner Insurrection, when they killed all those women and children, and then rose the hell-fire-for-all, bitter-'n-gall Abolition people stirring gunpowder with a lighted stick, holding on like grim death and in perfect safety fifteen hundred miles from where the explosion was due! And as they denounce without thinking, so a lot of men have risen with us to advocate without thinking. And underneath all the clamour, there goes on, all the time, quiet and steady, a freeing of negroes by deed and will, a settling them in communities in free States, a belonging to and supporting Colonization Societies. There are now forty thousand free negroes in Virginia, and Heaven knows how many have been freed and established elsewhere! It is our best people who make these wills, freeing their slaves, and in Virginia, at least, everybody, sooner or later, follows the best people. 'Gradual manumission, Mr. Green,' that's what Colonel Anderson said, 'with colonization in Africa if possible. The difficulties are enough to turn a man's hair grey, but,' said he, 'slavery's knell has struck, and we'll put an end to it in Virginia peacefully and with some approach to wisdom — if only they'll stop stirring the gunpowder!'"

The miller raised his large head, with its effect of white powder from the mill, and regarded the landscape. "'We're all mighty blind, poor creatures,' as the preacher says, but I reckon one day we'll find the right way, both for us and for that half million poor, dark-skinned, lovable, never-knew-any-better, pretty-happy-on-the-whole, way-behind-the-world people that King James and King Charles and King George saddled us with, not much to their betterment and to our certain hurt. I reckon we'll find it. But I'm damned if I'm going to take the North's word for it that she has the way! Her old way was to sell her negroes South."

"I've thought and thought," said Allan. "People mean well, and yet there's such a dreadful lot of tragedy in the world!"

"I agree with you there," quoth the miller. "And I certainly don't deny that slavery's responsible for a lot of bitter talk and a lot of red-hot feeling ; for some suffering to some negroes, too, and for a deal of harm to almost all whites. And I, for one, will be powerful glad when every negro, man and woman, is free. They can never really grow until they are free — I'll acknowledge that. And if they want to go back to their own country I'd pay my mite to help them along. I think I owe it to them — even though as far as I know I have n't a forbear that ever did them wrong. Trouble is, don't any of them want to go back! You could n't scare them worse than to tell them you were going to help them back to their fatherland! The Lauderdale negroes, for instance — never see one that he is n't laughing! And Tullius at Three Oaks, — *he 'd* say he could n't possibly think of going — must stay at Three Oaks and look after Miss Margaret and the children! No, it is n't an easy subject, look at it any way you will. But as between us and the North, it ain't the main subject of quarrel — not by a long shot it ain't! The quarrel's that a man wants to take all the grist, mine as well as his, and grind it in his mill! Well, I won't let him — that's all. And here's your road to Thunder Run."

Allan strode on alone over the frozen hills. Before him sprang the rampart of the mountains, magnificently drawn against the eastern sky. To either hand lay the fallow fields, rolled the brown hills, rose the shadowy bulk of forest trees, showed the green of winter wheat. The evening was cold, but without wind and soundless. The birds had flown south, the cattle were stalled, the sheep folded. There was only the earth, field and hill and mountain, the up and down of a narrow road, and the glimmer of a distant stream. The sunset had been red, and it left a colour that flared to the zenith. The young man, tall, blond, with grey-blue eyes and short, fair beard, covered with long strides the frozen road. It led him over a lofty hill whose summit commanded a wide prospect. Allan, reaching this height, hesitated a moment, then crossed to a grey zigzag of rail fence, and, leaning his arms upon it, looked forth over hill and vale, forest and stream. The afterglow was upon the land. He looked at the mountains, the great mountains, long and clean of line as the marching rollers of a giant sea, not split or jagged, but even, unbroken, and old, old, the oldest almost in the world. Now the ancient forest clothed them, while they were given, by some constant trick of the light, the distant, dreamy blue from which they took their name. The Blue Ridge — the Blue Ridge — and then the hills and the valleys, and all the rushing creeks, and the grandeur of the trees, and to the east, steel clear between the sycamores and the willows, the river — the upper reaches of the river James.

The glow deepened. From a farmhouse in the valley came the sound of a bell. Allan straightened himself, lifting his arms from the grey old rails. He spoke aloud.

Breathes there the man with soul so dead, —

The bell rang again, the rose suffused the sky to the zenith. The young man drew a long breath, and, turning, began to descend the hill.

Before him, at a turn of the road and overhanging a precipitous hollow, in the spring carpeted with bloodroot, but now thick with dead leaves, lay a giant oak, long ago struck down by lightning. The branches had been cut away, but the blackened trunk remained, and from it as vantage point one received another great view of the rolling mountains and the valleys between. Allan Gold, coming down the hill, became aware, first of a horse fastened to a wayside sapling, then of a man seated upon the fallen oak, his back to the road, his face to the darkening prospect. Below him the winter wind made a rustling in the dead leaves. Evidently another had paused to admire the view, or to collect and mould between the hands of the soul the crowding impressions of a decisive day. It was, apparently, the latter purpose; for as Allan approached the ravine there came to him out of the dusk, in a controlled but vibrant voice, the following statement, repeated three times: "We are going to have war. — We are going to have war. — We are going to have war."

Allan sent his own voice before him. "I trust in God that's not true! — It's Richard Cleave, there, is n't it?"

The figure on the oak, swinging itself around, sat outlined against the violet sky. "Yes, Richard Cleave. It's a night to make one think, Allan — to make one think — to make one think!" Laying his hand on the trunk beside him, he sprang lightly down to the roadside, where he proceeded to brush dead leaf and bark from his clothing with an old gauntlet. When he spoke it was still in the same moved, vibrating voice. "War's my *métier*. That's a curious thing to be said by a country lawyer in peaceful old Virginia in this year of grace! But like many another curious thing, it's true! I was never on a field of battle, but I know all about a field of battle."

He shook his head, lifted his hand, and flung it out toward the mountains. "I don't want war, mind you, Allan! That is, the great stream at the bottom does n't want it. War is a word that means agony to many and a set-back to all. Reason tells me that, and my heart wishes the world neither agony nor set-back, and I give my word for peace. Only — only — before this life I must have fought all along the line!"

His eyes lightened. Against the paling sky, in the wintry air, his powerful frame, not tall, but deep-chested, broad-shouldered, looked larger than life. "I don't talk this way often — as you'll grant!" he said, and laughed. "But I suppose to-day loosed all our tongues, lifted every man out of himself!"

"If war came," said Allan, "it could n't be a long war, could it? After the first battle we'd come to an understanding."

"Would we?" answered the other. "Would we? — God knows! In the past it has been that the more equal the tinge of blood, the fiercer was the war."

As he spoke he moved across to the sapling where was fastened his horse, loosed him, and sprang into the saddle. The horse, a magnificent bay, took the road, and the three began the long descent. It was very cold and still, a crescent moon in the sky, and lights beginning to shine from the farmhouses in the valley.

"Though I teach school," said Allan, "I like the open. I like to do things with my hands, and I like to go in and out of the woods. Perhaps, all the way behind us, I was a hunter, with a taste for books! My grandfather was a scout in the Revolution, and his father was a ranger. . . . God knows, *I* don't want war! But if it comes I'll go. We'll all go, I reckon."

"Yes, we'll all go," said Cleave. "We'll need to go."

The one rode, the other walked in silence for a time; then said the first, "I shall ride to Lauderdale after supper and talk to Fauquier Cary."

"You and he are cousins, are n't you?"

"Third cousins. His mother was a Dandridge — Unity Dandridge."

"I like him. It's like old wine and blue steel and a cavalier poet — that type."

"Yes, it is old and fine, in men and in women."

"He does not want war."

"No."

"Hairston Breckinridge says that he won't discuss the possibility at all — he'll only say what he said to-day, that every one should work for peace, and that war between brothers is horrible."

"It is. No. He wears a uniform. He cannot talk."

They went on in silence for a time, over the winter road, through the crystal air. Between the branches of the trees the sky showed intense and cold, the crescent moon, above a black mass of mountains, golden and sharp, the lights in the valley near enough to be gathered.

"If there should be war," asked Allan, "what will they do, all the Virginians in the army — Lee and Johnston and Stuart, Maury and Thomas and the rest?"

"They'll come home."

"Resigning their commissions?"

"Resigning their commissions."

Allan sighed. "That would be a hard thing to have to do."

"They'll do it. Would n't you?"

The teacher from Thunder Run looked from the dim valley and the household lamps up to the marching stars. "Yes. If my State called, I would do it."

"This is what will happen," said Cleave. "There are times when a man sees clearly, and I see clearly to-day. The North does not intend to evacuate Fort Sumter. Instead, sooner or later, she'll try to reinforce it. That will be the beginning of the end. South Carolina will reduce the fort. The North will preach a holy war. War there will be — whether holy or not remains to be seen. Virginia will be called upon to furnish her quota of troops with which to coerce South Carolina and the Gulf States back into the Union. Well — do you think she will give them?"

Allan gave a short laugh. "No!"

"That is what will happen. And then — and then a greater State than any will be forced into secession! And then the Virginians in the army will come home."

The wood gave way to open country, softly swelling fields, willow copses, and clear running streams. In the crystal air the mountain walls seemed near at hand, above shone Orion, icily brilliant. The lawyer from a dim old house in a grove of oaks and the school-teacher from Thunder Run went on in silence for a time; then the latter spoke.

"Hairston Breckinridge says that Major Cary's niece is with him at Lauderdale."

"Yes. Judith Cary."

"That's the beautiful one, is n't it?"

"They are all said to be beautiful — the three Greenwood Carys. But — Yes, that is the beautiful one."

He began to hum a song, and as he did so he lifted his wide soft hat and rode bareheaded.

"It's strange to me," said Allan presently, "that any one should be gay to-day."

As he spoke he glanced up at the face of the man riding beside him on the great bay. There was yet upon the road a faint after-light — enough light to reveal that there were tears on Cleave's cheek. Involuntarily Allan uttered an exclamation.

The other, breaking off his chant, quite simply put up a gauntleted hand and wiped the moisture away. "Gay!" he repeated. "I 'm not gay. What gave you such an idea? I tell you that though I 've never been in a war, I know all about war!"

CHAPTER III

THREE OAKS

AVING left behind him Allan Gold and the road to Thunder Run, Richard Cleave came, a little later, to his own house, old and not large, crowning a grassy slope above a running stream. He left the highway, opened a five-barred gate, and passed between fallow fields to a second gate, opened this and, skirting a knoll upon which were set three gigantic oaks, rode up a short and grass-grown drive. It led him to the back of the house, and afar off his dogs began to give him welcome. When he had dismounted before the porch, a negro boy with a lantern took his horse. "Hit's tuhnin' powerful cold, Marse Dick!"

"It is that, Jim. Give Dundee his supper at once and bring him around again. Down, Bugle! Down, Moira! Down, Baron!"

The hall was cold and in semi-darkness, but through the half-opened door of his mother's chamber came a gush of firelight warm and bright. Her voice reached him — "Richard!" He entered. She was sitting in a great old chair by the fire, idle for a wonder, her hands, fine and slender, clasped over her knees. The light struck up against her fair, brooding face. "It is late!" she said. "Late and cold! Come to the fire. Ailsy will have supper ready in a minute."

He came and knelt beside her on the braided rug. "It is always warm in here. Where are the children?"

"Down at Tullius's cabin. — Tell me all about it. Who spoke?"

Cleave drew before the fire the chair that had been his father's, sank into it, and taking the ash stick from the corner, stirred the glowing logs. "Judge Allen's Resolutions were read and carried. Fauquier Cary spoke — many others."

"Did not you?"

"No. They asked me to, but with so many there was no need. People were much moved — "

He broke off, sitting stirring the fire. His mother watched the deep hollows with him. Closely resembling as he did his long dead father, the inner tie, strong and fine, was rather between him and the woman who had given him birth. Wedded ere she was seventeen, a mother at eighteen, she sat now beside her first-born, still beautiful, and crowned by a lovely life. She had kept her youth, and he had come early to a man's responsibilities. For years now they had walked together, caring for the farm, which was not large, for the handful of servants, for the two younger children, Will and Miriam. The eighteen years between them was cancelled by their common interests, his maturity of thought, her quality of the summer time. She broke the silence. "What did Fauquier Cary say?"

"He spoke strongly for patience, moderation, peace — I am going to Lauderdale after supper."

"To see Judith?"

"No. To talk to Fauquier. . . . Maury Stafford is at Silver Hill." He straightened himself, put down the ash stick, and rose to his feet. "The bell will ring directly. I'll go upstairs for a moment."

Margaret Cleave put out a detaining hand. "One moment — Richard, are you quite, quite sure that she likes Maury Stafford so well?"

"Why should she not like him? He's a likable fellow."

"So are many people. So are you."

Cleave gave a short and wintry laugh. "I? I am only her cousin — rather a dull cousin, too, who does nothing much in the law, and is not even a very good farmer! Am I sure? Yes, I am sure enough!" His hand closed on the back of her chair; the wood shook under the sombre energy of his grasp. "Did I not see how it was last summer that week I spent at Greenwood? Was he not always with her? — supple and keen, easy and strong, with his face like a picture, with all the advantages I did not have — education, travel, wealth! — Why, Edward told me — and could I not see for myself? It was in the air of the place — not a servant but knew he had come a-wooing!"

"But there was no engagement then. Had there been we should have known it."

"No engagement then, perhaps, but certainly no discouragement! He was there again in the autumn. He was with her to-day." The chair shook again. "And this morning Fauquier Cary, talking to me, laughed and said that Albemarle had set their wedding day!"

His mother sighed. "Oh, I am sorry — sorry!"

"I should never have gone to Greenwood last summer — never have spent there that unhappy week! Before that it was just a fancy — and then I must go and let it bite into heart and brain and life —" He dropped his hand abruptly and turned to the door. "Well, I've got to try now to think only of the country! God knows, things have come to that pass that her sons should think only of her! It is winter time, Mother; the birds are n't mating now — save those two — save those two!"

Upstairs, in his bare, high-ceiled room, his hasty toilet made, he stood upon the hearth, beside the leaping fire, and looked about him. Of late — since the summer — everything was clarifying. There was at work some great solvent making into naught the dross of custom and habitude. The glass had turned; outlines were clearer than they had been, the light was strong, and striking from a changed angle. To-day both the sight of a face and the thought of an endangered State had worked to make the light intenser. His old, familiar room looked strange to him to-night. A tall bookcase faced him. He went across and stood before it, staring through the diamond panes at the backs of the books. Here were his Coke and Blackstone, Vattel, Henning, Kent, and Tucker, and here were other books of which he was fonder than of those, and here were a few volumes of the poets. Of them all, only the poets managed to keep to-night a familiar look. He took out a volume, old, tawny-backed, gold-lettered, and opened it at random —

> Her face so faire, as flesh it seemed not,
> But hevenly pourtraict of bright angels hew,
> Cleare as the sky, withouten blame or blot —

A bell rang below. Youthful and gay, shattering the quiet of the house, a burst of voices proclaimed " the children's " return from Tullius's cabin. When, in another moment, Cleave came downstairs, it was to find them both in wait at the foot, illumined by the light from the dining-room door. Miriam laid hold of him. "Richard, Richard! tell me quick! Which was the greatest, Achilles or Hector?"

Will, slight and fair, home for the holidays from Lexington and, by virtue of his cadetship in the Virginia Military Institute, an authority on most things, had a movement of impatience. "Girls are so stupid! Tell her it was Hector, and let's go to supper! She'll believe you.''

Within the dining-room, at the round table, before the few pieces of tall, beaded silver and the gilt-banded china, while Mehalah the waitress brought the cakes from the kitchen and the fire burned softly on the hearth below the Saint Memin of a general and lawgiver, talk fell at once upon the event of the day, the meeting that had passed the Botetourt Resolutions. Miriam, with her wide, sensitive mouth, her tip-tilted nose, her hazel eyes, her air of some quaint, bright garden flower swaying on its stem, was for war and music, and both her brothers to become generals. "Or Richard can be the general, and you be a cavalryman like Cousin Fauquier! Richard can fight like Napoleon and you may fight like Ney!"

The cadet stiffened. "Thank you for nothing, Missy! Anyhow, I shan't sulk in my tents like your precious Achilles — just for a girl! Richard! 'Old Jack' says —''

"I wish, Will," murmured his mother, "that you'd say 'Major Jackson.' ''

The boy laughed. "'Old Jack' is what we call him, ma'am! The other would n't be respectful. He's never 'Major Jackson' except when he's trying to teach natural philosophy. On the drill ground he's 'Old Jack.' Richard, he says — Old Jack says — that not a man since Napoleon has understood the use of cavalry.''

Cleave, sitting with his eyes upon the portrait of his grandfather, answered dreamily: "Old Jack is probably in the right of it, Will. Cavalry is a great arm, but I shall choose the artillery.''

His mother set down her coffee cup with a little noise, Miriam shook her hair out of her eyes and came back from her own dream of the story she was reading, and Will turned as sharply as if he were on the parade ground at Lexington. "You don't think, then, that it is just all talk, Richard! You are sure that we're going to fight!"

"You fight!" cried Miriam. "Why, you are n't sixteen!"

Will flared up. "Plenty of soldiers have *died* at sixteen, Missy! 'Old Jack' knows, if you don't —''

"Children, children!" said Margaret Cleave, in a quivering voice. "It is enough to know that not a man of this family but would fight now for Virginia, just as they fought eighty odd years ago! Yes, and we women did our part then, and we would do it now! But I pray God, night and day — and Miriam, you should pray too — that this storm will not burst! As for you two who've always been sheltered and fed, who've never had a blow struck you, who've grown like tended plants in a garden — you don't know what war is! It's a great and deep Cup of Trembling! It's a scourge that reaches the backs of all! It's universal destruction — and the gift that the world should pray for is to build in peace! That is true, is n't it, Richard?"

"Yes, it is true," said Richard. "Don't, Will," as the boy began to speak. "Don't let's talk any more about it to-night. After all, a deal of storms go by — and it's a wise man who can read Time's order-book." He rose from the table. "It's like the fable. The King may die, the Ass may die, the Philosopher may die — and next Christmas may be the peacefullest on record! I'm going to ride to Lauderdale for a little while, and, if you like, I'll ask about that shotgun for you."

A few minutes later and he was out on the starlit road to Lauderdale. As he rode he thought, not of the Botetourt Resolutions, nor of Fauquier Cary, nor of Allan Gold, nor of the supper table at Three Oaks, nor of a case which he must fight through at the court house three days hence, but of Judith Cary. Dundee's hoofs beat it out on the frosty ground. *Judith Cary — Judith Cary — Judith Cary!* He thought of Greenwood, of the garden there, of a week last summer, of Maury Stafford — Stafford whom at first meeting he had thought most likable! He did not think him so to-night, there at Silver Hill, ready to go to Lauderdale to-morrow! — *Judith Cary — Judith Cary — Judith Cary.* He saw Stafford beside her — Stafford beside her — Stafford beside her —

"If she love him," said Cleave, half aloud, "he must be worthy. I will not be so petty nor so bitter! I wish her happiness. — *Judith Cary — Judith Cary.* If she love him —"

To the left a little stream brawled through frosty meadows; to the right rose a low hill black with cedars. Along the southern horizon stretched the Blue Ridge, a wall of the Titans, a rampart in the night. The line was long and clean; behind it was an effect of light, a steel-like gleaming. Above blazed the winter stars. "If she love him — if she love him —" He determined that to-night at Lauder-

dale he would try to see her alone for a minute. He would find out
— he must find out — if there were any doubt he would resolve it.
The air was very still and clear. He heard a carriage before him
on the road. It was coming toward him — a horseman, too, evidently riding beside it. Just ahead the road crossed a bridge — not a
good place for passing in the night-time. Cleave drew a little aside,
reining in Dundee. With a hollow rumbling the carriage passed the
streams. It proved to be an old-fashioned coach with lamps, drawn
by strong, slow grey horses. Cleave recognized the Silver Hill equipage. Silver Hill must have been supping with Lauderdale. Immediately he divined who was the horseman. The carriage drew alongside, the lamps making a small ring of light. "Good-evening, Mr.
Stafford!" said Cleave. The other raised his hat. "Mr. Cleave, is
it not? Good-evening, sir!" A voice spoke within the coach. "It's
Richard Cleave now! Stop, Ephraim!"

The slow grey horses came to a stand. Cleave dismounted, and
came, hat in hand, to the coach window. The mistress of Silver Hill,
a young married woman, frank and sweet, put out a hand. "Good-
evening, Mr. Cleave! You are on your way to Lauderdale? My
sister and Maury Stafford and I are carrying Judith off to Silver Hill
for the night. — She wants to give you a message —"

She moved aside and Judith took her place — Judith in fur cap
and cloak, her beautiful face just lit by the coach lamp. "It's not a
message, Richard. I — I did not know that you were coming to
Lauderdale to-night. Had I known it, I — Give my love, my dear
love, to Cousin Margaret. I would have come to Three Oaks,
only —"

"You are going home to-morrow?"

"Yes. Fauquier wishes to get back to Albemarle —"

"Will you start from Lauderdale?"

"No, from Silver Hill. He will come by for me. But had I
known," said Judith clearly, "had I known that you would ride to
Lauderdale to-night —"

"You would dutifully have stayed to see a cousin," thought
Cleave in savage pain. He spoke quietly, in the controlled but vibrant voice he had used on the hilltop. "I am sorry that I will not
see you to-night. I will ride on, however, and talk to Fauquier. You
will give my love, will you not, to all my cousins at Greenwood? I

do not forget how good all were to me last summer! — Good-bye, Judith."

She gave him her hand. It trembled a little in her glove. "Come again to Greenwood! Winter or summer, it will be glad to see you! — Good-bye, Richard."

Fur cap, cloak, beautiful face, drew back. "Go on, Ephraim!" said the mistress of Silver Hill.

The slow grey horses put themselves into motion, the coach passed on. Maury Stafford waited until Cleave had remounted. "It has been an exciting day!" he said. "I think that we are at the parting of the ways."

"I think so. You will be at Silver Hill throughout the week?"

"No, I think that I, too, will ride toward Albemarle to-morrow. It is worth something to be with Fauquier Cary a little longer."

"That is quite true," said Cleave slowly. "I do not ride to Albemarle to-morrow, and so I will pursue my road to Lauderdale and make the most of him to-night!" He turned his horse, lifted his hat. Stafford did likewise. They parted, and Cleave presently heard the rapid hoofbeat overtake the Silver Hill coach and at once change to a slower rhythm. "Now *he* is speaking with her through the window!" The sound of wheel and hoof died away. Cleave shook Dundee's reins and went on toward Lauderdale. *Judith Cary — Judith Cary — There are other things in life than love — other things than love — other things than love. . . . Judith Cary — Judith Cary. . . .*

At Three Oaks Margaret Cleave rested upon her couch by the fire. Miriam was curled on the rug with a book, an apple, and Tabitha the cat. Will mended a skate-strap and discoursed of "Old Jack."

"It's a fact, ma'am! Wilson worked the problem, gave the solution, and got from Old Jack a regular withering up! They'll all tell you, ma'am, that he excels in withering up! 'You are wrong, Mr. Wilson,' says he, in that tone of his — dry as tinder, and makes you stop like a musket-shot! 'You are always wrong. Go to your seat, sir.' Well, old Wilson went, of course, and sat there so angry he was shivering. You see he was right, and he knew it. Well, the day went on about as usual. It set in to snow, and by night there was what a western man we've got calls a 'blizzard.' Barracks like an ice house, and snowing so you couldn't see across the Campus! 'T was so

deadly cold and the lights so dismal that we rather looked forward
to taps. Up comes an orderly. 'Mr. Wilson to the Commandant's
office!' — Well, old Wilson looked startled, for he had n't done anything; but off he marches, the rest of us predicting hanging. Well,
whom d' ye reckon he found in the Commandant's office?"

"Old Jack?"

"Good marksmanship! It was Old Jack — snow all over, snow
on his coat, on his big boots, on his beard, on his cap. He lives most
a mile from the Institute, and the weather was bad, sure enough!
Well, old Wilson did n't know what to expect — most likely hot
shot, grape and canister with musketry fire thrown in — but he
saluted and stood fast. 'Mr. Wilson,' says Old Jack, 'upon returning home and going over with closed eyes after supper as is my custom the day's work, I discovered that you were right this morning
and I was wrong. Your solution was correct. I felt it to be your due
that I should tell you of my mistake as soon as I discovered it. I
apologise for the statement that you were always wrong. You may
go, sir.' Well, old Wilson never could tell what he said, but anyhow
he accepted the apology, and saluted, and got out of the room somehow and back to barracks, and we breathed on the window and
made a place through which we watched Old Jack over the Campus,
ploughing back to Mrs. Jack through the blizzard! So you see,
ma'am, things like that make us lenient to Old Jack sometimes —
though he is awfully dull and has very peculiar notions."

Margaret Cleave sat up. "Is that you, Richard?" Miriam put
down Tabitha and rose to her knees. "Did you see Cousin Judith?
Is she as beautiful as ever?" Will hospitably gave up the big chair.
"You must have galloped Dundee both ways! Did you ask about
the shotgun?"

Cleave took his seat at the foot of his mother's couch. "Yes, Will,
you may have it. — Fauquier sent his love to you, Mother, and to
Miriam. They leave for Greenwood to-morrow."

"And Cousin Judith," persisted Miriam. "What did she have on?
Did she sing to you?"

Cleave picked up her fallen book and smoothed the leaves. "She
was not there. The Silver Hill people had taken her for the night.
I passed them on the road. . . . There'll be thick ice, Will, if this
weather lasts."

Later, when good-night had been said and he was alone in his bare, high-ceiled room, he looked, not at his law books nor at the poet's words, left lying on the table, but he drew a chair before the fireplace, and from its depths he raised his eyes to his grandfather's sword slung above the mantel-shelf. He sat there, long, with the sword before him; then he rose, took a book from the case, trimmed the candles, and for an hour read of the campaigns of Fabius and Hannibal.

CHAPTER IV

GREENWOOD

THE April sunshine, streaming in at the long windows, filled the Greenwood drawing-room with dreamy gold. It lit the ancient wall-paper where the shepherds and shepherdesses wooed between garlands of roses, and it aided the tone of time among the portraits. The boughs of peach and cherry blossoms in the old potpourri jars made it welcome, and the dark, waxed floor let it lie in faded pools. Miss Lucy Cary was glad to see it as she sat by the fire knitting fine white wool into a sacque for a baby. There was a fire of hickory, but it burned low, as though it knew the winter was over. The knitter's needles glinted in the sunshine. She was forty-eight and unmarried, and it was her delight to make beautiful, soft little sacques and shoes and coverlets for every actual or prospective baby in all the wide circle of her kindred and friends.

A tap at the door, and the old Greenwood butler entered with the mail-bag. Miss Lucy, laying down her knitting, took it from him with eager fingers. *Place à la poste* — in eighteen hundred and sixty-one! She untied the string, emptied letters and papers upon the table beside her, and began to sort them. Julius, a spare and venerable piece of grey-headed ebony, an autocrat of exquisite manners and great family pride, stood back a little and waited for directions.

Miss Lucy, taking up one after another the contents of the bag, made her comments half aloud. "Newspapers, newspapers! Nothing but the twelfth and Fort Sumter! *The Whig.* — 'South Carolina is too hot-headed! — but when all's said, the North remains the aggressor.' *The Examiner.* — 'Seward's promises are not worth the paper they are written upon.' *'Faith as to Sumter fully kept — wait and see.'* That which was seen was a fleet of eleven vessels, with two hundred and eighty-five guns and twenty-four hundred men — *'carrying provisions to a starving garrison!'* Have done with cant, and welcome open war! *The Enquirer.* — 'Virginia will still succeed in mediating. Virginia from her curule chair, tranquil and fast in the

Union, will persuade, will reconcile these differences!' Amen to that!" said Miss Lucy, and took up another bundle. "*The Staunton Gazette — The Farmer's Magazine — The Literary Messenger —* My *Blackwood —* Julius!"

"Yaas, Miss Lucy."

"Julius, the Reverend Mr. Corbin Wood will be here for supper and to spend the night. Let Car'line know."

"Yaas, Miss Lucy. Easter's Jim hab obsarved to me dat Marse Edward am conducin' home a gent'man from Kentucky."

"Very well," said Miss Lucy, still sorting. "*The Winchester Times — The Baltimore Sun.* — The mint's best, Julius, in the lower bed. I walked by there this morning. — Letters for my brother! I'll readdress these, and Easter's Jim must take them to town in time for the Richmond train."

"Yaas, Miss Lucy. Easter's Jim hab imported dat Marse Berkeley Cyarter done recompense him on de road dis mahnin' ter know when Marster's comin' home."

"Just as soon," said Miss Lucy, "as the Convention brings everybody to their senses. — Three letters for Edward — one in young Beaufort Porcher's writing. Now we'll hear the Charleston version — probably he fired the first shot! — A note for me. — Julius, the Palo Alto ladies will stop by for dinner to-morrow. Tell Car'line."

"Yaas, Miss Lucy."

Miss Lucy took up a thick, bluish envelope. "From Fauquier at last — from the Red River." She opened the letter, ran rapidly over the half-dozen sheets, then laid them aside for a more leisurely perusal. "It's one of his swift, light, amusing letters! He hasn't heard about Sumter. — There'll be a message for you, Julius. There always is."

Julius's smile was as bland as sunshine. "Yaas, Miss Lucy. I 'spects dar'll be some excommunication fer me. Marse Fauquier sho' do favour Old Marster in dat. — He don' never forgit! 'Pears ter me he'd better come home — all dis heah congratulatin' backwards an' forwards wid gunpowder over de kintry! Gunpowder gwine burn ef folk git reckless!"

Miss Lucy sighed. "It will that, Julius, — it's burning now. Edward from Sally Hampton. More Charleston news! — One for Molly, three for Unity, five for Judith —"

"Miss Judith jes' sont er 'lumination by one of de chillern at de gate. She an' Marse Maury Stafford 'll be back by five. Dey ain' gwine ride furder 'n Monticello."

"Very well. Mr. Stafford will be here to supper, then. Hairston Breckinridge, too, I imagine. Tell Car'line."

Miss Lucy readdressed the letters for her brother, a year older than herself, and the master of Greenwood, a strong Whig influence in his section of the State, and now in Richmond, in the Convention there, speaking earnestly for amity, a better understanding between Sovereign States, and a happily restored Union. His wife, upon whom he had lavished an intense and chivalric devotion, was long dead, and for years his sister had taken the head of his table and cared like a mother for his children.

She sat now, at work, beneath the portrait of her own mother. As good as gold, as true as steel, warm-hearted and large-natured, active, capable, and of a sunny humour, she kept her place in the hearts of all who knew her. Not a great beauty as had been her mother, she was yet a handsome woman, clear brunette with bright, dark eyes and a most likable mouth. Miss Lucy never undertook to explain why she had not married, but her brothers thought they knew. She finished the letters and gave them to Julius. "Let Easter's Jim take them right away, in time for the evening train. — Have you seen Miss Unity?"

"Yaas, ma'am. Miss Unity am in de flower gyarden wid Marse Hairston Breckinridge. Dey 're training roses."

"Where is Miss Molly?"

"Miss Molly am in er reverence over er big book in de library."

The youngest Miss Cary's voice floated in from the hall. "No, I 'm not, Uncle Julius. Open the door wider, please!" Julius obeyed, and she entered the drawing-room with a great atlas outspread upon her arms. "Aunt Lucy, where are all these places? I can't find them. The Island and Fort Moultrie and Fort Sumter and Fort Pickens, and the rest of them! I wish when bombardments and surrenders and exciting things happen they 'd happen nearer home!"

"Child, child!" cried Miss Lucy, "don't you ever say such a thing as that again! The way you young people talk is enough to bring down a judgment upon us! It 's like Sir Walter crying 'Bonny bonny!' to the jagged lightnings. You are eighty years away from a great war, and you don't know what you are talking about, and may you never be any nearer! — Yes, Julius, that's all. Tell Easter's Jim to go right away. — Now, Molly, this is the island, and here is Fort Moultrie and here Fort Sumter. I used to know Charleston, when I was a girl. I can see now the Battery, and the blue sky, and the roses, — and the roses."

She took up her knitting and made a few stitches mechanically, then laid it down and applied herself to Fauquier Cary's letter. Molly, ensconced in a window, was already busy with her own. Presently she spoke. "Miriam Cleave says that Will passed his examination higher than any one."

"That is good!" said Miss Lucy. "They all have fine minds — the Cleaves. What else does she say?"

"She says that Richard has given her a silk dress for her birthday, and she's going to have it made with angel sleeves, and wear a hoop with it. She's sixteen — just like me."

"Richard's a good brother."

"She says that Richard has gone to Richmond — something about arms for his Company of Volunteers. Aunt Lucy —"

"Yes, dear."

"I think that Richard loves Judith."

"Molly, Molly, stop romancing!"

"I am not romancing. I don't believe in it. That week last summer he used to watch her and Mr. Stafford — and there was a look in his eyes like the knight's in the ' Arcadia '—"

"Molly! Molly!"

"And everybody knew that Mr. Stafford was a suitor. *I* knew it — Easter told me. And everybody thought that Judith was going to make him happy, only she does n't seem to have done so — at least, not yet. And there was the big tournament, and Richard and Dundee took all the rings, though I know that Mr. Stafford had expected to, and Judith let Richard crown her queen, but she looked just as pale and still! and Richard had a line between his brows, and I think he thought she would rather have had the Maid of Honour's crown that Mr. Stafford won and gave to just a little girl —"

"Molly, I am going to lock up every poetry book in the house —"

"And that was one day, and the next morning Richard looked

stern and fine, and rode away. He is n't really handsome — not like Edward, that is — only he has a way of looking so. And Judith —"
"Molly, you 're uncanny —"
"I 'm not uncanny. I can't help seeing. And the night after the tournament I slept in Judith's room, and I woke up three times, and each time there was Judith still sitting in the window, in the moonlight, and the roses Richard had crowned her with beside her in grandmother's Lowestoft bowl. And each time I asked her, 'Why don't you come to bed, Judith?' and each time she said, 'I 'm not sleepy.' Then in the morning Richard rode away, and the next day was Sunday, and Judith went to church both morning and evening, and that night she took so long to say her prayers she must have been praying for the whole world —"

Miss Lucy rose with energy. "Stop, Molly! I should n't have let you ever begin. It 's not kind to watch people like that."

"I was n't watching Judith," said Molly. "I 'd scorn to do such a thing! I was just seeing. And I never said a word about her and Richard until this instant when the sunshine came in somehow and started it. And I don't know that she likes Richard any more. I think she's trying hard to like Mr. Stafford — he wants her to so much!"

"Stop talking, honey, and don't have so many fancies, and don't read so much poetry! — Who is it coming up the drive?"

"It 's Mr. Wood on his old grey horse — like a nice, quiet knight out of the 'Faery Queen.' Did n't you ever notice, Aunt Lucy, how everybody really belongs in a book?"

On the old, broad, pillared porch the two found the second Miss Cary and young Hairston Breckinridge. Apparently in training the roses they had discovered a thorn. They sat in silence — at opposite sides of the steps — nursing the recollection. Breckinridge regarded the toe of his boot, Unity the distant Blue Ridge, until, Mr. Corbin Wood and his grey horse coming into view between the oaks, they regarded him.

"The air," said Miss Lucy, from the doorway, "is turning cold. What did you fall out about?"

"South Carolina," answered Unity, with serenity. "It 's not unlikely that our grandchildren will be falling out about South Carolina. Mr. Breckinridge is a Democrat and a fire-eater. Anyhow, Virginia is not going to secede just because he wants her to!"

The angry young disciple of Calhoun opposite was moved to reply, but at that moment Mr. Corbin Wood arriving before the steps, he must perforce run down to greet him and help him dismount. A negro had hardly taken the grey, and Mr. Wood was yet speaking to the ladies upon the porch, when two other horsemen appeared, mounted on much more fiery steeds, and coming at a gait that approached the ancient "planter's pace." "Edward and Hilary Preston," said Miss Lucy, "and away down the road, I see Judith and Mr. Stafford."

The two in advance riding up the drive beneath the mighty oaks and dismounting, the gravel space before the white-pillared porch became a scene of animation, with beautiful, spirited horses, leaping dogs, negro servants, and gay horsemen. Edward Cary sprang up the steps. "Aunt Lucy, you remember Hilary Preston! — and this is my sister Unity, Preston, — the Quakeress we call her! and this is Molly, the little one! — Mr. Wood, I am very glad to see you, sir! Aunt Lucy! Virginia Page, the two Masons, and Nancy Carter are coming over after supper with Cousin William, and I fancy that Peyton and Dabney and Rives and Lee will arrive about the same time. We might have a little dance, eh? Here's Stafford with Judith, now!"

In the Greenwood drawing-room, after candle-light, they had the little dance. Negro fiddlers, two of them, born musicians, came from the quarter. They were dressed in an elaborate best, they were as suavely happy as tropical children, and beamingly eager for the credit in the dance, as in all things else, of " de fambly." Down came the bow upon the strings, out upon the April night floated " Money Musk!" All the furniture was pushed aside, the polished floor gave back the lights. From the walls men and women of the past smiled upon a stage they no longer trod, and between garlands of roses the shepherds and shepherdesses pursued their long, long courtship. The night was mild, the windows partly open, the young girls dancing in gowns of summery stuff. Their very wide skirts were printed over with pale flowers, their bodices were cut low, with a fall of lace against the white bosom. The hair was worn smooth and drawn over the ear, with on either side a bright cluster of blossoms. The fiddlers played " Malbrook s'en va-t-en guerre." Laughter, quick and gay, or low and ripplingly sweet, flowed through the old room. The dances were all square, for there existed in the country a prejudice against round dancing. Once Edward Cary pushed a friend down on the piano stool, and whirled with Nancy Carter into the middle of the room in a waltz. But Miss Lucy shook her head at her nephew, and Cousin William gazed sternly at Nancy, and the fiddlers looked scandalized. Scipio, the old, old one, who could remember the Lafayette ball, held his bow awfully poised.

Judith Cary, dressed in a soft, strange, dull blue, and wearing a little crown of rosy flowers, danced along like the lady of Saint Agnes Eve. Maury Stafford marked how absent was her gaze, and he hoped that she was dreaming of their ride that afternoon, of the clear green woods and the dogwood stars, and of some words that he had said. In these days he was hoping against hope. Well off and well-bred, good to look at, pleasant of speech, at times indolent, at times ardent, a little silent on the whole, and never failing to match the occasion with just the right shade of intelligence, a certain grip and essence in this man made itself felt like the firm bed of a river beneath the flowing water. He was not of Albemarle; he was of a tide-water county, but he came to Albemarle and stayed with kindred, and no one doubted that he strove for an Albemarle bride. It was the opinion of the county people that he would win her. It was hard to see why he should not. He was desperately in love, and far too determined to take the first " No " for an answer. Until the last eight months it had been his own conclusion that he would win.

The old clock in the hall struck ten; in an interval between the dances Judith slipped away. Stafford wished to follow her, but Cousin William held him like the Ancient Mariner and talked of the long past on the Eastern Shore. Judith, entering the library, came upon the Reverend Mr. Corbin Wood, deep in a great chair and a calf-bound volume. " Come in, come in, Judith my dear, and tell me about the dance."

" It is a pretty dance," said Judith. " Do you think it would be very wrong of you to watch it ? "

Mr. Wood, the long thin fingers of one hand lightly touching the long thin fingers of the other hand, considered the matter. " Why, no," he said in a mellow and genial voice. " Why, no — it is always hard for me to think that anything beautiful is wrong. It is this way. I go into the drawing-room and watch you. It is, as you say, a very pretty sight! But if I find it so and still keep a long face, I am to myself something of a hypocrite. And if I testify my delight, if I am absorbed in your evolutions, and think only of springtime and growing things, and show my thought, then to every one of you, and indeed to myself too, my dear, I am something out of my character! So it seems better to sit here and read Jeremy Taylor."

"You have the book upside down," said Judith softly. Her old friend put on his glasses, gravely looked, and reversed the volume. He laughed, and then he sighed. "I was thinking of the country, Judith. It's the only book that is interesting now — and the recital's tragic, my dear; the recital's tragic!"

From the hall came Edward Cary's voice, " Judith, Judith, we want you for the reel!"

In the drawing-room the music quickened. Scipio played with all his soul, his eyes uprolled, his lips parted, his woolly head nodding, his vast foot beating time; young Eli, black and shining, seconded him ably; without the doors and windows gathered the house servants, absorbed, admiring, laughing without noise. The April wind, fragrant of greening forests, ploughed land, and fruit trees, blew in and out the long, thin curtains. Faster went the bow upon the fiddle, the room became more brilliant and more dreamy. The flowers in the old, old blue jars grew pinker, mistier, the lights had halos, the portraits smiled forthright; but from greater distances, the loud ticking of the clock without the door changed to a great rhythm, as though Time were using a violin string. The laughter swelled, waves of brightness went through the ancient room. They danced the " Virginia Reel."

Miss Lucy, sitting beside Cousin William on the sofa, raised her head. "Horses are coming up the drive!"

"That's not unusual," said Cousin William, with a smile. "Why do you look so startled?"

"I don't know. I thought — but that's not possible." Miss Lucy half rose, then took her seat again. Cousin William listened. "The air's very clear to-night, and there must be an echo. It does sound like a great body of horsemen coming out of the distance."

"Balance corners!" called Eli. "Swing yo' partners! — *Sachay!*"

The music drew to a height, the lights burned with a fuller power, the odour of the flowers spread, subtle and intense. The dancers moved more and more quickly. "There are only three horses," said Cousin William, "two in front and one behind. Two gentlemen and a servant. Now they are crossing the little bridge. Shall I go see who they are?"

Miss Lucy rose. Outside a dog had begun an excited and joyous barking. "That's Gelert! It's my brother he is welcoming!" From the porch came a burst of negro voices. "Who dat comin' up de drive? Who dat, Gelert? — Dat's marster! — Go 'way, 'ooman! don' tell me he in Richmon'! Dat's marster!"

The reel ended suddenly. There was a sound of dismounting, a step upon the porch, a voice. "Father, father!" cried Judith, and ran into the hall.

A minute later the master of Greenwood, his children about him, entered the drawing-room. Behind him came Richard Cleave. There was a momentary confusion of greeting; it passed, and from the two men, travel-stained, fatigued, pale with some suppressed emotion, there sped to the gayer company a subtle wave of expectation and alarm. Miss Lucy was the first whom it reached. "What is it, brother?" she said quickly. Cousin William followed, "For God's sake, Cary, what has happened?" Edward spoke from beside the piano, "Has it come, father?" With his words his hand fell upon the keys, suddenly and startlingly upon the bass.

The vibrations died away. "Yes, it has come, Edward," said the master. Holding up his hand for silence, he moved to the middle of the room, and stood there, beneath the lit candles, the swinging prisms of the chandelier. Peale's portrait of his father hung upon the wall. The resemblance was strong between the dead and the living.

"Be quiet, every one," he said now, speaking very quietly himself. "Is all the household here? Open the window wide, Julius. Let the house servants come inside. If there are men and women from the quarter on the porch, tell them to come closer, so that all may hear." Julius opened the long windows, the negroes came in, Mammy in her turban, Easter and Chloe the seamstresses, Car'line the cook, the housemaids, the dining-room boys, the young girls who waited upon the daughters of the house, Isham the coachman, Shirley the master's body-servant, Edward's boy Jeames, and the nondescript half dozen who helped the others. The ruder sort upon the porch, "outdoor" negroes drawn by the music and the spectacle from the quarter, approached the windows. Together they made a background, dark and exotic, splashed with bright colour, for the Aryan stock ranged to the front. The drawing-room was filled. Mr. Corbin Wood had come noiselessly in from the library, none was missing. Guests, family, and servants stood motionless. There was that in the bearing of the master which seemed, in the silence, to detach itself, and to come toward them like an emanation, cold, pure, and quiet, determined and imposing. He spoke. "I supposed that you had heard the news. Along the railroad and in Charlottesville it was known; there were great crowds. I see it has not reached you. Mr. Lincoln has called for seventy-five thousand troops with which to procure South Carolina and the Gulf States' return into the Union. He — the North — demands of Virginia eight thousand men to be used for this purpose. She will not give them. We have fought long and patiently for peace; now we fight no more on that field. Matters have brought me for a few hours to Albemarle. To-morrow I return to Richmond, to the Convention, to do that which I never thought to do, to give my voice for the secession of Virginia."

There was a general movement throughout the room. "So!" said Corbin Wood very softly. Cousin William rose from the sofa, drew a long breath, and smote his hands together. "It had to come, Cary, it had to come! North and South, we've pulled in different directions for sixty years! The cord had to snap." From among the awed servants came the voice of old Isham the coachman, "'Secession!' What dat wuhd 'Secession,' marster?"

"That word," answered Warwick Cary, "means, Isham, that Virginia leaves of her free will a Union that she entered of her free will. The terms of that Union have been broken; she cannot, within it, preserve her integrity, her dignity, and her liberty. Therefore she uses the right which she reserved — the right of self-preservation. Unterrified she entered the Union, unterrified she leaves it."

He paused, standing in the white light of the candles, among his children, kinsmen, friends, and slaves. To the last, if ingrained affection, tolerance, and understanding, quiet guidance, patient care, a kindly heart, a ready ear, a wise and simple dealing with a simple, not wise folk, are true constituents of friendship, he was then their friend as well as their master. They with all the room hung now upon his words. The light wind blew the curtains out like streamers, the candles flickered, petals from the blossoms in the jars fell on the floor, the clock that had ticked in the hall for a hundred years struck eleven. "There will be war," said the master. "There should not be, but there will be. How long it will last, how deadly its nature, no man can tell! The North has not thought us in earnest, but the North is mistaken. We are in earnest. War will be for us a desperate thing. We are utterly unprepared; we are seven million against twenty million, an agricultural country against a manufacturing one. We have little shipping, they have much. They will gain command of the sea. If we can get our cotton to Europe we will have gold; therefore, if they can block our ports they will do it. There are those who think the powers will intervene and that we will have England or France for our ally. I am not of them. The odds are greatly against us. We have struggled for peace; apparently we cannot have it; now we will fight for the conviction that is in us. It will be for us a war of defence, with the North for the invader, and Virginia will prove the battle-ground. I hold it very probable that there are men here to-night who will die in battle. You women are going to suffer — to suffer more than we. I think of my mother and of my wife, and I know that you will neither hold us back nor murmur. All that is courageous, all that is heroically devoted, Virginia expects and will receive from you." He turned to face more fully the crowding negroes. "To every man and woman of you here, not the less my friends that you are called my servants, emancipated at my death, every one of you, by that will which I read to you years ago, each of you having long known that you have but to ask for your freedom in my lifetime to have it — to you all I speak. Julius, Shirley, Isham, Scipio, Mammy, and the rest of you, there are hard times coming! My son and I will go to war. Much will be left in your trust. As I and mine have tried to deal by you, so do you deal by us —"

Shirley raised his voice. "Don' leave nothin' in trus' ter me, marster! Kase I's gwine wid you! Sho! Don' I know dat when gent'men fight dey gwine want dey bes' shu't, an dey hat breshed jes' right! I'se gwine wid you!" A face as dark as charcoal, with rolling eyes, looked over mammy's shoulder. "Ain' Marse Edward gwine? 'Cose he gwine! Den Jeames gwine, too!" A murmuring sound came from the band of servants. They began to rock themselves, to strike with the tongue the roof of the mouth, to work toward a camp-meeting excitement. Out on the porch Big Mimy, the washerwoman, made herself heard. "Des' let um *dar* ter come fightin' Greenwood folk! Des' let me hab at um with er tub er hot water!" Scipio, old and withered as a last year's reed, began to sway violently. Suddenly he broke into a chant. "Ain' I done heard about hit er million times? Dar wuz Gineral Lafayette an' dar wuz Gineral Rochambeau, an' dar wuz Gineral Washington! An' dar wuz Light Horse Harry Lee, an' dar wuz Marse Fauquier Cary dat wuz marster's gran'father, an' Marse Edward Churchill! An' dey took de swords, an' dey made to stack de ahms, an' dey druv — an' dey druv King Pharaoh into de sea! Ain' dey gwine ter do hit ergain? Tell me dat! Ain' dey gwine ter do hit ergain?"

The master signed with his hand. "I trust you — one and all. I'll speak to you again before I go away to-morrow, but now we'll say good-night. Good-night, Mammy, Isham, Scipio, Easter, all of you!"

They went, one by one, each with his bow or her curtsy. Mammy paused a moment to deliver her pronunciamento. "Don' you fret, marster! I ain' gwine let er soul *tech* one er my chillern!" Julius followed her. "Dat's so, marster! An' Gawd Ermoughty knows I'se gwine always prohibit jes' de same care ob de fambly an' de silver!"

When they were gone came the leave-taking of the guests, of all who were not to sleep that night at Greenwood. Maury Stafford was to stay, and Mr. Corbin Wood. Of those going Cousin William was the only one of years; the others were all young, — young men, young women on the edge of an unthought-of experience, on the brink of a bitter, tempestuous, wintry sea. They did not see it so; there was danger, of course, but they thought of splendour and heroism, of trumpet calls and waving banners. They were much excited; the young girls half frightened, the men wild to be at home, with plans for volunteering. "Good-bye, and good-bye, and good-bye again! and when it's all over — it will be over in three months, will it not, sir? — we'll finish the 'Virginia Reel!'"

The large, old coach and the saddle horses were brought around.

They drove or rode away, through the April night, by the forsythia and the flowering almond, between the towering oaks, over the bridge with a hollow sound. Those left behind upon the Greenwood porch, clustered at the top of the steps, between the white pillars, stood in silence until the noise of departure had died away. Warwick Cary, his arm around Molly, his hand in Judith's, Unity's cheek resting against his shoulder, then spoke. "It is the last merrymaking, poor children! Well — 'Time and tide run through the longest day!'" He disengaged himself, kissed each of his daughters, and turned toward the lighted hall. "There are papers in the library which I must go over to-night. Edward, you had best come with me."

Father and son left the porch. Miss Lucy, too, went indoors, called Julius, and began to give directions. Ready and energetic, she never wasted time in wonder at events. The event once squarely met, she struck immediately into the course it demanded, cheerfully, without repining, and with as little attention as possible to forebodings. Her voice died away toward the back of the house. The moon was shining, and the lawn lay chequered beneath the trees. Corbin Wood, who had been standing in a brown study, began to descend the steps. "I'll take a little walk, Judith, my dear," he said, "and think it over! I'll let myself in." He was gone walking rapidly, not toward the big gate and the road, but across to the fields, a little stream, and a strip that had been left of primeval forest. Unity and Molly, moving back to the doorstep, sat there whispering together in the light from the hall. Judith and Richard were left almost alone, Judith leaning against a white pillar, Cleave standing a step or two below her.

"You have been in Richmond?" she said. "Molly had a letter from Miriam —"

"Yes, I went to find, if possible, rifled muskets for my company. I did not do as well as I had hoped — the supply is dreadfully small — but I secured a few. Two thirds of us will have to manage, until we can do better, with the smoothbore and even with the old flintlock. I have seen a breech-loader made in the North. I wish to God we had it!"

"You are going back to Botetourt?"

"As soon as it is dawn. The company will at once offer its services to the governor. Every moment now is important."

"At dawn. . . . You will be its captain?"

"I suppose so. We will hold immediately an election of officers — and that's as pernicious a method of officering companies and regiments as can be imagined! 'They are volunteers, offering all— they can be trusted to choose their leaders.' I don't perceive the sequence."

"I think that you will make a good captain."

He smiled. "Why, then, the clumsy thing will work for once! I'll try to be a good captain. — The clock is striking. I do not know when nor how I shall see Greenwood again. Judith, you'll wish me well?"

"Will I wish you well, Richard? Yes, I will wish you well. Do not go at dawn."

He looked at her. "Do you ask me to wait?"

"Yes, I ask you. Wait till — till later in the morning. It is so sad to say good-bye."

"I will wait then." The light from the hall lay unbroken on the doorstep. Molly and Unity had disappeared. A little in yellow lamplight, chiefly in silver moonlight the porch lay deserted and quiet before the murmuring oaks, above the fair downward sweep of grass and flowers. "It is long," said Cleave, "since I have been here. The day after the tournament —"

"Yes."

He came nearer. "Judith, was it so hard to forgive — that tournament? You had both crowns, after all."

"I do not know," said Judith, "what you mean."

"Do you remember — do you remember last Christmas when, going to Lauderdale, I passed you on your way to Silver Hill?"

"Yes, I remember."

"I was on my way to Lauderdale, not to see Fauquier, but to see you. I wished to ask you a question — I wished to make certain. And then you passed me going to Silver Hill, and I said, 'It is certainly so.' I have believed it to be so. I believe it now. And yet I ask you to-night — Judith —"

"You ask me what?" said Judith. "Here is Mr. Stafford."

Maury Stafford came into the silver space before the house, glanced upward, and mounted the steps. "I walked as far as the gate with Breckinridge. He tells me, Mr. Cleave, that he is of your Company of Volunteers."

"Yes."

"I shall turn my face toward the sea to-morrow. Heigho! War is folly at the best. And you? —"

"I leave Greenwood in the morning."

The other, leaning against a pillar, drew toward him a branch of climbing rose. The light from the hall struck against him. He always achieved the looking as though he had stepped from out a master-canvas. To-night this was strongly so. "In the morning! You waste no time. Unfortunately I cannot get away for another twenty-four hours." He let the rose bough go and turned to Judith. His voice when he spoke to her became at once low and musical. There was light enough to see the flush in his cheek, the ardour in his eye. "'Unfortunately!' What a word to use in leaving Greenwood! No! For me most fortunately I must wait another four and twenty hours."

"Greenwood," said Judith, "will be lonely without old friends." As she spoke, she moved toward the house door. In passing a great porch chair her dress caught on the twisted wood. Both men started forward, but Stafford was much the nearer to her. Released, she thanked him with grave kindness, went on to the doorway, and there turned, standing a moment in her drapery of dim blue, in the two lights. She had about her a long scarf of black lace, and now she drew it closer, holding it beneath her chin with a hand slender, fine, and strong. "Good-night," she said. "It is not long to morning, now. Good-night, Mr. Stafford. Good-night, Richard."

The "good-night" that Stafford breathed after her needed no commentary. It was that of the lover confessed. Cleave, from his side of the porch, looked across and thought, "I will be a fool no longer. She was merely kind to me — a kindness she could afford. 'Do not go till morning — dear cousin!'" There was a silence on the Greenwood porch, a white-pillared rose-embowered space, paced ere this by lovers and rivals. It was broken by Mr. Corbin Wood, returning from the fields and mounting the moonlit steps. "I have thought it out," he said. "I am going as chaplain." He touched Stafford, of whom he was fond, on the shoulder. "It's the sweetest night, and as I came along I loved every leaf of the trees and every blade of grass. It's home, it's fatherland, it's sacred soil, it's mother, dear Virginia —"

He broke off, said good-night, and entered the house.

The younger men prepared to follow. "The next time that we meet," said Stafford, "may be in the thunder of the fight. I have an idea that I'll know it if you're there. I'll look out for you."

"And I for you," said Cleave. Each had spoken with entire courtesy and a marked lack of amity. There was a moment's pause, a feeling as of the edge of things. Cleave, not tall, but strongly made, with his thick dark hair, his tanned, clean shaven, squarely cut face, stood very straight, in earnest and formidable. The other, leaning against the pillar, was the fairer to look at, and certainly not without his own strength. The one thought, "I will know," and the other thought, "I believe you to be my foe of foes. If I can make you leave this place early, without speaking to her, I will do it."

Cleave turned squarely. "You have reason to regret leaving Greenwood —"

Stafford straightened himself against the pillar, studied for a moment the seal ring which he wore, then spoke with deliberation. "Yes. It is hard to quit Paradise for even such a tourney as we have before us. Ah well! when one comes riding back the welcome will be the sweeter!"

They went indoors. Later, alone in a pleasant bedroom, the man who had put a face upon matters which the facts did not justify, opened wide the window and looked out upon moon-flooded hill and vale. "Do I despise myself?" he thought. "If it was false to-night I may yet make it truth to-morrow. All's fair in love and war, and God knows my all is in this war! Judith! Judith! Judith! look my way, not his!" He stared into the night, moodily enough. His room was at the side of the house. Below lay a slope of flower garden, then a meadow, a little stream, and beyond, a low hilltop crowned by the old Greenwood burying-ground. "Why not sleep? . . . Love is war — the underlying, the primeval, the immemorial. . . . All the same, Maury Stafford —"

In her room upon the other side of the house, Judith had found the candles burning on the dressing-table. She blew them out, parted the window curtains of flowered dimity, and curling herself on the window-seat, became a part of the April night. Crouching there in the scented air, beneath the large, mild stars, she tried to think of Virginia and the coming war, but at the end of every avenue she came upon a morning hour. Perhaps it would be in the flower garden, perhaps in the summer-house, perhaps in the plantation woods where the windflower and the Judas tree were in bloom. Her heart was hopeful. So lifted and swept was the world to-night, so ready for great things, that her great thing also ought to happen, her rose of happiness ought to bloom. "After to-morrow," she said to herself, "I will think of Virginia, and I'll begin to help."

Toward daybreak, lying in the large four-post bed beneath the white tasselled canopy, she fell asleep. The sun was an hour high when she awoke. Hagar, the girl who waited upon her, came in and flung wide the shutters. "Dar's er mockin' bird singin' mighty neah dish-yer window! Reckon he gwine mek er nes' in de honeysuckle."

"I meant to wake up very early," said Judith. "Is any one downstairs yet, Hagar? — No, not that dress. The one with the little flowers."

"Dar ain' nobody down yit," said Hagar. "Marse Richard Cleave, he done come down early, 'way 'bout daybreak. He got one of de stable-men ter saddle he horse an' he done rode er way. Easter, she come in de house jes' ez he wuz leavin', en he done tol' her ter tell marster dat he'd done been thinkin' ez how dar wuz so much ter do dat he'd better mek an early start, en he lef' good-bye fer de fambly. Easter, she ax him won't he wait 'twel the ladies come down, en he say No. 'T wuz better fer him ter go now. En he went. Dar ain' nobody else come down less'n hits Marse Maury Stafford. — Miss Judith, honey, yo' ain' got enny mo' blood in yo' face than dat ar counterpane! I gwine git yo' er cup er coffee!"

CHAPTER V

THUNDER RUN

ALLAN GOLD, teaching the school on Thunder Run, lodged at the tollgate halfway down the mountain. His parents were dead, his brothers moved away. The mountain girls were pretty and fain, and matches were early made. Allan made none; he taught with conscientiousness thirty tow-headed youngsters, read what books he could get, and worked in the toll-gate keeper's small, bright garden. He had a passion for flowers. He loved, too, to sit with his pipe upon the rude porch of the toll-house, fanned by the marvellous mountain air, and look down over ridges of chestnut and oak to the mighty valley below, and across to the far blue wall of the Alleghenies.

The one-roomed, log-built schoolhouse stood a mile from the road across the mountains, upon a higher level, in a fairy meadow below the mountain clearings. A walnut tree shaded it, Thunder Run leaped by in cascades, on either side the footpath Allan had planted larkspur and marigolds. Here, on a May morning, he rang the bell, then waited patiently until the last free-born imp elected to leave the delights of a minnow-filled pool, a newly discovered redbird's nest, and a blockhouse in process of construction against imaginary Indians. At last all were seated upon the rude benches in the dusky room, — small tow-headed Jacks and Jills, heirs to a field of wheat or oats, a diminutive tobacco patch, a log cabin, a piece of uncleared forest, or perhaps the blacksmith's forge, a small mountain store, or the sawmill down the stream. Allan read aloud the Parable of the Sower, and they all said the Lord's Prayer; then he called the Blue Back Speller class. The spelling done, they read from the same book about the Martyr and his Family. Geography followed, with an account of the Yang-tse-Kiang and an illustration of a pagoda, after which the ten-year-olds took the front bench and read of little Hugh and old Mr. Toil. This over, the whole school fell to ciphering. They ciphered for half an hour, and then they had a history lesson, which told of one Curtius who leaped into a gulf to save his country. History being followed by the writing lesson, all save the littlest present began laboriously to copy a proverb of Solomon.

Half-past eleven and recess drawing on! The scholars grew restless. Could the bird's nest still be there? Were the minnows gone from the pool? Had the blockhouse fallen down? Would writing go on forever? — The bell rang; the teacher, whom they liked well enough, was speaking. *No more school!* Recess forever — or until next year, which was the same thing! No more geography, reading, writing, arithmetic, and spelling; no more school! Hurrah! Of course the redbird's nest was swinging on the bough, and the minnows were in the pool, and the blockhouse was standing, and the sun shining with all its might! "All the men about here are going to fight," said Allan. "I am going, too. So we'll have to stop school until the war is over. Try not to forget what I've taught you, children, and try to be good boys and girls. You boys must learn now to be men, for you'll have to look after things and the women. And you girls must help your mothers all you can. It's going to be hard times, little folk! You've played a long time at fighting Indians, and latterly I've noticed you playing at fighting Yankees. Playtime's over now. It's time to work, to think, and to try to help. You can't fight for Virginia with guns and swords, but every woman and child, every young boy and old man in Virginia can make the hearts easier of those who go to fight. You be good boys and girls and do your duty here on Thunder Run, and God will count you as his soldiers just the same as if you were fighting down there in the valley, or before Richmond, or on the Potomac, or wherever we're going to fight. You're going to be good children; I know it!" He closed the book before him. "School's over now. When we take in again we'll finish the Roman History — I've marked the place." He left his rude old desk and the little platform, and stepping down amongst his pupils, gave to each his hand. Then he divided among them the scanty supply of books, patiently answered a scurry of questions, and outside, upon the sunshiny sward, with the wind in the walnut tree and the larkspur beginning to bloom, said good-bye once more. Jack and Jill gave no further thought to the bird's nest, the minnows in the pool, the unfinished blockhouse. Off they rushed, up the side of the mountain, over the wooded hills, along Thunder Run, where it leaped from pool to pool. They must be home with the news! No more school — no more school! And was father going — and were Johnny and Sam and Dave? Where were they going to fight? As far as the big sawmill? as far away as the *river*? Were the dogs going, too?

Allan Gold, left alone, locked the schoolhouse door, walked slowly along the footpath between the flowers he had planted, and, standing by Thunder Run, looked for awhile at the clear, brown water, then, with a long breath and a straightening of the shoulders, turned away. "Good-bye, little place!" he said, and strode down the ravine to the road and the toll-house.

The tollgate keeper, old and crippled, sat on the porch beside a wooden bucket of well-water. The county newspaper lay on his knee, and he was reading the items aloud to his wife, old, too, but active, standing at her ironing-board within the kitchen door. A cat purred in the sunshine, and all the lilac bushes were in bloom. "'Ten companies from this County,'" read the tollgate keeper; "'Ten companies from Old Botetourt, — The Mountain Rifles, the Fincastle Rifles, the Botetourt Dragoons, the Zion Hill Company, the Roaring Run men, the Thunder Run —' Air you listenin', Sairy?"

Sairy brought a fresh iron from the stove. "I am a-listenin', Tom. 'Pears to me I ain't done nothing but listen sence last December! It's got to be sech a habit that I ketch myself waking up at night to listen. But I've got to iron as well as listen, or Allan Gold won't have any shirts fit to fight in! Go on reading, I hear ye."

"It's an editorial," said Tom weightily. "'Three weeks have passed since war was declared. At once Governor Letcher called for troops; at once the call was answered. We have had in Botetourt, as all over Virginia, as through all the Southern States, days of excitement, sleepless nights, fanfare of preparation, drill, camp, orders, counter-orders, music, tears and laughter of high-hearted women —'"

Sairy touched her iron with a wet finger-tip. "This time next year thar'll be more tears, I reckon, and less laughter! I ain't a girl, and I don't hold with war — Well?"

"'Beat of drums and call of fife, heroic ardour and the cult of Mars —'"

"Of — ?"

"That's the name of the heathen idol they used to sacrifice men to. 'Parties have vanished from county and State. Whigs and Democrats, Unionists and Secessionists, Bell and Everett men and Breckinridge men — all are gone. There is now but one party — *the party of the invaded.* A month ago there was division of opinion; it does not exist to-day. It died in the hour when we were called upon to deny our convictions, to sacrifice our principles, to juggle with the Constitution, to play fast and loose, to blow hot and cold, to say one thing and do another, to fling our honour to the winds and to assist in coercing Sovereign States back into a Union which they find intolerable! It died in the moment when we saw, no longer the Confederation of Republics to which we had acceded, but a land whirling toward Empire. It is dead. There are no Union men to-day in Virginia. The ten Botetourt companies hold themselves under arms. At any moment may come the order to the front. The county has not spared her first-born — no, nor the darling of his mother! It is a rank and file different from the Old World's rank and file. The rich man marches, a private soldier, beside the poor man; the lettered beside the unlearned; the planter, the lawyer, the merchant, the divine, the student side by side with the man from the plough, the smith, the carpenter, the hunter, the boatman, the labourer by the day. Ay, rank and file, you are different; and the army that you make will yet stir the blood and warm the heart of the world!' "

The ironer stretched another garment upon the board. "If only we fight half as well as that thar newspaper talks! Is the editor going?"

"Yes, he is," said the old man. "It's fine talking, but it's mighty near God's truth all the same!" He moved restlessly, then took his crutch and beat a measure upon the sunken floor. His faded blue eyes, set in a thousand wrinkles, stared down upon and across the great view of ridge and spur and lovely valleys in between. The air at this height was clear and strong as wine, the noon sunshine bright, not hot, the murmur in the leaves and the sound of Thunder Run rather crisp and gay than slumbrous. "If it had to come," said Tom, "why couldn't it ha' come when I was younger? If 't weren't for that darned fall out o' Nofsinger's hayloft I'd go, anyhow!"

"Then I see," retorted Sairy, "what Brother Dame meant by good comin' out o' evil! — Here's Christianna."

A girl in a homespun gown and a blue sunbonnet came up the road and unlatched the little gate. She had upon her arm a small basket such as the mountain folk weave. "Good-mahnin', Mrs. Cole. Good-mahnin', Mr. Cole. It cert'ny is fine weather the mountain's having."

"Yes, it's fine weather, Christianna," answered the old man. "Come in, come in, and take a cheer!"

Christianna came up the tiny path and seated herself, not in the split-bottomed chair to which he waved her, but upon the edge of the porch, with her back to the sapling that served for a pillar, and with her small, ill-shod feet just touching a bed of heartsease. She pushed back her sunbonnet. "Dave an' Billy told us good-bye yesterday. Pap is going down the mountain to-day. Dave took the shotgun an' pap has grandpap's flintlock, but Billy did n't have a gun. He said he'd take one from the Yanks."

"Sho!" exclaimed Sairy. "Did n't he have no weapon at all?"

"He had a hunting-knife that was grandpap's. An' the blacksmith made him what he called a spear-head. He took a bit o' rawhide and tied it to an oak staff, an' he went down the mountain *so!*" Her drawling voice died, then rose again. "I'll miss Billy — I surely will!" It failed again, and the heartsease at her feet ran together into a little sea of purple and gold. She took the cape of her sunbonnet and with it wiped away the unaccustomed tears.

"Sho!" said Sairy. "We'll all miss Billy. I reckon we all that stay at home air going to have our fill o' missing! — What have you got in your basket, honey?"

Christianna lifted a coloured handkerchief and drew from the basket a little bag of flowered chintz, roses and tulips, drawn up with a blue ribbon. "My! that's pretty," exclaimed Sairy. "Whar did you get the stuff?"

The girl regarded the bag with soft pride. "Last summer I toted a bucket o' blackberries down to Three Oaks an' sold them to Mrs. Cleave. An' she was making a valance for her tester bed, an' I thought the stuff was mighty pretty, an' she gave me a big piece! an' I put it away in my picture box with my glass beads. For the ribbon — I'd saved a little o' my berry money, an' I walked to Buchanan an' bought it." She drew a long breath. "My land!

't was fine in the town — High Street just crowded with Volunteers, and the drums were beating." Her eyes shone like stars. "It's right hard on women to stay at home an' have all the excitement go away. There don't seem to be nothin' to make it up to us —"

Sairy put away the ironing-board. "Sho! We've just got the little end, as usual. What's in the bag, child?"

"Thar's thread and needles in a needle-case, an' an emery," said Christianna. "I wanted a little pair of scissors that was at Mr. Moelick's, but I didn't have enough. They'd be right useful, I reckon, to a soldier, but I couldn't get them. I wondered if the bag ought to be smaller — but he'll have room for it, I reckon? *I* think it's right pretty."

Old Tom Cole leaned over, took the tiny, flowery affair, and balanced it gently upon a horny hand. "Of course he'll have room for it! An' it's jest as pretty as they make them! — An' here he comes now, down the mountain, to thank ye himself!"

Allan Gold thanked Christianna with simplicity. He had never had so pretty a thing, and he would keep it always, and every time he looked at it he would see Thunder Run and hear the bees in the flowers. It was very kind of her to make it for him, and — and he would keep it always. Christianna listened, and then, with her eyes upon the heartsease, began to say good-bye in her soft, drawling voice. "You're going down the mountain to-day, Mrs. Cole says. Well, good-bye. An' pap's goin' too, an' Dave an' Billy have gone. I reckon the birds won't be singin' when you come again — thar'll be ice upon the creeks, I reckon." She drew her shoulders together as though she shivered for all the May sunshine. "Well, good-bye."

"I'll walk a piece of the road with you," said Allan, and the two went out of the gate together.

Sairy, a pan of biscuits for dinner in her hand, looked after them. "There's a deal of things I'd do differently if I was a man! What was the use in sayin' that every time he looked at that thar bag he'd see Thunder Run? Thunder Run ain't a-keerin' if he sees it or if he don't see it! He might ha' said that every time he laid eyes on them roses he'd see Christianna! — Thar's a wagon comin' up the road an' a man on horseback behind. Here, I'll take the toll —"

"No, I'll take it myself," said Tom, reaching for the tobacco box which served as bank. "If I can't 'list, I reckon I can get all the news that's goin'!" He hobbled out to the gate. "Mornin', Jake! Mornin', Mr. Robinson! Yes, 't is fine weather for the crops. What —"

"The Rockbridge companies are ordered off! Craig and Bedford are going, too. They say Botetourt's time will come next. Lord! we used to think forest fires and floods were exciting! Down there in camp the boys can't sleep at night — every time a rooster crows they think it's Johnny Mason's bugle and the order to the front! Ain't Allan Gold going?"

Sairy spoke from the path. "Course he's goin' — he and twenty more from Thunder Run. I reckon Thunder Run ain't goin' to lag behind! Even Steve Dagg's goin' — though I look for him back afore the battle. Jim's goin', too, to see what he can make out of it — 't won't harm no one, I reckon, if he makes six feet o' earth."

"They're the only trash in the lot," put in Tom. "The others are first-rate — though a heap of them are powerfully young."

"Thar's Billy Maydew, for instance," said Sairy. "Sho! Billy is too young to go —"

"All the cadets have gone from Lexington, remarked the man on horseback. "They've gone to Richmond to act as drill-masters — every boy of them with his head as high as General Washington's! I was at Lexington and saw them go. Good Lord! most of them just children — that Will Cleave, for instance, that used to beg a ride on my load of hay! Four companies of them marched away at noon, with their muskets shining in the sun. All the town was up and out — the minister blessing them, and the people crying and cheering! Major T. J. Jackson led them."

"The Thunder Run men are going in Richard Cleave's company. He sets a heap o' store by Allan, an' wanted him for second lieutenant, but the men elected Matthew Coffin —"

"Coffin's bright enough," said Tom, "but Allan's more dependable. — Well, good-day, gentlemen, an' thank ye both!"

The wagon lumbered down the springtime road and the man on horseback followed. The tollgate keeper hobbled back to his chair, and Sairy returned to her dinner. Allan was going away, and she was making gingerbread because he liked it. The spicy, warm fragrance permeated the air, homely and pleasant as the curl of blue smoke above the chimney, the little sunny porch, the buzzing of the bees in the lilacs. "Here's Allan now," said Tom. "Hey, Allan! you must have gone a good bit o' the way?"

"I went all the way," answered Allan, lifting the gourd of well-water to his lips. "Poor little thing! she is breaking her heart over Billy's going."

Sairy, cutting the gingerbread into squares, held the knife suspended. "Have ye been talkin' about Billy all this time?"

"Yes," said Allan. "I saw that she was unhappy and I tried to cheer her up. I'll look out for the boy in every way I can." He took the little bag of chintz from the bench where he had laid it when he went with Christianna, and turned to the rude stair that led to his room in the half story. He was not kin to the tollgate keepers, but he had lived long with them and was very fond of both. "I'll be down in a moment, Aunt Sairy," he said. "I wonder when I'll smell or taste your gingerbread again, and I don't see how I am going to tell you and Tom good-bye!" He was gone, humming "Annie Laurie" as he went.

"'T would be just right an' fittin'," remarked Mrs. Cole, "if half the men in the world went about with a piece of pasteboard round their necks an' written on it, 'Pity the Blind!' Dinner's most ready, Tom, — an' I don't see how I'm goin' to tell him good-bye myself."

An hour later, in his small bare room underneath the mossy roof, with the small square window through which the breezes blew, Allan stood and looked about him. Dinner was over. It had been something of a feast, with unusual dainties, and a bunch of lilacs upon the table. Sairy had on a Sunday apron. The three had not been silent either; they had talked a good deal, but without much thought of what was said. Perhaps it was because of this that the meal had seemed so vague, and that nothing had left a taste in the mouth. It was over, and Allan was making ready to depart.

On the floor, beside the chest of drawers, stood a small hair trunk. A neighbour with a road wagon had offered to take it, and Allan, too, down the mountain at three o'clock. In the spring of 1861, one out of every two Confederate privates had a trunk. One must preserve the decencies of life; one must make a good appearance in the field! Allan's was small and modest enough, God knows! but such as it was it had not occurred to him to doubt the propriety of taking it.

It stood there neatly packed, the shirts that Sairy had been ironing laid atop. The young man, kneeling beside it, placed in this or that corner the last few articles of his outfit. All was simple, clean, and new — only the books that he was taking with him were old. They were his Bible, his Shakespeare, a volume of Plutarch's Lives, and a Latin book or two beside. In a place to themselves were other treasures, a daguerreotype of his mother, a capacious huswife that Sairy had made and stocked for him, the little box of paper "to write home on" that had been Tom's present, various trifles that the three had agreed might come in handy. Among these he now placed Christianna's gift. It was soft and full and bright — he had the same pleasure in handling it that he would have felt in touching a damask rose. He shut it in and rose from his knees.

He had on his uniform. They had been slow in coming — the uniforms — from Richmond. It was only Cleave's patient insistence that had procured them at last. Some of the companies were not uniformed at all. So enormous was the press of business upon the authorities, so limited was the power of an almost purely agricultural, non-manufacturing world suddenly to clothe alike these thousands of volunteers, suddenly to arm them with something better than a fowling-piece or a Revolutionary flintlock, that the wonder is, not that they did so badly, but that they did so well. Pending the arrival of the uniforms the men had drilled in strange array. With an attempt at similarity and a picturesque taste of their own, most of them wore linsey shirts and big black hats, tucked up on one side with a rosette of green ribbon. One man donned his grandfather's Continental blue and buff — on the breast was a dark stain, won at King's Mountain. Others drilled, and were now ready to march, as they came from the plough, the mill, or the forge. But Cleave's company, by virtue of Cleave himself, was fairly equipped. The uniforms had come, and there was a decent showing of modern arms. Billy Maydew's hunting-knife and spear would be changed on the morrow for a musket, though in Billy's case the musket would certainly be the old smoothbore, calibre sixty-nine.

Allan's own gun, left him by his father, rested against the wall. The young man, for all his quietude, his conscientious ways, his daily work with children, his love of flowers, and his dreams of books, inherited from frontiersmen — whose lives had depended upon watchfulness — quickness of wit, accuracy of eye, and steadiness of aim. He rarely missed his mark, and he read intuitively and easily the language of wood, sky, and road. On the bed lay his slouch hat, his haversack, knapsack, and canteen, cartridge-box and belt, and slung over the back of a chair was his roll of blanket. All was in readiness. Allan went over to the window. Below him were the flowers he had tended, then the great forests in their May freshness, cataracts of green, falling down, down to the valley. Over all hung the sky, divinely blue. A wind went rustling through the forest, joining its voice to the voice of Thunder Run. Allan knelt, touching with his forehead the window-sill. "O Lord God," he said, "O Lord God, keep us all, North and South, and bring us through winding ways to Thy end at last." As he rose he heard the wagon coming down the road. He turned, put the roll of blanket over one shoulder, and beneath the other arm assumed knapsack, haversack, and canteen, dragged the hair trunk out upon the landing, returned, took up his musket, looked once again about the small, familiar room, then left it and went downstairs.

Sairy and Tom were upon the porch, the owner of the wagon with them. "I'll tote down yo' trunk," said the latter, and presently emerged from the house with that article upon his shoulder. "I reckon I'll volunteer myself, just as soon's harvest's over," he remarked genially. "But, gosh! you-all'll be back by then, telling how you did it!" He went down the path whistling, and tossed the trunk into the wagon.

"I hate good-byes," said Allan. "I wish I had stolen away last night."

"Don't ye get killed!" answered Sairy sharply. "That's what I'm afraid of. I know you'll go riskin' yourself!"

"God bless you," said Tom. "You've been like a son to us these five years. Don't you forget to write."

"I won't," answered Allan. "I'll write you long letters. And I won't get killed, Aunt Sairy. I'll take the best of care." He took the old woman in his arms. "You two have been just as good as a father and mother to me. Thank you for it. I'll never forget. Good-bye."

Toward five o'clock the wagon rolled into the village whence certain of the Botetourt companies were to march away. It was built beside the river — two long, parallel streets, one upon the water level, the other much higher, with intersecting lanes. There were brick and frame houses, modest enough; there were three small, white-spired churches, many locust and ailanthus trees, a covered bridge thrown across the river to a village upon the farther side and, surrounding all, a noble frame of mountains. There was, in those days, no railroad.

Cleave's hundred men, having the town at large for their friend, stood in no lack of quarters. Some had volunteered from this place or its neighbourhood, others had kinsmen and associates, not one was so forlorn as to be without a host. The village was in a high fever of hospitality; had the companies marching from Botetourt been so many brigades, it would still have done its utmost. From the Potomac to the Dan, from the Eastern Shore to the Alleghenies the flame of patriotism burned high and clear. There were skulkers, there were braggarts, there were knaves and fools in Virginia as elsewhere, but by comparison they were not many, and theirs was not the voice that was heard to-day. The mass of the people were very honest, stubbornly convinced, showing to the end a most heroic and devoted ardour. This village was not behindhand. All her young men were going; she had her company, too. She welcomed Cleave's men, gathered for the momentarily expected order to the front, and lavished upon them, as on two other companies within her bounds, every hospitable care.

The wagon driver deposited Allan Gold and his trunk before the porch of the old, red brick hotel, shook hands with a mighty grip, and rattled on toward the lower end of town. The host came out to greet the young man, two negro boys laid hold of his trunk, a passing volunteer in butternut, with a musket as long as Natty Bumpo's, hailed him, and a cluster of elderly men sitting with tilted chairs in the shade of a locust tree rose and gave him welcome. "It's Allan Gold from Thunder Run, is n't it? Good-day, sir, good-day! Can't have too many from Thunder Run; good giant stuff! Have you somewhere to stay to-night? If not, any one of us will be happy to look after you. — Mr. Harris, let us have juleps all round —"

"Thank you very kindly, sir," said Allan, "but I must go find my captain."

"I saw him," remarked a gray-haired gentleman, "just now down the street. He's seeing to the loading of his wagons, showing Jim Ball and the drivers just how to do it — and he says he is n't going to show them but this once. They seemed right prompt to learn."

"I was thar too," put in an old farmer. "'They're mighty heavy wagons,' I says, says I. 'Three times too heavy,' he says, says he. 'This company's got the largest part of its provisions for the whole war right here and now,' says he. 'Thar's a heap of trunks,' says I. 'More than would be needed for the White Sulphur,' he says, says he. 'This time two years we'll march lighter,' says he —"

There were exclamations. "Two years! Thunderation! — This war'll be over before persimmons are ripe! Why, the boys have n't volunteered but for one year — and even that seemed kind of senseless! Two years! He's daft!"

"I dunno," quoth the other. "If fighting's like farming it's all-fired slow work. Anyhow, that's what he said. 'This time two years we'll march lighter,' he says, says he, and then I came away. He's down by the old warehouse by the bridge, Mr. Gold — and I just met Matthew Coffin and he says thar's going to be a parade presently."

An hour later, in the sunset glow, in a meadow by the river, the three companies paraded. The new uniforms, the bright muskets, the silken colours, the bands playing "Dixie," the quick orders, the more or less practised evolutions, the universal martial mood, the sense of danger over all, as yet thrilling only, not leaden, the known faces, the loved faces, the imminent farewell, the flush of glory, the beckoning of great events — no wonder every woman, girl, and child, every old man and young boy who could reach the meadow were there, watching in the golden light, half wild with euthusiasm!

> Wish I was in de land ob cotton,
> Old times dar am not forgotten
> Look away! look away! Dixie Land.

At one side, beneath a great sugar maple, were clustered a number of women, mothers, wives, sisters, sweethearts, of those who were going forth to war. They swayed forward, absorbed in watching, not the companies as a whole, but one or two, sometimes three or four figures therein. They had not held them back; never in the

times of history were there more devotedly patriotic women than
they of the Southern States. They lent their plaudits; they were
high in the thoughts of the men moving with precision beneath
the great flag of Virginia, to the sound of music, in the green
meadow by the James. The colours of the several companies had
been sewed by women, sitting together in dim old parlours, behind
windows framed in roses. One banner had been made from a
wedding gown.

> Look away! look away!
> Look away down South to Dixie!

The throng wept and cheered. The negroes, slave and free,
belonging to this village and the surrounding country, were of an
excellent type, worthy and respectable men and women, honoured
by and honouring their "white people." A number of these were in
the meadow by the river, and they, too, clapped and cheered, borne
away by music and spectacle, gazing with fond eyes upon some
nursling, or playmate, or young, imperious, well-liked master in
those gleaming ranks. Isaac, son of Abraham, or Esau and Jacob,
sons of Isaac, marching with banners against Canaan or Moab, may
have heard some such acclaim from the servants left behind. Several were going with the company. Captain and lieutenants, and
more than one sergeant and corporal had their body-servants —
these were the proudest of the proud and the envied of their brethren.
The latter were voluble. "Des look at Wash, — des look at Washington Mayo! Actin' lak he own er co'te house an' er stage line! O
my Lawd! wish I wuz er gwine! An dat dar Tullius from Three Oaks
— he gwine march right behin' de captain, an' Marse Hairston
Breckinridge's boy he gwine march right behin' him! — Dar de big
drum ag'in!"

> In Dixie land I'll take my stand,
> To live and die in Dixie!
> Look away! Look away!
> Look away down South to Dixie!

The sun set behind the great mountain across the river. Parade
was over, ranks broken. The people and their heroes, some restless,
others tense, all flushed of cheek and bright of eye, all borne upon
a momentous upward wave of emotion, parted this way and that, to

supper, to divers preparations, fond talk, and farewells, to an indoor hour. Then, presently, out again in the mild May night, out into High Street and Low Street, in the moonlight, under the odour of the white locust clusters. The churches were lit and open; in each there was brief service, well attended. Later, from the porch of the old hotel, there was speaking. It drew toward eleven o'clock. The moon was high, the women and children all housed, the oldest men, spent with the strain of the day, also gone to their homes, or their friends' homes. The Volunteers and a faithful few were left. They could not sleep; if war was going to be always as exciting as this, how did soldiers ever sleep? There was not among them a man who had ever served in war, so the question remained unanswered. A Thunder Run man volunteered the information that the captain was asleep — he had been to the house where the captain lodged and his mother had come to the door with her finger on her lips, and he had looked past her and seen Captain Cleave lying on a sofa fast asleep. Thunder Run's comrades listened, but they rather doubted the correctness of his report. It surely was n't very sol- dier-like to sleep — even upon a sofa — the night before marching away! The lieutenants were n't asleep. Hairston Breckinridge had a map spread out upon a bench before the post office, and was demonstrating to an eager dozen the indubitable fact that the big victory would be either at Harper's Ferry or Alexandria. Young Matthew Coffin was in love, and might be seen through the hotel window writing, candles all around him, at a table, covering one pale blue sheet after another with impassioned farewells. Sergeants and corporals and men were wakeful. Some of these, too, were writ- ing letters, sending messages; others joined in the discussion as to the theatre of war, or made knots of their own, centres of conjec- tures and prophecy; others roamed the streets, or down by the river bank watched the dark stream. Of these, a few proposed to strip and have a swim — who knew when they'd see the old river again? But the notion was frowned upon. One must be dressed and ready. At that very moment, perhaps, a man might be riding into town with the order. The musicians were not asleep. Young Matthew Coffin, sealing his letter some time after midnight, and coming out into the moonlight and the fragrance of the locust trees, had an inspiration. All was in readiness for the order when it should come,

and who, in the meantime, wanted to do so prosaic a thing as rest?
"Boys, let us serenade the ladies!"

The silver night wore on. So many of the "boys" had sisters, that
there were many pretty ladies staying in the town or at the two
or three pleasant old houses upon its outskirts. Two o'clock, three
o'clock passed, and there were yet windows to sing beneath. Old
love songs floated through the soft and dreamy air; there was a sense
of angelic beings in the unlit rooms above, even of the flutter of their
wings. Then, at the music's dying fall, flowers were thrown; there
seemed to descend a breath, a whisper, "Adieu, heroes — adored,
adored heroes!" A scramble for the flowers, then out at the gate and
on to the next house, and so *da capo*.

Dawn, though the stars were yet shining, began to make itself felt.
A coldness was in the air, a mist arose from the river, there came a
sensation of arrest, of somewhere an icy finger upon the pulse of
life.

> Maxwelton's braes are bonnie,
> Where early fa's the dew,
> And 't was there that Annie Laurie
> Gie'd me her promise true, —

They were singing now before an old brick house in the lower
street. There were syringas in bloom in the yard. A faint light was
rising in the east, the stars were fading.

> Gie'd me her promise true
> Which ne'er forgot shall be —

Suddenly, from High Street, wrapped in mist, a bugle rang out.
The order — the order — the order to the front! It called again,
sounding the assembly. *Fall in, men, fall in!*

At sunrise Richard Cleave's company went away. There was a
dense crowd in the misty street, weeping, cheering. An old minister,
standing beside the captain, lifted his arms — the men uncovered,
the prayer was said, the blessing given. Again the bugle blew, the
women cried farewell. The band played "Virginia," the flag streamed
wide in the morning wind. Good-bye, good-bye, and again good-
bye! *Attention! Take arms! Shoulder arms! Right face!* FORWARD,
MARCH!

CHAPTER VI

BY ASHBY'S GAP

THE 65th Virginia Infantry, Colonel Valentine Brooke, was encamped to the north of Winchester in the Valley of Virginia, in a meadow through which ran a stream, and upon a hillside beneath a hundred chestnut trees, covered with white tassels of bloom. To its right lay the 2d, the 4th, the 5th, the 27th, and the 33d Virginia, forming with the 65th the First Brigade, General T. J. Jackson. The battery attached — the Rockbridge Artillery — occupied an adjacent apple orchard. To the left, in other July meadows and over other chestnut-shaded hills, were spread the brigades of Bee, Bartow, and Elzey. Somewhere in the distance, behind the screen of haze, were Stuart and his cavalry. Across the stream a brick farmhouse, ringed with mulberry trees, made the headquarters of Joseph E. Johnston, commanding the forces of the Confederacy — an experienced, able, and wary soldier, engaged just now, with eleven thousand men, in watching Patterson with fifteen thousand on the one hand, and McDowell with thirty-five thousand on the other, and in listening attentively for a voice from Beauregard with twenty thousand at Manassas. It was the middle of July, 1861.

First Brigade headquarters was a tree — an especially big tree — a little removed from the others. Beneath it stood a kitchen chair and a wooden table, requisitioned from the nearest cabin and scrupulously paid for. At one side was an extremely small tent, but Brigadier-General T. J. Jackson rarely occupied it. He sat beneath the tree, upon the kitchen chair, his feet, in enormous cavalry boots, planted precisely before him, his hands rigid at his sides. Here he transacted the business of each day, and here, when it was over, he sat facing the North. An awkward, inarticulate, and peculiar man, with strange notions about his health and other matters, there was about him no breath of grace, romance, or pomp of war. He was ungenial, ungainly, with large hands and feet, with poor eyesight and a stiff address. There did not lack spruce and handsome youths in his command who were vexed to the soul by the idea of being led to battle by such a figure. The facts that he had fought very bravely in Mexico, and that he had for the enemy a cold and formidable hatred were for him; most other things against him. He drilled his troops seven hours a day. His discipline was of the sternest, his censure a thing to make the boldest officer blench. A blunder, a slight negligence, any disobedience of orders — down came reprimand, suspension, arrest, with an iron certitude, a relentlessness quite 'like Nature's. Apparently he was without imagination. He had but little sense of humour, and no understanding of a joke. He drank water and sucked lemons for dyspepsia, and fancied that the use of pepper had caused a weakness in his left leg. He rode a rawboned nag named Little Sorrel, he carried his sabre in the oddest fashion, and said "oblike" instead of "oblique." He found his greatest pleasure in going to the Presbyterian Church twice on Sundays and to prayer meetings through the week. Now and then there was a gleam in his eye that promised something, but the battles had not begun, and his soldiers hardly knew what it promised. One or two observers claimed that he was ambitious, but these were chiefly laughed at. To the brigade at large he seemed prosaic, tedious, and strict enough, performing all duties with the exactitude, monotony, and expression of a clock, keeping all plans with the secrecy of the sepulchre, rarely sleeping, rising at dawn, and requiring his staff to do likewise, praying at all seasons, and demanding an implicity of obedience which might have been in order with some great and glorious captain, some idolized Napoleon, but which seemed hardly the due of the late professor of natural philosophy and artillery tactics at the Virginia Military Institute. True it was that at Harper's Ferry, where, as Colonel T. J. Jackson, he had commanded until Johnston's arrival, he had begun to bring order out of chaos and to weave from a high-spirited rabble of Volunteers a web that the world was to acknowledge remarkable; true, too, that on the second of July, in the small affair with Patterson at Falling Waters, he had seemed to the critics in the ranks not altogether unimposing. He emerged from Falling Waters Brigadier-General T. J. Jackson, and his men, though with some mental reservations, began to call him "Old Jack." The epithet implied approval, but approval hugely qualified. They might have said — in fact, they did say — that every fool knew that a crazy man could fight!

The Army of the Shenandoah was a civilian army, a high-spirited, slightly organized, more or less undisciplined, totally inexperienced in war, impatient and youthful body of men, with the lesson yet to learn that the shortest distance between two points is sometimes a curve. In its eyes Patterson at Bunker Hill was exclusively the blot upon the escutcheon, and the whole game of war consisted in somehow doing away with that blot. There was great chafing at the inaction. It was hot, argumentative July weather; the encampment to the north of Winchester in the Valley of Virginia hummed with the comments of the strategists in the ranks. Patterson should have been attacked after Falling Waters. What if he was entrenched behind stone walls at Martinsburg? Patterson should have been attacked upon the fifteenth at Bunker Hill. What if he has fifteen thousand men ? — what if he has *twenty* thousand ? — What if McDowell is preparing to cross the Potomac ? And now, on the seventeenth, Patterson is at Charlestown, creeping eastward, evidently going to surround the Army of the Shenandoah! Patterson is the burning reality and McDowell the dream — and yet Johnston won't move to the westward and attack! *Good Lord! we did n't come from home just to watch these chestnuts get ripe! All the generals are crazy, anyhow.*

It was nine, in the morning of Thursday the eighteenth, — a scorching day. The locusts were singing of the heat; the grass, wherever men, horses, and wagon wheels had not ground it into dust, was parched to a golden brown; the mint by the stream looked wilted. The morning drill was over, the 65th lounging beneath the trees. It was almost too hot to fuss about Patterson, almost too hot to pity the sentinels, almost too hot to wonder where Stuart's cavalry had gone that morning, and why "Old Joe" quartered behind the mulberries in the brick farmhouse, had sent a staff officer to "Old Jack," and why Bee's and Bartow's and Elzey's brigades had been similarly visited; almost too hot to play checkers, to whittle a set of chessmen, to finish that piece of Greek, to read "Ivanhoe" and resolve to fight like Brian de Bois Gilbert and Richard Cœur de Lion in one, to write home, to rout out knapsack and haversack, and look again at fifty precious trifles; too hot to smoke, to tease Company A's pet coon, to think about Thunder Run, to wonder how pap was gettin' on with that thar piece of corn, and what the girls were sayin'; too hot to borrow, too hot to swear, too hot to go down to the creek and wash a shirt, too hot — "What's that drum beginning for? *The long roll! The Army of the Valley is going to move! Boys, boys, boys! We are going north to Charlestown! Boys, boys, boys! We are going to lick Patterson!*"

At noon the Army of the Valley, the First Brigade leading, uncoiled itself, regiment by regiment, from the wide meadow and the chestnut wood, swept out upon the turnpike — and found its head turned toward the south! There was stupefaction, then tongues were loosed. "What's this — what's this, boys? Charlestown ain't in this direction. Old Joe's lost his bearings! Johnny Lemon, you go tell him so — go ask Old Jack if you can't. Whoa, there! The fool's going!! Come back here quick, Johnny, afore the captain sees you! O hell! we're going right back through Winchester!"

A wave of anger swept over the First Brigade. The 65th grew intractable, moved at a snail's pace. The company officers went to and fro. "Close up, men, close up! No, I don't know any more than you do — maybe it's some roundabout way. Close up — close up!" The colonel rode along the line. "What's the matter here? You are n't going to a funeral! Think it's a fox hunt, boys, and step out lively!" A courier arrived from the head of the column. "General Jackson's compliments to Colonel Brooke, and he says if this regiment is n't in step in three minutes he'll leave it with the sick in Winchester!"

The First Brigade, followed by Bee, Bartow, and Elzey, marched sullenly down the turnpike, into Winchester, and through its dusty streets. The people were all out, old men, boys, and women thronging the brick sidewalks. The army had seventeen hundred sick in the town. Pale faces looked out of upper windows; men just recovering from dysentery, from measles, from fever, stumbled out of shady front yards and fell into line; others, more helpless, started, then wavered back. "Boys, boys! you ain't never going to leave us here for the Yanks to take? Boys — boys —" The citizens, too, had their say. "Is Winchester to be left to Patterson? We've done our best by you — and you go marching away!" Several of the older women were weeping, the younger looked scornful. *Close up, men, close up — close up!*

The First Brigade was glad when it was through the town. Before it, leading southward through the Valley of Virginia, stretched the great pike, a hundred and twenty miles of road, traversing as fair, rich, and happy a region as war ever found a paradise and left a desolation. To the east towered the Blue Ridge, to west the Great North and Shenandoah Mountains, twenty miles to the south Massanutton rose like a Gibraltar from the rolling fields of wheat and corn, the orchard lands and pleasant pastures. The region was one of old mills, turning flashing wheels, of comfortable red brick houses and well-stored barns, of fair market towns, of a noble breed of horses, and of great, white-covered wagons, of clear waters and sweet gardens, of an honest, thrifty, brave, and intelligent people. It was a fair country, and many of the army were at home there, but the army had at the moment no taste for its beauties. It wanted to see Patterson's long, blue lines; it wanted to drive them out of Virginia, across the Potomac, back to where they came from.

The First Brigade was dispirited and critical, and as it had not yet learned to control its mood, it marched as a dispirited and critical person would be apt to march in the brazen middle of a July day. Every spring and rivulet, every blackberry bush and apple tree upon the road gathered recruits. The halts for no purpose were interminable, the perpetual *Close up, close up, men!* of the exasperated officers as unavailing as the droning in the heat of the burnished June-bugs. The brigade had no intention of not making known its reluctance to leave Patterson. It took an hour to make a mile from Winchester. General Jackson rode down the column on Little Sorrel and said something to the colonel of each regiment, which something the colonels passed on to the captains. The next mile was made in half an hour.

The July dust rose from the pike in clouds, hot, choking, thick as the rain of ash from a volcano. It lay heavy upon coat, cap, haversack, and knapsack, upon the muskets and upon the colours, drooping in the heat, drooping at the idea of turning back upon Patterson and going off, Heaven and Old Joe knew where! Tramp, tramp over the hot pike, sullenly southward, hot without and hot within! The knapsack was heavy, the haversack was heavy, the musket was heavy. Sweat ran down from under cap or felt hat, and made grimy trenches down cheek and chin. The men had too thick underwear. They carried overcoat and blanket — it was hot, hot, and every pound like ten! *To keep — to throw away? To keep — to throw away?* The beat of feet kept time to that pressing question, and to *Just marching to be marching! — reckon Old Joe thinks it's fun,* and to *Where in hell are we going, anyway?*

Through the enormous dust cloud that the army raised the trees of the valley appeared as brown smudges against an ochreish sky. The farther hills and the mountains were not seen at all. The stone fences on either side the road, the blackberry bushes, the elder, the occasional apple or cherry tree were all but dun lines and blotches. Oh, hot, hot! A man swung his arm and a rolled overcoat landed in the middle of a briar patch. A second followed suit — a third, a fourth. A great, raw-boned fellow from some mountain clearing jerked at the lacing of his shoes and in a moment was marching barefoot, the offending leather swinging from his arm. To right and left he found imitators. A corpulent man, a merchant used to a big chair set in the shady front of a village store, suffered greatly, pale about the lips, and with his breath coming in wheezing gasps. His overcoat went first, then his roll of blanket. Finally he gazed a moment, sorrowfully enough, at his knapsack, then dropped it, too, quietly, in a fence corner. *Close up, men — close up !*

A wind arose and blew the dust maddeningly to and fro. In the Colour Company of the 65th a boy began to cough, uncontrollably, with a hollow sound. Those near him looked askance. "You'd better run along home, sonny! Yo' ma had n't ought to let you come. Darn it all! if we march down this pike longer, we'll all land home! — If you listen right hard you can hear Thunder Run! — And that thar Yank hugging himself back thar at Charlestown! — dessay he's telegraphin' right this minute that we've run away —"

Richard Cleave passed along the line. "Don't be so downhearted, men! It's not really any hotter than at a barbecue at home. Who was that coughing?"

"Andrew Kerr, sir."

"Andrew Kerr, you go to the doctor the first thing after roll-call to-night. Cheer up, men! No one's going to send you home without fighting."

From the rear came a rumble, shouted orders, a cracking of whips. The column swerved to one side of the broad road, and the Rockbridge Artillery passed — a vision of horses, guns, and men, wrapped in a dun whirlwind and disappearing in the blast. They were gone in thunder through the heat and haze. The 65th Virginia wondered to a man why it had not chosen the artillery.

Out of a narrow way stretching westward, came suddenly at a gallop a handful of troopers, black plumed and magnificently mounted, swinging into the pike and disappearing in a pillar of dust toward the head of the column. Back out of the cloud sounded the jingling of accoutrements, the neighing of horses, a shouted order.

The infantry groaned. "Ten of the Black Horse! — where are the rest of them, I wonder? Oh, ain't they lucky dogs?"

"Stuart's men have the sweetest time! — just galloping over the country, and making love, and listening to Sweeney's banjo —

> If you want to have a good time —
> If you want to have a good time,
> Jine the cavalry! —

What's that road over there — the cool-looking one? The road to Ashby's Gap? Wish this pike was shady like that!"

A bugle blew; the command to halt ran down the column. The First Brigade came to a stand upon the dusty pike, in the heat and glare. The 65th was the third in column, the 4th and the 27th leading. Suddenly from the 4th there burst a cheer, a loud and high note of relief and exultation. A moment, and the infection had spread to the 27th; it, too, was cheering wildly. Apparently there were several couriers — No! staff officers, the 65th saw the gold lace — with some message or order from the commanding general, now well in advance with his guard of Black Horse. They were riding down the line — Old Jack was with them — the 4th and the 27th were cheering like mad. The colonel of the 65th rode forward. There was a minute's parley, then he turned, "Sixty-fifth! It isn't a fox hunt — it's a bear hunt! 'General Johnston to the 65th' —" He broke off and waved forward the aide-de-camp beside him. "Tell them, Captain Washington, tell them what a terror to corn-cribs we're going after!"

The aide, a young man, superbly mounted, laughed, raised his voice. "Sixty-fifth! The Army of the Valley is going through

Ashby's Gap to Piedmont, and from Piedmont by rail to Manassas Junction. General Stuart is still at Winchester amusing General Patterson. At Manassas our gallant army under General Beauregard is attacked by McDowell with overwhelming numbers. The commanding general hopes that his troops will step out like men and make a forced march to save the country!"

He was gone — the other staff officers were gone — Old Jack was gone. They passed the shouting 65th, and presently from down the line came the cheers of the 2d, 21st, and 33d Virginia. Old Jack rode back alone the length of his brigade; and so overflowing was the enthusiasm of the men that they cheered him, cheered lustily! He touched his old forage cap, went stiffly by upon Little Sorrel. From the rear, far down the road, could be heard the voices of Bee, Bartow, and Elzey. Ardour, elasticity, strength returned to the Army of the Shenandoah. With a triumphant cry the First Brigade wheeled into the road that led eastward through the Blue Ridge by Ashby's Gap.

Two o'clock, three o'clock, four o'clock came and passed. Enthusiasm carried the men fast and far, but they were raw troops and they suffered. The sun, too, was enthusiastic, burning with all its might. The road proved neither cool nor shady. All the springs seemed suddenly to have dried up. Out of every hour there was a halt of ten minutes, and it was needed. The men dropped by the roadside, upon the parched grass, beneath the shadow of the sumach and the elder bushes, and lay without speaking. The small farmers, the mountaineers, the hunters, the ploughmen fared not so badly; but the planters of many acres, the lawyers, the doctors, the divines, the merchants, the millers, and the innkeepers, the undergraduates from the University, the youths from classical academies, county stores, village banks, lawyers' offices, all who led a horseback or sedentary existence, and the elderly men and the very young, — these suffered heavily. The mounted officers were not foot-weary, but they also had heat, thirst, and hunger, and, in addition, responsibility, inexperience, and the glance of their brigadier. The ten minutes were soon over. *Fall in — fall in, men !* The short rest made the going worse, the soldiers rose so stiff and sore.

The men had eaten before leaving the camp above Winchester — but that was days ago. Now, as they went through Clarke County, there appeared at cross-roads, at plantation gates, at stiles leading into green fields, ladies young and old, bearing baskets of good things hastily snatched from pantry and table. They had pitchers, too, of iced tea, of cold milk, even of raspberry acid and sangaree. How good it all was! and how impossible to go around! But, fed or hungry, refreshed or thirsty, the men blessed the donors, and that reverently, with a purity of thought, a chivalrousness of regard, a shade of feeling, youthful and sweet and yet virile enough, which went with the Confederate soldier into the service and abode to the end.

The long afternoon wore to a close. The heat decreased, but the dust remained and the weariness grew to gigantic proportions. The First Brigade was well ahead of Bee, Bartow, and Elzey. It had started in advance and it had increased the distance. If there was any marching in men, Jackson forced it out; they went a league for him where another would have procured but a mile, but even he, even enthusiasm and the necessity of relieving Beauregard got upon this march less than two miles an hour. Most happily, McDowell, advancing on Beauregard and Bull Run and fearing "masked batteries," marched much more slowly. At sunset the First Brigade reached the Shenandoah.

The mounted officers took up one and sometimes two men beside them, and the horses struggled bravely through the cold, rapid, breast-deep current. Behind them, company by company, the men stripped off coat and trousers, piled clothing and ammunition upon their heads, held high their muskets, and so crossed. The guns and wagons followed. Before the river was passed the night fell dark.

The heat was now gone by, the dust was washed away, the men had drunk their fill. From the haversacks they took the remnant of the food cooked that morning. The biscuit and the bacon tasted very good; not enough of either, it was true, but still something. The road above the river rose steeply, for here was the Blue Ridge, lofty and dark, rude with rock, and shaggy with untouched forests. This was the pass through the mountains, this was Ashby's Gap. The brigade climbed with the road, tired and silent and grim. The day had somehow been a foretaste of war; the men had a new idea of the draught and of the depth of the cup. They felt older, and the air, blowing down from the mountains, seemed the air of a far country toward which they had been travelling almost without knowing it. They saw now that it was a strange country, much unlike that in which they had hitherto lived. They climbed slowly between dark crag and tree, and wearily. All song and jest had died; they were tired soldiers, hungry now for sleep. *Close up, men, close up!*

They came to the height of the pass, marked by a giant poplar whose roots struck deep into four counties. Here again there was a ten minutes' halt; the men sank down upon the soft beds of leaf and mould. Their eyelids drooped; they were in a dream at once, and in a dream heard the *Fall in — fall in, men!* The column stumbled to its feet and began the descent of the mountain.

Clouds came up; at midnight when they reached the lower slope, it was raining. Later they came to the outskirts of the village of Paris, to a grove of mighty oaks, and here the brigade was halted for the night. The men fell upon the ground and slept. No food was taken, and no sentries were posted. An aide, very heavy-eyed, asked if guard should not be set. "No, sir," answered the general. "Let them sleep." "And you, sir?" "I don't feel like it. I'll see that there is no alarm." With his cloak about him, with his old cadet cap pulled down over his eyes, awkward and simple and plain, he paced out the night beneath the trees, or sat upon a broken rail fence, watching his sleeping soldiers and, the aide thought, praying.

The light rain ceased, the sky cleared, the pale dawn came up from the east. In the first pink light the bugles sounded. Up rose the First Brigade, cooked and ate its breakfast, swung out from the oak grove upon the highroad, and faced the rising sun. The morning was divinely cool, the men in high spirits, Piedmont and the railway were but six miles down the road. The First Brigade covered the distance by eight o'clock. There was the station, there was the old Manassas Gap railroad, there was the train of freight and cattle cars — ever so many freight and cattle cars! Company after company the men piled in; by ten o'clock every car was filled, and the platforms and roofs had their quota. The crazy old engine blew its whistle, the First Brigade was off for Manassas. Bee, Bartow, and Elzey, arriving at Piedmont in the course of the morning, were not so fortunate. The railroad had promised, barring unheard-of accident, to place the four brigades in Manassas by sunrise of the twentieth.

The accident duly arrived. There was a collision, the track was obstructed, and only the 7th and 8th Georgia got through. The remainder of the infantry waited perforce at Piedmont, a portion of it for two mortal days, and that without rations. The artillery and the cavalry — the latter having now come up — marched by the wagon road and arrived in fair time.

From ten in the morning until sunset the First Brigade and the Manassas Gap train crept like a tortoise through the July weather, by rustling cornfields, by stream and wood, by farmhouse and village. It was hot in the freight and cattle cars, hot, cinderish, and noisy. With here and there an exception the men took off their coats, loosened the shoes from their feet, made themselves easy in any way that suggested itself. The subtle *give*, the slip out of convention and restraint back toward a less trammelled existence, the faint return of the more purely physical, the slight withdrawal of the more purely mental, the rapid breaking down of the sheer artificial — these and other marks of one of the many predicates of war began to show themselves in this journey. But at the village stations there came a change. Women and girls were gathered here, in muslin freshness, with food and drink for "our heroes." The apparel discarded between stations was assiduously reassumed whenever the whistle blew. "Our heroes" looked out of freight and cattle car, somewhat grimy, perhaps, but clothed and in their right mind, with a becoming bloom upon them of eagerness, deference, and patriotic willingness to die in Virginia's defence. The dispensers of nectar and ambrosia loved them all, sped them on to Manassas with many a prayer and God bless you!

At sunset the whistle shrieked its loudest. It was their destination. The train jolted and jerked to a halt. Regiment by regiment, out poured the First Brigade, fell into line, and was double-quicked four miles to Mitchell's Ford and a pine wood, where, hungry, thirsty, dirty, and exhausted, the ranks were broken.

This was the night of the nineteenth. At Piedmont the brigade had heard of yesterday's minor affair at this ford between Tyler's division and Longstreet, the honours of the engagement resting with the Confederate. In the pine wood there was a line of fresh graves; on the brown needles lay boughs that shell had cut from the trees; there were certain stains upon the ground. The First Brigade ate and slept — the last somewhat feverishly. The night passed without alarm. An attack in force was expected in the morning, but it did not come. McDowell, amazingly enough, still rested confident that Patterson had detained Johnston in the valley. Possessed by this belief he was now engaged in a "reconnoissance by stealth," his object being to discover a road whereby to cross Bull Run above the Stone Bridge and turn Beauregard's left. This proceeding and an afternoon rest in camp occupied him the whole of the twentieth. On this day Johnston himself reached Manassas, bringing with him Bee's 2d Mississippi and 4th Alabama, and Bartow's 7th and 8th Georgia. Stuart, having successfully amused Patterson, was also on hand. The remainder of the Army of the Shenandoah, detained by the break upon the Manassas Gap, was yet missing, and many an anxious glance the generals cast that way.

The First Brigade, undiscovered by the "reconnoissance by stealth," rested all day Saturday beneath the pines at Mitchell's Ford, and at night slept quietly, no longer minding the row of graves. At dawn of Sunday a cannon woke the men, loud and startling, McDowell's signal gun, fired from Centreville, and announcing to the Federal host that the interrupted march, the "On to Richmond" blazoned on banners and chalked on trunks, would now be resumed, willy nilly the "rebel horde" on the southern bank of Bull Run.

CHAPTER VII

THE DOGS OF WAR

IN the east was a great flare of pink with small golden clouds floating across, all seen uncertainly between branches of pine. A mist lay above Bull Run — on the high, opposite bank the woods rose huddled, indistinct, and dream-like. The air was still, cool, and pure, a Sunday morning waiting for church bells. There were no bells; the silence was shattered by all the drums of the brigade beating the long roll. Men rose from the pine needles, shook themselves, caught up musket and ammunition belt. The echoes from McDowell's signal cannon had hardly died when, upon the wooded banks of Bull Run, the First Brigade stood in arms.

Minutes passed. Mitchell's Ford marked the Confederate centre. Here, and at Blackburn's Ford, were Bonham, Bee, Bartow, Longstreet, and Jackson. Down the stream, at MacLean's Ford and Union Mills, Early and Ewell and D. R. Jones held the right. To the left, up Bull Run, beyond Bee and beyond Stuart, at the Island, Ball and Lewis fords, were Cocke's Brigade and Hampton's Legion, and farther yet, at the Stone Bridge, Evans with a small brigade. Upon the northern bank of the Run, in the thick woods opposite Mitchell's and Blackburn's fords, was believed to be the mass of the invaders. There had been a certitude that the battle would join about these fords. Beauregard's plan was to cross at MacLean's and fall upon the Federal left. Johnston had acceded, and with the first light orders had gone to the brigadiers. "Hold yourselves in readiness to cross and to attack."

Now suddenly from the extreme left, away in the direction of the Stone Bridge, burst an unexpected sound both of musketry and artillery. It was distant, it waxed and waned and waxed again. The First Brigade, nervous, impatient, chilled by the dawn, peered across its own reach of misty stream, and saw naught but the dream-like woods. Tyler's division was over there, it knew. When would firing begin along this line? When would the brigade have orders to move, when would it cross, when would things begin to happen?

An hour passed. Ranks were broken and the men allowed to cook and eat a hasty breakfast. How good, in the mist-drenched wood, tasted the scalding coffee, how good the cornbread and the bacon! The last crumb swallowed, they waited again, lying on the brown earth beneath the pines. The mounted officers, advanced upon the bank of the stream and seen through the mist, loomed larger, man and horse, than life. Jackson sat very quiet upon Little Sorrel, his lips moving. Far up the stream the firing continued. The 2d, 4th, 5th, 27th, 33d, and 65th Virginia fidgeted, groaned, swore with impatience.

Suddenly the nearer echoes awoke. A Federal battery, posted on the hills beyond the fringe of thick wood on the northern bank, opened a slow and ineffective fire against the hills and woods across the stream. The Confederates kept their position masked, made no reply. The shells fell short, and did harm only to the forest and its creatures. Nearly all fell short, but one, a shell from a thirty-pounder Parrott, entered the pine wood by Mitchell's Ford, fell among the wagons of the 65th, and exploded.

A driver was killed, a mule mangled so that it must be shot, and an ambulance split into kindling wood. Few in the First Brigade had seen such a thing before. The men brushed the pine needles and the earth from their coats, and looked at the furrowed ground and at the headless body of the driver with a startled curiosity. There was a sense of a sudden and vivid flash from behind the veil, and they as suddenly perceived that the veil was both cold and dark. This, then, was one of the ways in which death came, shrieking like this, ugly and resistless! The July morning was warm and bright, but more than one of the volunteers in that wood shivered as though it were winter. Jackson rode along the front. "They don't attack in force at the Stone Bridge. A feint, I think." He stopped before the colour company of the 65th. "Captain Cleave."

"Yes, sir."

"You have hunters from the mountains. After the battle send me the man you think would make the best scout — an intelligent man."

"Very well, sir."

The other turned Little Sorrel's head toward the stream and stood listening. The sound of the distant cannonade increased. The pine wood ran back from the water, grew thinner, and gave place to mere copse and a field of broomsedge. From this edge of the forest came now a noise of mounted men. "Black Horse, I reckon!" said the 65th. "Wish they'd go ask Old Joe what he and Beauregard have got against us! — No, 't aint Black Horse — I see them through the trees — gray slouch hats and no feathers in them! Infantry, too — more infantry than horse. Hampton, maybe — No, they look like home folk —" A horseman appeared in the wood, guiding a powerful black stallion with a light hand between the pines, and checking him with a touch beside the bank upon which Little Sorrel was planted. "General Jackson?" inquired a dry, agreeable voice.

"Yes, sir, I am General Jackson. What troops have you over there?"

"The Virginia Legion."

Jackson put out a large hand. "Then you are Colonel Fauquier Cary? I am glad to see you, sir. We never met in Mexico, but I heard of you — I heard of you!"

The other gave his smile, quick and magnetic. "And I of you, general. Magruder chanted your praises day and night — our good old Fuss and Feathers, too! Oh, Mexico!"

Jackson's countenance, so rigid, plain, restrained, altered as through some effect of soft and sunny light. The blue of the eye deepened, the iris enlarged, a smile came to his lips. His stiffly held, awkwardly erect figure relaxed, though very slightly. "I loved it in Mexico. I have never forgotten it. *Dear land of the daughters of Spain!*" The light went indoors again. "That demonstration up-stream is increasing. Colonel Evans will need support."

"Yes, we must have orders shortly." Turning in his saddle, Cary gazed across the stream. "Andrew Porter and Burnside are some-where over there. I wonder if Burnside remembers the last time he was in Virginia!" He laughed. "Dabney Maury's wedding in '52 at Cleveland, and Burnside happy as a king singing 'Old Virginia never tire!' stealing kisses from the bridesmaids, hunting with the hardest, dancing till cockcrow, and asking, twenty times a day, 'Why don't we do like this in Indiana?' I wonder — I wonder!" He laughed again. "Good old Burnside! It's an odd world we live in, general!"

"The world, sir, is as God made it and as Satan darkened it."

Cary regarded him somewhat whimsically. "Well, we'll agree on God now, and perhaps before this struggle's over, we'll agree on Satan. That firing's growing louder, I think. There's a cousin of mine in the 65th — yonder by the colours! May I speak to him?"

"Certainly, sir. I have noticed Captain Cleave. His men obey him with readiness." He beckoned, and when Cleave came up, turned away with Little Sorrel to the edge of the stream. The kinsmen clasped hands.

"How are you, Richard?"

"Very well, Fauquier. And you?"

"Very well, too, I suppose. I have n't asked. You've got a fine, tall company!"

Cleave, turning, regarded his men with almost a love-light in his eyes. "By God, Fauquier, we'll win if stock can do it! It's going to make a legend — this army!"

"I believe that you are right. When you were a boy you used to dream artillery."

"I dream it still. Sooner or later, by hook or by crook, I'll get into that arm. It was n't feasible this spring."

His cousin looked at him with the affection, half humorous and wholly tender, with which he regarded most of his belongings in life. "I always liked you, Richard. Now don't you go get killed in this unnatural war! The South's going to need every good man she's got — and more beside! Where is Will?"

"In the 2d. I wanted him nearer me, but 't would have broken his heart to leave his company. Edward is with the Rifles?"

"Yes, adding lustre to the ranks. I came upon him yesterday cutting wood for his mess. 'Why don't you make Jeames cut the wood?' I asked. 'Why,' said he, 'you see it hurts his pride — and, beside, some one must cook. Jeames cooks.'" Cary laughed. "I left him getting up his load and hurrying off to roll call. Phœbus Apollo swincking for Mars! — I was at Greenwood the other day. They all sent you their love."

A colour came into Cleave's dark cheek. "Thank them for me when you write. Only the ladies are there?"

"Yes. I told them it had the air of a Spanish nunnery. Maury Stafford is with Magruder on the Peninsula."

"Yes."

"Judith had a letter from him. He was in the affair at Bethel. — What's this? Orders for us all to move, I hope!"

A courier had galloped into the wood. "General Jackson? Where is General Jackson?" A hundred hands having pointed out Little Sorrel and his rider, he arrived breathless, saluted, and extended a gauntleted hand with a folded bit of paper. Jackson took and opened the missive with his usual deliberation, glanced over the contents, and pushed Little Sorrel nearer to Fauquier Cary. "*General*," he read aloud, though in a low voice. "*the signal officer reports a turning column of the enemy approaching Sudley Ford two miles above the Stone Bridge. You will advance with all speed to the support of the endangered left. Bee and Bartow, the Hampton Legion and the Virginia Legion will receive like orders. J. E. Johnston, General Commanding.*"

The commander of the Virginia Legion gathered up his reins. "Thank you, general! *Au revoir* — and laurels to us all!" With a wave of his hand to Cleave, he was gone, crashing through the thinning pines to the broomsedge field and his waiting men.

It was nine o'clock, hot and clear, the Stone Bridge three miles away. The First Brigade went at a double quick, guided by the sound of musketry, growing in volume. The pines were left behind; oak copse succeeded, then the up and down of grassy fields. Wooden fences stretched across the way, streamlets presented themselves, here and there gaped a ravine, ragged and deep. On and on and over all! Bee and Bartow were ahead, and Hampton and the Virginia Legion. The sound of the guns grew louder. "Evans has n't got but six regiments. *Get on, men, get on!*"

The fields were very rough, all things uneven and retarding. Only the sun had no obstacles: he rose high, and there set in a scorching day. The men climbed a bank of red earth, and struck across a great cornfield. They stumbled over the furrows, they broke down the stalks, they tore aside the intertwining small, blue morning-glories. Wet with the dew of the field, they left it and dipped again into woods. The shade did not hold; now they were traversing an immense and wasted stretch where the dewberry caught at their ankles and the sun had an unchecked sway. Ahead the firing grew louder. *Get on, men, get on !*

Allan Gold, hurrying with his hurrying world, found in life this July morning something he had not found before. Apparently there were cracks in the firmament through which streamed a dazzling light, an invigorating air. After all, there was something wide, it seemed, in war, something sweet. It was bright and hot — they were going, clean and childlike, to help their fellows at the bridge. When, near at hand, a bugle blew, high as a lark above the stress, he followed the sound with a clear delight. He felt no fatigue, and he had never seen the sky so blue, the woods so green. Chance brought him for a moment in line with his captain. "Well, Allan?"

"I seem to have waked up," said Allan, then, very soberly. "I am going to like this thing."

Cleave laughed. "You have n't the air of a Norse sea king for nothing!" They dipped into a bare, red gully, scrambled up the opposite bank, and fought again with the dewberry vines. "When the battle's over you're to report to General Jackson. Say that I sent you — that you're the man he asked for this morning."

The entangling vines abruptly gave up the fight. A soft hillside of pasturage succeeded, down which the men ran like schoolboys. A gray zigzag of rail fence, a little plashy stream, another hillside, and at the top, planted against a horizon of haze and sound, a courier, hatless, upon a reeking horse. "General Jackson?"

"Yes, sir."

"McDowell has crossed at Sudley Ford. The attack on the Stone Bridge is a feint. Colonel Evans has left four companies there, and with the 4th South Carolina and the Louisiana Tigers is getting into position across Young's Branch, upon the Mathews Hill. Colonel Evans's compliments, and he says for God's sake to come on!"

"Very good, sir. General Jackson's compliments, and I am coming."

The courier turned, spurred his horse, and was gone. Jackson rode down the column. "You're doing well, men, but you've got to do better. Colonel Evans says for God's sake to come on!"

That hilltop crossed at a run, they plunged again into the trough of those low waves. The First Brigade had proved its mettle, but here it began to lose. Men gasped, wavered, fell out of line and were left behind. In Virginia the July sunshine is no bagatelle. It beat hard to-day, and to many in these ranks there was in this July Sunday an awful strangeness. At home — ah, at home! — crushed ice and cooling fans, a pleasant and shady ride to a pleasant, shady church, a little dozing through a comfortable sermon, then friends and crops and politics in the twilight dells of an old churchyard, then home, and dinner, and wide porches — Ah, that was the way, that was the way. *Close up, there! Don't straggle, men, don't straggle!*

They were out now upon another high field, carpeted with yellowing sedge, dotted over with young pines. The 65th headed the column. Lieutenant Coffin of Company A was a busy officer, active as a jumping-jack, half liked and half distasted by the men. The need of some breathing time, however slight, was now so imperative that at a stake and rider fence, overgrown with creepers, a five minutes' halt was ordered. The fence ran at right angles, and all along the column the men dropped upon the ground, in the shadow of the vines. Coffin threw himself down by the Thunder Run men. "Billy Maydew!"

"Yaas, sir."

"What have you got that stick tied to your gun for? Throw it away! I should think you'd find that old flintlock heavy enough without shouldering a sapling besides!"

Billy regarded with large blue eyes his staff for a young Hercules. "'T ain't a mite in my way, lieutenant. I air a-goin' to make a notch on it for every Yank I kill. When we get back to Thunder Run I air a-goin' to hang it over the fireplace. I reckon it air a-goin' to look right interestin'. Pap, he has a saplin' marked for b'ar an' wolves, an' gran'pap he has one his pap marked for Indians —"

"Throw it away!" said Coffin sharply. "It is n't regular. Do as I tell you."

Billy stared. "But I don't want to. It air my stick, an' I air a-goin' to hang it over the fireplace —"

The heat, the sound in front, all things, made Coffin fretful. He rose from the fence corner. "Throw that stick away, or I'll put you in the guardhouse! This ain't Thunder Run — and you men have got to learn a thing or two! Come now!"

"I won't," said Billy. "An' if 't were Thunder Run, you would n't dar' —"

Allan Gold drew himself over the grass and touched the boy's arm. "Look here, Billy! We're going into battle in a minute, and you want to be there, don't you? The lieutenant's right — that oak tree surely will get in your way! Let's see how far you can throw it. There's plenty more saplings in the woods!"

"Let him alone, Gold," said the lieutenant sharply. "Do as I order you, Billy Maydew!"

Billy rose, eighteen years old, and six feet tall. "If it's jest the same to you, lieutenant," he said politely, "I'll break it into bits first. Thar are time when I jest hone to feel my hands on somethin' brittle!" He put the thick sapling across his knee like a sword, broke it in twain, broke in their turn the two halves, and tossed the four pieces over the fence. "Thar, now! It's did." Moving back to Allan's side, he threw himself down upon the grass. "When's this hell-fired fightin' goin' to begin? I don't ask anything better, jest at this minute, than to encounter a rattler!"

The sound ahead swelled suddenly into loud and continuous firing. Apparently Evans had met the turning column. *Fall in, men, fall in!*

The First Brigade rose to its feet, left the friendly fence, and found itself upon a stretch of road, in a dust cloud that neatly capped all previous ills. At some distance rose the low hill, covered, upon this side, by a second growth of pines. "That's the Henry Hill," said the guide with the 65th. "The house just this side is the Lewis house — 'Portici,' they call it. The top of the hill is a kind of plateau, with deep gulleys across it. Nearly in the middle is the Widow Henry's house, and beyond it the house of the free negro Robinson. Chinn's house is on the other side, near Chinn's Branch. It's called the Henry Hill, and Mrs. Henry is old and bedridden. I don't know what she'll do, anyway! The hill's most level on top, as I said, but beyond the Henry House it falls right down, quite steep, to the Warrenton turnpike. Across that there's marshy ground, and Young's Branch, with the Stone House upon it, and beyond the branch there's Mathews Hill, just around the branch. Yes, sir, this back side's wooded, but you see the cleared ground when you get on top."

A bowshot from the wood, the head of the column was met by a second courier, a boy from the Alabama River, riding like Jehu, pale with excitement. "When you get to the top of the hill you'll see! They're thicker than bees from a sweet gum — they're thicker than bolls in a cotton-field! They've got three thousand Regulars, and fifteen thousand of the other kind, and they're cutting Evans to pieces!" He pulled himself together and saluted. "General Bee's compliments to General Jackson, and he is going into action."

"General Jackson's compliments, and I will support him."

The 65th entered the wood. The trees were small — bundles of hard, bright green needles aloft on slender trunks, out of which, in the strong sunshine, resin was oozing. They were set well apart, the grass beneath dry and slippery, strewn with cones. The sky was intensely blue, the air hot and without moisture, the scent of the pines strong in the nostril. Another step and the 65th came upon the wounded of Evans's brigade. An invisible line joined with suddenness the early morning picture, the torn and dying mule, the headless driver, to this. Breathless, heated, excited, the 65th swept on, yet it felt the cold air from the cavern. It had, of course, seen accidents, men injured in various ways, but never had it viewed so many, nor so much blood, and never before had it rushed past the helpless and the agonizing. There were surgeons and ambulances — there seemed to be a table of planks on which the worst cases were laid — the sufferers had help, of course, a little help. A Creole from Bayou Têche lay writhing, shot through the stomach, beneath a pine. He was raving. "Mélanie, Mélanie, donnez-moi de l'eau! Mélanie, Mélanie! donnez-moi de l'eau!"

Stragglers were coming over the hilltop — froth and spume thrown from a great wave somewhere beyond that cover — men limping, men supported by their comrades, men gasping and covered with sweat, men livid with nausea, men without arms, men carrying it off with bluster, and men too honestly frightened for any pretence. A number were legitimately there, wounded, ill, exhausted, useless on the field of battle; others were malingerers, and some were cowards — cowards for all time, or cowards for this time only. A minority was voluble. "You all think yo' going to a Sunday-school picnic, don't you? Well, you ain't. Just *you* all wait until you get to the top of the hill! What are you going to see? You're going to see hell's mouth, and the devil wearing blue! We've been there — we've been in hell since daybreak — damned if we have n't! Evans all cut to pieces! Bee and Bartow have gone in now. They'll find it hell, jest like we did. Twenty thousand of them dressed in blue." A man began to weep. "All cut to pieces. Major Wheat's lying there in a little piney wood. He was bleeding and bleeding — I saw him — but I reckon the blood has stopped. And we were all so hungry. I did n't get no breakfast. There's a plateau and the Henry House, and then there's a dip and Young's Branch, and then there's a hill called the Mathews Hill. We were there — on the Mathews Hill — we ain't on it now." Two officers appeared, one on foot, the other mounted, both pale with rage. "You'll be on it again, if you have to be dragged by the heels! Get back there, you damned, roustabout cowards!" The mounted man laid about him with his sabre; the lieutenant, afoot, wrenched from a strapping fellow his Belgian musket and applied the stock to the recreant's shoulders. The 65th left the clamour, swept onward between the pines, and presently, in the narrow road, met a braver sort, men falling back, but without panic. "Hot as hell, sir, on the other side of the hill! No, we're not running. I'll get the men back. It's just that Sykes was in front of us with his damned Regulars. Beg your pardon, general — ? General Jackson. I'll get the men back — damned — blessed — if I don't, sir! Form right here, men! The present's the best time, and here's the best place."

At the crest of the hill the 65th came upon Imboden's battery — the Staunton Artillery — four smoothbore, brass six-pounders, guns, and caissons drawn by half the proper number of horses — the rest being killed — and conducted by wounded, exhausted, powder-grimed and swearing artillerymen. Imboden, in front, was setting the pitch. "—— ——! —— ——! —— —— ——!" Jackson checked Little Sorrel and withered the battery and its captain. "What are you doing here, sir, blaspheming and retreating? Out-facing your God with your back to the enemy! What —"

Imboden, an entirely gallant man, hastened to explain. "Beg pardon, general! Bad habit, I acknowledge, but the occasion excuses — My battery has spent the morning, sir, on the Henry Hill, and damn me, if it has n't been as lonely there as the Ancient Mariner! No support — not a damned infantryman in sight for the last half hour! Alone down there by the Robinson House, and Ricketts and Griffin — Regulars by the Lord! — and the devil knows how many batteries beside playing on us with Parrotts and twelve-pounder howitzers like all the fountains at Versailles! The ground looks as though it had been rooted by hogs! No support, and no orders, and on the turnpike a bank of blue massing to rush my guns! And my ammunition out, and half my horses down — and if General Bee sent me orders to move I never got them!" He stamped upon the ground, wiping the blood from a wound in his head. "*I* could n't hold the Henry Hill! *I* could n't fight McDowell with one battery — no, by God, not even if 't was the Staunton Artillery! We had to move out."

Jackson eyed him, unmollified. "I have never seen the occasion, Captain Imboden, that justified profanity. As for support — I will support your battery. Unlimber right here."

Imboden unlimbered, placing his guns below the pine wood upon the summit. The First Brigade wheeled into line to the left. Here it was met by an aide. "General Jackson, hold your troops in reserve until Bee and Bartow need support — then give it to them!" The First Brigade deployed in the wood. About the men was still the pine thicket, blazed upon by the sun, shrilled in by winged legions; before them was the field of Bull Run. A tableland, cut by gullies, furred with knots of pine and oak, held in the middle a flower garden, a few locust trees, and a small house — the Henry House — in which, too old and ill to be borne away to safety, lay a withered woman, awaiting death. Beyond the house the ground fell sharply. At the foot of the hill ran the road, and beyond the road were the marshy banks of a little stream, and on the other side of the stream rose the Mathews Hill. Ranged upon this height Ricketts and Griffin and Arnold and many another Federal battery were sending shrieking shells against the Henry Hill. North and east and west of the batteries ran long radii of blue, pointed with bright banners, and out of the hollow between the hills came a smoke and noise as of the nethermost pit. There, beneath that sulphurous cloud, the North and the South were locked in an embrace that was not of love.

CHAPTER VIII

A CHRISTENING

I MBODEN had been joined by the Rockbridge Artillery and the Alexandria and Loudoun batteries. A little later there came up two of the New Orleans guns. All unlimbered in front of the pine wood where was couched the First Brigade, trained the sixteen guns upon the Mathews Hill and began firing. Griffin and Ricketts and Arnold answered with Parrotts and howitzers, throwing elongated, cylindrical shell that came with the screech of a banshee. But the Federal range was too long, and the fuses of many shells were uncut. Two of Rockbridge's horses were killed, a caisson of Stanard's exploded, scorching the gunners, a lieutenant was wounded in the thigh, but the batteries suffered less than did the infantry in the background. Here, more than one exploding horror wrought destruction. Immediately in rear of the guns were posted the 4th, the 27th, and the 65th. To the right hand was the 5th, to the left the 2d and the 33d. In all the men lay down in ranks, just sheltered by the final fringe of pines. The younger officers stood up, or, stepping into the clearing, seated themselves not without ostentation upon pine stumps, to the laudable end that the enemy should know where to find them. Jackson rode back and forth behind the guns.

The thundering voices grew louder, shaking the hills. The First Brigade could not see the infantry, swept now from the Mathews Hill and engaged about the turnpike and the stream. By stretching necks it saw a roof of smoke, dun-coloured, hiding pandemonium. Beneath that deeper thunder of the guns, the crackling, unintermittent sound of musketry affected the ear like the stridulation of giant insects. The men awaiting their turn beneath the pines, breathing quick, watching the shells, moved their heads slightly to and fro. In front, outdrawn upon a little ridge, stood the guns and boomed defiance. Rockbridge, Staunton, Loudoun, Alexandria, and New Orleans did well this day. The guns themselves were something ancient, growing obsolete; but those striplings about them, beardless, powder-grimed, bare of arm and chest, silent and swift and steady of eye and hand, sponging, ramming, priming, aiming, firing, showed in the van of Time a brood of Mars, a band of whom foe-quelling Hector might say "They will do well."

General T. J. Jackson on Little Sorrel went up and down between the speaking guns and the waiting infantry. The men, from their couch upon the needles, watched him. Before their eyes war was transfiguring him, and his soldiers called him "Old Jack" and made no reservation. The awkward figure took on a stalwart grace, the old uniform, the boots, the cap, grew classically right. The inner came outward, the atmosphere altered, and the man was seen as he rode in the plane above. A shell from Ricketts came screaming, struck and cut down a young pine. In falling, the tree caught and hurt a man or two. Another terror followed and exploded overhead, a fragment inflicting upon a bugler of the 65th a ghastly wound. "Steady, men, steady! — all's well," said Old Jack. He threw up his left hand, palm out, — an usual gesture, — and turned to speak to Imboden, whose profanity he had apparently forgiven. As in any other July hour a cloud of gnats might have swum above that hill, so, on this one summer day, death-dealing missiles filled the air. Some splinter from one of these struck the lifted hand. Jackson let it fall, the blood streaming. Imboden uttered an ejaculation. "It's nothing," said the other; then, with slow earnestness, "Captain Imboden, I would give — I will give — for this cause every drop of blood that courses through my heart." He drew out a handkerchief, wrapped it around the wound, and rode on down the right of his line.

Up to meet him from the foot of the hill, out of the dun smoke hiding the wrestle, came at a gallop a roan horse bearing a rider tall and well made, black-eyed and long-haired, a bright sash about his waist, a plumed hat upon his head. Panting, he drew rein beside Little Sorrel. "I am Bee. — General Jackson, we are driven — we are overwhelmed! My God! only Evans and Bartow and I against the whole North and the Regulars! We are being pushed back — you must support. — In three minutes the battle will be upon this hill — Hunter and Heintzleman's divisions. They're hot and huzzaing — they think they've got us fast! They have, by God! if our troops don't come up!" He turned his horse. "But you'll support — we count on you — "

"Count only upon God, General Bee," said Jackson. "But I will give them the bayonet."

Bee struck spur into the roan and galloped across the plateau. Out of one of the furrowing ravines, a sunbaked and wrinkled trough springing from the turnpike below and running up and across the Henry Hill toward the crest of pine and oak, came now a handful of men, grey shadows, reeling, seeking the forest and night. Another followed — another — then a stream, a grey runlet of defeat which grew in proportions. A moment more, and the ravine, fed from the battle-ground below, overflowed. The red light shifted to the Henry Hill. It was as though a closed fan, laid upon that uneven ground, had suddenly opened. The rout was not hideous. The men had fought long and boldly, against great odds; they fled now before the storm, but all cohesion was not lost, nor presence of mind. Some turned and fired, some listened to their shouting officer, and strove to form about the tossed colours, some gave and took advice. But every gun of the Federal batteries poured shot and shell upon that hilltop, and the lines of blue had begun to climb. The disorder increased; panic might come like the wind in the grass. Bee reached the choked ravine, pulled up his great roan. He was a man tall and large, and as he rose in his stirrups and held his sword aloft, standing against the sky, upon the rim of the ravine, he looked colossal, a bronze designed to point the way. He cried aloud, "Look! Yonder is Jackson standing like a stone wall! Rally behind the Virginians!" As he spoke a shell struck him. He fell, mortally wounded.

The eyes of the men in the cleft below had followed the pointed sword. The hilltop was above them, and along the summit, just in advance of a pine wood, ran a stone wall, grey, irregular, touched here by sunlight, there by shadow, and shrouded in part by the battle smoke. Some one had planted upon it a flag. For a full moment the illusion held, then the wall moved. A captain of the 4th Alabama, hoarse with shouting, found voice once more. "God! We are n't beaten! Talk of Birnam wood! The stone wall's coming!"

Up and out of the ravine, widening like an opening fan, pressed the disordered troops. The plateau was covered by chaos come again. Officers, raging, shouted orders, ran to and fro, gesticulated with their swords. A short line was formed, another; they dissolved before a third could be added. All voices were raised; there was a tumult of cries, commands, protestations, adjurations, and refusals. Over all screamed the shells, settled the smoke. Franklin, Willcox, Sherman, and Porter, pressing the Federal advantage, were now across the turnpike. Beneath their feet was the rising ground — a moment more, and they would leap victorious up the ragged slope. The moment was delayed. With a rending sound as of a giant web torn asunder, the legions of Hampton and Cary, posted near the house of the free negro Robinson, came into action and held in check the four brigades.

High upon the plateau, near Jackson's line, above the wild confusion of the retreating troops, appeared in the blaze of the midday sun, hatless, on steeds reeking from the four miles' gallop from that centre where the battle did not join to this left where it did, the generals Johnston and Beauregard. Out of the red lightning, the thunder, the dust and the smoke, above the frenzied shouting and the crying of the wounded, their presence was electrically known. A cheer rushed from the First Brigade; at the guns Rockbridge, Staunton, Loudoun, Alexandria, and New Orleans took up the cry, tossed it with grape and canister across to the opposite hill. Bee, Bartow, and Evans, exhausted, shattered, wavering upwards toward the forest, rest, cessation from long struggle, heard the names and took fresh heart. The two were not idle, but in the crucial moment turned the scale. Black danger hemmed their cause. The missing brigade of the Shenandoah was no man knew where. At Mitchell's and Blackburn's fords, Ewell, D. R. Jones, Bonham, and Longstreet were engaged in a demonstration in force, retaining upon that front the enemy's reserve. Holmes and Jubal Early were on their way to the imperilled left, but the dust cloud that they raised was yet distant. Below the two generals were broken troops, men raw to the field, repulsed, driven, bleeding, and haggard, full on the edge of headlong flight; lower, in the hollow land, McDowell's advance, filling the little valley, islanding the two fighting legions, and now, a mounting tide, attacking the Henry Hill. At Beauregard's order the regimental colours were advanced, and the men adjured to rally about them. Fiery, eloquent, of French descent and impassioned, Pierre Gustave Toutant Beauregard rose in his stirrups and talked of *la gloire*, of home, and of country. Georgia, Alabama, Mississippi, and Louisiana listened, cheered, and began to reform. Johnston,

Scotch, correct, military, the Regular in person, trusted to the hilt by the men he led, seized the colours of the 4th Alabama, raised them above his grey head, spurred his war horse, and in the hail of shot and shell established the line of battle. Decimated as they were, raw volunteers as they were, drawn from peaceful ways to meet the purple dragon, fold on fold of war, the troops of Bee, Bartow, and Evans rallied, fell into line, and stood. The 49th Virginia came upon the plateau from Lewis Ford — at its head Ex-Governor William Smith. "Extra Billy," old political hero, sat twisted in his saddle, and addressed his regiment. "Now, boys, you've just got to kill the ox for this barbecue! Now, mind you, I ain't going to have any backing out! We ain't West P'inters, but, thank the Lord, we're men! When it's all over we'll have a torchlight procession and write to the girls! Now, boys, you be good to me, and I'll be good to you. Lord, children, I want to be proud of you! And I ain't Regular, but I know Old Virginny. Tom Scott, you beat the drum real loud, and James, you swing that flag so high the good Lord's got to see it! — Here's the West P'inters — here's the generals! Now, boys, just see how loud you can holler!"

The 49th went into line upon Gartrell's right, who was upon Jackson's left. Beauregard paused to speak to that brigadier, advanced upon Little Sorrel in front of the 65th. An aide addressed the latter's colonel. "General Bee christened this brigade just before he fell. He called it a stone wall. If he turns out a true prophet I reckon the name will stick." A shell came hurtling, fell, exploded, and killed under him Beauregard's horse. He mounted the aide's and galloped back to Johnston, near the Henry House. Here there was a short council. Had the missing brigade, the watched for, the hoped for, reached Manassas? Ewell and Early had been ordered up from Union Mills. Would they arrive upon this hill in time? What of the Stone Bridge, now left almost undefended? What of Blackburn and Mitchell's fords, and Longstreet's demonstration, and the enemy's reserves across Bull Run? What best disposition of the strength that might arrive? The conference was short. Johnston, the senior with the command of the whole field, galloped off to the Lewis House, while Beauregard retained the direction of the contest on the Henry Hill. Below it the two legions still held the blue wave from mounting.

Ricketts and Griffin upon the Mathews Hill ceased firing —
greatly to the excitement of Rockbridge, Staunton, Loudoun, Alexandria, and New Orleans. The smoke slightly lifted. "What're
they doing? They've got their horses — they're limbering up! What
in hell! — d' ye suppose they've had enough? No! Great day in
the morning! They're coming up here!"

Ricketts and Griffin, cannoneers on caissons, horses urged to a
gallop, thundered down the opposite slope, across Young's Branch
and the turnpike. A moment and they were lost to sight, another
and the straining horses and the dust and the guns and the fighting
men about them showed above the brow of the Henry Hill. Out
they thundered upon the plateau and wheeled into battery very
near to the Henry House. Magnificence but not war! They had no
business there, but they had been ordered and they came. With a
crash as of all the thunders they opened at a thousand feet, full upon
the Confederate batteries and upon the pine wood where lay the
First Brigade.

Rockbridge, Staunton, Loudoun, Alexandria, and New Orleans,
wet with sweat, black with powder, sponging, ramming, priming,
aiming, firing, did well with the bass of that hill-echoing tune. A
lieutenant of the Washington Artillery made himself heard above
the roar. "Short range! We've got short range at last! Now, old
smoothbores, show what you are made of!" The smoothbores
showed. Griffin and Ricketts answered, Jackson's sharpshooters
took a part, the uproar became frightful. The captain of the Rockbridge Artillery was a great-nephew of Edmund Pendleton, a gradu-
ate of West Point and the rector of the Episcopal Church in Lexington. He went back and forth among his guns. "Fire! and the Lord
have mercy upon their souls. — Fire! and the Lord have mercy
upon their souls." With noise and a rolling smoke and a scorching breath and a mad excitement that annihilated time and reduced with a thunderclap every series of happenings into one all-
embracing moment, the battle mounted and the day swung past
its burning noon.

The 11th and 14th New York had been pushed up the hill to the
support of Ricketts and Griffin. Behind them showed in strength
other climbing muskets. In the vale below Hampton and Cary had
made diversion, had held the brigades in check, while upon the pla-

teau the Confederates rallied. The two legions, stubborn and gallant, suffered heavily. With many dead and many wounded they drew off at last. The goal of the Henry Hill lay clear before Mc-Dowell.

He had brigades enough for the advance that should set all the bells of Washington ringing for victory. His turning column at Sudley Ford had numbered eighteen thousand men. But Howard was somewhere in the vague distance, Burnside was "resting," Keyes, who had taken part in the action against Hampton, was now astray in the Bull Run Valley, and Schenck had not even crossed the stream. There were the dead, too, the wounded and the stragglers. All told, perhaps eleven thousand men attacked the Henry Hill. They came on confidently, flushed with victory, brilliant as tropical birds in the uniforms so bright and new, in the blue, in the gold, in the fiery, zouave dress, in the Garibaldi shirt, in the fez, the Scotch bonnet, the plume, in all the militia pomp and circumstance of that somewhat theatrical "On to Richmond." With gleaming muskets and gleaming swords and with the stars and stripes above them, they advanced, huzzaing. Above them, on that plateau, ranged beneath the stars and bars, there awaited the impact six thousand and five hundred Confederates with sixteen guns. Three thousand of the troops were fresh; three thousand had been long and heavily engaged, and driven from their first position.

Rockbridge and New Orleans and their fellows worked like grey automata about their belching guns. They made a dead line for the advance to cross. Ricketts and Griffin answered with their howling shells — shells that burst above the First Brigade. One stopped short of the men in battle. It entered the Henry House, burst, and gave five wounds to the woman cowering in her bed. Now she lay there, dying, above the armies, and the flower-beds outside were trampled, and the boughs of the locust trees strewn upon the earth.

Hunter and Heintzleman mounted the ridge of the hill. With an immense volley of musketry the battle joined upon the plateau that was but five hundred yards across. The Fire Zouaves, all red, advanced like a flame against the 4th Alabama, crouched behind scrub oak to the left of the field. The 4th Alabama fired, loaded, fired again. The zouaves broke, fleeing in disorder toward a piece of woods. Out from the shadow of the trees came Jeb Stuart with two hundred cavalrymen. The smoke was very thick; it was not with ease that one told friend from foe. In the instant of encounter the *beau sabreur* thought that he spoke to Confederates. He made his horse to bound, he rose in his stirrups, he waved his plumed hat, he shouted aloud in his rich and happy voice, "Don't run, boys! We are here!" To his disappointment the magic fell short. The "boys" ran all the faster. Behind him, a trooper lifted his voice. "They're not ours! They're Yankees! Charge them, sir, charge!" Stuart charged.

Along the crest of the Henry Hill the kneeling ranks of the First Brigade fired and loaded and fired again. Men and horses fell around the guns of Ricketts and Griffin, but the guns were not silenced. Rockbridge and Loudoun and their fellows answered with their Virginia Military Institute six-pounders, with their howitzers, with their one or two Napoleons, but Ricketts and Griffin held fast. The great shells came hurtling, death screaming its message and sweeping the pine wood. The stone wall suffered; here and there the units dropped from place. Jackson, holding up his wounded hand, came to the artillery. "Get these guns out of my way. I am going to give them the bayonet." The bugler put the bugle to his lips. The guns limbered up, moving out by the right flank and taking position elsewhere upon the plateau. Jackson returned to his troops. "Fix bayonets! Now, men, charge and take those batteries!"

The First Brigade rose from beneath the pines. It rose, it advanced between the moving guns, it shouted. The stone wall became an avalanche, and started down the slope. It began crescent-wise, for the pine wood where it had lain curved around Ricketts and Griffin like a giant's half-closed hand. From the finger nearest the doomed batteries sprang the 33d Virginia. In the dust of the field all uniforms were now of one neutral hue. Griffin trained his guns upon the approaching body, but his chief stopped him. "They're our own, man! — a supporting regiment!" The 33d Virginia came on, halted at two hundred feet, and poured upon the batteries a withering fire. Alas for Ricketts and Griffin, brave men handling brave guns! Their cannoneers fell, and the scream of their horses shocked the field. Ricketts was badly wounded; his lieutenant Ramsay lay dead. The stone wall blazed again. The Federal infantry supporting the guns broke and fled in confusion. Other regiments — Michigan and Minnesota this time — came up the hill. A grey-haired officer — Heintzleman — seated sideways in his saddle upon a hillock, appealing, cheering, commanding, was conspicuous for his gallant bearing. The 33d, hotly pushed, fell back into the curving wood, only to emerge again and bear down upon the prize of the guns. The whole of the First Brigade was now in action and the plateau of the Henry Hill roared like the forge of Vulcan when it welded the armour of Mars. It was three in the afternoon of midmost July. There arose smoke and shouts and shrieks, the thunder from the Mathews Hill of the North's uncrippled artillery, and from the plateau the answering thunder of the Southern, with the under song, incessant, of the muskets. Men's tongues clave to the roofs of their mouths, the sweat streamed forth, and the sweat dried, black cartridge marks were about their lips, and their eyes felt metallic, heated balls distending the socket. There was a smell of burnt cloth, of powder, of all heated and brazen things, indescribable, unforgettable, the effluvia of the battlefield. The palate savoured brass, and there was not a man of those thousands who was not thirsty — oh, very, very thirsty! Time went in waves with hollows between of negation. A movement took hours — surely we have been at it since last year! Another passed in a lightning flash. We were there beneath the pines, on the ground red-breeched Zouaves and United States Marines, above us a noisy shell, the voice of the general coming dry and far like a grasshopper's through the din — we are here in a trampled flower garden, beside the stumps of locust trees, in the midst of yells and trampling, hands again upon the guns! There was no time between. The men who were left of Ricketts and Griffin fought well; they were brave fighters. The 2d Wisconsin came up the hill, then the 79th and 69th New York. An impact followed that seemed to rock the globe. Wisconsin and New York retired whence they came, and it was all done in a moment. Other regiments took their places. McDowell was making a frontal attack and sending in his brigades piecemeal. The plateau was uneven; low ridges, shallow hollows, with clumps of pine and oak; one saw at a time but a segment of the field. The nature of the ground split the troops as with wedges; over all the Henry Hill the fighting now became from hand to hand, in the woods and in the open, small squad against small squad. That night a man insisted that this phase had lasted twelve hours. He said that he remembered how the sun rose over the Henry House, and how, when it went down, it left a red wall behind a gun on the Mathews Hill — and he had seen both events from a ring of pines out of which he, with two others, was keeping twenty Rhode Islanders.

Ricketts and Griffin, forty men upon the ground, twice that number of horses dead or disabled, tried to drag away the guns. Down upon them roared the 65th, no alignment, broken and fierce as a mountain torrent, as Thunder Run when the rains were out and the snows had melted. It took again the guns; it met a regiment from the Northwest, also stark fighters and hunters, and turned it back; it seized the guns and drew them toward the pine wood. On the other side Howard's Brigade came into action, rising, a cloud of stinging bees, over the ridge. Maine and Vermont fell into line, fired, each man, twenty rounds. The First Brigade answered at close range. All the Henry plateau blazed and thundered.

From headquarters at the Lewis House a most able mind had directed the several points of entrance into battle of the troops drawn from the lower fords. The 8th, the 18th, and 28th Virginia, Cash and Kershaw of Bonham's, Fisher's North Carolina — each had come at a happy moment and had given support where support was most needed. Out of the southeast arose a cloud of dust, a great cloud as of many marching men. It moved rapidly. It approached at a double quick, apparently it had several guns at trail. Early had not yet come up from Union Mills; was it Early? Could it be — *could it be from Manassas? Could it be the missing brigade?* Beauregard, flashing across the plateau like a meteor, lifted himself in his stirrups, raised with a shaking hand his field-glasses to his eyes. Stonewall Jackson held higher his wounded hand, wrapped in a handkerchief no longer white. "It ain't for the pain, — he's praying," thought the orderly by his side. Over on the left, guarding that flank, Jeb Stuart, mounted on a hillock, likewise addressed the heavens. "Good Lord, I hope it's Elzey! Oh, good Lord, let it be Elzey!" The 49th Virginia was strung behind a rail fence, firing from between the grey bars. "Extra Billy," whose horse had been shot an hour before, suddenly appeared in an angle erect upon the topmost rails. He gazed, then turned and harangued. "Did n't I tell you, boys? Did n't I say that the old Manassas Gap ain't half so black as she's painted? The president of that road is my friend, gentlemen, and a better man never mixed a julep! The old Manassas Gap's got them through! It's a road to be patronized, gentlemen! The old Manassas Gap — "

A hand plucked at his boot. "For the Lord's sake, governor, come down from there, or you'll be travelling on the Angels' Express!"

The dust rose higher; there came out of it a sound, a low, hoarse din. Maine and Vermont, Michigan, Wisconsin and Minnesota, New York and Rhode Island, saw and heard. There was a waver as of grain beneath wind over the field, then the grain stood stiff against the wind, and all the muskets flamed again.

The lost brigade of the Army of the Shenandoah, seventeen hundred infantry and Beckham's Battery swept by the Lewis House, received instructions from Johnston in person, and advanced against the enemy's right flank. Kirby Smith led them. Heated, exhausted, parched with thirst, the regiments came upon the plateau. Not till then did they see the enemy, the awaited, the dreamed-of foe, the giant whose voice they had heard at Manassas. They saw him now, and they yelled recognition. From a thousand dusty throats came a cry, involuntary, individual, indescribably fierce, a high and shrill and wild expression of anger and personal opinion. There was the enemy. They saw him, they yelled, — without premeditation, without coöperation, each man for himself, *Yaai, Yai . . . Yaai, Yaai, Yai. . . . Yaai!* That cry was to be heard on more than two thousand battlefields. It lasts with the voice of Stentor, and with the horn of Roland. It has gone down to history as the "Rebel yell."

As they reached the oak woods Kirby Smith was shot. Desperately wounded, he fell from his horse. Elzey took command; the troops swept out by the Chinn House upon the plateau. Beckham's battery unlimbered and came, with decisive effect, into action.

McDowell, with a last desperate rally, formed a line of battle, a gleaming, formidable crescent, half hid by a cloud of skirmishers. Out of the woods by the Chinn House now came Jubal Early, with Kemper's 7th Virginia, Harry Hays's Louisianians, and Barksdale's 13th Mississippi. They took position under fire and opened upon the enemy's right. As they did so Elzey's brigade, the 10th Virginia, the 1st Maryland, the 3d Tennessee, the 8th and 2d South

Carolina, the 18th and 28th Virginia, and Hampton's and Cary's legions charged. The First Brigade came down upon the guns for the third time, and held them. Stuart, standing in his stirrups and chanting his commands, rounded the base of the hill, and completed the rout.

The Federals turned. Almost to a man their officers did well. There were many privates of a like complexion. Sykes' Regulars, not now upon the Henry Hill, but massed across the branch, behaved throughout the day like trained and disciplined soldiers. No field could have witnessed more gallant conduct than that of Griffin and Ricketts. Heintzleman had been conspicuously energetic, Franklin and Willcox had done their best. McDowell himself had not lacked in dash and grit, nor, to say sooth, in strategy. It was the Federal tactics that were at fault. But all the troops, barring Sykes and Ricketts and the quite unused cavalry, were raw, untried, undisciplined. Few were good marksmen, and, to tell the truth, few were possessed of a patriotism that would stand strain. That virtue awoke later in the Army of the Potomac; it was not present in force on the field of Bull Run. Many were three-months men, their term of service about to expire, and in their minds no slightest intention of reënlistment. They were close kin to the troops whose term expiring on the eve of battle had this morning "marched to the rear to the sound of the enemy's cannon." Many were men and boys merely out for a lark and almost ludicrously astonished at the nature of the business. New Englanders had come to battle as to a town meeting; placid farmers and village youths of the Middle States had never placed in the meadows of their imaginations events like these, while the more alert and restless folk of the cities discovered that the newspapers had been hardly explicit. The men of the Northwest had a more adequate conception; there was promise in these of stark fighting. To all is to be added a rabble of camp followers, of sutlers, musicians, teamsters, servants, congressmen in carriages, even here and there a congressman's wife, all the hurrah and vain parade, the strut and folly and civilian ignorance, the unwarlike softness and the misdirected pride with which these Greeks had set out to take in a night that four-years-distant Troy. Now a confusion fell upon them, and a rout such as was never seen again in that war. They left the ten guns, mute enough now, they gave no heed to their frantic officers, they turned and fled. One moment they stood that charge, the next the slopes of the Henry Hill were dark blue with fugitives. There was no cohesion; mere inability to find each an unencumbered path crowded them thus. They looked a swarm of bees, but there was no Spirit of the Hive. The Confederate batteries strewed their path with shot and shell, the wild and singular cry, first heard upon that field, rang still within their ears. They reached the foot of the hill, the Warrenton turnpike, the Sudley and Newmarket road, and the marshy fields through which flowed Young's Branch. Up to this moment courtesy might have called the movement a not too disorderly retreat, but now, upon the crowded roads and through the bordering meadows, it became mere rout, a panic quite simple, naked, and unashamed. In vain the officers commanded and implored, in vain Sykes' Regulars took position on the Mathews Hill, a nucleus around which the broken troops might have reformed. The mob had neither instinct nor desire for order. The Regulars, retreating finally with the rest, could only guard the rear and hinder the Confederate pursuit. The panic grew. Ravens in the air brought news, true and false, of the victors. Beckham's battery, screaming upon the heels of the rout, was magnified a hundred-fold; there was no doubt that battalions of artillery were hurling unknown and deadly missiles, blocking the way to the Potomac! Jeb Stuart was following on the Sudley Road, and another cavalry fiend — Munford — on the turnpike. Four hundred troopers between them? No! *Four thousand* — and each riding like the Headless Horseman with terror in his hand! There was Confederate infantry upon the turnpike — a couple of regiments, a legion, a battery — they were making for a point they knew, this side Centreville, where they might intercept the fleeing army. It behoved the army to get there first, to cross Bull Run, to cross Cub Run, and to reach Centreville with the utmost possible expedition. The ravens croaked of the Confederate troops four miles down Bull Run, at the lower fords. They would cross, they would fall upon Miles and Tyler, they would devour alive the Federal reserves, they would get first to Centreville! That catastrophe, at least, the mob did its best to prevent. It threw away its muskets, it dropped its colours, it lightened itself of accoutrements, it fled as if each tired and inexperienced grey soldier behind it had been Death in the Apocalypse.

Each man ran for himself, swore for himself, prayed for himself, found in Fate a personal foe, and strove to propitiate her with the rags of his courage. The men stumbled and fell, lifted themselves, and ran again. Ambulances, wagons, carriages, blocked the road; they streamed around and under these. Riderless horses tore the veil of blue. Artillery teams, unguided, maddened, infected by all this human fear, rent it further, and behind them the folds heard again the Confederate yell. Centreville — Centreville first, and a little food — all the haversacks had been thrown away — but no stopping at Centreville! No! Beyond Centreville the Potomac — Washington — *home !* Home and safety, Maine or Massachusetts, New York or Vermont, as the case might be! The sun went down and left the fleeing army streaming northward by every road or footpath which it conceived might lead to the Potomac.

In the summer dusk, back at the Lewis House, a breathless courier brought to Beauregard a circumstantial statement. "From Major Rhett at Manassas, general! The Federal Reserves have been observed crossing below MacLean's. A strong column — they'll take us in the rear, or they'll fall upon Manassas!" That McDowell would use his numerous reserves was so probable a card that Bonham and Longstreet, started upon the pursuit, were recalled. Ewell and Holmes had just reached the battlefield. They were faced about, and, Beauregard with them, double-quicked back to Mac-Lean's Ford — to find no Miles or Richardson or Runyon for them to attack! It was a mistake and a confusion of identity. The crossing troops were Confederates — D. R. Jones returning from the position he had held throughout the day to the southern bank of Bull Run. The dark had come, the troops were much exhausted, the routed army by now at Centreville. Beauregard did the only thing that could be done, — ordered the men to halt and bivouac for the night in the woods about the stream.

Back upon the Sudley Road Stuart and his troopers followed for twelve miles the fugitive army. There was a running fight; here and there the enemy was cut off; great spoil and many prisoners were taken. Encumbered with all of these, Stuart at Sudley Church called off the chase and halted for the night. At the bridge over Cub Run Munford with a handful of the Black Horse and the Chester-field Troop, a part of Kershaw's regiment and Kemper's battery meeting the retreat as it debouched into the Warrenton turnpike, heaped rout on rout, and confounded confusion. A wagon was upset upon the bridge, it became impassable, and Panic found that she must get away as best she might. She left her congressmen's carriages, her wagons of subsistence, and her wagons of ammunition, her guns and their caissons, her flags and her wounded in ambulances; she cut the traces of the horses and freed them from pleasure carriage, gun carriage, ammunition wagon, and ambulance; with these horses and afoot, she dashed through the water of Cub Run, and with the long wail of the helpless behind her, fled northward through the dusk. A little later, bugles, sounding here and there beneath the stars, called off the pursuit.

The spoil of Manassas included twenty-eight fieldpieces with a hundred rounds of ammunition to each gun, thirty-seven caissons, six forges, four battery wagons, sixty-four artillery horses, five hundred thousand rounds of small arm ammunition, four thousand five hundred sets of accoutrements, four thousand muskets, nine regimental and garrison flags, pistols, swords, musical instruments, knapsacks, canteens, blankets, tents, officers' luggage, rope, handcuffs, axes, and intrenching tools, wagons, horses, camp and garrison equipage, hospital stores and subsistence, and one thousand four hundred and twenty-one prisoners.

History has not been backward with a question. Why did not the Confederate forces press the pursuit to the Potomac, twenty-five miles away? Why did they not cross that river? Why did they not take Washington? History depones that it was a terror-stricken city and that it might have been stormed, and so, perhaps, the great war ended ere it had well begun. Why did you not pursue from Manassas to Washington?

The tongue of the case answers thus: "We were a victorious army, but we had fought long and hard. We had not many fresh troops. Even those which were not engaged had been marching and countermarching. The enemy had many more than we — heavy reserves to whom panic might or might not have been communicated. These were between us and Centreville, and the night had fallen. Our cavalry was the best in the land, but cruelly small in force, and very weary by that midnight. We were scant of provisions, scant of transportation, scant of ammunition. What if the Federal reserves had not stood, but had fled with the rest, and we had in some fashion achieved the Potomac? There were strong works at Arlington and Alexandria, lined with troops, and in easy distance were Patterson and his unused men. There was a river a mile wide, patrolled by gunboats, and beyond it a city with how many troops we knew not, certainly with strong earthworks and mounted guns. Being only men and not clairvoyants we did not know that the city was so crazed with fear that perhaps, after all, had we ever gotten there we might have stormed it with a few weary regiments. We never saw the like in our own capital at any after date, and we did not know. We were under arms from dawn until the stars came out, we had fought through the heat of a July day in Virginia, we were hungry, we were thirsty, we were drunk with need of rest. Most of us were under twenty-four. We had met and vanquished heavy odds, but we ourselves, like those who fled, were soldiers all untried. Victory disorganized us, as defeat disorganized them. Not in the same measure, but to the extent that all commands were much broken, men astray in the darkness, seeking their companies, companies calling out the number of their regiments. Most of us went hungry that night. And all around were the dead and wounded, and above us, like a pall, the strangeness of this war at last. The July night passed like a fevered dream; men sleeping on the earth, men seeking their commands, men riding to and fro, men wandering with lanterns over the battlefield. At three came down the rain. It was as though the heavens were opened. No one had ever seen such a downpour. All day long it rained, and in the rain we buried our comrades. There were two brothers, Holmes and Tucker Conrad, boys from the University. Holmes was shot through the heart, just on the edge of a ravine on the Henry Hill. Tucker, across the ravine, saw him fall. He was down one side and up the other before a man could draw breath. He lifted Holmes, and as he did so, he, too, was killed. We found them lying in each other's arms, Holmes smiling, and we buried them so. We buried many friends and comrades and kindred — we were all more or less akin — and perhaps, being young to war, that solemn battlefield loomed to us so large that it obstructed the view of the routed invasion now across the Potomac, out of Virginia. We held then and we hold still, that our generals that day were sagacious and brave, and we think history may take their word for it that any effective pursuit, looking to the crossing of the Potomac, was a military impossibility. It is true that Stonewall Jackson, as history reminds us, was heard to exclaim while the surgeon was dressing his hand, "Give me ten thousand fresh troops, and I will be in Washington to-morrow!" But there were not the ten thousand troops to give.

CHAPTER IX

WINCHESTER

THE December afternoon was drawing to a quiet close. The season had proved extraordinarily mild — it seemed Indian summer still rather than only a fortnight from Christmas. Farming folk prophesied a cold January, while the neighbourhood negroes held that the unusual warmth proceeded from the comet which blazed this year in the skies. An old woman whom the children called a witch sat in the sun on her doorstep, and shook her head at every passer-by. "A green Christmas makes a fat grave-yard. — Down, pussy, down, down! — A green Christmas makes a fat graveyard. Did ye hear the firing yesterday?"

An amethyst haze filled the valley town of Winchester. Ordinarily, in weather such as this, the wide streets had a dream quality and the gardens where the chrysanthemums yet lingered and the brick sidewalks all strewn with russet leaves, and the faint smell of wood smoke, and the old gilt of the sunshine, all carried back as to some vanished song or story, sweet while it lasted. But if this was true once of Winchester, and might be true again, it was hardly true of to-day, of Winchester in December 1861; of Winchester with Major-General T. J. Jackson, commanding the Department of the Valley, quartered in the town, and the Stonewall Brigade, commanded by Garnett, encamped upon its edge, and the Valley Troopers commanded by Ashby, flashing by on their way to reconnoitre the Federal General Banks; of Winchester, with bands playing "Dixie," with great white-topped wagons going endlessly through the streets, with soldiers passing and repassing, or drilling, drilling, drilling in the fields without, or thronging the Taylor House, or coming to supper in the hospitable brick mansions where the pretty girls could never, never, never look aught but kindly on any man who wore the grey — of Winchester, in short, in war time.

The sun slipped low in the heavens. Out of the purple haze to the south, a wagon from Staunton way, drawn by oxen and piled high with forage, came up a side street. The ancient negro who drove was singing, —

> "I saw de beam in my sistah's eye,
> Cyarn see de beam in mine!
> Yo 'd better lef' yo' sistah's doah,
> An' keep yo' own doah fine! –
> An' I had er mighty battle lak Jacob an' de angel —"

The wagon passed on. A picket squad swung up the middle of the street, turned, and went marching toward the sunset. The corner house was a warehouse fitted for a hospital. Faces showed at the windows; when, for a moment, a sash was lifted, a racking cough made itself heard. Just now no wounded lodged in the warehouse, but all the diseases were there with which raw troops are scourged. There were measles and mumps, there were fevers, typhoid and malarial, there were intestinal troubles, there were pleurisy and pneumonia. Some of the illnesses were slight, and some of the men would be discharged by Death. The glow of the sun made the window glass red. It was well, for the place needed every touch of cheer.

The door opened, and two ladies came out, the younger with an empty basket. The oppression of the place they were leaving stayed with them for some distance down the wider street, but at last, in the rosy light, with a bugle sounding from the camp without the town, the spirits of the younger, at least, revived. She drew a long breath. "Well! As long as Will is in a more comfortable place, and is getting better, and Richard is well and strong, and they all say he is a born soldier and his men adore him, and there is n't a battle, and if there were, we 'd win, and this weather lasts, and a colonel and a captain and two privates are coming to supper, and one of them draws and the other has a voice like an angel, and my silk dress is almost as good as new, I can't be terribly unhappy, mother!"

Margaret Cleave laughed. "I don't want you to be! I am not 'terribly' unhappy myself — despite those poor, poor boys in the warehouse! I am thankful about Will and I am thankful about Richard, and war is war, and we must all stand it. We must stand it with just as high and exquisite a courage as we can muster. If we can add a gaiety that is n't thoughtless, so much the better! We 've got to do it for Virginia and for the South — yes, and for every soul who is dear to us, and for ourselves! I 'll lace your silk dress, and

I'll play Mr. Fairfax's accompaniments with much pleasure — and to-morrow we'll come back to the warehouse with a full basket! I wish the coffee was not getting so low."

A soldier, a staff officer equipped for the road, came rapidly up the brick sidewalk, overtook the two, and spoke their names, holding out his hand. "I was sure 't was you! Nowadays one meets one's world in no matter how unlikely a place! Not that Winchester is an unlikely place — dear and hospitable little town! Nor, perhaps, should I be surprised. I knew that Captain Cleave was in the Stonewall Brigade." He took the basket from Miriam and walked beside them.

"My youngest son has been ill," said Margaret. "He is in the 2d. Kind friends took him home and cared for him, but Miriam and I were unhappy at Three Oaks. So we closed the house and came."

"Will always was a baby," volunteered Miriam. "When the fever made him delirious and they thought he was going to die, he kept calling for mother, and sometimes he called for me. Now he's better, and the sister of a man in his mess is reading 'Kenilworth' aloud to him, and he's spoiled to death! Richard always did spoil him —"

Her mother smiled. "I don't think he's really spoiled; not, that is, by Richard. — When did you come to town, Major Stafford?"

"Last night," answered Stafford. "From General Loring, near Monterey. I am the advance of the Army of the Northwest. We are ordered to join General Jackson, and ten days or so should see the troops in Winchester. What is going to happen then? Dear madam, I do not know!"

Miriam chose to remain petulant. "General Jackson is the most dreadful martinet! He drills and drills and drills the poor men until they're too tired to stand. He makes people get up at dawn in December, and he won't let officers leave camp without a pass, and he has prayer meetings all the time! Ever so many people think he's crazy!"

"Miriam!"

"But they do, mother! Of course, not Richard. Richard knows how to be a soldier. And Will — Will would be loyal to a piece of cement out of the Virginia Military Institute! And of course the Stonewall Brigade does n't say it, nor the Rockbridge Artillery, nor any of Ashby's men — they're soldiers, too! But I've heard the *militia* say it —"

Maury Stafford laughed. "Then I won't! I'll only confide to you that the Army of the Northwest thinks that General Jackson is — is — well, is General Jackson! — To burn our stores of subsistence, to leave unguarded the passes along a hundred miles of mountain, to abandon quarters just established, to get our sick somehow to the rear, and to come up here upon some wild winter campaign or other — all on the representation of the rather singular Commander of the Army of the Valley!" He took off his gold-braided cap, and lifted his handsome head to the breeze from the west. "But what can you do with professors of military institutes and generals with one battle to their credit? Nothing — when they have managed to convert to their way of thinking both the commanding general and the government at Richmond! — You look grave, Mrs. Cleave! I should not have said that, I know. Pray forget it — and don't believe that I am given to such indiscretions!" He laughed. "There were representations which I was to make to General Jackson. Well, I made them! In point of fact, I made them but an hour ago. Hence this unbecoming temper. They were received quite in the manner of a stone wall — without comment and without removal from the ground occupied! Well! Why not expect the thing to show its nature? — Is this pleasant old house your goal?"

They had come to a white, old mansion, with steps running up to a narrow yard and a small porch. "Yes, we are staying here. Will you not come in?"

"Thank you, no. I ride as far as Woodstock to-night. I have not seen Captain Cleave. Indeed, I have not seen him since last spring."

"He is acting just now as aide to General Jackson. You have been all this while with General Magruder on the Peninsula?"

"Yes, until lately. We missed Manassas." He stood beside the garden wall, his gauntleted hand on the gatepost. A creeper bearing yet a few leaves hung from a tree above, and one of the crimson points touched his grey cap. "I am now on General Loring's staff. Where he goes at present I go. And where General Jackson goes, apparently we all go! Heigho! How do you like war, Miss Miriam?"

Miriam regarded him with her air of a brown and gold gilliflower. She thought him very handsome, and oh, she liked the gold-braided cap and the fine white gauntlet! "There is something to be said on both sides," she stated sedately. "I should like it very much did not you all run into danger."

Stafford looked at her, amused. "But some of us run out again Ah!"

Cleave came from the house and down the path to the gate, moving in a red sunset glow, beneath trees on which yet hung a few russet leaves. He greeted his mother and sister, then turned with courtesy to Stafford. "Sandy Pendleton told me you were in town. From General Loring, are you not? You low-countrymen are gathering all our mountain laurels! Gauley River and Greenbriar and to-day, news of the Allegheny engagement —"

"You seem to be bent," said Stafford, "on drawing us from the Monterey line before we can gather any more! We will be here next week."

"You do not like the idea?"

The other shrugged. "I? Why should I care? It is war to go where you are sent. But this weather is much too good to last, and I fail to see what can be done to the northward when winter is once let loose! And we leave the passes open. There is nothing to prevent Rosecrans from pushing a force through to Staunton!"

"That is the best thing that could happen. Draw them into the middle valley and they are ours."

Stafford made a gesture. "*Ducdame, ducdame, ducdame!* Mrs. Cleave, there is no help for it! We are bewitched — and all by a stone wall in an old cadet cap!"

Cleave laughed. "No, no! but it is, I think, apparent — You will not go in? I will walk with you, then, as far as the hotel."

Margaret Cleave held out her hand. "Good-bye, Major Stafford. We think day and night of all you soldiers. God bless you all, wherever you may be!"

In the sunset light the two men turned their faces toward the Taylor House. "It is a good thing to have a mother," said Stafford. "Mine died when I was a little boy. — Well, what do you think of affairs in general?"

"I think that last summer we won a Pyrrhic victory."

"I share your opinion. It was disastrous. How confident we are with our 'One to Four,' our 'Quality, not Quantity,' our contempt for 'Brute Mass'! To listen to the newspapers one would suppose that the fighting animal was never bred north of the Potomac — Maryland, alone, an honourable exception! France and England, too! They'll be our active allies not a minute later than April Fool's Day!"

"You are bitter."

"It is the case, is it not?"

"Yes," said Cleave gravely. "And the blockade is daily growing more effective, and yet before we are closed in a ring of fire we do not get our cotton out nor our muskets in! Send the cotton to Europe and sell it and so fill the treasury with honest gold! — not with this delusion of wealth, these sheafs of Promises to Pay the Government is issuing. Five million bales of cotton idle in the South! With every nerve strained, with daring commensurate to the prize, we could get them out — even now! To-morrow it will be too late. The blockade will be complete, and we shall rest as isolated as the other side of the moon. Well! Few countries or men are wise till after the event."

"You are not bitter."

Cleave shook his head. "I do not believe in bitterness. And if the government is not altogether wise, so are few others. The people are heroic. We will see what we will see. I had a letter from the Peninsula the other day. Fauquier Cary is there with his legion. He says that McClellan will organize and organize and organize again until springtime. It's what he does best. Then, if only he can be set going, he will bring into the field an army that is an army. And if he's not thwarted by his own government he'll try to reach Richmond from the correct direction — and that's by sea to Old Point and up both banks of the James. All of which means heavy fighting on the Peninsula. So Cary thinks, and I dare say he knows his man. They were classmates and served together in Mexico."

They approached the old colonnaded hotel. Stafford's horse stood at the rack. A few soldiers were about the place and down the street, in the warm dusk a band was playing. "You ride up the valley to-night?" said Cleave. "When you return to Winchester you must let me serve you in any way I can."

"You are very good. How red the sunsets are! Look at that bough across the sky!"

"Were you," asked Cleave, "were you in Albemarle this autumn?"

"Yes. For one day in October. The country looked its loveliest. The old ride through the woods, by the mill —"

"I remember," said Cleave. "My cousins were well?"

"Quite well. Enchanted princesses guarded by the sable Julius. The old place was all one drift of red and yellow leaves."

They reached the hotel. Cleave spoke abruptly. "I am to report presently at headquarters, so I will say good-bye here." The two touched hands. "A pleasant gallop! You'll have a moon and the road is good. If you see Randolph of Taliaferro's, tell him to bring that book of mine he has."

He walked away, stalwart in the afterglow. Stafford watched him from the porch. "Under other circumstances," he thought, "I might have liked you well enough. Now I do not care if you lead your mad general's next mad charge."

The night fell, mild as milk, with a great white moon above the treetops. It made like mother-of-pearl the small grey house with pointed windows occupied, this December, by Stonewall Jackson. A clock in the hall was striking nine as Cleave lifted the knocker. An old negro came to the door. "Good-evening, Jim. Will you tell the general —"

Some one spoke from down the hall. "Is that Captain Cleave? Come here, sir."

Passing an open door through which could be seen a clerk writing and an aide with his hands behind him studying an engraving of Washington crossing the Delaware, Cleave went on to the room whence the voice had issued. "Come in, and close the door," it said again.

The room was small, furnished with a Spartan simplicity, but with two good lamps and with a log of hickory burning on the hearth. A table held a number of outspread maps and three books — the Bible, a dictionary, and Napoleon's "Maxims." General Jackson was seated on a small, rush-bottomed chair beside the table. By the window stood a soldier in nondescript grey attire, much the worse for mud and brambles. "Captain Cleave," said the general, "were you ever on the Chesapeake and Ohio Canal?"

"No, sir."

"Do you know the stretch of the Potomac north of us ? "

"I have ridden over the country between Harper's Ferry and Bath."

"Do you know where is Dam No. 5 ? "

"Yes, sir."

"Come nearer, Gold," said the general. "Go on with your report."

"I counted thirty boats going up, general," said Allan. "All empty. There's a pretty constant stream of them just now. They'll get the coal at Cumberland and turn back toward Washington in about ten days. It is estimated that a thousand tons a day will go down the canal — some of it for private use in Washington, but the greater part for the warships and the factories. The flatboats carry a large amount of forage. The Yankees are using them, too, to transport troops. There is no attempt to rebuild the section of the Baltimore and Ohio that we destroyed. They seem willing to depend upon the canal. But if Dam No. 5 were cut it would dry that canal like a bone for miles. The river men say that if any considerable breach were made it could not be mended this winter. As for the troops on the other side of the river —" He drew out a slip of paper and read from it: "'Yankees upon the Maryland side of the Potomac from Point of Rocks to Hancock — say thirty-five hundred men. Two thirds of this force above Dam No. 4. At Williamsport Colonel Leonard with three regiments and several guns. At Four Locks a troop. At Dam No. 5 several companies of infantry encamped. At Hancock a considerable force — perhaps two regiments. A detachment at Clear Spring. Cavalry over against Sleepy Creek, Cherry Run, and Sir John's Run. Concentration easy at any point up and down the river. A system of signals both for the other side and for any of their scouts who may have crossed to this. Troops reported below Point of Rocks and at the mouth of the Monocacy. The remainder of General Banks's division — perhaps fifteen thousand men — in winter quarters at Frederick City.' — That is all I have to report, general."

"Very good," said Jackson. "Give me your memorandum. Captain Cleave —"

"Yes, sir."

Stonewall Jackson rose from the rush-bottomed chair and walked with his slow stiff stride to the mantelpiece. From behind a china vase he took a saucer holding a lemon which had been cut in two, then, standing very rigidly before the fire, he slowly and meditatively sucked the lemon. Cleave, beside the table, had a whimsical thought. The general, about to open slightly the door of reticence and impart information, was stimulating himself to the effort. He put the lemon down and returned to the table. "Captain Cleave, while I am waiting for General Loring, I propose to break this dam — Dam No. 5."

"Yes, sir."

"I shall go almost immediately to Martinsburg, taking with me General Garnett's brigade and two of the Rockbridge guns. It will be necessary to cover the operation. The work may take several days. By the time the dam is broken General Loring will be up."

His eyes moved toward the mantel. Allan Gold stepped noiselessly across the room and brought back the saucer with the lemon, setting it on the table. "Thank you," said Jackson gently, and sucked the acid treasure. "With this reinforcement I am going against Kelly at Romney. If God gives us the victory there, I shall strike past Kelly at Rosecrans."

"I hope that He will give it, sir. That part of Virginia is worth making an effort for."

"That is my opinion, sir. While I march toward Romney the government at Washington may thrust General Banks across the Potomac. I do not want him in my rear, nor between me and General Johnston." He again sucked the lemon. "The Secretary of War writes that our spies report a clamour at Washington for some movement before spring. It is thought at Richmond that General Banks has been ordered to cross the Potomac as soon as practicable, effecting if possible a junction with Kelly and descending upon Winchester; General McClellan at the same time to advance against General Johnston at Manassas. Maybe it is so, maybe not. Of one thing I am sure — General McClellan will not move until General Banks is on this side of the river. Yesterday Colonel Ashby captured a courier of Kelly's bearing a letter to Banks. The letter, which demands an answer, asks to know explicitly what are Banks's instructions from Washington."

He put the lemon down. "Captain Cleave, I very particularly wish to know what are General Banks's instructions from Washington. Were Jarrow here he would find out for me, but I have sent Jarrow on other business. I want to know within four days."

There was a moment's stillness in the room; then, "Very well, sir," said Cleave.

"I remember," said Jackson, "that you sent me the scout here. He does good service. He is at your disposal for the next few days." Drawing ink and paper toward him, he wrote a few lines. "Go to the adjutant for anything you may need. *Captain Cleave on Special Service.* Here, too, is the name and address of a Catholic priest in Frederick City. He may be depended upon for some readiness of mind, and for good-will. That is all, I think. Good-night, captain. In four days, if you please. You will find me somewhere between Martinsburg and the river."

"You spoke, sir," said Cleave, "of a captured dispatch from General Kelly. May I see it?"

Jackson took it from a box upon the table. "There it is."

"Do you object, sir, to its reaching General Banks?"

The other retook the paper, glanced over it, and gave it back. "No, not if it goes by a proper courier."

"Has the former courier been sent to Richmond?"

"Not yet." He wrote another line. "This, if you wish to see the courier."

"That is all, sir?"

"That is all, captain. Within four days, near Martinsburg. Good-night."

The two soldiers saluted and left the room, going softly through the hall, past the door where the aide was now studying the Capture of André and out into the moonlight. They walked down the long board path to the gate, unlatched this, and turned their faces toward the camp. For some distance they were as silent as the street before them; then, "If ever you had taught school," said Allan, "you would know how headings out of reading books and sentences that you set for the children to copy have a way of starting up before you at every corner. *The Post of Honour is the Post of Danger.* I can see that in round hand. But what I can't see is how you are going to do it."

"I want," said the other, "one half-hour quite to myself. Then I think I'll know. Here's the picket. The word's *Bethel*."

The Stonewall Brigade was encamped in the fields just without the town. It was early in the war and there were yet tents — long line of canvas "A's" stretching in the moonlight far over the rolling ground. Where the tents failed there had been erected tiny cabins, very rude, with abundant ventilation and the strangest chimneys. A few field officers were quartered in the town and Jackson had with him there his permanent staff. But captains and lieutenants stayed with the men. The general of them all ruled with a rod of iron. For the most part it swayed lightly, with a certain moral effect only over the head of the rank and file, but it grew to a crushing beam for the *officer* who did not with alacrity habitually attend to his every duty, great or small. The do-nothing, the popinjay, the intractable, the self-important, the remonstrant, the *I thought, sir* — the *It is due to my dignity, sir* — none of these flourished in the Army of the Valley. The tendencies had been there, of course; they came up like the flowers of spring, but each poor bloom as it appeared met an icy blast. The root beneath learned to send up to the sky a sturdier growth.

Company A, 65th Virginia, numbered in its ranks men who knew all about log cabins. It was well lodged, and the captain's hut did it credit. Richard Cleave and Allan, entering, found a fire, and Tullius nodding beside it. At their step he roused himself, rose, and put on another log. He was a negro of sixty years, tall and hale, a dignified master of foraging, a being simple and taciturn and strong, with a love for every clod of earth at Three Oaks where he had been born.

Cleave spoke. "Where is Lieutenant Breckinridge, Tullius?"

Tullius straightened himself. "Lieutenant Breckinridge is at the colonel's, sah. An' Lieutenant Coffin, he's at the Debatin' Society in Company C."

Cleave sat down before the pine table. "Give Allan Gold something to eat, and don't either of you speak to me for twenty minutes." He propped his head on his hands and stared at the boards. Allan seated himself on a box beside the fire. Tullius took from a flat, heated stone a battered tin coffee-pot, poured into an earthenware cup some smoking mixture, and brought it to the scout. "Hit ain't moh'n half chicory, sah." From an impromptu cupboard he brought a plate of small round cakes. "Mis' Miriam, she done mek 'em fer us."

Cleave spoke from the table. His voice was dreamy, his eyes fixed upon the surface before him as though he were studying ocean depths. "Tullius, give me a dozen coffee berries."

"Er *cup* of coffee, you mean, Marse Dick?"

"No, coffee berries. Have n't you any there?"

Tullius brought a small tin box, tilted it, and poured on the table something like the required number. "Thar's all thar is." He returned to his corner of the fire, and it purred and flamed upon the crazy hearth between him and the scout. The latter, his rifle across his knees, now watched the flames, now the man at the table. Cleave had strung the coffee berries along a crack between the boards. Now he advanced one small brown object, now retired another, now crossed them from one side to the other. Following these manœuvres, he sat with his chin upon his hand for five minutes, then began to make a circle with the berries. He worked slowly, dropping point after point in place. The two ends met. He rose from the table. "That's all right. I am going to brigade headquarters for a little, Allan. Suppose you come along. There are some things I want to know — those signals, for instance." He took up his hat and sword. "Tullius, you'll have Dundee saddled at four o'clock. I'll see Lieutenant Breckinridge and the colonel. I won't be back until after taps. Cover the fire, but wait up for me."

He and Allan went out together. Tullius restored the coffee berries to the tin box, and the box to the cupboard, sat down by the fire, and fell again into a nodding dream of Three Oaks, of the garden, and of his grandchildren in the quarter.

CHAPTER X

LIEUTENANT MCNEIL

THE Williamsport ferry-boat came slowly across the Potomac, from the Maryland to the Virginia side. The clear, deep water lay faintly blue beneath the winter sky, and the woods came so close that long branches of sycamore swept the flood. In that mild season every leaf had not fallen; up and down the river here the dull red of an oak met the eye, and there the faded gold of a willow.

The flatboat, a brown shadow beneath a creaking wire and pulley, came slowly to the southern side of the stream. The craft, squat to the water and railed on either side, was in the charge of an old negro. Clustered in the middle of the boat appeared a tall Marylander in blue jeans, two soldiers in blue cloth, and a small darky in a shirt of blue gingham. All these stared at a few yards of Virginia road, shelving, and overarched by an oak that was yet touched with maroon, and stared at a horseman in high boots, a blue army overcoat, and a blue and gold cap, who, mounted upon a great bay horse, was waiting at the water's edge. The boat crept into the shadow of the trees.

One of the blue soldiers stood watchfully, his hands upon an Enfield rifle. The other, a middle-aged, weather-beaten sergeant-major who had been leaning against the rail, straightened himself and spoke, being now within a few feet of the man on horseback.

"Your signal was all right," he said. "And your coat's all right. But how did your coat get on this side of the river?"

"It's been on this side for some time," explained the man on horseback, with a smile. "Ever since Uncle Sam presented it to me at Wheeling — and that was before Bull Run." He addressed the negro. "Is this the fastest this boat can travel? I've been waiting here half an hour."

The sergeant-major persisted. "Your coat's all right, and your signal's all right, and if it had n't ha' been, our sharpshooters would n't ha' left much of you by now — Your coat's all right, and your signal's all right, but I'm damned if your voice ain't Southern —" The head of the boat touched the shore and the dress of the horseman was seen more closely. — "Lieutenant," ended the speaker, with a change of tone.

The rider, dismounting, led his horse down the yard or two of road and into the boat. "So, Dandy! Just think it's the South Branch, and come on! Thirty miles since breakfast, and still so gaily!"

Horse and man entered the boat, which moved out into the stream.

"I was once," stated the sergeant-major, though still in the proper tone of respect toward a lieutenant, "I was once in Virginia for a month, down on the Pamunkey — and the people all said 'gaily.'"

"They say it still," answered the rider. "Not so much, though, in my part of Virginia. It's Tuckahoe, not Cohee. I'm from the valley of the South Branch, between Romney and Moorefield."

The heretofore silent blue soldier shifted his rifle. "What in hell —" he muttered. The sergeant-major looked at the Virginia shore, looked at the stranger, standing with his arm around his horse's neck, and looked at the Williamsport landing, and the cannon frowning from Doubleday's Hill. In the back of his head there formed a little picture — a drumhead court-martial, a provost guard, a tree and a rope. Then came the hand of reason, and wiped the picture away. "Pshaw! spies don't *say* they're Southern. And, by jiminy! one might smile with his lips, but he could n't smile with his eyes iike that. And he's lieutenant, and there's such a thing, Tom Miller, as being too smart! —" He leaned upon the rail, and, being an observant fellow, he looked to see if the lieutenant's hand trembled at all where it lay upon the horse's neck. It did not; it rested as quiet as an empty glove. The tall Marylander began to speak with a slow volubility. "There was a man from the Great Kanawha to Williamsport 't other day — a storekeeper — a big, fat man with a beard like Abraham's in the 'lustrated Bible. I heard him a-talking to the colonel. 'All the Union men in northwestern Virginia are on the Ohio side of the mountains,' said he. 'Toward the Ohio we're all for the Union,' said he. 'There's more Northern blood than Southern in that section, anyway,' said he. 'But all this side of the Alleghenies is different, and as for the Valley of the South Branch — the Valley of the South Branch is a hotbed of rebels.' That's what he said — 'a hotbed of rebels.' 'As for the mountain folk in between,' he says, 'they hunt with guns, and the men in the valley hunt with dogs, and there ain't any love lost between them at the best of times. Then, too, it's the feud that settles it. If a mountain man's hereditary enemy names his baby Jefferson Davis, then the first man, he names his Abraham Lincoln, and shoots at the other man from behind a bush. And *vice versa*. So it goes. But the valley of the South Branch is old stock,' he says, 'and a hotbed of rebels.'"

"When it's taken by and large, that is true," said the horseman with coolness. "But there are exceptions to all rules, and there are some Union men along the South Branch." He stroked his horse's neck. "So, Dandy! Are n't there exceptions to all rules?"

"He's a plumb beauty, that horse," remarked the sergeant-major. "I don't ride much myself, but if I had a horse like that, and a straight road, and weather like this, I would n't ask any odds between here and Milikenville, Illinois! I guess he's a jim dandy to travel, Lieutenant —"

"McNeill," said the Virginian. "It is lovely weather. You don't often have a December like this in your part of the world."

"No, we don't. And I only hope 't will last."

"I hope it will," assented McNeill. "It's bad marching in bad weather."

"I don't guess," said the sergeant-major, "that we'll do much marching before springtime."

"No, I reckon not," answered the man from the South Branch. "I came from Romney yesterday. General Kelly is letting the men build cabins there. That does n't look like moving."

"We're doing the same here," said the sergeant-major, "and they say that the army's just as cosy at Frederick as a bug in a rug. Yes, sir; it's in the air that we'll give the rebels rope till springtime."

The ferry-boat touched the northern bank. Here were a little, rocky shore, an expanse of swampy ground, a towpath, a canal, a road cut between two hills, and in the background a village with one or two church spires. The two hills were white with tents, and upon the brow cannon were planted to rake the river. Here and there, between the river and the hills, were knots of blue soldiers. A freight boat loaded with hay passed snail-like down the canal. It was a splendid early afternoon, cool, still, and bright. The tall Marylander and the three blue soldiers left the boat, the man from Romney leading his horse. "Where's headquarters?" he demanded. "I'll go report, and then get something to eat for both Dandy and myself. We've got to make Frederick City to-night."

"The large wall tents over there on the hill," directed the sergeant-major. "It's a long way to Frederick, but Lord! with that horse —" He hesitated for a moment, then spoke up in a courageous, middle-aged, weather-beaten fashion, "I hope you'll have a pleasant ride, lieutenant! I guess I was a little stiffer'n good manners calls for, just at first. You see there's been so much talk of — of — of *masquerading* — and your voice is Southern, if your politics ain't! 'T is n't my usual way."

Lieutenant McNeill smiled. "I am sure of that, sergeant! As you say, there has been a deal of masquerading, and this side of the river naturally looks askance at the other. But you see, General Kelly *is* over there, and he happens, just now, to want to communicate with General Banks." His smile grew broader. "It's perfectly natural, but it's right hard on the man acting courier! Lord knows I had trouble enough running Ashby's gauntlet without being fired on from this side!"

"That's so! that's so!" answered the sergeant cordially. "Well, good luck to you getting back! You may find some friends here. We've a company or two of Virginians from the Ohio."

General Kelly's messenger proceeded to climb the hill to the wall tents indicated. There was a short delay, then he found himself in the presence of the colonel commanding at Williamsport. "From General Kelly at Romney? How did you get here?"

"I left Romney, sir, yesterday morning, and I came by bridle paths through the mountains. I was sent because I have hunted over every mile of that country, and I could keep out of Ashby's way. I struck the river above Bath, and I worked down through the woods to the ferry. I have a letter for General Banks."

Drawing out a wallet, he opened it and handed to the other the missive in question. "If I was chased I was to destroy it before capture," he said. "The slip with it is a line General Kelly gave me."

The colonel commanding at Williamsport glanced at the latter document. "A native of the South Branch valley," he said crisply. "That's a disaffected region."

"Yes, sir. It is. But there are one or two loyal families."

"You wish to go on to Frederick this afternoon?"

"Yes, sir. As soon as my horse is a little rested. My orders are to use all dispatch back to Romney with General Banks's answer."

The colonel, seated at a table, weighed General Kelly's letter in his hand, looked at the superscription, turned it over, and studied the seal. "Do the rebels on the other side show any signs of coming activity? Our secret service men have not been very successful — they make statements that it is hard to credit. I should be glad of any reliable information. What did you see or hear coming through?"

The lieutenant studied the floor a moment, shrugged, and spoke out. "Ashby's active enough, sir. Since yesterday I have just grazed three picket posts. He has vedettes everywhere. The report is that he has fifteen hundred troopers — nearly all valley men, born to the saddle and knowing every crook and cranny of the land. They move like a whirlwind and deal in surprises —

The Assyrian came down like the wolf on the fold —

Only these cohorts are grey, not purple and gold. That's Ashby. On the other hand, Jackson at Winchester need not, perhaps, be taken into account. The general impression is that he'll stay where he is until spring. I managed to extract some information from a mountain man above Sleepy Creek. Jackson is drilling his men from daylight until dark. It is said that he is crazy on the subject — on most subjects, in fact; that he thinks himself a Cromwell, and is bent upon turning his troops into Ironsides. Of course, should General Banks make any movement to cross — preparatory, say, to joining with General Kelly — Jackson might swing out of Winchester and give him check. Otherwise, he'll probably keep on drilling —"

"The winter's too far advanced," said the colonel, "for any such movement upon our part. As soon as it is spring we'll go over there and trample out this rebellion." He weighed Kelly's letter once more in his hand, then restored it to the bearer. "It's all right, Lieutenant McNeill. I'll pass you through. — You read Byron?"

"Yes," said Lieutenant McNeill briefly. "He's a great poet. 'Don Juan,' now, and Suvaroff at Ismail —

> He made no answer, but he took the city.

The bivouac, too, in Mazeppa." He restored General Kelly's letter and the accompanying slip to his wallet. "Thank you, sir. If I am to make Frederick before bedtime I had better be going —"

"An aide of General Banks," remarked the colonel, "is here, and is returning to Frederick this afternoon. He is an Englishman, I believe, of birth. You might ride together — Very opportunely; here he is!"

A tall, blond being, cap-à-pie for the road, had loomed in dark blue before the tent door. "Captain Marchmont," said the colonel, "let me make you acquainted with Lieutenant McNeill, a *loyal* Virginian bearing a letter from General Kelly to General Banks — a gentleman with a taste, too, for your great poet Byron. As you are both riding to Frederick, you may find it pleasant to ride in company."

"I must ride rapidly," said McNeill, "but if Captain Marchmont —"

"I always ride rapidly," answered the captain. "Learned it in Texas in 1843. At your service, lieutenant, whenever you're ready."

The road to Frederick lay clear over hill and dale, past forest and stream, through a gap in the mountain, by mill and barn and farmhouse, straight through a number of miles of crystal afternoon. Out of Williamsport conversation began. "When you want a purchaser for that horse, I'm your man," said the aide. "By any chance, *do* you want to sell?"

McNeill laughed. "Not to-day, captain!" He stroked the brown shoulder. "Not to-day, Dun — Dandy!"

"What's his name? Dundandy?"

"No," replied the lieutenant. "Just Dandy. I'm rather fond of him. I think we'll see it out together."

"Yes, they aren't bad comrades," said the other amicably. "In '53, when I was with Lopez in Cuba, I had a little black mare that was just as well worth dying for as a woman or a man or most causes, but, damn me! she died for me — carried me past a murderous ambuscade, got a bullet for her pains, and never dropped until she reached our camp!" He coughed. "What pleasant weather! Was it difficult getting through Jackson's lines?"

"Yes, rather."

They rode for a time in silence between fields of dead aster and goldenrod. "When I was in Italy with Garibaldi," said Captain Marchmont thoughtfully, "I saw something of kinsmen divided in war. It looked a very unnatural thing. You're a Virginian, now?"

"Yes, I am a Virginian."

"And you are fighting against Virginia. Curious!"

The other smiled. "To be where you are you must believe in the inviolability of the Union."

"Oh, I?" answered Marchmont coolly. "I believe in it, of course. I am fighting for it. It chanced, you see, that I was in France — and out of service and damnably out at elbows, too! — when Europe heard of Bull Run. I took passage at once in a merchant ship from Havre. It was my understanding that she was bound for New Orleans, but instead she put into Boston Harbour. I had no marked preference, fighting being fighting under whatever banner it occurs, so the next day I offered my sword to the Governor of Massachusetts. North and South, they're none of mine. But were I in England — where I have n't been of late years — and a row turned up, I should fight with England."

"No doubt," answered the other. "Your mind travels along the broad and simple lines of the matter. But with us there are many subtle and intricate considerations."

Passing now through woods they started a covey of partridges. The small brown and white shapes vanished in a skurry of dead leaves. "No doubt, no doubt!" said the soldier of fortune. "At any rate, I have rubbed off particularity in such matters. Live and let live — and each man to run the great race according to his inner vision! If he really conflicts with me, I'll let him know it."

They rode on, now talking, now silent. To either side, beyond stone walls, the fields ran bare and brown to distant woods. The shadow of the wayside trees grew longer and the air more deep and cold. They passed a string of white-covered wagons bearing forage for the army. The sun touched the western hills, rimming them as with a forest fire. The horsemen entered a defile between the hills, travelled through twilight for a while, then emerged upon a world still softly lighted. "In the country at home," said the Englishman, "the waits are practicing Christmas carols."

"I wish," answered the Virginian, "that we had kept that old custom. I should like once to hear English carols sung beneath the windows on a snowy night." As he rode he began to sing aloud, in a voice not remarkable, but good enough to give pleasure —

> "As Joseph was a-walking,
> He heard an angel sing,
> 'This night shall be born
> Our Heavenly King —'"

"Yes, I remember that one quite well," said Captain Marchmont, and proceeded to sing in an excellent bass, —

> "He neither shall be born
> In housen nor in hall,
> Nor in the place of Paradise,
> But in an ox's stall —

"Do you know the next verse?"

"Yes," said McNeill.

> "He neither shall be clothed
> In purple nor in pall,
> But all in fair linen
> As are babies all!"

"That's it," nodded the other. "And the next goes, —

> "He neither shall be rocked
> In silver nor in gold
> But in a wooden cradle
> That rocks on the mould —"

Alternately they sang the carol through. The sun went down, but the pink stayed in the sky and was mirrored in a tranquil stream which they crossed. It faded at last into the quiet dusk. A cricket chirped from a field of dried Michaelmas daisies. They overtook and passed an infantry regiment, coming up, an officer told them, from Harper's Ferry. The night fell, cold and still, with many stars. "We are not far from Frederick," said Marchmont. "You were never here before?"

"No."

"I'll take you at once to General Banks. You go back to Kelly at Romney to-morrow."

"Just as soon as General Banks shall have answered General Kelly's letter."

"You have an occasional fight over there?"

"Yes, up and down the line. Ashby's command is rather active."

"By George! I wish I were returning with you! When you've reported I'll look after you if you'll allow me. Pleasant enough mess. — Major Hertz, whom I knew in Prussia, Captain Wingate of your old army and one or two others."

"I'm exceedingly obliged," said McNeill, "but I have ridden hard of late, and slept little, and I should prove dull company. Moreover there's a good priest in Frederick who is a friend of a friend of mine. I have a message for him, and if General Banks permits, I shall sleep soundly and quietly at his house to-night."

"Very good," said Marchmont. "You'll get a better night there, though I'm sorry not to have you with us.— There are the lights of Frederick, and here's the picket. You have your pass from Williamsport?"

McNeill gave it to a blue soldier, who called a corporal, who read it by a swinging lantern. "Very good. Pass, Lieutenant McNeill."

The two rode on. To left and right were lighted streets of tents, varied here and there by substantial cabins. Commissary quarters appeared, sutlers' shops, booths, places of entertainment, guard-houses, a chapel. Soldiers were everywhere, dimly seen within the tents where the door flap was fastened back, plain to view about the camp-fires in open places, clustering like bees in the small squares from which ran the camp streets, thronging the trodden places before the sutlers, everywhere apparent in the foreground and divined in the distance. From somewhere came the strains of "Yankee Doodle." A gust of wind blew out the folds of the stars and stripes, fastened above some regimental headquarters. The city of tents and of frame structures hasty and crude, of fires in open places, of sutlers' shops and cantines, and booths of strolling players, of chapels and hospitals, of fluttering flags and wandering music, of restless blue soldiers, oscillating like motes in some search-light of the giants, persisted for a long distance. At last it died away; there came a quiet field or two, then the old Maryland town of Frederick.

CHAPTER XI

" AS JOSEPH WAS A-WALKING "

AT eleven that night by the Frederick clocks an orderly found an Englishman, a Prussian, a New Yorker, and a man from somewhere west of the Mississippi playing poker. "General Banks would like to speak to Captain Marchmont for a moment, sir."

The aide laid down his cards, and adjusted his plumage before a long mirror. "Lieber Gott!" said Major Hertz, "I wish our general would go sleep and leafe us play the game."

Captain Marchmont, proceeding to a handsomely furnished apartment, knocked, entered, saluted, and was greeted by a general in a disturbed frame of mind. "Look here, captain, you rode from Williamsport with that fellow of Kelly's. Did you notice anything out of the usual?"

The aide deliberated. "He had a splendid horse, sir. And the man himself seemed rather a mettled personage. If that's out of the usual, I noticed that."

"Oh, of course he's all right!" said the general. "Kelly's letter is perfectly *bona fide*, and so I make no doubt are McNeill's passport and paper of instructions. I gave the letter back or I'd show you the signatures. It's only that I got to thinking, awhile ago, after he'd gone." He took a turn across the roses upon the carpet. "A man that's been in politics knows there are so many dodges. Our spies say that General Jackson is very acute. I got to thinking —" He came back to the red-covered table. "Did you talk of the military situation coming along?"

"Very little, sir."

"He wasn't inquisitive? Didn't criticise, or draw you on to talk — didn't ask about my troops and my movements?"

"He did not, sir."

The general sighed. "It's all right, of course. You see, he seemed an intelligent man, and we got to talking. I wrote my answer to General Kelly. He has it now, is to start to Romney with it at dawn. Then I asked some questions, and we got to talking. It's all straight, of course, but on looking back I find that I said some things. He seemed an intelligent man, and in his general's confidence. Well, I dismissed him at last, and he saluted and went off to get some rest before starting. And then, somehow, I got to thinking. I have never been South, and all these places are only names to me, but —" He unrolled upon the table a map of large dimensions. "Look here a moment, captain! This is a map the department furnishes us. It's black, you see, for the utterly disloyal sections, shaded for the doubtful, and white where there are Unionists. All Virginia's black except this northwest section, and that's largely shaded."

"What," asked Marchmont, "is this long black patch in the midst of the shading?"

"That's the valley of the South Branch of the Potomac — see, it's marked! Now, this man's from that locality."

"H—m! Dark as Erebus, apparently, along the South Branch!"

"Just so." General Banks paced again the roses. "Pshaw! It's all right. I never saw a straighter looking fellow. I just thought I would ask you the nature of his talk along the road —"

"It was hardly of military matters, sir. But if you wish to detain him —"

"General Kelly must have my letter. I'm not to move, and it's important that he should know it."

"Why not question him again?"

The general came back to the big chair beside the table. "I have no doubt he's as honest as I am." He looked at the clock. "After midnight! — and I've been reviewing troops all day. Do you think it's worth while, captain?"

"In war very little things are worth while, sir."

"But you were with him all afternoon, and he seemed perfectly all right —"

"Yes, sir, I liked him very well." He pulled at his long yellow moustache. "There was only one little circumstance. . . . If you are doubtful, sir — The papers, of course, might be forged."

The late Governor of Massachusetts rested irresolute. "Except that he was born in Virginia there isn't a reason for suspecting him.

And it's our policy to conciliate all this shaded corner up here."
The clock struck the half-hour. General Banks looked longingly
toward his bedroom. "I've been through the mill to-day. It's
pretty hard on a man, this working over time. — Where's he
lodging?"

"McNeill, sir? He said he would find quarters with some connection or other — a Catholic priest —"

"A Catholic — There again!" The general looked perturbed.
Rising, he took from a desk two or three pages of blue official paper, covered with writing. "I got that from Washington to-day,
from the Secret Service Department. Read it."

Captain Marchmont read: "'Distrust without exception the
Catholic priests in Frederick City. There is reason to believe that
the Catholics throughout Maryland are Secessionists. Distrust all
Maryland, in fact. The Jesuits have a house at Frederick City.
They are suspected of furnishing information. Keep them under
such surveillance as your judgment shall indicate.' — Humph!"

General Banks sighed, poured out something from a decanter, and
drank it. "I guess, captain, you had better go and bring that man
from the South Branch back here. Take a few men and do it
quietly. He seems a gentleman, and there may be absolutely nothing wrong. Tell him I've something to add to General Kelly's
letter. Here's a list of the priests in Frederick. Father Tierney
seems the most looked up to, and I gave him a subscription yesterday for his orphan asylum."

Half an hour later Marchmont and two men found themselves
before a small, square stone house, standing apart from its neighbours in a small, square yard. From without the moonbeams
flooded it, from within came no pinpoint of light. It was past the
middle of the night, and almost all the town lay still and dark.
Marchmont lifted the brass knocker and let it fall. The sound, deep
and reverberant, should have reached every ear within, however
inattentive. He waited, but there came no answering footfall. He
knocked again — no light nor sound; again — only interstellar
quiet. He shook the door. "Go around to the back, Roberts, and
see if you can get in." Roberts departed. Marchmont picked
up some pieces of gravel from the path and threw them against
the window panes, to no effect. Roberts came back. "That's an

awful heavy door, sir, heavier than this. And the windows are high up."

"Very good," said the captain. "This one looks stronger than it really is. Stand back, you two."

He put his shoulder to the door — "Wait a minute, sir! Somebody's lit a candle upstairs."

The candle passed leisurely from window to window, was lost for a minute, and then, through a small fan-light above the door, was observed descending the stairs. A bolt creaked, then another. The door opened, and Father Tierney, hastily gowned and blinking, stood before the invaders. He shaded his candle with his hand, and the light struck back, showing a strong and rosy and likable face. "Faith!" he said, "an' I thought I was after hearin' a noise. Goodevenin', gentlemen — or rather good-morning, for it must be toward cockcrow. What —"

"It's not so late as that," interrupted Marchmont. "I wish I had your recipe for sleeping, father. It would be invaluable when a man did n't want to be waked up. However, my business is not with you, but —"

"Holy powers!" said Father Tierney, "did ye not know that I live here by myself? Father Lavalle is at the other end of town, and Father O'Hara lives by the Noviciate. Sure, and any one could have told you —"

"Father Lavalle and Father O'Hara," said the aide, "are nothing to the question. You have a guest with you —"

Father Tierney looked enlightened. "Oh! Av coorse! There's always business on hand between soldiers. Was it Lieutenant McNeill you'll be looking after?"

Marchmont nodded. "There are some instructions that General Banks neglected to give him. It is late, but the general wishes to get it all straight before he sleeps. I am sorry to disturb Lieutenant McNeill, for he must be fatigued. But orders are orders, you know —"

"Av coorse, av coorse!" agreed Father Tierney. "'A man having authority,' 'I say unto this man, Go, and he goeth; and to another, Come, and he cometh —'"

"So, father, if you'll be good enough to explain to Lieutenant McNeill — or if you'll tell me which is his room —"

The light of the candle showed a faint trouble in Father Tierney's face. "Sure, it's too bad! Do you think, my son, the matter is of importance? 'T would be after being just a little left-over of directions?"

"Perhaps," said Marchmont. "But orders are orders, father, and I must awaken Lieutenant McNeill. Indeed, it's hard to think that he's asleep —"

"He is n't aslape."

"Then will you be so good as to tell him —"

"Indeed, and I wish I could do that same thing, my son, but it is n't in nature —"

General Banks's aide made a gesture of impatience. "I can't dawdle here any longer! Either you or I, father." He pushed into the hall. "Where is his room?"

"Holy Virgin!" exclaimed Father Tierney. "It's vexed he'll be when he learns that the general was n't done with him! There's the room, captain darlint, but —"

Marchmont's eyes followed the pointing of the candlestick. "There!" he exclaimed. The door was immediately upon the left, not five feet from the portal he had lately belaboured. "Then 't was against his window that I flung the gravel!"

With an oath he crossed the hall and struck his hand against the panel indicated. No answer. He knocked again with peremptoriness, then tried the door. It was unlocked, and opened quietly to his touch. All beyond was silent and dark. "Father Tierney, I'll thank you for that candle!" The priest gave it, and the aide held it up, displaying a chill and vacant chamber, furnished with monastic spareness. There was a narrow couch that had been slept in. Marchmont crossed the bare floor, bent, and felt the bedclothing. "Quite cold. You've been gone some time, my friend. H—m! things look rather black for you!"

Father Tierney spoke from the middle of the room. "It's sorry the lieutenant will be! Sure, and he thought he had the general's last word! 'Slape until you wake, my son,' says I. 'Judy will give us breakfast at eight.' 'No, no, father,' says he. 'General Kelly is wearying for this letter from General Banks. If I get it through prompt it will be remembered for me,' he says. ''T will be a point toward promotion,' he says. 'My horse has had a couple of hours' rest, and he's a Trojan beside,' he says. 'I'll sleep an hour myself, and then I'll be taking the road back to Romney. Ashby's over on the other side,' he says, 'and the sooner I get Ashby off my mind, the better pleased I'll be,' he says. And thereupon he slept for an hour —"

Marchmont still regarded the bed. "I'll be damned if I know, my friend, whether you're blue or grey! How long has he been gone?"

Father Tierney pondered the question. "By the seven holy candles, my son, I was that deep asleep when you knocked that I don't rightly know the time of night! Maybe he has been gone an hour, maybe more —"

"And how did he know the countersign?"

"Faith, and I understood that the general himself gave him the word —"

"H—m!" said Marchmont, and tugged at his moustache. He stood in silence for a moment, then turned sharply. "Blue or grey, which? I'll be damned if I don't find out! Your horse may be a Trojan, my friend, but by this time he's a tired Trojan! Roberts!"

"Yes, sir."

"You two go at once to headquarters' stables. Saddle my horse — not the black I rode yesterday — the fresh one, Caliph. Get your own horses. Double-quick now! Ten minutes is all I give you."

The men departed. Marchmont stalked out of the chamber and to the open front door. Father Tierney, repossessed of the candle, followed him. "Sure, and the night's amazing chill! By good luck, I've a fine old bottle or two — one of the brigadiers, that's a good son of the church, having sent me a present. Whist, captain! a little glass to cheer the heart av ye —"

"I'll not stop now, father," said the aide dryly. "Perhaps, upon my return to Frederick I may call upon you."

"Do so, do so, my son," said Father Tierney. "And ye're going to overtake the lieutenant with the general's last words? — Faith, and while I think of it — he let drop that he'd be after not going by the pike. The old road by the forge, that goes south, and then turns. It's a dirt road, and easier on his horse, the poor crathur —"

"Thanks. I'll try the pike," said Marchmont, from the doorstep. "Bah! it's turning cold! Had you noticed, father, what exceedingly thin ice you have around this house?"

"By all the powers, my son!" answered Father Tierney. "The moonlight's desaving you! That is n't water — that's firm ground. Look out for the flagstaff at the gate, and presint my respects to the general. Sure, 't was a fine donation for the orphans he donated!"

It was two o'clock of a moonlight night when Captain March-mont and his troopers took the road to Williamsport. They passed through the silent camp, gave the word to the last sentry, and emerged upon the quiet countryside. "Was a courier before them?" "Yes, sir — a man on a great bay horse. Said he had important dispatches."

The moon-flooded road, hard beneath the hoofs of the horses, stretched south and west, unmarked by any moving creature. Marchmont rode in advance. His horse was strong and fresh; clear of the pickets, he put him to the gallop. An hour went by. Nothing but the cold, still moonshine, the sound of hoofs upon the metalled road, and now and then, in some wayside house, the stealthy lifting of a sash, as man or woman looked forth upon the riders. At a toll-gate the aide drew rein, leaned from his saddle, and struck against the door with a pistol butt. A man opened a window. "Has a courier passed, going to Williamsport?"

"Yes, sir. A man on a great bay horse. Three quarters of an hour ago."

"Was he riding fast?"

"Yes. Riding fast."

Marchmont galloped on, his two troopers behind him. Their steeds were good, but not so good as was his. He left them some way behind. The night grew old. The moon, which had risen late, was high in the heavens. The Englishman traversed a shadowy wood, then went by silvered fields. A cabin door creaked; an old negro put out a cautious head. "Has a courier passed, going to Williamsport?"

"Yaas, sah. Er big man on er big bay. 'Bout half er hour ergo, sah."

Marchmont galloped on. He looked back over his shoulder — his men were a mile in the rear. "And when I come up with you, my friend, what then? On the whole I don't think I'll ask you to turn with me. We'll go on to Williamsport, and there we'll hold the court of inquiry."

He touched his horse with the spur. The miles of road ran past, the air, eager and cold, pressed sharply; there came a feeling of the morning. He was now upon a level stretch of road, before him, a mile away, a long, bare hill. He crossed a bridge, hollowly sounding through the night, and neared the hill. His vision was a trained one, exercised by war in many lands. There was a dark object on the road before him; it grew in size, but it grew very slowly; it, too, was moving. "You've a tired horse, though, lieutenant!" said the aide. "Strain as you may, I'll catch you up!" His own horse devoured the ground, steadily galloping by the frosty fields, through the air of earliest dawn. Suddenly, before him, the courier from Kelly halted. Mounted against a faint light in the southwestern sky, he stood upon the hilltop and waited for the horseman from Frederick. The latter took at a gallop the remainder of the level road, but at the foot of the hill changed to a trot. Above him, the waiting horseman grew life-size. He waited, very quietly, Marchmont observed, sitting, turned in his saddle, against the sky of dawn. "Damned if I know if you're truly blue or grey!" thought the aide. "Did you stop to disarm suspicion, because you saw you'd be overtaken —"

Another minute and the two were in speaking distance; another, and they were together on the hilltop. "Good-morning!" said McNeill. "What haste to Williamsport?" He bent forward in the light that was just strong enough to see by. "Why — It is yesterday's comrade! Good-morning, Captain Marchmont!"

"We must have started," said Marchmont, "somewhere near the same hour. I have a communication from General Banks for the commander at Williamsport."

If the other raised his brows over the aide's acting courier twice in twenty-four hours, the action did not appear in the yet uncertain light. Apparently McNeill took the statement easily, upon its face value. "In that case," he said with amicableness, "I shall have the pleasure of your company a little longer. We must be about six miles out, I should think."

"About that distance," agreed the other. "And as at this unearthly hour I certainly cannot see the colonel, and as your horse is evidently spent, why go the rest of the way at a gallop?"

"It was my idea," said McNeill, "to pass the river early. If I can gain the big woods before the day is old, so much the better. Dandy is tired, it is true, but he has a certain staying quality. However, we will go more slowly now."

They put themselves in motion. "Two men are behind us," remarked the man from Romney.

"Yes. There they come through the fields. Two troopers who are riding with me — Regulars. They'll accommodate their pace to ours."

"Very good," said the other with serenity, and the two rode on, Marchmont's men a little way behind. By now the stars had faded, the moon looked wan, there was a faint rose in the east. Far in a vale to the left a cock crew, and was answered from across a stream. To the south, visible between and above the fringing trees, a ribbon of mist proclaimed the river. The two men rode, not in silence, but still not with yesterday's freedom of speech. There was, however, no quietude that the chill ebb of the hour and the weariness of over-work might not account for. They spoke of this and that briefly, but amicably. "Will you report at headquarters?" asked Marchmont, "before attempting the Virginia shore?"

"I do not yet know. There is no occasion, as I have all instructions from General Banks. I wish to make no unnecessary delay."

"Have you the countersign?"

"Yes."

"Will you cross by the ferry?"

"I hardly think so. Ashby may be watching that and the ford below. There is a place farther up the river that I may try."

"That is, after you pass through Williamsport?"

"Yes, a mile or two beyond."

The light increased. Gold clouds barred the east, the cocks crew, and crows came cawing from the woods to the vast, brown corn-fields. The road now ran at no great distance from the canal and the river. First came the canal, mirroring between trodden banks the red east, then the towpath, a cornfield, a fringe of sycamore, oak, and willow, then the Potomac veiled with mist. They were drawing near to Williamsport. The day's travel had begun. They met or overtook workers upon the road, sutlers' carts, ordnance wagons, a squad of artillerymen conducting a gun, a country doctor in an old buggy, two boys driving calves yoked together. The road made a curve to the north, like a sickle. On the inland side it ran beneath a bluff; on the other a rail fence rimmed a twelve-foot embankment dropping to a streamlet and a wide field where the corn stood in shocks. Here, at a cross-roads debouching from the north into the pike, they encountered a company of infantry.

Marchmont checked his horse. "I'm not sure, but I think I know the officer. Be so good as to await me a moment, lieutenant."

He rode up to the captain in blue, and the two talked in low voices. The infantrymen broke lines a little, leaned on their rifles, and discussed arrangements for breakfast. Among them were a number of tall men, lean and sinewy, with a sweep of line and unconstraint of gesture that smacked of hunters' ways and mountain exercise. The two troopers from Frederick City came up. The place of the cross-roads showed animated and blue. The sun pushed its golden ball above the hilltops, and all the rifle barrels gleamed in the light. Marchmont and the new-met captain approached the courier from Kelly, sitting his horse in the middle of the road. "Lieutenant McNeill," said the aide with quietness, "there seemed, at Frederick, some irregularity in your papers. Doubtless everything can be explained, and your delay in reaching Romney will be slight. It is my duty to conduct you to Williamsport headquarters, and to report the matter to the colonel commanding. I regret the interruption — not a long continued one, I trust — to our pleasant relations."

McNeill had made a movement of surprise, and his brows had come together. It was but for an instant, then he smiled, and smiled with his eyes. "If such are your orders, sir, neither you nor I can help the matter. To headquarters, of course — the sooner the better! I can have no possible objection."

He touched his horse and advanced a little farther into the road. All the blue soldiers were about him. A sergeant-major, brought for the moment opposite him, uttered an exclamation. "You know this officer, Miller?" called the captain of infantry.

Miller saluted. "No, sir. But I was in the ferry-boat when he crossed yesterday. We talked a little. 'You've got a Southern voice,' says I, and he says, 'Yes. I was born in the valley of the South Branch.' 'You'll find company here,' says I, 'for we've got some northwestern Virginians —'"

"By jingo!" cried the captain, "that's true! There's a squad of them here." He raised his voice. "Men from northwest Virginia, advance!"

A detachment swung forward, lean men and tall, stamped as hunters, eighteenth-century frontiersmen projected to the middle of the nineteenth. "Do any of you men know the South Branch of the Potomac?"

Three voices made themselves heard. "Know it like a book." — "Don't know it like a book — know it like I know my gun and dawg." — "Don't know any good of it — they-uns air all rebels down that-a-way!"

"Especially," said a fourth voice, "the McNeills."

The courier from Kelly glanced at him sharply. "And what have you got, my man, against the McNeills?"

"I've got something," stated the mountaineer doggedly. "Something ever since afore the Mexican War. Root and branch, I've got something against them. When I heard, over there in Grant, that they was hell-bent for the Confederacy, I just went, hell-bent, for the other side. Root and branch, I know them, and root and branch they're damned rebels —"

"Do you know," demanded the captain, "this one? This is Lieutenant McNeill."

The man looked, General Kelly's courier facing him squarely. There was a silence upon the road to Williamsport. The mountaineer spat. "He may be a lieutenant, but he ain't a McNeill. Not from the South Branch valley, he ain't."

"He says he is."

"Do you think, my friend," asked the man in question, and he looked amused, "that you really know all the McNeills, or their party? The valley of the South Branch is long and wide, and the families are large. One McNeill has simply escaped your observation."

"There ain't," said the man, with grimness, "a damned one of them that has escaped my observation, and there ain't one of them that ain't a damned rebel. They're with Ashby now, and those of them that ain't with Ashby are with Jackson. And you may be Abraham Lincoln or General Banks, but you ain't a McNeill!"

The ranks opened and there emerged a stout German musician.

"Herr Captain! I was in Winchester before I ran away and joined der Union. Herr Captain, I haf seen this man. I haf seen him in der grey uniform, with der gold sword and der sash. And, lieber Gott, dot horse is knòwn! Dot horse is der horse of Captain Richard Cleave. Dot horse is named Dundee."

" 'Dundee —' " exclaimed Marchmont. "That's the circumstance. You started to say ' Dundee.' "

He gave an abrupt laugh. "On the whole, I like you even better than I did — but it's a question now for a drumhead and a provost guard. I'm sorry —"

The other's hand had been resting upon his horse's neck. Suddenly there was a motion of his knee, a pressure of this hand, a curious sound, half speech, half cry, addressed to the bay beneath him. Dundee backed, gathered himself together, arose in air, cleared the rail fence, overpassed the embankment and the rivulet beneath, touched the frosted earth of the cornfield, and was away like an arrow toward the misty white river. Out of the tumult upon the road rang a shot. Marchmont, the smoking pistol still in hand, urged his horse to the leap, touched in turn the field below, and at top speed followed the bay. He shouted to the troopers behind him; their horses made some difficulty, but in another moment they, too, were in pursuit. Rifles flashed from the road, but the bay had reached a copse that gave a moment's shelter. Horse and rider emerged unhurt from the friendly walls of cedar and locust. "Forward, sharpshooters!" cried the infantry captain. A lieutenant and half a dozen men made all haste across the fence, down the low bluff, and over the field. As they ran one fired, then another, but the fleeing horse kept on, the rider close to the neck, in their sight, beyond the water, the Virginia shore. The bay moved as though he knew not fatigue, but only a friend's dire need. The stock told; many a race had been won by his forefathers. What his rider's hand and voice conveyed cannot be precisely known, but that which was effected was an access of love, courage, and understanding of the end desired. He moved with every power drawn to the point in hand. Marchmont, only a few lengths behind, fired again. The ball went through Cleave's sleeve, grazing his arm and Dundee's shoulder. The two shot on, Marchmont behind, then the two mounted men, then the sharpshooters, running afoot. From the road the remainder of the company watched with immemorial, white-heat interest the immemorial incident. "He's wounded — the bay's wounded, too! They'll get him at the canal! — Thar's a bridge around the bend, but he don't know it! — Climb atop the fence; ye can see better —"

The canal, deep between willowy banks, a moat to be overpassed without drawbridge, lay ahead of the foremost horse and rider. A moment and the two burst through the screen of willows, another, and from the high, bare bank they had leaped into the narrow, deep, and sluggish stream. "That horse's wounded — he's sinking! No, by God, he ain't! Whar's the captain from Frederick! Thar he is — thar he is!" Marchmont vanished into the belt of willows. The two troopers had swerved; they knew of the bridge beyond the turn. Dundee swam the canal. The bank before him, up to the towpath, was of loose earth and stone, steep and difficult. He climbed it like a cat-o'-mountain. As he reached the towpath Marchmont appeared before the willows. His horse, a powerful sorrel, took the water unhesitatingly, but the opposite bank made trouble. It was but a short delay; while the soldiers on the road held their breath he was up and away, across the wide field between canal and river. The troopers, too, had thundered across the bridge. The sharpshooters were behind them, blue moving points between the shocked corn. The field was wide, rough, and furrowed, bordered on its southern side by a line of sycamores, leafless and tall, a lacework of white branches against the now brilliant sky. Beyond the sycamores lay the wide river, beyond the river lay Virginia. Dundee, red of eye and nostril, foam streaked and quivering, raced on, his rider talking to him as to a lover. But the bay was sore tired, and the sorrel gained. Marchmont sent his voice before him. "Surrender! You'll never reach the other side!"

"I'll try mighty hard," answered Cleave between his teeth. He caressed his horse, he made their two hearts one, he talked to him, he crooned an air the stallion knew, —

> Then fling ope your gates, and let me go free,
> For it's up with the bonnets of Bonnie Dundee!

Superbly the bay answered. But the sorrel, too, was a thorough-bred, fresh when he left Frederick. Stride by stride he gained. Cleave crashed into the belt of sycamores. Before him was the

Potomac, cold, wide, mist-veiled. He heard Marchmont break into the wood and turned. The aide's arm was raised, and a shaft of red sunlight struck the barrel of his pistol. Before his finger could move Cleave fired.

The sorrel, pierced through the shoulder, swerved violently, reared, and plunged, all but unseating his rider. Marchmont's ball passed harmlessly between the branches of trees. The bay and his master sprang from the low bank into the flood. So veiled was it by the heavy mist that, six strokes from shore, all outlines grew indistinct.

The two troopers reached the shore. "Where is he, sir? — Out there?" They emptied their pistols — it was firing into a cloud. The sharpshooters arrived. Skilful and grim, they raised their rifles, scanned the expanse of woolly white before them, and fired at what, now here, now there, they conceived might be a moving object. The mist lay close to the river, like a pall. They fired and fired again. Other infantrymen, arriving, talked excitedly. "Thar! — No, thar! That's him, downstream! Fire! — Darn it! 'T was a piece of drift." Across the river, tall against the south, wreathed and linked by lianas of grape, showed, far withdrawn and shadowy, the trees of the Virginia shore. The rifles continued to blaze, but the mist held, and there came no answering scream of horse or cry of man. Marchmont spoke at last, curtly. "That's enough! He's either hit and drowned, or he has reached home. I wish we were on the same side."

One of the troopers uttered an exclamation. "Hear that, sir! He's across! Damned if he is n't halloaing to tell us so!"

Faintly, from the southern shore, came a voice. It was raised in a line of song, —

> " As Joseph was a-walking,
> He heard the angels sing " —

CHAPTER XII

"THE BATH AND ROMNEY TRIP"

RICHARD CLEAVE and his horse, two tired wights, turned a corner in the wood and came with suddenness upon a vedette, posted beneath a beech tree. The vedette brought his short rifle to bear upon the apparition. "Halt! Halt, you in blue! Halt, I say, or I'll blow your head off."

Down an aisle of the woods, deep in russet leaves, appeared a grey figure. "Hello, Company F! It's all right! It's all right! It's Captain Cleave, 65th Virginia. Special service." Musket in hand, Allan came at a run through the slanting sunshine of the forest. "It's all right, Cuninghame — Colonel Ashby will understand."

"Here," said the vedette, "is Colonel Ashby now."

From another direction, out of the filmy and amethyst haze that closed each forest vista, came a milk-white horse, stepping high over the fallen leaves. The rider, not tall, black-bearded, with a pale, handsome face, sat like a study for some great sculptor's equestrian masterpiece. In a land where all rode well, his was superb horsemanship. The cape of his grey coat was lined with scarlet, his soft wide hat had a black plume; he wore long boots and white gauntlets. The three beneath the beech saluted. He spoke in a pensive and musical voice. "A prisoner, Cuninghame? Where did you get him? — Ah, it's Richard Cleave!"

The bright December day wore on, sunny and cold in the woods, sunny and cold above the river. The water, clear now of mist, sparkled, a stream of diamonds, from shore to shore, except where rose Dam No. 5. Here the diamonds fell in cataracts. A space of crib-work, then falling gems, another bit of dry logs in the sun, then again brilliancy and thunder of water over the dam; this in sequence to the Maryland side. That side reached, there came a mere ribbon of brown earth, and beyond this ran the Chesapeake and Ohio Canal. To-day boats from Cumberland were going down the canal with coal and forage, and boats from Harper's Ferry were coming up with a reinforcing regiment of soldiers for Lander at Hancock. It was bright and lively weather, and the negroes talked to the mules on the towpath, and the conductors of coal and forage hailed the soldiers, and the soldiers shouted back. The banks rang to laughter and voices. "Where're you fellows going?" — "Going to Hancock, — no, don't know where it is!" — "Purty day! Seen any rebels crost the river?" — "At Williamsport they told us there was a rebel spy got away this morning — galloped down a cliff like Israel Putnam and took to the river, and if he was drowned or not they don't know —" "No, he wasn't drowned; he got away, but he was shot. Anyhow, they say he hadn't been there long enough to find out anything." — "Wish *I* could find out something — wish I could find out when we're going to fight!" — "Low braidge!" — "That's a pretty big dam. What's the troops over there in the field? Indiana? That's a right nice picnic-ground —

> ' Kiss me good-bye, my dear,' he said;
> 'When I come back, we will be wed.'
> Crying, she kissed him, 'Good-bye, Ned!'
> And the soldier followed the drum,
> The drum,
> The echoing, echoing drum!"

Over on the Virginia side, behind the friendly woods paced through by Ashby's men, the height of the afternoon saw the arrival of the advance guard of that portion of the Army of the Valley which was to cover operations against Dam No. 5. Later in the day came Garnett with the remainder of the Stonewall Brigade and a two-gun detachment of the Rockbridge Artillery, and by sunset the militia regiments were up. Camp was pitched behind a line of hills, within the peninsula made by the curve of the river. This rising ground masked the movement; moreover, with Ashby between any body of infantry and an enemy not in unreasonable force, that body worked and ate and slept in peace of mind. Six miles down the river, over on the Maryland side, was Williamsport, with an infantry command and with artillery. Opposite Dam No. 5 in the Maryland fields beyond the canal, troops were posted, guarding that very stretch of river. From a little hill above the tents frowned their cannon. At Hancock, at Hagerstown, and at Frederick were other thousands, and all, from the general of the division to the corporal drilling an awkward squad in the fields beside the canal, thought of the Army of the Valley as at Winchester.

With the Confederate advance guard, riding Little Sorrel, his cadet cap over his eyes, his uniform whole and clean, but discoloured like a November leaf from rain and dust and dust and rain, with great boots and heavy cavalry spurs, with his auburn beard and his deep-set grey-blue eyes, with his forehead broad and high, and his aquiline nose, and his mouth, wide and thin-lipped, came Jackson. The general's tent was a rude affair. His soldiers pitched it beneath a pine, beside a small trickling stream half choked with leaves. The staff was quartered to right and left, and a clump of pines in the rear served for an Arcadian kitchen. A camp-stool and a table made of a board laid upon two stumps of trees furnished the leaf-strewn terrace before the tent. Here, Cleave, coming to report, found his commander.

Jackson was sitting, feet planted as usual, arms at side as usual, listening to his chief of staff. He acknowledged Cleave's salute, with a glance, a slight nod of the head, and a motion of the hand to one side. The young man waited, standing by a black haw upon the bank of the little stream. The respectful murmur of the chief of staff came to an end. "Very good, major. You will send a courier back to Falling Waters to halt General Carson there. He is to be prepared to make a diversion against Williamsport in the morning. I will give precise instructions later. What of this mill by the river?"

"It is a very strong, old, stone mill, sir, with windows. It would command any short-range attack upon the workers."

"Good! good! We will put riflemen there. As soon as General Garnett is up, send him to me."

From the not-distant road came a heavy rumble of wheels and the sound of horses' feet. "There are the guns, now, sir."

"Yes. They must wait until nightfall to get into position. Send Captain McLaughlin to me in half an hour's time."

"Yes, sir. Captain Colston of the 2d is here —"

"Very good. I will see him now. That is all, major."

The chief of staff withdrew. Captain Colston of the 2d approached from the shadows beyond the big pine and saluted. "You are from this region, captain?"

"Yes, sir. The *Honeywood* Colstons."

"This stone mill is upon your land?"

"Yes, sir. My mother owns it."

"You have been about the dam as a boy?"

"Yes, sir. In the water above it and in the water below it. I know every log, I reckon. It works the mill."

"If we break it, it will work the mill no longer. In addition, if the enemy cross, they will probably destroy the property."

"Yes, sir. My mother and I would not let that weigh with us. As I know the construction I should esteem it an honour, sir, if I might lead the party. I think I may say that I know where the cribs could be most easily cut."

"Very good then, sir. You will report for duty at nine to-night. Captain Holliday of the 33d and Captain Robinson of the 27th, with a number of their men, have volunteered for this service. It is not without danger, as you know. That is all."

Captain Colston departed. "Now, Captain Cleave," said the general.

A few minutes later, the report ended, Jackson refolded General Banks's letter to General Kelly and put it into his pocketbook. "Good! good!" he said, and turned slightly on the camp-stool so as to face the river and the north. "It's all right, captain, it's all right!"

"I wish, sir," said Cleave, "that with ten times the numbers you have, you were leading us across the river. We might force a peace, I think, and that right quickly."

Jackson nodded. "Yes, sir, I ought to have every soldier in Virginia — if they could be gotten here in time every soldier in the Carolinas. There would then be but a streamlet of blood where now there is going to be a great river. The streamlet should run through the land of them with whom we are righteously at war. As it is, the great river will run through ours." He rose. "You have done your mission well, sir. The 65th will be up presently."

It took three days to cut Dam No. 5. On the fourth the brigade went back to Winchester. A week later came Loring with the Army of the Kanawha, and on the third of January the whole force found itself again upon the road.

In the afternoon the weather changed. The New Year had come

in smiling, mild as April, dust in the roads, a blue sky overhead. The withered goldenrod and gaunt mullein stalks and dead asters by the wayside almost seemed to bloom again, while the winter wheat gave an actual vernal touch. The long column, winding somewhere — no one knew where, but anyhow on the Pugh Town Road and in a northwesterly direction (even Old Jack could n't keep them from knowing that they were going northwest!) — was in high spirits. At least, the Stonewall Brigade was in spirits. It was said that Loring's men did n't want to come, anyhow. The men whistled and sang, laughed, joked, were lavish of opinions as to all the world in general and the Confederate service in particular. They were sarcastic. The Confederate private was always sarcastic, but throughout the morning there had been small sting in their remarks. Breakfast — "at early dawn" — was good and plentiful. Three days' rations had been served and cooked, and stowed in haversacks. But, so lovely was the weather, so oppressive in the sunshine would be a heavy weight to carry, so obliging were the wagon drivers, so easy in many regiments the Confederate discipline, that overcoats, blankets, and, in very many instances haversacks, had been consigned before starting to the friendly care of the wagons in the rear. The troops marched light, and in a good humour. True, Old Jack seemed bent on getting there — wherever "there" was — in a tremendous hurry. Over every smooth stretch the men were double-timed, and there was an unusual animus against stragglers. There grew, too, a moral certitude that from the ten minutes' lawful rest in each hour at least five minutes was being filched. Another and still more certain conclusion was that the wagon train was getting very far behind. However, the morning was still sweet, and the column, as a whole, cheerful. It was a long column — the Stonewall Brigade, three brigades of Loring's, five batteries, and a few cavalry companies; eight thousand, five hundred men in all.

Mid-day arrived, and the halt for dinner. Alas for the men without haversacks! They looked as though they had borne all the burdens of the march. There was hunger within and scant sympathy without. "Did n't the damned fools know that Old Jack always keeps five miles ahead of wagon trains and hell fire?" "Here, Saunders! take these corn pones over to those damned idiots with the complipliments of Mess No. 4. We know that they have Cherrystone oysters, canvas-back ducks, terrapin, and peach brandy in their haversacks, and that they meant to ask us to join them. So unfortunate!"

The cavalry marched on, the artillery marched on, the infantry marched on. The bright skies subtly changed. The blue grew fainter; a haze, white, harsh, and cold, formed gradually, and a slight wind began to blow. The aster and goldenrod, the dried ironweed and sumach, the red rose hips and magenta pokeberry stalks looked dead enough now, dead and dreary upon the weary, weary road. The men sang no more; the more weakly shivered. Before long the sky was an even greyish-white, and the wind had much increased. Coming from the northwest, it struck the column in the face; moreover, it grew colder and colder. All types shivered now, the strong and the weak, the mounted officer and the leg-weary private, the men with overcoats, and the men without. The column moved slower and slower, all heads bent before the wind, which now blew with violence. It raised, too, a blinding dust. A curt order ran down the lines for less delay. The regiments changed gait, tried quick time along a level stretch, and left behind a large number of stragglers. The burst of speed was for naught, they went the slower thereafter, and coming to a long, bleak hill, crept up it like tortoises — but without protecting shells. By sunset the cold was intense. Word came back that the head of the column was going into camp, and a sigh of approbation arose from all. But when brigade by brigade halted, deployed, and broke ranks, it appeared that "going into camp" was rather a barren phrase. The wagons had not come up; there were no tents, no blankets, no provisions. A northwester was blowing, and the weather-wise said that there would be snow ere morning. The regiments spread over bare fields, enclosed by rail fences. There were a small, rapidly freezing stream and thick woods, skirting the fields. In the woods were fallen boughs and pine cones enough to make the axes in the company wagons not greatly missed, and detachments were sent to gather fagots. The men, cold and exhausted, went, but they looked wistfully at the rail fences all around them, so easy to demolish, so splendid to burn! Orders on the subject were stringent. *Officers will be held responsible for any destruction of property. We are here to protect and defend, not to destroy.* The men gathered dead branches and broke down others, heaped them together in the open fields, and made their camp-fires. The Rockbridge Artillery occupied a fallow field covered with fox grass, dead Michaelmas daisy, and drifted leaves. It was a good place for the poor horses, the battery thought. But the high wind blew sparks from the fires and lighted the grass. The flames spread and the horses neighed with terror. The battery was forced to move, taking up position at last in a ploughed field where the frozen furrows cut the feet, and the wind had the sweep of an unchained demon. An infantry regiment fared better. It was in a stretch of fenced field between the road and the freezing brook. A captain, native of that region, spoke to the lieutenant-colonel, and the latter spoke to the men. "Captain —— says that we are camping upon his land, and he's sorry he can't give us a better welcome! But we can have his fence rails. Give him a cheer, and build your fires!" The men cheered lustily, and tore the rails apart, and had rousing fires and were comfortable; but the next morning Stonewall Jackson suspended from duty the donor of his own fences. The brigades of Loring undoubtedly suffered the most. They had seen, upon the Monterey line, on the Kanawha, the Gauley, and the Greenbriar, rough and exhausting service. And then, just when they were happy at last in winter quarters, they must pull up stakes and hurry down the Valley to join "Fool Tom Jackson" of the Virginia Military Institute and one brief day of glory at Manassas! Loring, a gallant and dashing officer, was popular with them. "Fool Tom Jackson" was not. They complained, and they very honestly thought that they had upon their side justice, common sense, and common humanity — to say nothing of military insight! The bitter night was bitterer to them for their discontent. Many were from eastern Virginia or from the states to the south, not yet inured to the winter heights and Stonewall Jackson's way. They slept on frozen ground, surrounded by grim mountains, and they dreamed uneasily of the milder lowlands, of the yet green tangles of bay and myrtle, of quiet marshes and wide, unfreezing waters. In the nighttime the clouds thickened, and there came down a fine rain, mixed with snow. In the morning, fields, hillsides, and road appeared glazed with ice — and the wagons were not up!

The country grew rougher, lonelier, a series of low mountains and

partly cleared levels. To a few in the creeping column it may have
occurred that Jackson chose unfrequented roads, therefore narrow,
therefore worse than other roads, to the end that his policy of utter
secrecy might be the better served; but to the majority his course
seemed sprung from a certain cold wilfulness, a harshness without
object, unless his object were to wear out flesh and bone. The road,
such as it was, was sheeted with ice. The wind blew steadily from
the northwest, striking the face like a whip, and the fine rain and
snow continued to fall and to freeze as it fell. What, the evening
before, had been hardship, now grew to actual misery.   The column
faltered, delayed, halted, and still the order came back, "The general commanding wishes the army to press on." The army stumbled to its now bleeding feet, and did its best with a hill like Calvary.
Up and down the column was heard the report of muskets, men falling and accidentally discharging their pieces. The company officers
lifted monotonous voices, weary and harsh as reeds by a winter
pond. *Close up, men — close up — close up!*

In the afternoon Loring, riding at the head of his brigades, sent a
staff officer forward with representations. The latter spurred his
horse, but rapid travelling was impossible upon that ice-sheathed
road. It was long before he overtook the rear of the Stonewall
Brigade. Buffeted by the wind, the grey uniforms pale under a glaze
of sleet, the red of the colours the only gleam of cheer, the line
crawled over a long hill, icy, unwooded, swept by the shrieking
wind. Stafford in passing exchanged greetings with several of the
mounted officers. These were in as bad case as their men, nigh
frozen themselves, distressed for the horses beneath them, and for
the staggering ranks, striving for anger with the many stragglers and
finding only compunction, in blank ignorance as to where they were
going and for what, knowing only that whereas they had made
seventeen miles the day before, they were not likely to make seven
to-day. He passed the infantry and came up with the artillery. The
steep road was ice, the horses were smooth shod. The poor brutes
slipped and fell, cutting themselves cruelly. The men were down in
the road, lifting the horses, dragging with them at gun and caisson.
The crest of the hill reached, the carriages must be held back, kept
from sliding sideways in the descent. Going down was worse than
coming up. The horses slipped and fell; the weight of gun and cais-

son came upon them; together they rolled to the foot, where they must be helped up and urged to the next ascent. Oaths went here and there upon the wind, hurt whinnies, words of encouragement, cracking of whips, straining and groaning of gun carriages.

Stafford left the artillery behind, slowly climbed another hill, and more slowly yet picked his way down the glassy slope. Before him lay a great stretch of meadow, white with sleet, and beyond it he saw the advance guard disappearing in a fold of the wrinkled hills. As he rode he tried to turn his thoughts from the physical cold and wretchedness to some more genial chamber of the brain. He had imaginative power, ability to build for himself out of the void. It had served him well in the past — but not so well the last year or two. He tried now to turn the ring and pass from the bitter day and road into some haunt of warmth and peace. Albemarle and summer — Greenwood and a quiet garden. That did not answer! Harassment, longing, sore desire, check and bitterness — unhappiness there as here! He tried other resting places that once had answered, poets' meadows of asphodel, days and nights culled like a bouquet from years spent in a foreign land, old snatches out of boyhood. These answered no longer, nor did a closing of the eyes and a sinking downward, downward through the stratas of being into some cavern, reckonless and quiet, of the under-man. It as little served to front the future and try to climb, like Jack of the Beanstalk, to some plane above and beyond war and disappointment and denying. He was unhappy, and he spoke wearily to his horse, then shut his lips and faced the Siberian road. Entering in his turn the fold of the hills, he soon came up with the advance. As he passed the men on foot a sudden swirl of snow came in larger flakes from the leaden skies. Before him were a dozen horsemen, riding slowly. The air was now filled with the great white flakes; the men ahead, in their caped overcoats, with their hats drawn low, plodding on tired horses between the hills, all seen vaguely through the snow veil, had a sudden wintry, desolate, and far-away seeming. He said to himself that they were ghosts from fifty years back, ghosts of the Grand Army in the grasp of General January. He made what haste he could and came up with Stonewall Jackson, riding with Ashby and with his staff. All checked their horses, the general a little advanced, Stafford facing him. "From General Loring, sir,"

"Good! What does he want?"

"There is much suffering amóng his men, sir. They have seen hard service and they have faced it gallantly —"

"Are his men insubordinate?"

"Not at all, sir. But —"

"You are, I believe, the officer whom General Loring sent me once before?"

"Yes, general. Many of the men are without rations. Others are almost barefoot. The great number are unused to mountain work or to so rigorous a climate."

The commanding general sat regarding the emissary with a curious chill blankness. In peace, to the outward eye he was a commonplace man; in war he changed. The authority with which he was clothed went, no doubt, for much, but it was rather, perhaps, that a door had been opened for him. His inner self became visible, and that imposingly. The man was there; a firm man, indomitable, a thunderbolt of war, a close-mouthed, far-seeing, praying and worshipping, more or less ambitious, not always just, patriotically devoted fatalist and enthusiast, a mysterious and commanding genius of an iron sort. When he was angered it was as though the offender had managed to antagonize some natural law, or force or mass. Such an one had to face, not an irritated human organism, but a Gibraltar armed for the encounter. The men who found themselves confronted by this anger could and did brace themselves against it, but it was with some hopelessness of feeling, as of hostility upon a plane where they were at a disadvantage. The man now sitting his horse before him on the endless winter road was one not easily daunted by outward aspects. Nevertheless he had at this moment, in the back of his head, a weary consciousness that war was roseate only to young boys and girls, that the day was cold and drear, the general hostile, the earth overlaid with dull misery, that the immortals, if there were any, must be clamouring for the curtain to descend forever upon this shabby human stage, painful and sordid, with its strutting tragedians and its bellman's cry of *World Drama!* The snow came down thickly, in large flakes; a horse shook himself, rubbed his nose against his fellow's neck, and whinnied mournfully. The pause, which had seemed long, was not really so. Jackson turned toward the group of waiting officers. "Major Cleave."

Cleave pushed his horse a little into the road. "Sir."

"You will return with this officer to General Loring's command. It is far in the rear. You will give General Loring this note." As he spoke he wrote upon a leaf torn from his pocket-book. The words as he traced them read: "*General Jackson's compliments to General Loring. He has some fault to find with the zeal of General Loring, his officers and men. General Loring will represent to himself that in war soldiers are occasionally called upon to travel in winter weather. Campaigns cannot always be conducted in seasons of roses. General Loring will urge his men forward, without further complaint. T. J. Jackson, Major-General.*"

He folded the leaf and gave it to Richard Cleave, then touched Little Sorrel with his heavy spur and with Ashby and the staff rode on through the falling snow, between the hills. The small cavalry advance passed, too, grey and ghost-like in the grasp of General January, disappearing within the immense and floating veil of the snow. When all were gone Stafford and Cleave turned their horses' heads toward the distant column, vaguely seen in the falling day. Stafford made an expressive sound.

"I am sorry," said Cleave gravely. "But when you have been with him longer you will understand him better."

"I think that he is really mad."

The other shook his head. "He is not mad. Don't get that idea, Stafford. It *is* hard on the troops, poor fellows! How the snow falls! We had better turn out and let the guns pass."

They moved into the untrodden snow lying in the fence corners and watched the guns, the horses, and men strain past with a sombre noise. Officers and men knew Richard Cleave, and several hailed him. "Where in hell are we going, Cleave? Old Jack likes you! Tell him, won't you, that it's damned hard on the horses, and we have n't much to eat ourselves? Tell him even the guns are complaining! Tell him — Yes, sir! Get up there, Selim! Pull, Flora, pull! — Whoa! — Damnation! Come lay a hand to this gun, boys! Where's Hetterich! Hetterich, this damned wheel's off again!"

The delay threatening to be considerable, the two men rode on, picking their way, keeping to the low bank, or using the verge of the crowded road. At last they left the artillery, and found themselves again upon a lonely way. "I love that arm," said Cleave. "There is n't a gun there that is n't alive to me." He turned in his saddle and looked back at the last caisson vanishing over the hill.

"Shall you remain with the staff?"

"No. Only through this campaign. I prefer the line."

The snow fell so fast that the trampled and discoloured road was again whitening beneath it. Half a mile ahead was visible the Stonewall Brigade, coming very slowly, beaten by the wind, blinded by the snow, a spectral grey serpent upon the winding road.

Stafford spoke abruptly. "I am in your debt for the arrangements I found made for me in Winchester. I have had no opportunity to thank you. You were extremely good so to trouble yourself —"

"It was no trouble. As I told you once before, I am anxious to serve you."

They met the brigade, Garnett riding at the head. "Good-day, Richard Cleave," he said. "We are all bound for Siberia, I think!" Company by company the regiments staggered by, in the whirling snow, the colours gripped by stiffening hands. There were blood stains on the frozen ground. Oh, the shoes, the shoes that a non-manufacturing country with closed ports had to make in haste and send its soldiers! Oh, the muskets, heavy, dull, ungleaming, weighting the fiercely aching shoulders! Oh, the snow, mounded on cap, on cartridge box, on rolled blanket and haversack. Oh, the northwest wind like a lash, the pinched stomach, the dry lips, the wavering sight, the weariness excessive! The strong men were breathing hard, their brows drawn together and upward. The weaker soldiers had a ghastly look, as of life shrunk to a point. *Close up, men! Close up — close up!*

Farther down the line, on the white bank to which they tried to keep, the column almost filling the narrow road, Cleave checked his horse. "I have a brother in this regiment, and he has been ill —"

A company came stumbling by, heads bent before the bitter wind. He spoke to its captain, the captain spoke to a lieutenant, the lieutenant to a private in the colour guard, who at once fell out of line and sprang somewhat stiffly across the wayside depression to the two horsemen drawn up upon the bank. "Well, Richard! It's snowing."

"Have you had anything to eat, Will?"

"Loads. I had a pone of cornbread and a Mr. Rat in my file had a piece of bacon. We added them and then divided them, and it was lovely, so far as it went!" He laughed ruefully. "Only I've still that typhoid fever appetite —"

His brother took from under the cape of his coat a small parcel. "Here are some slices of bread and meat. I hoped I would see you, and so I saved them. Where is that comforter Miriam knitted you?"

The boy's eyes glistened as he put out a gaunt young hand and took the parcel. "Won't Mr. Rat and I have a feast! We were just talking of old Judge at the Institute, and of how good his warm loaves used to taste! Seems like an answer to prayer. Thank you, Richard! Miriam's comforter? There's a fellow, a clerk from the store at Balcony Falls, who hasn't much stamina and no shoes at all. They were bad when he started, and one fell to pieces yesterday, and he left most of the other on that bad piece of road this morning. So at the last halt we cut my comforter in two and tied up his feet with it — I didn't need it, anyway." He looked over his shoulder. "Well, I'd better be catching up!"

Richard put a hand upon his arm. "Don't give away any more clothing. You have your blanket, I see."

"Yes, and Mr. Rat has an oilcloth. Oh, we'll sleep. I could sleep now —" he spoke dreamily; "right in that fence corner. Doesn't it look soft and white? — like a feather bed with lovely clean sheets. The fence rails make it look like my old crib at home —" He pulled himself together with a jerk. "You take care of yourself, Richard! I'm all right. Mr. Rat and I were soldiers before the war broke out!" He was gone, stumbling stiffly across to the road, running stiffly to overtake his company. His brother looked after him with troubled eyes, then with a sigh picked up the reins and followed Stafford toward the darkening east.

The two going one way, the haggard regiments another, the line that seemed interminable came at last toward its end. The 65th held the rear. There were greetings from many throats, and from Company A a cheer. Hairston Breckinridge, now its captain, came across. "*Judge Allen's Resolutions* — hey, Richard! The world has moved since then! I wish Fincastle could see us now — or rather I don't wish it! Oh, we're holding out all right! The men are trumps."

Mathew Coffin, too, came up. "It does n't look much, Major Cleave, like the day we marched away! All the serenading and the flowers — we never thought war could be ugly." He glanced disconsolately down at a torn cuff and a great smear of frozen mire adorning his coat. "I'm rather glad the ladies can't see us."

The Stonewall Brigade went by. There was again a stretch of horribly cut road, empty save for here and there poor stragglers, sitting dismally huddled together beneath a cedar, or limping on painful feet, hoping somewhere to overtake "the boys." A horse had fallen dead and had been dragged out of the road and through a gap in the fencing into a narrow field. Beyond this, on the farther boundary of grey rails, three buzzards were sitting, seen like hobgoblins through the veiling snow. The afternoon was closing in; it could only be said that the world was a dreary one.

The Army of the Kanawha, Loring's three brigades, with the batteries attached, came into view a long way off, grey streaks upon the road. Before the two horsemen reached it it had halted for the night, broken ranks, and flowed into the desolate fields. There was yet an hour of daylight, but discontent had grown marked, the murmuring loud, and the halt was made. A few of the wagons were up, and a dark and heavy wood filling a ravine gave fagots for the gathering. The two aides found Loring himself, middle-aged and imposing, old Indian fighter, hero of Contreras, Churubusco, Chapultepec, and Garita de Belen, commander, since the transference of General Robert E. Lee to South Carolina, of the Army of the Kanawha, gallant and dashing, with an arm left in Mexico, with a gift for picturesque phrases, with a past full of variety and a future of a like composition, with a genuine tenderness and care for his men, and an entire conviction that both he and his troops were at present in the convoy of a madman — they found Loring seated on a log beside a small fire and engaged in cooling in the snow a too-hot tin cup of coffee. His negro servant busily toasted hardtack; a brigadier seated on an opposite log was detailing, half fiercely, half plaintively, the conditions under which his brigade was travelling. The two from Jackson dismounted, crunched their way over the snow and saluted. The general looked up. "Good-evening, gentlemen! Is that you, Stafford? Well, did you do your prettiest — and did he respond?"

"Yes, sir, he responded," replied Stafford, with grimness. "But not by me. — Major Cleave, sir, of his staff."

Cleave came forward, out of the whirling snow, and gave Jackson's missive. It was so dull and dark a late afternoon that all things were indistinct. "Give me a light here, Jupiter!" said Loring, and the negro by the fire lit a great sliver of pine and held it like a torch above the page. Loring read, and his face grew purple. With a suppressed oath he sat a moment, staring at the paper, then with his one hand folded it against his knee. His fingers shook, not with cold, but with rage. "Very good, very good! That's what he says, is n't it, all the time? 'Very good!' or is it 'Good, good!'" He felt himself growing incoherent, pulled himself sharply together, and with his one hand thrust the paper into his breast pocket. "It's all right, Stafford. Major Cleave, the Army of the Kanawha welcomes you. Will you stay with us to-night, or have you fifty miles to make ere dawn?"

Cleave, it appeared, had not fifty miles to make, but four. He must report at the appointed bivouac. Loring tore with his one hand a leaf from his pocket-book, found his pencil, and using a booted knee for a table, wrote a line, folded and superscribed it. "This for General Jackson. Ugh, what freezing weather! Sit down and drink a cup of coffee before you go. You, too, Maury. Here, Jupiter! hot coffee. Major Cleave, do you remember Æsop's fables?"

"Yes, sir, — a number of them."

"A deal of knowledge there of damned human nature! The frog that swelled and swelled and thought himself an ox. Curious how your boyhood books come back into your mind! Sit down, gentlemen, sit down! Reardon's got a box of cigars tucked away somewhere or he is n't Reardon —"

Along the edge of the not-distant ravine other small fires had been built. From the circle about one of these arose a quavering voice — a soldier trying to sing cheer into company.

Dere was an old niggah, dey called him Uncle Ned —
 He 's dead long ago, long ago!
He had no wool on de top ob his head,
 De place whar de wool ought to grow.
  Den lay down de shubble an de hoe,
  Hang up de fiddle an de bow —

CHAPTER XIII

FOOL TOM JACKSON

THE REVEREND MR. CORBIN WOOD, chaplain to one of Loring's regiments, coming down from the hillside where he had spent the night, very literally like a shepherd, found the little stream at its foot frozen to the bottom. No morning bath for a lover of cleanliness! There had been little water, indeed, to expend on any toilet since leaving Winchester. Corbin Wood tried snow for his face and hands, but the snow was no longer soft, as it had fallen the day before. It was frozen and harsh. "And the holy hermits and the saints on pillars never had a bath — apparently never wanted one!"

Reveille sounded drearily enough from the surrounding mountains. The fires sprang up, but they did not burn brightly in the livid day. The little there was to eat was warmed and eaten. When, afterwards, the rolls were called, there were silences. Mr. Ready-to-halt, Mr. Faint Heart, Mr. Fearing, and also Mr. Honesty, really too ill to march, were somewhere on the backward road to Winchester. Length by length, like a serpent grey and cold, sluggish, unburnished, dull, and bewildered, the column took the road. Deeply cut the day before by the cavalry, by Garnett's brigade, and by the artillery, the road was horrible. What had been ridged snow was now ridged ice.

Corbin Wood and his old grey horse were loved by their regiment. The chaplain was not, physically, a strong man, and his ways were those of a scholar, but the regiment found them lovable. Pluto the horse was very wise, very old, very strong and gentle. Upon the march he was of use to many beside his master. The regiment had grown accustomed to the sight of the chaplain walking through dust or mud at the bridle of the grey, saying now and then a word in a sober and cheerful fashion to the half-sick or wholly weary private seated in his saddle. He was forever giving some one a lift along the road. Certain things that have had small place in the armies of the world were commonplaces in the Confederate service. The man on horseback was a more fortunate, but not a better man — not even a better born or educated man — than he on foot. The long grey lines saw nothing strange in a dismounted officer giving a cast of the road to a comrade in the ranks. So, to-day, the chaplain's horse was rather for everybody than for the chaplain himself. An old college mate slipping stiffly to earth after five inestimable minutes, remonstrated. "I'd like to see you riding, Corbin! Just give yourself a lift, won't you? Look at Pluto looking at that rent in your shoe! You'll never be a bishop if you go on this way."

The sleet fell and fell, and it was intensely cold. The wagons were invisible. It was rumoured that they had taken another road. The country was almost a wilderness. At long intervals the troops came upon a lonely farmhouse, or a wayside cabin, a mill, a smithy. Loring sent ahead a foraging party, with orders to purchase all supplies. Hardly anything was gotten. Little had been made this year and little stored. Moreover, latterly, the Yankees at Bath had taken all the stock and poultry and corn — and without paying for it either. "Yes, sir, there are Yankees at Bath. More'n you can shake a stick at!"

The foragers brought back the news. "There are Yankees at Bath — eight miles away! Any number of them. Just as certain as it's sleeting, that's where Old Jack's going!"

The news running along the column awoke a small flare of interest. But it filled no empty stomachs, nor dissipated the numbing cold. The momentary enthusiasm passed. "Eight miles! Have we got to go eight miles to-day? We haven't made three miles since dawn. If George Washington, Napoleon Bonaparte, and Julius Cæsar were here they couldn't get this army eight miles to-day!"

The cavalry, the artillery, the Stonewall Brigade, Meems and Carson's Militia, the three brigades of Loring — on wound the sick and sluggish column. The hills were now grey glass, and all the horses smooth-shod. In advance a corps of pioneers broke with pickaxes the solid and treacherous surface, roughening the road so that the poor brutes might gain foothold. The vanguard, stumbling around a bend of the road, stumbled upon a Federal ambush, horse and foot. To either side a wood of cedars blazed and rang. A lieutenant of the

21st Virginia threw up his arms and pitched forward, dead. A private was badly wounded. The company charged, but the blue outposts fired another volley and got away, crashing through the woods to some by-road. It was impossible to follow; chase could not be given over grey glass.

With the closing in of the ghostly day, in a stretch of fields beside a frozen stream, the column halted. There were no tents, and there was scarcely anything to eat. One of the fields was covered by stacked corn, and it was discovered that the ear had been left. In the driving sleet the men tore apart the shocks and with numbed fingers stripped from the grain the sere, rough, and icy husks. They and the horses ate the yellow corn. All night, stupid with misery, the soldiers dozed and muttered beside the wretched fires. One, a lawyer's clerk, cried like a child, with his hands scored till they bled by the frozen corn husks. Down the stream stood a deserted sawmill, and here the Rockbridge men found planks with which they made for themselves little pens. The sleet sounded for hours on the boards that served for roof, but at last it died away. The exhausted army slept, but when in the grey dawn it stirred and rose to the wailing of the bugles, it threw off a weight of snow. All the world was white again beneath a livid sky.

This day they made four miles. The grey trees were draped with ice, the grey zigzag of the fences was gliding ice under the hands that caught at it, the hands of the sick and weak. Motion resolved itself into a Dead March; few notes and slow, with rests. The army moved and halted, moved and halted with a weird stateliness. Couriers came back from the man riding ahead, cadet cap drawn over eyes that saw only what a giant and iron race might do under a giant and iron dictatorship. General Jackson says, " Press Forward! " General Jackson says, " Press Forward, men! "

They did not reach Bath that night. They lay down and slept behind a screen of hills and awoke in an amethyst dawn to a sky of promise. The light, streaming from the east, made glorious the ice-laden trees and the far and dazzling wastes of snow. The sunshine cheered the troops. Bath was just ahead — Bath and the Yankees! The 1st Tennessee and the 48th Virginia suddenly swung from the main road, and moved across the fields to the ridges overlooking the town. Apparently they had gathered their strength into a ball, for

they went with energy, double-quickening over the snow. The afternoon before Carson and Meems had been detached, disappearing to
the right. A rumour ran through the ranks. This force would be
now on the other side of Bath. "It's like a cup, all of us on the rim,
and the Yanks at the bottom. If Carson can hold the roads on the
other side we've got them, just like so many coffee grounds! Fifteen hundred of them in blue, and two guns? — Boys, I feel better!"

Old Jack — the men began with suddenness again to call him
Old Jack — Old Jack divulged nothing. Information, if information it was, came from scouts, couriers, Ashby's vedettes, chance-
met men and women of the region. Something electric flashed from
van to rear. The line went up the hill with rapidity. When they
reached the crest the men saw the cavalry far before and below
them, charging upon the town and shouting. After the horse came a
body of skirmishers, then, pouring down the hillside the 1st Tennessee and the 48th Virginia, yelling as they ran. From the town
burst a loud rattle of musketry, and from a height beyond a cannon
thundered. All the white sides of the cup echoed the sound.

The infantry swerved to let the artillery by. The guns, grim
beneath their ice coats, the yelling men, the drivers loudly encourag-
ing the horses, the horses, red-nostrilled, wide-eyed — all came somehow, helter-skelter down the long windings of the ridge. The infantry followed; the town was entered; the Federals retreated, firing as
they went, streaming out by two roads. One led toward Sir John's
Run, the other direct to the Potomac with Hancock on the Maryland shore, and at Hancock General Lander with a considerable
force. Carson's men, alack! had found the winter hills no bagatelle.
They were not in time to secure the roads.

The Confederate cavalry, dividing, followed, full tilt, the retreating foe. A courier brought back to the artillery a curt order from
Jackson to push on by the Hancock road. As he turned, his mare
slipped, and the two came crashing down upon the icy road. When
they had struggled up and out of the way the batteries passed rumbling through the town. Old men and boys were out upon the trampled sidewalks, and at window and door women and children waved
handkerchiefs, clapped hands. At a corner, in the middle of the
street, lay a horse, just lifeless, covered with blood. The sight maddened the battery horses. They reared and plunged, but at last

went trembling by. From the patriarchs and the eager boys came information. The Yankees were gone, but not their baggage and stores. Everything had been left behind. There were army blankets, tents, oilcloths, clothing, *shoes*, cords of firewood, forage for the horses, flour, and fresh meat, sugar, coffee, sutlers' stores of every kind, wines, spirits, cigars — oh, everything! The artillery groaned and swore, but obeyed orders. Leaving Capua behind, it strained along the Hancock road in the wake of the pursuing cavalry and the fleeing Federals.

The main body of the latter, well in advance and with no exhausting march behind them to weaken horse and man, reached the Potomac by the Hancock road at a point where they had boats moored, and got clean away, joining Lander on the Maryland shore. The lesser number, making for Sir John's Run and the Big Cacapon and followed by some companies of Ashby's, did not so quickly escape. The Confederate advance came, artillery, horse, and skirmishers, upon the river bank at sunset. All around were great rolling hills, quite bare of trees and covered with snow, over which the setting sun threw a crimson tinge. Below was the river, hoarsely murmuring, and immediately upon the other side, the clustering Maryland village, with a church spire tall and tapering against the northern sky. About the village was another village of tents, and upon a hilltop frowned a line of guns. Dusk as it was, the Confederate batteries unlimbered, and there opened an artillery duel, shells screaming from north to south and south to north across the river yet stained with the sunset glow.

That night the infantry remained at Bath, warmed and· comforted by the captured stores. They came like a gift from the gods, and as is usual with that gift they disappeared in a twinkling. In the afternoon the three arms met on the river bank. The sky was again a level grey; it was evident that a snowstorm was brewing. There was not a house; except for the fringe along the water's edge there was hardly a tree. The hills were all bare. The snow was packed so hard and so mingled with ice that when, in the cannonading, the Federal missiles struck and tore it up the fragments were as keen and troublesome, almost, as splinters of shell. There was no shelter, little wood for burning. The men gazed about them with a frown of uneasiness. The storm set in with a whirl of snow and with a wind that raved like a madman and broke the spectral white arms of the sycamores by the river. In a short time there was a shifting, wonderful, numbing veil streaming silent from the grey heavens. It was almost a relief when dark came and wrapped the great, lonely, ghostly countryside. This night the men disregarded the taboo and burned every available fence rail.

In the morning a boat was put across the half-frozen river. It bore a summons to Lander to surrender, the alternative being a bombardment of the town. " Retaliation for Shepherdstown " read Jackson's missive. Ashby bore the summons and was led blindfold through the streets to headquarters. Lander, looking momently for reinforcements from Williamsport, declined to surrender. Ashby passed blindfolded out of the town, entered the boat, and came back to Stonewall Jackson. The latter waited two hours, then began to throw shells into the town. Since early morning a force had been engaged in constructing, two miles up the river, a rude bridge by which the troops might cross. The evening before there had been skirmishes at Sir John's Run and at the Big Cacapon. A regiment of Loring's destroyed the railroad bridge over the latter stream. The Federals withdrew across the river, leaving no command in Morgan County.

Throughout the afternoon McLaughlin's battery dropped shells into Hancock, but an hour before dark came orders to cease firing. A scout — Allan Gold — brought tidings of heavy reinforcements pouring into the town from Williamsport and Hagerstown. So heavy were they that Jackson, after standing for five minutes with his face to the north, sent orders to discontinue work upon the bridge. Romney, when all was said, not Hancock, was his destination — Kelly's eight thousand in Virginia, not Lander's brigades across the line. Doubtless it had been his hope to capture every Federal in Bath, to reach and cross the Potomac, inflict damage, and retire before those reinforcements could come up. But the infantry which he commanded was not yet his "foot cavalry," and neither knew nor trusted him as it was to know and trust. The forces about him to-day were not homogeneous. They pulled two ways, they were not moulded and coloured as they were to be moulded and coloured, not instinct with the one man view as they were to become instinct. They were not iron as he was iron, nor yet thunderbolts of war. They could not divine the point and hour of attack, and, sooth to say, they received scant assistance from the actual wizard. They were patriot forces, simple and manly souls ready enough to die for their cause, but few were yet at the arrowhead of concentration as was this man. They were to attain it, but not yet. He looked at the north and he looked at his complaining legions, and he strode off to his bivouac beneath a solitary tree. Here, a little later he gave orders to his brigadiers. The Army of the Northwest would resume the march "at early dawn."

In the harsh coldness of the morning they retraced the road to Bath, a frightful road, a road over which an army had passed. At noon they came to Bath, but there was hardly a pause in the town. Beneath a sky of lead, in a harsh and freezing wind, the troops swung slowly into a narrow road running west through a meagre valley. Low hills were on either side — low and bleak. Scrub oak and pine grew sparsely, and along the edges of the road dead milkweed and mullein stood gaunt above the snow. The troops passed an old cider press and a cabin or two out of which negroes stared.

Before long they crossed a creek and began to climb. All the landscape was now mountainous. To the right, as the way mounted, opened a great view, white dales and meadows, far winter forests, and the long, long wall of North Mountain. There was small care for the view among the struggling soldiers. The hills seemed perpendicular, the earth treacherous glass. Going up, the artillerymen must drag with the horses at gun and caisson; going down the carriages must be held back, else they would slide sideways and go crashing over the embankment. Again and again, going down, the horses slipped and fell. The weight of metal behind coming upon them, the whole slid in a heap to the bottom. There they must be gotten to their feet, the poor trembling brutes! and set to the task of another hill. The long, grey, halting, stumbling, creeping line saw no beauty in the winter woods, in the arched fern over the snow, in the vivid, fairy plots of moss, in the smooth, tall ailanthus stems by the wayside, in the swinging, leafless lianas of grape, pendent from the highest trees, in the imposing view of the mountains. The line was sick, sick to the heart, numbed and shivering, full of pain. Every ambulance and wagon used as ambulance was heavy laden; at every infrequent cabin or lonely farmhouse were left the too ill to travel farther. The poor servants, of whom there were some in each company, were in pitiable plight. No negro likes the cold; for him all the hot sunshine he can get! They shivered now, in the rear of the companies, their bodies drawn together, their faces grey. The nature of most was of an abounding cheerfulness, but it was not possible to be cheerful on this January road to Romney.

The army crossed Sleepy Creek. It was frozen to the bottom. The cedars along its shore stood so funereally, so crape-like and dark, the sycamores were so clay-white and long of arm, the great birds slowly circling above a neighbouring wood of so dreary a significance, that the heart sank and sank. Was this war? — war, heroic and glorious, with banners, trumpets, and rewarded enterprise? Manassas had been war — for one brief summer day! But ever since there was only marching, tenting, suffering, and fatigue — and fatigue — and fatigue.

Maury Stafford and the Reverend Mr. Corbin Wood found themselves riding side by side, with other mounted officers, in advance of Loring's leading regiment. The chaplain had experienced, the day before, an ugly fall. His knee was badly wrenched, and so, perforce, he rode to-day, though, as often as he thought the grey could stand it, he took up a man behind him. Now, however, he was riding single. Indeed, for the last mile he had uttered no pitiful comment and given no invitation. Moreover, he talked persistently and was forever calling his companion's attention to the beauty of the view. At last, after a series of short answers, it occurred to Stafford to regard him more closely. There was a colour in the chaplain's cheek and he swayed ever so slightly and rhythmically in his saddle. Stafford checked his horse, drew his hand out of an ice-caked gauntlet, and leaning over laid it on the other's which was bare. The chaplain's skin was burning hot. Stafford made a sound of concern and rode forward to the colonel. In a minute he returned. "Now you and I, Mr. Wood, will fall out here and just quietly wait until the wagons come by. Then the doctor will fix you up nicely in the ambulance. . . . Oh, yes, you are! You're ill enough to want to lie down for awhile. Some one else, you know, can ride Pluto."

Corbin Wood pondered the matter. "That's true, that's very true, my dear Maury. Fontaine, now, behind us in the ranks, his shoes are all worn out. Fontaine, eh? Fontaine knows more Greek than any man — and he'll be good to Pluto. Pluto's almost worn out himself — he's not immortal like Xanthius and Balius. Do you know, Maury, it's little wonder that Gulliver found the Houyhnhnms so detesting war? Horses have a dreadful lot in war — and the quarrel never theirs. Do but look at that stream! — how cool and pleasant, winding between the willows —"

Stafford got him to one side of the road, to a small plateau beneath an overhanging bank. The column was now crawling through a ravine with a sheer descent on the right to the frozen creek below. To the left, covering the mountain-side, were masses of evergreen kalmia, and above them tall and leafless trees in whose branches the wind made a grating sound. The sleet was falling again — a veil of sleet. The two waiting for the ambulance looked down upon the grey soldiers, grey, weary, and bent before the wind. "Who would ever have thought," said the chaplain, "that Dante took an idea from Virginia in the middle of the nineteenth century? I remember things being so happy and comfortable — but it must have been long ago. Yes, my people, long ago." Dropping the bridle, he raised his arm in a gesture usual with him in the pulpit. In the fading light there was about him an illusion of black and white; he moved his arm as though it were clad in the sleeve of a surplice. "I am not often denunciatory," he said, "but I denounce this weary going to and fro, this turning like a dervish, this finding that every straight line is but a fraction of a circle, this squirrel cage with the greenwood never reached, this interminable drama, this dance of midges, —

> Through a circle that ever returneth in
>   To the selfsame spot,
> And much of Madness and more of Sin
>   And Horror the soul of the plot —

Is it not wonderful, the gold light on the mountains?"

At last the ambulance appeared — a good one, captured at Manassas. The chaplain, still talking, was persuaded stiffly to dismount, to give Pluto's bridle into Stafford's hand, and to enter. There were other occupants, two rows of them. Stafford saw his old friend laid in a corner, on a wisp of straw; then, finding Fontaine in the ranks, gave over the grey, and joined the staff creeping, creeping on tired horses through the sleet.

Cavalry and infantry and wagon train wound at the close of day over a vast bare hilltop toward Unger's Store where, it was known, would be the bivouac. The artillery in the rear found it impossible to finish out the march. Two miles from Unger's the halt was ordered. It was full dark; neither man nor brute could stumble farther. All came to a stand high up on the wind-swept hill. The guns were left in the road, the horses led down the slope and picketted in the lee of a poor stable, placed there, it seemed, by some pitying chance. In the stable there was even found some hay and corn. The men had no supper, or only such crumbs as were found in the haversacks. They made their fires on the hillside and crouched around them, nodding uneasily, trying to sleep with faces scorched by the flame and freezing backs. They put their feet in the sodden shoes to the fire, and the poor, worn-out leather fell into yet greater holes. There was some conjecture as to how far the thermometer stood below zero. Some put it at forty, but the more conservative declared for twenty. It was impossible to sleep, and every one was hungry, and the tobacco was all out. *What were they doing at home, by the fire, after supper, with the children playing about?*

At dawn the bugles blew. Stiff and sore, racked with pains and aches, coughing, limping, savagely hungry, the men rose. Time was to come when even a dawn like this would be met by the Confederate soldier with whimsical cheer, with greetings as to an oft-encountered friend, with a courage quaint, pathetic, and divinely high — but the time was not yet. The men swore and groaned. The haversacks were quite empty; there would be no breakfast until the wagons were caught up with at Unger's. The drivers went down the hillside for the horses. When they came to the strength that had drawn the guns and looked, there was a moment's silence. Hetterich the blacksmith was with the party, and Hetterich wept. "If I was God, I would n't have it — I would n't have a horse treated so! Just look at Flora — just look at her knees! Ah, the poor brute!" So frequent had been the falls of the day before, so often had the animals been cut by the carriages coming upon them, that many were scarred in a dreadful fashion. The knees of Flora had been badly cut, and what Hetterich pointed at were long red icicles hanging from the wounds.

At Unger's the evening before, in a narrow valley between the silver hills, the infantry stacked arms, broke ranks, and listened with sullen brows to two pieces of news. At Hanging Rock, between Unger's and Romney, the advance, composed of a regiment of militia and a section of artillery, had come into touch with the enemy. The militia had broken, the two guns had been lost. "Fool Tom Jackson" was reported to have said, "Good! good!" and lifted that right hand of his to the sky. The other tidings were to the effect that the troops would rest at Unger's for three days, to the end, chiefly, that the horses might be rough-shod. Rest — delicious sound! But Unger's! To the east the unutterably bleak hills over which they had toiled, to the west Capon Mountain high and stark against the livid skies, to the south a dark forest with the snow beneath the trees, to the north long, low hills, with faded broom-sedge waving in the wind. Upon a hilltop perched a country store, a blacksmith shop, and one or two farmhouses, forlorn and lonely in the twilight, and by the woods ran Buffalo Run, ice upon the shallows to either bank.

In the morning, when the artillery was up, when breakfast was over, roll called, orders read, the army fell to the duties upon which paramount stress had been laid. All the farriers, the drivers, the men who had to do with horses, went to work with these poor, wretched, lame, and wounded friends, feeding them, currying them, dressing their hurts and, above all, rough-shoeing them in preparation for the icy mountains ahead. The clink of iron against iron made a pleasant sound; moreover, this morning, the sun shone. Very cold as it was, there was cheer in the sky. Even the crows cawing above the woods did not sound so dolefully. A Thunder Run man found a tree laden with shrivelled persimmons. He was up it like a squirrel. "Simmon tree! Simmon tree!" Comrades came hurrying over the snow; the fruit was dropped into upheld caps, lifted toward eager mouths. Suddenly there flamed a generous impulse. "Boys! them poor sick fellows with nothing but hard-tack —" The persimmons were carried to the hospital tents.

Before the sun was halfway to the meridian a curious spectacle appeared along the banks of Buffalo Run. Every hundred feet or so was built a large fire. Over it hung a camp kettle, full of water — water hot as the fire could make it. Up and down the stream an improvised laundry went into operation, while, squad by squad, the men performed their personal ablutions. It was the eighth of January; they had left Winchester upon the first, and small, indeed, since then had been the use of washing water. In the dire cold, with the streams frozen, cleanliness had not tempted the majority, and indeed, latterly, the men had been too worn out to care. Sleep and food and warmth had represented the sum of earthly desire. A number, with ostentation, had each morning broken the ice from some pool or other and bathed face and hands, but few extended the laved area. The General Order appointing a Washerman's Day came none too soon. Up and down Buffalo Run, in the zero weather, the men stripped and bathed. Soap was not yet the scarce and valuable commodity it was to become; there was soap enough for all and the camp kettles were filled from the stream as soon as emptied. Underclothing, too, flannel and cotton, must be washed. . . . There came discoveries, made amid "Ughs!" of disgust. The more fastidious threw the whole business, undergarment and parasites into the fire; others, more reasonable, or without a change of clothing, scalded their apparel with anxious care. The episode marked a stage in warfare. That night Lieutenant Coffin, writing a letter on his last scrap of pale blue paper, sat with scrupulously washed hands well back from the board he was using as a table. His boyish face flushed, his lips quivered as he wrote. He wrote of lilies and moss rose-buds and the purity of women, and he said there was a side of war which Walter Scott had never painted.

Three bleak, pinched days later the army again took the road to Romney. Four miles from Unger's they began to climb Sleepy Creek Mountain, mounting the great, sparsely wooded slope like a long line of warrior ants. To either hand the view was very fine, North Mountain to the left, Capon Mountain to the right, in between a sea of hills and long deep vales — very fine and utterly unappreciated. The earth was hostile, the sky was hostile, the commanding general was hostile. Snow began to fall.

Allan Gold, marching with Company A, began to think of Thunder Run, the schoolhouse, and the tollgate. The 65th was now high upon the mountain-side and the view had vastly widened. The men looked out and over toward the great main Valley of Virginia, and they looked wistfully. To many of the men home was over there — home, wife, child, mother — all hopelessly out of reach.

Allan Gold had no wife nor child nor mother, but he thought of Sairy and Tom, and he wondered if Sairy were making ginger-bread. He tried to smell it again, and to feel the warmth of her kitchen — but then he knew too well that she was not making gingerbread! Tom's last letter had spoken of the growing scarcity; flour so high, sugar so high. Everybody was living very plainly, and the poor were going to suffer. Allan thought of the school-house. It was closed. He could see just how it looked; a small unused building, mournful, deserted, crumbling, while past it rushed the strong and wintry torrent. He thought suddenly of Christianna. He saw her plainly, more plainly than ever he had done before. She looked starved, defeated. He thought of the Country. How long would the war last? In May they had thought "Three months." In the flush of triumph after Manassas they had said "It is over." But it wasn't over. Marching and camping had followed, fights on the Peninsula, fights on the Kanawha, at Lees-burg, at Cheat Mountain, affairs in the far South; and now Mc-Clellan drilling, organizing, organizing below Washington! with rumours of another "On to Richmond." When would the war be over? Allan wondered.

The column, turning to the right, began to descend the mountain, a long, slipping, stumbling downward going, with the snow falling heavily and the wind screaming like a banshee. At the foot was a stretch of bottom land, then, steep and rocky, grimly waiting to be crossed, rose Bear Garden Ridge. High Top loomed behind. The infantry could see the cavalry, creeping up Bear Garden, moving slowly, slowly, bent before the blast, wraithlike through the falling snow. From far in the rear, back of the Stonewall Brigade, back of Loring, came a dull sound — the artillery and the wagon train climbing Sleepy Creek Mountain. It was three o'clock in the after-noon — oh, leaden weariness, hunger, cold, sickness, worn-out shoes —

Back upon the mountain top, in the ambulance taken at Manas-sas, Mr. Corbin Wood, better than he had been for several days, but still feverish, propped himself upon the straw and smiled across at Will Cleave, who, half carried by his brother, had appeared beside the ambulance an hour before. Swaying as he stood, the boy pro-tested to the last that he could march just as well as the other fel-

lows, that they would think him a baby, that Richard would ruin his
reputation, that he was n't giddy, that the doctor in Winchester had
told him that after you got well from typhoid fever you were
stronger than you ever had been before, that Mr. Rat would think
he was malingering, that — that — that — Richard lifted him into
the ambulance and laid him upon the straw which several of the
sick pushed forward and patted into place. The surgeon gave a
restorative. The elder brother waited until the boy's eyes opened,
stooped and kissed him on the forehead, and went away. Now Will
said that he was rested, and that it was all a fuss about nothing anyway, and it was funny, travelling like animals in a circus, and was n't
it most feeding time anyway? Corbin Wood had a bit of bread
which he shared, and two or three convalescents in a corner took up
the circus idea. "There ain't going to be another performance this
year! We're going into winter quarters — that's where we're
going. Yes, siree, up with the polar bears —" "And the living
skeletons —" "Gosh! I'm a warm weather crittur! I'd jest like to
peacefully fold the equator in my arms an' go to sleep." "Oh,
hell! — Beg your pardon, sir, it just slipped out, like one of the
snake charmer's rattlers!" "Boys, jes' think of a real circus, with
all the women folk, an' the tarletan, an' the spangles, an' the pink
lemonade, an' the little fellers slipping under the ropes, an' the
Grand Parade coming in, an' the big tent so hot everybody's fan-
ning with their hats — Oh, Lord!" "Yes, and the clown — and the
ring master —" "*What d'ye think of our ring master?*" "Who d' ye
mean? *Him?* Think of him? I think he's a damned clown! Don't
they call him Fool Tom —"

Will rose from the straw. "While I am by, I'll allow no man to
reflect upon the general commanding this army —"

A Georgian of Loring's, tall, gaunt, parched, haggard, a college
man and high private astray from his own brigade, rose to a sitting
posture. "What in hell is that young cockerel crowing about? Is
it about the damned individual at the head of this army? I take it
that it is. Then I will answer him. The individual at the head of
this army is not a general; he is a schoolmaster. Napoleon, or Cæsar,
or Marlborough, or Eugène, or Cromwell, or Turenne, or Frederick
would n't turn their heads to look at him as they passed! But every
little school-yard martinet would! He's a pedagogue — by God, he's

the Falerian pedagogue who sold his pupils to the Romans! Oh, the lamb-like pupils, trooping after him through flowers and sunshine — straight into the hands of Kelly at Romney, with Rosecrans and twenty thousand just beyond! Yaaah! A schoolmaster leading Loring and all of us! Let him go back to Lexington and teach the Rule of Three, for by God, he'll never demonstrate the Rule of One!"

He waved a claw-like hand. "Kindly do not interrupt. Stiff, fanatic, inhuman, callous, cold, half mad and wholly rash, without military capacity, ambitious as Lucifer and absurd as Hudibras — I ask again what is this person doing at the head of this army? Has any one confidence in him? Has any one pride in him? Has any one love for him? In all this frozen waste through which he is dragging us, you could n't find an echo to say 'One!' Oh, you need n't shout 'One!' You're not an echo; you're only a misguided V. M. I. cadet! And you don't count either, chaplain! With all respect to you, you're a non-combatant. And that Valley man over there — he does n't count either. He belongs to the Stonewall Brigade. He's one of Major-General T. J. Jackson's pet lambs. They're school-teachers' favourites. All they've got to do is to cheer for their master. — Hip, hip, hooray! Here's Old Jack with his hand lifted and his old cap pulled low, and his sabre carried *oblikely*, and his 'God has been very good to us to-day, men!' Yaaah — Look out! What are you about?"

The cadet and the Valley man threw themselves across the straw, upon the Georgian. Corbin Wood crawled over and separated them. "Boys, boys! You're quarrelling just because you're sick and tired and cold and fretful! Try to be good children. I predict there'll come a day when we'll *all* cheer like mad — our friend from Georgia, too — all cheer like mad when General Jackson goes by, leading us to victory! Be good now. I was at the circus once, when I was a little boy, when the animals got to fighting —"

The way over Bear Garden was steep, the road a mere track among boulders. There were many fallen trees. In places they lay across the road, abatis thrown there by the storm to be removed by half-frozen hands while the horses stood and whinnied. The winter day was failing when Stonewall Jackson, Ashby, and a portion of the cavalry with the small infantry advance, came down by precipitous paths into Bloomery Gap. Here, in a dim hollow and pass of the mountains, beside a shallow, frozen creek, they bivouacked.

From the other side of Bear Garden, General Loring again sent Stafford forward with a statement, couched in terms of courtesy three-piled and icy. The aide — a favourite with his general — had ventured to demur. "I don't think General Jackson likes me, sir. Would not some other —" Loring, the Old Blizzard of two years later — had sworn. "Damn you, Maury, whom does he like? Not any one out of the Stonewall Brigade! You've got a limberer wit than most, and he can't make you cower — by the Lord, I've seen him make others do it! You go ahead, and when you're there talk indigo Presbyterian!"

"There" was a space of trampled snow underneath a giant pine. A picket on the eastern side of the stream pointed it out, three hundred yards away, a dark sentinel towering above the forest. "He's thar. His staff's this side, by the pawpaw bushes." Stafford crossed the stream, shallow and filled with floating ice, climbed the shelving bank, and coming to the pawpaw bushes found Richard Cleave stooping over the small flame that Tullius had kindled and was watchfully feeding with pine cones. Cleave straightened himself. "Good-evening, Stafford! Come to my tiny, tiny fire. I can't give you coffee — worse luck! — but Tullius has a couple of sweet potatoes."

"I can't stay, thank you," said the other. "General Jackson is over yonder?"

"Yes, by the great pine. I will take you to him." The two stepped from out the ring of pawpaws, Stafford, walking, leading his horse. "General Loring complains again?"

"Has he not reason to?" Stafford looked about him. "Ugh! steppes of Russia!"

"You think it a Moscow march? Perhaps it is. But I doubt if Ney complained."

"You think that we complain too much?"

"What do you think of it?"

Stafford stood still. They were beside a dark line of cedars, skirting the forest, stretching toward the great pine. It was twilight; all the narrow valley drear and mournful; horses and men like phantoms on the muffled earth. "I think," said Stafford deliberately, "that to a Napoleon General Loring would not complain, nor I bear his message of complaint, but to General Jackson we will, in the interests of all, continue to make representations."

"In the interests of all!" exclaimed Cleave. "I beg that you will qualify that statement. Garnett's Brigade and Ashby's Cavalry have not complained."

"No. Many disagreeable duties are left to the brigades of General Loring."

"I challenge that statement, sir. It is not true."

Stafford laughed. "Not true! You will not get us to believe that. I think you will find that representations will be forwarded to the government at Richmond —"

"Representations of disaffected soldiers?"

"No, sir! Representations of gentlemen and patriots. Remonstrances of brave men against the leadership of a petty tyrant — a diseased mind — a Presbyterian deacon crazed for personal distinction —"

Cleave let his hand fall on the other's wrist. "Stop, sir! You will remember that I am of Garnett's Brigade, and, at present, of General Jackson's military family —"

Stafford jerked his wrist away. He breathed hard. All the pent weariness, irritation, wrath, of the past most wretched days, all the chill discomfort of the hour, the enmity toward Cleave of which he was increasingly conscious, the very unsoundness of his position and dissatisfaction with his errand, pushed him on. Quarrel was in the air. Eight thousand men had, to-day, found their temper on edge. It was not surprising that between these two a flame leaped. "Member of Garnett's Brigade and member of General Jackson's military family to the contrary," said Stafford, "these are Russian steppes, and this is a march from Moscow, and the general in command is no Napoleon, but a fool and a pedant —"

"I give you warning!"

"A crazy Barebones masquerading as a Cromwell —"

The other's two hands on the shoulders of General Loring's aide had undoubtedly — the weight of the body being thrown forward — the appearance of an assault. Stafford's foot slipped upon the freezing snow. Down he came to the earth, Cleave upon him. A voice behind them spoke with a kind of steely curtness, "Stand up, and let me see who you are!"

The two arose and faced Stonewall Jackson. He had come upon them silently, out from the screen of blackening cedars. Now he blocked their path, his lips iron, his eyes a mere gleaming line. "Two squabblers rolling in the snow — two staff officers brawling before a disheartened army! What have you to say for yourselves? Nothing!"

Stafford broke the silence. "Major Cleave has my leave to explain his action, sir."

Jackson's eyes drew to a yet narrower line. "Your leave is not necessary, sir. What was this brawl about, Major Cleave?"

"We quarrelled, sir," said Cleave slowly. "Major Stafford gave utterance to certain sentiments with which I did not agree, and . . . we quarrelled."

"What sentiments? Yes, sir, I order you to answer."

"Major Stafford made certain statements as to the army and the campaign — statements which I begged to contradict. I can say no more, sir."

"You will tell me what statements, major."

"It is impossible for me to do that, sir."

"My orders are always possible of execution, sir. You will answer me."

Cleave kept silence. The twilight settled closer; the dark wall of the cedars seemed to advance; a hollow wind blew through the forest. "Why, I will tell you, sir!" said Stafford impatiently. "I said —"

Jackson cut him short. "Be silent, sir! I have not asked you for your report. Major Cleave, I am waiting."

Cleave made a slight gesture, sullen, weary, and determined. "I am very sorry, sir. Major Stafford made certain comments which I resented. Hence the action of a moment. That is all that I can say, sir."

Stafford spoke with curt rapidity. "I said that these were Russian steppes and that this was a march from Moscow, but that we had not a Napoleon to soften privation for us. I said that the Stonewall Brigade was unduly favoured, that the general commanding was —"

He got no further. "Silence, sir," said Jackson, "or I will bring you before a court martial! You will come with me now to my tent.

I will hear General Loring's latest communication there." He turned upon Cleave. "As for you, sir, you will consider yourself under arrest, first for disobedience of orders, second for brawling in camp. You will march to-morrow in the rear of your regiment."

He towered a moment, then with a jerk of his hand went away, taking with him the officer from Loring. Stafford had a moment in which to make a gesture of anger and deprecation — a gesture which the other acknowledged with a nod; then he was gone, looking back once. Cleave returned to Tullius and the small fire by the pawpaw bushes.

An hour later when his regiment came down into Bloomery Gap, he found the colonel and made his report. "Why, damn it all!" said the colonel. "We were backing you for the brush. Hunting weather, and a clean run and all the dogs of war to fawn upon you at the end! And here's a paltry three-foot hedge and a bad tumble! Never you mind! You'll pick yourself up. Old Jack likes you first-rate."

Cleave laughed. "It does n't much look like it, sir! Well — I'm back with the regiment, anyway!"

All that night it snowed, snowed hard. When the day broke the valley had the seeming of a crowded graveyard — numberless white mounds stretching north and south in the feeble light. A bugle blew, silver chill; — the men beneath the snow stirred, moaned, arose all white. All that day they marched, and at dusk crossed the Capon and bivouacked below the shoulder of Sand Mountain. In the morning they went up the mountain. The road was deep sand, intolerably toilsome. The column ascended in long curves, through a wood of oak and hickory, with vast tangles of grape hanging from the trees. Cavalry, infantry, artillery, wagon train, stragglers, the army came slowly, slowly down Sand Mountain, crossed the slender levels, and climbed Lovett's Mountain. Lovett's was long and high, but at last Lovett's, too, was overpassed. The column crept through a ravine with a stream to the left. Grey cliffs appeared; fern and laurel growing in the clefts. Below lay deep snowdrifts with blue shadows. Ahead, overarching the road, appeared a grey mass that all but choked the gorge. "Hanging Rock!" quoth some one. "That's where the guns were lost!" The army woke to interest. "Hanging Rock! . . . How're we going to get by?

That ain't a road, it's just a cow path! — Powerful good place for an ambush — "

The column passed the rock, and leaving the pass came into open country. Before the leading brigade was a creek, an old covered bridge now almost burned away, and the charred ruin of a house. By the roadside lay a dead cow; in the field were others, and buzzards were circling above a piece of woods. A little farther a dog — a big, brown shepherd — lay in the middle of the road. Its throat had been cut. By the blackened chimney, on the stone hearth drifted over by the snow, stood a child's cradle. Nothing living was to be seen; all the out-houses of the farm and the barn were burned.

It was the beginning of a track of desolation. From Hanging Rock to Romney the Confederate column traversed a country where Kelly's troops had been before it. To well-nigh all of the grey rank and file the vision came with strangeness. They were to grow used to such sights, used, used! but now they flamed white with wrath, they exclaimed, they stammered. "What! what! Just look at that thar tannery! They've slit the hides to ribbons! — That po' ole white horse! What'd he done, I wonder? . . . What's that trampled in the mud? That's a doll baby. O Lord! Pick it up, Tom! — Maybe 't was a mill once, but won't never any more water go over that wheel! . . . Making war on children and doll babies and dumb animals and mills!"

Now as hereafter the immediate effect was almost that of warmth and rest, food and wine. Suddenly the men began to say, "Old Jack. Wait till Old Jack gets there! Just wait till Old Jack and us gets there. I reckon there'll be something doing! There'll be some shooting, I reckon, that ain't practised on a man's oxen! — I reckon we'd better step up, boys! — Naw, my foot don't hurt no more!"

A mounted officer came by. "General Jackson says, 'Press forward, men!'"

The men did their best. It was very cold, with a high, bitter wind. Another low mountain presented itself; the road edged by banks of purplish slate, to either hand great stretches of dogwood showing scarlet berries, or sumach lifting torches in which colour yet smouldered. The column came down a steep descent, crossed a creek, and saw before it Jersey Mountain. Jersey Mountain proved ghastly;

long, high, bare, blown against by all the winds. There had been
upon Jersey a few cabins, a smithy, a mountain school — now there
were only blackened chimneys. The men panted as they climbed;
the wind howled along the crest, the snow began to swirl. At a turn
of the road where had been a cabin, high upon the bank above the
men, stood a mountain woman, her linsey skirt wrapped about her
by the wind, her thick, pale Saxon hair lifted and carried out to its
full length, her arms raised above her head. "Air ye going against
them? Air ye going against them? The lightning go with ye —
and the fire go with ye — and the hearts of your mothers go with
ye! Oh-h! — Oh-h-h-h! — Oh-h! Shoot them down!"

It was as though Jersey would never be overpassed. There grew
before the men's eyes, upon the treeless plateau which marked the
summit, a small country church and graveyard. Inexpressibly lonely
they looked against the stormy sky, lonely and beckoning. From
company to company ran a statement. "When you get to that
church you're just three miles from Romney." Up and up they
mounted. The cavalry and advance guard, seen for a moment
against a level horizon, disappeared beyond the church, over the
brink of the hill. The main column climbed on through the wind
and the snow; the rear came far behind. The Stonewall Brigade
led the main body. As it reached the crest of Jersey, a horse and
rider, a courier of Jackson's coming from the west, met it, rose in his
stirrups, and shouted, "The damned vandals have gone! The
Yankees have gone! They've gotten across the river, away to Cumberland! You were n't quick enough. General Jackson says, 'By
God, you are too slow!' The courier even in his anger caught himself. "I say, 'By God!' General Jackson says, 'You are too slow.'
They've gone — only Ashby at their heels! They've left their
stores in Romney, but they've gone, every devil of them! By God,
General Jackson says, 'you should have marched faster!'"

He was gone, past the brigade, on to Loring's with his tidings.
The Stonewall Brigade left behind the graveyard and the church and
began the long descent. At first a great flame of anger kept up the
hearts of the men. But as they marched, as they toiled down
Jersey, as the realization of the facts pressed upon them, there came
a change. The enemy had been gone from Bath; the enemy had
been inaccessible at Hancock; now the enemy was not at Romney.

Cumberland! Cumberland was many a wintry mile away, on the other side of the Potomac. Here, here on Jersey, there were cold, hunger, weariness, sickness, clothing grown ragged, shoes between a laugh and a groan, the snow falling, the wind rising, the day declining, and misery flapping dark wings above the head of the Army of the Northwest! Over the troops flowed, resistless, a wave of reaction, nausea, disappointment, melancholy. The step changed. Toward the foot of Jersey came another courier. "Yes, sir. On toward New Creek. General Jackson says, 'Press forward!'"

The Stonewall Brigade tried to obey, and somewhat dismally failed. How could it quicken step again? Night was coming, the snow was falling, everybody was sick at heart, hobbling, limping, dog-tired. The *Close up, men*, the *Get on, men!* of the officers, thin, like a child's fretful wail, was taken up by the wind and lost. With Romney well in sight came a third courier. "General Jackson says, 'Press forward!' — No, sir. He did n't say anything else. But I 've been speaking with a courier of Ashby's. *He* says there are three railroad bridges, — one across Patterson's Creek and two across the river. If they were destroyed the enemy's communications would be cut. He thinks we 're headed that way. It's miles the other side of Romney." He passed down the column. "General Jackson says, 'Press forward!'"

Press forward — Press forward! It went like the tolling of a bell, on and on toward the rear, past the Stonewall Brigade, past the artillery, on to Loring yet climbing Jersey. Miles beyond Romney! Railroad bridges to cut! — Frozen creeks, frozen rivers, steel in a world of snow — Kelly probably already at Cumberland, and Rosecrans beyond at Wheeling — hunger, cold, winter in the spurs of the Alleghenies, disease, stragglers, weariness, worn-out shoes, broken-down horses, disappointment, disillusion, a very, very strange commanding general — Suddenly confidence, heretofore a somewhat limping attendant of the army, vanished quite away. The shrill, derisive wind, the grey wraiths of snow, the dusk of the mountains took her, conveyed her from sight, and left the Army of the Northwest to the task of following without her "Fool Tom Jackson."

CHAPTER XIV

THE IRON-CLADS

Miss Lucy Cary, knitting in hand, stood beside the hearth and surveyed the large Greenwood parlour. "The lining of the window curtains," she said, "is good, stout, small figured chintz. My mother got it from England. Four windows — four yards to a side — say thirty-two yards. That's enough for a dozen good shirts. The damask itself? — I don't know what use they could make of it, but they can surely do something. The net curtains will do to stretch over hospital beds. Call one of the boys, Julius, and have them all taken down. — Well, what is it?"

"Miss Lucy, chile, when you done sont de curtains ter Richmon', how is you gwine surmantle de windows?"

"We will leave them bare, Julius. All the more sunlight."

Unity came in, knitting. "Aunt Lucy, the velvet piano cover could go."

"That's a good idea, dear. A capital blanket!"

"A soldier won't mind the embroidery. What is it, Julius?"

"Miss Unity, when you done sont dat kiver ter Richmon', what you gwine investigate dat piano wif?"

"Why, we'll leave it bare, Julius! The grain of the wood shows better so."

"The bishop," said Miss Lucy thoughtfully — "the bishop sent his study carpet last week. What do you think, Unity?"

Unity, her head to one side, studied the carpet. "Do you reckon they would really sleep under those roses and tulips, Aunt Lucy? Just imagine Edward! — But if you think it would do any good —"

"We might wait awhile, seeing that spring is here. If the war should last until next winter, of course we shall send it."

Unity laughed. "Julius looks ten years younger! Why, Uncle Julius, we have bare floors in summer, anyhow!"

"Yaas, Miss Unity," said Julius solemnly. "An' on de hottes' day ob July you hab in de back ob yo' haid dat de cyarpets is superimposin' in de garret, in de cedar closet, ready fer de fust day ob November. How you gwine feel when you see November on de road, an' de cedar closet bar ez er bone? Hit ain' right ter take de Greenwood cyarpets an' curtains, an' my tablecloths an' de blankets an' sheets an' Ole Miss's fringed counterpanes — no'm, hit ain't right eben if de ginerals do sequesterate supplies! How de house gwine look when marster come home?"

Molly entered with her knitting. "The forsythia is in bloom! Aunt Lucy, please show me how to turn this heel. Car'line says you told her not to make sugar cakes for Sunday?"

"Yes, dear, I did. I am sorry, for I know that you like them. But everything is so hard to get — and the armies — and the poor people. I've told Car'line to give us no more desserts."

"Oh!" cried Molly. "I wasn't complaining! It was Car'line who was fussing. I'd give the army every loaf of sugar, and all the flour. Is that the way you turn it?

> Knit — knit — knit —
> The soldiers' feet to fit!"

She curled herself up on the long sofa, and her needles went click, click! Unity lifted the music from the piano lid, drew off the velvet cover, and began to fold it. Muttering and shaking his head, Julius left the room. Miss Lucy went over and stood before the portrait of her mother. "Unity," she said, "would you send the great coffee urn to Richmond for the Gunboat Fair, or would you send lace?"

Unity pondered the question. "The lace would be easier to send, but maybe they would rather have the silver. I don't see who is to buy at the Fair — every one is *giving*. Oh, I wish we had a thousand gunboats and a hundred *Virginias* —"

A door banged in the distance and the windows of the parlour rattled. The room grew darker. "I knew we should have a storm!" said Miss Lucy. "If it lightens, put by your needles."

Judith came in suddenly. "There's going to be a great storm! The wind is blowing the elms almost to the ground! There are black clouds in the east. I hope that there are clouds over the ocean, and over Chesapeake, and over Hampton Roads — except where the Merrimac lies! I hope that there it is still and sunny. Clouds, and a wind like a hurricane, a wind that will make high waves and drive the ships — and drive the Monitor! There will be a great storm. If the elms break, masts would break, too! Oh, if this night the Federal fleet would only go to the bottom of the sea!"

She crossed the room, opened the French window, and stood, a hand on either side of the window frame, facing the darkened sky and the wind-tossed oaks. Behind her, in the large old parlour, there was an instant's silence. Molly broke it with a shocked cry, "Judith Jacqueline Cary!"

Judith did not answer. She stood with her hair lifted by the wind, her hands wide, touching the window sides, her dark eyes upon the bending oaks. In the room behind her Miss Lucy spoke. "It is they or us, Molly! They or all we love. The sooner they suffer the sooner they will let us alone. They have shut up all our ports. God forgive me, but I am blithe when I hear of their ships gone down at sea!"

"Yes," said Judith, without turning. "Not stranded as they were before Roanoke Island, but wrecked and sunken. Come, look, Unity, at the wild storm!"

Unity came and stood beside her. The oaks outside, like the elms at the back of the house, were moving in the blast. Over them hurried the clouds, black, large, and low. Down the driveway the yellow forsythias, the red pyrus japonicas showed in blurs of colours. The lightning flashed, and a long roll of thunder jarred the room. "You were the dreamer," said Unity, "and you had most of the milk of human kindness, and now you have been caught up beyond us all!"

Her sister looked at her, but with a distant gaze. "It is because I can dream — no, not dream, see! I follow all the time — I follow with my mind the troops upon the march, and the ships on the sea. I do not hate the ships — they are beautiful, with the green waves about them and the sea-gulls with shining wings. And yet I wish that they would sink — down, down quickly, before there was much suffering, before the men on them had time for thought. They should go like a stone to the bottom, without suffering, and they should lie there, peacefully, until their spirits are called again. And our ports should be open, and less blood would be shed. Less blood, less anger, less wretchedness, less pain, less shedding of tears, less watching, watching, watching —"

"Look!" cried Unity. "The great oak bough is going!"

A vast spreading bough, large itself as a tree, snapped by the wind from the trunk, came crashing down and out upon the lawn. The thunder rolled again, and large raindrops began to splash on the gravel paths.

"Some one is coming up the drive," exclaimed Unity. "It's a soldier! He's singing!"

The wind, blowing toward the house, brought the air and the quality of the voice that sang it.

> "Beau chevalier qui partez pour la guerre,
>   Qu'allez-vous faire
>   Si loin d'ici?
> Voyez-vous pas que la nuit est profonde,
>   Et que le monde
>   N'est que souci?"

"Edward!" cried Judith. "It is Edward!"

The Greenwood ladies ran out on the front porch. Around the house appeared the dogs, then, in the storm, two or three turbaned negresses. Mammy, coifed and kerchiefed, came down the stairs and through the house. "O my Lawd! Hit's my baby! O glory be! Singin' jes' lak he uster sing, layin' in my lap — mammy singin' ter him, an' he singin' ter mammy! O Marse Jesus! let me look at him —"

> "Beau chevalier qui partez pour la guerre,
>   Qu'allez-vous faire
>   Si loin de nous? — "

Judith ran down the steps and over the grass, through the storm. Beyond the nearer trees, by the great pyrus japonica bush, flamered, she met a ragged spectre, an Orpheus afoot and travel-stained, a demigod showing signs of service in the trenches, Edward Cary, in short, beautiful still, but gaunt as any wolf. The two embraced; they had always been comrades. "Edward, Edward —"

"Eleven months," said Edward. "Judith, Judith, if you knew how good home looks —"

"How thin you are, and brown! And walking! — Where is Prince John — and Jeames?"

"Did n't I tell you in my last letter? Prince John was killed in a fight we had on the Warwick River. . . . Jeames is in Richmond down with fever. He cried to come, but the doctor said he must n't. I've only three days myself. Furloughs are hard to get, but just now the government will do anything for anybody who was on the Merrimac — You're worn yourself, Judith, and your eyes are so big and dark! — Is it Maury Stafford or Richard Cleave?"

Amid the leaping of the dogs they reached the gravelled space before the house. Miss Lucy folded her nephew in her arms. "God bless you, Edward —" She held him off and looked at him. "I never saw it before — but you're like your grandfather, my dear; you're like my dear father! — O child, how thin you are!"

Unity and Molly hung upon him. "The papers told us that you were on the Merrimac — though we don't know how you got there! Did you come from Richmond? Have you seen father?"

"Yes, for a few moments. He has come up from the south with General Lee. General Lee is to be commander of all the forces of the Confederacy. Father is well. He sent his dear love to you all. I saw Fauquier, too —"

Mammy met him at the top of the steps. "Oh, my lamb! O glory hallelujah! What you doin' wid dem worn-out close? An' yo' sh'ut tohn dat-er-way? What dey been doin' ter you — dat's what I wants ter know? My po' lamb! — Marse Edward, don' you laugh kaze mammy done fergit you ain' er baby still —"

Edward hugged her. "One night in the trenches, not long ago, I swear I heard you singing, mammy! I could n't sleep. And at last I said, 'I'll put my head in mammy's lap, and she'll sing me

The Buzzards and the Butterflies —

and I'll go to sleep.' I did it, and I went off like a baby — Well, Julius, and how are you?"

Within the parlour there were explanations, ejaculations, questions, and answers. "So short a furlough — when we have not seen you for almost a year! Never mind — of course, you must get back. We'll have a little party for you to-morrow night. Oh, how brown you are, and your uniform's so ragged! Never mind — we've got a bolt of Confederate cloth and Johnny Bates shall come out to-morrow. . . . All well. Knitting and watching, watching and knitting. The house has been full of refugees — Fairfaxes and Fauntleroys. They've gone on to Richmond, and we're alone just now. We take turn about at the hospitals in Charlottesville — there are three hundred sick — and we look after the servants and the place and the poor families whose men are gone, and we read the papers over and over, every word — and we learn letters off by heart, and we make lint, and we twist and turn and manage, and we knit and knit and wait and wait — Here's Julius with the wine! And your room's ready — fire and hot water, and young Cato to take Jeames's place. Car'line is making sugar cakes, and we shall have coffee for supper. . . . Hurry down, Edward, Edward *darling!*"

Edward darling came down clean, faintly perfumed, shaven, thin, extremely handsome and debonair. Supper went off beautifully, with the last of the coffee poured from the urn that had not yet gone to the Gunboat Fair, with the Greenwood ladies dressed in the best of their last year's gowns, with flowers in Judith's hair and at Unity's throat, with a reckless use of candles, with Julius and Tom, the dining-room boy, duskily smiling in the background, with the spring rain beating against the panes, with the light-wood burning on the hearth, with Churchill and Cary and Dandridge portraits, now in shadow, now in gleam upon the walls — with all the cheer, the light, the gracious warmth of Home. None of the women spoke of how seldom they burned candles now, of how the coffee had been saved against an emergency, and of the luxury white bread was becoming. They ignored, too, the troubles of the plantation. They would not trouble their soldier with the growing difficulty of finding food for the servants and for the stock, of the plough horses gone, and no seed for the sowing, of the problem it was to clothe the men, women, and children, with osnaburgh at thirty-eight cents a yard, with the difficulties of healing the sick, medicine having been declared contraband of war and the home supply failing. They would not trouble him with the makeshifts of women, their forebodings as to shoes, as to letter paper, their windings here and there through a maze of difficulties strange to them as a landscape of the moon. They would learn, and it was but little harder than being in the field. Not that they thought of it in that light; they thought the field as much harder as it was more glorious. Nothing was too good for their soldier; they would have starved a week to have given him the white bread, the loaf sugar, and the Mocha.

Supper over, he went down to the house quarter to speak to the men and women there; then, in the parlour, at the piano, he played with his masterly touch "The Last Waltz," and then he came to the fire, took his grandfather's chair, and described to the women the battle at sea.

"We were encamped on the Warwick River — infantry, and a cavalry company, and a battalion from New Orleans. Around us were green flats, black mud, winding creeks, waterfowl, earthworks, and what guns they could give us. At the mouth of the river, across the channel, we had sunk twenty canal boats, to the end that Burnside should not get by. Besides the canal boats and the guns and the waterfowl there was a deal of fever — malarial — of exposure, of wet, of mouldy bread, of homesickness and general desolation. Some courage existed, too, and singing at times. We had been down there a long time among the marshes — all winter, in fact. About two weeks ago —"

"Oh, Edward, were you very homesick?"

"Devilish. For the certain production of a very curious feeling, give me picket duty on a wet marsh underneath the stars! Poetic places — marshes — with a strong suggestion about them of The Last Man. . . . Where was I? Down to our camp one morning about two weeks ago came El Capitan Colorado — General Magruder, you know — gold lace, stars, and black plume! With him came Lieutenant Wood, C. S. N. We were paraded —"

"Edward, try as I may, I cannot get over the strangeness of your being in the ranks!"

Edward laughed. "There's many a better man than I in them, Aunt Lucy! They make the best of crows'-nests from which to spy on life, and that is what I always wanted to do — to spy on life! — The men were paraded, and Lieutenant Wood made us a speech. 'The old Merrimac, you know, men, that was burnt last year when the Yankees left Norfolk? — well, we've raised her, and cut her down to her berth deck, and made of her what we call an iron-clad. An iron-clad is a new man-of-war that's going to take the place of the old. The Merrimac is not a frigate any longer; she's the iron-clad Virginia, and we rather think she's going to make her name remembered. She's over there at the Gosport Navy Yard, and she's almost ready. She's covered over with iron plates, and she's got an iron beak, or ram, and she carries ten guns. On the whole, she's the ugliest beauty that you ever saw! She's almost ready to send to Davy Jones's locker a Yankee ship or two. Commodore Buchanan commands her, and you know who he is! She's got her full quota of officers, and, the speaker excepted, they're as fine a set as you'll find on the high seas! But man-of-war's men are scarcer, my friends, than hen's teeth! It's what comes of having no maritime population. Every man Jack that isn't on our few little ships is in the army — and the Virginia wants a crew of three hundred of the bravest of the brave! Now, I am talking to Virginians and Louisianians. Many of you are from New Orleans, and that means that some of you may very well have been seamen — seamen at an emergency, anyhow! Anyhow, when it comes to an emergency Virginians and Louisianians are there to meet it — on sea or on land! Just now there is an emergency — the Virginia's got to have a crew. General Magruder, for all he's got only a small force with which to hold a long line — General Magruder, like the patriot that he is, has said that I may ask this morning for volunteers. Men! any seaman among you has the chance to gather laurels from the strangest deck of the strangest ship that ever you saw! No fear for the laurels! They're fresh and green even under our belching smokestack. The Merrimac is up like the phœnix; and the last state of her is greater than the first, and her name is going down in history! Louisianians and Virginians, who volunteers?'

"About two hundred volunteered —"

"Edward, what did you know about seamanship?"

"Precious little. Chiefly, Unity, what you have read to me from novels. But the laurels sounded enticing, and I was curious about the ship. Well, Wood chose about eighty — all who had been seamen or gunners and a baker's dozen of ignoramuses beside. I came in with that portion of the elect. And off we went, in boats, across the James to the southern shore and to the Gosport Navy Yard. That was a week before the battle."

"What does it look like, Edward — the Merrimac?"

"It looks, Judith, like Hamlet's cloud. Sometimes there is an appearance of a barn with everything but the roof submerged — or of Noah's Ark, three fourths under water! Sometimes, when the flag is flying, she has the air of a piece of earthworks, mysteriously floated off into the river. Ordinarily, though, she is rather like a turtle, with a chimney sticking up from her shell. The shell is made of pitch pine and oak, and it is covered with two-inch thick plates of Tredegar iron. The beak is of cast iron, standing four feet out from the bow; that, with the rest of the old berth deck, is just awash. Both ends of the shell are rounded for pivot guns. Over the gun deck is an iron grating on which you can walk at need. There is the pilot-house covered with iron, and there is the smokestack. Below are the engines and boilers, condemned after the Merrimac's last cruise, and, since then, lying in the ooze at the bottom of the river. They are very wheezy, trembling, poor old men of the sea! It was hard work to get the coal for them to eat; it was brought at last from away out in Montgomery County, from the Price coal-fields. The guns are two 7-inch rifles, two 6-inch rifles, and six 9-inch smoothbores; ten in all. — Yes, call her a turtle, plated with iron; she looks as much like that as like anything else.

"When we eighty men from the Warwick first saw her, she was swarming with workmen. They continued to cover her over, and to make impossible any drill or exercise upon her. Hammer, hammer upon belated plates from the Tredegar! Tinker, tinker with the poor old engines! Make shift here and make shift there; work through the day and work through the night, for there was a rumour abroad that the Ericsson, that we knew was building, was coming down the coast! There was no chance to drill, to become acquainted with the turtle and her temperament. Her species had never gone to war before, and when you looked at her there was room for doubt as to how she would behave! Officers and men were strange to one another — and the gunners could not try the guns for the swarming workmen. There was n't so much of the Montgomery coal that it could be wasted on experiments in firing up — and, indeed, it seemed wise not to experiment at all with the ancient engines! So we stood about the navy yard, and looked down the Elizabeth and across the flats to Hampton Roads, where we could see the Cumberland, the Congress, and the Minnesota, Federal ships lying off Newport News — and the workmen rivetted the last plates — and smoke began to come out of the smokestack — and suddenly Commodore Buchanan, with his lieutenants behind him, appeared between us and the Merrimac — or the Virginia. Most of us still call her the Merrimac. It was the morning of the eighth.

The sun shone brightly and the water was very blue — blue and still. There were sea-gulls, I remember, flying overhead, screaming as they flew — and the marshes were growing emerald —"

"Yes, yes! What did Commodore Buchanan want?"

"Don't be impatient, Molly! You women don't in the least look like Griseldas! Aunt Lucy has the air of her pioneer great-grandmother who has heard an Indian calling! And as for Judith — Judith!"

"Yes, Edward."

"Come back to Greenwood. You looked a listening Jeanne d'Arc. What did you hear?"

"I heard the engines working, and the sea fowl screaming, and the wind in the rigging of the Cumberland. Go on, Edward."

"We soldiers turned seamen came to attention. 'Get on board, men,' said Commodore Buchanan. 'We are going out in the Roads and introduce a new era.' So off the workmen came and on we went — the flag officers and the lieutenants and the midshipmen and the surgeons and the volunteer aides and the men. The engineers were already below and the gunners were looking at the guns. The smoke rolled up very black, the ropes were cast off, a bugle blew, out streamed the stars and bars, all the workmen on the dock swung their hats, and down the Elizabeth moved the Merrimac. She moved slowly enough with her poor old engines, and she steered badly, and she drew twenty-two feet, and she was ugly, ugly, ugly, — poor thing!

"Now we were opposite Craney Island, at the mouth of the Elizabeth. There's a battery there, you know, part of General Colston's line, and there are forts upon the main along the James. All these were now crowded with men, hurrahing, waving their caps. . . . As we passed Craney they were singing 'Dixie.' So we came out into the James to Hampton Roads.

"Now all the southern shore from Willoughby's Spit to Ragged Island is as grey as a dove, and all the northern shore from Old Point Comfort to Newport News is blue where the enemy has settled. In between are the shining Roads. Between the Rip Raps and Old Point swung at anchor the Roanoke, the Saint Lawrence, a number of gunboats, store ships, and transports, and also a French man-of-war. Far and near over the Roads were many small craft.

The Minnesota, a large ship, lay halfway between Old Point and Newport News. At the latter place there is a large Federal garrison, and almost in the shadow of its batteries rode at anchor the frigate Congress and the sloop Cumberland. The first had fifty guns, the second thirty. The Virginia, or the Merrimac, or the turtle, creeping out from the Elizabeth, crept slowly and puffing black smoke into the South Channel. The pilot, in his iron-clad pilot-house no bigger than a hickory nut, put her head to the northwest. The turtle began to swim toward Newport News.

"Until now not a few of us within her shell, and almost all of the soldiers and the forts along the shore, had thought her upon a trial trip only, — down the Elizabeth, past Craney Island, turn at Sewell's Point, and back to the dock of the Gosport Navy Yard! When she did not turn, the cheering on the shore stopped; you felt the breathlessness. When she passed the point and took to the South Channel, when her head turned upstream, when she came abreast of the Middle Ground, when they saw that the turtle was going to fight, from along the shore to Craney and from Sewell's Point there arose a yell. Every man in grey yelled. They swung hat or cap; they shouted themselves hoarse. All the flags streamed suddenly out, trumpets blared, the sky lifted, and we drank the sunshine in like wine; that is, some of us did. To others it came cold like hemlock against the lip. Fear is a horrible sensation. I was dreadfully afraid —"

"Edward!"

"Dreadfully. But you see I did n't tell any one I was afraid, and that makes all the difference! Besides, it wore off. . . . It was a spring day and high tide, and the Federal works at Newport News and the Congress and the Cumberland and the more distant Minnesota all looked asleep in the calm, sweet weather. Washing day it was on the Congress, and clothes were drying in the rigging. That aspect as of painted ships, painted breastworks, a painted sea-piece, lasted until the turtle reached mid-channel. Then the other side woke up. Upon the shore appeared a blue swarm — men running to and fro. Bugles signalled. A commotion, too, arose upon the Congress and the Cumberland. Her head toward the latter ship, the turtle puffed forth black smoke and wallowed across the channel. An uglier poor thing you never saw, nor a bolder! Squat to the water, belching black smoke, her engines wheezing and repining, unwieldy of management, her bottom scraping every hummock of sand in all the shoaly Roads — ah, she was ugly and courageous! Our two small gunboats, the Raleigh and the Beaufort, coming from Norfolk, now overtook us, — we went on together. I was forward with the crew of the 7-inch pivot gun. I could see through the port, above the muzzle. Officers and men, we were all cooped under the turtle's shell; in order by the open ports, and the guns all ready. . . . We came to within a mile of the Cumberland, tall and graceful with her masts and spars and all the blue sky above. She looked a swan, and we, the Ugly Duckling. . . . Our ram, you know, was under water — seventy feet of the old berth deck, ending in a four-foot beak of cast iron. . . . We came nearer. At three quarters of a mile, we opened with the bow gun. The Cumberland answered, and the Congress, and their gunboats and shore batteries. Then began a frightful uproar that shook the marshes and sent the sea birds screaming. Smoke arose, and flashing fire, and an excitement — an excitement — an excitement. — Then it was, ladies, that I forgot to be afraid. The turtle swam on, toward the Cumberland, swimming as fast as Montgomery coal and the engines that had lain at the bottom of the sea could make her go. There was a frightful noise within her shell, a humming, a shaking. The Congress, the gunboats and the shore batteries kept firing broadsides. There was an enormous, thundering noise, and the air was grown sulphurous cloud. Their shot came pattering like hail, and like hail it rebounded from the iron-clad. We passed the Congress — very close to her tall side. She gave us a withering fire. We returned it, and steered on for the Cumberland. A word ran from end to end of the turtle's shell, 'We are going to ram her — stand by, men!'

"Within easy range we fired the pivot gun. I was of her crew; half naked we were, powder-blackened and streaming with sweat. The shell she sent burst above the Cumberland's stern pivot, killing or wounding most of her crew that served it. . . . We went on. . . . Through the port I could now see the Cumberland plainly, her starboard side just ahead of us, men in the shrouds and running to and fro on her deck. When we were all but on her, her starboard blazed. That broadside tore up the carriage of our pivot gun, cut another off at the trunnions, and the muzzle from a third, riddled the smokestack and steam-pipe, carried away an anchor, and killed or wounded nineteen men. The Virginia answered with three guns; a cloud of smoke came between the iron-clad and the armed sloop; it lifted — and we were on her. We struck her under the fore rigging with a dull and grinding sound. The iron beak with which we were armed was wrested off.

" The Virginia shivered, hung a moment, then backed clear of the Cumberland, in whose side there was now a ragged and a gaping hole. The pilot in the iron-clad pilot-house turned her head up-stream. The water was shoal; she had to run up the James some way before she could turn and come back to attack the Congress. Her keel was in the mud; she was creeping now like a land turtle, and all the iron shore was firing at her. . . . She turned at last in freer water and came down the Roads. Through the port we could see the Cumberland that we had rammed. She had listed to port and was sinking. The water had reached her main deck; all her men were now on the spar deck, where they yet served the pivot guns. She fought to the last. A man of ours, stepping for one moment through a port to the outside of the turtle's shell, was cut in two. As the water rose and rose, the sound of her guns was like a lessening thunder. One by one they stopped. . . . To the last she flew her colours. The Cumberland went down.

" By now there had joined us the small, small James River squadron that had been anchored far up the river. The Patrick Henry had twelve guns, the Jamestown had two, and the Teaser one. Down they scurried like three valiant marsh hens to aid the turtle. With the Beaufort and the Raleigh there were five valiant pygmies, and they fired at the shore batteries, and the shore batteries answered like an angry Jove with solid shot, with shell, with grape, and with canister! A shot wrecked the boiler of the Patrick Henry, scalding to death the men who were near. . . . The turtle sank a transport steamer lying alongside the wharf at Newport News, and then she rounded the point and bore down upon the Congress.

" The frigate had showed discretion, which is the better part of valour. Noting how deeply we drew, she had slipped her cables and run aground in the shallows where she was safe from the ram of the Merrimac. We could get no nearer than two hundred feet. There we took up position, and there we began to rake her, the Beaufort, the Raleigh, and the Jamestown giving us what aid they might. She had fifty guns, and there were the heavy shore batteries, and below her the Minnesota. This ship, also aground in the Middle Channel, now came into action with a roar. A hundred guns were trained upon the Merrimac. The iron hail beat down every point, not iron-clad, that showed above our shell. The muzzle of two guns were shot away, the stanchions, the boat davits, the flagstaff. Again and again the flagstaff fell, and again and again we replaced it. At last we tied the colours to the smokestack. Beside the nineteen poor fellows that the Cumberland's guns had mowed down, we now had other killed and wounded. Commodore Buchanan was badly hurt, and the flag lieutenant, Minor. The hundred guns thundered against the Merrimac, and the Merrimac thundered against the Congress. The tall frigate and her fifty guns wished herself an iron-clad; the swan would have blithely changed with the ugly duckling. We brought down her mainmast, we disabled her guns, we strewed her decks with blood and anguish (war is a wild beast, nothing more, and I'll hail the day when it lies slain). We smashed in her sides and we set her afire. She hauled down her colours and ran up a white flag. The Merrimac ceased firing and signalled to the Beaufort. The Beaufort ran alongside, and the frigate's ranking officer gave up his colours and his sword. The Beaufort's and the Congress's own boats removed the crew and the wounded. . . . The shore batteries, the Minnesota, the picket boat Zouave, kept up a heavy firing all the while upon the Merrimac, upon the Raleigh and the Jamestown, and also upon the Beaufort. We waited until the crew was clear of the Congress, and then we gave her a round of hot shot that presently set her afire from stem to stern. This done, we turned to other work.

"The Minnesota lay aground in the North Channel. To her aid hurrying up from Old Point came the Roanoke and the Saint Lawrence. Our own batteries at Sewell's Point opened upon these two ships as they passed, and they answered with broadsides. We fed our engines, and under a billow of black smoke ran down to the Minnesota. Like the Congress, she lay upon a sand bar, beyond fear of ramming. We could only manœuvre for deep water, near enough to her to be deadly. It was now late afternoon. I could see through the port of the bow pivot the slant sunlight upon the water, and how the blue of the sky was paling. The Minnesota lay just ahead; very tall she looked, another of the Congress breed; the old warships singing their death song. As we came on we fired the bow gun, then, lying nearer her, began with broadsides. But we could not get near enough; she was lifted high upon the sand, the tide was going out, and we drew twenty-three feet. We did her great harm, but we were not disabling her. An hour passed and the sun drew on to setting. The Roanoke turned and went back under the guns of Old Point, but the Saint Lawrence remained to thunder at the turtle's iron shell. The Merrimac was most unhandy, and on the ebb tide there would be shoals enough between us and a berth for the night. . . . The Minnesota could not get away, at dawn she would be yet aground, and we would then take her for our prize. 'Stay till dusk, and the blessed old iron box will ground herself where Noah's flood won't float her!' The pilot ruled, and in the gold and purple sunset we drew off. As we passed, the Minnesota blazed with all her guns; we answered her, and answered, too, the Saint Lawrence. The evening star was shining when we anchored off Sewell's Point. The wounded were taken ashore, for we had no place for wounded men under the turtle's shell. Commodore Buchanan leaving us, Lieutenant Catesby Ap Rice Jones took command.

"I do not remember what we had for supper. We had not eaten since early morning, so we must have had something. But we were too tired to think or to reason or to remember. We dropped beside our guns and slept, but not for long. Three hours, perhaps, we slept, and then a whisper seemed to run through the Merrimac. It was as though the iron-clad herself had spoken, 'Come! watch the Congress die!' Most of us arose from beside the guns and mounted to the iron grating above, to the top of the turtle's shell. It was a night as soft as silk; the water smooth, in long, faint, olive swells; a half-moon in the sky. There were lights across at Old Point, lights on the battery at the Rip Raps, lights in the frightened shipping, huddled under the guns of Fortress Monroe, lights along either shore. There were lanterns in the rigging of the Minnesota where she lay upon the sand bar, and lanterns on the Saint Lawrence and the Roanoke. As we looked a small moving light, as low as possible to the water, appeared between the Saint

Lawrence and the Minnesota. A man said, 'What's that? Must be a rowboat.' Another answered, 'It's going too fast for a rowboat — funny! right on the water like that!' 'A launch, I reckon,' said a third, 'with plenty of rowers. Now it's behind the Minnesota.' — 'Shut up, you talkers,' said a midshipman, 'I want to look at the Congress!'

"Four miles away, off Newport News, lay the burning Congress. In the still, clear night, she seemed almost at hand. All her masts, her spars, and her rigging showed black in the heart of a great ring of firelight. Her hull, lifted high by the sand bank which held her, had round red eyes. Her ports were windows lit from within. She made a vision of beauty and of horror. One by one, as they were reached by the flame, her guns exploded — a loud and awful sound in the night above the Roads. We stood and watched that sea picture, and we watched in silence. We are seeing giant things, and ere this war is ended we shall see more. At two o'clock in the morning the fire reached her powder magazine. She blew up. A column like the Israelite's Pillar shot to the zenith; there came an earthquake sound, sullen and deep; when all cleared there was only her hull upborne by the sand and still burning. It burned until the dawn, when it smouldered and went out."

The narrator arose, walked the length of the parlour, and came back to the four women. "Have n't you had enough for to-night? Unity looks sleepy, and Judith's knitting has lain this half-hour on the floor. Judith!"

Molly spoke. "Judith says that if there is fighting around Richmond she is going there to the hospitals, to be a nurse. The doctors here say that she does better than any one —"

"Go on, Edward," said Judith. "What happened at dawn?"

"We got the turtle in order, and those ancient mariners, our engines, began to work, wheezing and slow. We ran up a new flagstaff, and every man stood to the guns, and the Merrimac moved from Sewell's Point, her head turned to the Minnesota, away across, grounded on a sand bank in the North Channel. The sky was as pink as the inside of a shell, and a thin white mist hung over the marshes and the shore and the great stretch of Hampton Roads. It was so thin that the masts of the ships huddled below Fortress Monroe rose clear of it into the flush of the coming sun. All their pennants were flying — the French man-of-war, and the northern ships. At that hour the sea-gulls are abroad, searching for their food. They went past the ports, screaming and moving their silver wings.

"The Minnesota grew in size. Every man of us looked eagerly — from the pilot-house, from the bow ports, and as we drew parallel with her from the ports of the side. We fired the bow gun as we came on and the shot told. There was some cheering; the morning air was so fine and the prize so sure! The turtle was in spirits — poor old turtle with her battered shell and her flag put back as fast as it was torn away! Her engines, this morning, were mortal slow and weak; they wheezed and whined, and she drew so deep that, in that shoaly water, she went aground twice between Sewell's Point and the stretch she had now reached of smooth pink water, with the sea-gulls dipping between her and the Minnesota. Despite the engines she was happy, and the gunners were all ready at the starboard ports —"

Leaning over, he took the poker and stirred the fire.

> "The best laid plans of mice and men
> Do aften gang agley — "

Miss Lucy's needles clicked. "Yes, the papers told us. The Ericsson."

"There came," said Edward, "there came from behind the Minnesota a cheese-box on a shingle. It had lain there hidden by her bulk since midnight. It was its single light that we had watched and thought no more of! A cheese-box on a shingle — and now it darted into the open as though a boy's arm had sent it! It was little beside the Minnesota. It was little even beside the turtle. There was a silence when we saw it, a silence of astonishment. It had come so quietly upon the scene — a *deus ex machina*, indeed, dropped from the clouds between us and our prey. In a moment we knew it for the Ericsson — the looked-for other iron-clad we knew to be a-building. The Monitor, they call it. . . . The shingle was just awash; the cheese-box turned out to be a revolving turret, mail-clad and carrying two large, modern guns — 11-inch. The whole thing was armoured, had the best of engines, and drew only twelve feet. . . . Well, the Merrimac had a startled breath, to be sure — there is no denying the drama of the Monitor's appearance — and then she righted and began firing. She gave to the cheese-box, or to the armoured turret, one after the other, three broadsides. The turret blazed and answered, and the balls rebounded from each armoured champion." He laughed. "By Heaven! it was like our old favourites, Ivanhoe and De Bois Guilbert — the ugliest squat gnomes of an Ivanhoe and of a Brian de Bois Guilbert that ever came out of a nightmare! We thundered in the lists, and then we passed each other, turned, and again encountered. Sometimes we were a long way apart, and sometimes there was not ten feet of water between those sunken decks from which arose the iron shell of the Merrimac and the iron turret of the Monitor. She fired every seven minutes; we as rapidly as we could load. Now it was the bow gun, now the after pivot, now a full broadside. Once or twice we thought her done for, but always her turret revolved, and her 11-inch guns opened again. In her lighter draught she had a great advantage; she could turn and wind where we could not. The Minnesota took a hand, and an iron battery from the shore. We were striving to ram the Ericsson, but we could not get close to her; our iron beak, too, was sticking in the side of the sunken Cumberland — we could only ram with the blunt prow. The Minnesota, as we passed, gave us all her broadside guns—a tremendous fusillade at point-blank range, which would have sunk any ship of the swan breed. The turtle shook off shot and shell, grape and canister, and answered with her bow gun. The shell which it threw entered the side of the frigate, and, bursting amidship, exploded a store of powder and set the ship on fire. Leaving disaster aboard the Minnesota, we turned and sunk the tugboat Dragon. Then came manœuvre and manœuvre to gain position where we could ram the Monitor. . . .

"We got it at last. The engines made an effort like the leap of the spirit before expiring. 'Go ahead! Full speed!' We went; we bore down upon the Monitor, now in deeper water. But at the moment that we saw victory she turned. Our bow, lacking the iron beak, gave but a glancing stroke. It was heavy as it was; the Monitor shook like a man with the ague, but she did not share the fate of the Cumberland. There was no ragged hole in her side; her armour was good, and held. She backed, gathered herself together, then rushed forward, striving to ram us in her turn. But our armour, too, was good, and held. Then she came upon the Merrimac's quarter, laid her bow against the shell, and fired her 11-inch guns twice in succession. We were so close, each to the other, that it was as though two duelists were standing upon the same cloak. Frightful enough was the concussion of those guns.

"That charge drove in the Merrimac's iron side three inches or more. The shots struck above the ports of the after guns, and every man at those guns was knocked down by the impact and bled at the nose and ears. The Monitor dropped astern, and again we turned and tried to ram her. But her far lighter draught put her where we could not go; our bow, too, was now twisted and splintered. Our powder was getting low. We did not spare it, we could not; we sent shot and shell continuously against the Monitor, and she answered in kind. Monitor and Merrimac, we went now this way, now that, the Ericsson much the lighter and quickest, the Merrimac fettered by her poor old engines, and her great length, and her twenty-three feet draught. It was two o'clock in the afternoon. . . . The duelists stepped from off the cloak, tried operations at a distance, hung for a moment in the wind of indecision, then put down the match from the gunners' hands. The Monitor darted from us, her head toward the shoal water known as the Middle Ground. She reached it and rested triumphant, out of all danger from our ram, and yet where she could still protect the Minnesota. . . . A curious silence fell upon the Roads; sullen like the hush before a thunderstorm, and yet not like that, for we had had the thunderstorm. It was the stillness, perhaps, of exhaustion. It was late afternoon, the fighting had been heavy. The air was filled with smoke; in the water were floating spars and wreckage of the ships we had destroyed. The weather was sultry and still. The dogged booming of a gun from a shore battery sounded lonely and remote as a bell buoy. The tide was falling; there were sand-bars enough between us and Sewell's Point. We waited an hour. The Monitor was rightly content with the Middle Ground, and would not come back for all our charming. We fired at intervals, upon her and upon the Minnesota, but at last our powder grew so low that we ceased. The tide continued to fall, and the pilot had much to say. . . . The red sun sank in the west; the engineers fed the ancient mariners with Montgomery coal; black smoke gushed forth and pilots felt their way into the South Channel, and slowly, slowly back toward Sewell's Point. The day closed in a murky evening with a taste of smoke in the air. In the night-time the Monitor went down the Roads to Fortress Monroe, and in the morning we took the Merrimac into dry dock at Norfolk. Her armour was dented all over, though not pierced. Her bow was bent and twisted, the iron beak lost in the side of the Cumberland. Her boats were gone, and her smokestack as full of holes as any colander, and the engines at the last gasp. Several of the guns were injured, and coal and powder and ammunition all lacked. We put her there — the dear and ugly warship, the first of the iron-clads — we put her there in dry dock, and there she's apt to stay for some weeks to come. Lieutenant Wood was sent to Richmond with the report for the president and the secretary of the navy. He carried, too, the flag of the Congress, and I was one of the men detailed for its charge. . . . And now I have told you of the Merrimac and the Monitor."

Rising, he went to the piano, sat down and played "Malbrook s'en va-t-en guerre." Miss Lucy took up her knitting, and knitted very rapidly, her eyes now upon her nephew, now upon her father's portrait. Judith, rising from the old cross-stitch tabouret where she had been sitting, laid a fresh log on the fire, then went and stood beside the long window, looking out upon the rainy night.

"What," asked Edward between two chords, "what do you hear from the Valley?"

Unity answered: "General Banks has crossed the Potomac and entered Winchester — poor, poor Winchester! General Jackson has n't quite five thousand men. He has withdrawn toward Woodstock. In spite of that dreadful Romney march, General Johnston and the soldiers seem to have confidence in him —"

Molly came in with her soft little voice. "Major Stafford has been transferred. He is with General Ewell on the Rappahannock. He writes to Judith every week. They are beautiful letters — they make you see everything that is done."

"What do you hear from Richard Cleave?"

"He never writes."

Judith came back from the window. "It is raining, raining! The petals are falling from the pyrus japonica, and all the trees are bending! Edward, war is terrible, but it lifts you up. . . ." She locked her hands behind her head. "It lifts you up, out in the storm or listening to what the ships have done, or to the stories that are told! And then you look at the unploughed land, and you wait for the bulletins, and you go to the hospital down there, . . . and you say, 'Never—oh, nevermore let us have war!'"

CHAPTER XV

KERNSTOWN

THE brigade was halted before a stretch of forest white with dogwood. Ahead began a slow cannonade. Puffs of smoke rose above the hill that hid the iron combatants. "Ashby's Horse Artillery," said the men. "That's the Blakeley now! Boys, I reckon we're in for it!"

An aide passed at a gallop. "Shields and nine thousand men. Ashby was misinformed — more than we thought — Shields and nine thousand men."

Along the line the soldiers slightly moved their feet, moistened their lips. The 65th occupied a fairy dell where Quaker ladies, blue as the heavens, bloomed by every stone. A Federal battery opened from a hill to the right. A screaming shell entered the wood, dug into earth, and exploded, showering all around with mould. There came a great burst of music — the Northern bands playing as the regiments deployed. "That's 'Yankee Doodle!'" said the men. "Everybody's cartridge-box full? Johnny Lemon, don't you forgit to take your ramrod out before you fire!"

The colonel came along the line. "Boys, there is going to be a considerable deer drive! — Now, I am going to tell you about this quarry. Its name is Banks, and it wants to get across country to the Shenandoah, and so out of the Valley to join McClellan. Now General Johnston's moving from the Rapidan toward Richmond, and he doesn't want Banks bothering him. He says, 'Delay the enemy as long as you can.' Now General Jackson's undertaken to do it. We've got thirty-five hundred men, and that ought to be enough. — *Right face! Forward march!*"

As the troops crossed the Valley pike the men hailed it. "Howdy, old Road! Pleased to meet you again. Lord! jest as fresh as a daisy — jest as though we hadn't tramped them thirty-six miles from New Market since yesterday daybreak! My Lord! wish I had your staying qualities — *Au re-vo-ree!*"

Stone fences bordered the pike. The infantry, moving in double column, climbed them and entered another strip of springtime woods. The artillery — McLaughlin's, Carpenter's, and Waters's batteries — found a cross-roads and thundered by, straining to the front. Ashby, together with Chew's battery of horse artillery, kept the pike the other side of Kernstown. In front of the infantry stretched a great open marshy meadow, utterly without cover. Beyond this to the north, rose low hills, and they were crowned with Federal batteries, while along the slopes and in the vales between showed masses of blue infantry, clearly visible, in imposing strength and with bright battle-flags. It was high noon, beneath a brilliant sky. There were persistent musicians on the northern side; all the blue regiments came into battle to the sound of first-rate military bands. The grey listened. "They sure are fond of 'Yankee Doodle!' There are three bands playing it at once. . . . There's the 'Star Spangled Banner' —

> Oh, say can you see,
> Through the blue shades of evening —

I used to love it! . . . Good Lord, how long ago!"

Hairston Breckinridge spoke, walking in front of his company. "We're waiting for the artillery to get ahead. We're going to turn the enemy's right—Shields's division, Kimball commanding. You see that wooded ridge away across there? That's our objective. That's Pritchard's Hill, where all the flags are — How many men have they got? Oh, about nine thousand. — There goes the artillery now — there goes Rockbridge! — Yes, sir! — *Attention! Fall in!*"

In double column almost the entire fighting force of the Army of the Valley crossed the endless open meadow beneath Kimball's batteries. That the latter's range was poor was a piece of golden fortune. The shells crossed to the wood or exploded high in blue air. Harmless they might be, but undeniably they were trying. Involuntarily the men stared, fascinated, at each round white cloud above them; involuntarily jerked their heads at each rending explosion. From a furrowed ridge below the guns, musketry took a hand. The Army of the Valley here first met with minie balls. The sound with which they came curdled the blood. "What's that? What's that? . . . That's something new. *The infernal things!*" Billy Maydew, walking with his eyes on the minies, stumbled over a fairy's ring and came to his knees. Lieutenant Coffin swore at him. "—— ——! Gawking and gaping as though 't were Christmas and Roman candles going off! Get up!" Billy arose and marched on. "I air a-going to kill him. Yes, sir; I air a-going to kill him yet." "Shoo!" said the man beside him. "He don't mean no harm. He's jest as nervous as a two-year filly, and he's got to take it out on some one! Next 'lection of officers he'll be down and out. — Sho! how them things do screech!"

The meadow closed with a wooded hill. The grey lines, reaching shelter, gasped with relief. The way was steep, however, and the shells still rained. An oak, struck and split by solid shot, fell across the way. A line of ambulances coming somehow upon the hillside fared badly. Up the men strained to the top, which proved to be a wide level. The Rockbridge battery passed them at a gallop, to be greeted by a shell thrown from a thirty-two pounder on the Federal right. It struck a wheel horse of one of the howitzers, burst, and made fearful havoc. Torn flesh and blood were everywhere; a second horse was mangled, only less horribly than the first; the third, a strong white mare, was so covered with the blood of her fellows and from a wound of her own, that she looked a roan. The driver's spine was crushed, the foot of a gunner was taken off — clean at the ankle as by a scythe. The noise was dreadful; the shriek that the mare gave echoed through the March woods. The other guns of the battery, together with Carpenter's and Waters's, swept round the ruin and over the high open ground toward a stone wall that ran diagonally across. The infantry followed and came out on an old field, strewn with rocks and blackberry bushes. In the distance stretched another long stone wall. Beyond it, on the gentle slopes, were guns enough and blue soldiers enough — blue soldiers, with bright flags above them and somewhere still that insistent music. They huzzahed when they saw the Confederates, and the Confederates answered with that strangest battle shout, that wild and high and ringing cry called the "rebel yell."

In the woods along the ridge and in the old field itself the infantry deployed. There were portions of three brigades, — Fulkerson's, Burk's, and the Stonewall. Fulkerson held the left, Burk with the Irish Battalion the right, and Garnett the centre. The position was commanding, the Confederate strength massed before the Federal right, Shields's centre well to the eastward, and his left under Sullivan in the air, on the other side of the pike. It was Stonewall Jackson's desire to turn that right flank, to crumple it back upon the centre, and to sweep by on the road to Winchester — the loved valley town so near that one might see its bourgeoning trees, hear its church bells.

He rode, on Little Sorrel, up and down the forming lines, and he spoke only to give orders, quiet and curt, much in his class-room tone. He was all brown like a leaf with Valley dust and sun and rain. The old cadet cap was older yet, the ancient boots as grotesquely large, the curious lift of his hand to Heaven no less curious than it had always been. He was as awkward, as hypochondriac, as literal, as strict as ever. Moreover, there should have hung about him the cloud of disfavour and hostility raised by that icy march to Romney less than three months ago. And yet — and yet! What had happened since then? Not much, indeed. The return of the Stonewall Brigade to Winchester, Loring's representations, the War Department's interference, and Major-General T. J. Jackson's resignation from the service and request to be returned to the Virginia Military Institute. General Johnston's remonstrance, Mr. Benjamin's *amende honorable*, and the withdrawal of "Old Jack's" resignation. There had been some surprise among the men at the effect upon themselves of this withdrawal. They had greeted the news with hurrahs; they had been all that day in extraordinary spirits. Why? To save them they could not have told. He had not won any battles. He had been harsh, hostile, pedantic, suspected, and detested upon that unutterable Bath and Romney trip. And yet — and yet! He was cheered when, at Winchester, it was known that the Army of the Valley and not the Virginia Military Institute was to have Major-General T. J. Jackson's services. He was cheered when, at short intervals, in the month or two there in camp, he reviewed his army. He was cheered when, a month ago, the army left Winchester, left the whole-hearted, loving, and loved town to be occupied by the enemy, left it and moved southward to New Market! He was cheered loudly when, two days before, had come the order to march — to march northward, back along the pike, back toward Winchester.

He was cheered now as he rode quietly to and fro, forming his line of battle — Fulkerson's 23d and 37th Virginia on the left, then the 27th supported by the 21st, in the second line the 4th, the 33d, the 2d, the 65th, a little back the Irish Battalion, and at the bottom of the ridge the 5th, keeping touch with Ashby toward the pike. It was two of the afternoon, beautiful and bright. A brigadier, meeting him, said, "We were not sure, general, that you would fight to-day! It is Sunday."

The other fastened upon him his steady grey-blue eyes. "The God of Battles, sir, as a great general, will understand. I trust that every regiment may have service to-morrow in Winchester. Advance your skirmishers, and send a regiment to support Carpenter's battery."

The 27th Virginia, target for a withering artillery fire, crossed the open and disappeared in a strip of March wood, high and keen and brown against the fleckless sky. Behind it two long grey lines moved slowly forward, out now in the old field. The men talked as they went. "Wish there was nice ripe blackberries on these bushes! Wish I was a little boy again with a straw hat and a tin bucket, gathering blackberries and listenin' to the June bugs! *Zoon — Zoon — Zoon!* O Lord! listen to that shell! — Sho! that was n't much. I'm getting to kind of like the fuss. There ain't so many of them screeching now, anyhow!"

A lieutenant raised his voice. "Their fire is slackening. — Don't reckon they're tired of it, sir? Hope their ammunition's out!"

From the rear galloped a courier. "Where's General Jackson? — They're drawing off! — a big body, horse and foot, is backing toward Winchester —"

"Glory hallelujah!" said the men. "Maybe we won't have to fight on Sunday after all!"

Out of the March woods ahead broke a thunderclap of sound, settling into a roar of musketry. It endured for some minutes, then forth from the thickets and shadow of the forest, back from Barton's Woods into the ragged old field, reeled the 27th Virginia. Its colonel, Colonel John Echols, was down; badly hurt and half carried now by his men; there were fifty others, officers and men, killed or wounded. The wounded, most of them, were helped back by their comrades. The dead lay where they fell in Barton's Woods, where the arbutus was in bloom and the purple violets.

The 21st swept forward. The 27th rallied, joined the 21st. The two charged the wood that was now filling with clouds of blue skirmishers. Behind came hurrying Garnett with the 2d, the 4th, and the 33d.

Fulkerson on the left, facing Tyler, had two regiments, the 23d and 37th Virginia. He deployed his men under cover, but now they were out in a great and ragged field, all up and down, with boggy hollows, scarred too by rail fences and blurred by low-growing briar patches. Diagonally across it, many yards away, ran one of the stone fences of the region, a long dike of loosely piled and rounded rock. Beyond it the ground kept the same nature, but gradually lifted to a fringe of tall trees. Emerging from this wood came now a Federal line of battle. It came with pomp and circumstance. The sun shone on a thousand bayonets; bright colours tossed in the breeze, drums rolled and bugles blew. Kimball, commanding in Shields's absence, had divined the Confederate intention. He knew that the man they called Stonewall Jackson meant to turn his right, and he began to mass his regiments, and he sent for Sullivan from the left.

The 23d and 37th Virginia eyed the on-coming line and eyed the stone fence. "That's good cover!" quoth a hunter from the hills. "We'd a long sight better have it than those fellows! — Sh! the colonel's speaking."

Fulkerson's speech was a shout, for there had arisen a deafening noise of artillery. "Run for your lives, men — toward the enemy! Forward, and take the stone fence!"

The two regiments ran, the Federal line of battle ran, the stone cover the prize. As they ran the grey threw forward their muskets and fired. That volley was at close range, and it was discharged by born marksmen. The grey fired again; yet closer. Many a blue soldier fell; the colour-bearer pitched forward, the line wavered, gave back. The charging grey reached and took the wall. It was good cover. They knelt behind it, laid their musket barrels along the stones, and fired. The blue line withstood that volley, even continued its advance, but a second fusillade poured in their very faces gave them check at last. In disorder, colours left upon the field, they surged back to the wood and to the cover of a fence at right angles with that held by the Confederates. Now began upon the left the fight of the stone wall — hours of raging battle, of high quarrel for this barrier. The regiments composing the grey centre found time to cheer for Fulkerson; the rumour of the fight reached the right where Ashby's squadron held the pike. Jackson himself came on Little Sorrel, looked at the wall and the line of men, powder grimed about the lips, plying the ramrods, shouldering the muskets, keeping back Tyler's regiments, and said "Good! good!"

Across a mile of field thundered an artillery duel, loud and prolonged. The blue had many guns; the grey eighteen in action. There were indeed but seventeen, for a Tredegar iron gun was disabled in crossing the meadow. The blue were the stronger cannon, modern, powerful. The grey were inferior there; also the grey must reach deeper and deeper into caisson and limber chest, must cast anxious backward glances toward ordnance wagons growing woefully light. The fire of the blue was extremely heavy; the fire of the grey as heavy as possible considering the question of ammunition. Rockbridge worked its guns in a narrow clearing dotted with straw stacks. A section under Lieutenant Poague was sent at a gallop, half a mile forward, to a point that seemed of vantage. Here the unlimbering guns found themselves in infantry company, a regiment lying flat, awaiting orders. "Hello, 65th!" said the gunners. "Wish people going to church at home could see us!"

A shell fell beside the howitzer and burst with appalling sound. The gun was blown from position, and out of the smoke came a fearful cry of wounded men. "O God! — O God!" The smoke cleared. All who had served that gun were down. Their fellows about the six-pounder, the other gun of the section, stood stupefied, staring, their lips parted, sponge staff or rammer or lanyard idle in their hands. A horse came galloping. An aide of Jackson's — Sandy Pendleton it was said — leaped to the ground. He was joined by Richard Cleave. The two came through the ring of the wounded and laid hold of the howitzer. "Mind the six-pounder, Poague! We'll serve here. Thunder Run men, three of you, come here and help!"

They drew the howitzer in position, charged it, and fired. In a very few moments after the horror of the shell, she was steadily sending canister against the great Parrott on the opposite hill. The six-pounder beside her worked as steadily. A surgeon came with his helpers, gathered up the wounded, and carried them beneath a whistling storm of shot and shell to a field hospital behind the ridge.

Out of the woods came fresh regiments of the enemy. These bore down upon the guns and upon the 5th Virginia now forming behind them. Poague's section opened with canister at one hundred and fifty yards. All the Valley marksmen of the 5th let fall the lids of their cartridge boxes, lifted their muskets, and fired. The blue withstood the first volley and the second, but at the third they went back to the wood. An order arrived from McLaughlin of the Rockbridge, "Lieutenant Poague back to the straw stacks!" The battery horses, quiet and steadfast, were brought from where they had stood and cropped the grass, the guns were limbered up, Jackson's aide and the men of the 65th fell back, the six-pounder shared its men with the howitzer, off thundered the guns. There was a stir in the 65th. "Boys, I heard say that when those fellows show again, we're going to charge!"

The battle was now general — Fulkerson on the left behind the stone wall, Garnett in the centre, the artillery and Burk with three battalions on the right. Against them poured the regiments of Kimball and Tyler, with Sullivan coming up. The sun, could it have been seen through the rolling smoke, would have showed low in the heavens. The musketry was continuous, and the sound of the cannon shook the heart of Winchester three miles away.

The 65th moved forward. Halfway up the slope, its colonel received an ugly wound. He staggered and sank. "Go on! go on, men! Fine hunt! Don't let the stag —" The 65th went on, led by Richard Cleave.

Before it stretched a long bank of springtime turf, a natural breastwork seized by the blue soldiers as the stone fence on the left had been taken by Fulkerson. From behind this now came a line of leaping flame. Several of the grey fell, among them the colour-bearer. The man nearest snatched the staff. Again the earthwork blazed and rang, and again the colour-bearer fell, pitching forward, shot through the heart. Billy Maydew caught the colours. "Thar's a durned sharpshooter a-settin' in that thar tree! Dave, you pick him off."

Again the bank blazed. A western regiment was behind it, a regiment of hunters and marksmen. Moreover a fresh body of troops could be seen through the smoke, hurrying down from the tall brown woods. The grey line broke, then rallied and swept on. The breastwork was now but a few hundred feet away. A flag waved upon it, the staff planted in the soft earth. Billy, moving side by side with Allan Gold, clutched closer the great red battle-flag with the blue cross. His young face was set, his eyes alight. Iron-sinewed he ran easily, without panting. "I air a-goin'," he announced, "I air a-goin' to put this here one in the place of that thar one."

"'T is n't going to be easy work," said Allan soberly. "What's the use of ducking, Steve Dagg? If a bullet's going to hit you it's going to hit you, and if it is n't going to hit you it is n't —"

A minie ball cut the staff of the flag in two just above Billy's head. He caught the colours as they came swaying down, Allan jerked a musket from a dead man's grasp, and together he and Billy somehow fastened the flag to the bayonet and lifted it high. The line halted under a momentary cover, made by the rising side of a hollow rimmed by a few young locust trees. Cleave came along it. "Close ranks! — Men, all of you! that earthwork must be taken. The 2d, the 4th, and the 33d are behind us looking to see us do it. General Jackson himself is looking. *Attention! Fix bayonets! Forward! Charge!*"

Up out of the hollow, and over the field went the 65th in a wild charge. The noise of a thousand seas was in the air, and the smoke of the bottomless pit. The yellow flashes of the guns came through it, and a blur of colour — the flag on the bank. On went their own great battle-flag, slanting forward as Billy Maydew ran. The bank flamed and roared. A bullet passed through the fleshy part of the boy's arm. He looked sideways at the blood. "Those durned bees sure do sting! I air a-goin' to plant this here flag on that thar bank, jest the same as if 't was a hop pole in Christianna's garden!"

Fulkerson fought on grimly by the stone wall; Garnett and the other Stonewall regiments struggled with desperation to hold the centre, the artillery thundered from every height. The 65th touched the earthwork. Cleave mounted first; Allan followed, then Billy and the Thunder Run men, the regiment pouring after. Hot was the welcome they got, and fierce was their answering grip. In places men could load and fire, but bayonet and musket butt did much of the work. There was a great clamour, the acrid smell of powder, the indescribable taste of battle. The flag was down; the red battle-flag with the blue cross in its place. There was a surge of the western regiment toward it, a battle around it that strewed the bank and the shallow ditch beneath with many a blue figure, many a grey. Step by step the grey pushed the blue back, away from the bank, back toward the wood arising, shadowy, from a base of eddying smoke.

Out of the smoke, suddenly, came hurrahing. It was deep and loud, issuing from many throats. The western regiment began to hurrah, too. "They're coming to help! They're coming to help! Indiana, ain't it? — Now, you rebs, you go back on the other side!"

The blue wave from the wood came to reinforce the blue wave in front. The 65th struggled with thrice its numbers, and there was a noise from the wood which portended more. Back, inch by inch, gave the grey, fighting desperately. They loaded, fired, loaded, fired. They used bayonet and musket stock. The blue fell thick, but always others came to take their places. The grey fell, and the ranks must close with none to reinforce. In the field to the left the 4th and the 33d had their hands very full; the 2d was gone to Fulkerson's support, the 5th and the 42d were not yet up. Out of the wood came a third huzzahing blue line. Cleave, hatless, bleeding from a bayonet thrust in the arm, ordered the retreat.

On the crest of the bank there was confusion and clamour, shots and shouts, the groans of the fallen, a horrible uproar. Out of the storm came a high voice, "It air a-goin' to stay, and I air a-goin' to stay with it!"

Billy Maydew had the flag. He stood defiant, half enveloped in its folds, his torn shirt showing throat and breast, his young head thrown back against the red ground. "I ain't a-goin' to quit — I ain't a-goin' to quit! Thunder Run and Thunder Mountain hear me what I am a-sayin'! I ain't a-goin' to quit!"

Allan Gold laid hold of him. "Why, Billy, we're coming back! There's got to be a lot of times like this in a big war! You come on and carry the colours out safe. You don't want those fellows to take them!"

Billy chanted on, "I ain't a-goin' to quit! I put it here jest like I was putting a hop pole in Christianna's garden, and I ain't a-goin' to dig it up again —"

Dave appeared. "Billy boy, don't be such a damned fool! You jest skeedaddle with the rest of us and take it out of them next time. Don't ye want to see Christianna again, an' maw an' the dogs? — Thar, now!"

A bullet split the standard, another — a spent ball coming from the hillside — struck the bearer in the chest. Billy came to his knees, the great crimson folds about him. Cleave appeared in the red-lit murk. "Pick him up, Allan, and bring him away."

It was almost dusk to the green and rolling world about the field of Kernstown. Upon that field, beneath the sulphurous battle cloud, it was dusk indeed. The fighting line was everywhere, and for the Confederates there were no reinforcements. Fulkerson yet held the left, Garnett with conspicuous gallantry the centre with the Stonewall regiments. The batteries yet thundered upon the right. But ammunition was low, and for three hours Ashby's mistake as to the enemy's numbers had received full demonstration. Shields's brigadiers did well and the blue soldiers did well.

A body of troops coming from the wood and crowding through a gap in a stone fence descended upon the Rockbridge battery. Four regiments of the Stonewall brigade clung desperately to the great uneven field which marked the centre. The musket barrels were burningly hot to the touch of the men, their fingers must grope for the cartridges rattling in the cartridge boxes, their weariness was horrible, their eyes were glazed, their lips baked with thirst. Long ago they had fought in a great, bright, glaring daytime; then again, long ago, they had begun to fight in a period of dusk, an age of dusk. The men loaded, fired, loaded, rammed, fired quite automatically. They had been doing this for a long, long time. Probably they would do it for a long time to come. Only the cartridges were not automatically supplied. It even seemed that they might one day come to an end. The dusk deepened. They had, beneath the red-lit battle clouds, a glimpse of Garnett, a general chivalric and loved, standing in his stirrups, looking out and upward toward the dark wood and Sullivan's fresh regiments.

A sergeant came along the line stretching a haversack open with his hands. In it were cartridges. "I gathered all the dead had.

'T is n't many. You've got to shoot to kill, boys!" A man with a ball through the end of his spine, lying not far from a hollow of the earth, half pool, half bog, began to cry aloud in an agonizing fashion, "Water! water! Oh, some one give me water! Water! For the love of God, water!" A grey soldier started out of line toward him; in a second both were killed. Garnett settled down in his saddle and came back to the irregular, smoke-wreathed, swaying line. He spoke to his colonels. "There are three thousand fresh bayonets at the back of these woods. General Jackson does not wish a massacre. I will withdraw the brigade."

The troops were ready to go. They had held the centre very long; the cartridges were all but spent, the loss was heavy, they were deadly tired. They wanted water to drink and to hear the command, *Break ranks!* Garnett was gallant and brave; they saw that he did what he did with reason, and their judgment acquiesced. There was momently a fresh foe. Without much alignment, fighting in squads or singly, firing as they went from thicket and hollow at the heavy on-coming masses, the Stonewall Brigade fell back upon the wood to the south. The blue wave saw victory and burst into a shout of triumph. Kimball's batteries, too, began a jubilant thunder.

Over the field, from Fulkerson on the left to the broken centre and the withdrawing troops came a raw-bone sorrel urged to a furious gallop; upon it a figure all dusk in the dusk, a Cromwell-Quixote of a man, angered now to a degree, with an eye like steel and a voice like ice. He rode up to Garnett, as though he would ride him down. "General Garnett, what are you doing? Go back at once, sir!"

As he spoke he threw himself from the saddle and closed his gauntleted hand with force on the arm of a drummer boy. "Beat the rally!" he commanded.

The rapid and continuous rolling filled like a sound of the sea the ears of the Stonewall Brigade. Garnett, in a strange voice, gave the counter-order. The men uttered a hard and painful gasp. They looked and saw Stonewall Jackson lifted above them, an iron figure in a storm of shot and shell. He jerked his hand into the air; he shouted, "Back, men! Give them the bayonet!" The drum beat on. Colonels and captains and lieutenants strove to aid him and to change the retreat into an advance. In vain! the commands were shattered; the fighting line all broken and dispersed. The men did not shamefully flee; they retreated sullenly, staying here and there where there were yet cartridges, to fire upon the on-coming foe, but they continued to go back.

The 5th and the 42d with Funsten's small cavalry command came hastening to the broken centre and there made a desperate fight. The 5th Virginia and the 5th Ohio clanged shields. The 84th Pennsylvania broke twice, rallied twice, finally gave way. Two Indiana regiments came up; the 5th Virginia was flanked; other blue reinforcements poured in. The last grey commands gave way. Fulkerson, too, on the left, his right now uncovered, must leave his stone fence and save his men as best he might. Rockbridge and Carpenter and Waters no longer thundered from the heights. The grey infantry, wildly scattered, came in a slow surge back through the woods where dead men lay among the spring flowers, and down the ridge and through the fields, grey and dank in the March twilight, toward the Valley pike. Night and the lost battle weighed upon the army. The shadowy ambulances, the lights of the gatherers of the wounded flitting few and far over the smoke-clouded field, made for a ghastly depression. Sick at heart, in a daze of weariness, hunger and thirst, drunk with sleep, mad for rest, command by command stumbled down the pike or through the fields to where, several miles to the south, stretched the meadows where their trains were parked. There was no pursuit. Woods and fields were rough and pathless; it was now dark night, and Ashby held the pike above.

A camp-fire was built for Stonewall Jackson in a field to the right of the road, three miles from Kernstown. Here he stood, summoned Garnett, and put him under arrest. The army understood next day that heavy charges would be preferred against this general.

To right and left of the pike camp-fires flamed in the windy night. Passing one of these, Richard Cleave cut short some bewailing on the part of the ring about it. "Don't be so downcast, people! Sometimes a defeat in one place equals a victory in another. I don't believe that General Banks will join General McClellan just now. Indeed, it's not impossible that McClellan will have to part with another division. Their government's dreadfully uneasy about Washington and the road to Washington. They did n't beat us

easily, and if we can lead them up and down this Valley for a
while — I imagine that's what General Johnston wants, and what
General Jackson will procure. — And now you'd better all go to
sleep."

"Where are you going, Cleave?"

"To see about the colonel. They've just brought him to the
farmhouse yonder. Dr. McGuire says he will get well — dear old
Brooke!"

He went, striding over the furrowed field past groups of men
sleeping and moaning as they slept. The stars were very bright in
the clear, cold, windy night. He looked at them and thought of the
battle and of the dead and the wounded, and of Judith and of his
mother and sister, and of Will in the 2d, and of to-morrow's movements, and of Stonewall Jackson. A dark figure came wandering up
to him. It proved to be that of an old negro. "Marster, is you seen
Marse Charlie?"

"Marse Charlie whom, uncle?"

"Marse Charlie Armetage, sah, mah young marster. I 'spec you
done seed him? I 'spec he come marchin' wif you down de pike f'om
dat damn battlefield? I sure would be 'bleeged ef you could tell me,
sah."

"I wish I could," said Cleave, with gentleness. "I have n't seen
him, but maybe some one else has."

The old negro drew one hand through the other. "I 's asked erbout
fifty gent'men. . . . Reckon Marse Charlie so damn tired he jes'
lain down somewhere an' gone ter sleep. Reckon he come down
de pike in de mahnin', shoutin' fer Daniel. Don' you reckon so,
marster?"

"It's not impossible, Daniel. Maybe you'll find him yet."

"I 'specs ter," said Daniel. "I 'spec ter fin' him howsomever he 's
a-lyin'." He wandered off in the darkness, and Cleave heard him
speaking to a picket, "Marster, is you seen Marse Charlie?"

CHAPTER XVI

RUDE'S HILL

STONEWALL JACKSON and his army in slow retreat up the valley came, the second day after Kernstown, to the gorge of Cedar Creek. A bridge had once been here; there remained the blackened cross-timbers and a portion of the flooring. The water below was cold, deep, and rapid. Rather than breast it, the army made shift to cross on the charred wood. An infantry command, stepping gingerly, heard behind it shots and shouts — a Federal cavalry charge upon the rear guard. Several of the men, listening too absorbedly, or not content with the present snail-like motion, suddenly left the timbers and entered the rough and swollen creek that poured beneath. Their exclamations in this berth were piteous, and their comrades fished them out with bayonets and laughter.

Upon the night of the 26th Banks's troopers occupied the northern shore of Tom's Brook. Ashby held the southern side, and held it fast. Behind that safe and vigilant and valiant screen the Army of the Valley moved quietly and in good spirits to the points its general had in mind. The army never knew what were these points until it found itself actually upon the ground. It is morally certain that had he lived, a recalcitrant, in former days, no amount of *peine forte et dure* would have opened the lips of Stonewall Jackson had he willed to keep them closed. During their earlier acquaintance officers and men alike had made many an ingenious endeavour to learn the plans they thought they ought to know. They set quaint traps, they made innocent-seeming remarks, they guided right, they guided left, they blazed beautiful trails straight, they thought, to the moment of revelation. It never came. He walked past and around and over their traps. Inquisitive officers found themselves not only without a straw of information, but under displeasure. Brilliant leading remarks shone a moment by their own brilliancy, then went out. The troops conjectured one road — they went by another; natives described the beauties of the village before which they were sure to break ranks — at eve they experienced the hospitalities of quite another town. Generals in the ranks demonstrated that they were going to turn on Shields, or that they were going east by the old Manassas Gap and whip Geary, or northeast and whip Abercrombie. They did none of the three. They marched on up the valley to Rude's Hill near Mount Jackson. About this time, or a little later, men and officers gave it up, began to admire, and to follow blindly. A sergeant, one evening, put it to his mess. "If we don't know, then Banks and Shields and Frémont and Milroy and McClellan and Lincoln and Stanton don't know, either!" The mess grew thoughtful; presently it took the pipe from its mouth to answer, "Dog-gone it, Martin, that's true! Never saw it just that way before."

Rude's Hill formed a strong natural position. There was water, there were woods, there was an excellent space for a drill-ground. Jackson's directions as to drill-grounds were always characteristically explicit. *"Major: You will see that a camp is chosen where there are wood, water, and a drill-ground —"* emphasis on the drill-ground. At Rude's Hill they drilled and drilled and drilled. Every morning rang out adjutant's call, every morning there were infantry evolutions, artillery evolutions. The artillery had some respite, for, turn by turn, the sections went forward ten miles to do picket duty for Ashby, Chew's Horse Artillery being continually engaged with the Federal outposts. But the infantry drilled on, drilled and wondered at Banks. One week — two weeks! — and the general in blue with nineteen thousand men still on the farther side of Tom's Brook!

Despite the drilling the Army of the Valley had a good time at Rude's Hill. Below brawled the Shenandoah, just to the east sprang the Massanuttens. There was much rain, but, day by day, through the silver veil or the shattered golden light, lovelier and more lovely grew the spring. The army liked to see her coming. In its heart it felt a springtime, too; a gush of hope and ardour. The men hardly counted Kernstown a defeat. It was known that Old Jack had said to one of the aides, "I may say that I am satisfied, sir." And Congress had thanked the Army of the Valley. And all the newspapers sang its praises. The battle of Pea Ridge in Arkansas, the shelling of Newbern in North Carolina, the exploits of the Merrimac in Hampton Roads, the battle of Kernstown in the Valley — so at the moment ran the newspapers. And day by day recruits were coming in; comrades as well who had been in hospital or home on furlough. In that fortnight the Army of the Valley grew to number nearly six thousand men.

At Rude's Hill there was an election of company officers. The proceedings — amazing enough to the professional soldier — put into camp life three days of excitement and salt. Given a people of strong political proclivities suddenly turned soldier; given human grudges and likings, admirations and contempts; given the ballot in military as in civil life; given a chance to inject champagne into the ennui of camp existence, and in lieu of gun practice to send off sky-rockets and catherine wheels; given a warm personal interest in each private's bosom as to whom, for the next twelfth month (if the war lasted that long), he was going to obey — and there resulted a shattering of monotony comparable to a pitched battle.

The elections were held in beautiful, vernal groves. That there would be changes it was believed; change was in the air! For days beforehand the character for conduct, courage, and general agree-ableness of every man who wore three bars on his collar, or two, or one, or who carried chevrons of silk or chevrons of worsted, had been strictly in the zone of fire. Certain officers nearing certain camp-fires felt caucuses dissolving at their approach into an inno-cence of debating societies engaged with Fabius Maximus or Scipio Africanus. Certain sergeants and corporals dreamed bars instead of chevrons, and certain high privates, conscious of merit, saw worsted chevrons, silk chevrons, and gold bars all in one blissful night.

But when election day dawned bright and clear, with a fine chorus of birds and an especial performance by the regimental bands, when roll call was over, and camp duties were over, and morning drill was over (no relaxation here! There was only one day in the week on which Old Jack let up on drill, and that was n't elec-tion day!) and the pickets had reluctantly marched away, leaving their votes behind them, and a section of artillery had gone off, swearing, to relieve Chew, and the men could at last get down to work, to happy babbling, happy speechifying, happy minding the polls, and when in the cool of the afternoon the returns were an-nounced, there were fewer changes than had been predicted. After all, most of the officers were satisfactory; why let them down with a jolt? And the privates were satisfactory, too. Why take a capital comrade, a good cook and forager and story-teller, and make him uncomfortable by turning him into an officer? He was nice enough as he was. Not that there were no alterations. Several companies had new captains, some lieutenants stepped down, and there was a shifting of non-commissioned officers. In Company A of the 65th Lieutenant Mathew Coffin lost out. The men wished to put up Allan Gold for the lieutenancy, but Allan declined. He had rather, he said, be scout than lieutenant — and what was the use in changing, anyhow? Lieutenant Coffin was all right. Had n't he been as brave as a lion at Kernstown — and any man is liable to lose his temper at times — and would n't we hate him to have to write back to that young lady at home —? The last plea almost settled it, for the Confederate heart might be trusted to melt at the mention of any young lady at home. But all the Thunder Run men were against Coffin, and Thunder Run turned the scale. In the main, however, throughout the army, company officers were retained, and retained because they were efficient. The election was first-rate fun, and the men cheered the returns, then listened to the orders of the evening from the same old bars and chevrons. The sun went down on a veritable love feast — special rations, special music, special fires, and, between supper and tattoo, an entertainment in each regiment.

The 65th had a beautiful programme, its debating and literary societies, its glee clubs, chess and checker circles, old sledge associations, Thespians and Greek Letter men all joining forces. The stage was a piece of earth, purple brown with pine needles. Two huge fires, one at either side, made a strong, copper-red illumination. The soldier audience sat in a deep semicircle, and sat at ease, being accustomed by now to the posture of tailor or Turk. Only recruits sought logs or stones upon which to sit. Tobacco smoke rose like incense.

The chief musician "sounded on the bugle horn." The Glee Club of Company C filed on the stage with three banjos and two guitars, bowed elegantly, and sang the "Bonny Blue Flag." The applause was thunderous. A large bearded man in the front row lifted a voice that boomed like one of Ashby's cannon. "Encore! Encore!"

Company C sang "Listen to the Mocking Bird." The audience gently sighed, took the pipe from its lips, and joined in —

"Listen to the mocking bird — Listen to the mocking bird. . . .
The mocking bird still singing o'er her grave.
Listen to the mocking bird — Listen to the mocking bird. . . .
Still singing where the weeping willows wave."

The pine trees took it up, and the hazel copses and the hurrying Shenandoah.

"T was in the mild September — September — September,
And the mocking bird was singing far and wide."

"*Far and wide.* . . . That's grand, but it sure is gloomy. Next!" The chief musician, having a carrying voice, made announcements. "No. 2. Debate. Which will first recognize the Confederacy, England or France? With the historic reasons for both doing so. England, Sergeant Smith. France, Sergeant Duval. — The audience is not expected to participate in the debate otherwise than judicially, at the close."

The close saw it decided by a rising vote that England would come first — Sergeant Smith, indeed, who chanced to be a professor of belles-lettres at a great school, having declared, with the gesture of Saint John on Patmos, that he saw approaching our shores a white winged ship bearing her declaration of amity. "No. 3," intoned the first musician. "Recitation by Private Edwin Horsemanden."

Private Edwin Horsemanden gave the title of his selection, a poetic selection. Some of his fellow privates looked puzzled. "'Oz Etaliahn?' — What does 'Oz Etaliahn' mean? Cherokee or Choctaw, which? Explain it to us, Eddy. Is it something to eat — or to drink? ''T is true, 't is pity, 't is pity 't is 't is true' — but most of us never went to college! . . . Oh, an opera house! — In Paris, do you say? Go on, Eddy, go on!"

"At Paris it was, at the opera there, —
And she looked like a queen in a book that night —"

"Never saw one out of a book, did you? . . . Yes, I saw a gypsy queen once. . . . And the queen of the circus. . . . There's a man in Company D once saw the queen of England, saw her just as plain! She was wearing a scoop bonnet with pink roses around her face. . . . Sh! Shh!"

"Of all the operas that Verdi wrote,"

"Who's Verdi?"

"The best, to my taste, is the 'Trovatore.' "

" 'Trovatore?' Eddy, is n't that the serenading fellow who goes on singing till they hang him? Oh, Lord, yes! And the anvil chorus! The anvil chorus comes in there. Go on, Eddy. We feel perfectly at home."

"And Mario"

"Hm! stumped again."

"can sooth with a tenor note
The souls in Purgatory."

The large bearded man was up once more. "I rise to object. There is n't any such place. The com — commanding general 'll put him in irons for misrepresenting the sidereal system. There's only heaven, hell, and the enemy. — *Yaaaaih, Yaai. . . . Yaaai, yaaaah, yaaaaih!* Certainly, sergeant. The pleasure is mine, sir. Don't mention it, I beg. Mum's the word!"

"The moon on the tower slept soft as snow " —

"Gee-whiz! what a snowball! Did n't the tower break down? No! You amaze me. Go on, Eddy, go on. We know the natural feelings of a sophomore."

"And who was not thrilled in the strangest way
As we heard him sing, while the gas burned low,
'*Non ti scordar di me?*' "

"What's that? Wait a minute, Eddy! Let's get the words. I always did want a chance at German. — Now you say them slowly and we'll repeat. . . . Why, man alive, you ought to be proud of your linguistic accomplishments! . . . Well, I'll begin, and we'll fire by platoons.

"Non ti scordar di me? — "

"Attention! Company A!"

"Non ti scordar di me? —
Non ti scordar di me?"

"Very good! We'll get the meaning after we learn the words. Company B!"

"Non ti scordar di me?"

"Well roared, Bottom! Company C!"

"Non ti scordar di me?"

"Look out, or General Banks'll be sending over Tom's Brook to know what's the matter! Company D!"

"Non ti scordar di me?"

"Company D goes to the head of the class! Company E!"

"Non ti scordar di me?"

"'Ware pine cones! Company E's shaking them down. . . . This class's getting too big. Let's all learn the words together, so's Private Horsemanden can go on with his piece! Attention, 65th! Make ready! Take aim! Fire!"

"NON TI SCORDAR DI ME?"

"Now Eddy. . . . Oh, yes, you go on! You are n't going to cheat us that way. We want to know what happened when they stopped talking German! Has n't anything happened yet."

"Non ti —"

"Sh! Go on, Eddy boy, and tell us exactly what occurred."

Private Edwin Horsemanden had pluck as well as sentiment, and he went on. Moreover he had his revenge, for at bottom the 65th was itself tender-hearted, not to say sentimental. It believed in lost loves and lost blossoms, muslin dresses, and golden chains, cypress shades and jasmine flowers,

> "And the one bird singing alone to his nest,
> And the one star over the tower."

The 65th sighed and propped its chin on its hand. Presently the 65th grew misty-eyed.

> "Then I smelt the smell of that jasmine flower
> She used to wear in her breast
> It smelt so faint and it smelt so sweet. —"

The pipe dropped from the 65th's hand. It sat sorry and pleased. Private Edwin Horsemanden went on without interruption and finished with éclat. The chief musician cleared his throat. "The Glee Club of Company H will now —"

The Glee Club of Company H was a large and popular organization. It took the stage amid applause. The leader bowed. "Gentlemen, we thank you. Gentlemen, you have just listened to a beautiful novelty — a pretty little foreign song bird brought by the trade-wind, an English nightingale singing in Virginian forests. — Gentlemen, the Glee Club of Company H will give you what by now is devil a bit of a novelty — what promises to be as old as the hills before we have done with it — what our grandchildren's grandchildren may sing with pride — what to the end of time will carry with it a breath of our armies. Gentlemen, the Glee Club of Company H gives you the Marseillaise of the South. *Attention!*"

> "Way down South in the land of cotton,
> 'Simmon seed and sandy bottom —"

The 65th rose to its feet. Its neighbour to the right was the 2d Virginia, encamped in a great open field; to the left the 5th, occupying a grove of oaks. These regiments were busied with their own genial hour, but when the loudly sung air streamed across from the 65th they suspended their work in hand. They also sung "Dixie." Thence it was taken up by the 4th and the 33d, and then it spread to Burk and Fulkerson. The batteries held the top of Rude's Hill, up among the night wind and the stars. The artillerymen took the air from the infantry. Headquarters was situated on the green bank of the Shenandoah. Staff and couriers and orderlies hummed or sang. Stonewall Jackson came to the door of his tent and stood, looking out. All Rude's Hill throbbed to "Dixie."

On went the programme. "Marco Bozzaris" was well spoken. A blacksmith and a mule driver wrestled for a prize. "Marmion Quitting the Douglas's Hall" was followed by "Lula, Lula, Lula is Gone," and "Lula" by "Lorena," and "Lorena" by a fencing match. The Thespians played capitally an act from "The Rivals," and a man who had seen Macready gave Hamlet's Soliloquy. Then they sang a song lately written by James Randall and already very popular, —

"I hear the distant thunder hum,
Maryland!
The Old Line bugle, fife and drum —"

An orderly from headquarters found Richard Cleave. "General Jackson wishes to see you, sir."

The general's tent was not large. There were a table and two stools, on one of which sat Jackson in his characteristic position, large feet accurately paralleled. On the table, beside the candle, lay three books — the Bible, a dictionary, and "Napoleon's Maxims." Jackson was writing, his hand travelling slowly across a sheet of dim blue, lined, official paper. The door flap of the tent was fastened back. Cleave, standing in the opening, saluted.

"Take a seat, sir," said the general, and went on to the end of his page. Having here signed his name, he dropped the quill and slightly turned so as to face the waiting officer. From under his high bronzed forehead his blue eyes looked quietly upon Cleave.

The younger man returned the gaze as quietly. This was the first time he had been thus summoned since that unlucky winter evening at Bloomery Gap. He remembered that evening, and he did not suppose that his general had forgotten it. He did not suppose that Jackson forgot anything. But apparently it was no longer to be counted against him. Jackson's face wore the quiet, friendly, somewhat sweet expression usual to it when all was calm within. As for Cleave himself, his nature owned a certain primal flow and bigness. There were few fixed and rigid barriers. Injured pride and resentment did not lift themselves into reefs against which the mind must break in torment. Rather, his being swept fluid, making no great account of obstacles, accepting all turns of affairs, drawing them into its main current, and moving onward toward some goal, hardly self-conjectured, but simple, humane, and universal. The anger he might have felt at Bloomery Gap had long passed away. He sat now attentive, collected, broad-browed, and quiet.

"Major Cleave," said Jackson, "you will take an orderly with you and ride across the mountains. General Ewell is at Gordonsville with a somewhat larger force than my own. You will take this letter to him," he folded it as he spoke, "and you will talk to him as one intelligent man to another."

"Do you mean, sir, that I am to answer his questions?"

"Yes, sir. To the best of your ability. There is impending a junction between General Ewell and myself. He wishes to know many things, and seems to think it natural that I should tell him them. I am not a great letter writer. You will give him all the information that is common to the army."

Cleave smiled. "That, sir, is not a great deal."

"Perhaps it is not, sir. You are at liberty to give to General Ewell your own observations and expectations. You will, however, represent them as your own."

"May I ask, sir, when this junction is to occur?"

"I have not decided, sir."

"Does General Ewell know when it will occur?"

"Not precisely. He will be told in good time."

"Whether, when you move, you move north or west or south or east, is, I suppose, sir, purely a matter of conjecture?"

"Purely, sir."

"But the *morale* of the army, its efficiency and spirit, may be freely praised and imparted?"

"Yes, sir, freely. Upon your return I shall want from you your impression of General Ewell and the troops he commands." He drew toward him a map which lay on the table. "You will ride through Massanutton Gap by Conrad's Store and Swift Run Gap. Thence you will make a détour to Charlottesville. There are stores there that I wish reported upon and sent on to Major Harman at Staunton. You will spend one day upon that business, then go on to Ewell."

CHAPTER XVII

CLEAVE AND JUDITH

THE hospital at Charlottesville, unlovely and lovely, ghastly and vital, brutal, spiritual, a hell of pain and weakness, another region of endeavour and helpfulness, a place of horror, and also of strange smiling, even of faint laughter, a country as chill as death and as warm as love — the hospital at Charlottesville saw the weary morning grow to weary noon, the weary noon change toward the weary latter day. The women who nursed the soldiers said that it was lovely outside, and that all the peach trees were in bloom. "We'll raise you a little higher," they said, "and you can see for yourself. And look! here is your broth, so good and strengthening! And did you hear? We won on the Peninsula to-day!"

At four o'clock Judith Cary gave to another her place beside a typhoid pallet and came out into the emerald and rose, the freshness and fragrance of the spring. The Greenwood carriage was waiting. "We'll go, Isham," said Judith, "by the University for Miss Lucy."

Isham held open the door. "No'm, Miss Judith. Miss Lucy done sont wuhd dat de ladies'll be cuttin' out nuniforms clean 'twel dark. She say don' wait fer her — Mrs. Carter'll bring her home."

Judith entered the carriage. An old acquaintance, passing, paused to speak to her. "Is n't there a greater stir than usual?" she asked.

"Some of General Ewell's men are over from Gordonsville. There goes General Dick Taylor now — the one in grey and white! He's a son, you know, of Zachary — Old Rough and Ready. General Jackson, too, has an officer here to-day, checking the stores that came from Richmond. — How is it at the hospital?"

"It is very bad," said Judith. "When the bands begin to play I laugh and cry like all the rest, and I wave and clap my hands, and I would fight on and on like the rest of you, and I do not see that, given people as they are, the war could have been avoided, and I would die to win, and I am, I hope, a patriot — and yet I do not see any sense in it! It hurts me as I think it may hurt the earth. She would like, I believe, something better than being a battlefield. — There is music again! Yesterday a man died, crying for the band to hush. He said it drowned something he needed to hear."

"Yes, yes," replied her friend, nodding his head. "That is perfectly true. That is very true, indeed! — That band's coming from the station. They're looking for a regiment from Richmond. — That's a good band! What are they playing —?"

> " Bright flowers spring from the hero's grave,
>   The craven knows no rest, —
> Thrice cursed the traitor and the knave,
>   The hero thrice is blessed — "

The Greenwood carriage rolled out of the town into the April country. The fruit trees were in bloom, the woods feathering green, the quiet and the golden light inestimable after the moaning wards. The carriage went slowly, for the roads were heavy; moreover the former carriage horses were gone to the war. These were two from the farm, somewhat old and stiff, willing, but plodders. They went half asleep in the soft sunshine, and Isham on the box went half asleep too. Judith would have been willing to sleep, but she could not. She sat with her gaze upon the fair spring woods and the amethystine hills rising to blue skies. The carriage stopped. Isham bent down from the box. "Miss Judith, honey, er gent'man's on de road behin' us, ridin' ter overtek de kerridge."

"Wait for him, then," said Judith. "There is some message, perhaps."

While they waited she sat with folded hands, her eyes upon the purple hills, her thoughts away from Albemarle. The sound that Isham made of surprise and satisfaction did not reach her. Until she saw Cleave's face at the window she thought him somewhere in the Valley — fighting, fighting! in battle and danger, perhaps, that very day.

Her eyes widened, her face had the hush of dawn; it was turned toward him, but she sat perfectly still, without speaking. Only the door was between them, the glass down. He rested his clasped hands on the ledge, and his dark, moved face looked in upon her. "Judith," he said, "I did not know. — I thought it was one of the others. . . . I hope that you are a little glad to see me."

Judith looked at him a moment longer, then swayed a little forward. She bent her head. Her cheek touched his clasped hands, he felt her kiss upon them, and her forehead resting there.

There was a moment's silence, deep, breathless, then Cleave spoke. "Judith . . . Am I mad?"

"I believe that you love me," she said. "If you do not, it does not matter. . . . I have loved you for two years."

"Maury Stafford?"

"I have never believed that you understood — though what it was that made you misunderstand I have never guessed. . . . There is no Maury Stafford. There never was."

He opened the door. "Come out," he said. "Come out with me into the light. Send the carriage on."

She did so. The road was quiet, deserted, a wide bright path between the evening hills. Dundee following them, they walked a little way until they came to a great rock, sunk in the velvet sward that edged a wood. Here they sat down, the gold light bathing them, behind them fairy vistas, fountains of living green, stars of the dogwood and purple sprays of Judas tree. "How I misunderstood is no matter now," said Cleave. "I love you, and you say that you love me. Thank God for it!"

They sat with clasped hands, their cheeks touching, their breath mingling. "Judith, Judith, how lovely are you! I have seen you always, always! . . . Only I called it 'vision,' 'ideal.' At the top of every deed I have seen your eyes; from the height of every thought you have beckoned further! Now — now — It is like a wonderful home-coming . . . and yet you are still there, above the mountains, beckoning, drawing — There and here, here in my arms! . . . Judith — What does 'Judith' mean?"

"It means 'praised.' Oh, Richard, I heard that you were wounded at Kernstown!"

"It was nothing. It is healed. . . . I will write to your father at once."

"He will be glad, I think. He likes you. . . . Have you a furlough? How long can you stay?"

"Love, I cannot stay at all. I am on General Jackson's errand. I must ride on to Gordonsville — It would be sweet to stay!"

"When will you come again?"

"I do not know. There will be battles—many battles, perhaps—up and down the Valley. Every man is needed. I am not willing to ask even a short furlough."

"I am not willing that you should. . . . I know that you are in danger every day! I hear it in the wind, I see it in every waving bough. . . . Oh, come back to me, Richard!"

"I?" he answered, "I feel immortal. I will come back."

They rose from the rock. "The sun is setting. Would you rather I went on to the house? I must turn at once, but I could speak to them —"

"No. Aunt Lucy is in town, Unity, too. . . . Let's say good-bye before we reach the carriage."

They went slowly by the quiet road beneath the flowering trees. The light was now only on the hilltops; the birds were silent; only the frogs in the lush meadows kept up their quiring, a sound quaintly mournful, weirdly charming. A bend of the road showed them Isham, the farm horses, and the great old carriage waiting beneath a tulip tree. The lovers stopped, took hands, moved nearer each to the other, rested each in the other's arms. Her head was thrown back, his lips touched her hair, her forehead, her lips. "Good-bye, good-bye, good-bye!"

He put her in the carriage, kissed her hands as they lay on the door ledge, and stood back. It was not far to the Greenwood gates; the old, slow horses moved on, the carriage rounded a leafy turn, the road was left to the soldier and his horse.

Cleave rode to Gordonsville that night as though he carried Heaven with him. The road was fair, the moon was high. Far-flung, beautiful odours filled the air; the red ploughed earth sent its share, the flowering fruit trees theirs, the flowers in the wood, the mint by the stream. A light wind swung them as from a censer; the moved air touched the young man's forehead. He took off his hat; he rode rapidly with head held high. He rode for hours, Dundee taking the way with even power, a magnificently silent friend. Behind, on an iron grey, came the orderly. Riding thus together, away from organization and discipline, the relations between the two men, officer and private, were perfectly democratic. From Rude's Hill across the Massanuttons and from Swift Run Gap to Charlottesville they had been simply comrades and fellow Virginians. They were from adjoining counties, where the one had practised law and the other had driven a stage. There were differences in breeding, education, and employment; but around these, recognized by both, stretched the enormous plane of humanity. They met there in simple brotherliness. To-night, however, Cleave had spoken for silence. "I want to be quiet for a while, Harris. — There is something I have to think of."

The night was all too short for what he had to think of. The pink flush of dawn, the distant view of Ewell's tents, came too soon. It was hard to lower the height and swell of the mind, to push back the surging thoughts, to leave the lift and wonder, the moonlight, and the flowering way. Here, however, were the pickets; and while he waited for the corporal of the guard, standing with Harris on a little hill, before them the pink sky, below them a peach orchard, pink too, with a lace-like mist wreathing the trees, he put golden afternoon and moonlight night in the bottom of his heart and laid duty atop.

Ewell's camp, spread over the rolling hills and lighted by a splendid sunrise, lay imposingly. To the eyes of the men from the Valley the ordered white tents of Trimble's and Taylor's and the Maryland line had an air luxuriously martial. Everything seemed to gleam and shine. The guns of the parked batteries gave back the light, the colours seemed silken and fine, the very sunrise gun had a sonorousness lacking to Chew's Blakeley, or to McLaughlin's six-pounders, and the bugles blowing reveille a silvery quality most remarkable. As for the smoke from the camp-fires — "Lord save us!" said Harris, "I believe they're broiling partridges! Of all the dandy places!"

Cleave laughed. "It's not that they are so fine, but that we are so weather-beaten and rusty! They're only in good working-day trim. We'll have to polish up at Rude's Hill."

"This is the 1st Maryland on the hillside," said the guide the corporal had given; " there with the blue flag. Mighty fine feathers, but I reckon they're gamecocks all right! Elzey's Brigade's over beside the woods — Virginian to the backbone. Trimble's got a fine lot — Georgians and Alabamians and Mississippians. Here come some of the 2d Virginia Cavalry! Ain't they pretty?"

They were. But Harris stood up for the absent Valley. "Huh!

Ashby's good enough for me! Ashby's got three stallions — the white he's fondest of, and a black like a piece of coal, and a red roan —"

The guide nodded energetically. "Oh, we think a heap of Ashby ourselves! There ain't anybody that the men listen about more eagerly. We ain't setting up on this side of the mountains to beat *him!* But I reckon the 2d and the 6th'll do right well when they get a chance. Yes, sir, General Taylor's Brigade. He's got a lot of Frenchmen from Louisiana — Acadians I've heard them called — and they can't speak a word of English, poor souls! — There goes their band again. They're always playing, dancing, and cooking rice. We call them Parlavoos — name of their county, I reckon. — He's got Wheat's Battalion, too. Sorrow a bit of a Frenchman there — they're Irish Tartars! — That's headquarters, sir. By the apple orchard."

An aide brought Cleave to a fair-sized central tent, set beside a great wine sap just coming into bloom. Around it was a space of trodden earth, to one side a cheerful fire and a darky cook, in front a pine table, over which a coloured boy was spreading a very clean tablecloth. Out of the tent came a high, piping voice. "Good-morning, Hamilton! What is it? What is it? — An officer from General Jackson? All right! All right! glad to see him. Tell him to wait — Jim, you black idiot, what have I done with that button?"

The aide smiled, Cleave smiled. There was something in the voice that announced the person, quaintly rough, lovable and gallant, — "dear Dick Ewell." He came out presently, a small man with a round bald head, hook nose and bright eyes.

"This the officer? Glad to see you, Major — Major Cleave? Stay to breakfast. Bob, you black rascal, another plate! Can't give you much, — mysterious inward complaint, myself, — can't eat anything but frumenty. — Well, sir, how is General Jackson?"

"Quite well, general."

"Most remarkable man! Wants to tie a bandage round everybody's eyes but his own!" — all this plaintively treble. "Would ask to have it off if I was facing a firing party, and in the present circumstances don't like it at all! — Did you happen to meet any of my couriers?"

"Yes, general. One at the foot of the Massanuttons, one in Elk Run Valley."

"Got to send them. Got to ask what to do. By God, out on the plains with fifty dragoons I'd know! And here President Davis has made me a major-general, and I don't know! — Draw up to the table, sir, draw up! You can drink coffee; I can't. Can't sleep at night; don't want to lie down; curl up on the ground and think of my fifty dragoons. — Well, sir, and what does General Jackson say?"

"I have a letter for you, sir."

He presented it. Ewell, head on one side like a bird, took and opened the paper. "I really do believe the sun's up at last! What does he say? '*Move in three days by Stanardsville. Take a week's rations. Rest on Sunday. Other directions will be given as needed.*' Hm! Highly characteristic! Never anything more than a damned dark lantern! — Well, it's something to know that we're going by Stanardsville and are to rest on Sunday! Where is Stanardsville?"

"It is a few miles this side of Swift Run Gap."

The general helped his guest to cornbread and himself began upon frumenty. "All right! I'll move, and I suppose when I get there old Jackson'll vouchsafe another gleam. — Bob, you damned Ethiopian, where are your wits? Fill Major Cleave's cup. — Glad to welcome you, major, to Camp Ewell. Pretty tidy place, don't you think?"

"I do indeed, sir."

"Have you seen Dick Taylor's beauties — his Creoles and Tigers and Harry Hayes, 7th Louisiana? The Maryland Line, too, and Trimble and Elzey? Damned fine army! How about yours over there?" He indicated the Blue Ridge with a bird-like jerk, and helped himself again to frumenty.

"Your description applies there, too, sir. It's a little rough and ready, but — it's a damned fine army!"

"Kernstown did n't shake it?"

"Kernstown was as much a victory as a defeat, sir. No, it did n't shake it."

"*Morale* good?"

"Extraordinarily so. That army is all right, sir."

"I wish," said Ewell plaintively, "that I knew what to make of General Jackson. What do you make of him, major?"

"I make a genius, sir."

Ewell raised his shoulder and ducked his head, his bright round eyes much like a robin's. "And he is n't crazy?"

"Not in the very least."

"Well, I've had my doubts. I am glad to hear you say that. I want to think mighty well of the man who leads me. That Romney trip now? — of course, I only heard Loring's side. He does n't just wind in and out of mountains for the fun of doing it?"

"I think that, generally speaking, he has some other object in view, sir. I think that acquaintance with General Jackson will show you what I mean. It develops confidence in a very marked fashion."

Ewell listened bright-eyed. "I am glad to hear you say that, for damn me, confidence is what I want! I want, sir, to be world-without-end-sure that my commanding officer is forever and eternally right, and then I want to be let go ahead! — I want to be let feel just as though I were a captain of fifty dragoons, and nothing to do but to get back to post by the sunset gun and report the work done! — And so you think that when my force and old Jackson's force get together we'll do big things?"

"Fairly big, sir. It is fortunate to expect them. They will arrive the sooner."

Ewell bobbed his head. "Yes, yes, that's true! Now, major, I'm going to review the troops this morning, and then I'll write an answer for General Jackson, and you'll take it to him and tell him I'm coming on by Stanardsville, just as he says, and that I'll rest on Sunday. Maybe even we'll find a church — Presbyterian." He rose. "You'd better come with me. — I've got some more questions to ask. Better see my troops, too. Old Jackson might as well know what beautiful children I've got. Have you any idea yourself what I'm expected to do at Stanardsville?"

"I don't know what General Jackson expects, sir. But my own idea is that you'll not be long at Stanardsville."

"He'll whistle again, will he?"

"I think so. But I speak without authority."

"There's an idea abroad that he means to leave the Valley — come east — cross the mountains himself instead of my crossing them. What do you think of that?"

"I am not in his council, sir. The Valley people would hate to see him go."

"Well, all that I can say is that I hope Banks is puzzled, too! — Jim, Jim! damn you, where's my sword and sash?"

As they went Ewell talked on in his piping voice. "General Jackson must n't fling my brigades against windmills or lose them in the mountains! I'm fair to confess I feel anxious. Out on the plains when we chase Apaches we chase 'em! We don't go deviating like a love vine all over creation. — That's Harry Hayes's band — playing some Frenchy thing or other! Cavalry's over there — I know you've got Ashby, but Flournoy and Munford are right wicked, too!"

"The — Virginia is with you, sir?"

"Yes. Fine regiment. You know it?"

"I know one of its officers — Major Stafford."

"Oh, we all know Maury Stafford! Fine fellow, but damned restless. General Taylor says he is in love. I was in love once myself, but I don't remember that I was restless. He is. He was with Loring but transferred. — You went to Romney together?"

"Yes, we went together."

"Fine fellow, but unhappy. Canker somewhere, I should say. Here we are, and if General Jackson don't treat my army well, I'll — I'll — I'll know he's crazy!"

The review was at last over. Back under the wine sap Ewell wrote his answer to Jackson, then, curled in a remarkable attitude on the bench beneath the tree ("I'm a nervous major-general, sir. Can't help it. Did n't sleep. Can't sleep."), put Cleave through a catechism searching and shrewd. His piping, treble voice, his varied oaths and quaintly petulant talk, his roughness of rind and inner sweetness made him, crumpled under the apple tree, in his grey garb and cavalry boots, with his bright sash and bright eyes, a figure mellow and olden out of an ancient story. Cleave also, more largely built, more muscular, a little taller, with a dark, thin, keen face, the face of a thinking man-at-arms, clad in grey, clean but worn, seated on a low stool beneath the tinted boughs, his sword between his knees, his hands clasped over the hilt, his chin on his hands — Cleave, too, speaking of skirmishes, of guns and horsemen, of the massed enemy, of mountain passes and fordable rivers, had the value of a figure from a Flemish or Venetian canvas. The form of the moment was of old time, old as the smell of apple blossoms or the buzzing of the bees; old as these and yet persistently, too, of the present as were these. The day wore on to afternoon, and at last the messenger from Jackson was released.

The — Virginia had its encampment upon the edge of a thick and venerable wood, beech and oak, walnut and hickory. Regimental headquarters was indeed within the forest, half a dozen tents pitched in a glade sylvan enough for Robin Hood. Here Cleave found Stafford sitting, writing, before the adjutant's tent. He looked up, laid down his pen and rose. "Ah! Where did you come from? I thought you in the Valley, in training for a brigadier!" He came forward, holding out his hand. "I am glad to see you. Welcome to Camp Ewell!"

Cleave's hand made no motion from his side. "Thank you," he said. "It is good when a man can feel that he is truly welcome."

The other was not dull, nor did he usually travel by indirection. "You will not shake hands," he said. "I think we have not been thrown together since that wretched evening at Bloomery Gap. Do you bear malice for that?"

"Do you think that I do?"

The other shrugged. "Why, I should not have thought so. What is it, then?"

"Let us go where we can speak without interruption. The woods down there?"

They moved down one of the forest aisles. The earth was carpeted with dead leaves from beneath which rose the wild flowers. The oak was putting forth tufts of rose velvet, the beech a veil of pale and satiny green. The sky above was blue, but, the sun being low, the space beneath the lacing boughs was shadowy enough. The two men stopped beside the bole of a giant beech, silver-grey, splashed with lichens. "Quiet enough here," said Stafford. "Well, what is it, Richard Cleave?"

"I have not much to say," said Cleave. "I will not keep you many moments. I will ask you to recall to mind the evening of the seventeenth of last April."

"Well, I have done so. It is not difficult."

"No. It would, I imagine, come readily. Upon that evening, Maury Stafford, you lied to me."

"I —"

"Don't!" said Cleave. "Why should you make it worse? The impression which, that evening, you deliberately gave me, you on every after occasion as deliberately strengthened. Your action, then and since, brands you, sir, for what you are!"

"And where," demanded Stafford hoarsely, "where did you get this precious information — or misinformation? Who was at the pains to persuade you — no hard matter, I warrant! — that I was dealing falsely? Your informant, sir, was mistaken, and I —"

A shaft of sunshine, striking between the boughs, flooded the space in which they stood. It lit Cleave's head and face as by a candle closely held. The other uttered a sound, a hard and painful gasp. "You have seen her!"

"Yes."

"Did she tell you that?"

"No. She does not know why I misunderstood. Nor shall I tell her."

"You have seen her — You are happy?"

"Yes, I am happy."

"She loves you — She is going to marry you?"

"Yes."

The wood stood very quiet. The shaft of light drew up among the boughs. Stafford leaned against the trunk of the beech. He was breathing heavily; he looked, veritably, a wounded man. "I will go now," said Cleave. "I had to speak to you and I had to warn you. Good-day."

He turned, the leaves crisp beneath his footfall. "Wait," said Stafford. "One moment — " He drew himself up against the beech. "I wish to tell you why I — as you phrase it — lied to you. I allowed you to rest under that impression which I am not sure that I myself gave you, because I thought her yet trembling between us, and that your withdrawal would be advantageous to my cause. Not for all of Heaven would I have had her turn to you! Now that, apparently, I have lost her irrevocably, I will tell you that you do not love her as I do. Have I not watched you? Did she die to-day, you would go on to-morrow with your *Duty — Duty — Duty — * ! For me, I would kill myself on her grave. Where you and I were rivals and enemies, now we are enemies. Look out for me, Richard

Cleave!" He began to laugh, a broken and mirthless sound. "Look out for me, Richard Cleave. Go!"

"I shall," said Cleave. "I will not keep a watch upon you in such a moment, nor remember it. I doubt neither your passion nor your suffering. But in one thing, Maury Stafford, you have lied again. I love as strongly, and I love more highly than you do! As for your threats —threatened men live long."

He turned, left the forest glade and came out into the camp lying now beneath the last rays of the sun. That evening he spent with Ewell and his staff, passed the night in a friendly tent, and at dawn turned Dundee's head toward the Blue Ridge.

CHAPTER XVIII

McDOWELL

A T Stanardsville he heard from a breathless crowd about the small hotel news from over the mountains. Banks was at last in motion — was marching, nineteen thousand strong, up the Valley — had seized New Market, and, most astounding and terrific of all to the village boys, had captured a whole company of Ashby's! "General Jackson?" General Jackson had burned the railway station at Mt. Jackson and fallen back — was believed to be somewhere about Harrisonburg.

"Any other news?"

"Yes, sir! Frémont's pressing south from Moorefield, Milroy east from Monterey! General Edward Johnson's had to fall back from the Alleghenies! — he's just west of Staunton. He has n't got but a brigade and a half."

"Anything more?"

"Stage's just brought the Richmond papers. All about Albert Sydney Johnston's death at Shiloh. He led the charge and a minie ball struck him, and he said 'Lay me down. Fight on.'"

"Fort Pulaski's taken! The darned gunboats battered down the wall. All of the garrison that ain't dead are prisoners."

"News from New Orleans ain't hilarious. Damned mortar boats bombard and bombard! — four ships, they say, against Fort Saint Philip, more against Fort Jackson. Air full of shells. Farragut may try to run forts and batteries, Chalmette and all —"

"What else?"

"Looks downright bad down t' Richmond. McClellan's landed seventy-five thousand men. Magruder lost a skirmish at Yorktown. All the Richmond women are making sandbags for the fortifications. Papers talk awful calm and large, but if Magruder gives way and Johnston can't keep McClellan back, I reckon there'll be hell to pay! I reckon Richmond'll fall."

"Anything more?"

"That's all to-day."

The village wag stepped forth, half innocent and half knave. "Saay, colonel! The prospects of this here Confederacy look rather *blue*."

"It is wonderful," said Cleave, "how quickly blue can turn to grey."

A portion of that night he spent at a farmhouse at the western mouth of Swift Run Gap. Between two and three he and Harris and Dundee and the grey were again upon the road. It wound through forests and by great mountains, all wreathed in a ghostly mist. The moon shone bright, but the cold was clinging. It had rained and on the soft wood road the horses feet fell noiselessly. The two men rode in silence, cloaks drawn close, hats over their eyes.

Behind them in the east grew slowly the pallor of the dawn. The stars waned, the moon lost her glitter, in the woods to either side began a faint peeping of birds. The two came to Conrad's Store, where the three or four houses lay yet asleep. An old negro, sweeping the ground before a smithy, hobbled forward at Harris's call. "Lawd, marster, enny news? I specs, sah, I'll hab ter ax you 'bout dat. I ain' heard none but dat dar wuz er skirmish at Rude's Hill, en er skirmish at New Market, en er-nurr skirmish at Sparta, en dat Gineral Jackson hold de foht, sah, at Harrisonburg, en dat de Yankees comin', lickerty-split, up de Valley, en dat de folk at Magaheysville air powerful oneasy in dey minds fer fear dey'll deviate dis way. Howsomever, we's got er home guard ef dey do come, wid ole Mr. Smith what knew Gin'ral Washington at de haid. En dar wuz some bridges burnt, I hearn, en Gineral Ashby he had er fight on de South Fork, en I cyarn think ob no mo' jes now, sah! But Gineral Jackson he sholy holdin' de foht at Harrisonburg. — Yes, sah, dat's de Magaheysville road."

The South Fork of the Shenandoah lay beneath a bed of mist. They crossed by a wooden bridge and came up again to the chill woods. Dim purple streaks showed behind them in the east, but there was yet no glory and no warmth. Before them rose a long, low mountain ridge, a road running along the crest. "That certainly is damn funny!" said Harris; "unless I've taken to seeing sights."

Cleave checked his horse. Above them, along the ridge top, was moving an army. It made no noise on the soft, moist road, artillery wheel and horse's hoof quiet alike. It seemed to wish to move quietly, without voice. The quarter of the sky above the ridge was coldly violet, palely luminous. All these figures stood out against it, soldiers with their muskets, colour-bearer with furled colours, officers on foot, officers on horseback, guns, caissons, gunners, horses, forges, ordnance wagons, commissary — van, main body and rear, an army against the daybreak sky.

"Well, if ever I saw the like of that!" breathed the orderly. "What d' ye reckon it means, sir?"

"It means that General Jackson is moving east from Harrisonburg."

"Not a sound — D' ye reckon they're ghosts, sir?"

"No. They're the Army of the Valley — There! the advance has made the turn."

Toward them swung the long column, through the stillness of the dawn, down the side of the ridge, over the soundless road, into the mist of the bottom lands. The leading regiment chanced to be the 2d; colonel and adjutant and others riding at the head. "Hello! It's Richard Cleave! — The top of the morning to you, Cleave! — knew that Old Jack had sent you off somewhere, but did n't know where. — Where are we going? By God, if you'll tell us, we'll tell you! Apparently we're leaving the Valley — damn it all! Train to Richmond by night, I reckon. We've left Fourth of July, Christmas, and New Year behind us — Banks rubbing his hands, Frémont doing a scalp dance, Milroy choosing headquarters in Staunton! Well, it does n't stand thinking of. You had as well waited for us at the Gap. The general? Just behind, head of main column. He's jerked that right hand of his into the air sixteen times since we left Harrisonburg day before yesterday, and the staff says he prays at night most powerful. Done a little praying myself; hope the Lord will look after the Valley, seeing we are n't going to do it ourselves!"

Cleave drew his horse to one side. "I'll wait here until he comes up — no, not the Lord; General Jackson. I want, too, to speak to Will. Where in column is the 65th?"

"Fourth, I think. He's a nice boy — Will. It was pretty to

watch him at Kernstown — V. M. I. airs and precision, and
gallantry enough for a dozen!"

"I'll tell him you said so, colonel! Good-bye!"

Will, too, wanted to know — he said that Mr. Rat wanted to
know — all the fellows wanted to know, what — ("I wish you'd let
me swear, Richard!") what it all meant? "Mr. Rat and I don't
believe he's responsible — it is n't in the least like his usual conduct! Old Jack backing away from cannons and such — quitting
parade ground before it's time! — marching off to barracks with
a beautiful rumpus behind him! It ain't natural! Mark my words,
Richard, and Mr. Rat thinks so, too, it's General Lee or General
Johnston, and he's got to obey and can't help himself! — What do
you think?"

"I think it will turn out all right. Now march on, boy! The
colonel says he watched you at Kernstown; says you did mighty
well — 'gallant for a dozen!'"

General Jackson on Little Sorrel was met with further on. Imperturbable and self-absorbed, with his weather-stained uniform,
his great boots, his dreadful cap, he exhibited as he rode a demeanour
in which there was neither heaviness nor lightness. Never jovial,
seldom genial, he was on one day much what he was on another —
saving always battle days. Riding with his steadfast grey-blue
eyes level before him, he communed with himself or with Heaven —
certainly not with his dissatisfied troops.

He acknowledged Cleave's salute, and took the letter which the
other produced. "Good! good! What did you do at Charlottesville?"

"I sent the stores on to Major Harman at Staunton, sir. There
was a good deal of munition." He gave a memorandum.

> One hundred rifled muskets with bayonets.
>   "   "   Belgian   "   "   "
> Fifty flintlocks.
> Two hundred pikes.
> Five hundred pounds cannon powder.
> Two   "   "   musket   "
> Five thousand rounds of cartridge.
> Eight sets artillery harness.
> Ten artillery sabres.
> One large package of lint.
> One small case drugs and surgical instruments.

"Good, good," said Jackson. "What day?"

"Monday, sir. Virginia Central that afternoon. I telegraphed to Major Harman."

"Good!" He folded the slip of paper between his large fingers and transferred it to his pocket. "I will read General Ewell's letter. Later I may wish to ask you some questions. That is all, major."

Cleave rode back to the 65th. Presently, the sun now brilliantly up, the Army of the Valley, in no sunny mood, crossed the bridge over the Shenandoah. There was a short halt. A company of Ashby's galloped from the rear and drew off into a strip of level beside the bridge. A section of artillery followed suit. The army understood that for some reason or other and for some length of time or other the bridge was to be guarded, but it understood nothing more. Presently the troops passed Conrad's Store, where the old negro, reinforced now by the dozen white inhabitants, gaped at the tramping column. The white men asked stuttering questions, and as the situation dawned upon them they indulged in irritating comment. "Say, boys, where in the Lord's name air you going? We want you on this side of the Blue Ridge — you ain't got any call to go on the other! — if you've got any Tuckahoes, let them go, but you Cohees stay in your native land — Valley men ain't got no *right* to go! *What'd the women say to you along the road?* Clearing out like a passel of yaller dogs afore there's trouble and leavin' them an' the children to entertain the Yankees!"

Harris, coming up with the orderlies, found the old negro at his mare's bridle. "Well, marster, I sholy did think I wuz tellin' de truf, sah, 'bout Gin'ral Jackson holdin' de foht at Harrisonburg! En now he done 'vacuate hit, en Gin'ral Banks he prance right in! Hit look powerful cu'rous, hit sho do. But dar! I done seed de stars all fallin' way back in '33, en dat wuz powerful cu'rous too, fer de worl' did n't come ter an eend — Mebbe, sah, he jes' er drawin' dat gent'man on?"

Sullen and sorry, the army marched on, and at noon came to Elk Run Valley on the edge of Swift Run Gap. When the men stacked arms and broke ranks, it was upon the supposition that, dinner over, they would resume the march. They did not so; they stayed ten days in Elk Run Valley.

All around were the mountains, heavily timbered, bold and path-less. Beyond Conrad's Store, covering Jackson's front, rushed the Shenandoah, the bridge guarded by Ashby's men. There were pick-ets enough between the river and the camp; north, south, and east rose the mountains, and on the other side of Swift Run Gap, near Stanardsville, lay Ewell and his eight thousand. The encampment occupied low and flat ground, through which ran a swollen creek. The spring had been on the whole inclement, and now, with sudden-ness, winter came back for a final word. One day there was a whirl of snow, another was cold and harsh, on the third there set in a chilly rain. It rained and rained, and all the mountain streams came down in torrents and still further swelled the turbid creek. One night, about halfway through their stay, the creek came out of its banks and flooded the surrounding land. All tents, huts, and shelters of boughs for a hundred feet each side acquired a liquid flooring. There arose an outcry on the midnight air. Wet and cursing, half naked and all a-shiver, men disentangled themselves from their soaked blankets, snatched up clothing and accoutrements, and splashed through a foot of icy water to slightly dryer quarters on the rising ground.

Snow, rain, freeze, thaw, impatience, listlessness, rabid con-jecture, apathetic acquiescence, quarrels, makeups, discomfort, ennui, a deal of swearing (carefully suppressed around headquarters) drill whenever practicable, two Sunday services and one prayer meeting! — the last week of April 1862 in Elk Run Valley was one to be forgotten without a pang. There was an old barn which the artillery had seized upon, that leaked like a sieve, and there was a deserted tannery that still filled the air with an evil odour, and there was change of pickets, and there were rain-sodden couriers to be observed coming and going (never anything to be gotten out of them), and there were the mountains hung with grey clouds. The wood was always wet and would not burn. Coffee was so low that it was served only every other day, besides being half chicory, and the commissary had been cheated into getting a lot of poor tobacco. The guardhouse accommodated more men than usual. A squad of Ashby's brought in five deserters, all found on the back-ward road to the Valley. One said that he was sick and that his mother had always nursed him; another that he was only going to see that the Yankees had n't touched the farm, and meant to come right back; another that the war was over, anyhow; another that he had had a bad dream and could n't rest until he saw that his wife was alive; the fifth that he was tired of living; and the sixth said nothing at all. Jackson had the six put in irons, and it was thought that after the court martial they would be shot.

On the twenty-ninth Ashby, from the other side of the Shenandoah, made a demonstration in force against the enemy at Harrisonburg, and the next day, encountering the Federal cavalry, drove them back to the town. That same afternoon the Army of the Valley, quitting without regret Elk Run Valley, found itself travelling an apparently bottomless road that wound along the base of the mountains.

"For the Lord's sake, where are we going now?"

"This is the worst road to Port Republic."

"Why are we going to Port Republic?"

"Boys, I don't know. Anyway, we ain't going through the Gap. We're still in the Valley."

"By gosh, I've heard the captain give some mighty good guesses! I'm going to ask him. — Captain, what d' ye reckon we camped ten days in that mud hole for?"

Hairston Breckinridge gave the question consideration. "Well, Tom, maybe there were reasons, after all. General Ewell, for instance — he could have joined us there any minute. They say he's going to take our place at Elk Run to-night!"

"That so? Wish him joy of the mud hole!"

"And we could have been quickly reinforced from Richmond. General Banks would know all that, and 't would make him even less eager than he seems to be to leave the beaten way and come east himself. Nobody wants *him*, you know, on the other side of the Blue Ridge."

"That's so — "

"And for all he knew, if he moved north and west to join Frémont we might pile out and strike Milroy, and if he went south and west to meet Milroy he might hear of something happening to Frémont."

"That's so — "

"And if he moved south on Staunton he might find himself

caught like a scalybark in a nut cracker — Edward Johnson on one side and the Army of the Valley on the other."

"That's so — "

"The other day I asked Major Cleave if General Jackson never amused himself in any way — never played any game, chess for instance. He said, 'Not at all — which was lucky for the other chess player.' "

"Well, he ought to know, for he's a mighty good chess player himself. And you think —"

"I think General Banks has had to stay where he is."

"And where are we going now — besides Port Republic?"

"I have n't any idea. But I'm willing to bet that we're going somewhere."

The dirt roads, after the incessant rains, were mud, mud, mud! ordinarily to the ankles, extraordinarily to the knees of the marching infantry. The wagon train moved in front, and the heavy wheels made for the rest a track something like Christian's through the Slough of Despond. The artillery brought up the rear and fared worst of all. Guns and caissons slid heavily into deep mud holes. The horses strained — poor brutes! but their iron charges stuck fast. The drivers used whip and voice, the officers swore, there arose calls for Sergeant Jordan. Appearing, that steed tamer picked his way to the horses' heads, spoke to them, patted them, and in a reasonable voice said, "Get up!" They did it, and the train dragged on to the next bog, deeper than before. Then *da capo* — stuck wheels, straining teams, oaths, adjuration, at last "Sergeant Jordan!"

So abominable was the road that the army went like a tortoise, a mud tortoise. Twilight found it little more than five miles from its starting-point, and the bivouac that night was by the comfortless roadside, in the miry bushes, with fires of wet wood, and small and poor rations. Clouds were lowering and a chilly wind fretted the forests of the Blue Ridge. Around one of the dismal, smoky fires an especially dejected mess found a spokesman with a vocabulary rich in comminations.

"Sh!" breathed one of the ring. "Officer coming by. Heard you too, Williams — all that about Old Jack."

A figure wrapped in a cloak passed just upon the rim of the firelight. "I don't think, men," said a voice, "that you are in a position to judge. If I have brought you by this road it is for your own good."

He passed on, the darkness taking him. Day dawned as best it might through grey sheets of rain. Breakfast was a mockery, damp hardtack holding the centre of the stage. A very few men had cold coffee in their canteens, but when they tried to heat it the miserable fire went out. On marched the Army of the Valley, in and out of the great rain-drenched, mist-hidden mountains, on the worst road to Port Republic. Road, surrounding levels, and creek-bed had somehow lost identity. One was like the other, and none had any bottom. Each gun had now a corps of pioneers, who, casting stone and brushwood into the morass, laboriously built a road for the piece. Whole companies of infantry were put at this work. The officers helped, the staff dismounted and helped, the commanding general was encountered, rain-dripping, mud-spattered, a log on his shoulder or a great stone in his hands. All this day they made but five miles, and at night they slept in something like a lake, with a gibing wind above to whisper *What 's it for ? — What 's it for ?*

May the second was of a piece with May the first. On the morning of May the third the clouds broke and the sun came out. It found the troops bivouacked just east of the village of Port Republic, and it put into them life and cheer. Something else helped, and that was the fact that before them, clear and shining in the morning light, stretched, not the neglected mountain road they had been travelling, but a fair Valley road, the road to Staunton.

Jackson and his staff had their quarters at the neighbouring house of General Lewis. At breakfast one of the ladies remarked that the Staunton road was in good condition, and asked the guest of honour how long it would take the army to march the eighteen miles.

"Is that the exact distance?" asked the general. "Eighteen miles?"

"Yes, sir; just about eighteen. You should get there, should you not, by night?"

"You are fortunate," said the general, "in having a great natural curiosity at your very doors. I have long wanted to see Weyers's Cave. A vast cavern like that, hollowed out by God's finger, hung with stalactites, with shells and banners of stone, filled with sounding aisles, run through by dark rivers in which swim blind fish — how wonderful a piece of His handiwork! I have always wished to see it — the more so that my wife has viewed it and told me of its marvels. I always wish, madam, to rest my eyes where my wife's have rested."

The bugles ringing "Fall in!" were positively sweet to the ears of the soldiers of the Valley. "Fall in? with pleasure, sir! Eighteen miles? What's eighteen miles when you're going home? It's a fine old road anyhow, with more butterflies on it! We'll double-quick it all the way if Old Jack wants us!"

"That man back there says Staunton's awfully anxious. Says people all think we've gone to reinforce Richmond without caring a damn what becomes of the Valley. Says Milroy is within ten miles of Staunton, and Banks's just waiting a little longer before he pulls up stakes at Harrisonburg and comes down the pike to join him. Says Edward Johnson ain't got but a handful, and that the Staunton women are hiding their silver. Says — Here's Old Jack, boys! going to lead us himself back to Goshen! One cheer ain't enough — *three cheers for General Jackson!*"

Jackson, stiffly lifting the old forage cap, galloped by upon Little Sorrel. His staff behind him, he came to the head of the column where it was drawn up on the fair road leading through Port Republic, south and west to Staunton. Close on the eastern horizon rose the Blue Ridge. To this side turned off a rougher, narrower way, piercing at Brown's Gap the great mountain barrier between the Valley and Piedmont Virginia.

The column was put into motion, the troops stepping out briskly. Warm and lovely was the sunshine, mildly still the air. Big cherry trees were in bloom by the wayside: there was a buzzing of honey bees, a slow fluttering of yellow butterflies above the fast drying mud puddles. Throughout the ranks sounded a clearing of throats; it was evident that the men felt like singing, presently would sing. The head of the column came to the Brown's Gap Road.

"What's that stony old road?" asked a Winchester man.

"That's a road over the mountains into Albemarle. Thank the Lord — "

"*Column left.* MARCH!"

It rang infernally. *Column left.* MARCH! — Not a freight boat horn winding up the James at night, not the minie's long screech, not Gabriel's trump, not anything could have sounded at this moment so mournfully in the ears of the Army of the Valley. It wheeled to the left, it turned its back to the Valley, it took the stony road to Brown's Gap, it deeply tasted the spring of tragic disappointment.

The road climbed and climbed through the brilliant weather. Spur and wall, the Blue Ridge shimmered in May greenery, was wrapped in happy light and in sweet odours, was carpeted with wild flowers and ecstatic with singing birds. Only the Army of the Valley was melancholy — desperately melancholy. Here and there through openings, like great casements in the foliage, wide views might be had of the Valley they were leaving. Town and farm and mill with turning wheel were there, ploughed land and wheat fields, Valley roads and Valley orchards, green hills and vales and noble woods, all the great vale between mountain chains, two hundred miles from north to south, twenty-five from Blue Ridge to Alleghenies! The men looked wistfully, with grieved, children's faces.

At the top of the mountain there was a short halt. The up-hill pull had been hard enough, heavy hearts and all! The men dropped upon the earth between the pine trees of the crest. For the most part they lay in the sullen silence with which they had climbed. Some put their heads upon their arms, tilted hat or cap over their eyes. Others chewed a twig or stalk of grass and gazed upon the Valley they were leaving, or upon the vast eastward stretch of Piedmont, visible also from the mountain top. It was bright and quiet up here above the world. The sunshine drew out the strong, life-giving odour of the pines, the ground was dry and warm, it should have been a pleasant place to drowse in and be happy. But the Valley soldiers were not happy. Jackson, riding by a recumbent group, spoke from the saddle. "That's right, men! You rest all over, lying down." In the morning this group had cheered him loudly; now it saluted in a genuine "Bath to Romney" silence. He rode by, imperturbable. His chief engineer was with him, and they went on to a flat rock commanding both the great views, east and west. Here they dismounted, and between them unfurled a large map, weighting its corners with pine cones. The soldiers below

them gazed dully. Old Jack — or Major-General T. J. Jackson —
or Fool Tom Jackson was forever looking at maps. It was a trick
of his, as useless as saying " Good! good! " or jerking his hand in
the air in that old way.

That evening the Army of the Valley slept in emerald meadows
beside Meechum's River in Albemarle. Coming down the mountain it had caught distant glimpses of white spirals of smoke floating from the overworked engines of the Virginia Central; and now
it lay near a small country station, and there on the switch were
empty cars and empty cars! — *cars to go to Richmond on.* The army
groaned and got its supper, took out its pipe and began, though reluctantly enough, to regard the situation with a philosophic eye.
What was done was done! The Blue Ridge lay between it and the
Valley, and after all Old Joe must be wanting soldiers pretty badly
down at Richmond! The landscape was lovely, the evening tranquil and sweet. The army went to bed early, and went in a frame
of mind approaching resignation. This was Saturday evening; Old
Jack would rest to-morrow.

Sunday dawned clear and sweet. Pleasant morning — no drill,
and light camp duties — coffee, hot biscuits, good smoke — general
Sunday atmosphere — bugler getting ready to sound " Church! "
— regimental chaplains moving toward chosen groves — " Old Hundred " in the air. — " Oh, come on and go! All the people are going
at home."

And, after all, no one in the Army of the Valley went to church!
The bugler blew another call, the chaplains stopped short in their
sedate stride, short as if they had been shot, " Old Hundred " was
not sung. *Break camp — Break camp!*

The regiments, marching down to Meechum's Station, were of
one mind. *Old Jack was losing his religion.* Manassas on Sunday —
Kernstown on Sunday — forced marches on Sunday — Sunday train
to Richmond. Language failed.

There were long lines of cars, some upon the main track, others
on the siding. The infantry piled in, piled atop. Out of each
window came three or four heads. "You fellows on the roof,
you're taller'n we are! Air we the first train? That's good, we'll
be the first to say howdy to McClellan. You all up there, don't

dangle your legs that-a-way! You're as hard to see through as Old Jack!"

Company after company filed into the poor old cars that were none too large, whose ante-bellum days were their best days, who never had time now to be repaired or repainted, or properly cleaned. Squad by squad swung itself up to the cindery roof and sat there in rows, feet over the edge, the central space between heaped with haversacks and muskets.

"2d — 4th — 5th — 65th — Jerusalem! the whole brigade's going on this train! Another's coming right behind — why don't they wait for it? Crowding gentlemen in this inconsiderate fashion! Oh, ain't it hot? Wish I was going to Niagara, to a Know-Nothing Convention! Our train's full. There's the engine coming down the siding! You all on top, can you see the artillery and the wagons?"

"Yes. Way over there. Going along a road — nice shady road. Rockbridge 's leading — "

"That's the road to Rockfish Gap."

"Rockfish Gap? Go 'way! You've put your compass in the wrong pocket. Rockfish Gap's back where we came from. Look out!"

The backing engine and the waiting cars came together with a grinding bump. An instant's pause, a gathering of force, a mighty puffing and, slow and jerkily, the cars began to move. The ground about Meechum's Station was grey with soldiers — part of the Stonewall, most of Burk's and Fulkerson's brigades, waiting for the second train and the third train and their turn to fill the cars. They stood or leaned against the station platform, or they sat upon the warm red earth beneath the locust trees, white and sweet with hanging bloom. "Good-bye, boys! See you in Richmond — Richmond on the James! Don't fight McClellan till we get there! That engine's just pulling them beyond the switch. Then that one below there will back up and hitch on at the eastern end. — That's funny!" The men sitting on the warm red earth beneath the locust trees sprang to their feet. "That train ain't coming back! Before the Lord, they're going *west!*"

Back to Meechum's Station, from body and top of the out-going train floated wild cheering. "Staunton! We're going to Staunton! We're going back to the Valley! We're going home!

We're going to get there first! We're going to whip Banks! We've got Old Jack with *us*. You all hurry up. Banks thinks we've gone to Richmond, but we ain't! *Yaaaih! Yaaaaihhh! Yaaaih! Yaaaaaaih!* "

At Meechum's Station, beneath the locust trees, it was like bees swarming. Another train was on the main track, the head beautifully, gloriously westward! "Staunton! Good-bye, you little old Richmond, we ain't going to see you this summer! — Feel good? I feel like a shouting Methodist! My grandmother was a shouting Methodist. I feel I'm going to shout — anyhow, I've got to sing — "

A chaplain came by with a beaming face. "Why don't we all sing, boys? I'm sure I feel like it. It's Sunday."

How firm a foundation, ye saints of the Lord —

In Staunton it had been a day of indigo gloom. The comfortable Valley town, fair-sized and prosperous, with its pillared court house, its old hotel, its stores, its up and down hill streets, its many and shady trees, its good brick houses, and above the town its quaintly named mountains — Staunton had had, in the past twelve months, many an unwonted throb and thrill. To-day it was in a condition of genuine, dull, steady anxiety, now and then shot through by a fiercer pang. There had been in town a number of sick and convalescent soldiers. All these were sent several days before, eastward, across the mountains. In the place were public and military stores. At the same time, a movement was made toward hiding these in the woods on the other side of the twin mountains Betsy Bell and Mary Grey. It was stopped by a courier from the direction of Swift Run Gap with a peremptory order. *Leave those stores where they are.* Staunton grumbled and wondered, but obeyed. And now the evening before, had come from Port Republic, eighteen miles toward the Blue Ridge, a breathless boy on a breathless horse, with tidings that Jackson was at last and finally gone from the Valley — had crossed at Brown's Gap that morning! "Called to Richmond!" groaned the crowd that accompanied the boy on his progress toward official Staunton. "Reckon Old Joe and General Lee think we're small potatoes and few in a row. They ain't, either of them, a Valley man. Reckon this time to-mor-

row Banks and Milroy'll saunter along and dig us up! There's old
Watkin's bugle! Home Guard, come along and drill!"

Staunton did little sleeping that Saturday night. Jackson was
gone — Ashby with him. There was not a Confederate vedette
between the town and Banks at Harrisonburg — the latter was
probably moving down the pike this very night, in the dark of the
moon. Soldiers of Edward Johnson — tall Georgians and 44th
Virginians — had been in town that Saturday, but they two were
gone, suddenly recalled to their camp, seven miles west, on the
Parkersburg road. Scouts had reported to Johnson that Milroy
was concentrating at M'Dowell, twenty miles to the westward, and
that Schenck, sent on by Frémont, had joined or would join him.
Any hour they might move eastward on Staunton. Banks — Frémont — Milroy — three armies, forty thousand men — all converging on Staunton and its Home Guard, with the intent to
make it even as Winchester! Staunton felt itself the mark of
the gods, a mournful Rome, an endangered Athens, a tottering
Carthage.

Sunday morning, clear and fine, had its church bells. The children
went to Sunday School, where they learned of Goliath and the
brook Hebron, and David and his sling. At church time the pews
were well filled — chiefly old men and women and young boys. The
singing was fervent, the prayers were yet more so. The people
prayed very humbly and heartily for their Confederacy, for their
President and his Cabinet, and for Congress, for their Capital, so
endangered, for their armies and their generals, for every soldier
who wore the grey, for their blocked ports, for New Orleans, fallen
last week, for Norfolk that the authorities said must be abandoned, for Johnston and Magruder on the Peninsula — at that
very hour, had they known it, in grips with Hancock at Williamsburg.

Benediction pronounced, the congregation came out of the
churchyards in time to greet with delight, not unmixed with a sense
of the pathos of it, certain just arrived reinforcements. Four companies of Virginia Military Institute cadets, who, their teachers at
their head, had been marched down for the emergency from Lexington, thirty-eight miles away. Flushed, boyish, trig, grey and white
uniformed, with shining muskets, seventeen years old at most,

beautifully marching with their band and their colours, amidst plaudits, tears, laughter, flowers, thrown kisses, they came down the street, wheeled, and before the court house were received by the Home Guard, an organization of greyheaded men.

Sunday afternoon brought many rumours. Milroy would march from McDowell to-morrow — Banks was coming down the turnpike — Frémont hovering closer. Excited country people flocked into town. Farmers whose sons were with Jackson came for advice from leading citizens. Ought they to bring in the women and children? — no end of foreigners with the blue coats, and foreigners are rough customers! And stock? Better drive the cows up into the mountains and hide the horses? "Tom Watson says they're awful wanton, — take what they want and kill the rest, and no more think of paying! — Says, too, they're burning barns. What d'you think we'd better do, sir?" There were Dunkards in the Valley who refused to go to war, esteeming it a sin. Some of these were in town, coming in on horseback or in their white-covered wagons, and bringing wife or daughter. The men were long-bearded and venerable of aspect; the women had peaceful Quaker faces, framed by the prim close bonnet of their peculiar garb. These quiet folk, too, were anxious-eyed. They would not resist evil, but their homes and barns were dear to their hearts.

By rights the cadets should have been too leg weary for parade, but if Staunton (and the young ladies) wished to see how the V. M. I. did things, why, of course! In the rich afternoon light, band playing, Major Smith at their head, the newly-arrived Corps of Defence marched down the street toward a green field fit for evolutions. With it, on either sidewalk, went the town at large, specifically the supremely happy, small boy. The pretty girls were already in the field, seated, full skirted beneath the sweet locust trees.

V. M. I., Home Guard, and attendant throng neared the Virginia Central. A whistle shrieked down the line, shrieked with enormous vigour — "What's that? Train due?" — "No. Not due for an hour — always late then! Better halt until it pulls in. Can't imagine —"

The engine appeared, an old timer of the Virginia Central, excitedly puffing dark smoke, straining in, like a racer to the goal.

Behind it cars and cars — *cars with men atop!* They were all in grey — they were all yelling — the first car had a flag, the battle-flag of the Confederacy, the dear red ground, and the blue Saint Andrew's Cross and the white stars. There were hundreds of men! hundreds and hundreds, companies, regiments, on the roof, on the platforms, half out of the windows, waving, shouting — no! singing —

> "We're the Stonewall.
>   Zoom! Zoom!
>   We're the openers of the ball.
>   Zoom! Zoom!

> "Fix bayonets! Charge!
>   Rip! Rip!
>   N. P. Banks for our targe.
>   Zip! Zip!

> "We wrote it on the way.
>   Zoom! Zoom!
>   Hope you like our little lay.
>   Zoom! Zoom!
> For we did n't go to Richmond and we're coming home to stay!"

Four days later, on Sitlington's Hill, on the Bull Pasture Mountain, thirty miles to the west of Staunton, a man sat at nightfall in the light of a great camp-fire and wrote a dispatch to his Government. There waited for it a swift rider — watching the stars while the general wrote, or the surgeons' lanterns, like fireflies, wandering up and down the long green slopes where the litter bearers lifted the wounded, friend and foe.

The man seated on the log wrote with slow precision a long dispatch, covering several pages of paper. Then he read it over, and then he looked for a minute or two at the flitting lanterns, and then he slowly tore the dispatch in two, and fed the fire with the pieces. The courier, watching him write a much shorter message, half put forth his hand to take it, for his horse whinnied upon the road far below, and the way to Staunton was long and dark. However, Jackson's eyes again dwelt on the grey slopes before him and on the Alleghenies, visited by stars, and then, as slowly as before, he tore this dispatch also across and across and dropped the pieces on the brands. When they were burned he wrote a single line, signed and folded it, and gave it to the courier. The latter, in the first pink light, in the midst of a jubilant Staunton, read it to the excited operator in the little telegraph station.

"God blessed our arms with victory at McDowell yesterday.
"T. J. JACKSON
"*Major-General.*"

CHAPTER XIX

THE FLOWERING WOOD

THANK you, ma'am," said Allan. "I reckon just so long as there are such women in the Valley there'll be worth-while men there, too! You've all surely done your share."

"Now, you've got the pot of apple butter, and the bucket with the honeycomb, and the piece of bacon and the light bread. If you'd come a little earlier I could have let you have some eggs —"

"I've got a feast for a king. — All these fighting men going up and down the Valley are going to eat you out of house and home. — I got some pay two months ago, and I've enough left to make it fairer — "

He drew out a Confederate note. The woman on the doorstep looked at it admiringly, and, taking it from him, examined either side. "They make them pretty as a picture," she said. "Once't I was in Richmond and saw the Capitol. That's a good picture of it. And that statue of General Washington! — My! his horse's just dancing as they say Ashby's does to music. One of those bronze men around the base is a forebear of mine." She gave back the note. "I had a little mite of real coffee that I'd have liked to give you — but it's all gone. Howsoever, you won't go hungry with what you've got. Have you a nice place to sleep in?"

"The nicest in the world. A bed of oak leaves and a roof all stars."

"You could stay here to-night. I've got a spare room."

"You're just as good as gold," said Allan. "But I want to be out where I can hear the news. I'm a scout, you see."

"I thought that, watching you come up the path. We're learning fast. Used to be I just thought a soldier was a soldier! I never thought of there being different kinds. Do you think the army'll come this way?"

"I shouldn't be surprised," said Allan. "Indeed, I'm rather expecting it. But you never know. How many of your people are in it?"

"A lot of cousins. But my sons are with Johnston. Richmond's more 'n a hundred miles away, I reckon, but all last night I thought I heard the cannon. Well, good-bye! I'm mighty glad to see you all again in the Valley. Be sure to come back for your breakfast — and if the army passes I've got enough for one or two besides. Good-bye — God bless you."

Allan left behind the small brick farmhouse, stopped for a drink at the spring, then climbed a rail fence and made across a rolling field of bright green clover to a width of blossoming woods, beyond which ran the Mt. Solon and Bridgewater road. From the forest issued a curl of blue vapour and a smell of wood smoke. The scout, entering, found a cheerful, unnecessarily large fire. Stretched beside it, upon the carpet of last year's leaves, lay Billy Maydew, for whose company he had applied upon quitting, a week before, the army between McDowell and Franklin. Allan snuffed the air. "You build too big a fire, Billy! 'T is n't a good scout's way of doing."

Billy laid down horizontally upon the leaves the stick he had been whittling. "Thar ain't anybody but home folks to smell it. Did n't we see Ashby on the black stallion draw a line like that thar stick across the Valley with a picket post for every knot?" He sat up. "Did you get anything to eat?"

"I certainly did. There surely are good women in the land!" Allan disburdened himself. "Rake the coals out and get the skillet."

Afterwards they lay prone upon the leaves and talked. They had much of life in common; they were as at home with each other as two squirrels frequenting the same tree. Now, as they lay beneath two clouds from two briar-roots, they dwelt for some time upon Thunder Run, then from that delectable region turned to the here and now. Allan had taught Billy, finding him a most unsatisfactory pupil. Billy had in those days acquired little book learning, but a very real respect for the blond giant now lying opposite to him. Since coming to the army he had been led to deplore his deficiencies, and, a week ago, he had suggested to Allan that in the interim of active scouting the latter should continue his education. "When thar air a chance I want to swap into the artillery. Three bands of red thar," he drew a long finger across his sleeve, "air my ambition. I reckon then Christianna and all the Thunder Run girls would stop saying 'Billy.' They'd say 'Sergeant Maydew.' An artillery sergeant's got to be head in ciphering, and he's got to be able to read words of mor'n one — one —"

"Syllable."

"That's it. Now they are n't any printed books hereabouts, but you've got it all in your head —"

"I can't teach you much," Allan had said soberly, "whispering under bushes and listening for Schenck's cavalry! We might do something, though. You were an awful poor speller. Spell 'sergeant' — now 'ordnance' — now 'ammunition' — 'battery' — 'caisson' — 'Howitzer' — 'Napoleon' — 'Tredegar' — 'limber' — 'trail' — 'cannon-powder' — ."

In the week Billy had made progress — more progress than in a session on Thunder Run. Now, lying in the woods a little west of Mt. Solon, waiting for the army moving back to the Valley, this time from the west, from the Allegheny fastnesses, he accomplished with éclat some oral arithmetic — "If two Yankee Parrotts are fired every eight minutes, and in our battery we serve the howitzer every nine minutes, the Napoleon every ten, the two six-pounders every eleven, and if the Yankees limber up and leave at the end of an hour, how many shells will have been thrown?" — "If it is a hundred and ten miles from Harrisonburg to the Potomac, and if Old Jack's foot cavalry advances twenty-two miles a day, and if we lay off a day for a battle, and if we have three skirmishes each occupying two hours, and if Banks makes a stand of half a day at Winchester, and if Frémont executes a flank movement and delays us six hours, just how long will it be before Old Jack pushes Banks into the Potomac?" — "If Company A had ninety men when it started ('thar war a full hundred') and five men died of measles and pneumonia (''t were six'), and if we recruited three at Falling Springs, and six were killed at Manassas and sixteen wounded, half of whom never came back, and we got twelve recruits at Centreville and seven more at Winchester, and if five straggled on the Bath and Romney trip and were never heard of more, and if five were killed at Kernstown and a dozen are still in the hospital, and if ten more recruits came in at Rude's Hill and if we left four sick at Magaheysville, and if we lost none at McDowell, not being engaged, but two in a skirmish since, and if Steve Dagg straggled three times but was brought back and tried to desert twice but never got any further than the guardhouse — how many men are in Company A?" — "If" — this was Billy's — "if I have any luck in the next battle, and if I air found to have a speaking acquaintance with every damned thousand-legged word the captain asks me about, and I get to be a sergeant, and I air swapped into the artillery, and thar's a big fight, and my battery and Company A are near, and Sergeant Mathew Coffin gets into trouble right next door to me, and he cried out a hundred times (lying right thar in the zone of fire), 'Boys, come take me out of hell!' and the company all was forced back, and all the gunners, and I was left thar serving my gun, just as pretty and straight, and he cried out anoth'r hundred times, 'Billy Maydew, come pick me up and carry me out of hell' — and I just served on a hundred times, only looking at him every time the gun thundered and I straightened up—"

"For shame!" cried Allan. "I've heard Steve Dagg say something like that about Richard Cleave." Billy sat up indignant. "It air not like that at all! The major air what he is, and Steve Dagg air what he is! Sergeant Mathew Coffin air what somebody or other called somebody else in that thar old history book you used to make us learn! He air 'a petty tyrant.' He air that, and Thunder Run don't like that kind. He air not going to tyrannize much longer over Billy Maydew. And don't you be comparing me to Steve Dagg. I ain't like that, and I never was."

He lay prone again, insulted, and would not go on with the lesson. Allan took it calmly, made a placating remark or two, and lapsed into a friendly silence. It was pleasant in the woods, where the birds flitted to and fro, and the pink honeysuckle grew around, and from a safe distance a chipmunk daintily watched the intruders. The scout lay, drowsily happy, the sunshine making spun gold of his hair and beard, his carbine resting near. Back on Thunder Run, at the moment, Christianna in her pink sunbonnet, a pansy from the tollgate at her throat, rested upon her hoe in the garden she was making and looked out over the great sea of mountains visible from the Thunder Run eyrie. Shadows of clouds moved over them; then the sun shone out and they lay beneath in an amethystine dream; Christianna had had her dream the night before. In her sleep she had come upon a dark pool beneath alders, and she had knelt upon the black bank and plunged her arms to the shoulders into the water. It seemed in her dream that there was something at the bottom that she wanted — a breastpin or a piece of money. And she had drawn up something that weighed heavily and filled her arms. When she had lifted it halfway out of the water the moon came out, and it was Allan Gold. She stood now in her steep mountain garden bordered with phlox and larkspur and looked far out over the long and many ridges. She knew in which general direction to look, and with her mind's eye she tried to see the fighting men, the fighting men; and then she shook her head and bent to her hoeing — far back and high up on Thunder Run.

Thirty leagues away, in the flowering wood by the Mt. Solon road Allan sat up. "I was nearly asleep," he said, "back on the mountain-side above Thunder Run." He listened. "Horses' hoofs — a squad at a trot, coming east! some of Ashby's of course, but you stay here and put earth on the fire while I take a look." Rifle in hand, he threaded the thick undergrowth between the camp and the road.

It was late in the afternoon, but the road lay yet in sunshine between the clover and the wheat, the bloomy orchards and the woods of May. Allan's precautions had been largely instinctive; there were no Federals, he had reason to be sure, south of Strasburg. He looked to see some changing picket post of Ashby's. But the five horsemen who came in sight, three riding abreast, two a little behind, had not a Valley air. "Tidewater men," said Allan to himself. "How far is it to Swift Run Gap? Should n't wonder if General Ewell —"

A minute later the party came in line with the woods. Allan, after another deliberate look, stepped from behind a flowering thorn. The party drew up. "Good-afternoon, my man," said the stars and wreath in the centre in a high, piping voice. "Alone, are you? — Ain't straggling, I hope? Far too many stragglers — curse of this service — civilians turned soldiers and all that. What's that? You know him, Stafford? One of General Jackson's scouts? — Then do you know, pray, where is General Jackson? for, by God, I don't!"

"I came across country myself to-day, sir — I and a boy that's with me. We've been ahead with Ashby, fending off Frémont. General Jackson is marching very rapidly, and I expect him to-night."

"Where's he going, then?"

"I haven't the least idea, sir."

"Well," piped Ewell, "I'll be glad to see him. God knows, I don't know what I'm to do! Am I to strengthen Johnston at Richmond? Am I to cross into the Valley — by God, it's lovely! — and reinforce Jackson? Damn it, gentlemen, I'm a major-general on a seesaw! Richmond in danger — Valley in danger. 'Better come to me!' says Johnston. Quite right! He needs every man. 'Better stay with Jackson,' says Lee. Quite right again! Old Jackson has three armies before him and only a handful. 'Better gallop across and find out the crazy man's own mind,' says the major-general in the middle." He turned with the suddenness of a bird to Allan. "By God, I'm hungry as a coyote! Have you got anything to eat?"

"I've some bread and bacon and a few eggs and half a pot of apple butter and a piece of honeycomb, sir —"

Ewell dismounted. "You're the foster brother I've been in search of for thirty-five years! Maury and John, it sounds as though there were enough for four. Deane and Edmondson, you ride on to that mill I see in front of us, and ask if the folks won't give you supper. We'll pick you up in an hour or so. Now, my friend in need, we'll build a fire and if you've got a skillet I'll show you how an omelette ought to be made and generally is n't!"

Within the covert Billy made up the fire again, and General Ewell, beneath the amused eyes of his aides, sliced bacon, broke eggs into the skillet and produced an omelette which was a triumph. He was, in truth, a master cook — and everything was good and savoury — and the trio was very hungry. Ewell had cigars, and smoked them like a Spaniard — generous, too — giving freely to the others. As often as it burned low Billy threw dried sticks upon the fire. The evening was cool, the shadows advancing; the crackling light and warmth grateful enough. The newcomers asked questions. They were eager to know — all the country was keen-set to know — eye-witnesses of events were duly appreciated. The scout had been at McDowell?

"Yes, but not in the battle, the Stonewall Brigade not being engaged. 12th Georgia did best — and the 44th Virginia. 12th

Georgia held the crest. There was one man, just a boy like Billy there ('I'm eighteen!' from Billy) — could n't anybody keep him back, behind the rise where our troops were lying down. 'We did n't come all this way to hide from Yankees,' he cried, and he rushed out and down upon them — poor fellow!"

"That's the spirit. In the morning you followed on?"

"Yes, but Milroy and Schenck did not do badly. That was a good fetch of theirs — firing the forest! Everywhere a great murk with tongues of flame — smoke in nostril and eyes and the wind blowing fast. It looked like the end of the world. Old Jack — beg pardon, sir, General Jackson — General Jackson could n't but smile, it was such excellent tactics. We drew off at last, near Franklin, and the army went into camp for a bit. Billy and I have been with a squadron of Ashby's."

"Keeping Frémont back?"

"Yes. General Jackson wanted the passes blocked. We did it pretty thoroughly."

"How?"

"Burned all the bridges; cut down trees — in one place a mile of them — and made abatis, toppled boulders over the cliffs and choked the roads. If Frémont wants to get through he'll have to go round Robin Hood's Barn to do it! He's out of the counting for awhile, I reckon. At least he won't interfere with our communications. Ashby has three companies toward the mountains. He's picketed the Valley straight across below Woodstock. Banks can't get even a spy through from Strasburg. I've heard an officer say — you know him, Major Stafford — Major Cleave — I've heard him say that General Jackson uses cavalry as Napoleon did and as no one has done since."

Ewell lit another cigar. "Well, I'm free to confess that old Jackson is n't as crazy as an idiot called Dick Ewell thought him! As Milton says, 'There's method in his madness' — Shakespeare, was it, Morris? Don't read much out on the plains."

The younger aide had been gleeful throughout the recital. "Stonewall's a good name, by George! but, by George! they ought to call him the Artful Dodger —"

Maury Stafford burst into laughter. "By Heaven. Morris, you'd better tell him that! Have you ever seen him?"

"No. They say he's real pious and as simple as they make them — but Lord! there has n't been anything simple about his late proceedings."

Stafford laughed again. "Religious as Cromwell, and artless as Macchiavelli! Begins his orders with an honourable mention of God, closes them with 'Put all deserters in irons,' and in between gives points to Reynard the Fox —"

Ewell took his cigar from his lips. "Don't be so damned sarcastic, Maury! It's worse than drink — Well, Deane?"

One of his troopers had appeared. "A courier has arrived, general, with a letter from General Jackson. I left him at the mill and came back to report. There's a nice little office there with a light and writing materials."

Dusk filled the forest, the night came, and the stars shone between the branches. A large white moon uprose and made the neighbouring road a milky ribbon stretched east and west. A zephyr just stirred the myriad leaves. Somewhere, deeper in the woods, an owl hooted at intervals, very solemnly. Billy heaped wood upon the fire, laid his gun carefully, just so, stretched himself beside it and in three minutes reached the deepest basin of sleep. Allan sat with his back to the hickory, and the firelight falling upon the leaves of a book he had borrowed from some student in the ranks. It was a volume of Shelley, and the young man read with serious appreciation. He was a lover of poetry, and he was glad to meet with this poet whose works he had not been able as yet to put upon his book-shelf, back in the little room, under the eaves of the tollgate. He read on, bent forward, the firelight upon his ample frame, gold of hair and beard, and barrel of the musket lying on the leaves beside him.

> O Love! who bewailest
> The frailty of all things here,
> Why choose you the frailest
> For your cradle, your home, and your bier?

Allan made the fire yet brighter, listened a moment to the hooting of the owl, then read on: —

> Its passions will rock thee
> As the storms rock the ravens on high;
> Bright reason will mock thee —

He ceased to read, turning his head, for he heard a horse upon the road, coming from the direction of the mill. It came slowly, with much of weariness in the very hoof sounds, then left the road for the woodside and stopped. Ensued a pause while the rider fastened it to some sapling, then, through the bushes, the former came toward the camp-fire. He proved to be Maury Stafford. "The courier says General Jackson will reach Mt. Solon about midnight. General Ewell is getting an hour's sleep at the mill. I am not sleepy and your fire is attractive. May I keep you company for awhile?"

Allan was entirely hospitable. "Certainly, sir! Spread your cloak just there — the wind will blow the smoke the other way. Well, we'll all be glad to see the army!"

"What are you reading?"

Allan showed him. "Humph! —

> Its passions will rock thee
> As the storms rock the ravens on high;
> Bright reason will mock thee —

Well — we all know the man was a seer."

He laid the book down upon the grey cloak lined with red and sat with his chin in his hand, staring at the fire. Some moments elapsed before he spoke; then, "You have known Richard Cleave for a long time?"

"Yes. Ever since we were both younger than we are now. I like him better than any one I know — and I think he's fond of me."

"He seems to have warm friends."

"He has. He 's true as steel, and big-minded. He's strong-thewed — in and out."

"A little clumsily simple sometimes, do you not think? Lawyer and soldier grafted on Piers Ploughman, and the seams not well hidden? I would say there's a lack of grace —"

"I have not noticed it," said Allan dryly. "He's a very good leader."

The other smiled, though only with the lips. "Oh, I am not decrying him! Why should I? I have heard excellent things of him. He is a favourite, is he not, with General Jackson?"

"I don't think that General Jackson has favourites."

"At least, he is no longer in disfavour. I remember toward the close of the Romney expedition —"

"Oh, that!" said Allan, "that was nothing." He put down his pipe. "Let me see if I can explain to you the ways of this army. You don't know General Jackson as we do, who have been with him ever since a year ago and Harper's Ferry! In any number of things he's as gentle as a woman; in a few others he — is n't. In some things he's like iron. He's rigid in his discipline, and he'll tolerate no shade of insubordination, or disobedience, or neglect of duty. He's got the defect of his quality, and sometimes he'll see those things where they are not. He does n't understand making allowances or forgiving. He'll rebuke a man in general orders, hold him up — if he's an officer — before the troops, and all for something that another general would hardly notice! He'll make an officer march without his sword for whole days in the rear of his regiment, and all for something that just a reprimand would have done for! As you say, he made the very man we're talking of do that from Bloomery Gap to Romney — and nobody ever knew why. Just the other day there were some poor fools of twelve-month men in one of our regiments who concluded they did n't want to reënlist. They said they'd go home and cried out for their discharge. And they had forgotten all about the conscription act that Congress had just passed. So, when the discharge was refused they got dreadfully angry, and threw down their arms. The colonel went to the general, and the general almost put him under arrest. 'Why does Colonel Grigsby come to me to learn how to deal with mutineers? Shoot them where they stand.' — Kernstown, too. There's hardly a man of the Stonewall that does n't think General Garnett justified in ordering that retreat, and yet look at Garnett! Under arrest, and the commanding general preferring charges against him! Says he did not wait for orders, lost the battle and so on. With Garnett it is a deadly serious matter — rank and fame and name for courage all in peril —"

"I see. But with Richard Cleave it was not serious?"

"Not in the least. These smaller arrests and censures — not even the best can avoid them. I should n't think they were pleasant, for sometimes they are mentioned in reports, and sometimes they get home to the womenfolk. But his officers understand him by now, and they keep good discipline, and they had rather be led by Stonewall Jackson than by an easier man. As for Richard

Cleave, I was with him on the march to McDowell and he looked a happy man."

"Ah!"

The conversation dropped. The scout, having said his say, easily relapsed into silence. His visitor, half reclining upon his cloak beneath an old, gnarled tree, was still. The firelight played strangely over his face, for now it seemed the face of one man, now that of another. In the one aspect he looked intent, as though in his mind he mapped a course. In the other he showed only weariness, dashed with something tragic — a handsome, brooding, melancholy face. They stayed like this for some time, the fire burning before them, the moon flooding the forest, the owl hooting from his hole in some decaying tree.

At last, however, another sound intruded, a very low, subdued sound like a distant ground swell or like thunder without resonance. It grew; dull yet, it became deep. Allan knocked the ashes from his pipe. "That is a sound," he said, "that when you have once heard you don't forget. The army's coming."

Stafford rose. "I must get back to General Ewell! Thank you, Gold, for your hospitality."

"Not at all! Not at all!" said Allan heartily. "I am glad that I could put that matter straight for you. It would blight like black frost to have Stonewall Jackson's hand and mind set against you — and Richard Cleave is not the least in that predicament!"

The Army of the Valley, advance and main column, and rearguard, artillery and wagon train, came down the moon-lighted road, having marched twenty miles since high noon. On either hand stretched pleasant pastures, a running stream, fair woods. Company by company the men left the road, were halted, stacked arms, broke ranks. Cessation from motion was sweet, sweet the feel of turf beneath their feet. They had had supper three hours before; now they wanted sleep, and without much previous ado they lay down and took it — Stonewall Jackson's "foot cavalry" sleeping under the round moon, by Mt. Solon.

At the mill there was a meeting and a conference. A figure in an old cloak and a shabby forage cap dismounted, ungracefully enough, from a tired nag, and crossed the uncovered porch to the wide mill door. There he was met by his future trusty and trusted lieutenant

— "dear Dick Ewell." Jackson's greeting was simple to baldness. Ewell's had the precision of a captain of dragoons. Together they entered the small mill office, where the aides placed lights and writing materials, then withdrew. The generals sat down, one on this side of the deal table, one on that. Jackson took from his pocket a lemon, very deliberately opened a knife, and, cutting the fruit in two, put one half of the sour treasure to his lips. Ewell fidgeted, then, as the other sucked on, determined to set the ball rolling. "Damn me, general! if I am not glad to have the pleasure at last —"

Jackson sent across the table a grey-blue glance, then gently put down one half of the lemon and took up the other. "Why the deuce should he look at me in that damned reproachful fashion?" thought Ewell. He made another start. "There's a damned criss-cross of advices from Richmond. I hate uncertainty like the devil, and so I thought I'd ride across —"

"General Ewell," said Jackson gently, "you will oblige me by not swearing. Profanity, sir, is most distasteful to me. Now, you rode across?"

Ewell swallowed. "Rode across — rode across — I rode across, sir, from Swift Run Gap, and I brought with me two late dispatches from General Johnston and General Lee. I thought some expression, perhaps, to them of your opinion — following the late victory and all —"

The other took and read, laid down the dispatches and applied himself to his lemon. Presently. "I will telegraph to-night to General Johnston and General Lee. I shall advise that you enter the Valley as first intended. As for Richmond — we may best serve Richmond by threatening Washington."

"Threatening Washington?"

"At present you are in my district and form part of my command. You will at once move your troops forward a day's march. Upon receipt of advices from General Johnston and General Lee — and if they are of the tenour I expect — you will move with promptness to Luray."

"And then?"

"With promptness to Luray. I strongly value swiftness of movement."

"I understand that, sir. Double the distance in half the time."

"Good! When instructions are given, it is desirable that those instructions be followed. I assume the responsibility of giving the proper instructions."

"I understand, general. Obey and ask no questions."

"Just so. Be careful of your ammunition wagons, but otherwise as little impedimenta as possible."

"I understand, sir. The road to glory cannot be followed with much baggage."

Jackson put out his long arm, and gently touched the other's hand. "Good! I should be surprised if we did n't get on very well together. Now I will write a telegram to General Lee and then you shall get back to Swift Run Gap. The fewer hours a general is away from his troops the better." He rose and opened the door. "Lieutenant Meade!" The aide appeared. "Send me a courier — the one with the freshest horse. Order General Ewell's horses to be saddled."

This was the seventeenth. Two days later the Army of the Valley, moving down the Valley pike in a beautiful confidence that it was hurling itself against Banks at Strasburg, swerved to the east about New Market, with a suddenness that made it dizzy. Straight across its path now ran the strange and bold wall of the Massanuttons, architectural freak of Nature's, planted midway of the smiling Valley. The army groaned. "Always climbing mountains! This time to-morrow, I reckon, we'll climb it back again. Nothing over on the other side but the Luray Valley!"

Up and up went the army, through luxuriant forests where the laurel was in bloom, by the cool dash of mountain waters, past one-time haunts of stag and doe, through fern, over pine needles, under azure sky, — then down it sank, long winding after winding, moss and fern and richest forest, here velvet shadow, there highest light, down and down to the lovely Luray Valley, to the crossing of the Shenandoah, to green meadows and the bugles ringing "halt"!

How short the time between tattoo and reveille! The dawn was rosy, still, not cold, the river running near, the men with leave to rid themselves of the dust of yesterday's long march. In they plunged, all along the south fork of the Shenandoah, into the cool and wholesome flood. There were laughters, shoutings, games of dolphins. Then out they came, and while they cooked their breakfasts they heard the drums and fifes of Ewell's eight thousand, marching down from Conrad's Store.

The night before at Washington, where there was much security and much triumph over the certain-to-occur-soon-if-not-already-occurred Fall of Richmond, the Secretary of War received a dispatch from General Banks at Strasburg in the Valley of Virginia, thirty miles from Winchester.

"My force at Strasburg is 4476 infantry, two brigades; 1600 cavalry, 10 Parrott guns and 6 smooth-bore pieces. I have on the Manassas Gap Railroad, between Strasburg and Manassas, 2500 infantry, 6 companies cavalry, and 6 pieces artillery. There are 5 companies cavalry, First Maine, near Strasburg. Of the enemy I received information last night, direct from New Market, that Jackson has returned to within 8 miles of Harrisonburg, west. I have no doubt that Jackson's force is near Harrisonburg, and that Ewell still remains at Swift Run Gap. I shall communicate more at length the condition of affairs and the probable plans of the enemy."

In pursuance of his promise General Banks wrote at length from Strasburg, the evening of the 22d: —

"SIR. The return of the rebel forces of General Jackson to the Valley after his forced march against Generals Milroy and Schenck increases my anxiety for the safety of the position I occupy. . . . That he has returned there can be no doubt. . . . From all the information I can gather — and I do not wish to excite alarm unnecessarily — I am compelled to believe that he meditates attack here. I regard it as certain that he will move north as far as New Market, a position which . . . enables him also to coöperate with General Ewell, who is still at Swift Run Gap. . . . Once at New Market they are within twenty-five miles of Strasburg. . . . I have forborne until the last moment to make this representation, well knowing how injurious to the public service unfounded alarms become. . . ."

The general signed and sent his letter. Standing for a moment, in the cool of the evening, at the door of headquarters, he looked toward the east where the first stars were shining. Fourteen miles over there was his strongest outpost, the village of Front Royal occupied by Colonel Kenly with a thousand men and two guns. The general could not see the place; it lay between the Massanuttons and the Blue Ridge, but it was in his mind. He spoke to an aide. "To-morrow I think I will recall Kenly and send him down the pike to develop the force of the enemy."

The small town of Strasburg pulsed with flaring lights and with the manifold sounds of the encamped army. Sutlers showed their wares, guard details went by, cavalrymen clanked their spurs through the streets, laughter and talk rang through the place. A company of strolling players had come down from the North, making its way from Washington to Harper's Ferry, held by three thousand Federals; from Harper's Ferry to Winchester, held by fifteen hundred; and from Winchester to Strasburg. The actors had a canvas booth, where by guttering candles and to the sound of squeaking fiddles they gave their lurid play of the night, and they played to a crowded house. Elsewhere there was gambling, elsewhere praying, elsewhere braggarts spoke of Ajax exploits, elsewhere there was moaning and tossing in the hospitals, elsewhere some private, raised above the heads of his fellows, read aloud the Northern papers. *McClellan has one hundred and twelve thousand men. Yesterday his advance reached the White House on the Pamunkey. McDowell has forty thousand men, and at last advice was but a few marches from the treasonable capital. Our gunboats are hurrying up the James. Presumably at the very hour this goes to press Richmond is fallen.*

> Fallen, fallen, fallen, fallen,
> Fallen from her high estate,
> And weltering in her blood.

Elsewhere brave, true, and simple men attended to their duties, wrote their letters home, and, going their rounds or walking their beats, looked upward to the silver stars. They looked at the stars in the west, over the Alleghenies where Frémont, where Milroy and Schenck should be; and at those in the south, over the long leagues of the great Valley, over Harrisonburg, somewhere the other side of which Stonewall Jackson must be; and at those in the east, over the Massanuttons, with the Blue Ridge beyond, and Front Royal in between, where Colonel Kenly was; and at the bright stars in the North, over home, over Connecticut and Pennsylvania and Massachusetts, over Wisconsin, Indiana, and Maine.

They who watched the stars from Strasburg dwelt least of all, perhaps, upon the stars in the east. Yet under those lay that night, ten miles from Front Royal, Stonewall Jackson and seventeen thousand men.

CHAPTER XX

FRONT ROYAL

I N the hot, bright morning Cleave, commanding four companies
of the 65th thrown out as skirmishers, entered the band of forest
lying between the Blue Ridge and Front Royal. The day was
hot, the odour of the pines strong and heady; high in heaven, in a
still and intense blue, the buzzards were slowly sailing. A long, thin
line of picked men, keen, watchful, the reserve a hundred yards or
two behind, the skirmishers moved forward over a rough cart track
and over the opposing banks. Each man stepped lightly as a cat,
each held his gun in the fashion most convenient to himself, each
meant to do good hunting. Ahead was a thicker belt of trees, and
beyond that a gleam of sky, a promise of a clearing. Suddenly, out
of this blue space, rose the neigh of a horse.

The skirmishers halted beneath the trees. The men waited, bent
forward, holding breath, recognizing the pause on the rim of action,
the moment before the moment. The clearing appeared to be
several hundred yards away. Back from it, upon the idle air, floated
loud and careless talking, then laughter. Allan Gold came out of the
thicker wood, moved, a tawny shadow, across the moss and reported
to Cleave. "Two companies, sir — infantry — scattered along a
little branch. Arms stacked."

The line entered the wood, the laughter and talking before it
growing louder. Each grey marksman twitched his cartridge box in
place, glanced at his musket, glanced toward his immediate officer.
Across the intervals ran an indefinable spark, a bracing, a tension.
Some of the men moistened their lips, one or two uttered a little sigh,
the hearts of all beat faster. The step had quickened. The trees
grew more thinly, came down to a mere bordering fringe of sumach.
Cleave motioned to the bugler; the latter raised the bugle to his
lips. *Forward! — Commence — Firing!* The two companies in blue,
marched down that morning superfluously to picket a region where
was no danger, received that blast and had their moment of stupour.

Laughter died suddenly. A clock might have ticked twice while they sat or stood as though that were all there was to do. The woods blazed, a long crackle of musketry broke the spell. A blue soldier pitched forward, lay with his head in the water. Another, seated in the shade, his back to a sugar maple, never more of his own motion left that resting place; a third, undressing for a bath, ran when the others ran, but haltingly, a red mark upon his naked thigh. All ran now, ran with cries and oaths toward the stacked rifles. Ere they could snatch the guns, drop upon their knees, aim at the shaken sumach bushes and fire, came a second blaze and rattle and a leaden hail.

Out of the wood burst the long skirmish line. It yelled; it gave the "rebel yell." It rushed on, firing as it came. It leaped the stream, it swallowed up the verdant mead, it came on, each of its units yelling death, to envelop the luckless two companies. One of these was very near at hand, the other, for the moment more fortunate, a little way down the stream, near the Front Royal road. Cleave reached, a grey brand, the foremost of the two. "Surrender!"

The blue captain's sword lay with other paraphernalia on the grass beneath the trees, but he signified assent to the inevitable. The reserve, hurrying down from the wood, took the captured in charge. The attack swept on, tearing across the meadow to the Front Royal road, where the second company had made a moment's stand, as brave as futile. It fired two rounds, then broke and tore down the dusty road or through the bordering fields toward Front Royal. Cleave and his skirmishers gained. They were mountain men, long of limb; they went like Greek runners, and they tossed before them round messengers of death. The greater number of blue soldiers, exhausted, slackened in their pace, halted, threw down their arms. Presently, trailing their feet, they returned to the streamlet and their companions in misfortune.

The grey swept on, near now to Front Royal; before them a few blue fugitives, centre of a swiftly moving cloud of dust, a cloud into which the Thunder Run men fired at short intervals. Behind them they heard the tramp of the army. The Louisiana Brigade, leading, was coming at a double-quick. On a parallel road to the left a dust cloud and dull thunder proclaimed a battery, making for the front.

Out of the wood which the skirmishers had left came like a whirlwind the 65th Virginia, Jackson riding with Flournoy at the head.

Little Sorrel swerved toward the skirmishers and paused a moment abreast of Cleave. Jackson spoke from the saddle. "How
many?"

"Two companies, sir. Several killed, the rest prisoners, save six
or eight who will reach the town."

"Good! Press on. If they open with artillery, get under cover
until our guns are placed." He jerked his hand into the air and rode
on, galloping stiffly, his feet stuck out from the nag's sides. The
cavalry disappeared to the right in a storm of yellow dust.

The village of Front Royal that had been dozing all the summer
forenoon, woke with a vengeance. Kenly's camp lay a mile or two
west, but in the town was quartered a company or so. Soldiers off
duty were lounging on the shady side of the village street, missing
the larger delights of Strasburg, wondering if Richmond had fallen
and where was Stonewall Jackson, when the fracas, a mile away,
broke upon their ears. Secure indolence woke with a start. Front
Royal buzzed like an overturned hive. In the camp beyond the
town bugles blared and the long roll was furiously beaten. The lounging soldiers jerked up their muskets; others poured out of houses
where they had been billeted. All put their legs to good use, down
the road, back to the camp! Out, too, came the village people,
though not to flee the village. In an instant men and women were in
street or porch or yard, laughing, crying, hurrahing, clapping hands,
waving anything that might serve as a welcoming banner. "Stonewall Jackson! It's Jackson! Stonewall Jackson! Bless the Lord,
O my soul! — Can't you all stop and tell a body? — No; you
can't, of course. Go along, and God bless you! — Their camp's
this side the North Fork — about a thousand of them. — Guns?
Yes, they've got two guns. Cavalry? No, no cavalry. — Don't let
them get away! If they fall back they'll try to burn the bridges.
Don't let them do that. The North Fork's awful rough and swollen.
It'll be hard to get across. — Yes, the railroad bridge and the
wagon bridge. I can't keep up with you any longer. I ain't as
young as I once was. You're welcome, sir."

Cleave and his men came out of the village street at a run.
Before them stretched level fields, gold with sunshine and with

blossoming mustard, crossed and cumbered with numerous rail
fences. Beyond these, from behind rolling ground lightly wooded,
rang a great noise of preparation, drums, trumpets, confused voices.
As the skirmishers poured into the open and again deployed, a cannon planted on a knoll ahead spoke with vehemence. The shell that
it sent struck the road just in front of the grey, exploded, fright-
fully tore a man's arm and covered all with a dun mantle of dust.
Another followed, digging up the earth in the field, uprooting and
ruining clover and mustard. A third burst overhead. A stone wall,
overtopped by rusty cedars, ran at right angles with the road. To
this cover Cleave brought the men, and they lay behind it panting,
welcoming the moment's rest and shelter, waiting for the battery
straining across the fields. The Louisianians, led by Taylor, were
pouring through the village — Ewell was behind — Jackson and the
cavalry had quite disappeared.

Lying in the shadow of the wall, waiting for the order forward,
Cleave suddenly saw again and plainly what at the moment he had
seen without noting — Stafford's face, very handsome beneath soft
hat and plume, riding with the 6th. It came now as though between
eyelid and ball. The eyes, weary and tragic, had rested upon him
with intentness as he stood and spoke with Jackson. Maury Stafford — Maury Stafford! Cleave's hand struck the sun-warmed
stone impatiently. He was not fond of deep unhappiness — no, not
even in the face of his foe! Why was it necessary that the man
should have felt thus, have thought thus, acted thus? The fact that
he himself could not contemplate without hot anger that other fact
of Stafford's thought still dwelling, dwelling upon Judith had made
him fight with determination any thought of the man at all. He
could not hurt Judith, thank God! nor make between them more
misunderstanding and mischief! Then let him go — let him go! with
his beauty and his fatal look, like a figure out of an old, master canvas! — Cleave wrenched his thought to matters more near at hand.

The battery first seen and heard was now up. It took position on
a rise of ground and began firing, but the guns were but smooth-bore
six-pounders and the ammunition was ghastly bad. The shells exploded well before they reached the enemy's lines. The opposing
blue battery — Atwell's — strongly posted and throwing canister
from ten-pounder Parrotts — might have laughed had there not

been — had there not been more and more and yet more of grey infantry! Taylor with his Louisianians, the First Maryland, Ewell, Winder with the Stonewall, grey, grey, with gleaming steel, with glints of red, pouring from the woods, through the fields — the Pennsylvanians, working the battery, did not laugh; they were pale, perhaps, beneath the powder grime. But pale or sanguine they bravely served their guns and threw their canister, well directed, against the mediæval engines on the opposite knoll.

Shouting an order, there now galloped to these Jackson's Chief of Artillery, Colonel Crutchfield. The outclassed smooth-bores limbered up and drew sulkily away; Courtenay's Battery, including a rifled gun, arrived in dust and thunder to take their place. Behind came Brockenborough. The reeking battery horses bent to it; the drivers yelled. The rumbling wheels, the leaping harness, the dust that all raised, made a cortège and a din as of Dis himself. The wheel stopped, the men leaped to the ground, the guns were planted, the limbers dropped, the horses loosed and taken below the hill. A loud cannonade began.

Behind the screen of smoke, in the level fields, four Louisiana regiments formed in line of battle. A fifth moved to the left, its purpose to flank the Federal battery. As for the cavalry, it appeared to have sunk into the earth — and yet, even with the thought, out of the blue distance toward McCoy's Ford, on the South Fork arose a tremendous racket! A railway station, Buckton — was there, and a telegraph line, and two companies of Pennsylvania infantry, and two locomotives with steam up. At the moment there were also Ashby and the 7th Virginia, bent upon burning the railroad bridge, cutting the telegraph, staying the locomotives, and capturing the Pennsylvanians. The latter tried to escape by the locomotives; tried twice and failed twice. The forming infantry before Front Royal knew by the rumpus that Ashby was over there, below the Massanuttons. There ran a rumour, too, that the 2d Virginia cavalry under Munford was somewhere to the northeast, blocking the road to Manassas Gap, closing the steel trap on that quarter. The 6th with Jackson remained sunken.

In the hot sunshine blared the Louisianian trumpets. An aide, stretched like an Indian along the neck of his galloping horse, came to the skirmishers. "All right, Cleave! Go ahead! The Louisianians are pawing the ground!—Shade of Alexander Hamilton, listen to that!"

"That" was the "Marseillaise," grandly played. *Tramp, tramp!* the Louisianians came on to its strains. The skirmish line left the sunny stone fence where slender ferns filled the chinks, and lizards ran like frightened flames, and brown ants, anxious travellers, sought a way home. Cleave, quitting the shadow of a young locust tree, touched with his foot a wren's nest, shaken from the bough above. The eggs lay in it, unbroken. He stooped swiftly, caught it up and set it on the bough again, then ran on, he and all his men, under a storm of shot and shell.

Kenly, a gallant soldier, caught, through no fault of his, in a powerful trap, manœuvred ably. His guns were well served, and while they stayed for a moment the Confederate advance, he made dispositions for a determined stand. The longer delay here, the greater chance at Strasburg! A courier dispatched in hot haste to warn the general there encountered and hurried forward a detachment of the 7th New York Cavalry as well as a small troop of picked men, led by a sometime aide of General Banks. These, crossing the wagon bridge over the Shenandoah and coming down the road at a double, reported to Kenly and were received by the anxious troops with cheering. The ground hereabouts was rolling, green eminences at all points breaking the view. Kenly used the cavalry skilfully, making them appear now here, now there between the hills, to the end that to the attackers they might appear a regiment. His guns thundered, and his few companies of infantry fired with steadiness, greeting with hurrahs every fall of a grey skirmisher.

But the skirmishers pressed on, and behind them came the chanters of the "Marseillaise." Moreover a gasping courier brought news to Kenly. "A great force of cavalry, sir — Ashby, I reckon, or the devil himself — on the right! If they get to the river first —" There was small need of further saying. If Ashby or the devil got to the river first, then indeed was the trap closed on the thousand men!

Face to the Rear! March! ordered Kenly. Atwell's Battery limbered up in hot haste, turned, and dashed in thunder up the road. It must cross the bridge, seize some height, from there defend the crossing. Where the battery had been the cavalry now formed the screen, thin enough and ragged, yet menacing the grey infantry.

The grey skirmishers rallied, fixed bayonets and advanced, the Louisianians close behind. The blue horsemen attempted a charge, an action more bold than wise, they were so small a force. The men in grey sprang at the bridles of the foremost, wrapped long mountain arms about the riders. Despite sabre, despite pistol, several were dragged down, horse and man made captive. The most got back to safer ground. Kenly's bugles rang out again, palpably alarmed, shrilly insistent. Horse and foot must get across the Shenandoah or there would be the devil to pay! Beside the imperious trumpet came something else, an acrid smell and smoke, then a great flame and crackle. Torch had been put to the camp; all the Federal tents and forage and stores were burning. *To the rear! To the rear!*

In the middle of the road, out of one of the scuffling groups, a whirling pillar of dust and clamour, sabre strokes, rifle and pistol cracks, oaths, cries, plunging of a maddened horse, Cleave saw a flushed face lift itself from the ground, a powerful shoulder thrust away the surging grey shapes, a sabre flash in the sun, a hand from which blood was streaming catch at the horse's mane. The owner of the hand swung himself again into the saddle from which Dave Maydew had plucked him. Remounted, he made a downward thrust with his sabre. Dave, keeping warily out of reach of the horse's lashing heels, struck up the arm with his bayonet. The sabre clattered to the ground; with an oath the man — an officer — drew a revolver. The ball whizzed past Cleave's temple; a second might have found his heart but that Allan Gold, entering somehow the cleared circle made by the furious horse, hung upon the arm sleeved in fine blue cloth, and wrenched the Colt's from the gauntleted hand. Cleave, at the bridle, laughed and took his hands away. "Christmas Carols again!" he said.

> God save you, merry gentlemen!
> Let nothing you dismay —

"Give him way, men! He's a friend of mine."

Marchmont's horse bounded. "Lieutenant McNeill," said the rider. "I profess that in all this dust and smoke I did not at first recognize you. I am your obedient servant. If my foe, sir, then I dub you my dearest foe! To our next meeting!"

He backed the furious horse, wheeled and was gone like a bolt from a catapult toward his broken and retiring troop. As he rode he turned in his saddle, raised his cap, and sang, —

> "As the Yankees were a-marching,
> They heard the rebel yell — "

Close at the heels of Kenly's whole command poured, resistlessly, the skirmish line, the Louisiana troops, the First Maryland. A light wind blew before them the dun and rolling smoke from the burning camp. For all their haste the men found tongue as they passed that dismal pyre. They sniffed the air. "Coffee burning! — good Lord, ain't it a sin? — Look at those boxes — shoes as I am a Christian man! — And all the wall tents — like 'Laddin's palaces! Geewhilikins! what was that? That was oil. There might be gunpowder somewhere! Captain, honey, don't you want us to *treble-quick* it?" They passed the fire and waste and ruin, rounded a curve, and came upon the long downward slope to the river. "Oh, here we are! Thar they are! Thar's the river. Thar's the Shenandoah! Thar's the covered bridge! They're on it — they're halfway over! Their guns are over! — We ain't ever going to let them all get across? — Ain't we going down the hill at them? — Yes. *Forward!* — Yaaaih! — Yaaih! — Yaaaaaaaihh! — Yaaaaaih! — Thar's the cavalry! Thar's Old Jack!"

Jackson and the 6th Virginia came at a gallop out of the woods, down the eastern bank of the stream. The skirmishers, First Maryland, — Louisiana, — poured down the slope, firing on Kenly as they ran. A number of his men dropped, but he was halfway across and he pressed on, the New York cavalry and Marchmont's small troop acting as rear guard. The battery was already over. The western bank rose steep and high, commanding the eastern. Up this strained the guns, were planted, and opened with canister upon the swarming grey upon the other shore. Company by company Kenly's infantry got across — got across, and once upon the rising ground faced about and opened a determined fire under cover of which his cavalry entered the bridge. The last trooper over, his pioneers brought brush and hay, thrust it into the mouth of the bridge and set all on fire.

Jackson was up just in time to witness the burst of flames. He turned to the nearest regiment — the 8th Louisiana, Acadians from the Attakapas. There was in him no longer any slow stiffness of action; his body moved as though every joint were oiled. He looked a different creature. He pointed to the railroad bridge just above the wagon bridge. "Cross at once on the ties." The colonel looked, nodded, waved his sword and explained to his Acadians. "*Mes enfans! Nous allons traverser le pont là-bas. En avant!*" In column of twos he led his men out on the ties of the trestle bridge. Below, dark, rapid, cold, rushed the swollen Shenandoah. Musketry and artillery, Kenly opened upon them. Many a poor fellow, who until this war had never seen a railroad bridge, threw up his arms, stumbled, slipped between the ties, went down into the flood and disappeared.

Stonewall Jackson continued his orders. "Skirmishers forward! Clear those combustibles out of the bridge. Cross, Wheat's Battalion! First Maryland, follow!" He looked from beneath the forage cap at the steep opposite shore, from the narrow level at the water's edge to the ridge top held by the Federal guns. Rank by rank on this staircase, showed Kenly's troops, stubbornly firing, trying to break the trap. "Artillery's the need. We must take more of their guns."

It was hot work, as the men of the 65th and Wheat's Tigers speedily found, crossing the wagon bridge over the Shenandoah! One span was all afire. The flooring burned their feet, flames licked the wooden sides of the structure, thick, choking smoke canopied the rafters. With musket butts the men beat away the planking, hurled into the flood below burning scantling and brand, and trampled the red out of the charring cross timbers. Some came out of the western mouth of the bridge stamping with the pain of burned hands, but the point was that they did come out — the four companies of the 65th, Wheat's Tigers, the First Maryland. Back to Jackson, however, went a messenger. "Not safe, sir, for horse! We broke step and got across, but at one place the supports are burned away —"

"Good! good!" said Jackson. "We will cross rougher rivers ere we are done." He turned to Flournoy's bugler. "*Squadrons. Right front into line. March!*"

Kenly, stubbornly firing upon the two columns, that one now quitting, with a breath of relief, the railway bridge, and that issuing under an arch of smoke from the wagon bridge, was hailed by a wild-eyed lieutenant. "Colonel Kenly, sir, look at that!" As he spoke, he tried to point, but his hand waved up and down. The Shenandoah, below the two bridges, was thick with swimming horses.

Kenly looked, pressed his lips together, opened them and gave the order. "*Face to the rear. Forward. March!*" Discretion was at last entirely the better part of valour. Strasburg was fourteen miles away; over hill and dale rose and fell the road that ran that way. Off, off! and some might yet escape — or it might please the gods to let him meet with reinforcements! His guns ceased with their canister and limbering up thundered away toward the sun, now low and red in the heavens. The infantry followed; the small cavalry force bringing up the rear, now deployed as skirmishers, now rallying and threatening the grey footmen.

The Shenandoah was impetuous, deep, turbid, with many eddies, lifted by the spring rains almost level with its banks. The horses liked it not — poor brutes! They shuddered, whinnied, glared with distended, bloodshot eyes. Once in, they patiently did their best. Each was owned by its rider, and was his good friend as well as servant. The understanding between the two could not be disturbed, no, not even by the swollen Shenandoah! The trooper, floating free upon the down-stream side, one hand on mane, or knees upgathered, and carbine held high, squatting in the saddle on the crossed stirrups, kept up a stream of encouragement — soft words, pet names, cooing mention of sugar (little enough in the commissariat!) and of apples. The steed responded. The god above or beside him wished it thus, and certainly should be obeyed, and that with love. The rough torrent, the eddies, the violent current were nothing — at least, not much! In column of twos the horses breasted the river, the gods above them singing of praise and reward. They neared the western shore and the green, overhanging trees, touched bottom, plunged a little and came out, wet and shining, every inch of metal about them glinting in the level rays of the sun.

High on the bank Stonewall Jackson with Flournoy and his aides, the first to cross, watched that passage of the squadrons. Little

Sorrel, slow and patient, had perhaps been, in his own traversing, the one steed to hear no especial word of endearment nor much of promise. He did not seem to miss them; he and Jackson apparently understood each other. The men said that he could run only one way and that toward the enemy.

Far down the Front Royal and Winchester turnpike, through a fair farming country, among cornfields and orchards, the running fight continued. It was almost sunset; long shadows stretched across the earth. Scene and hour should have been tranquil-sweet — fall of dew, vesper song of birds, tinkling of cow bells coming home. It was not so; it was filled with noise and smoke, and in the fields and fence corners lay dead and wounded men, while in the farmhouses of the region, women drew the blinds, gathered the children about them and sat trembling.

The blue cavalry was hard put to it. The grey infantrymen were good marksmen, and their line was long, drawn across the road and the up and down of the fields. Here and there, now and again, a trooper went down to the dust, and the riderless horse, galloping to the rear, brought small comfort to Kenly's retreating companies. At last there rode back the major commanding the New York squadron. "We're losing too heavily, colonel! There's a feverishness — if they're reinforced I don't know if I can hold the men —"

Kenly debated within himself, then. "I'll make a stand at the cross-roads yonder. Atwell shall plant the guns and give them canister. It is nearly night — if we could hold them off one hour —"

Richard Cleave, pressing very close with his skirmishers, lost sight of the blue infantry now behind an orchard-clad undulation. "Billy Maydew! come climb this tree and tell me what you see."

Billy went up the roadside locust like a squirrel. "Thar air a man just tumbled off a black horse with a white star! 'T was Dave hit him, I reckon. They look powerful droopy, them cavalrymen! The big man you would n't let us take, he air waving his sabre and swearing —"

"The infantry?"

"The infantry air halted. The road air stuffed with them. One — two — three — six companies, stretched out like a black horse's tail."

"Faced which way?"

"That way. No! by Jiminy, they ain't! They air faced this way! They air going to make a stand!"

"They have done well, and they've got a brave officer, whoever he is. The guns?"

"Away ahead, but they air turning! They air making for a hill-top that hangs over the road. Thar's another man off his horse! Threw up his arm and fell, and his foot caught in the stirrup. I don't know if 't war Dave this time shot him — anyhow, 't war not Sergeant Coffin —"

"Is the infantry deploying?"

"They air still in column — black as flies in the road. They air tearing down the fence, so they can get into the fields."

"Look behind — toward the river."

Billy obediently turned upon the branch. "We air coming on in five lines — like the bean patch at home. I love them Lou-is-iana Tigers! What's that?"

"What?"

"An awful cloud of dust — and a trumpet out of it! The First Maryland's getting out of the way — Now the Tigers! — Oh-h-h!"

He scrambled down. "By the left flank!" shouted Cleave. "Double quick. March!"

The 65th, the Louisiana troops, the First Maryland, moved rapidly west of the road, leaving a space of trampled green between themselves and it. Out of the dust cloud toward the river now rose a thud of many hoofs — a body of horse coming at a trot. The sound deepened, drew nearer, changed measure. The horses were galloping, though not at full speed. They could be seen now, in two lines, under bright guidons, eating up the waves of earth, galloping toward the sunset in dust and heat and thunder. At first sight like toy figures, men and horses were now grown life-size. They threatened, in the act of passing, to become gigantic. The sun had set, but it left walls and portals of cloud tinged and rimmed with fire. The horsemen seemed some home-returning aerial race, so straight they rode into the west. The ground shook, the dust rose higher, the figures enlarged, the gallop increased. Energy at its height, of a sudden all the trumpets blew

Past the grey infantry, frantically yelling its welcome, swept a tremendous charge. Knee to knee, shouting, chanting, horse and man one war shaft, endued with soul and lifted to an ecstasy, they went by, flecked with foam, in a whirlwind of dust, in an infernal clangour, with the blare and fury, the port and horror of Mars attended. The horses stretched neck, shook mane, breathed fire; the horsemen drained to the lees the encrusted heirloom, the cup of warlike passion. Frenzied they all rode home.

The small cavalry force opposed, gasped at the apparition. Certainly their officers tried to rally the men, but certainly they knew it for futility! Some of the troopers fired their carbines at the approaching tide, hoar, yelling, coming now so swiftly that every man rode as a giant and every steed seemed a spectre horse — others did not. All turned, before the shock, and fled, in a mad gallop of their own.

Kenly's infantry, yet in column, was packed in a road none too wide, between ragged banks topped by rail fences. Two panels of these had been taken down preparatory to deploying in the fields, but the movement was not yet made. Kenly had his face turned to the west, straining his eyes for the guns or for the reinforcements which happily General Banks might send. A shout arose. "Look out! Look out! Oh, good Lord!"

First there was seen a horrible dust cloud, heard a great thunder of hoofs. Then out of all came bloodshot eyes of horses, stiffened manes, blue figures downward bent on the sweat-gleaming necks, oaths, prayers, sounds of unnerved Nature, here and there of grim fury, impotent in the torrent as a protesting straw. Into the blue infantry rode the blue cavalry. All down the soldier-crammed road ensued a dreadful confusion, danger and uproar. Men sprang for their lives to this side and that. They caught at jutting roots and pulled themselves out of the road up the crumbling banks. Where they could they reached the rail fences, tumbled over them and lay, gasping, close alongside. The majority could not get out of the road. They pressed themselves flat against the shelving banks, and let the wedge drive through. Many were caught, overturned, felt the fierce blows of the hoofs. Regardless of any wreck behind them, on and over and down the Winchester road tore the maddened horses, the appalled troopers.

The luckless infantry when, at last, their own had passed, had no time to form before the Confederate charge was upon them. At the highest key, the fiercest light, the extremest motion, sound and sight procuring for them a mighty bass and background, came Jackson's charging squadrons. They swallowed the road and the fields on either hand. Kenly, with the foremost company, fired once, a point-blank volley, received at twenty yards, and emptying ten saddles of the central squadron. It could not stay the unstayable; in a moment, in a twinkling of the eye, with indescribable noise, with roaring as of undammed waters, with a lapse of all colours into red, with smell of sweat and powder, hot metal and burning cloth, with savour of poisoned brass in furred mouths, with an impact of body, with sabre blow and pistol shot, with blood spilled and bone splintered, with pain and tremendous horror and invading nausea, with delirium, with resurgence of the brute, with jungle triumph, Berserker rage and battle ecstasy came the shock — then, in a moment, the mêlée.

Kenly, vainly striving to rally a handful about the colours, fell, all but mortally wounded. In the wild quarter of an hour that elapsed before the surrender of the whole, many of the blue were killed, many more wounded. Far and wide the men scattered, but far and wide they were ridden down. One of the guns was taken almost at once, the other a little later, overtaken a mile or two down the road. A few artillerymen, a squad or two of cavalry with several officers, Marchmont among them, got away. They were all who broke the trap. Kenly himself, twenty officers and nine hundred men, the dead, the wounded, the surrendered, together with a section of artillery, some unburned stores, and the Northern colours and guidons, rested in Jackson's hands. That night in Strasburg, when the stars came out, men looked toward those that shone in the east.

CHAPTER XXI

STEVEN DAGG

STEVEN DAGG, waked by the shrill reveille, groaned, raised himself from his dew-drenched couch, ran his fingers through his hair, kneaded neck, arms, and ankles, and groaned more heavily yet. He was dreadfully stiff and sore. In five days the "foot cavalry" had marched more than eighty miles. Yesterday the brigade had been afoot from dawn till dark. "And we didn't have the fun of the battle neither," remarked Steve, in a savagely injured tone. "Leastwise none of us but the damned three companies and a platoon of ours that went ahead to skirmish 'cause they knew the type of country! Don't I know the type of country, too? Yah!"

The man nearest him, combing his beard with ostentation, burst into a laugh. "Did you hear that, fellows? Steve's grumbling because he wasn't let to do it all! Poor Steve! poor Hotspur! poor Pistol!" He bent, chuckling, over the pool that served him for mirror. "You stop calling me dirty names!" growled Steve, and, his toilet ended well-nigh before begun, slouched across to fire and breakfast. The former was large, the latter small. Jackson's ammunition wagons, double-teamed, were up with the army, but all others back somewhere east of Front Royal.

Breakfast was soon over — "sorry breakfast!" The *assembly* sounded, the column was formed, Winder made his brigade a short speech. Steve listened with growing indignation. "General Banks, falling back from Strasburg, is trying to get off clear to Winchester. ('Well, let him! I don't give a damn!') We want to intercept him at Middletown. ('Oh, do we?') We want to get there before the head of his column appears, and then to turn and strike him full. ('O Lord! I ain't a rattler!') We want to beat him in the middle Valley — never let him get to Winchester at all! ('I ain't objecting, if you'll give the other brigades a show and let them do it!') It's only ten miles to Middletown. ('Only!') A forced march needed. ('O Gawd!') Ashby and Chew's Battery and a section of the Rockbridge and the skirmishers and Wheat's Tigers are ahead. ('Well, if they're so brash, let them wipe out Banks and welcome! And if one damned officer that's ahead gits killed, I won't mourn him.') Ewell with Trimble's Brigade and the First Maryland, Courtenay and Brockenborough are off, making as the bird flies for Winchester! ('We ain't birds. We're men, and awful tired men, too.') Steuart with the 2d and 6th cavalry are already at Newtown. ('What in hell do I care if they air?') Campbell and Taliaferro and Elzey and Scott and the Stonewall and the balance of the guns form the main column, and at Middletown we're going to turn and meet Banks. ('Gawd! more fighting, on an empty stomach, and dog-tired!') General Jackson says, '*Men, we're going to rid the Valley of Virginia of the enemy. Press on.*' You know what an avalanche is. ('Knowed it before you was born. It's a place where you hide till the man you hate worse than pison oak comes by!') Let the Stonewall now turn avalanche; fall on Banks at Middletown and grind him small! — *Fours right! Forward! March!* ('Oh, Gawd! my cut foot! It's my lasting hope that — sh! — Fool Tom Jackson'll break you same as he broke Garnett')."

The morning, at first divinely cool and sweet, turned hot and languid, humid and without air. It made the perspiration stream, and then the dust rose from the road, and the two together caused the most discomfortable grime! It marked all faces, and it lodged between neck and neckband and wrist and wristband where it chafed the skin. It got deep into the shoes — through holes enough, God knows! — and there the matter became serious, for many a foot was galled and raw. It got into eyes and they grew red and smarting. It stopped ear and nostril. It lined the mouth; it sifted down the neck and made the body miserable. At the starting, as the men quit the green banks of Shenandoah, several of the æsthetic sort had been heard to comment upon the beauty of the scenery. Possibly the soul for beauty lasted, but as for the scenery, it vanished. The brigade was now upon the Front Royal and Winchester pike, moving in the foot and wheel prints of the advance, and under and through an extended cirrhus cloud of dirty saffron. The scenery could not be viewed through it — mere red blotches and blurs. It was so heavy that it served for darkness. Men saw each other dimly at the distance of ten feet, and mounted officers and couriers went by, dun and shapeless, through the thick powder.

Steve could not be said to mind grime (Sergeant Mathew Coffin did; he was forever wiping it away with what remained to him of a handkerchief), but the stuff in his shoes made his feet hurt horribly. It was in his mouth besides, where it made him thirsty. He eyed an object dangling from the belt of the man next him, and since from long habit it had become easy to him to break the tenth commandment he broke it again — into a thousand pieces. At last, "Where did you get that canteen?"

"Picked it up at McDowell. Ef 't war n't covered with dust you could see the U. S."

"Empty, I reckon?"

"Nop. Buttermilk."

"O Gawd! I could drink Thunder Run dry!"

"Sorry. Reckon we'll come to a stream bimeby. Saving the milk 'gainst an emergency."

It did not appear that we would come to a stream, or a spring, or a well, or anything liquid — to anything but awful miles of dust and heat, trudged over by anything but three-leagued boots. Despite the spur of Winder's speech the brigade moved with dispiriting slowness. It was not the first in column; there were troops ahead and troops behind, and it would perhaps have said that it was not its part to overpass the one and outstrip the other. The whole line lagged. "Close up, men! close up!" cried the officers, through dust-lined throats. "If it's as hot as ginger, then let the ginger show! Step out!" Back from the head of the column came peremptory aides. "Press on! General Jackson says, 'Press on!' — Yes; he knows you marched twenty-six miles yesterday, and that it's hot weather! All the same we've got to get there! — Thank you, colonel, I will take a swallow! I'm damned tired myself."

Between nine and ten they came to a village. Boys and women stood in the dusty street with buckets of water — a few buckets, a little water. The women looked pale, as though they would swoon; beads of sweat stood on the boys' brows and their lips worked. Thousands of soldiers had passed or were passing; all thirsty, all crying, "Water, please! water, please!" Women and boys had with haste drawn bucket after bucket from the wells of the place, pumped them full from a cistern, or run to a near-by spring and come panting back to the road — and not one soldier in ten could get his tin cup filled! They went by, an endless line, a few refreshed, the vast majority thirstier for the Tantalus failure. The water bearers were more deadly tired than they; after it was all over, the last regiment passed, the women went indoors trembling in every limb. "O Jesus! this war is going to be a dreadful thing!" The column marching on and passing a sign-post, each unit read what it had to say. "*Seven miles to Middletown.* — Seven miles to hell!"

Some time later, the brigade made a discovery. "They are willows — yes, they are! — running cross field, through the blur! Whoever's toting the water bucket, get it ready!"

The halt came — Jackson's ten minutes out of an hour "lie-down-men. You-rest-all-over-lying-down" halt. The water buckets were ready, and there were the willows that the dust had made as sere as autumn, — but where was the stream? The thin trickle of water had been overpassed, churned, trampled into mire and dirt, by half the army, horse and foot. The men stared in blank disappointment. "A polecat couldn't drink here!" "Try it up and down," said the colonel. "It will be clearer away from the road. But every one of you listen for the *Fall-In.*"

Steve wandered off. He did not wait for clean water. There was a puddle, not half so bad as thirst! Settling down upon his hands, he leaned forward and well-nigh drank it up. Refreshed, he rose, got out of the mire back to the bank, and considered a deeper belt of willows farther down the stream. They were on the edge of the dust belt, they had an air faintly green, extremely restful. Steve looked over his shoulder. All the boys were drinking, or seeking a place to drink, and the dust was like a red twilight! Furtively swift as any Thunder Run "crittur," he made for the willows. They formed a deep little copse; nobody within their round and, oh joy! shade and a little miry pool! Steve sat down and drew off his shoes, taking some pains lest in the action side and sole part company. Undoubtedly his feet were sore and swollen, red and fevered. He drank from the miry pool, and then, trousers rolled to his knees, sunk foot and ankle in the delicious coolness. Presently he lay back, feet yet in mud and water, body flat upon cool black earth, overhead a thick screen of willow leaves. "Ef I had a corn pone and never had to move I would n't change for heaven. O Gawd! that damned bugle!"

Fall in! Fall in! — Fall in! Fall in! With a deep groan Steve picked up his shoes and dragged himself to the edge of the copse. He looked out. "Danged fools! running back to line like chicks when the hen squawks 'Hawk!' O Gawd! my foot's too sore to run." He stood looking cautiously out of an opening he had made in the willow branches. The regiments were already in column, the leading one, the 4th, formed and disappearing in the dust of the turnpike. "Air ye going now and have every damned officer swearing at you? What do they care if your foot's cut and your back aches? and you could n't come no sooner. *I ain't a-going.*" Steve's eyes filled with tears. He felt sublimely virtuous; a martyr from the first. "What does anybody there care for *me!* They would n't care if I dropped dead right in line. Well, I ain't a-going to gratify them! What's war, anyhow? It's a trap to catch decent folk in! and the decenter you are the quicker you try to get out of it!" He closed the willow branches and stepped back to his lair. "Let 'em bellow for Steve just as loud as they like! I ain't got no call to fight Banks on this here foot. If a damned provost-guard comes along, why I just fell asleep and could n't help it."

So tired was he, and so soothing still his retreat, that to fall asleep was precisely what he did. The sun was twenty minutes nearer the zenith when noise roused him — voices up and down the stream. He crawled across the black earth and looked out. "Taliaferro's Brigade getting watered! All I ask is you'll just let me and my willows alone."

He might ask, but Taliaferro's seemed hardly likely to grant. Taliaferro's had a harder time even than the Stonewall finding water. There was less there to find and it was muddier. The men, swearing at their luck, ranged up and down the stream. It was presently evident that the search might bring any number around or through Steve's cool harbour. He cursed them, then, in a sudden panic, picked up his shoes and slipped out at the copse's back door. Able-bodied stragglers, when caught, were liable to be carried on and summarily deposited with their rightful companies. Deserters fared worse. On the whole, Steve concluded to seek safety in flight. At a little distance rose a belt of woods roughly parallel with the road.

Steve took to the woods, and found sanctuary behind the bole of an oak. His eye advanced just beyond the bark, he observed the movement of troops with something like a grin. On the whole he thought, perhaps, he wouldn't rejoin. Taliaferro's men hardly seemed happy, up and down the trodden, miry runlet. "Wuz a time they wouldn't think a dog could drink there, and now just look at them lapping it up! So many fine, stuck-up fellows, too — gentlemen and such. — Yah!"

The brigade moved on as had done the Stonewall. There grew in the wood a sound. "What's that?" Scrambling up, he went forward between the trees and presently came full upon a narrow wood road, with a thin growth of forest upon the other side. The sound increased. Steve knew it well. He stamped upon the moss with the foot that hurt him least. "Artillery coming! — and all them damned gunners with eyes like lynxes —"

He crossed the road and the farther strip of woods. Behind him the approaching wheels rumbled loudly; before him a narrow lane stretched through a ploughed field, to a grassy dooryard and a small house. On the edge of the wood was a mass of elderbush just coming into bloom. He worked his way into the centre of this, squatted down and regarded the house from between the green stems. Smoke rose from the chimney. "It must be near eleven o'clock," thought Steve. "She's getting dinner."

Behind him, through the wood, on toward Middletown rumbled the passing battery. The heavy sound brought a young woman to the door. She stood looking out, her hands shading her eyes; then, the train disappearing, went back to her work. Steve waited until the sound was almost dead, then left the elder, went up the lane and made his appearance before the open door. The woman turned from the hearth where she was baking bread. "Good-morning, sir."

"Morning, miss," said Steve. "Could you spare a poor sick soldier a bite to eat?"

He ended with a hollow groan and the weight of his body against the lintel. The young woman dragged forward a split-bottomed armchair. "Sit right down there! Of course I'll give you something to eat. It ain't anything catching, is it?"

Steve sank into the chair. "It was pneumonia, and my strength ain't come back yet."

"I only asked because I have to think of my baby." She glanced toward a cradle by the window. "Pneumonia is dreadful weakening! How come they let you march?"

"Why, I did n't," said Steve, "want to be left behind. I wanted to be in the fight with the rest of the boys. So the captain said, says he, 'Well, you can try it, for we need all the good fighters we've got, but if you find you're too weak to go on, fall out! Maybe some good Seraphim will give you 'commodation —'"

"I can't give you 'commodation, because there's just the baby and myself, James being with Ashby. But I can give you dinner (I have n't got much, but what I've got you're quite welcome to). You kin rest here till evening. Maybe a wagon'll come along and give you a lift, so's you can get there in time —"

"Get where, ma'am?"

"Why, wherever the battle's going to be!"

"Yaas, yaas," said Steve. "It's surely hard lines when those who kin fight have to take a back seat 'cause of illness and watch the other kind go front!" He groaned again and closed his eyes. "I don't suppose you've got a drop of spirits handy?"

The woman — she was hardly more than a girl — hesitated. Because the most were heroic, and for the sake of that most, all Confederate soldiers wore the garland. It was not in this or any year of the war that Confederate women lightly doubted the entire heroism of the least of individuals, so that he wore the grey. It was to them, most nobly, most pathetically, a sacred investiture. Priest without but brute within, wolf in shepherd's clothing, were to them not more unlooked-for nor abhorrent than were coward, traitor, or shirk enwrapped in the pall and purple of the grey. Fine lines came into the forehead of the girl standing between Steve and the hearth. She remembered suddenly that James had said there were plenty of scamps in the army and that not every straggler was lame or ill. Some were plain deserters.

"I have n't got any spirits," she answered. "I did have a little bottle but I gave it to a sick neighbour. Anyhow, it is n't good for weak lungs."

Steve looked at her with cunning eyes. "You did n't give it all away," he thought. "You've got a little hid somewhere. O Gawd! I want a drink so bad!"

"I was making potato soup for myself," said the girl, "and my father sent me half a barrel of flour from Harrisonburg and I was baking a small loaf of bread for to-morrow. It's Sunday. It's done now, and I'll slice it for you and give you a plate of soup. That's better for you than —. Where do you think we'll fight to-day?"

"Where? — Oh, anywhere the damned fools strike each other." He stumbled to the table which she was spreading. She glanced at him. "There's a basin and a roller towel on the back porch and the pump's handy. Would n't you like to wash your face and hands?"

Steve shook his tousled head. "Naw, I'm so burned the skin would come off. O Gawd! this soup is good."

"People getting over fevers and lung troubles don't usually burn. They stay white and peaked even out of doors in July."

"I reckon I ain't that kind. I'll take another plateful. Gawd, what a pretty arm you've got!"

The girl ladled out for him the last spoonful of soup, then went and stood with her foot upon the cradle rocker. "I reckon you ain't that kind," she said beneath her breath. "If you ever had pneumonia I bet it was before the war!"

Steve finished his dinner, leaned back in his chair and stretched himself. "Gawd! if I just had a nip. Look here, ma'am! I don't believe you gave all that apple brandy away. S'pose you look and see if you was n't mistaken."

"There is n't any."

"You've got too pretty a mouth to be lying that-a-way! Look-a-here, the doctor prescribed it."

"You've had dinner and you've rested. There's a wood road over there that cuts off a deal of distance to Middletown. It's rough but it's shady. I believe if you tried you could get to Middletown almost as soon as the army."

"Did n't I tell you I had a furlough? Where'd you keep that peach brandy when you had it?"

"I'm looking for James home any minute now. He's patrolling between here and the pike."

"You're lying. You said he was with Ashby, and Ashby's away north to Newtown — the damned West P'inter that marches at the head of the brigade said so! You have n't got the truth in you, and that's a pity, for otherwise I like your looks first-rate." He rose. "I'm going foraging for that mountain dew —"

The girl moved toward the door, pushing the cradle in front of her. Steve stepped between, slammed the door and locked it, putting the key in his pocket. "Now you jest stay still where you are or it'll be the worse for you and for the baby, too! Don't be figuring on the window or the back door, 'cause I've got eyes in the side of my head and I'll catch you before you get there! That thar cupboard looks promising."

The cupboard not only promised; it fulfilled. Steve's groping hand closed upon and drew forth a small old Revolutionary brandy bottle quite full. Over his shoulder he shot a final look at once precautionary and triumphant. "You purty liar! jest you wait till I've had my dram!" An old lustre mug stood upon the shelf. He filled this almost to the brim, then lifted it from the board. There was a sound from by the door, familiar enough to Steve — namely, the cocking of a trigger. "You put that mug down," said the voice of his hostess, "or I'll put a bullet through you! Shut that cupboard door. Go and sit down in that chair!"

"'T ain't loaded! I drew the cartridge."

"You don't remember whether you did or not! And you are n't willing for me to try and find out! You set down there! That's it; right there where I can see you! My grandmother's birthday mug! Yes, and she saw her mother kill an Indian right here, right where the old log cabin used to stand! Well, I reckon I can manage a dirty, sneaking hound like you. Grandmother's cup indeed, that I don't even let James drink out of! I'll have to scrub it with brick dust to get your finger marks off —"

"Won't you please put that gun down, ma'am, and listen to reason?"

"I'm listening to something else. There's three or four horses coming down the road —"

"Please put that gun down, ma'am. I'll say good-bye and go just as peaceable —"

"And whether they're blue or grey I hope to God they'll take you off my hands! There! They've turned up the lane. They're coming by the house!"

She raised a strong young voice. "Help! Help! Stop, please! O soldiers! Soldiers! Help! Soldiers! There! I've made them hear and waked the baby!"

"Won't you let me go, ma'am? I did n't mean no harm."

"No more did the Indian great-grandmother killed when he broke in the door! You're a coward and a deserter, and the South don't need you! Bye, bye, baby — bye, bye!"

A hand tried the door. "What's the matter here? Open!"

"It's locked, sir. Come round to the window — Bye, baby, bye!"

The dismounted cavalryman — an officer — appeared outside the open window. His eyes rested a moment upon the interior; then he put hands upon the sill and swung himself up and into the room.

"What's all this? Has this soldier annoyed you, madam?"

The girl set down the musket and took up the baby. "I'm downright glad somebody came, sir. He's a coward and a deserter and a drunkard and a frightener of women! He says he's had pneumonia, and I don't believe him. If I was the South I'd send every man like him right across Mason and Dixon as fast as they'd take them! — I reckon he's my prisoner, sir, and I give him up to you."

The officer smiled. "I'm not the provost, but I'll rid you of him somehow." He wiped the dust from his face. "Have you anything at all that we could eat? My men and I have had nothing since midnight."

"That coward's eaten all I had, sir. I'm sorry — If you could wait a little, I've some flour and I'll make a pan of biscuits —"

"No. We cannot wait. We must be up with the army before it strikes the Valley pike."

"I've got some cold potatoes, and some scraps of bread crust I was saving for the chickens —"

"Then won't you take both to the four men out there? Hungry soldiers *like* cold potatoes and bread crusts. I'll see to this fellow. — Now, sir, what have you got to say for yourself?"

"Major, my feet are so sore, and I was kind of light-headed! First thing I knew, I just somehow got separated from the brigade —"

"We'll try to find it again for you. What were you doing here?"

"Major, I just asked her for a little licker. And, being light-headed, maybe I happened to say something or other that she took up notions about. The first thing I knew — and I just as innocent as her baby — she up and turned my own musket against me —"

"Who locked the door?"

"Why — why —"

"Take the key out of your pocket and go open it. Faugh! — What's your brigade?"

"The Stonewall, sir."

"Humph! They'd better stone you out of it. Regiment?"

"65th, sir. Company A. — If you'd be so good just to look at my foot, sir, you'd see for yourself that I couldn't march —"

"We'll try it with the Rogue's March. — 65th. Company A. Richard Cleave's old company."

"He ain't my best witness, sir. He's got a grudge against me —"

Stafford looked at him. "Don't put yourself in a fury over it. Have you one against him?"

"I have," said Steve, "and I don't care who knows it! If he was as steady against you, sir, as he has proved himself against me —"

"I would do much, you mean. What is your name?"

"Steven Dagg."

The woman returned. "They've eaten it all, sir. I saved you a piece of bread. I wish it was something better."

Stafford took it from her with thanks. "As for this man, my orderly shall take him up behind, and when we reach Middletown I'll turn him over with my report to his captain. If any more of his kind come around, I would advise you just to shoot them at once. — Now you, sir! In front of me. — March!"

The five horsemen, detail of Flournoy's, sent upon some service the night before, mounted a hill from which was visible a great stretch of country. From the east came the Front Royal road; north and south stretched that great artery, the Valley turnpike. Dust lay over the Front Royal road. Dust hung above the Valley pike — hung from Strasburg to Middletown, and well beyond Middletown. Out of each extended cloud, now at right angles, came rumblings as of thunder. The column beneath the Front Royal cloud was moving rapidly, halts and delays apparently over, lassitude gone, energy raised to a forward blowing flame. That on the Valley pike, the six-mile-long retreat from Strasburg, was making, too, a progress not unrapid, considering the immensity of its wagon train and the uncertainty of the commanding general as to what, on the whole, it might be best to do. The Confederate advance, it was evident, would strike the pike at Middletown in less than fifteen minutes.

Stafford and his men left the hill, entered a body of woods running toward the village, and three minutes later encountered a detachment of blue horsemen, flankers of Hatch's large cavalry force convoying the Federal wagon train. There was a shout, and an interchange of pistol shots. The blue outnumbered the grey four to one. The latter wheeled their horses, used spur and voice, outstripped a shower of bullets and reached Middletown. When, breathless, they drew rein before a street down which grey infantry poured to the onslaught, one of the men, pressing up to Stafford, made his report. "That damned deserter, sir! — in the scrimmage a moment ago he must have slipped off. I'm sorry — but I don't reckon he's much loss."

Steve had taken refuge behind the lock of a rail fence draped with creeper. On the whole, he meant to stay there until the two armies had wended their ways. When it was all done and over, he would make a change somehow and creep to the southward and get a doctor's certificate. All this in the first gasp of relief, at the end of which moment it became apparent that the blue cavalry had seen him run to cover. A couple of troopers rode toward the rail fence. Steve stepped from behind the creepers and surrendered. "Thar are Daggs up North anyway," he explained to the man who took his musket. "I've a pack of third cousins in them parts somewhere. I shouldn't wonder if they weren't fighting on your side this doggoned minute! I reckon I'd as lief fight there myself."

The soldier took him to his officer. "It's a damned deserter, sir. Says he's got cousins with us. Says he'd as soon fight on one side as the other."

"I can't very well fight nowhere," whined Steve. "If you'd be so good as to look at my foot, sir —"

"I see. You deserted and they picked you up. Very well, Mr. Deserter, I want some information and you're the man to give it to me."

Steve gave it without undue reluctance. "What in hell does it matter, anyway?" he thought, "they'll find out damned quick anyhow about numbers and that we are n't only Ewell. Gawd! Old Jack's struck them this very minute! I hear the guns."

So did the company to which he had deserted. "Hell and damnation! Artillery to shake the earth! Middletown. All the wagons to pass and the cavalry. — It is n't just Ewell's division, he says. He says it's all of them and Stonewall Jackson! — Take the fellow up somebody and bring him along! — *Fours right! Forward!*"

Five minutes later they reached the pike, south of Middletown. It proved a seething stream of horse and foot and wagon train, forms shadowy and umber, moving in the whirling dust. Over all hung like a vast and black streamer a sense of panic. Underneath it every horse was restive and every voice had an edge. Steve gathered that there were teamsters who wished to turn and go back to Strasburg. He saw wagon masters plying long black whips about the shoulders of these unwilling; he heard officers shouting. The guns ahead boomed out, and there came a cry of "Ashby"! The next instant found him violently unseated and hurled into the dust of the middle road, from which he escaped by rolling with all the velocity of which he was capable into the depression at the side. He hardly knew what had happened — there had been, he thought, a runaway team dragging an ordnance wagon. He seemed to remember a moving thickness in the all-pervading dust, and, visible for an instant, a great U. S. painted on the wagon side. Then shouts, general scatteration, some kind of a crash — He rubbed a bump upon his forehead, large as a guinea hen's egg. "Gawd! I wish I'd never come into this here world!"

The world was, indeed, to-day rather like a bad dream — like one of those dim and tangled streams of things, strange and frightful, at once grotesquely unfamiliar and sickeningly real, which one neighbours for a time in sleep. Steve picked himself out of the ditch, being much in danger, even there, of trampling hoofs or wagons gone amuck, and attained, how he could not tell, a rank wayside clump of Jamestown weed and pokeberry. In the midst of this he squatted, gathered into as small a bunch as was physically possible. He was in a panic; the sweat cold upon the back of his hands. Action or inaction in this world, sitting, standing, or going seemed alike ugly and dangerous.

First of all, this world was blue-clad and he was dressed in grey.

It was in a wild hurry; the main stream striving somehow to gain Middletown, which must be passed, hook or crook, aid of devil or aid of saint, while a second current surged with increasing strength back toward Strasburg. All was confusion. They would never stop to listen to explanations as to a turned coat! Steve was sure that they would simply shoot him or cut him down before he could say "I am one of you!" They would kill him, like a stray bee in the hive, and go their way, one way or the other, whichever way they were going! The contending motions made him giddy.

An aide in blue, galloping madly from the front, encountered beside the pokeberry clump an officer, directing, with his sword. Steve was morally assured that they had seen him, had stopped, in short, to hale him forth. As they did not — only excitedly shouted each at the other — he drew breath again. He could see the two but dimly, close though they were, because of the dust. Suddenly there came to him a rose-coloured thought. That same veil must make him well-nigh invisible; more than that, the dust lay so thickly on all things that colour in any uniform was a debatable quality. He did n't believe anybody was noticing. The extreme height to which his courage ever attained, was at once his. He felt almost daredevil.

The aide was shouting, so that he might be heard through the uproar. "Where are the guns? Colonel Hatch says for the good Lord's sake hurry them up! Hell's broke loose and occupied Middletown. Ashby's there, and they say Jackson! They've planted guns — they've strung thousands of men behind stone fences — they're using our own wagons for breastworks! The cavalry was trying to get past. Listen to that!"

The other officer shouted also, waving his sword. "There's a battery behind — Here it comes! — We ought to have started last night. The general said he must develop the forces of the enemy —"

"He's developing them all right. Well, good-bye! Meet in Washington!"

The battery passed with uproar, clanging toward the front, scattering men to either side like spray. Steve's wayside bower was invaded. "Get out of here! This ain't no time to be sitting on your tail, thinking of going fishing! G'lang!"

Steve went, covered with dust, the shade of the uniform below never noticed in the furious excitement of the road. Life there was at fever point, aware that death was hovering, and struggling to escape. In the dust and uproar, the blare and panic, he was aware that he was moving toward Middletown where they were fighting. Fighting was not precisely that for which he was looking, and yet he was moving that way, and he could not help it. The noise in front was frightful. The head of the column of which he now formed an unwilling part, the head of the snake, must be somewhere near Newtown, the rattling tail just out of Strasburg. The snake was trying to get clear, trying to get out of the middle Valley to Winchester, fifteen miles away. It was trying to drag its painful length through the village just ahead. There were scorpions in the village, on both sides the pike, on the hills above. Stonewall Jackson with his old sabre, with his "Good! Good!" was hacking at the snake, just there, in its middle. The old sabre had not yet cut quite through, but there was hope — or fear — (the deserter positively did not know which) that presently it would be done. A tall soldier, beside whom, in the dream torrent, Steve found himself, began to talk. "Got any water? No. Nobody has. I guess it's pouring down rain in New Bedford this very minute! All the little streams running." He sighed. "'T ain't no use in fussing. I don't remember to have ever seen you before, but then we're all mixed up —"

"We are," said Steve. "Ain't the racket awful?"

"Awful. 'T is going to be like running the gauntlet, to run that town, and we're most there. If I don't get out alive, and if you ever go to New Bedford — Whoa, there! Look out!"

Steve, thrust by the press away from the pike into a Middletown street, looked for a cellar door through which he might descend and be in darkness. All the street was full of struggling forms. A man on horseback, tall and horrible in the nightmare, cut at him with a sabre as long as himself. Steve ducked, went under the horse's belly, and came up to have a pistol shot take the cap from his head. With a yell he ran beneath the second horse's arching neck. The animal reared; a third horseman raised his carbine. There was an overturned Conestoga wagon in the middle of the street, its white top like a bubble in all the wild swirl and eddy of the place. Steve and the ball from the carbine passed under the arch at the same instant, the bullet lodging somewhere in the wagon bed.

Steve at first thought he might be dead, for it was cool and dark under the tilted canvas, and there was a momentary effect of quietness. The carbine had been fired; perhaps the bullet was in his brain. The uncertainty held but a second; outside the fracas burst forth again, and beneath him something moved in the straw. It proved to be the driver of the wagon, wounded, and fallen back from the seat in front. He spoke now in a curious, dreamy voice. "Get off the top of my broken leg — damn you to everlasting hell!" Steve squirmed to one side. "Sorry. Gawd knows I wish I was n't any nearer it than the Peaks of Otter!" There was a triangular tear in the canvas. He drew down the flap and looked out. "They were Ashby's men — all those three!" He began to cry, though noiselessly. "They had n't ought to cut at me like that — shooting, too, without looking! They ought to ha' seen I was n't no damned Yank —" The figure in the straw moved. Steve turned sick with apprehension. "Did you hear what I said? I was just a-joking. Gawd! It's enough to make a man wish he was a Johnny Reb — Hey, what did you say?"

But the figure in blue said nothing, or only some useless thing about wanting water. Steve, reassured, looked again out of window. His refuge lay a few feet from the pike, and the pike was a road through pandemonium. He could see, upon a height, dimly, through the dust and smoke the Rockbridge battery. Yellow flashes came from it, then ear-splitting sound. A Federal force, horse, foot and guns, had hastily formed in the opposite fields, seized a crest, planted cannon. These sent screaming shells. In between the iron giants roared the mêlée — Ashby jousting with Hatch's convoying cavalry — the Louisiana troops firing in a long battle line, from behind the stone fences — a horrible jam of wagons, overturned or overturning, panic-stricken mules, drivers raving out oaths, using mercilessly long, snaky, black whips — heat, dust, thirst and thunder, wild excitement, blood and death! There were all manner of wagons. Ambulances were there with inmates, — fantastic sickrooms, with glare for shade, Tartarean heat for coolness, cannon thunder and shouting for quietness, grey enemies for nursing women, and for home a battlefield in a hostile land. Heavy ordnance wagons, far from the guns they were meant to feed, traces cut and horses gone, rested reef-like for the tides to break against. Travelling forges kept them company, and wagons bearing officers' luggage. Beneath several the mules were pinned; dreadful sight could any there have looked or pitied! Looming through there were the great supply wagons, with others of lighter stores, holding boxes and barrels of wines and fruits, commodities of all sorts, gold-leafed fripperies, luxuries of all manner, poured across the Potomac for her soldiers by the North. Sutlers' wagons did not lack, garishly stocked, forlorn as Harlequin in the day's stress. In and around and over all these stranded hulls roared the opposing forces. Steve saw Ashby, on the black stallion, directing with a gauntleted hand. Four great draught horses, drawing a loaded van, without a driver, maddened with fright, turned into this street up and down which there was much fighting. A shout arose. Carbines cracked. One of the leaders came down upon his knees. The other slipped in blood and fell. The van overturned, pinning beneath it one of the wheel horses. Its fall, immediately beside the Conestoga, blocked Steve's window. He turned to crawl to the other side. As he did so the wounded soldier in the straw had a remark to make. He made it in the dreamy voice he had used before. "Don't you smell cloth burning?"

Steve did; in an instant saw it burning as well, first the corner of the canvas cover, then the straw beneath. He gave a screech. "We're on fire! Gawd! I've got to get out of this!"

The man in the straw talked dreamily on. "I got a bullet through the end of my backbone. I can't sit up. I been lying here studying the scoop of this here old wagon. It looks to me like the firmament at night, with all the stars a-shining. There's no end of texts about stars. 'Like as one star differeth from another —'" He began to cough. "There seems to be smoke. I guess you'll have to drag me out, brother."

At the end of the village a stone fence ran between two houses, on the other side of a little garden slope planted with potatoes. In the shadow of the wall a line of men, kneeling, rested rifle barrel upon the coping and fired on Hatch's cavalry, now much broken, wavering toward dispersion. At first the line was hidden by a swirl of smoke; this lifted, and Steve recognized a guidon they had planted, then the men themselves. They were the Louisiana Tigers, Wheat's Battalion, upgathered from levee and wharf and New Orleans purlieu, among many of a better cast, not lacking rufflers and bravos,

soldiers of fortune whom Pappenheim might not have scorned.
Their stone wall leaped fire again.

Steve looked to heaven and earth and as far around as the dun
cloud permitted, then moved with swiftness across the potato patch.
All about in the mingled dust and smoke showed a shifting pageantry
of fighting men; upon the black earth below the rank green leaves
and purple blooms lay in postures hardly conceivable the dead and
wounded. In the line by the stone fence was here and there a gap.
Steve, head between shoulders, made for the breastwork and sank
into one of these openings, his neighbour upon one hand an Irish
roustabout, on the other a Creole from a sugar plantation. He explained his own presence. "I got kind of separated from my company — Company A, 65th Virginia. I had an awful fight with three
damned Yanks, and a fourth came in and dragged my gun away! If
you don't mind I'll just stay here and help you —"

"Sorra an objection," said the Irishman. "Pick up Tim's musket
behind you there and get to wurruk!"

"Bon jour!" said the other side. "One camarade ees always zee
welcome!"

An order rang down the line. "Sthop firing, is it?" remarked the
Irishman. "And that's the first dacint wurrud I've heard this half
hour! Wid all the plazure in life, captin!" He rested his musket
against the stones, drew himself up, and viewed the prospect.
"Holy Saint Pathrick! look at them sthramin' off into space! An'
look at the mile of wagons they're afther lavin! Refrishmint in
thim, my frind, for body and sowl!"

Steve pulled himself up beside the other. "Thar ain't any danger
now of stray bullets, I reckon? There's something awful in seeing a
road like that. There's a man that his mother would n't know! —
horse stepped on his face, I reckon. Gawd! we have gangs of prisoners! — Who's that coming out of the cloud?"

"Chew's Horse Artillery — with Ashby, the darlint!"

Ashby stopped before the stone house to the right. "There
are men in here — officers with them. Captain, go bid them surrender."

The captain, obeying, found a barred door and no answer. An
approach to the window revealed behind the closed blinds the gleam
of a musket barrel. "Go again! Tell them their column's cut and

their army dispersed. If they do not surrender at once I will plant a shell in the middle of that room."

The captain returned once more. "Well?"

"They said, 'Go to hell,' sir. They said General Banks would be here in a moment, and they'd taken the house for his headquarters. They've got something in there beside water, I think."

A sergeant put in a word. "There's a score of them. They seized this empty house, and they've been picking off our men —"

"Double canister, point-blank, Allen. — Well, sergeant?"

"It's not certain it was an empty house, sir. One of the Tigers, there, thinks there are women in it."

"Women!"

"He don't know — just thinks so. Thinks he heard a cry when the Yanks broke in — Ah! — Well, better your hat than you, sir! We'll blow that sharpshooter where he can look out of window sure enough! Match's ready, sir."

Ashby put back on his head the soft wide hat with a bullet hole beside the black plume. "No, no, West! We can't take chances like that! We'll break open the door instead."

"The others think that the Tiger was mistaken, sir. They say all the women went out of the other houses, and they're sure they went out of this one, too. Shan't we fire, sir?"

"No, no! We can't take chances. Limber up, lieutenant, and move on with the others. — Volunteers to break open that door!"

"Ain't nobody looking," thought Steve, behind the wall. "Gawd! I reckon I'll have to try my luck again. 'T won't do to stay here." To the big Irishman he said, "Reckon I'll try again to find my company! I don't want to be left behind. Old Jack's going to drive them, and he needs every fighter!"

CHAPTER XXII

THE VALLEY PIKE

A s he moved away from the stone house, the vicinity of Ashby and the line of Tigers behind the fence, he became aware that not a small portion of Wheat's Battalion had broken ranks and was looting the wagons. There were soldiers like grey ants about a sutler's wagon. Steve, struggling and shouldering boldly enough now, managed to get within hailing distance. Men were standing on the wheels, drawing out boxes and barrels and throwing them down into the road, where the ants swarmed to the attack. Not the Tigers alone, but a number of Ashby's men as well engaged in the general business. The latter, either not so hungry or more valiant to abstain from the smaller rifling, turned to the plunder of horses. There were horses enough, dead and wounded, along that frightful road. Others were unhurt, still harnessed to wagons, or corralled in fence corners, or huddled with prisoners in the trodden fields. Horses, to the trooper of the Valley, were as horses in the ten years' war at Troy — the prized spoil of battle, the valued trophies, utilities outweighing all filagree spoil. Each man of Ashby's owned the horse he rode, burned to provide himself with a second mount, and flamed to be able to say at home, " This horse I took at Middletown, just before we drove the Yankees out of the Valley and ended the war!" "Home," for many of them was not at all distant — gallop a few miles, deposit the prize, return, catch up before Winchester! Wild courage, much manliness, much chivalry, ardent devotion to Ashby and the cause, individualism of a citizen soldiery, and a naïve indiscipline all their own — such were Ashby's men! Not a few now acted upon the suggestion of the devil who tempts through horse flesh. In the dust they went by Steve like figures of a frieze.

Inefficient even in plundering, he found himself possessed of but a handful of crackers, a tin of sardines — a comestible he had never seen before and did not like when he tasted it — and a bottle of what he thought wine but proved vinegar. Disgusted, he moved to the next wagon, overswarmed like the first by grey ants. This time it was ale, unfamiliar still, but sufficiently to his liking. "Gawd! Jest to drink when you're thirsty, and eat when you're hungry, and sleep when you're sleepy —"

A drum beat, a bugle blew. *Fall in! Fall in!* Officers passed from wagon to wagon. They were ready enough with the flats of their swords. "For shame, men, for shame! *Fall in! Fall in!* General Jackson is beyond Newtown by now. You don't want him to have to *wait* for you, do you? *Fall in!*"

The Valley pike, in the region of Middletown, proved a cumbered path. From stone fence to stone fence, in the middle trough of dust, and on the bordering of what had been, that morning, dew-gemmed grass and flower, War the maniac had left marks. Overturned wagons formed barriers around which the column must wind. Some were afire; the smoke of burning straw and clothing and foodstuffs mingling with the yet low-lying powder smoke and with the pall of Valley dust. Horses lay stark across the way, or, dying, stared with piteous eyes. The sky was like a bowl of brass, and in the concave buzzards were sailing. All along there was underfoot much of soldiers' impedimenta — knapsacks, belts, accoutrements of all kinds, rolled blankets and oilcloths, canteens. Dead men did not lack. They lay in strange postures, and on all the dust was thick. There were many wounded; the greater number of these had somehow reached the foul grass and trampled flowers of the wayside. Prisoners were met; squads brought in from the road, from fields and woods. There was one group, men and horses covered with the dust of all time, disarmed, hatless, breathless, several bleeding from sabre cuts. One among them — a small man on a tall horse — indulged in bravado. "What are you going to do with us now you've got us? You've nowhere to take us to! Your damned capital's fallen — fell this morning! Yes, it did! News certain. Rebellion's over and Jack Ketch's waiting for you — waiting for every last dirty ragamuffin and slave-driver that calls himself general or president, and for the rest of you, too! Pity you didn't have just one neck so's he could do the whole damn thirteen millions of you at once! — Jeff Davis and Lee and Johnston were hanged at noon. This very moment Little Mac's in Richmond, marching down whatever your damned Pennsylvania Avenue's called —"

A negro body servant marching in the rear of one of the contemptuous companies broke ranks and rushed over to the reviling soldier. "You damn po' white trash, shet yo' mouf or I'll mek you! Callin' Main Street 'Pennsylvania Avenue,' and talkin' 'bout hangin' gent'men what you ain't got 'bility in you ter mek angry enuff ter swear at you! 'N Richmon' fallen! Richmon' ain' half as much fallen as you is! Richmon' ain' never gwine ter fall. I done wait on Marse Robert Lee once't at Shirley, an he ain't er gwine ter let it! '*Pennsylvania* Avenue!'"

Half a mile from Middletown they came up with a forlorn little company. On a high bank above the road, huddled beneath three cedars, appeared the theatrical troupe which had amused General Banks's army in Strasburg. Men and women there were, a dozen actors, and they had with them a cart bearing their canvas booth and the poor finery of their wardrobe. One of the women nursed a baby; they all looked down like wraiths upon the passing soldiers.

Firing broke out ahead. "Newtown," said the men beside Steve. "I've got friends there. Told 'em when we came up the Valley after Kernstown we'd come down again! 'N here we are, bigger'n life and twice as natural! That's Rockbridge making that awful noise. Must be a Yankee battery — There it opens! Oh, we're going to have a chance, too!"

They were moving at double-quick. Steve simulated a stumble, caught himself, groaned and fell out of line. The wall to the left blazed. He uttered a yell and sprang back. "That's right!" said the man. "It's taken most a year to learn it, but you feel a whole heap safer in line than out of it when firing's going on. That's a nice little — what d'ye call it? — they've planted there —"

"Avalanche," panted Steve. "O Gawd!" A minie ball had pierced the other's brain. He fell without a sound, and Steve went on.

The troops entered the hamlet at a run, passing two of the Rockbridge guns planted on a hillock and hurling shell against a Federal battery at the far end of the street. There was hot fighting through the place, then the enemy, rallied here, broke again and dispersed to the westward. The grey soldiers swept through the place, and the people with tears and laughter cried them welcome. On the porch of a comfortable house stood a comfortable, comely matron, pale with ardent patriotism, the happy tears running down her cheeks. Parched as were their throats the troops found voice to cheer, as always, when they passed through these Valley towns. They waved their colours vigorously; their ragged bit of a band played "Old Virginny never tire." The motherly soul on the porch, unconscious of self, uplifted, tremulous with emotion, opened wide her arms, "All of you run here and kiss me!"

Late afternoon came and the army yet skirmished, marched, marched, skirmished on the Valley pike. The heat decreased, but dust and thirst remained. Fatigue was the abominable thing. "Gawd!" thought Steve. "I can't stand it any longer. I got ter quit, and ef I could shoot that lieutenant, I would." The man whom the closing of the ranks had brought upon his left began to speak in a slow, refined voice. "There was a book published in England a year or so ago. It brings together old observations, shoots and theories, welds them, and produces a Thor's hammer that's likely to crack some heads. Once upon a time, it seems, we went on four feet. It's a pity to have lost so valuable a faculty. Oh, Jupiter! we are tired!"

A man behind put in his word. "To-morrow's Sunday. Two Sundays ago we were at Meechum's River, and since then we've marched most two hundred miles, and fought two battles and a heap of skirmishes! I reckon there'll be a big fight to-morrow, with Old Jack jerking his hand in the air as they say he's been doing! 'N all to the sound of church bells! Oh, Moses, I'm tired!"

At sunset the bugles blew halt. The men dropped down on the tarnished earth, on the vast, spectacular road to Winchester. They cared not so much for supper, faint as they were; they wanted sleep. Supper they had — all that could be obtained from the far corners of haversacks and all that, with abounding willingness, the neighbouring farmhouses could scrape together — but when it came to sleep —. With nodding heads the men waited longingly for roll call and tattoo, and instead there came an order from the front. "*A night march!* O Lord, have mercy, for Stonewall Jackson never does." *Fall in! Fall in! Column Forward!*

When they came to the Opequon they had a skirmish with a Massachusetts regiment which fired a heavy volley into the cavalry ahead, driving it back upon the 33d Virginia, next in column. The 33d broke, then rallied. Other of the Stonewall regiments deployed in the fields and the 27th advanced against the opposing force, part of Banks's rearguard. It gave way, disappearing in the darkness of the woods. The grey column, pushing across the Opequon, came into a zone of Federal skirmishers and sharpshooters ambushed behind stone fences.

Somewhere about midnight Steve, walking in about the worst dream he had ever had, determined that no effort was too great if directed toward waking. It was a magic lantern dream — black slides painted only with stars and fireflies, succeeded by slides in which there was a moment's violent illumination, stone fences leaping into being as the musket fire ran along. A halt — a company deployed — the foe dispersed, streaming off into the darkness — the hurt laid to one side for the ambulances—*Column Forward!* Sometimes a gun was unlimbered, trained upon the threatening breastwork and fired. Once a shell burst beneath a wagon that had been drawn into the fields. It held, it appeared, inflammable stores. Wagon and contents shot into the air with a great sound and glare, and out of the light about the place came a frightful crying. Men ran to right and left to escape the rain of missiles; then the light died out, and the crying ceased. The column went on slowly, past dark slides. Its progress seemed that of a snail army. Winchester lay the fewest of miles away, but somewhere there was legerdemain. The fewest of miles stretched like a rubber band. The troops marched for three minutes, halted, marched again, halted, marched, halted. To sleep—to sleep! *Column Forward!—Column Forward!*

There was a bridge to cross over a wide ditch. Steve hardly broke his dream, but here he changed the current. How he managed he could scarce have told, but he did find himself under the bridge where at once he lay down. The mire and weed was like a blissful bed. He closed his eyes. Three feet above was the flooring, and all the rearguard passing over. It was like lying curled in the hollow of a drum, a drum beaten draggingly and slow. "Gawd!" thought Steve. "It sounds like a Dead March."

He slept, despite the canopy of footsteps. He might have lain like a log till morning but that at last the flooring of the bridge rebelled. A section of a battery, kept for some hours at Middletown, found itself addressed by a courier, jaded, hoarse as a raven of the night. "General Jackson says, 'Bring up these guns.' He says, 'Make haste.'" The battery limbered up and came with a heavy noise down the pike, through the night. Before it was the rearguard; the artillery heard the changed sound as the men crossed the wooden bridge. The rearguard went on; the guns arrived also at the ditch and the overtaxed bridge. The Tredegar iron gun went over and on, gaining on the foot, with intent to pass. The howitzer, following, proved the last straw. The bridge broke. A gun wheel went down, and amid the oaths of the drivers a frightened screech came from below. "O Gawd! lemme get out of this!"

Pulled out, he gave an account of his cut foot, piteous enough. The lieutenant listened. "The 65th? Scamp, I reckon, but flesh is weak! Has n't been exactly a circus parade for any of us. Let him ride, men — if ever we get this damned wheel out! Keep an eye on him, Fleming! — Now, all together! — Pull, White Star! — Pull, Red Star!"

The column came to Kernstown about three o'clock in the morning. Dead as were the troops the field roused them. "Kernstown! Kernstown! We're back again."

"Here was where we crossed the pike — there's the old ridge. Griffin tearing up his cards — and Griffin's dead at McDowell."

"That was Fulkerson's wall — that shadow over there! There's the bank where the 65th fought. — Kernstown! I'm mighty tired, boys, but I've got a peaceful certainty that that was the only battle Old Jack's ever going to lose!"

"Old Jack did n't lose it. Garnett lost it."

"That ain't a Stonewall man said that! General Garnett's in trouble. I reckon did n't anybody lose it. Shields had nine thousand men, and he just gained it! — Shields the best man they've had in the Valley. Kernstown! — Heard what the boys at Middletown called Banks? *Mr. Commissary Banks.* Oh, law! that pesky rearguard again!"

The skirmish proved short and sharp. The Federal rearguard gave way, fell back on Winchester; the Confederate column, advance, main and rear, heard in the cold and hollow of the night the order: *Halt. Stack arms! Break ranks!* From regiment to regiment ran a further word. "One hour. You are to rest one hour, men. Lie down."

In the first grey streak of dawn a battery which had passed in turn each segment of the column, came up with the van, beyond Kernstown battlefield, and halted upon a little rise of ground. All around stretched grey, dew-wet fields and woods, and all around lay an army, sleeping, strange sight in the still and solemn light, with the birds cheeping overhead! The guns stopped, the men got down from limber and caisson, the horses were unhitched. "An hour's sleep — Kernstown battlefield!"

An officer whose command lay in the field to the left, just beyond a great breach that had been made in the stone fence, arose from the cloak he had spread in the opening and came over to the guns. "Good-morning, Randolph! Farmers and soldiers see the dawn!

> Light thickens; and the crow
> Makes wing to the rooky wood.

The poor guns! Even they look overmarched." As he spoke he stroked the howitzer as though it had been a living thing.

"We've got with us a stray of yours," said the artilleryman. "Says he has a cut foot, but looks like a skulker. Here you, Mr. Under-the-Bridge! come from behind that caisson —"

Out of a wood road, a misty opening overarched by tall and misty trees, came two or three horsemen, the foremost of whom rode up to the battery. "Good-morning, Randolph! General Jackson will be by in a moment. General Ewell lies over there on the Front Royal road. He has eaten breakfast, and is clanking his spurs and swearing as they swore in Flanders." He pointed with his gauntleted hand, turning as he did so in the saddle. The action brought recognition of Cleave's presence upon the road. Stafford ceased speaking and sat still, observing the other with narrowed eyes.

Cleave addressed the figure, which, there being no help for it, had come from behind the caisson. "You, Dagg, of course! Straggling or deserting — I wonder which this time! Are you not ashamed?"

"Gawd, major! I just could n't keep up. I got a cut foot —"

"Sit down on that rock. — Take off your shoe — what is left of it. Now, let me see. Is that the cut, that scratch above the ankle?"

"It ain't how deep it is. It's how it hurts."

"There is no infantryman to-day who is not footsore and tired. Only the straggler or deserter has as few marks as you to show. There is the company, down the road, in the field. To-night I shall find out if you have been with it all the day. Go! You disgrace the very mountains where you were born —"

Beyond the guns was a misty bend of the road. The light was stronger, in the east a slender streamer of carnation; the air dank, cool and still. On the edge of Kernstown battlefield a cock crew; a second horn came faintly. Very near at hand sounded a jingle of accoutrement; Stonewall Jackson, two or three of the staff with him, came around the turn and stopped beside the guns. The men about them and the horses, and on the roadside, drew themselves up and saluted. Jackson gave his slow quiet nod. He was all leaf bronze from head to foot, his eyes just glinting beneath the old forage cap. He addressed the lieutenant. "You will advance, sir, in just three quarters of an hour. There are batteries in place upon the ridge before us. You will take position there, and you will not leave until ordered." His eyes fell upon Stafford. "Have you come from General Ewell?"

"Yes, general. He sends his compliments, and says he is ready."

"Good! Good! — What is this soldier doing here?" He looked at Steve.

"It is a straggler, sir, from my regiment. Lieutenant Randolph picked him up —"

"Found him under a bridge, sir. I'd call him a deserter —"

Steve writhed as though, literally, the eyes were cold steel and had pinned him down. "Gawd, general! I did n't desert! Cross my heart and may I go to hell if I did! I was awful tired — hungry and thirsty — and my head swimming — I just dropped out, meaning to catch up after a bit! I had a sore foot. Major Cleave's awful hard on me —"

"You're a disgrace to your company," said Cleave. "If we did not need even shadows and half men you would be drummed home to Thunder Run, there to brag, loaf, and rot —"

Steve began to whine. "I meant to catch up, I truly did!" His eyes, shifting from side to side, met those of Stafford. "Gawd, I'm lost —"

Stafford regarded his quondam prisoner curiously enough. His gaze had in it something of cruelty, of pondering, and of question. Steve writhed. "I ain't any better 'n anybody else. Life's awful! Everybody in the world's agin me. Gawd knows Major Cleave's so —" Cleave made a sound of contempt.

Stafford spoke. "I do not think he's actually a deserter. I remember his face. I met him near Middletown, and he gave me his regiment and company. There are many stragglers."

Steve could have fallen and worshipped. "Don't care whether he did it for me, or jest 'cause he hates that other one! He does hate him! 'N I hate him, too — sending me to the guardhouse every whip-stitch!" This to himself; outside he tried to look as though he had carried the colours from Front Royal, only dropping them momentarily at that unfortunate bridge. Jackson regarded him with a grey-blue eye unreconciled, but finally made his peculiar gesture of dismissal. The Thunder Run man saluted and stumbled from the roadside into the field, the dead Tiger's musket in the hollow of his arm, his face turned toward Company A. Back in the road Jackson turned his eyes on Cleave. "Major, in half an hour you will advance with your skirmishers. Do as well as you have done heretofore and you will do well — very well. The effect of Colonel Brooke's wound is graver than was thought. He has asked to be retired. After Winchester you will have your promotion."

With his staff he rode away — a leaf brown figure, looming large in the misty half light, against the red guidons of the east. Stafford went with him. Randolph, his cannoneers and drivers dropped beside the pieces and were immediately asleep — half an hour now was all they had. The horses cropped the pearled wayside grass. Far away the cocks were crowing. In the east the red bannerols widened. There came a faint blowing of bugles. Cleave stooped and took up his cloak.

Steve, stumbling back over the wet field, between the ranks of sleeping men, found Company A — that portion of it not with the skirmishers. Every soul was asleep. The men lay heavily, some drawn into a knot, others with arms flung wide, others on their faces. They lay in the dank and chilly dawn as though death had reaped the field. Steve lay down beside them. "Gawd! when will this war be over?"

He dreamed that he was back at Thunder Run, crouching behind a certain boulder at a turn of the road that wound up from the Valley. He had an old flintlock, but in his dream he did not like it, and it changed to one of the beautiful modern rifles they were beginning to take from the Yankees. There were no Yankees on Thunder Run. Steve felt assured of that in his dream; very secure and comfortable. Richard Cleave came riding up the road on Dundee. Steve lifted the rifle to his shoulder and sighted very carefully. It seemed that he was not alone behind the boulder. A shadowy figure with a sword, and a star on his collar, said, "Aim at the heart." In the dream he fired, but before the smoke could clear so that he might know his luck the sound of the shot changed to clear trumpets, long and wailing. Steve turned on his side. "Reveille! O Gawd!"

The men arose, the ranks were formed. *No breakfast?* — Hairston Breckinridge explained the situation. "We're going to breakfast in Winchester, men! All the dear old cooks are getting ready for us — rolls and waffles and broiled chicken and poached eggs and coffee — and all the ladies in muslin and ribbons are putting flowers on the table and saying, 'The Army of the Valley is coming home!' — Isn't that a Sunday morning breakfast worth waiting for? The sooner we whip Banks the sooner we'll be eating it."

"All right. All right," said the men. "We'll whip him all right."

"We're sure to whip him now we've got Steve back!"

"That's so. Where've you been anyway, Steve, and how many did you kill on the road?"

"I killed three," said Steve. "General Ewell's over thar in the woods, and he's going to advance 'longside of us, on the Front Royal road. Rockbridge 'n the rest of the batteries are to hold the ridge up there, no matter what happens! Banks ain't got but six thousand men, and it ought ter be an easy job —"

"Good Lord! Steve's been absent at a council of war — talking familiarly with generals! Always thought there must be more in him than appeared, since there couldn't well be less —"

"Band's playing! 'The Girl I Left Behind Me'!"

"That's Winchester! Didn't we have a good time there 'fore and after Bath and Romney? 'Most the nicest Valley town!— and we had to go away and leave it blue as indigo —"

"I surely will be glad to see Miss Fanny again —"

"Company C over there's most crazy. It all lives there —"

"Three miles! That ain't much. I feel rested. There goes the 2d! Don't it swing off long and steady? Lord, we've got the hang of it at last!"

"Will Cleave's got to be sergeant. — 'N he's wild about a girl in Winchester. Says his mother and sister are there, too, and he can't sleep for thinking of the enemy all about them. Children sure do grow up quick in war time!"

"A lot of things grow up quick — and a lot of things don't grow at all. There goes the 4th — long and steady! Our turn next."

Steve again saw from afar the approach of the nightmare. It stood large on the opposite bank of Abraham's Creek, and he must go to meet it. He was wedged between comrades — Sergeant Coffin was looking straight at him with his melancholy, bad-tempered eyes—he could not fall out, drop behind! The backs of his hands began to grow cold and his unwashed forehead was damp beneath matted, red-brown elf locks. From considerable experience he knew that presently sick stomach would set in. When the company splashed through Abraham's Creek he would not look at the running water, but when he looked at the slopes he was expected presently to climb he saw that there was fighting there and that the nightmare attended! Steve closed his eyes. "O Gawd, take care of me —"

Later on, when the ridge was won he found himself, still in the company of the nightmare, cowering close to the lock of a rail fence that zigzagged along the crest. How he got there he really did not know. He had his musket still clutched — his mountaineer's instinct served for that. Presently he made the discovery that he had been firing, had fired thrice, it appeared from his cartridge box. He remembered neither firing nor loading, though he had some faint recollection of having been upon his knees behind a low stone wall—he saw it now at right angles with the rail fence. A clover field he remembered because some one had said something about four-leaved clovers, and then a shell had come by and the clover turned red. Seized with panic he bit a cartridge and loaded. The air was rocking; moreover, with the heavier waves came a sharp zzzz-*ip!* zzzzzz-*ip!* Heaven and earth blurred together, blended by the giant brush of eddying smoke. Steve tasted powder, smelled powder. On the other side of the fence, from a battery lower down the slope to the guns beyond him two men were running — running very swiftly, with bent heads. They ran like people in a pelting rain, and between them they carried a large bag or bundle, slung in an oilcloth. They were tall and hardy men, and they moved with a curious air of determination. "Carrying powder! Gawd! before I'd be sech a fool — " A shell came, and burst — burst between the two men. There was an explosion, ear-splitting, heart-rending. A part of the fence was wrecked; a small cedar tree torn into kindling. Steve put down his musket, laid his forehead upon the rail before him, and vomited.

The guns were but a few yards above him, planted just below the crest, their muzzles projecting over. Steve recognized Rockbridge. He must, he thought, have been running away, not knowing where he was going, and infernally managed to get up here. The nightmare abode with him. His joints felt like water, his heart was straightened, stretched, and corded in his bosom like a man upon the rack. He pressed close into the angle of the fence, made himself of as little compass as his long and gangling limbs allowed, and held himself still as an opossum feigning death. Only his watery blue eyes wandered — not for curiosity, but that he might see and dodge a coming harm.

Before him the ridge ran steeply down to a narrow depression, a little vale, two hundred yards across. On the further side the land rose again to as high a hill. Here was a stone fence, which even as he looked, leaped fire. Above it were ranged the blue cannon — three batteries, well served. North and South, muzzle to muzzle, the guns roared across the green hollow. The blue musketrymen behind the wall were using minies. Of all death-dealing things Steve most hated these. They came with so unearthly a sound — zzzz-ip! zzzzz-ip! — a devil noise, a death that shrieked, taunted, and triumphed. To-day they made his blood like water. He crouched close, a mere lump of demoralization, behind a veil of wild buckwheat.

Rockbridge was suffering heavily, both from the opposing Parrotts and from sharpshooters behind the wall. A belated gun came straining up the slope, the horses doing mightily, the men cheering. There was an opening in a low stone wall across the hillside, below

Steve. The gate had been wrenched away and thrown aside, but the thick gatepost remained, and it made the passage narrow — too narrow for the gun team and the carriage to pass. All stopped and there was a colloquy.

"We've got an axe?"

"Yes, captain."

"John Agnor, you've felled many a tree. Take the axe and cut that post down."

"Captain, I will be killed!"

"Then you will be killed doing your duty, John. Get down."

Agnor got the axe, swung it and began chopping. The stone wall across the hollow blazed more fiercely; the sharpshooters diverted their attention from the men and horses higher upon the hill. Agnor swung the axe with steadiness; the chips flew far. The post was cut almost through before his billet came. In falling he clutched the weakened obstruction, and the two came down together. The gun was free to pass, and it passed, each cannoneer and driver looking once at John Agnor, lying dead with a steady face. It found place a few yards above Steve in his corner, and joined in the roar of its fellows, throwing solid shot and canister.

A hundred yards and more to the rear stood a barn. The wounded from all the guns, strung like black beads along the crest, dragged themselves or were carried to this shelter. Hope rose in Steve's heart. "Gawd! I'll creep through the clover and git there myself." He started on hands and knees, but once out of his corner and the shrouding mass of wild buckwheat, terror took him. The minies were singing like so many birds. A line of blue musketrymen, posted behind cover, somewhat higher than the grey, were firing alike at gunners, horses, and the men passing to and fro behind the fighting line. Steve saw a soldier hobbling to the barn throw up his arms, and pitch forward. Two carrying a third between them were both struck. The three tried to drag themselves further, but only the one who had been borne by the others succeeded. A shell pierced the roof of the barn, burst and set the whole on fire. Steve turned like a lizard and went back to the lock of the fence and the tattered buckwheat. He could hear the men talking around the gun just beyond. They spoke very loud, because the air was shaken like an ocean in storm. They were all powder-grimed, clad only in trousers and shirt, the shirt open over the breast, and sleeves rolled up. They stood straight, or bent, or crept about the guns, all their movements swift and rhythmic. Sometimes they were seen clearly; sometimes the smoke swallowed them. When seen they looked larger than life, when only heard their voices came as though earth and air were speaking. "Sponge out. — All right. Fire! Hot while it lasts, but it won't last long. I have every confidence in Old Jack and Old Dick. Drat that primer! All right! — Three seconds! Jerusalem! that created a sensation. The Louisianians are coming up that cleft between the hills. All the Stonewall regiments in the centre. Ewell to flank their left. Did you ever hear Ewell swear? Look out! wheel's cut through. Lanyard's shot away. Take handkerchiefs. Haven't got any — tear somebody's shirt. Number 1! Number 2! Look out! look out — Give them hell. Good Heaven! here's Old Jack. General, we hope you'll go away from here! We'll stay it out — give you our word. Let them enfilade ahead! — but you'd better go back, sir."

"Thank you, captain, but I wish to see —"

A minie ball imbedded itself in a rail beside Steve's cheek. Before he could recover from this experience a shell burst immediately in front of his panel. He was covered with earth, a fragment of shell sheared away the protecting buckwheat and a piece of rail struck him in the back with force. He yelled, threw down his musket and ran.

He passed John Agnor lying dead by the gateway, and he reached somehow the foot of the hill and the wide fields between the embattled ridges and the Valley pike, the woods and the Front Royal road. He now could see the Federal line of battle, drawn on both sides of the pike, but preponderantly to the westward. They were there, horse and foot and bellowing artillery, and they did not look panic-stricken. Their flags were flying, their muskets gleaming. They had always vastly more and vastly better bands than had the grey, and they used them more frequently. They were playing now — a brisk and stirring air, sinking and swelling as the guns boomed or were silent. The mist was up, the sun shone bright. "Gawd!" thought Steve. "I'd better be there than here! We ain't a-goin' to win, anyhow. They've got more cannon, and a bigger country, and all the ships, and pockets full of money. Once't I had a chance to move North —"

He had landed in a fringe of small trees by a little runlet, and now, under this cover, he moved irresolutely forward. "Ef I walked toward them with my hands up, they surely would n't shoot. What's that? — Gawd! Look at Old Jack a-comin'! Reckon I'll stay — Told them once't on Thunder Run I would n't move North for nothing! *Yaaaihhhh! Yaaaaihhh —*"

Yaaihhhhh! Yaaihhhhh! Yaaaihh! Yaaaaaaaihhhh! Ten thousand grey soldiers with the sun on their bayonets —

There came by a riderless horse, gentle enough, unfrightened, wanting only to drink at the little stream. Steve caught him without difficulty, climbed into the saddle and followed the army. The army was a clanging, shouting, triumphant thing to follow — to follow into the Winchester streets, into a town that was mad with joy. A routed army was before it, pouring down Loudoun Street, pouring down Main Street, pouring down every street and lane, pouring out of the northern end of the town, out upon the Martinsburg pike, upon the road to the frontier, the road to the Potomac. There was yet firing in narrow side streets, a sweeping out of single and desperate knots of blue. Church bells were pealing, women young and old were out of doors, weeping for pure joy, laughing for the same, praising, blessing, greeting sons, husbands, lovers, brothers, friends, deliverers. A bearded figure, leaf brown, on a sorrel nag, answered with a gravity strangely enough not without sweetness the acclamation with which he was showered, sent an aide to hasten the batteries, sent another with an order to General George H. Steuart commanding cavalry, jerked his hand into the air and swept on in pursuit out by the Martinsburg pike. The infantry followed him, hurrahing. They tasted to-day the sweets of a patriot soldiery relieving a patriot town. The guns came thundering through, the horses doing well, the proud drivers, cannoneers, officers, waving caps and hats, bowing to half-sobbing hurrahs, thrown kisses, praises, blessings. Ewell's division poured through — Ewell on the flea-bitten grey, Rifle, swearing his men forward, pithily answering the happy people, all the while the church bells clanging. The town was in a clear flame of love, patriotism, martial spirit, every heart enlarged, every house thrown open to the wounded whom, grey and blue alike, the grey surgeons were bringing in.

For fear to keep him, Steve had left his captured horse's back and let him go loose. Now on foot and limping terribly, trying to look equal parts fire-eater and woe-begone, he applied to a grey-headed couple in the dooryard of a small clean home. Would they give a hurt soldier a bed and something to eat? Why, of course, of course they would! Come right in! What command?

"The Stonewall Brigade, sir. You see, 't was this a-way. I was helping serve a gun, most of the gunners being strewed around dead — and we infantrymen having to take a hand, and a thirty pound Parrott came and burst right over us! I was stooping, like this, my thumb on the vent, like that — and a great piece struck me in the back! I just kin hobble. Thank you, ma'am! You are better to me than I deserve."

CHAPTER XXIII

MARGARET CLEAVE drew her arms gently from under the wounded boy she had been tending. He was asleep; had gone to sleep calling her "Maman" and babbling of wild-fowl on the bayou. She kissed him lightly on the forehead "for Will" — Will, somewhere on the Martinsburg pike, battling in heat and dust, battling for the Confederacy, driving the foe out of Virginia, back across the Potomac — Will who, little more than a year ago, had been her "baby," whom she kissed each night when he went to sleep in his little room next hers at Three Oaks. She straightened herself and looked around for more work. The large room, the "chamber" of the old and quiet house in which she and Miriam had stayed on when in March the army had withdrawn from Win-chester, held three wounded. Upon the four-post bed, between white valance and tester, lay a dying officer. His wife was with him, and a surgeon, who had found the ball but could not stop the hemorrhage. A little girl sat on the bed, and every now and then put forth a hand and timidly stroked her father's clay-cold wrist. On the floor, on a mattress matching the one on which the boy lay, was stretched a gaunt giant from some backwoods or mountain clearing. Mar-garet knelt beside him and he smiled up at her. "I ain't much hurt, and I ain't sufferin' to amount to nothin'. Ef this pesky butternut would n't stick in this here hurt place—" She cut the shirt from a sabre wound with the scissors hanging at her waist, then bringing water bathed away the grime and dried blood. "You're right," she said. "It is n't much of a cut. It will soon heal." They spoke in whispers, not to disturb the central group. "But you don't look easy. You are still suffering. What is it?"

"It ain't nothing. It's my foot, that a shell kind of got in the way of. But don't you tell anybody — for fear they might want to cut it off, ma'am."

She looked and made a pitying sound. The officer on the bed had now breathed his last. She brought the unneeded surgeon to the crushed ankle, summoned to help him another of the women in the house, then moved to the four-poster and aided the tearless widow, young and soon again to become a mother, to lay the dead calm and straight. The little girl began to shake and shudder. She took her in her arms and carried her out of the room. She found Miriam helping in the storeroom. "Get the child's doll and take her into the garden for a little while. She is cold as ice; if she begins to cry don't stop her. When she is better, give her to Hannah and you go sit beside the boy who is lying on the floor in the chamber. If he wakes, give him water, but don't let him lift himself. He looks like Will."

In the hall a second surgeon met her. "Madam, will you come help? I've got to take off a poor fellow's leg." They entered a room together — the parlour this time, with the windows flung wide and the afternoon sunlight lying in pools among the roses of the carpet. Two mahogany tables had been put together, and the soldier lay atop, the crushed leg bared and waiting. The surgeon had an assistant and the young man's servant was praying in a corner. Margaret uttered a low, pained exclamation. This young lieutenant had been well liked last winter in Winchester. He had been much at this house. He had a good voice and she had played his accompaniments while he sang — oh, the most sentimental of ditties! Miriam had liked him very well — they had read together — "The Pilgrims of the Rhine" — Goldsmith — Bernardin de Saint Pierre. He had a trick of serenading — danced well. She put her cheek down to his hand. "My poor, poor boy! My poor, brave boy!"

The lieutenant smiled at her — rather a twisted smile, shining out of a drawn white face. "I've got to be brave on one leg. Anyhow, Mrs. Cleave, I can still sing and read. How is Miss Miriam?"

The assistant placed a basin and cloths. The surgeon gave a jerk of his head. "You come on this side, Mrs. Cleave."

"No chloroform?"

"No chloroform. Contraband of war. Damned chivalric contest."

Late in the afternoon, as she was crossing the hall upon some other of the long day's tasks she heard a group of soldiers talking. There

were infantry officers from the regiments left in town, and a dusty
cavalryman or two — riders from the front with dispatches or orders.
One with an old cut glass goblet of water in his hand talked and drank,
talked and drank.

"The aide came to George H. Steuart and said, 'General Jackson
orders you to pursue vigorously. He says lose no time. He says
kill and capture; let as few as possible get to the Potomac. Do
your best.'" He filled his glass again from the pitcher standing by.
"Steuart answers that he's of General Ewell's Division. Must take
his orders from General Ewell."

"West Point notions! Good Lord!"

"Says the aide, 'General Jackson commands General Ewell, and
so may command you. His orders are that you shall pursue vigorously' — Says Steuart, 'I will send a courier to find General Ewell.
If his orders are corroboratory I will at once press forward —'"

"Good God! did he think Banks would wait?"

"Old Dick was in front; he was n't behind. Took the aide two
hours to find him, sitting on Rifle, swearing because he did n't see
the cavalry! Well, he made the air around him blue, and sent back
highly 'corroboratory' orders. Steuart promptly 'pressed forward
vigorously,' but Lord! Banks was halfway to the Potomac, his
troops streaming by every cow path, Stonewall and the infantry advance behind him — but Little Sorrel could n't do it alone." He
put down the glass. "Steuart 'll catch it when Old Jack reports.
We might have penned and killed the snake, and now it's gotten
away!"

"Never mind! It's badly hurt and it's quitting Virginia at a
high rate of speed. It's left a good bit of its skin behind, too. Hawks
says he's damned if the army shan't have square meals for a week,
and Crutchfield's smiling over the guns —"

"Falligant says the men are nigh dead, officers nodding in their
saddles, giving orders in their sleep. Falligant says —"

Margaret touched one of the group upon the arm. He swung
round in the hall that was darkening toward sunset and swept
off his hat. "Do you think, sir, that there will be fighting to-
night?"

"I think not, madam. There may be skirmishes of course — our
men may cut off parties of the enemy. But there will be no general

battle. It is agreed that General Banks will get across the Potomac.
The troups will bivouac this side of Martinsburg."

The wounded in the house slept or did not sleep. The young
widow sat beside the dead officer. She would not be drawn away —
said that she was quite comfortable, not unhappy, there was so
much happiness to remember. Hannah found a nook for the little
girl and put her to bed. The officers went away. There were a
thousand things to do, and, also, they must snatch some sleep, or
the brain would reel. The surgeon, hollow-eyed, grey with fatigue,
dropping for sleep, spoke at the open front door to the elderly lady
of the house and to Margaret Cleave. "Lieutenant Waller will die,
I am afraid, though always while there is life there is hope. No,
there is nothing — I have given Mrs. Cleave directions, and his
boy is a good nurse. I'll come back myself about midnight. That
Louisiana youngster is all right. You might get two men and move
him from that room. No; the other won't lose the foot. He, too,
might be moved, if you can manage it. I'll be back —"

"I wish you might sleep yourself, doctor."

"Should n't mind it. I don't expect you women do much sleeping either. Got to do without like coffee for a while. Funny world,
funny life, funny death, funny universe. Could give whoever made
it a few points myself. Excuse me, ladies, I hardly know what I am
saying. Yes, thank you, I see the step. I'll come back about midnight."

The old yards up and down the old street were much trampled,
shrubbery broken, fences down, the street thick dust, and still
strewn with accoutrements that had been thrown away, with here
and there a broken wagon. Street and pavement, there was passing
and repassing — the life of the rear of an army, and the faring to
and fro on many errands of the people of the relieved town. There
were the hospitals and there were the wounded in private houses.
There were the dead, and all the burials for the morrow — the negroes digging in the old graveyard, and the children gathering
flowers. There were the living to be cared for, the many hungry
to be fed. All the town was exalted, devoted, bent on service — a
little city raised suddenly to a mountain platform, set in a strange,
high light, fanned by one of the oldest winds, and doing well with
a clear intensity.

Miriam came and stood beside her mother, leaning her head upon the other's breast. The two seemed like elder and younger sister, no more. There was a white jasmine over the porch, in the yard the fireflies were beginning to sparkle through the dusk. "Dear child, are you very tired?"

"I am not tired at all. That Louisiana boy called me 'Zephine' — 'Zephine!' 'Zephine, your eyes are darker, but your lips are not so red.' He said he kept all my letters over his heart — only he tore them up before the battle, tore them into little bits and gave them to the wind, so that if he fell into his hands 'l'ennemi' might not read them."

"The doctor says that he will do well."

"He is like Will. Oh, mother, I feel ten thousand years old! I feel as though I had always lived."

"I, too, dear. Always. I have always borne children and they have always gone forth to war. They say there will be no fighting to-night."

She put her daughter slightly from her and leaned forward, listening. "That is Richard. His foot strikes that way upon the street."

In the night, in his mother's chamber Cleave waked from three hours of dreamless sleep. She stood beside him. "My poor, dead man, I hated to keep my word."

He smiled. "It would have been as hard to wake up at the end of a week! — Mother, I am so dirty!"

"The servants have brought you plenty of hot water, and we have done the best we could with your uniform. Here is fresh underwear, and a beautiful shirt. I went myself down to the officer in charge of captured stores. He was extremely good and let me have all I wished. Tullius is here. He came in an hour ago with Dundee. I will send him up. When you are dressed come into the hall. I will have something there for you to eat."

Richard drew her hand to his lips. "I wonder who first thought of so blessed an institution as a mother? Only a mother could have thought of it, and so there you are again in the circle!"

When he was dressed he found in the wide upper hall without his door, spread upon a small leaf table, a meal frugal and delicate. A breeze came through the open window, and with it the scent of

jasmine. The wind blew the candle flame until his mother, stepping lightly, brought a glass shade and set it over the silver stick.
Small moths flew in and out, and like a distant ground swell came
the noise of the fevered town. The house itself was quiet after the
turmoil of the day; large halls and stair in dimness, the ill or
wounded quiet or at least not loudly complaining. Now and then a
door softly opened or closed; a woman's figure or that of some coloured servant passed from dimness to dimness. They passed and
the whole was quiet again. Mother and son spoke low. "I will not
wake Miriam until just time to say good-bye. She is overwrought,
poor child! She had counted so on seeing Will."

"We will press on now, I think, to Harper's Ferry. But events
may bring us this way again. The 2d is bivouacked by a little
stream, and I saw him fast asleep. He is growing strong, hardy,
bronzed. It is striking twelve. Tullius is saddling Dundee."

"There will be no fighting in the morning?"

"No. Not, perhaps, until we reach Harper's Ferry. Banks will
get across to Williamsport to-night. For the present he is off the
board. Saxton at Harper's Ferry has several thousand men, and he
will be at once heavily reinforced from Washington. It is well for
us and for Richmond that that city is so nervous."

"General Jackson is doing wonderful work, is he not, Richard?"

"Yes. It is strange to see how the heart of the army has turned
to him. 'Old Jack' can do no wrong. But he is not satisfied with
to-day's work."

"But if they are out of Virginia —"

"They should be in Virginia — prisoners of war. It was a cavalry failure. — Well, it cannot be helped."

"Will you cross at Harper's Ferry?"

"With all my heart I wish we might! Defensive war should
always be waged in the enemy's territory. But I am certain that we
are working with the explicit purpose of preventing McDowell's
junction with McClellan and the complete investment of Richmond
which would follow that junction. We are going to threaten Washington. The government there may be trusted, I think, to recall
McDowell. Probably also they will bring upon our rear Frémont from
the South Branch. That done, we must turn and meet them both."

"Oh, war! Over a year now it has lasted! There are so many

in black, and the church bells have always a tolling sound. And then the flowers bloom, and we hear laughter as we knit."

"All colours are brighter and all sounds are deeper. If there is horror, there is also much that is not horror. And there is nobility as well as baseness. And the mind adapts itself, and the ocean is deeper than we think. Somewhere, of course, lies the shore of Brotherhood, and beyond that the shore of Oneness. It is not unlikely, I think, that we may reinforce Johnston at Richmond."

"Then Miriam and I will make our way there also. How long will it last, Richard — the war?"

"It may last one year and it may last ten. The probability is perhaps five."

"Five years! All the country will be grey-haired."

"War is a forge, mother. Many things will be forged — more of iron perhaps than of gold."

"You have no doubt of the final victory?"

"If I ever have I put it from me. I do not doubt the armies nor the generals — and, God knows, I do not doubt the women at home! If I am not so sure in all ways of the government, at least no man doubts its integrity and its purpose. The President, if he is clear and narrow rather than clear and broad, if he sometimes plays the bigot, if he is a good field officer rather than the great man of affairs we need — yet he is earnest, disinterested, able, a patriot. And Congress does its best — is at least eloquent and fires the heart. Our crowding needs are great and our resources small; it does what it can. The departments work hard. Benjamin, Mallory, Randolph, Meminger — they are all good men. And the railroad men and the engineers and the chemists and the mechanics — all so wonderfully and pathetically ingenious, labouring day and night, working miracles without material, making bricks without straw. Arsenals, foundries, powder-mills, workshop, manufactories — all in a night, out of the wheat fields! And the runners of blockades, and the river steamer men, the special agents, the clerks, the workers of all kind — a territory large as Europe and every man and woman in the field in one aspect or another! If patriotism can save and ability, fortitude, endurance, we are saved. And yet I think of my old 'Plutarch's Lives,' and of all the causes that have been lost. And sometimes in the middle of the night, I see all our blocked ports — and the Mississippi, slipping from our hands. I do not believe that England will come to our help. There is a sentiment for us, undoubtedly, but like the island mists it stays at home."

He rose from the table. "And yet the brave man fights and must hope. Hope is the sky above him — and the skies have never really fallen. I do not know how I will come out of war! I know how I went into it, but no man knows with what inner change he will come out. Enough now, being in, to serve with every fibre."

She shaded her eyes with her hand. With her soft brown hair, with her slender maturity, with the thin fine bit of lace at her neck, against the blowing curtains and in the jasmine scent she suggested something fine and strong and sweet, of old time, of all time. "I know that you will serve with every fibre," she said. "I know it because I also shall serve that way." Presently she dropped her hand and looked up at him with a face, young, soft, and bright, lit from within. "And so at last, Richard, you are happy in the lovely ways!"

He put something in her hand. "Would you like to see it? She sent it to me, two weeks ago. It does not do her justice."

Margaret laughed. "They never do! But I agree with you — and yet, it is lovely! Her eyes were always wonderful, and she smiles like some old picture. I shall love her well, Richard."

"And she you. Mother, the country lies on my heart. I see a dark'ning sky and many graveyards, and I hear, now ' Dixie,' now a Dead March. And yet, through it all there runs a singing stream, under a blue Heaven —"

A little later, Miriam having waked, he said a lingering, fond good-bye, and leaving them both at the gate in the dead hour before the dawn, rode away on Dundee, Tullius following him, down the pike, toward the sleeping army. He passed the pickets and came to the first regiment before dawn; to the 65th just as the red signals showed in the east. It was a dawn like yesterday's. Far and wide lay the army, thousands of men, motionless on the dew-drenched earth, acorns fallen from the tree of war. He met an officer, plodding through the mist, trying to read in the dim light a sheaf of orders which he carried. "Good-morning, adjutant."

"Good-morning. Richard Cleave, isn't it? Hear you are going to be a general. Hear Old Jack said so."

Cleave laughed, a vibrant sound, jest and determination both.

"Of course I am! I settled that at sixteeen, one day when I was ploughing corn. How they all look, scattered wide like that!"

"Reveille not until six. The general's going to beat the devil round the stump. Going to have a Sunday on a Monday. Rest, clean up, divine service. Need all three, certainly need two. Good record the last few weeks — reason to be thankful. Well, good-bye! Always liked you, Cleave!"

Reveille sounded, and the army arose. Breakfast was a sumptuous thing, delicately flavoured with compliments upon the taste, range, and abundance of the Federal commissariat. Roll call followed, with the moment's full pause after names that were not answered to. A general order was read.

Within four weeks this army has made long and rapid marches, fought six combats and two battles, signally defeating the enemy in each one, captured several stands of colours and pieces of artillery, with numerous prisoners and vast medical, ordnance, and army stores; and finally driven the host that was ravaging our country into utter rout. The general commanding would warmly express to the officers and men under his command, his joy in their achievements and his thanks for their brilliant gallantry in action and their patient obedience under the hardship of forced marches; often more painful to the brave soldier than the dangers of battle. The explanation of the severe exertions to which the commanding general called the army, which were endured by them with such cheerful confidence in him, is now given, in the victory of yesterday. He receives this proof of their confidence in the past with pride and gratitude, and asks only a similar confidence in the future.

But his chief duty to-day, and that of the army, is to recognize devoutly the hand of a protecting providence in the brilliant successes of the last three days, and to make the oblation of our thanks to God for his mercies to us and to our country, in heartfelt acts of religious worship. For this purpose the troops will remain in camp to-day, suspending as far as practicable all military exercises; and the chaplains of regiments will hold divine service in their several charges at four o'clock P. M.

At four the general went to church with the 37th Virginia. The doxology sung, the benediction pronounced, he told the chaplain that he had been edified exceedingly, and he looked it. There were times when it might be said quite truly that his appearance was that of an awkward knight of the Holy Grail.

Headquarters was a farmhouse, a small, cosy place, islanded in a rolling sea of clover. About dusk Allan Gold, arriving here, found himself admitted to the farmer's parlour. Here were a round table with lamps, a clerk or two writing, and several members of Jackson's military family. The general himself came in presently, and sat down at the table. A dark, wiry man, with a highly intellectual face, who had been going over papers by a lamp in the corner of the room, came forward and saluted.

"Very well, Jarrow. Have you got the mail bag?"

"Yes, sir." He laid upon the table a small, old, war-worn leather pouch. "It won't hold much, but enough. Headquarters' mail. Service over the mountain, to the Manassas Gap for the first Richmond train. Profound ignorance on General Jackson's part of McDowell's whereabouts. The latter's pickets gobble up courier, and information meant for Richmond goes to Washington."

"Who is the volunteer, Gold?"

"A boy named Billy Maydew, sir. Company A, 65th. A Thunder Run man."

"He understands that he is to be captured?"

"Yes, sir. Both he and the mail bag, especially the mail bag. After it is safe prisoner, and he has given a straight story, he can get away if he is able. There's no object in his going North?"

"None at all. Let me see the contents, Jarrow."

Jarrow spread them on the table. "I thought it best, sir, to include a few of a general nature —"

"I thought of that. Here are copies of various letters received from Richmond. They are now of no special value. I will return them with a memorandum on the packet, 'Received on such a date and now returned.'" He drew out a packet, tied with red tape. "Run them over, Jarrow."

Jarrow read aloud, —

MOBILE, March 1st, 1862.

HIS EXCELLENCY JEFFERSON DAVIS,
    PRESIDENT OF THE CONFEDERATE STATES OF AMERICA:
    Sir, — The subject of permitting cotton to leave our Southern ports clandestinely has had some attention from me, and I have

come to the conclusion that it is a Yankee trick that should have immediate attention from the Governmental authorities of this country. The pretence is that we must let it go forward to buy arms and munitions of war, and I fear the fate of the steamer Calhoun illustrates the destination of these arms and munitions of war after they are bought with our cotton. Her commander set her on fire and the Yankees put her out just in time to secure the prize. This cotton power is a momentous question —

"Very good. The next, Jarrow."

RICHMOND, VA., February 22d.

HON. J. P. BENJAMIN,
  SECRETARY OF WAR:

Sir, — I have the honour to state there are now many volunteers from Maryland who are desirous of organizing themselves as soon as possible into companies, regiments, and brigades —

"Good! good! The next, Jarrow."

EXECUTIVE DEPARTMENT,
MILLEDGEVILLE, GA.

HIS EXCELLENCY JEFFERSON DAVIS:

Sir, — I have the pleasure to inform you that in response to your requisition on Georgia for twelve additional regiments of troops she now tenders you thirteen regiments and three battalions —

"Good! The next."

HAVANA, March 22d, 1862.

HON. J. P. BENJAMIN,
  SECRETARY OF WAR, RICHMOND.

Sir, — Our recent reverses in Tennessee and on the seacoast, magnified by the Northern press, have had a tendency to create doubt in the minds of our foreign friends here as to our ultimate success. I have resisted with all my power this ridiculous fear of the timid —

"Lay that aside. It might jeopardize the agent. The next."

" Copy of a proposed General Order.

" WAR DEPARTMENT
" ADJT. AND INSP. GENERAL'S OFFICE.

" No. 1. General officers and officers in command of departments, districts, and separate posts will make a detail of men from their commands to work the nitre caves which may be situated within the limits of their respective commands — "

" Good! The next."

SURGEON GENERAL'S OFFICE,
RICHMOND, VA.

It is the policy of all Nations at all times, especially such as at present exist in our Confederacy, to make every effort to develop its internal resources, and to diminish its tribute to foreigners by supplying its necessities from the productions of its own soil. This observation may be considered peculiarly applicable to the appropriation of our indigenous medicinal substances of the vegetable kingdom, and with the view of promoting this object the inclosed pamphlet embracing many of the more important medicinal plants has been issued for distribution to the medical officers of the Army of the Confederacy now in the field. You are particularly instructed to call the attention of those of your corps to the propriety of collecting and preparing with care such of the within enumerated remedial agents or others found valuable, as their respective charges may require during the present summer and coming winter. Our forests and Savannahs furnish our *materia medica* with a moderate number of narcotics and sedatives, and an abundant supply of tonics, astringents, aromatics and demulcents, while the list of anodynes, emetics and cathartics remains in a comparative degree incomplete —

" Very good! The next, Jarrow — "

RICHMOND, FREDERICKSBURG AND POTOMAC RR.
PRESIDENT'S OFFICE.

HON. GEORGE W. RANDOLPH:

Dear Sir, — At the risk of seeming tedious, permit me to say that my impression that you were mistaken last night in your recollection of the extent to which Louis Napoleon used railroads in transporting his army into Sardinia is this morning confirmed by a gentleman who is a most experienced and well-informed railroad officer, and is also the most devoted student of geography and military history, with the most accurate and extraordinary memory for every detail, however minute, of battles and all other military operations that I have ever met with. He is positive in his recollection that not less than 100,000 and probably more, of that army were gradually concentrated at Toulon and sent thence by sea to Genoa, and the rest were during some weeks being concentrated at a little town on the confines of France and Italy, whence they were transferred, partly on foot and partly on a double-track railroad, into Sardinia. The capacity of a double-track railroad, adequately equipped like the European railroads, may be moderately computed at five times that of a single-track road like those of the Confederate States. For the sudden and rapid movement of a vanguard of an army, to hold in check an enemy till reinforced, or of a rear guard to cover a retreat, or of any other portion of an army which must move suddenly and rapidly, and for the transportation of ordnance, ammunition, commissary and other military supplies, railroads are available and invaluable to an army. And when these objects of prime necessity are attained, they can advantageously carry more troops according to the amount of the other transportation required, the distance, their force, and equipment, etc. But to rely on them as a means of transporting any large body of troops beside what is needed to supply and maintain them, is certainly a most dangerous delusion, and must inevitably result in the most grievous disappointments and fatal consequence.

Very respectfully and truly yours, etc.

P. V. DANIEL, JR.

P. S. As a railroad officer, interest would prompt me to advocate the opposite theory about this matter, for troops constitute the most profitable, if not the only profitable, part of any transportation by railroads. But I cannot be less a citizen and patriot because I am a railroad officer.

"Good! good. The next, Jarrow."

"Copy of resolutions declaring the sense of Congress.

"Whereas the United States are waging war against the Confederate States with the avowed purpose of compelling the latter to reunite with them under the same constitution and government, and whereas the waging of war with such an object is in direct opposition to the sound Republican maxim that 'all government rests upon the consent of the governed' and can only tend to consolidation in the general government and the consequent destruction of the rights of the States, and whereas, this result being attained the two sections can only exist together in the relation of the oppressor and the oppressed, because of the great preponderance of power in the Northern section, coupled with dissimilarity of interest; and whereas we, the Representatives of the people of the Confederate States, in Congress assembled, may be presumed to know the sentiments of said people, having just been elected by them. Therefore,

" Be it resolved by the Congress of the Confederate States of America that this Congress do solemnly declare and publish to the world that it is the unalterable determination of the people of the Confederate States, in humble reliance upon Almighty God, to suffer all the calamities of the most protracted war —"

"Just so. That will do for this packet. Now what have you there ? "

"These are genuine soldiers' letters, sir — the usual thing — incidents of battle, wounds, messages, etc. They are all optimistic in tone, but for the rest tell no news. I have carefully opened, gone over, and reclosed them."

"Good! good! Let Robinson, there, take a list of the names. Lieutenant Willis, you will see each of the men and tell them they must rewrite their letters. These were lost. Now, Jarrow."

"These are the ones to the point, sir. I had two written this morning, one this afternoon. They are all properly addressed and signed, and dated from this bivouac. The first."

MY DEAR FATHER, — A glorious victory yesterday! Little cost to us and Banks swept from the Valley. We are in high spirits, confident that the tide has turned and that the seat of war will be changed. Of late the army has grown like a rolling snowball. Perhaps thirty thousand here —

An aide uttered a startled laugh. "Pray be quiet, gentlemen," said Jackson.

Thirty thousand here, and a large force nearer the mountains.
Recruits are coming in all the time; good, determined men. I truly
feel that we are invincible. I write in haste, to get this in the bag we
are sending to the nearest railway station. Dear love to all.

Aff'y your son,

JOHN SMITH.

"Good!" said Jackson. "Always deceive, mystify, and mislead
the enemy. You may thereby save your Capital city. The next."
"From one of Ashby's men, sir."

MY DEAR SISTER, — We are now about thirty companies — every
man from this region who owns or can beg, borrow, or steal a horse
is coming in. I got at Staunton the plume for my hat you sent. It is
beautifully long, black, and curling! Imagine me under it, riding
through Maryland! Forty thousand of us, and the bands playing
"Dixie"! Old Jack may stand like a stone wall, but by the Lord,
he moves like a thunderbolt! Best love. Your loving brother,

WILLIAM PATTERSON.

"Scratch out the oath, Jarrow. He is writing to a lady, nor
should it be used to a man. The next."

MY DEAR FITZHUGH, — Papers, reports, etc., will give you the
details. Suffice it, that we've had a lovely time. A minie drew some
blood from me — not much, and spilt in a good cause. As you see, I
am writing with my left hand — the other arm's in a sling. The
army's in the highest spirits — South going North on a visit.

All the grey bonnets are over the border!

We hear that all of you in and about Richmond are in excellent
health and spirits, and that in the face of the Young Napoleon!
Stronger, too, than he thinks. We hear that McDowell is somewhere between you and Fredericksburg. Just keep him there, will
you? We'd rather not have him up here just yet. Give my love to
all my cousins. Will write *from the other side of the water.*

Yours as ever,

PETER FRANCISCO.

P. S. Of course this is not official, but the impression is strong in the army that the defensive has been dropped and that the geese in the other Capitol ought to be cackling if they are not.

Jarrow drew the whole together. "I thought the three would be enough, sir. I never like to overdo."

"You have the correct idea, Jarrow. Bring the boy in, Gold. I want the bag captured early to-morrow."

On May the twenty-eighth, fifteen thousand in all, Winder still in advance, they moved by Summit Point toward Harper's Ferry, thirty miles away. Ewell on Rifle led the main column, Jackson and Little Sorrel marched to-day with the rear, Ashby on the black stallion went far ahead with his cavalry. The army moved with vigour, in high spirits and through fine weather, a bright, cool day with round white clouds in an intense blue sky. When halts were made and the generals rode by the resting troops they were loudly cheered. The men were talkative; they indulged in laughter and lifted voice in song. Speculation ran to and fro, but she wore no anxious mien. The army felt a calm confidence, a happy-go-lucky mood. It had come into a childlike trust in its commanding general, and that made all the difference in the world. "Where are we going? Into Maryland? Don't know and don't care! Old Jack knows. *I* think we're going to Washington — Always did want to see it. I think so, too. Going to take its attention off Richmond, as the Irishman said when he walked away with the widow at the wake. Look at that buzzard up there against that cloud! Kingbird's after him! Right at his eyes! — Say, boys, look at that fight!"

In the afternoon the Stonewall came to Charlestown, eight miles from Harper's Ferry. Here they found, strongly posted in a wood, fifteen hundred Federals with two guns, sent from Harper's Ferry by Saxton. A courier went back to Ewell. Winder, without waiting for reinforcements, attacked. The fight lasted twenty minutes, when the Federal line broke, retreating in considerable disorder. The Stonewall, pressing after, came into view, two miles from the Potomac, of the enemy's guns on Bolivar Heights.

Saxton, now commanding about seven thousand men, had strongly occupied the hills on the southern side of the Potomac. To the north the Maryland Heights were held by several regiments and a naval battery of Dahlgren guns. The brigadier commanding received and sent telegrams.

WASHINGTON.

BRIGADIER-GENERAL SAXTON,
  Harper's Ferry.

Copy of Secretary of War's dispatch to Governors of States.

"Send forward all the troops that you can immediately. Banks completely routed. Intelligence from various quarters leaves no doubt that the enemy, in great force, are advancing on Washington. You will please organize and forward immediately all the volunteer and militia force in your state."

In addition, the President has notified General McClellan that his return to Washington may be ordered. City in a panic.

X. Y.

HARPER'S FERRY, VIRGINIA, May 31.

The enemy moved up in force last evening about seven o'clock, in a shower of rain, to attack. I opened on them from the position which the troops occupy above the town, and from the Dahlgren battery on the mountains. The enemy then retired. Their pickets attacked ours twice last night within 300 yards of our works. A volley from General Slough's breastworks drove them back. We lost one man killed. Enemy had signal-lights on the mountains in every direction. Their system of night-signals seems to be perfect. They fire on our pickets in every case. My men are overworked. Stood by their guns all night in the rain. What has become of Generals Frémont and McDowell?

R. SAXTON.

HON. E. M. STANTON, *Secretary of War.*

At Williamsport on the Maryland side, twelve miles above, General Banks likewise sent a telegram to the Government at Washington.

WILLIAMSPORT, May 28, 1862.

Have received information to-day which I think should be transmitted, but not published over my name, as I do not credit it altogether. A merchant from Martinsburg, well known, came to inform me that in a confidential conversation with a very prominent secessionist, also merchant of that town, he was informed that the policy of the South was changed; that they would abandon Richmond, Virginia, everything South, and invade Maryland and Washington; that every Union soldier would be driven out of the Valley immediately. This was on Friday evening, the night of attack on Front Royal. Names are given me, and the party talking one who might know the rebel plans. A prisoner was captured near Martinsburg to-day. He told the truth I am satisfied, as far as he pretended to know. He was in the fight at Front Royal and passed through Winchester two hours after our engagement. He says the rebel force was very large — not less than twenty-five thousand at Winchester and 6000 or 7000 at Front Royal; that the idea was general among the men that they were to invade Maryland. He passed Ashby yesterday, who had twenty-eight companies of cavalry under his command; was returning from Martinsburg, and moving under orders, his men said, to Berryville. There were 2000 rebels at Martinsburg when he passed that town yesterday. These reports came to me at the same time I received General Saxton's dispatch and the statement from my own officer that 4000 rebels were near Falling Waters, in my front.

N. P. BANKS,
Major-General Commanding.

HON. E. M. STANTON.

Friday evening the thirtieth was as dark as Erebus. Clouds had been boiling up since dark. Huge portentous masses rose on all sides and blotted out the skies. The air was for a time oppressively hot and still. The smoke from the guns which had wrangled during the day, long and loud, hung low; the smell of powder clung. The grey troops massed on Loudoun Heights and along the Shenandoah wiped the sweat from their brows. Against the piled clouds signal-lights burned dull and red, stars of war communicating through the sultry night. The clouds rose higher yet and the lightnings began to play. A stir began in the leaves of the far-flung forests, blended with the murmur of the rivers and became rushing sound. Thunder burst, clap after clap, reverberating through the mountains. The air began to smell of rain, grew suddenly cool. Through the welcome freshness the grey troops advanced beyond Bolivar Heights; there followed a long crackle of musketry and a body of blue troops retreated across the river. The guns opened again; the grey cannon trained upon the Maryland Heights; the Maryland Heights answering sullenly. Down came the rain in torrents, the lightning flashed, the thunder rolled. The lightnings came jaggedly, bayonets of the storm, stabbing downward; the artillery of the skies dwarfed all sound below. For an hour there was desultory fighting, then it ceased. The grey troops awaiting orders, wondered, "Are n't we going to cross the river after them?" "Oh, let it alone. Old Jack knows."

Toward midnight, in the midst of a great access of lightning, rain, and thunder, fighting was renewed. It was not for long. The guns fell silent again upon Loudoun Heights; moreover the long lines of couching infantry saw by the vivid lightning the battery horses come up, wet and shining in the rain. From regiment to regiment, under the rolling thunder, ran the order. *Into column! By the left flank! March!*

A small stone hut on the side of a hill had formed the shelter of the general commanding. Here he wrote and gave to two couriers a message in duplicate.

HARPER'S FERRY,
VIRGINIA.
May 31. Midnight.

HON. GEORGE W. RANDOLPH, Secretary of War:

Under the guidance of God I have demonstrated toward the Potomac and drawn off McDowell, who is sending Shields by Front Royal. Moving now to meet him and Frémont who comes from the West.

T. J. JACKSON,
Major-General Commanding.

CHAPTER XXIV

THE FOOT CAVALRY

THREE armies had for their objective Strasburg in the Valley of Virginia, eighteen miles below Winchester. One came from the northwest, under Frémont, and counted ten thousand. One came from the southeast, Shields's Division from McDowell at Fredericksburg, and numbered fifteen thousand. These two were blue clad, moving under the stars and stripes. The third, grey, under the stars and bars, sixteen thousand muskets, led by a man on a sorrel nag, came from Harper's Ferry. Frémont, Indian fighter, moved fast; Shields, Irish born, veteran of the Mexican War, moved fast; but the man in grey, on the sorrel nag, moved infantry with the rapidity of cavalry. Around the three converging armies rested or advanced other bodies of blue troops, hovering, watchful of the chance to strike. Saxton at Harper's Ferry had seven thousand; Banks at Williamsport had seven thousand. Ord, commanding McDowell's second division, was at Manassas Gap with nine thousand. King, the third division, had ten thousand, near Catlett's Station. At Ashby's Gap was Geary with two thousand; at Thoroughfare, Bayard with two thousand.

Over a hundred miles away, southeast, tree-embowered upon her seven hills, lay Richmond, and at her eastern gates, on the marshy Chickahominy were gathered one hundred and forty thousand men, blue clad, led by McClellan. Bronzed, soldierly, chivalrous, an able if over-cautious general, he waited, irresolute, and at last postponed his battle. He would tarry for McDowell who, obeying orders from Washington, had turned aside to encounter and crush a sometime professor of natural philosophy with a gift for travelling like a meteor, for confusing like a Jack-o'-lantern, and for striking the bull's-eye of the moment like a silver bullet or a William Tell arrow. Between Richmond and the many and heavy blue lines, with their siege train, lay thinner lines of grey — sixty-five thousand men under the stars and bars. They, too, watched the turning aside of McDowell, watched Shields, Ord, King, and Frémont from the west, trappers hot on the path of the man with the old forage cap, and the sabre tucked under his arm! All Virginia watched, holding her breath.

Out of Virginia, before Corinth in Tennessee, and at Cumberland Gap, Armies of the Ohio, of the Mississippi, of the West — one hundred and ten thousand in blue, eighty thousand in grey, Halleck and Beauregard — listened for news from Virginia. "Has Richmond fallen?" "No. McClellan is cautious. Lee and Johnston are between him and the city. He will not attack until he is further strengthened by McDowell." "Where is McDowell?" "He was moving south from Fredericksburg. His outposts almost touched those of McClellan. But now he has been sent across the Blue Ridge to the Valley, there to put a period to the activities of Stonewall Jackson. That done, he will turn and join McClellan. The two will enfold Lee and Jackson — the Anaconda Scheme — and crush every bone in their bodies. Richmond will fall and the war end."

Tennessee watched and north Alabama. In Arkansas, on the White River were twelve thousand men in blue, and, arrayed against them, six thousand, white men and Indians, clad in grey. Far, far away, outer edges of the war, they, too, looked toward the east and wondered how it went in Virginia. Grey and blue, Missouri, Louisiana, New Mexico, Arizona — at lonely railway or telegraph stations, at river landings, wherever, in the intervals between skirmishes, papers might be received or messages read, soldiers in blue or soldiers in grey asked eagerly "What news from Richmond?" — "Stonewall Jackson? Valley of Virginia?" — "Valley of Virginia! I know! — saw it once. God's country."

At New Orleans, on the levees, in the hot streets, under old balconies and by walled gardens, six thousand men in blue under Butler watched, and a sad-eyed captive city watched. From the lower Mississippi, from the blue waters of the Gulf, from the long Atlantic swells, the ships looked to the land. All the blockading fleets, all the old line-of-battle ships, the screw-frigates, the corvettes, the old merchant steamers turned warrior, the strange new iron-clads and mortar boats, engaged in bottling up the Confederacy, they all looked for the fall of Richmond. There watched, too, the ram-fitted river boats, the double-enders, lurking beneath Spanish moss, rocking beside canebrakes, on the far, sluggish, southern rivers. And the other ships, the navy all too small, the scattered, shattered, despairing and courageous ships that flew the stars and bars, they listened, too, for a last great cry in the night. The blockade-runners listened, the Gladiators, the Ceciles, the Theodoras, the Ella Warleys faring at headlong peril to and fro between Nassau in the Bahamas and small and hidden harbours of the vast coast line, inlets of Georgia, Florida, Carolina. Danger flew with them always through the rushing brine, but with the fall of Richmond disaster might be trusted to swoop indeed. Then woe for all the wares below — the Enfield rifles, the cannon powder, the cartridges, the saltpetre, bar steel, nitric acid, leather, cloth, salt, medicines, surgical instruments! Their outlooks kept sharp watch for disaster, heaving in sight in the shape of a row of blue frigates released from patrol duty. Let Richmond fall, and the Confederacy, war and occupation, freedom, life, might be gone in a night, blown from existence by McClellan's siege guns!

Over seas the nations watched. Any day might bring a packet with news — Richmond fallen, fallen, fallen, the Confederacy vanquished, suing for peace — Richmond not fallen, some happy turn of affairs for the South, the Peace Party in the North prevailing, the Confederacy established, the olive planted between the two countries! Anyhow, anyhow! only end the war and set the cotton jennies spinning!

Most feverishly of all watched Washington on the Potomac. "The latest?" "It will surely fall to-day. The thing is absurd. It is a little city —" " From the Valley? Jackson has turned south from Harper's Ferry. Shields and Frémont will meet at Strasburg long before the rebels get there. Together they'll make Jackson pay — grind the stonewall small!"

The Army of the Valley had its orders from Strasburg the night of the thirtieth. The main body moved at once, back upon Winchester, where it gathered up stragglers, prisoners, and the train of captured stores. Winder with the Stonewall Brigade, left to make a final feint at Harper's Ferry, was not in motion southward till much later. Of the main army the 21st Virginia led the column, convoying prisoners and the prize of stores. There were twenty-three hundred prisoners, men in blue, tramping sullenly. Stonewall Jackson had made requisition of all wagons about Winchester. They were now in line, all manner of wagons, white-covered, uncovered, stout-bodied, ancient, rickety, in every condition but of fresh paint and new harness. Carts were brought, small vans of pedlars; there were stranded circus wagons with gold scrolls. Nor did there lack vehicles meant for human freight. Old family carriages, high-swung, capacious as the ark, were filled, not with women and children, belles and beaux, but with bags of powder and boxes of cartridges. Superannuated mail coaches carried blankets, oilcloths, sabres, shoes; light spring wagons held Enfield rifles; doctors' buggies medicine cases corded in with care. All these added themselves to the regular supply train of the army; great wagons marked C. S. A. in which, God knows! there was room for stores. The captures of the past days filled the vacancies; welcome enough were the thirty-five thousand pounds of bacon, the many barrels of flour, the hardtack, sugar, canned goods, coffee, the tea and strange delicacies kept for the sick. More welcome was the capture of the ammunition. The ordnance officers beamed lovingly upon it and upon the nine thousand excellent new small arms, and the prisoner Parrotts. There were two hundred beautiful wagons marked U. S. A.; the surgeons, too, congratulated themselves upon new ambulances. Horses and mules that had changed masters might be restless at first; but they soon knew the touch of experienced hands and turned contented up the Valley. A herd of cattle was driven bellowing into line.

Seven miles in length, train and convoying troops emerged from Winchester in the early light and began a rumbling, bellowing, singing, jesting, determined progress up the Valley pike. Ewell followed with his brigadiers — Taylor, Trimble, Elzey, Scott, and the Maryland Line. The old Army of the Valley came next in column — all save the Stonewall Brigade that was yet in the rear double-quicking it on the road from Harper's Ferry. As far in advance moved Stonewall Jackson's screen of cavalry, the Valley horsemen under Ashby, a supple, quick-travelling, keen-eyed, dare-devil horde, an effective cloud behind which to execute intricate manœuvres, a drawer-up of information like dew from every by-road, field, and wood, and an admirable mother of thunderbolts. Ashby and Ashby's men were alike smarting from a late rebuke, administered in General Orders. They felt it stingingly. The Confederate soldier enthroned on high his personal honour, and a slur there was a slur indeed. Now the memory of the reprimand was a strong spur to endeavour. The cavalry meant to distinguish itself, and pined for a sight of Frémont.

The day was showery with strong bursts of sunshine between the slanting summer rains. All along the great highway, in sun and shade, women, children, the coloured people, all the white men left by the drag-net of the war, were out in the ripening fields, by the roadside wall, before gates, in the village streets. They wept with pride and joy, they laughed, they embraced. They showered praises, blessings; they prophesied good fortune. The young women had made bouquets and garlands. Many a favourite officer rode with flowers at his saddle bow. Other women had ransacked their storerooms, and now offered delicate food on salvers — the lavish, brave, straightforward Valley women, with the men gone to the war, the horses gone to the war, the wagons taken for need, the crops like to be unreaped and the fields to be unplanted, with the clothes wearing out, with supplies hard to get, with the children, the old people, the servants, the sick, the wounded on their hands, in their hearts and minds! They brought food, blessings, flowers, "everything for the army! It has the work to do." The colours streamed in the wet breeze, glorious in shadow, splendid when the sun burst forth. The little old bands played

> In Dixie Land whar I was born in
> Early on one frosty mornin'!
> Look away, look away, look away, Dixie Land!

Long, steady, swinging tread, pace of the foot cavalry, the main column moved up the Valley pike, violet in the shadow, gold in the sun. The ten-minutes-out-of-an-hour halts were shortened to five minutes. During one of these rests Jackson came down the line. The men cheered him. "Thirty miles to-day. You must do thirty miles to-day, men." He went by, galloping forward to the immense and motley convoy. The men laughed, well pleased with themselves and with him. "Old Jack's got to see if his lemons are all right! If we don't get those lemon wagons through safe to Staunton there'll be hell to pay! Go 'way! we know he won't call it hell!"

> "The butcher had a little dog,
> And Bingo was his name.

B-i-n-g-o-go-! B-i-n-g-o-go!
And Bingo was his name!"

"*Fall in!* Oh, Lord, we just fell out!"

Advance, convoy, main column, camped that night around and in Strasburg, Strasburg jubilant, welcoming, restless through the summer night. Winder with the Stonewall Brigade bivouacked at Newtown, twelve miles north. He had made a wonderful march. The men, asleep the instant they touched the earth, lay like dead. The rest was not long; between one and two the bugles called and the regiments were again in motion. A courier had come from Jackson. "*General Winder, you will press forward.*"

Silent, with long, steady, swinging tread, the Stonewall moved up the Valley. Before it, pale, undulating, mysterious beneath the stars, ran the turnpike, the wonderful Valley road, the highway that had grown familiar to the army as its hand. The Army of the Valley endowed the Valley pike with personality. They spoke of it as "her." They blamed her for mud and dust, for shadeless, waterless stretches, for a habit she was acquiring of furrows and worn places, for the aid which she occasionally gave to hostile armies, for the hills which she presented, for the difficulties of her bordering stone walls when troops must be deployed, for the weeds and nettles, thistles, and briars, with which she had a trick of decking her sides, for her length. "You kin march most to Kingdom Come on this here old road!" for the heat of the sun, the chill of the frost, the strength of the blast. In blander moods they caressed her name. "Wish I could see the old pike once more!" — "Ain't any road in the world like the Valley pike, and never was! *She* never behaved herself like this damned out-of-corduroy-into-mud-hole, bayonet-narrow, drunken, zig-zag, world's-end-and-no-to-morrow cow track!"

It was not only the road. All nature had new aspects for the Confederate soldier; day by day a deeper shade of personality. So much of him was farmer that he was no stranger to the encampment of the earth. He was weather-wise, knew the soil, named the trees, could *orientate* himself, had a fighting knowledge, too, of blight and drouth, hail, frost, high wind, flood, too little and too much of sun fire. Probably he had thought that he knew all that was to be told. When he volunteered it was not with the expectation of learning any other manual than that of arms. As is generally the case, he learned that what he expected was but a mask for what he did not expect. He learned other manuals, among them that of earth, air, fire, and water. His ideas of the four underwent modification. First of all he learned that they were combatants, active participants in the warfare which he had thought a matter only of armies clad in blue and armies clad in grey. Apparently nothing was passive, nothing neutral. Bewilderingly, also, nothing was of a steadfast faith. Sun, moon, darkness and light, heat and cold, snow, rain, mud, dust, mountain, forest, hill, dale, stream, bridge, road, wall, house, hayrick, dew, mist, storm, everything! — they fought first on one side then on the other. Sometimes they did this in rapid succession, sometimes they seemed to fight on both sides at once; the only attitude they never took was one immaterial to the business in hand. Moreover they were vitally for or against the individual soldier; now his friend, now his foe, now flattering, caressing, bringing gifts, now snatching away, digging pitfalls, working wreck and ruin. They were stronger than he, strong and capricious beyond all reckoning. Sometimes he loved these powers; sometimes he cursed them. Indifference, only, was gone. He and they were alike sentient, active, conscious, inextricably mingled.

To-night the pike was cool and hard. There were clouds above, but not heavy; streams of stars ran between. To either side of the road lay fields of wheat, of clover, of corn, banded and broken by shadowy forest. Massanutton loomed ahead. There was a wind blowing. Together with the sound of marching feet, the jingle of accoutrements, the striking of the horses' hoofs against loose stones, the heavy noise of the guns in the rear, it filled the night like the roar of a distant cataract. The men marched along without speech; now and then a terse order, nothing more. The main army was before them at Strasburg; they must catch up. To the west, somewhat near at hand in the darkness, would be lying Frémont. Somewhere in the darkness to the east was Shields. Their junction was unmade, Stonewall Jackson and his army passing between the upper and the nether millstone which should have joined to crush.

The stars began to pale, the east to redden. Faintly, faintly the swell and roll of the earth gathered colour. A cock crew from some distant farmhouse. The Stonewall swung on, the 65th leading, its colonel, Richard Cleave, at its head. The regiment liked to see him there; it loved him well and obeyed him well, and he in his turn would have died for his men. Undoubtedly he was responsible for much of the regiment's tone and temper. It was good stuff in the beginning, but something of its firm modelling was due to the man now riding Dundee at its head. The 65th was acquiring a reputation, and that in a brigade whose deeds had been ringing, like a great bell, sonorously through the land. "The good conduct of the 65th —" "The 65th, reliable always —" "The 65th with its accustomed courage —" "The disciplined, intelligent, and courageous 65th —" "The gallantry of the 65th —"

The light strengthened; pickets were reached. They belonged to Taylor's Brigade, lying in the woods to either side of the pike. The Stonewall passed them, still figures, against the dawn. Ahead lay Strasburg, its church spires silver-slender in the morning air. Later, as the sun pushed a red rim above the hills, the brigade stacked arms in a fair green meadow. Between it and the town lay Taliaferro. Elzey and Campbell were in the fields to the east. General Jackson and his staff occupied a knoll just above the road.

The Stonewall fell to getting breakfast — big tin cups of scalding coffee! sugar! fresh meat! double allowance of meal! They broiled the meat on sharpened sticks, using the skillets for batter bread; they grinned at the sugar before they dropped it in, they purred over the coffee. Mingling with the entrancing odours was the consciousness of having marched well, fought well, deserved well. Down the pike, where Taylor kept the rear, burst a rattle of musketry. The Stonewall scrambled to its feet. "What's that? Darn it all! the Virginia Reel's beginning!" An officer hurried by. "Sit down, boys. It's just a minuet — reconnoissance of Frémont and Dick Taylor! It's all right. Those Louisianians are damned good dancers!" A courier quitting the knoll above the pike gave further information. "Skirmish back there, near the Capon road. Just a feeler of Frémont's — his army's three miles over there in the woods. Old Dick's with General Taylor. Don't need your help, boys — thank you all the same! Frémont won't attack in force. Old Jack says so — sitting up there on a hickory stump reading the Book of Kings!"

"All right," said the Stonewall. "We ain't the kind to go butting in without an invitation! We're as modest as we are brave. Listen! The blue coats are using minies."

Down the pike, during an hour of dewy morning, the Louisiana Brigade and Frémont's advance fired at each other. The woods hereabouts were dense. At intervals the blue showed; at intervals Ewell dispatched a regiment which drove them back to cover. "Old Dick" would have loved to follow, but he was under orders. He fidgeted to and fro on Rifle. "Old Jackson says I am not to go far from the pike! I want to go after those men. I want to chase them to the Rio Grande! I am sick of this fiddling about! Just listen to that, General Taylor! There's a lot of them in the woods! What's the good of being a major-general if you've got to stick close to the pike? If Old Jackson were here he would say Go! Why ain't he here? Bet you anything you like he's sucking a lemon and holding morning prayer meeting! — Oh, here are your men back with prisoners! Now, you men in blue, what command's that in the woods? Eh? — What?" " *Von Bayern bin ich nach diesem Lande gekommen.*" " *Am Rhein habe ich gehört dass viel bezahlt wird für* . . ." "Take 'em away! Semmes, you go and tell General Jackson all Europe's here. — Mean you to go? Of course I don't mean you to go, you thundering idiot! Always could pick Cæsar out of the crowd. When I find him I obey him, I don't send him messages. ——! —— ——! They've developed sharpshooters. Send Wheat over there, General Taylor — tell him to shake the pig-nuts out of those trees!"

Toward mid-day the army marched. All the long afternoon it moved to the sound of musketry up the Valley pike. There was skirmishing in plenty — dashes by Frémont's cavalry, repulsed by the grey, a short stampede of Munford's troopers, driven up the pike and into the infantry of the rear guard, rapid recovery and a Roland for an Oliver. The Valley, shimmering in the June light, lay in anything but Sabbath calm. Farmhouse and village, mill, smithy, tavern, cross-roads store, held their breath — Stonewall Jackson coming up the pike, holding Frémont off with one hand while he passes Shields.

Sunset came, a splendid flare of colour behind the Great North Mountain. The army halted for the night. The Louisiana Brigade still formed the rear guard. Drawn upon high ground to either side of the pike, it lighted no fires and rested on its arms. Next it to the south lay Winder. The night was clear and dark, the pike a pale limestone gleam between the shadowy hills. Hour by hour there sounded a clattering of hoofs, squads of cavalry, reports, couriers, staff. There was, too, a sense of Stonewall Jackson somewhere on the pike, alert with grey-blue eyes piercing the dark. Toward one o'clock firing burst out on the north. It proved an affair of outposts. Later, shots rang out close at hand, Frémont having ordered a cavalry reconnoissance. The grey met it with clangour and pushed it back. Wheat's battalion was ordered northward and went swinging down the pike. The blue cavalry swarmed again, whereupon the Louisianians deployed, knelt first rank, fired rear rank, rose and went forward, knelt, fired and dispersed the swarm. From a ridge to the west opened a Federal gun. It had intent to rake the pike, but was trained too high. The shells hurtled overhead, exploding high in air. The cannonade ceased as suddenly as it had begun. Day began to break in violet and daffodil.

As the hours went on they became fiery hot and dry. The dust cloud was high again over advance with great wagon train, over main column and rear. Water was scarce, the men horribly weary; all suffered. Suffering or ease, pain or pleasure, there was no resting this day. Frémont, using parallel roads, hung upon the right; he must be pushed back to the mountains as they passed up the Valley pike. All morning blue cavalry menaced the Stonewall; to the north a dense southward moving cloud proclaimed a larger force. Mid-day found Winder deployed on both sides of the pike, with four guns in position. The Louisianians sent back to know if they could help. "No — we'll manage." A minute later Jackson appeared. Wherever matters drew suddenly to a point, there he was miraculously found. He looked at the guns and jerked his hand in the air. "General Winder, I do not wish an engagement here. Withdraw your brigade, sir, regiment by regiment. General Ashby is here. He will keep the rear."

Ashby came at the moment with a body of horse out of the wood to the east. He checked the black stallion, saluted and made his report. "I have burned the Conrad Store, White House and Columbia bridges, sir. If Shields wishes to cross he must swim the Shenandoah. It is much swollen. I have left Massanutton Gap strongly guarded."

"Good! good! General Winder, you will follow General Taylor. Tell the men that I wish them to press on. General Ashby, the march is now to proceed undisturbed."

The second of June burned onward to its close, through heat, dust, thirst, and relentlessly rapid marching. In the late afternoon occurred a monstrous piling up of thunder clouds, a whistling of wind, and a great downpour of rain. It beat down the wheat and pattered like elfin bullets on the forest leaves. Through this fusillade the army came down to the west fork of the Shenandoah. Pioneers laid a bridge of wagons, and, brigade by brigade, the army crossed. High on the bank in the loud wind and dashing rain, Jackson on Little Sorrel watched the transit. By dusk all were over and the bridge was taken up.

On the further shore Ashby now kept guard between Frémont and the host in grey. As for Shields, he was on the far side of the Massanuttons, before him a bridgeless, swollen torrent and a guarded mountain pass. Before becoming dangerous he must move south and round the Massanuttons. Far from achieving junction, space had widened between Shields and Frémont. The Army of the Valley had run the gauntlet, and in doing so had pushed the walls apart. The men, climbing from the Shenandoah, saluting their general, above them there in the wind and the rain, thought the voice with which he answered them unusually gentle. He almost always spoke to his troops gently, but to-night there was almost a fatherly tone. And though he jerked his hand into the air, it was meditatively done, a quiet salute to some observant commander up there.

Later, in the deep darkness, the army bivouacked near New Market. Headquarters was established in an old mill. Here a dripping courier unwrapped from a bit of cloth several leaves of the whitey-brown telegraph paper of the Confederacy and gave them into the general's hand.

Next morning, at roll call, each colonel spoke to his regiment. "Men! There has been a great battle before Richmond — at a place called Seven Pines. Day before yesterday General Johnston attacked General McClellan. The battle raged all day with varying fortune. At sunset General Johnston, in the thickest of the fight, was struck from his horse by a shell. He is desperately wounded; the country prays not mortally. General Lee is now in command of the Armies of Virginia. The battle was resumed yesterday morning and lasted until late in the day. Each side claims the victory. Our loss is perhaps five thousand; we hold that the enemy's was as great. General McClellan has returned to his camp upon the banks of the Chickahominy. Richmond is not taken. — The general commanding the Army of the Valley congratulates his men upon the part they have played in the operations before our capital. At seven in the morning the chaplains of the respective regiments will hold divine services."

CHAPTER XXV

ASHBY

FLOURNOY and Munford, transferred to Ashby's command, kept with him in the Confederate rear. The army marching from the Shenandoah left the cavalry behind in the wind and rain to burn the bridge and delay Frémont. Ashby, high on the eastern bank, watched the slow flames seize the timbers, fight with the wet, prevail and mount. The black stallion planted his fore feet, shook his head, snuffed the air. The wind blew out his rider's cloak. In the light from the burning bridge the scarlet lining glowed and gleamed like the battle-flag. The stallion neighed. Ashby's voice rose ringingly. "Chew, get the Blakeley ready! Wyndham's on the other side!"

The flames mounted high, a great pyre streaming up, reddening the night, the roaring Shenandoah, the wet and glistening woods. Out of the darkness to the north came Maury Stafford with a scouting party. He saluted. "There is a considerable force over there, sir, double-quicking through the woods to save the bridge. Cavalry in front — Wyndham, I suppose, still bent on 'bagging' you."

"Here they are!" said Ashby. "But you are too late, Colonel Sir Percy Wyndham!"

The blazing arch across the river threw a wine-red light up and down and showed cavalry massing beneath walnut, oak, and pine. There were trumpet signals and a great trampling of hoofs, but the roaring flames, the swollen torrent, the pattering rain, the flaws of wind somewhat dulled other sounds. A tall man with sash and sabre, thigh boots and marvellously long moustaches, sat his horse beneath a dripping, wind-tossed pine. He pointed to the grey troopers up and down the southern bank. "There's the quarry! *Fire!*"

Two could play at that game. The flash from the northern bank and the rattle of the carbines were met from the southern by as vivid a leaping spark, as loud a sound. With the New Jersey squadrons was a Parrott gun. It was brought up, placed and fired. The shell exploded as it touched the red-lit water. There was a Versailles fountain costing nothing. The Blakeley answered. The grey began to sing.

> "If you want to have a good time —
> If you want to have a good time —
> If you want to catch the devil,
>   Jine the cavalry!"

A courier appeared beside Ashby. "General Jackson wants to know, sir, if they can cross?"

"Look at the bridge and tell him, No."

"Then he says to fall back. Ammunition's precious."

The cavalry leader put to his lips the fairy clarion slung from his shoulder and sounded the retreat. The flaming bridge lit all the place and showed the great black horse and him upon it. The English adventurer across the water had with him sharpshooters. In the light that wavered, leaped and died, and sprang again, these had striven in vain to reach that high-placed target. Now one succeeded.

The ball entered the black's side. He had stood like a rock, now he veered like a ship in a storm. Ashby dropped the bugle, threw his leg over the saddle, and sprang to the earth as the great horse sank. Those near him came about him. "No! I am not hurt, but Black Conrad is. My poor friend!" He stroked Black Conrad, kissed him between the eyes and drew his pistol. Chew fired the Blakeley again, drowning all lesser sound. Suddenly the supports of the bridge gave way. A great part of the roaring mass fell into the stream; the remainder, toward the southern shore, flamed higher and higher. The long rattle of the Federal carbines had an angry sound. They might have marched more swiftly after all, seeing that Stonewall Jackson would not march more slowly! Build a bridge! How could they build a bridge over the wide stream, angry itself, hoarsely and violently thrusting its way under an inky, tempestuous sky! They had no need to spare ammunition, and so they fired recklessly, cannon, carbine, and revolvers into the night after the grey, retiring squadrons.

Stafford, no great favourite with the mass of the men, but well liked by some, rode beside a fellow officer. This was a man genial and shrewd, who played the game of war as he played that of whist, eyes half closed and memory holding every card. He spoke cheerfully. "Shenandoah beautifully swollen! Don't believe Frémont has pontoons. He's out of the reckoning for at least a day and a night — probably longer. Nice for us all!"

"It has been a remarkable campaign."

"'Remarkable'! Tell you what it's like, Stafford. It's like 1796 — Napoleon's Italian campaign."

"You think so? Well, it may be true. Hear the wind in the pines!"

"Tell you what you lack, Stafford. You lack interest in the war. You are too damned perfunctory. You take orders like an automaton, and you go execute them like an automaton. I don't say that they're not beautifully executed; they are. But the soul's not there. The other day at Tom's Brook I watched you walk your horse up to the muzzle of that fellow Wyndham's guns, and, by God! I don't believe you knew any more than an automaton that the guns were there!"

"Yes, I did —"

"Well, you may have known it with one half of your brain. You didn't with the other half. To a certain extent, I can read your hand. You've got a big war of your own, in a country of your own — eh?"

"Perhaps you are not altogether wrong. Such things happen sometimes."

"Yes, they do. But I think it a pity! This war" — he jerked his head toward the environing night — "is big enough, with horribly big stakes. If I were you, I'd drum the individual out of camp."

"Think only of the general? I wish I could!"

"Well, can't you?"

"No, not yet."

"There are only two things — barring disease — which can so split the brain in two — send the biggest part off, knight-errant or Saracen, into some No-Man's Country, and keep the other piece here in Virginia to crack invaders' skulls! One's love and one's hate —"

"Never both?"

"Knight-errant and Saracen in one? That's difficult."

"Nothing is so difficult as life, nor so strange. And, perhaps, love and hate are both illnesses. Sometimes I think so."

"A happy recovery then! You are too good a fellow —"

"I am not a good fellow."

"You are not at least an amiable one to-night! Don't let the fever get too high!"

"Will you listen," said Stafford, "to the wind in the pines? and did you ever see the automatic chess-player?"

Two days later, Frémont, having bridged the Shenandoah, crossed, and pushed his cavalry with an infantry support southward by the pike. About three in the afternoon of the sixth, Ashby's horses were grazing in the green fields south of Harrisonburg, on the Port Republic road. To the west stretched a belt of woodland, eastward rose a low ridge clad with beech and oak. The green valley lay between. The air, to-day, was soft and sweet, the long billows of the Blue Ridge seen dreamily, through an amethyst haze. The men lay among dandelions. Some watched the horses; others read letters from home, or, haversack for desk, wrote some vivid, short-sentenced scrawl. A number were engaged by the rim of the clear pool. Naked to the waist, they knelt like washerwomen, and rubbed the soapless linen against smooth stones, or wrung it wrathfully, or turning, spread it, grey-white, upon the grass to dry. Four played poker beneath a tree, one read a Greek New Testament, six had found a small turtle, and with the happy importance of boys were preparing a brushwood fire and the camp kettle. Others slept, head pillowed on arm, soft felt hat drawn over eyes. The rolling woodland toward Harrisonburg and Frémont was heavily picketed. A man rose from beside the pool, straightened himself, and holding up the shirt he had been washing looked at it critically. Apparently it passed muster, for he painstakingly stretched it upon the grass and taking a pair of cotton drawers turned again to the water. A blue-eyed Loudoun youth whistling "Swanee River" brought a brimming bucket from the stream that made the pool and poured it gleefully into the kettle. A Prince Edward man, lying chest downward, blew the fire, another lifted the turtle. The horses moved toward what seemed lusher grass, one of the poker players said "Damn!" the reader turned a leaf of the Greek Testament. One of the sleepers sat up. "I thought I heard a shot —"

Perhaps he had heard one; at any rate he now heard many. Down the road and out from under the great trees of the forest in front

burst the pickets driven in by a sudden, well-directed onslaught of
blue cavalry — Frémont's advance with a brigade of infantry behind. In a moment all was haste and noise in the green vale. Men
leaped to their feet, left their washing, left the turtle simmering in
the pot, the gay cards upon the greensward, put up the Greek Testament, the home letters, snatched belt and carbine, caught the
horses, saddled them with speed, swung themselves up, and trotted
into line, eyes front — Ashby's men.

The pickets had their tale to tell. "Burst out of the wood — the
damned Briton again, sir, with his squadrons from New Jersey!
Rode us down — John Ferrar killed — Gilbert captured — You
can see from the hilltop there. They are forming for a charge.
There's infantry behind — Blinker's Dutch from the looks of
them!"

"Blinker's Dutch," said the troopers. "'Hooney,' 'Nix furstay,'
'Bag Jackson,' 'Kiss und steal,' 'Hide under bed,' 'Rifle bureau
drawers,' 'Take lockets und rings' — Blinker's Dutch! We should
have dog whips!"

To the rear was the little ridge clothed with beech and oak. The
road wound up and over it. Ashby's bugle sounded. "*Right face.
Trot! March!*" The road went gently up, grass on either side with
here and there a clump of small pines. Butterflies fluttered; all was
gay and sweet in the June sunshine. Ashby rode before on the bay
stallion. The Horse Artillery came also from the meadow where it
had been camped — Captain Chew, aged nineteen, and his three
guns and his threescore men, four of them among the best gunners
in the whole army. All mounted the ridge, halted and deployed.
The guns were posted advantageously, the 6th, the 7th, and the 2d
Virginia Cavalry in two ranks along the ridge. Wide-spreading
beech boughs, growing low, small oak scrub and branchy dogwood
made a screen of the best; they looked down, hidden, upon a gentle
slope and the Port Republic road. Ashby's post was in front of the
silver bole of a great beech. With one gauntleted hand he held the
bay stallion quiet, with the other he shaded his eyes and gazed at the
westerly wood into which ran the road. Chew, to his right, touched
the Blakeley lovingly. Gunner number 1 handed the powder. Number 2 rammed it home, took the shell from Number 1 and put it in.
All along the ridge the horsemen handled their carbines, spoke each

in a quiet, genial tone to his horse. Sound of the approaching force made itself heard and increased.

"About a thousand, should n't you think, sir?" asked an aide.

"No. Between seven and eight hundred. Do you remember in 'Ivanhoe' —"

Out of the western wood, in order of charge, issued a body of horse. It was yet a little distant, horses at a trot, the declining sun making a stirring picture. Rapidly crescent to eye and ear, they came on. Their colours flew, the sound of their bugles raised the blood. Their pace changed to a gallop. The thundering hoofs, the braying trumpets, shook the air. Colours and guidons grew large.

"By God, sir, Wyndham is coming to eat you up! This time he knows he's caught the hare."

"Do all John Bulls ride like that? Shades of the Revolution! did we all ride like that before we came to Virginia?"

"God! what a noise!"

Ashby spoke. "Don't fire till you see the whites of their eyes."

The charge began to swallow up the gentle slope, the sunny road, the green grass to either hand. The bugles blew at height, the sabres gleamed, the tall man in front rode rising in his stirrups, his sabre overhead. "Huzzah! huzzah! huzzah!" shouted the blue cavalry.

"Are you ready, Captain Chew?" demanded Ashby. "Very well, then, let them have it!"

The Blakeley and the two Parrott guns spoke in one breath. While the echoes were yet thundering, burst a fierce volley from all the Confederate short rifles. Down went the Federal colour-bearer, down went other troopers in the front rank, down went the great gaunt horse beneath the Englishman! Those behind could not at once check their headlong gallop; they surged upon and over the fallen. The Blakeley blazed again and the grey carbines rang. The Englishman was on his feet, had a trooper's horse and was shouting like a savage, urging the squadrons on and up. For the third time the woods flamed and rang. The blue lines wavered. Some horsemen turned. "Damn you! On!" raged Wyndham.

Ashby put his bugle to his lips. Clear and sweet rose the notes, a silver tempest. *"Ashby! Ashby!"* shouted the grey lines and

charged. "*Ashby! Ashby!*" Out of the woods and down the hill
they came like undyked waters. The two tides met and clashed.
There followed a wild mêlée, a shouting, an unconscious putting
forth of great muscular energy, a seeing as through red glasses be-
smirched with powder smoke, a poisonous odour, a sense of cotton in the mouth, a feeling as of struggle on a turret, far, far up,
with empty space around and below. The grey prevailed, the blue
turned and fled. For a moment it seemed as though they were
flying through the air, falling, falling! the grey had a sense of
dizziness as they struck spur in flank and pursued headlong. All
seemed to be sinking through the air, then, suddenly, they felt
ground, exhaled breath, and went thundering up the Port Republic
road, toward Harrisonburg. In front strained the blue, presently
reaching the wood. A gun boomed from a slope beyond. Ashby
checked the pursuit and listened to the report of a vedette. "Frémont pushing forward. Horse and guns and the German division.
Hm!" He sat the bay stallion, looking about him, then, "Cuninghame, you go back to General Ewell. Rear guard can't be more
than three miles away. Tell General Ewell about the Germans
and ask him to give me a little infantry. Hurry now, and if he gives
them, bring them up quickly!"

The vedette galloped eastward. Ashby and his men rode back to
the ridge, the Horse Artillery, the dead, the wounded, and the prisoners. The latter numbered four officers and forty men. They were
all in a group in the sunshine, which lay with softness upon the short
grass and the little pine trees. The dead lay huddled, while over them
flitted the butterflies. Ashby's surgeons were busy with the wounded.
A man with a shattered jaw was making signs, deliberately talking
in the deaf-and-dumb alphabet, which perhaps he had learned for
some friend or relative's sake. A younger man, his hand clenched
over a wound in the breast, said monotonously, over and over again,
"I am from Trenton, New Jersey, I am from Trenton, New Jersey."
A third with glazing eyes made the sign of the cross, drew himself
out of the sun, under one of the little pine trees, and died. Some
of the prisoners were silent. Others talked with bravado to their
captors. "Salisbury, North Carolina! That's not far. Five hundred miles not far — Besides, Frémont will make a rescue presently. And if he does n't, Shields will to-morrow! Then off you

fellows go to Johnson's Island!" The officer who had led the charge sat on a bank above the road. In the onset he had raged like a Berserker, now he sat imperturbable, ruddy and stolid, an English philosopher on a fallen pine. Ashby came back to the road, dismounting, and leading the bay stallion, advanced. "Good-day, Colonel Wyndham."

"Good-day, General Ashby. War's a game. Somebody's got to lose. Only way to stop loss is to stop war. You held the trumps— Damn me! You played them well, too." His sword lay across his knees. He took it up and held it out. Ashby made a gesture of refusal. "No. I don't want it. I am about to send you to the rear. If there is anything I can do for you —"

"Thank you, general, there is nothing. Soldier of fortune. Fortune of war. Bad place for a charge. Ought to have been more wary. Served me right. You've got Bob Wheat with you? Know Bob Wheat. Find him in the rear?"

"Yes. With General Ewell. And now as I am somewhat in haste —"

"You must bid me good-day! See you are caring for my wounded. Much obliged. Dead will take care of themselves. Pretty little place! Flowers, butterflies — large bronze one on your hat. — This our escort? Perfectly true you'll have a fight presently. There's the New York cavalry as well as the New Jersey — plenty of infantry — Pennsylvania Bucktails and so forth. Wish I could see the scrimmage! Curious world! Can't wish you good luck. Must wish you ill. However, good luck's wrapped up in all kinds of curious bundles. Ready, men! General Ashby, may I present Major Markham, Captain Bondurant, Captain Schmidt, Lieutenant Colter? They will wish to remember having met you. — Now, gentlemen, at your service!"

Prisoners and escort vanished over the hill. Ashby, remounting, proceeded to make his dispositions, beginning with the Horse Artillery which he posted on a rise of ground, behind a mask of black thorn and dogwood. From the east arose the strains of fife and drum. "Maryland Line," said the 6th, the 7th, and the 2d Virginia Cavalry.

> I hear the distant thunder hum,
> Maryland!

> The old line bugle, fife and drum,
> > Maryland!
> She breathes! She burns! she'll come! she'll come —

"Oh! here's the 58th, too! Give them a cheer, boys! Hurrah! 58th Virginia! Hurrah! The Maryland Line!"

The two infantry regiments came forward at a double-quick, bright and brisk, rifle barrels and bayonets gleaming in the now late sunshine, their regimental flags azure and white, and beside them streaming the red battle-flag with the blue cross. As they approached there also began to show, at the edge of the forest which cut the western horizon, the Federal horse and foot. Before these was a space of rolling fields, then a ragged line of timber, a straggling copse of underbrush and tall trees cresting a wave of earth. A body of blue cavalry started out of the wood, across the field. At once Chew opened with the Blakeley and the two Parrotts. There ensued confusion and the horse fell back. A blue infantry regiment issued at a run, crossed the open and attained the cover of the coppice which commanded the road and the eastern stretch of fields. A second prepared to follow. The Maryland Line swung through the woods with orders to flank this movement. Ashby galloped to the 58th. "Forward, 58th, and clear that wood!" He rode on to Munford at the head of the squadrons. "I am going to dislodge them from that cover. The moment they leave it sound the charge!"

The 58th advanced steadily over the open. When it was almost upon the coppice it fired, then fixed bayonets. The discharge had been aimed at the wood merely. The shadows were lengthening, the undergrowth was thick; they could not see their opponents. Suddenly the coppice blazed, a well-directed and fatal volley. The regiment that held this wood had a good record and meant to-day to better it. Its target was visible enough, and close, full before it in the last golden light. A grey officer fell, the sword that he had brandished described a shining curve before it plunged into a clump of sumach. Five men lay upon the earth; the colour-bearer reeled, then pitched forward. The man behind him caught the colours. The 58th fired again, then, desperately, continued its advance. Smoke and flame burst again from the coppice. A voice of Stentor was heard. "Now Pennsylvania Bucktails, you're making history! Do your durndest!"

"Close ranks!" shouted the officer of the 58th. "Close ranks! Forward!" There came a withering volley. The second colour-bearer sank; a third seized the standard. Another officer was down; there were gaps in the ranks and under feet the wounded. The regiment wavered.

From the left came a bay stallion, devouring the earth, legs and head one tawny line, distended nostril and red-lit eye. The rider loosened from his shoulders a scarlet-lined cloak, lifted and shook it in the air. It flared out with the wind of his coming, like a banner, or a torch. He sent his voice before him, "Charge, men, charge!"

Spasmodically the 58th started forward. The copse, all dim and smoky, flowered again, three hundred red points of fire. The sound was crushing, startling, beating at the ear drum. The Bucktails were shouting, "Come on, Johnny Reb! Go back, Johnny Reb! Don't know what you want to do, do you, Johnny Reb?"

Ashby and the bay reached the front of the regiment. There was disorder, wavering, from underfoot groans and cries. So wrapped in smoke was the scene, so dusk, with the ragged and mournful woods hiding the low sun, that it was hard to distinguish the wounded. It seemed as though it was the earth herself complaining.

"On, on, men!" cried Ashby. "Help's coming — the Maryland Line!" There was a wavering answer, half cheer, half-wailing cry, "*Ashby! Ashby!*" Two balls pierced the bay stallion. He reared, screamed loudly, and fell backward. Before he touched the earth the great horseman of the Valley was clear of him. In the smoke and din Ashby leaped forward, waving the red-lined cloak above his head. "Charge, men!" he cried. "For God's sake, charge!" A bullet found his heart. He fell without a groan, his hand and arm wrapped in the red folds.

From rank to rank there passed something like a sobbing cry. The 58th charged. Bradley Johnson with the Maryland Line dislodged the Bucktails, captured their colonel and many others, killed and wounded many. The coppice, from soaked mould to smoky treetop, hung in the twilight like a wood in Hades. It was full dusk when Frémont's advance drew back, retreating sullenly to its camp at Harrisonburg. The stars were all out when, having placed the body on a litter, Ashby's men carried Ashby to Port Republic.

He lay at midnight in a room of an old house of the place. They had laid him upon a narrow bed, an old, single four-poster, with tester and valance. The white canopy above, the fall of the white below had an effect of sculptured stone. The whole looked like an old tomb in some dim abbey. The room was half in light, half in darkness. The village women had brought flowers; of these there was no lack. All the blossoms of June were heaped about him. He lay in uniform, upon the red-lined cloak, his plumed hat beside him, his sword in his hand. His staff watched in the room, seated with bowed heads beside the open window. An hour before dawn some one spoke to the sentry without the door, then gently turned the handle and entered the chamber. The watchers arose, stood at salute. "Kindly leave General Ashby and me alone together for a little while, gentlemen," said the visitor. The officers filed out. The last one turning softly to close the door saw Jackson kneel.

CHAPTER XXVI

THE BRIDGE AT PORT REPUBLIC

THE seventh of June was passed by the Army of the Valley in a quiet that seemed unnatural. For fifteen days, north from Front Royal to Harper's Ferry, south from Harper's Ferry to Port Republic, cannon had thundered, musketry rattled. Battle here and battle there, and endless skirmishing! "One male and three foights a day," said Wheat's Irishmen. But this Saturday there was no fighting. The cavalry watched both flanks of the Massanuttons. The main army rested in the rich woods that covered the hills above the North Fork of the Shenandoah. Headquarters were in the village across the river, spanned by a covered bridge. Three miles to the northwest Ewell's division was strongly posted near the hamlet of Cross Keys. From the great south peak of the Massanuttons a signal party looked down upon Frémont's road from Harrisonburg, and upon the road by which Shields must emerge from the Luray Valley. The signal officer, looking through his glass, saw also a road that ran from Port Republic by Brown's Gap over the Blue Ridge into Albemarle, and along this road moved a cortège — soldiers with the body of Ashby. The dead general's mother was in Winchester. They would have taken him there, but could not, for Frémont's army was between. So, as seemed next most fit, they carried him across the mountains into Albemarle, to the University of Virginia. Up on Massanutton the signal officer's hand shook. He lowered his glass and cleared his throat: "War's a short word to say all it says —"

Frémont rested at Harrisonburg after yesterday's repulse. On the other side of Massanutton was Shields, moving south from Luray under the remarkable impression that Jackson was at Rude's Hill and Frémont effectively dealing with the "demoralized rebels." On the sixth he began to concentrate his troops near where had been Columbia Bridge. On the seventh he issued instructions to his advance guard.

"The enemy passed New Market on the 5th. Benker's Division in pursuit. The enemy has flung away everything, and their stragglers fill the mountains. They need only a movement on the flank to panic-strike them, and break them into fragments. No man has had such a chance since the war commenced. You are within thirty miles of a broken, retreating enemy, who still hangs together. Ten thousand Germans are on his rear, who hang on like bull dogs. You have only to throw yourself down on Waynesborough before him, and your cavalry will capture thousands, seize his train and abundant supplies."

In chase of this so beautiful a chance Shields set forth down the eastern side of Massanutton, with intent to round the mountain at Port Republic, turn north again, and somewhere on the Valley pike make that will-o'-the-wisp junction with Frémont and stamp out rebellion. But of late it had rained much, and the roads were muddy and the streams swollen. His army was split into sections; here a brigade and there a brigade, the advance south of Conrad's Store, the rear yet at Luray. He had, however, the advantage of moving through leagues of forest, heavy, shaggy, dense. It was not easy to observe the details of his operations.

Sunday morning dawned. A pearly mist wrapped the North Fork and the South Fork of the Shenandoah, and clung to the shingle roofs and bowery trees of the village between. The South Fork was shallow and could be forded. The North Fork was deep and strong and crossed by a covered bridge. Toward the bridge now, winding down from the near-by height on which the brigade had camped, came a detail from the 65th — twenty men led by Sergeant Mathew Coffin. They were chiefly Company A men, and they were going to relieve the pickets along the South Fork. Thanks to Mr. Commissary Banks, they had breakfasted well. The men were happy, not hilariously so, but in a placid, equable fashion. As they came down, over the wet grass, from the bluff, they talked. "Mist over the Shenandoah's just like mist over the James" — "No, 't is n't! Nothing's like mist over the James." — "Well, the bridge's like the bridge at home, anyway!" — "'T is n't much like it. Has n't got sidewalks inside." — "Yes, it has!" — "No, it has n't!" — "I know better, I've been through it." — "I've been through it twice't — was through it after Elk Run, a month ago!" — "Well, it has n't got sidewalks, anyway." — "I tell you it has." — "You're

mistaken!" — "I'm not." — "You never did see straight nohow!"
— "If I was at home I'd thrash you!"

Mathew Coffin turned his head. "Who's that jowering back
there? Stop it! Sunday morning and all!"

He went on, holding his head straight, a trig, slender figure,
breathing irritation. His oval face with its little black moustache
was set as hard as its boyish curves permitted, and his handsome
dark eyes had two parallel lines above them. He marched as he
marched always nowadays, with a mien aggrieved and haughty. He
never lost the consciousness that he was wearing chevrons who
had worn bars, and he was quite convinced that the men continually compared his two states.

The progress down hill to the bridge was short. Before the party
the long, tunnel-like, weather-beaten structure loomed through the
mist. The men entered and found it dusk and warm, smelling of
horses, the river, fifteen feet below, showing through the cracks between the heavy logs of the floor. The marching feet sounded hollowly, voices reverberated. "Just like our bridge — told you 't was
— Ain't it like, Billy Maydew?"

"It air," said Billy. "I air certainly glad that we air a-crossing on
a bridge. The Shenandoah air a prop-o-si-tion to swim."

"How did you feel, Billy, when you got away?"

"At first, just like school was out," said Billy. "But when a whole
picket post started after me, 'n' I run fer it, 'n' the trees put out arms
to stop me, 'n' the dewberry, crawling on the ground, said to itself,
'Hello! Let's make a trap'; 'n' when the rail fences all hollered out,
'We're goin' to turn agin you!' 'n' when a bit of swamp hollered
louder than any, 'Let's suck down Billy Maydew — suck down
Billy Maydew!' 'n' when a lot o' bamboo vines running over cedars,
up with 'Hold him fast until you hear a bullet whizzing!' 'n' I got to
the Shenandoah and there wa'n't no bridge, 'n' the Shenandoah says
'I'd just as soon drown men as look at them!' — when all them
things talked so, I knew just how the critturs feel in the woods; 'n'
I ain't so crazy about hunting as I was — and I say again this here
air a most con-ve-ni-ent bridge."

With his musket butt he struck the boarded side. The noise was
so resoundingly greater than he had expected that he laughed and
the men with him. Now Sergeant Mathew Coffin was as nervous as

a witch. He had been marching along with his thoughts moodily hovering over the battery he would take almost single-handed, or the ambush he would dislodge and so procure promotion indeed. At the noise of the stick he started violently. "Who did that? Oh, I see, and I might have known it! I'll report you for extra duty —"

"Report ahead," said Billy, under his breath.

Coffin halted. "What was that you said, Maydew?"

"I did n't speak to you — sir."

"Well, you'll speak to me now. What was it you said then?" He came nearer, his arm thrown up, though but in an angry gesture. "If I struck you," thought Billy, "I'd be sorry for it, so I won't do it. But one thing's sure — I certainly should like to!"

"If you don't answer me," said Coffin thickly, "I'll report you for disobedience as well as for disorderly conduct! What was it you said then?"

"I said, 'Report ahead — and be damned to you!'"

Coffin's lips shut hard. "Very good! We'll see how three days of guardhouse tastes to you! — Forward!"

The party cleared the bridge and almost immediately found itself in the straggling village street. The mist clung here as elsewhere, houses and trees dim shapes, the surrounding hills and the dense woods beyond the South Fork hardly seen at all. Coffin marched with flushed face and his brows drawn together. He was mentally writing a letter on pale blue paper, and in it he was enlarging upon ingratitude. The men sympathized with Billy and their feet sounded resentfully upon the stones. Billy alone marched with elaborate lightness, quite as though he were walking on air and loved the very thought of the guardhouse.

Headquarters was an old corner house that had flung open its doors to General Jackson with an almost tremulous eagerness. A flag waved before the door, and there was a knot beneath of couriers and orderlies, with staff officers coming and going. Opposite was a store, closed of course upon Sunday, but boasting a deep porch with benches, to say nothing of convenient kegs and boxes. Here the village youth and age alike found business to detain them. The grey-headed exchanged remarks. "Sleep? No, I could n't sleep! Might as well see what's to be seen! I ain't got long to see anything, and so I told Susan. When's he coming out? — Once't when I was a little shaver like Bob, sitting on the scales there, I went with my father in the stage-coach to Fredericksburg, I remember just as well — and I was sitting before the tavern on a man's knee, — old man 't was, for he said he had fought the Indians, — and somebody came riding down the street, with two or three others. I jus' remember a blue coat and a cocked hat and that his hair was powdered — and the man put me down and got up, and everybody else before the tavern got up — and somebody holloaed out 'Hurrah for General Washington —' "

There was a stir about the opposite door. An aide came out, mounted and rode off toward the bridge. An orderly brought a horse from the neighbouring stable. "That's his! That's General Jackson's! — Don't look like the war horse in Job, does he now? — Looks like a doctor's horse — Little Sorrel's his name." The small boy surged forward. "He's coming out!" — "How do you know him?" — "G' way! You always know generals when you see them! Great, big men, all trimmed up with gold. Besides, I saw him last night." — "You did n't!" — "Yes, I did! Saw his shadow on the curtain." — "How did you know 't was his?" — "My mother said, 'Look, John, and don't never forget. That's Stonewall Jackson.' And it was a big shadow walking up and down, and it raised its hand —"

The church bell rang. A chaplain came out of the house. He had a Bible in his hand, and he beamed on all around. "There's the first bell, gentlemen — the bell, children! Church in a church, just like before we went to fighting! Trust you'll all come, gentlemen, and you, too, boys! The general hopes you'll all come."

Within headquarters, in a large bare room, Jackson was having his customary morning half-hour with his heads of departments — an invariably recurring period in his quiet and ordered existence. It was omitted only when he fought in the morning. He sat as usual, bolt upright, large feet squarely planted, large hands stiff at sides. On the table before him were his sabre and Bible. Before him stood a group of officers. The adjutant, Colonel Paxton, finished his report. The general nodded. "Good! good! Well, Major Harman?"

The chief quartermaster saluted. "The trains, sir, had a good night. There are clover fields on either side of the Staunton road and the horses are eating their fill. A few have sore hoof and may have to be left behind. I had the ordnance moved as you ordered, nearer the river. An orderly came back last night from the convoy on the way to Staunton. Sick and wounded standing it well. Prisoners slow marchers, but marching. I sent this morning a string of wagons to Cross Keys, to General Ewell. We had a stampede last night among the negro teamsters. They were sitting in a ring around the fire, and an owl hooted or a bat flitted. They had been telling stories of ha'nts, and they swore they saw General Ashby galloping by on the white stallion."

"Poor, simple, ignorant creatures!" said Jackson. "There is no witch of Endor can raise that horse and rider! — Major Hawks!"

The chief commissary came forward. "General Banks's stores are holding out well, sir. We are issuing special rations to the men to-day — Sunday dinner — fresh beef, rice and beans, canned fruits, coffee, sugar —"

"Good! good! They deserve the best. — Colonel Crutchfield —"

"I have posted Wooding's battery as you ordered, sir, on the brow of the hill commanding the bridge. There's a gun of Courtney's disabled. I have thought he might have the Parrott we captured day before yesterday. Ammunition has been issued as ordered. Caissons all filled."

"Good! — Captain Boswell — Ah, Mr. Hotchkiss."

"Captain Boswell is examining the South Fork, sir, with a view to finding the best place for the foot bridge you ordered constructed. I have here the map you ordered me to draw."

"Good! Put it here on the table. — Now, Doctor McGuire."

"Very few reported sick this morning, sir. The good women of the village are caring for those. Three cases of fever, two of pneumonia, some dysentery, measles among the recruits. The medicines we got at Winchester are invaluable; they and the better fare the men are getting. Best of all is the consciousness of victory, — the confidence and exaltation that all feel."

"Yes, doctor. God's shield is over us. — Captain Wilbourne —"

"I brought the signal party in from Peaked Mountain last night, sir. A Yankee cavalry company threatened to cut us off. Had we stayed we should have been captured. I trust, sir, that I acted rightly?"

"You acted rightly. You saw nothing of General Shields?"

"Nothing, sir. It is true that the woods for miles are extremely thick. It would perhaps be possible for a small force to move unseen. But we made out nothing."

Jackson rose and drew closer the sabre and the Bible. "That is all, gentlemen. After religious services you will return to your respective duties."

The sun was now above the mountain tops, the mist beginning to lift. It lay heavily, however, over the deep woods and the bottom lands of the South Fork, through which ran the Luray road, and on the South Fork itself. — Clatter, clatter! Shots and cries! Shouting the alarm as they came, splashing through the ford, stopping on the hither bank for one scattering volley back into the woolly veil, came Confederate infantry pickets and vedettes. "Yankee cavalry! Look out! Look out! Yankees!" In the mist the foremost man ran against the detail from the 65th. Coffin seized him. "Where? where?" The other gasped. "Coming! Drove us in! Whole lot of them! Got two guns. All of Shields, I reckon, right behind!" He broke away, tearing with his fellows into the village.

Sergeant Coffin and his men stared into the mist. They heard a great splashing, a jingling and shouting, and in another instant were aware of something looming like a herd of elephants. From the village behind them burst the braying of their own bugles — headquarters summoning, baggage train on the Staunton road summoning. The sound was shrill, insistent. The shapes in the mist grew larger. There came a flash of rifles, pale yellow through the drift as of lawn. Zzzzzz! Zzzzzz! sang the balls. The twenty men of the 65th proceeded to save themselves. Some of them tore down a side street, straight before the looming onrush. Others leaped fences and brushed through gardens, rich and dank. Others found house doors suddenly and quietly opening before them, houses with capacious dark garrets and cellars. All the dim horde, more and more of it, came splashing through the ford. A brazen rumbling arose, announcing guns. The foremost of the horde, blurred of outline, preternaturally large, huzzaing and firing, charged into the streets of Port Republic.

In a twinkling the village passed from her Sunday atmosphere to one of a highly work-a-day Monday. The blue cavalry began to harry the place. The townspeople hurried home, trumpets blared, shots rang out, oaths, shouts of warning! Men in grey belonging with the wagon train ran headlong toward their posts, others made for headquarters where the flag was and Stonewall Jackson. A number, headed off, were captured at once. Others, indoors when the alarm arose, were hidden by the women. Three staff officers had walked, after leaving Jackson's council, toward a house holding pretty daughters whom they meant to take to church. When the clangour broke out they had their first stupefied moment, after which they turned and ran with all their might toward headquarters. There was fighting up and down the street. Half a dozen huzzaing and sabring troopers saw the three and shouted to others nearer yet. "Officers! Cut them off, you there!" The three were taken. A captain, astride of a great reeking horse, towered above them. "Staff? You're staff? Is Jackson in the town? — and where? Quick now! Eh — what!"

"That's a lovely horse. Looks exactly, I imagine, like Rozinante —"

"On the whole I should say that McClellan might be finding Richmond like those mirages travellers tell about. The nearer he gets to it the further it is away."

"It has occurred to me that if after the evacuation of Corinth Beauregard should come back to Virginia —"

The captain in blue, hot and breathless, bewildered by the very success of the dash into town, kept saying, "Where is Jackson? What? Quick there, you! Where —" Behind him a corporal spoke out cavalierly. "They are n't going to tell you, sir. There's a large house down there that's got something like a flag before it — I think, too, that we ought to go take the bridge."

The streams of blue troopers flowed toward the principal street and united there. Some one saw the flag more plainly. "That's a headquarters! — What if Jackson were there? Good Lord! what if we took Jackson?" A bugler blew a vehement rally. "*All of you, come on! All of you, come on!*" The stream increased in volume, began to move, a compact body, down the street. "There are horses before that door! Look at that nag! That's Jackson's horse! — No." — "Yes! Saw it at Kernstown! Forward!"

Stonewall Jackson came out of the house with the flag before it. Behind him were those of his staff who had not left headquarters when the invasion occurred, while, holding the horses before the door, waited, white-lipped, a knot of most anxious orderlies. One brought Little Sorrel. Jackson mounted with his usual slow deliberation, then, turning in the saddle, looked back to the shouting blue horsemen. They saw him and dug spurs into flanks. First he pulled the forage cap over his eyes and then he jerked his hand into the air. These gestures executed he touched Little Sorrel with the rowel and, his suite behind him, started off down the street toward the bridge over the Shenandoah. One would not have said that he went like a swift arrow. There was, indeed, an effect of slowness, of a man traversing, in deep thought, a solitary plain. But for all that, he went so fast that the space between him and the enemy did not decrease. They came thunderingly on, a whole Federal charge — but he kept ahead. Seeing that he did so, they began to discharge carbine and pistol, some aiming at Little Sorrel, some at the grey figure riding stiffly, bolt upright and elbows out. Little Sorrel shook his head, snorted, and went on. Ahead loomed the bridge, a dusky, warm, gold-shot tunnel below an arch of weather-beaten wood. Under it rolled with a heavy sound the Shenandoah. Across the river, upon the green hilltops, had arisen a commotion. All the drums were beating the long roll. Stonewall Jackson and Little Sorrel came on the trodden rise of earth leading to the bridge mouth. The blue cavalry shouted and spurred. Their carbines cracked. The balls pockmarked the wooden arch. Jackson dragged the forage cap lower and disappeared within the bridge. The four or five with him turned and drew across the gaping mouth.

The blue cavalry came on, firing as they came. Staff and orderlies, the grey answered with pistols. Behind, in the bridge, sounded the hollow thunder of Little Sorrel's hoofs. The sound grew fainter. Horse and rider were nearly across. Staff and orderlies fired once again, then, just as the blue were upon them, turned, dug spur, shouted, and disappeared beneath the arch.

The Federal cavalry, massed before the bridge and in the field to either side, swore and swore, "He's out! — Jackson's out! There he goes — up the road! Fire! — Damn it all, what's the use? He's charmed. We almost got him! Good Lord! We'd all have been major-generals!"

A patrol galloped up. "They've got a great wagon train, sir, at the other end of the village — ordnance reserve, supply, everything! It is in motion. It's trying to get off by the Staunton road."

The cavalry divided. A strong body stayed by the bridge, while one as large turned and galloped away. Those staying chafed with impatience. "Why don't the infantry come up — damned creeping snails!" — "Yes, we could cross, but when we got to the other side, what then? — No, don't dare to burn the bridge — don't know what the general would say." — "Listen to those drums over there! If Stonewall Jackson brings all those hornets down on us!" — "If we had a gun — Speak of the angels! — Unlimber right here, lieutenant! — Got plenty of canister? Now if the damned infantry would only come on! Thought it was just behind us when we crossed the ford — What's that off there?"

"That" was a sharp sputter of musketry. "Firing! Who are they firing at? There aren't any rebels — we took them all prisoners —"

"There's fighting, anyway — wagon escort, maybe. The devil! Look across the river! Look! All the hornets are coming down —"

Of the detail from the 65th Coffin and two others stood their ground until the foremost of the herd was crossing the ford near at hand, large, threatening, trumpeting. Then the three ran like hares, hearts pounding at their sides, the ocean roaring in their ears, and in every cell in their bodies an accurate impression that they had been seen, and that the trumpeting herd meant to run down, kill or capture every grey soldier in Port Republic! Underfoot was wet knot grass, difficult and slippery; around was the shrouding mist. They thought the lane ran through to another street, but it proved a cul-de-sac. Something rose mistily before them; it turned out to be a cowshed. They flung themselves against the door, but the door was padlocked. Behind the shed, between it and a stout board fence, sprang a great clump of wet elder, tall and rank, with spreading leaves; underneath, black, miry earth. Into this they crowded, squatted on the earth, turned face toward the passage up which they had come, and brought their rifles to the front. A hundred yards away the main herd went by, gigantic in the mist. The three in the elder breathed deep. "All gone. Gone! — No. There's a squad coming up here."

The three kneeling in the mire, watching through triangular spaces between the branchy leaves, grew suddenly, amazingly calm.

What was the sense in being frightened? You could n't get away. Was there anywhere to go to one might feel agitation enough, but there was n't! Coffin handled his rifle with the deliberation of a woman smoothing her long hair. The man next him — Jim Watts — even while he settled forward on his knees and raised his musket, turned his head aside and spat. "Derned old fog always gits in my throat!" A branch of elder was cutting Billy Maydew's line of vision. He broke it off with noiseless care and raised to his shoulder the Enfield rifle which he had acquired at Winchester. There loomed, at thirty feet away, colossal beasts bestridden by giants.

Suddenly the mist thinned, lifted. The demon steeds and riders resolved themselves into six formidable looking Federal troopers. From the main street rang the Federal bugles, vehemently rallying, imperative. Shouting, too, broke out, savage, triumphant, pointed with pistol shots. The bugle called again, *Rally to the colours! Rally!*

"I calculate," said one of the six blue horsemen, "that the boys have found Stonewall."

"Then they'll need us all!" swore the trooper leading. "If anybody's in the cow-house they can wait." — *Right about face! Forward! Trot!*

The men within the elder settled down on the wet black earth. "Might as well stay here, I suppose," said Coffin. Jim Watts began to shiver. "It's awful damp and cold. I've got an awful pain in the pit of my stomach." He rolled over and lay groaning. "Can't I go, sir?" asked Billy. "I kind of feel more natural in the open."

Now Mathew Coffin had just been thinking that while this elder bush springing from muddy earth, with a manure heap near, was damned uncomfortable, it was better than being outside while those devils were slashing and shooting. Perhaps they would ride away, or the army might come over the bridge, and there would be final salvation. He had even added a line to the letter he was writing, "An elder bush afforded me some slight cover from which to fire —" And now Billy Maydew wanted to go outside and be taken prisoner! Immediately he became angry again. "You're no fonder of the open than I am!" he said, and his upper lip twitched one side away from his white teeth.

Billy, his legs already out of the bush, looked at him with large, calm grey eyes. "Kin I go?"

"Go where? You'll get killed."

"You would n't grieve if I did, would you? I kinder thought I might get by a back street to the wagons. A cousin of mine's a wagon master and he ain't going ter give up easy. I kinder thought I might help —"

"I'm just waiting," said Coffin, "until Jim here gets over his spasm. Then I'll give the word."

Jim groaned. "I feel sicker'n a yaller dog after a fight — 'n' you know I did n't mind 'em at all when they were really here! You two go on, 'n' I'll come after awhile."

Coffin and Billy found the back street. It lay clear, warm, sunny, empty. "They're all down at the bridge," said Billy. "Bang! bang! bang!" They came to a house, blinds all closed, shrinking behind its trees. Houses, like everything else, had personality in this war. A town occupied changed its mien according to the colour of the uniform in possession. As the two hurrying grey figures approached, a woman, starting from the window beside which she had been kneeling, watching through a crevice, ran out of the house and through the yard to the gate. "You two men, come right in here! Don't you know the Yankees are in town?"

She was young and pretty. Coffin swept off his cap. "That's the reason we're trying to get to the edge of town — to help the men with the wagon train."

Her eyes grew luminous. "How brave you are! Go, and God bless you!"

The two ran on. Mathew Coffin added another line to his letter: "A lady besought me to enter her house, saying that I would surely be killed, and that she could conceal me until the enemy was gone. But I —"

They were nearly out of town — they could see the long train hurriedly moving on the Staunton road. There was a sudden burst of musketry. A voice reached them from the street below. "Halt, you two Confeds running there! Come on over here! Rally to the colours!" There was a flash of the stars and bars, waved vigorously. "Oh, ha, ha!" cried Billy, "thar was some of us was n't taken! Are n't you glad we did n't stay behind the cowshed?"

It came into Coffin's head that Billy might tell that his sergeant had wished to stay behind the cowshed. The blood rushed to his face; he saw the difficulty of impressing men who knew about the cowshed with his abilities in the way of storming batteries single-handed. He had really a very considerable share of physical courage, and naturally he esteemed it something larger than it was. He began to burn with the injustice of Billy Maydew's thinking him backward in daring and so reporting him around camp-fires. As he ran he grew angrier and angrier, and not far from the shaken flag, in a little grassy hollow which hid them from view, he called upon the other to halt. Billy's sense of discipline brought him to a stop, but did not keep him from saying, "What for?" They were only two soldiers, out of the presence of others and in a pretty tight place together — Mathew Coffin but three years older than he, and no great shakes anyhow. "What for?" asked Billy.

"I just want to say to you," said Coffin thickly, "that as to that shed, it was my duty to protect my men; just as it is my duty as an officer to report you for disobedience and bad language addressed to an officer —"

Billy's brow clouded. "I had forgotten all about that. I was going along very nicely with you. You were really behaving yourself — like a — like a gentleman. The cow-house was all right. You are brave enough when it comes to fighting. And now you're bringing it all up again —"

"'*Gentleman.*' — Who are you to judge of a gentleman?"

Billy looked at him calmly. "I air one of them. — I air a-judging from that-a stand."

"You are going to the guardhouse for disobedience and bad language and impertinence."

"It would be right hard," said Billy, "if I had to leave su-pe-ri-or-i-ty outside with my musket. But I don't."

Coffin, red in the face, made at him. The Thunder Run man, supple as a moccasin, swerved aside. "Air you finished speaking, sergeant? Fer if you have, 'n' if you don't mind, I think I'll run along — I air only fighting Yankees this mornin'!"

An aide of Jackson's, cut off from headquarters and taking shelter in the upper part of the town, crept presently out of hiding, and finding the invaders' eyes turned toward the bridge, proceeded with dispatch and quietness to gather others from dark havens. When he had a score or more he proceeded to bolder operations. In the field and on the Staunton road all was commotion; wagons with their teams moving in double column up the road, negro teamsters clamouring with ashen looks, "Dose damn Yanks! Knowed we did n't see dat ghos' fer nothin' las' night!" Wagon masters shouted, guards and sentries looked townward with anxious eyes. The aide got a flag from the quartermaster's tent; found moreover a very few artillery reserves and an old cranky howitzer. With all of these he returned to the head of the main street, and about the moment the cavalry at the bridge divided, succeeded in getting his forces admirably placed in a strong defensive position: Coffin and Billy Maydew joined just as an outpost brought a statement that about two hundred Yankee cavalry were coming up the street.

The two guns, Federal Parrott, Confederate howitzer, belching smoke, made in twenty minutes the head of the street all murk. In the first charge Coffin received a sabre cut over the head. The blood blinded him at first, and when he had wiped it away, and tied a beautiful new handkerchief from a Broadway shop about the wound, he found it still affected sight and hearing. He understood that their first musketry fire had driven the cavalry back, indeed he saw two or three riderless horses galloping away. He understood also that the Yankees had brought up a gun, and that the captain was answering with the superannuated howitzer. He was sure, too, that he himself was firing his musket with great precision. *Fire!* — *load, fire!* — *load, fire! One, two,* — *one, two!* but his head, he was equally sure, was growing larger. It was now larger than the globe pictured on the first page of the geography he had studied at school. It was the globe, and he was Atlas holding it. *Fire* — *load, fire* — *load!* Now the head was everything, and all life was within it. There was a handsome young man named Coffin, very brave, but misunderstood by all save one. He was brave and handsome. He could take a tower by himself — *Fire, load* — *Fire, load* — *One, two.* The enemy knew his fame. They said, "Coffin! Which is Coffin?" — *Fire, load, one, two.* The grey armies knew this young hero. They cheered when he went by. They cheered — they cheered — when he went by to take the tower. They wrote home and lovely women envied the loveliest woman. "Coffin! Coffin! Coffin's going to take the tower! Watch him! *Yaaaaih! Yaaaih!*" — He struck the tower and looked to see it go down. Instead, with a roar, it sprang, triple brass, height on height to the skies. The stars fell, and suddenly, in the darkness, an ocean appeared and went over him. He lay beneath the overturned Federal gun, and the grey rush that had silenced the gunners and taken the piece went on.

For a long time he lay in a night without a star, then day began to break. It broke curiously, palely light for an instant, then obscured by thick clouds, then faint light again. Some part of his brain began to think. His head was not now the world; the world was lying on his shoulder and arm, crushing it. With one piece of his brain he began to appeal to people; with another piece to answer the first. "Mother, take this thing away! Mother, take this thing away! She's dead. She can't, however much she wants to. Father! He's dead, too. Rob, Carter — Jack! Grown up and moved away. Judge Allen, sir! — Mr. Boyd! — would you just give a hand? Here I am, under Purgatory Mountain. Darling — take this thing away! Darling — Darling! Men! — Colonel Cleave! — Boys — boys —" All the brain began to think. "O God, send somebody!"

When Purgatory Mountain was lifted from his shoulder and arm he fainted. Water, brought in a cap from a neighbouring puddle and dashed in his face, brought him to. "Thar now!" said Billy, "I certainly air glad to see that you air alive!" Coffin groaned. "It must ha' hurt awful! S'pose you let me look before I move you?" He took out a knife and gently slit the coat away. "Sho! I know that hurts! But you got first to the gun! You ran like you was possessed, and you yelled, and you was the first to touch the gun. Thar now! I air a-tying the han'kerchief from your head around your arm, 'cause there's more blood —"

"They'll have to cut it off," moaned Coffin.

"No, they won't. Don't you let 'em! Now I air a-going to lift you and carry you to the nearest house. All the boys have run on after the Yanks."

He took up his sergeant and moved off with an easy step. Coffin uttered a short and piteous moaning like a child. They presently met a number of grey soldiers. "We've druv them — we've druv them! The 37th's down there. Just listen to Rockbridge! — Who've you got there?"

"Sergeant Coffin," said Billy. "He air right badly hurt! He was the first man at the gun. He fired, an' then he got hold of the sponge staff and laid about him — he was that gallant. The men ought to 'lect him back. He sure did well."

The nearest house flung open its doors. "Bring him right in here — oh, poor soldier! Right here in the best room! — Run, Maria, and turn down the bed. Oh, poor boy! He looks like my Robert down at Richmond! This way — get a little blackberry wine, Betty, and the scissors and my roll of lint —"

Billy laid him on the bed in the best room. "Thar now! You air all right. The doctor'll come just as soon as I can find him, 'n' then I'll get back to the boys — Wait — I did n't hear, I'll put my ear down. You could n't lose all that blood and not be awful weak —"

"I'd be ashamed to report now!" whispered Coffin. "Maybe I was wrong —"

"Sho!" said Billy. "We're all wrong more or less. Here, darn you, drink your wine, and stop bothering!"

Across the Shenandoah Stonewall Jackson and the 37th Virginia came down from the heights with the impetuosity of a torrent. Behind them poured other grey troops. On the cliff heads Poague and Carpenter came into position and began with grape and canister. The blue Parrott, full before the bridge mouth, menacing the lane within, answered with a shriek of shells. The 37th and Jackson left the road, plunged down the ragged slope of grass and vines, and came obliquely toward the dark tunnel. Jackson and Little Sorrel had slipped into their battle aspect. You would have said that every auburn hair of the general's head and beard was a vital thing. His eyes glowed as though there were lamps behind, and his voice rose like a trumpet of promise and doom. "Halt! — Aim at the gunners! — Fire! Fix bayonets! Charge!"

The 37th rushed in column through the bridge. The blue cavalry fired one volley. The unwounded among the blue artillerymen strove to plant a shell within the dusky lane. But most of the gunners were down, or the fuse was wrong. The grey torrent leaped out of the tunnel and upon the gun. They took it and turned it against the horsemen. The blue cavalry fled. On the bluff heads above the river three grey batteries came into action. The 37th Virginia began to sweep the streets of Port Republic.

The blue cavalry, leaving the guns, leaving prisoners they had taken and their wounded, turned alike from the upper end of the village and rode, pell-mell, for the South Fork. One and all they splashed through, not now in covering mist, but in hot sunshine, the 37th volleying at their heels and from the bluffs above the Shenandoah, Poague and Carpenter and Wooding strewing their path with grape and canister.

A mile or two in the deep woods they met Shields's infantry advance. There followed a movement toward the town — futile enough, for as the vanguard approached, the Confederate batteries across the river limbered up, trotted or galloped to other positions on the green bluff heads, and trained the guns on the ground between Port Republic and the head of the Federal column. Winder's brigade came also and took position on the heights commanding Lewiston, and Taliaferro's swung across the bridge and formed upon the townward side of South Fork. Shields halted. All day he halted, listening to the guns at Cross Keys.

Sitting Little Sorrel at the northern end of the bridge, Stonewall Jackson watched Taliaferro's men break step and cross. A staff officer ventured to inquire what the general thought General Shields would do.

"I think, sir, that he will stay where he is."

"All day, sir?"

"All day."

"He has ten thousand men. Will he not try to attack?"

"No, sir! No! He cannot do it. I should tear him to pieces."

A heavy sound came into being. The staff officer swung round on his horse. "Listen, sir!"

"Yes. Artillery firing to the northwest. Frémont will act without Shields."

A courier came at a gallop. "General Ewell's compliments, sir, and the battle of Cross Keys is beginning."

"Good! good! My compliments to General Ewell, and I expect him to win it."

CHAPTER XXVII

JUDITH AND STAFFORD

THE cortège bearing Ashby to his grave wound up and up to the pass in the Blue Ridge. At the top it halted. The ambulance rested beside a grey boulder, while the cavalry escort dismounted and let the horses crop the sweet mountain grass. Below them, to the east, rolled Piedmont Virginia; below them to the west lay the great Valley whence they had come. As they rested they heard the cannon of Cross Keys, and with a glass made out the battle smoke.

For an hour they gazed and listened, anxious and eager; then the horsemen remounted, the ambulance moved from the boulder, and all went slowly down the long loops of road. Down and down they wound, from the cool, blowing air of the heights into the warm June region of red roads, shady trees and clear streams, tall wheat and ripening cherries, old houses and gardens. They were moving toward the Virginia Central, toward Meechum's Station.

A courier had ridden far in advance. At Meechum's was a little crowd of country people. "They're coming! That's an ambulance! — Is he in the ambulance? Everybody take off their hats. Is that his horse behind? Yes, it is a horse that he sometimes rode, but the three stallions were killed. How mournful they come! Albert Sidney Johnston is dead, and Old Joe may die, he is so badly hurt — and Bee is dead, and Ashby is dead." Three women got out of an old carryall. "One of you men come help us lift the flowers! We were up at dawn and gathered all there were —"

The train from Staunton came in — box cars and a passenger coach. The coffin, made at Port Republic, was lifted from the ambulance, out of a bed of fading flowers. It was wrapped in the battle-flag. The crowd bowed its head. An old minister lifted trembling hand. "God — this Thy servant! God — this Thy servant!" The three women brought their lilies, their great sprays of citron aloes. The coffin was placed in the aisle of the passenger coach, and four officers followed as its guard. The escort was slight. Never were there many men spared for these duties. The dead would have been the first to speak against it. Every man in life was needed at the front. The dozen troopers stalled their horses in two of the box cars and themselves took possession of a third. The bell rang, slowly and tollingly. The train moved toward Charlottesville, and the little crowd of country folk was left in the June sunshine with the empty ambulance. In the gold afternoon, the bell slowly ringing, the train crept into Charlottesville.

In this town, convenient for hospitals and stores, midway between Richmond and the Valley, a halting place for troops moving east and west, there were soldiers enough for a soldier's escort to his resting place. The concourse at the station was large, and a long train followed the bier of the dead general out through the town to the University of Virginia, and the graveyard beyond.

There were no students now at the University. In the white-pillared rotunda surgeons held council and divided supplies. In the ranges, where were the cell-like students' rooms, and in the white-pillared professors' houses, lay the sick and wounded. From room to room, between the pillars, moved the nursing women. To-day the rotunda was cleared. Surgeons and nurses snatched one half-hour, and, with the families from the professors' houses, and the men about the place and the servants, gathered upon the rotunda steps, or upon the surrounding grassy slopes, to watch the return of an old student. It was not long before they heard the Dead March.

For an hour the body lay between the white columns before the rotunda that Jefferson had built. Soldiers and civilians, women and children, passing before the bier, looked upon the marble face and the hand that clasped the sword. Then, toward sunset, the coffin lid was closed, the bearers took the coffin up, the Dead March began again, and all moved toward the graveyard.

Dusk gathered, soft and warm, and filled with fireflies. The Greenwood carriage, with the three sisters and Miss Lucy, drew slowly through the scented air up to the dim old house. Julius opened the door. The ladies stepped out, and in silence went up the steps. Molly had been crying. The little handkerchief which she dropped, and which was restored to her by Julius, was quite wet.

Julius, closing the carriage door, looked after the climbing figures,

"Fo' de Lawd, you useter could hear dem laughin' befo' dey got to de big oaks, and when dey outer de kerriage an' went up de steps dey was chatterin' lak de birds at daybreak! An' now I heah dem sighin' an' Miss Molly's handkerchief ez wet ez ef 't was in de washtub! De ol' times is evaporated."

"Dat sholy so," agreed Isham, from the box. "Des look at me er-drivin' horses dat once I'd er scorned to tech! — An' all de worl' er-mournin'. Graveyards gitting full an' ginerals lyin' daid. What de use of dis heah war, anyhow? W'ite folk ought ter hab more sence."

In the Greenwood dining-room they sat at table in silence, scarcely touching Car'line's supper, but in the parlour afterward Judith turned at bay. "Even Aunt Lucy — of all people in the world! Aunt Lucy, if you do not smile this instant, I hope all the Greenwood shepherdesses will step from out the roses and disown you! And Unity, if you don't play, sing, look cheerful, my heart will break! Who calls it loss this afternoon? He left a thought of him that will guide men on! Who doubts that to-morrow morning we shall hear that Cross Keys was won? Oh, I know that you are thinking most of General Ashby! — but I am thinking most of Cross Keys!"

"Judith, Judith, you are the strongest of us all —"

"Judith, darling, nothing's going to hurt Richard! I just feel it —"

"Hush, Molly! Judith's not afraid."

"No. I am not afraid. I think the cannon have stopped at Cross Keys, and that they are resting on the field. — Now, for us women. I do not think that we do badly now. We serve all day and half the night, and we keep up the general heart. I think that if in any old romance we read of women like the women of the South in this war we would say, 'Those women were heroic.' We have been at war for a year and two months. I see no end of it. It is a desert, and no one knows how wide it is. We may travel for years. Beside every marching soldier, there marches invisible a woman soldier too. We are in the field as they are in the field, and doing our part. No — we have not done at all badly, but now let us give it all! There is a plane where every fibre is heroic. Let us draw to full height, lift eyes, and travel boldly! We have to cross the desert, but from the desert one sees all the stars! Let us be too wise for such another drooping hour!" She came and kissed her aunt, and clung to her. "I was n't scolding, Aunt Lucy! How could I? But to-night I simply have to be strong. I have to look at the stars, for the desert is full of terrible shapes. Some one said that the battle with Shields may be fought to-morrow. I have to look at the stars." She lifted herself. "We finished 'Villette,' did n't we? — Oh, yes! I did n't like the ending. Well, let us begin 'Mansfield Park' — Molly, have you seen my knitting?"

Having with his fellows of the escort from Port Republic seen the earth heaped over the dead cavalry leader, Maury Stafford lay that night in Charlottesville at an old friend's house. He slept little; the friend heard him walking up and down in the night. By nine in the morning he was at the University. "Miss Cary? She'll be here in about half an hour. If you'll wait —"

"I'll wait," said Stafford. He sat down beneath an elm and, with his eyes upon the road by which must approach the Greenwood carriage, waited the half-hour. It passed; the carriage drew up and Judith stepped from it. Her eyes rested upon him with a quiet friendliness. He had been her suitor; but he was so no longer. Months ago he had his answer. All the agitation, the strong, controlling interest of his world must, perforce, have made him forget. She touched his hand. "I saw you yesterday afternoon. I did not know if you had ridden back —"

"No. I shall be kept here until to-morrow. Will you be Sister of Mercy all day?"

"I go home to-day about four o'clock."

"If I ride over at five may I see you?"

"Yes, if you wish. I must go now — I am late. Is it true that we won the battle yesterday? Tell me —"

"We do not know the details yet. It seems that only Ewell's division was engaged. Trimble's brigade suffered heavily, but it was largely an artillery battle. I saw a copy of General Jackson's characteristic telegram to Richmond. 'God gave us the victory to-day at Cross Keys.' — Frémont has drawn off to Harrisonburg. There is a rumour of a battle to-day with Shields."

He thought that afternoon, as he passed through the road gates and into the drive between the oaks, that he had never seen the Greenwood place look so fair. The sun was low and there were shadows, but where the light rays touched, all lay mellow and warm, golden and gay and sweet. On the porch he found Unity, sitting with her guitar, singing to a ragged grey youth, thin and pale, with big hollow eyes. She smiled and put out her hand. "Judith said you were coming. She will be down in a moment. Major Stafford — Captain Howard — Go on singing? Very well, —

"Soft o'er the fountain, lingering falls the southern moon — "

"Why is it that convalescent soldiers want the very most sentimental ditties that can be sung?

"Far o'er the mountain, breaks the day too soon!"

"I know that string is going to snap presently! Then where would I buy guitar strings in a land without a port?

"Nita! Juanita! Ask thy soul if we should part — Nita! Juanita! Lean thou on my heart!"

Judith came down in a soft old muslin, pale violet, open at the throat. It went well with that warm column, with the clear beauty of her face and her dark liquid eyes. She had a scarf in her hand; it chanced to be the long piece of black lace that Stafford remembered her wearing that April night. — "It is a lovely evening. Suppose we walk."

There was a path through the flower garden, down a slope of grass, across a streamlet in a meadow, then gently up through an ancient wood, and more steeply to the top of a green hill — a hill of hills from which to watch the sunset. Stafford unlatched the flower-garden gate. "The roses are blooming as though there were no war!" said Judith. "Look at George the Fourth and the Seven Sisters and my old Giant of Battle!"

"Sometimes you are like one flower," answered Stafford, "and sometimes like another. To-day, in that dress, you are like heliotrope."

Judith wondered. "Is it wise to go on — if he has forgotten so little as that?" She spoke aloud. "I have hardly been in the garden for days. Suppose we rest on the arbour steps and talk? There is so much I want to know about the Valley —"

Stafford looked pleadingly. "No, no! let us go the old path and see the sunset over Greenwood. Always when I ride from here I say to myself, 'I may never see this place again!'"

They walked on between the box. "The box has not been clipped this year. I do not know why, except that all things go unpruned. The garden itself may go back to wilderness."

"You have noticed that? It is always so in times like these. We leave the artificial. Things have a hardier growth — feeling breaks its banks — custom is not listened to —"

"It is not so bad as that!" said Judith, smiling. "And we will not really let the box grow out of all proportion! — Now tell me of the Valley."

They left the garden and dipped into the green meadow. Stafford talked of battles and marches, but he spoke in a monotone, distrait and careless, as of a day-dreaming scholar reciting his lesson. Such as it was, the recital lasted across the meadow, into the wood, yet lit by yellow light, a place itself for day dreams. "No. I did not see him fall. He was leading an infantry regiment. He was happy in his death, I think. One whom the gods loved. — Wait! your scarf has caught."

He loosed it from the branch. She lifted the lace, put it over her head, and held it with her slender hand beneath her chin. He looked at her, and his breath came sharply. A shaft of light, deeply gold, struck across the woodland path. He stood within it, on slightly rising ground that lifted him above her. The quality of the light gave him a singular aspect. He looked a visitant from another world, a worn spirit, of fine temper, but somewhat haggard, somewhat stained. Lines came into Judith's brow. She stepped more quickly, and they passed from out the wood to a bare hillside, grass and field flowers to the summit. The little path that zigzagged upward was not wide enough for two. He moved through the grass and flowers beside her, a little higher still, and between her and the sun. His figure was dark; no longer lighted as it was in the wood. Judith sighed inwardly. "I am so tired that I am fanciful. I should not have come." She talked on. "When we were children and read 'Pilgrim's Progress' Unity and I named this the Hill Difficulty. And we named the Blue Ridge the Delectable Mountains — War puts a stop to reading."

"Yes. The Hill Difficulty! On the other side was the Valley of Humiliation, was it not?"

"Yes: where Christian met Apollyon. We are nearly up, and the sunset will be beautiful."

At the top, around a solitary tree, had been built a bench. The two sat down. The sun was sinking behind the Blue Ridge. Above the mountains sailed a fleet of little clouds, in a sea of pale gold shut in by purple headlands. Here and there on the earth the yellow light lingered. Judith sat with her head thrown back against the bark of the tree, her eyes upon the long purple coast and the golden sea. Stafford, his sword drawn forward, rested his clasped hands upon the hilt and his cheek on his hands. "Are they not like the Delectable Mountains?" she said. "Almost you can see the shepherds and the flocks — hear the pilgrims singing. Look where that shaft of light is striking!"

"There is heliotrope all around me," he answered. "I see nothing, know nothing but that!"

"You do very wrongly," she said. "You pain me and you anger me!"

"Judith! Judith! I cannot help it. If the wildest tempest were blowing about this hilltop, a leaf upon this tree might strive and strive to cling to the bough, to remain with its larger self — yet would it be twisted off and carried whither the wind willed! My passion is that tempest and my soul is that leaf."

"It is more than a year since first I told you that I could not return your feeling. Last October — that day we rode to the old mill — I told you so again, and told you that if we were to remain friends it could only be on condition that you accepted the truth as truth and let the storm you speak of die! You promised —"

"Even pale friendship, Judith — I wanted that!"

"If you wish it still, all talk like this must cease. After October I thought it was quite over. All through the winter those gay, wonderful letters that you wrote kept us up at Greenwood —"

"I could hear from you only on those terms. I kept them until they, too, were of no use —"

"When I wrote to you last month —"

"I knew of your happiness — before you wrote. I learned it from one nearly concerned. I — I — " He put his hand to his throat as if he were choking, arose, and walked a few paces and came back. "It was over there near Gordonsville — under a sunset sky much like this. What did I do that night? I have a memory of all the hours of blackness that men have ever passed, lying under forest trees with their faces against the earth. You see me standing here, but I tell you my face is against the earth, at your feet —"

"It is madness!" said Judith. "You see not me, but a goddess of your own making. It is a chain of the imagination. Break it! True goddesses do not wish such love — at least, true women do not!"

"I cannot break it. It is too strong. Sometimes I wish to break it, sometimes not."

Judith rose. "Let us go. The sun is down."

She took the narrow path and he walked beside and above her as before. Darker crimson had come into the west, but the earth beneath had yet a glow and warmth. They took a path which led, not by way of the wood, but by the old Greenwood graveyard, the burying-place of the Carys. At the foot of the lone tree hill they came again side by side, and so mounted the next low rise of ground. "Forgive me," said Stafford. "I have angered you. I am very wretched. Forgive me."

They were beside the low graveyard wall. She turned, leaning against it. There were tears in her eyes. "You all come, and you go away, and the next day brings news that such and such an one is dead! With the sound of Death's wings always in the air, how can any one — I do not wish to be angry. If you choose we will talk like friends — like a man and a woman of the South. If you do not, I can but shut my ears and hasten home and henceforth be too wise to give you opportunity —"

"I go back to the front to-morrow. Be patient with me these few minutes. And I, Judith — I will cling with all my might to the tree —"

A touch like sunlight came upon him of his old fine grace, charming, light, and strong. "I won't let go! How lovely it is, and still — the elm tops dreaming! And beyond that gold sky and the mountains all the fighting! Let us go through the graveyard. It is so still — and all their troubles are over."

Within the graveyard, too, was an old bench around an elm. "A few minutes only!" pleaded Stafford. "Presently I must ride back to town — and in the morning I return to the Valley." They sat down. Before them was a flat tombstone sunk in ivy, a white rose at the head. Stafford, leaning forward, drew aside with the point of his scabbard the dark sprays that mantled the graved coat of arms.

LUDWELL CARY

In part I sleep. I wake within the whole.

He let the ivy swing back. "I have seen many die this year who wished to live. If death were forgetfulness! I do not believe it. I shall persist, and still feel the blowing wind —"

"Listen to the cow-bells!" said Judith. "There shows the evening star."

"Can a woman know what love is? This envelope of the soul — If I could but tear it! Judith, Judith! Power and longing grow in the very air I breathe! — will to move the universe if thereby I might gain you! — your presence always with me in waves of light and sound! and you cannot truly see nor hear me! Could you do so, deep would surely answer deep!"

"Do you not know," she said clearly, "that I love Richard Cleave? You do not attract me. You repel me. There are many souls and many deeps, and the ocean to which I answer knows not your quarter of the universe!"

"Do you love him so? I will work him harm if I can!"

She rose. "I have been patient long enough. — No! not with me, if you please! I will go alone. Let me pass, Major Stafford! —"

She was gone, over the dark trailing periwinkle, through the little gate canopied with honeysuckle. For a minute he stayed beneath the elms, calling himself fool and treble fool; then he followed, though at a little distance. She went before him, in her pale violet, through the gathering dusk, unlatched for herself the garden gate and passed into the shadow of the box. A few moments later he, too, entered the scented alley and saw her waiting for him at the gate that gave upon the lawn. He joined her, and they moved without speaking to the house.

They found the family gathered on the porch, an old horse waiting on the gravel below, and an elderly, plain man, a neighbouring farmer, standing halfway up the steps. He was speaking excitedly. Molly beckoned from above. "Oh, Judith, it's news of the battle —"

"Yes'm," said the farmer. "Straight from Staunton — telegram to the colonel in Charlottesville. '*Big fighting at Port Republic. Jackson whipped Shields. Stonewall Brigade suffered heavily.*' — No'm — That was all. We won't hear details till to-morrow. — My boy John's in the Stonewall, you know — but Lord! John always was a keerful fellow! I reckon he's safe enough — but I ain't going to tell his mother about the battle till to-morrow; she might as well have her sleep. — War's pernicious hard on mothers. I reckon we'll see the bulletin to-morrow."

He was gone, riding in a sturdy, elderly fashion toward his home in a cleft of the hills. "Major Stafford cannot stay to supper, Aunt Lucy," said Judith clearly. "Is that Julius in the hall? Tell one of the boys to bring Major Stafford's horse around."

As she spoke she turned and went into the house. The group upon the porch heard her step upon the polished stair. Unity proceeded to make conversation. A negro brought the horse around. Judith did not return. Stafford, still and handsome, courteous and self-possessed, left farewell for her, said good-bye to the other Greenwood ladies, mounted and rode away. Unity, sitting watching him unlatch the lower gate and pass out upon the road, hummed a line —

"Nita! Juanita! Ask thy soul if we should part!"

"I have a curious feeling about that man," said Miss Lucy, "and yet it is the rarest thing that I distrust anybody! — What is it, Molly?"

"It's no use saying that I romance," said Molly, "for I don't. And when Mr. Hodge said 'the Stonewall Brigade suffered heavily' he looked *glad* —"

"Who looked glad?"

"Major Stafford. It's no use looking incredulous, for he did! There was the most curious light came into his face. And Judith saw it —"

"Molly — Molly —"

"She did! You know how Edward looks when he's white-hot angry — still and Greek looking? Well, Judith looked like that. And she and Major Stafford crossed looks, and it was like crossed swords. And then she sent for his horse and went away, upstairs to her room. She's up there now praying for the Stonewall Brigade and for Richard."

"Molly, you're uncanny!" said Unity. "Oh me ! Love and Hate
— North and South — and we'll not have the bulletin until to-
morrow —"

Miss Lucy rose. "I am going upstairs to Judith and tell her that I
simply know Richard is safe. There are too many broken love
stories in the world, and the Carys have had more than their
share."

XXVIII

THE LONGEST WAY ROUND

HAVING, in a month and ten days, marched four hundred miles, fought four pitched battles and a whole rosary of skirmishes, made of naught the operations of four armies, threatened its enemy's capital and relieved its own, the Army of the Valley wound upward toward the Blue Ridge from the field of Port Republic. It had attended Shields some distance down the Luray road. "Drive them! — drive them!" had said Jackson. It had driven them then, turning on its steps it had passed again the battlefield. Frémont's army, darkening the heights upon the further side of that river of burned bridges, looked impotently on. Frémont shelled the meadow and the wheat fields over which ambulances and surgeons were yet moving, on which yet lay his own wounded, but his shells could not reach the marching foe. Brigade after brigade, van, main and rear, cavalry, infantry, artillery, quartermaster, commissary and ordnance trains, all disappeared in the climbing forest. A cold and chilling rain came on; night fell, and a drifting mist hid the Army of the Valley. The next morning Frémont withdrew down the Valley toward Strasburg. Shields tarried at Luray, and the order from Washington directing McDowell to make at once his long delayed junction with McClellan upon the Chickahominy was rescinded.

The rear guard of the Army of the Valley buried the dead of Port Republic in trenches, and then it, too, vanished. To the last wagon wheel, to the last poor straggler, all was gone. It was an idiosyncrasy of Jackson's to gather and take with him every filing. He travelled like a magnet; all that belonged to him went with him. Long after dark, high on the mountain-side, an aide appeared in the rain, facing the head of the rear brigade.

"The general says have you brought off every inch of the captured guns?"

"Tell him all but one unserviceable caisson. We did not have horses for that."

THE LONGEST WAY ROUND

The aide galloped forward, reported, turned, and galloped back. " General Jackson says, sir, that if it takes every horse in your command, that caisson is to be brought up before daylight."

The other swore. " All those miles — dark and raining! — Lieutenant Parke! — Something told me I'd better do it in the first place! "

Brigade after brigade the Army of the Valley climbed the Blue Ridge. At first the rain had been welcome, so weary and heated were the men. But it never took long for the novelty of rain to wear off. Wet and silent the troops climbed through the darkness. They had won a victory; they were going to win others. Old Jack was as great a general as Napoleon, and two or three hours ago it had seemed possible to his soldiers that history might rank them with the Old Guard. But the rain was chill and the night mournfully dark. When had they eaten ? They hardly remembered, and it was an effort to lift one leg after the other. Numbers of men were dropping with sleep. All shivered; all felt the reaction. Back on the plain by the river lay in trenches some hundreds of their comrades. In the rear toiled upwards ambulances filled with wounded. There were not ambulances enough; the wounded rode wherever there was room in any wagon. The less badly hurt sat or lay, dully suffering, on caissons. All as they toiled upward had visions of the field behind them. It had not been a great battlefield, as to extent and numbers engaged, but a horrible one. The height where the six guns had been, the gun which the Louisianians took — the old charcoal kiln where the guns had been planted, the ground around, the side of the ravine — these made an ugly sight between eyelid and ball! So many dead horses! — eighty of them in one place — one standing upright where he had reared and, dying, had been caught and propped by a blasted pine. So many dead men, grey and blue, lying as in pattern! And then the plain beneath, and the Stonewall's desperate fight, and the battle in the wheat! The Federal cannon had sheared the heads from the men. The soldiers, mounting through the darkness in the whistling wind and rain, saw again these headless bodies. One only, the body of a young soldier of the 2d Virginia, a brother of the colonel of the 65th, the army was carrying with it. The brother, wounded himself, had begged the body. At the first village where the army halted, he would get a coffin and lay the boy in a grave he could mark. His mother and sister could visit it then. Permission was given. It lay now in an ambulance, covered with a flag. Cleave lay upon the straw beside it, his arm flung across the breast. At its feet sat a dark and mournful figure, old Tullius with his chin propped on his knees.

The rain came down, fine as needles' points and cold. Somewhere far below a mountain stream was rushing, and in the darkness the wind was sighing. The road wound higher. The lead horses, drawing a gun, stepped too near the edge of the road. The wet earth gave way. The unfortunate brutes plunged, struggled, went down and over the embankment, dragging the wheel horses after them. Gun, carriage, and caisson followed. The echoes awoke dismally. The infantry, climbing above, looked down the far wooded slopes, but incuriously. The infantry was tired, cold, and famished; it was not interested in artillery accidents. Perhaps at times the Old Guard had felt thus, with a sick and cold depression, kibed spirits as well as heels, empty of enthusiasm as of food, resolution lost somewhere in the darkness, sonority gone even from " l'empereur " and " la France." Slowly, amid drizzling rain, brigade after brigade made Brown's Gap and bivouacked within the dripping forest.

Morning brought a change. The rain yet fell, but the army was recovering from the battlefield. It took not long, nowadays, to recover. The army was learning to let the past drop into the abyss and not to listen for the echoes. It seemed a long time that the country had been at war, and each day's events drove across and hid the event of the day before. Speculation as to the morrow remained, but even this hung loosely upon the Army of the Valley. Wonderment as to the next move partook less of deep anxiety than of the tantalization of guessing at a riddle with the answer always just eluding you. The army guessed and guessed — bothering with the riddle made its chief occupation while it rested for two days and nights, beside smoky camp-fires, in a cold June rain, in the cramped area of Brown's Gap; but so assured was it that Old Jack knew the proper answer, and would give it in his own good time, that the guessing had little fretfulness or edge of temper. By now, officers and men, the confidence was implicit. "Tell General Jackson that we will go wherever he wishes us to go, and do whatever he wishes us to do."

On the morning of the twelfth "at early dawn" the army found itself again in column. The rain had ceased, the clouds were gone, presently up rose the sun. The army turned its back upon the sun; the army went down the western side of the mountains, down again into the great Valley. The men who had guessed "Richmond" were crestfallen. They who had stoutly held that Old Jack had mounted to this eyrie merely the better again to swoop down upon Frémont, Shields, or Banks crowed triumphantly. "Knew it Tuesday, when the ambulances obliqued at the top and went on down toward Staunton! He sends his wounded in front, he never leaves them behind! Knew it was n't Richmond!"

Brigade by brigade the army wound down the mountain, passed below Port Republic, and came into a lovely verdurous country, soft green grass and stately trees set well apart. Here it rested five days, and here the commanding general received letters from Lee.

"*Your recent successes have been the cause of the liveliest joy in this army as well as in the country. The admiration excited by your skill and boldness has been constantly mingled with solicitude for your situation. The practicability of reinforcing you has been the subject of the gravest consideration. It has been determined to do so at the expense of weakening this army. Brigadier-General Lawton with six regiments from Georgia is on his way to you, and Brigadier-General Whiting with eight veteran regiments leaves here to-day. The object is to enable you to crush the forces opposed to you. Leave your enfeebled troops to watch the country and guard the passes covered by your artillery and cavalry, and with your main body, including Ewell's Division and Lawton's and Whiting's commands, move rapidly to Ashland, by rail or otherwise as you find most advantageous, and sweep down between the Chickahominy and the Pamunkey, cutting up the enemy's communications, etc., while this army attacks McClellan in front. He will then, I think, be forced to come out of his entrenchments where he is strongly posted on the Chickahominy, and apparently preparing to move by gradual approaches on Richmond.*"

And of a slightly earlier date.

"*Should there be nothing requiring your attention in the Valley, so as to prevent your leaving it in a few days, and you can make arrangements to deceive the enemy and impress him with the idea of your presence, please let me know, that you may unite at the decisive moment with the army near Richmond.*"

It may be safely assumed that these directions could have been given to no man more scrupulously truthful in the least of his personal relations, and to no commander in war more gifted in all that pertains to " deceiving the enemy and impressing him with an idea of your presence." Infantry and artillery, the Army of the Valley rested at Mt. Meridian under noble trees. The cavalry moved to Harrisonburg. Munford had succeeded Ashby in command, and Munford came to take his orders from his general. He found him with the dictionary, the Bible, the Maxims, and a lemon.

" You will draw a cordon quite across, north of Harrisonburg. See, from here to here." He drew a map toward him and touched two points with a strong, brown finger.

" Very well, sir."

" You will arrest all travellers up and down the Valley. None is to pass, going north or going south."

" Very well, sir."

" I wish the cavalry outposts to have no communication with the infantry. If they know nothing of the latter's movements they cannot accidentally transmit information. You will give this order, and you will be held accountable for its non-obedience."

" Very well, sir."

" You will proceed to act with boldness masking caution. Press the outposts of the enemy and, if possible, drive him still further northward." He broke off and sucked the lemon.

" Very well, sir."

" Create in him the impression that you are strongly supported. Drive it into his mind that I am about to advance against him. General Lee is sending reinforcements from Richmond. I do not object to his knowing this, nor to his having an exaggerated idea of their number. You will regard these instructions as important."

" I will do my best, sir."

" Good, good! That is all, colonel."

Munford returned to Harrisonburg, drew his cordon across the Valley, and pushed his outposts twelve miles to the northward. Here they encountered a Federal flag of truce, an officer with several surgeons, and a demand from Frémont for the release of his wounded men. The outposts passed the embassy on to Munford's headquarters at Harrisonburg. That cavalryman stated that he would take pleasure in forwarding General Frémont's demand to General Jackson. "Far? Oh, no! it is not far." In the mean time it was hoped that the Federal officers would find such and such a room comfortable lodging. They found it so, discovered, too, that it was next to Munford's own quarters, and that the wall between was thin — nothing more, indeed, than a slight partition. An hour or two later the Federal officers, sitting quietly, heard the Confederate cavalryman enter, ask for writing materials, demand of an aide if the courier had yet returned from General Jackson, place himself at a table and fall to writing. One of the blue soldiers tiptoed to the wall, found a chair conveniently placed and sat down with his ear to the boards. For five minutes, scratch, scratch! went Munford's pen. At the expiration of this time there was heard in the hall without a jingling of spurs and a clanking of a sabre. The scratching ceased; the pen was evidently suspended. "Come in!" The listeners in the next room heard more jingling, a heavy entrance, Munford's voice again.

"Very good, Gilmer. What did the general say?"

"He says, sir, that General Frémont is to be told that our surgeons will continue to attend their wounded. As we are not monsters they will be as carefully attended to as are our own. The only lack in the matter will be medicines and anæsthetics."

"Very good, Gilmer, I will so report to the officer in charge of the flag of truce. — Well, what is it, man? You look as though you were bursting with news!"

"I am, sir! Whiting, and Hood, and Lawton, and the Lord knows who besides, are coming over the Rockfish Gap! I saw them with my own eyes on the Staunton road. About fifteen thousand, I reckon, of Lee's best. Gorgeous batteries — gorgeous troops — Hood's Texans — thousands of Georgians — all of them playing 'Dixie,' and hurrahing, and asking everybody they see to point out Jackson! — No, sir, I'm not dreaming! I know we thought that they could n't get here for several days yet — but here they are! Good Lord! I would n't, for a pretty, miss the hunting down the Valley!"

The blue soldiers heard Munford and the courier go out. An hour later they were conducted to the colonel's presence. "I am sorry, major, but General Jackson declines acceding to General Frémont's request. He says — "

The party with the flag of truce went back to Frémont. They

went like Lieutenant Gilmer,"bursting with news." The next day Munford pushed his advance to New Market. Frémont promptly broke up his camp, retired to Strasburg, and began to throw up fortifications. His spies brought bewilderingly conflicting reports. A deserter, who a little later deserted back again, confided to him that Stonewall Jackson was simply another Cromwell; that he was making his soldiers into Ironsides: that they were Presbyterian to a man, and believed that God Almighty had planned this campaign and sent Jackson to execute it; that he — the deserter — being of cavalier descent, could n't stand it and "got out." There was an affair of outposts, in which several prisoners were taken. These acknowledged that a very large force of cavalry occupied Harrisonburg, and that Jackson was close behind, having rebuilt the bridge at Fort Republic across the Shenandoah, and advanced by the Keezletown road. An old negro shambled one morning into the lines. "Yaas, sah, dat's de truf! I ain' moughty unlike ol' Brer Eel. I cert'ny slipped t'roo dat 'cordion Gineral Jackson am er stretchin'! How many on de oder side, sah? 'Bout er half er million." Frémont telegraphed and wrote to Washington. "The condition of affairs here imperatively requires that some position be immediately made strong enough to be maintained. Reinforcements should be sent here without an hour's delay. Whether from Richmond or elsewhere, forces of the enemy are certainly coming into this region. Casualties have reduced my force. The small corps scattered about the country are exposed to sudden attack by greatly superior force of an enemy to whom intimate knowledge of country and universal friendship of inhabitants give the advantage of rapidity and secrecy of movements. I respectfully submit this representation to the President, taking it for granted that it is the duty of his generals to offer for his consideration such impressions as are made by knowledge gained in operations on the ground."

South of the impenetrable grey curtain stretched across the Valley began a curious series of moves. A number of Federal prisoners on their way from Port Republic to Richmond, saw pass them three veteran brigades. The guards were good-naturedly communicative. "Who are those? Those are Whiting and Hood and Lawton on their way to reinforce Stonewall. If we did n't have to leave this railroad you might see Longstreet's Division — it's just behind. How can Lee spare it? — Oh, Beauregard's up from the South to take its place!" The prisoners arrived in Richmond. To their surprise and gratification the officers found themselves paroled, and that at once. They had a glimpse of an imposing review; they passed, under escort, lines of entrenchments, batteries, and troops; their passage northward to McDowell's lines at Fredericksburg was facilitated. In a remarkably short space of time they were in Washington, insisting that Longstreet had gone to the Valley, and that Beauregard was up from the South — they had an impression that in that glimpse of a big review they had seen him! Certainly they had seen somebody who looked as though his name ought to be Pierre Gustave Toutant Beauregard!

In the mean time Hood, Lawton, and Whiting actually arrived in the Valley. They came into Staunton, in good order, veteran troops, ready to march against Shields or Frémont or Banks or Sigel, to keep the Valley or to proceed against Washington, quite as Stonewall Jackson should desire! Seven thousand troops, Georgia, Texas, North Carolina, and Virginia, lean, bronzed, growing ragged, tall men, with eyes set well apart, good marchers, good fighters, good lovers, and good haters. — There suddenly appeared before them on the pike at Staunton Stonewall Jackson, ridden through the night from Mt. Meridian.

The three brigades paraded. Jackson rode up and down the line. His fame had mounted high. To do with a few men and at a little cost what, by all the rules of war, should have involved strong armies and much bloodshed — that took a generalship for which the world was beginning to give him credit. With Cross Keys and Port Republic began that sustained enthusiasm which accompanied him to the end. Now, on the march and on the battlefield, when he passed his men cheered him wildly, and throughout the South the eyes of men and women kindled at his name. At Staunton the reinforcing troops, the greater number of whom saw him for the first time, shouted for him and woke the echoes. Grave and unsmiling, he lifted the forage cap, touched Little Sorrel with the spur and went on by. It is not to be doubted that he was ambitious, and it lies not in ambitious man, no, nor in man of any type, to feel no joy in such a cry of recognition! If he felt it, however, he did not evince it. He only jerked his hand into the air and went by.

Two hours later he rode back to Mt. Meridian. The three brigades under orders to follow, stayed only to cook a day's rations and to repack their wagons. Their certainty was absolute. "We will join the Army of the Valley *wherever it may be.* Then we will march against Shields or Frémont, or maybe against Banks or Sigel."

Breaking camp in the afternoon, they moved down the pike, through a country marvellous to the Georgians and Texans. Sunset came, and still they marched; dark, and still they marched; midnight, and, extremely weary, they halted in a region of hills running up to the stars. Reveille sounded startlingly soon. The troops had breakfast while the stars were fading, and found themselves in column on the pike under the first pink streakings of the dawn. They looked around for the Army of the Valley. A little to the northeast showed a few light curls of smoke, such as might be made by picket fires. They fancied, too, that they heard, from behind the screen of hills, faint bugle-calls, bugle answering bugle, like the cocks at morn. If it were so, they were thin and far away, "horns of elfland." Evidently the three brigades must restrain their impatience for an hour or two.

In the upshot it proved that they were not yet to fraternize with the Army of the Valley. When presently, they marched, it was *up* the Valley, back along the pike toward Staunton. The three briga-diers conferred together. Whiting, the senior, a veteran soldier, staunch and determined, was angry. "Reasonable men should not be treated so! 'You will start at four, General Whiting, and march until midnight, when you will bivouac. At early dawn a courier will bring you further instructions.' Very good! We march and bivouac, and here's the courier. 'The brigades of Whiting, Hood, and Lawton will return to Staunton. There they will receive further instruc-tions.'" Whiting swore. "We are getting a taste of his quality with a vengeance! Very well! very well! It's all right — if he wins through I'll applaud, too — but, by God! he ought n't to treat reasonable men so! — *Column Forward!*"

Under the stately trees at Mt. Meridian, in the golden June weather, the Army of the Valley settled to its satisfaction that it was about to invade Maryland. Quite an unusual number of straws showed which way the wind was blowing. Northern news arrived by grapevine, and Northern papers told the army that was what it was going to do, — "invade Maryland and move on Washington — sixty thousand bloody-minded rebels!" — "Look here, boys, look here. Multiplication by division! The Yanks have split each of us into four!" Richmond papers, received by way of Staunton, divulged the fact that troops had been sent to the Valley, and opined that the other side of Mason and Dixon needed all the men at home. The engineers received an order to prepare a new and elaborate series of maps of the Valley. They were not told to say nothing about it, so presently the army knew that Old Jack was having every rabbit track and rail fence put down on paper. "Poor old Valley! won't she have a scouring!"

The sole question was, when would the operations begin. The "foot cavalry" grew tired of verdant meads, June flowers, and warbling birds. True, there were clear streams and Mr. Commissary Banks's soap, and the clothes got gloriously washed! Uniforms, too, got cleaned and patched. "Going calling. Must make a show!" and shoes were cobbled. (Cartridge boxes surreptitiously cut to pieces for this.) Morning drills occurred of course, and camp duties and divine services; but for all these diversions the army wearied of Mt. Meridian, and wanted to march. Twenty miles a day — twenty-five — even thirty if Old Jack put a point on it! The foot cavalry drew the line at thirty-five. It had tried this once, and once was enough! In small clasped diaries, the front leaves given over to a calendar, a table of weights and measures, a few 1850 census returns, and the list of presidents of the United States, stopping at James Buchanan, the army recorded that nothing of interest happened at Mt. Meridian and that the boys were tired of loafing.

"How long were they going to stay?" The men pestered the company officers, the company asked the regimental, field asked staff, staff shook its head and had no idea, a brigadier put the question to Major-General Ewell and Old Dick made a statement which reached the drummer boys that evening. "We are resting here for just a few days until all the reinforcements are in, and then we will proceed to beat up Banks's quarters again about Strasburg and Winchester."

On the morning of the seventeenth there was read a general order. "*Camp to be more strictly policed. Regimental and brigade drill ordered. Bridge to be constructed across the Shenandoah. Chapel to be erected. Day of fasting and prayer for the success of our arms on the Mississippi."* — "Why, we are going to stay here forever!" The regimental commanders, walking away from drill, each found himself summoned to the presence of his brigadier. "Good-morning, colonel! Just received this order. 'Cook two days' rations and pack your wagons. Do it quietly.'"

By evening the troops were in motion, Ewell's leading brigade standing under arms upon a country road, the red sunset thrown back from every musket barrel. The brigadier approached Old Dick where he sat Rifle beneath a locust tree. "Might I be told in which direction, sir —"

Ewell looked at him with his bright round eyes, bobbed his head and swore. "By God! General Taylor! I do not know whether we are to march north, south, east, or west, or to march at all!" There was shouting down the line. "Either Old Jack or a rabbit!" Five minutes, and Jackson came by. "You will march south, General Ewell."

The three brigades of Whiting, Hood, and Lawton, having, like the King of France, though not with thirty thousand men, marched up the hill and down again, found at Staunton lines of beautifully shabby Virginia Central cars, the faithful, rickety engines, the faithful, overworked, thin-faced railroad men, and a sealed order from General Jackson. *"Take the cars and go to Gordonsville. Go at once."* The reinforcements from Lee left the Valley of Virginia without having laid eyes upon the army they were supposed to strengthen. They had heard its bugles over the hilltops — that was all.

The Army of the Valley marched south, and at Waynesboro struck the road through Rockfish Gap. Moving east through magnificent scenery, it passed the wall of the Blue Ridge and left for a time the Valley of Virginia. Cavalry went before the main body, cavalry guarded the rear, far out on the northern flank rode Munford's troopers. At night picket duty proved heavy. In the morning, before the bivouacs were left, the troops were ordered to have no conversation with chance-met people upon the road. "If anybody asks you questions, you are to answer, I don't know." The troops went on through lovely country, through the June weather, and they did not know whither they were going. "Wandering in the wilderness!" said the men. "Good Lord! they wandered in the wilderness for forty years!" "Oh, that was Moses! Old Jack'll double-quick us through on half-rations in three days!"

The morning of the nineteenth found the army bivouacked near Charlottesville. An impression prevailed — Heaven knows how or why — that Banks had also crossed the Blue Ridge, and that the army was about to move to meet him in Madison County. In reality, it moved to Gordonsville. Here it found Whiting, Hood, and Lawton come in by train from Staunton. Now they fraternized, and now the army numbered twenty-two thousand men. At Gordonsville some hours were spent in wondering. One of the chaplains was, however, content. The Presbyterian pastor of the place told him in deep confidence that he had gathered at headquarters that at early dawn the army would move toward Orange Court House and Culpeper, thence on to Washington. The army moved at early dawn, but it was toward Louisa Court House.

Cavalry, artillery, and wagon trains proceeded by the red and heavy roads, but from Gordonsville on the Virginia Central helped the infantry as best it might. The cars were few and the engine almost as overworked as the train men, but the road did its best. The trains moved back and forth, took up in succession the rear brigade and forwarded them on the march. The men enjoyed these lifts. They scrambled aboard, hung out of the window, from the platform and from roof, encouraged the engine, offered to push the train, and made slighting remarks on the tameness of the scenery. "Not like God's country, back over the mountains!" They yelled encouragement to the toiling column on the red roads. "Step spryer! Your turn next!"

Being largely Valley of Virginia Virginians, Louisianians, Georgians, Texans, and North Carolinians, the army had acquaintance slight or none with the country through which it was passing. Gordonsville left behind, unfamiliarity began. "What's this county? What's that place over there? What's that river? Can't be the Potomac, can it? Naw, 't aint wide enough!" — "Gentlemen, I think it is the Rappahannock." — " Go away! it is the headwaters of the York." — "Rapidan maybe, or Rivanna." — "Probably Pamunkey, or the Piankatank,

Where the bullfrogs jump from bank to bank."

"Why not say the James?" — "Because it isn't. We know the James." — "Maybe it's the Chickahominy! I'm sure we've marched far enough! Think I hear McClellan's cannon, anyhow!" — "Say, captain, is that the river Dan?" — "*Forbidden to give names!*" — "Good Lord! I'd like to see — no, I wouldn't like to see Old Jack in the Inquisition!" — "I was down here once and I think it is the South Anna." — "It couldn't be — it couldn't be Acquia Creek, boys?" — "Acquia Creek! Absurd! You aren't even warm!" — "It might be the North Anna." — "Gentlemen, cease this idle discussion. It is the Tiber!"

On a sunny morning, somewhere in this *terra incognita*, one of Hood's Texans chanced, during a halt, to stray into a by-road where an ox-heart cherry tree rose lusciously, above a stake and rider fence. The Texan looked, set his musket against the rails, and proceeded to mount to a green and leafy world where the cherries bobbed against his nose. A voice came to him from below. "What are you doing up there, sir?"

The Texan settled himself astride a bough. "I don't really know."

"Don't know! To what command do you belong?"

"I don't know."

"You don't know! What is your State?"

"Really and truly, I don't — O Lord!" The Texan scrambled down, saluted most shamefacedly. The horseman looked hard and grim enough. "Well, sir, what is the meaning of this? And can you give me any reason why you should not mount guard for a month?"

Tears were in the Texan's eyes. "General, general! I didn't know 't was you! Give you my word, sir, I thought it was just anybody! We've had orders every morning to say, 'I don't know' — and it's gotten to be a joke — and I was just fooling. Of course, sir, I don't mean that it has gotten to be a joke — only that we all say 'I don't know' when we ask each other questions, and I hope, sir, that you'll understand that I didn't know that 't was you —".

"I understand," said Jackson. "You might get me a handful of cherries."

On the twenty-first the leading brigades reached Fredericksburg. "To-morrow is Sunday," said the men. "That ought to mean a battle!" While wood and water were being gotten that evening, a rumour went like a zephyr from company to company: "We'll wait here until every regiment is up. Then we'll move north to Fredericksburg and meet McDowell."

The morrow came, a warm, bright Sunday. The last brigade got up, the artillery arrived, the head of the ammunition train appeared down the road. There were divine services, but no battle. The men rested, guessing Fredericksburg and McDowell, guessing Richmond and McClellan, guessing return to the Valley and Shields, Frémont, Banks, and Sigel. They knew now that they were within fifty miles of Richmond; but if they were going there anyhow, why — why — why in the name of common sense had General Lee sent Whiting, Hood, and Lawton to the Valley? Was it reasonable to suppose that he had marched them a hundred and twenty miles just to march them back a hundred and twenty miles? The men agreed that it was n't common sense. Still, a number had Richmond firmly fixed in their minds. Others conceived it not impossible that the Army of the Valley might be on its way to Tennessee to take Memphis, or even to Vicksburg, to sweep the foe from Mississippi. The men lounged beneath the trees, or watched the weary Virginia Central bringing in the fag end of things. Fredericksburg was now the road's terminus; beyond, the line had been destroyed by a cavalry raid of McClellan's.

Stonewall Jackson made his headquarters in a quiet home, shaded with trees and with flowers in the yard. Sunday evening the lady of the house sent a servant to the room where he sat with his chief of staff. "Ole Miss, she say, gineral, dat she hope fer de honour ob yo' brekfastin' wif her —"

The general rolled a map and tied it with a bit of pink tape. "Tell Mrs. Harris, with my compliments, that if I am here at breakfast time I shall be most happy to take it with her."

"Thank you, sah. An' what hour she say, gineral, will suit you bes'?"

"Tell her, with my compliments, that I trust she will breakfast at the usual hour."

Morning came and breakfast time. "Ole Miss" sent to notify the general. The servant found the room empty and the bed unslept in — only the dictionary and Napoleon's Maxims (the Bible was gone) on the table to testify to its late occupancy. Jim, the general's body servant, emerged from an inner room. "Gineral Jackson? Fo' de

Lawd, niggah! yo' ain't looking ter fin' de gineral heah at dis heah hour? He done clar out 'roun' er bout midnight. Reckon by now he's whipping de Yankees in de Valley!"

In the dark night, several miles from Frederic'shall, two riders, one leading, one following, came upon a picket. "Halt!" There sounded the click of a musket. The two halted.

"Jest two of you? Advance, number one, and give the counter-sign!"

"I am an officer bearing dispatches —"

"That air not the point! Give the countersign!"

"I have a pass from General Whiting —"

"This air a Stonewall picket. Ef you've got the word, give it, and ef you have n't got it my hand air getting mighty wobbly on this gun!"

"I am upon an important mission from General Jackson —"

"It air not any more important than my orders air! You get down from that thar horse and mark time!"

"That is not necessary. Call your officer of guard."

"Thank you for the sug-ges-tion," said Billy politely. "And don't you move while I carry it out!" He put his fingers to his lips and whistled shrilly. A sergeant and two men came tumbling out of the darkness. "What is it, Maydew?"

"It air a man trying to get by without the countersign."

The first horseman moved a little to one side. "Come here, sergeant! Have you got a light? Wait, I will strike a match."

He struck it, and it flared up, making for an instant a space of light. Both the sergeant and Billy saw his face. The sergeant's hand went up to his cap with an involuntary jerk; he fell back from the rein he had been holding. Billy almost dropped his musket. He gasped weakly, then grew burning red. Jackson threw down the match. "Good! good! I see that I can trust my pickets. What is the young man named?"

"Billy Maydew, sir. Company A, 65th Virginia."

"Good! good! Obedience to orders is a soldier's first, last, and best lesson! He will do well." He gathered up the reins. "There are four men here. You will all forget that you have seen me, sergeant."

"Yes, sir."

"Good! Good-night."

He was gone, followed by the courier. Billy drew an almost sobbing breath. "I gave him such a damned lot of impudence! He was hiding his voice, and not riding Little Sorrel, or I would have known him."

The sergeant comforted him. "Just so you were obeying orders and watching and handling your gun all right, he did n't care! I gather you did n't use any cuss words. He seemed kind of satisfied with you."

The night was dark, Louisa County roads none of the best. As the cocks were crowing, a worthy farmer, living near the road, was awakened by the sound of horses. "Wonder who's that? — Tired horses — one of them's gone lame. They're stopping here."

He slipped out of bed and went to the window. Just light enough to see by. "Who's there?"

"Two Confederate officers on important business. Our horses are tired. Have you two good fresh ones?"

"If I've got them, I don't lend them to every straggler claiming to be a Confederate officer on important business! You'd better go further. Good-night!"

"I have an order from General Whiting authorizing me to impress horses."

The farmer came out of the house, into the chill dawn. One of the two strangers took the stable key and went off to the building looming in the background. The other sat stark and stiff in the grey light. The first returned. "Two in very good condition, sir. If you'll dismount I'll change saddles and leave our two in the stalls."

The officer addressed took his large feet out of the stirrups, tucked his sabre under his arm, and stiffly dismounted. Waiting for the fresh horses, he looked at the angry farmer. "It is for the good of the State, sir. Moreover, we leave you ours in their places."

"I am as good a Virginian as any, sir, with plenty of my folks in the army! And one horse ain't as good as another — not when one of yours is your daughter's and you've ridden the other to the Court House and to church for twelve years —"

"That is so true, sir," answered the officer, "that I shall take pleasure in seeing that, when this need is past, your horses are returned to you. I promise you that you shall have them back in a very few days. What church do you attend?"

The second soldier returned with the horses. The first mounted stiffly, pulled a forage cap over his eyes, and gathered up the reins. The light had now really strengthened. All things were less like shadows. The Louisa County man saw his visitor somewhat plainly, and it came into his mind that he had seen him before, though where or when— He was all wrapped up in a cloak, with a cap over his eyes. The two hurried away, down the Richmond road, and the despoiled farmer began to think: "Where'd I see him—Richmond? No, 't was n't Richmond. After Manassas, when I went to look for Hugh? Rappahannock? No, 't was n't there. Lexington? Good God! That was Stonewall Jackson!"

CHAPTER XXIX

THE NINE–MILE ROAD

In the golden afternoon light of the twenty-third of June, the city of Richmond, forty thousand souls, lay, fevered enough, on her seven hills. Over her floated the stars and bars. In her streets rolled the drum. Here it beat quick and bright, marking the passage of some regiment from the defences east or south to the defences north. There it beat deep and slow, a muffled drum, a Dead March — some officer killed in a skirmish, or dying in a hospital, borne now to Hollywood. Elsewhere, quick and bright again, it meant Home Guards going to drill. From the outskirts of the town might be heard the cavalry bugles blowing, — from the Brook turnpike and the Deep Run turnpike, from Meadow Bridge road and Mechanicsville road, from Nine-Mile and Darbytown and Williamsburg stage roads and Osborne's old turnpike, and across the river from the road to Fort Darling. From the hilltops, from the portico or the roof of the Capitol, might be seen the camp-fires of Lee's fifty thousand men — the Confederate Army of the Potomac, the Army of the Rappahannock, the Army of Norfolk, the Army of the Peninsula — four armies waiting for the arrival of the Army of the Valley to coalesce and become the Army of Northern Virginia. The curls of smoke went up, straight, white, and feathery. With a glass might be seen at various points the crimson flag, with the blue St. Andrew's cross and the stars, eleven stars, a star for each great State of the Confederacy. By the size you knew the arm — four feet square for infantry, three feet square for artillery, two and a half by two and a half for cavalry.

The light lay warm on the Richmond houses — on mellow red brick, on pale grey stucco. It touched old iron-work balconies and ivy-topped walls, and it gilded the many sycamore trees, and lay in pools on the heavy leaves of the magnolias. Below the pillared Capitol, in the green up and down of the Capitol Square, in Main Street, in Grace Street by St. Paul's, before the Exchange, the

Ballard House, the Spotswood, on Shockoe Hill by the President's House, through all the leafy streets there was vivid movement. In this time and place Life was so near to Death; the ocean of pain and ruin so evidently beat against its shores, that from very contrast and threatened doom Life took a higher light, a deeper splendour. All its notes resounded, nor did it easily relinquish the major key.

In the town were many hospitals. These were being cleaned, aired, and put in order against the impending battles. The wounded in them now, chiefly men from the field of Seven Pines, looked on and hoped for the best. Taking them by and large, the wounded were a cheerful set. Many could sit by the windows, in the perfumed air, and watch the women of the South, in their soft, full gowns, going about their country's business. Many of the gowns were black.

About the hotels, the President's House, the governor's mansion, and the Capitol, the movement was of the official world. Here were handsome men in broadcloth, grown somewhat thin, somewhat rusty, but carefully preserved and brushed. Some were of the old school and still affected stocks and ruffled shirts. As a rule they were slender and tall, and as a rule wore their hair a little long. Many were good Latinists, most were good speakers. One and all they served their states as best they knew how, overworked and anxious, facing privation here in Richmond with the knowledge that things were going badly at home, sitting long hours in Congress, in the Hall of Delegates, in courts or offices, struggling there with Herculean difficulties, rising to go out and listen to telegrams or to read bulletins. Sons, brothers, kinsmen, and friends were in the field.

This golden afternoon, certain of the latter had ridden in from the lines upon this or that business connected with their commands. They were not many, for all the world knew there would be a deadly fighting presently, deadly and prolonged. Men and officers must stay within drumbeat. Those who were for an hour in Richmond, in their worn grey uniforms, with the gold lace grown tarnished (impossible of replacement!), with their swords not tarnished, their netted silk sashes, their clear bright eyes and keen thin faces, found friends enough as they went to and fro — more eager questioners and eager listeners than they could well attend to. One, a general officer, a man of twenty-nine, in a hat with a long black plume, with the most charming blue eyes, and a long bronze, silky, rippling beard which he constantly stroked, could hardly move for the throng about him. Finally, in the Capitol Square, he backed his horse against the railing about the great equestrian Washington. The horse, a noble animal, arched his neck. There was around it a wreath of bright flowers. The rider spoke in an enchanting voice. "Now if I tell you in three words how it was and what we did, will you let me go? I've got to ride this afternoon to Yellow Tavern."

"Yes, yes! Tell us, General Stuart."

"My dear people, it was the simplest thing in the world! A man in the First has made a song about it, and Sweeney has set it to the banjo — if you'll come out to the camp after the battle you shall hear it! General Lee wanted to know certain things about the country behind McClellan. Now the only way to know a thing is to go and look at it. He ordered a reconnoissance in force. I took twelve hundred cavalrymen and two guns of the horse artillery and made the reconnoissance. Is there anything else that you want to know?"

"Be good, general, and tell us what you did."

"I am always good — just born so! I rode round McClellan's army — Don't cheer like that! The town'll think it's Jackson, come from the Valley!"

"Tell us, general, how you did it!"

"Gentlemen, I have n't time. If you like, I'll repeat the man in the First's verses, and then I'm going. You'll excuse the metre? A poor, rough, unlearned cavalryman did it.

> "Fitz Lee, Roony Lee, Breathed and Stuart,
>   Martin to help, and Heros von Borcke,
>   First Virginia, Fourth, Ninth, two guns and a Legion —
>   From Hungary Run to Laurel Hill Fork,
>
> "By Ashland, Winston, Hanover, Cash Corner,
>   Enon Church, Salem Church, Totopotomoy, Old Church,

"You observe that we are trotting.

> "By Hamstead, Garlick, Tunstall Station, Talleyville,
>   Forge Mill, Chickahominy, Sycamore, White Birch.

"Here we change gait.

> " By Hopewell and Christian, Wilcox and Westover,
>   Turkey Bridge, Malvern Hill, Deep Bottom and Balls
> Four days, forty leagues, we rode round McClellan
>   As Jeremiah paced round Jericho's walls. — "

" It was n't Jeremiah, general! It was Joshua."
" Is that so? I 'll tell Sweeney. Anyhow, the walls fell.

> " Halt! Advance! Firing! Engagement at Hanover.
>   Skirmish at Taliaferro's. Skirmish at Hawes.
> Tragic was Totopotomoy, for there we lost Latané
>   Hampden-like, noble, dead for his Cause.

> " At Old Church broke up meeting. Faith! 't was a pity
>   But indigo azure was pulpit and pew!
> Fitz Lee did the job. Sent his love to Fitz Porter.
>   Good Lord! Of Mac's Army the noble review!

" There is n't anything our horses can't do.

> " Tunstall Station was all bubbly white with wagons.
>   We fired those trains, those stores, those sheltering sheds!
> And then we burned three transports on Pamunkey
>   And shook the troops at White House from their beds!

> " Loud roars across our path the swollen Chickahominy
>   ' Plunge in, Confeds! you were not born to drown.'
> We danced past White Oak swamp, we danced past Fighting Joseph
>   Hooker!
> We rode round McClellan from his sole to his crown!

> " There are strange, strange folk who like the Infantry!
>   Men have been found to love Artillery.
> McClellan's quoted thus ' In every family
>   There should exist a gunboat ' — ah, but we,
> Whom all arms else do heap with calumny,
>   Saying, ' Daily those damned centaurs put us up a tree!'
> We insist upon the virtues of the Cavalry!

" Now, friends, I 'm going! It was a beautiful raid! I always liked
Little Mac. He 's a gentleman, and he 's got a fine army. Except
for poor Latané we did not lose a man. But I left a general behind
me."
" A general? General who — "
Stuart gave his golden laugh. " General Consternation."
The sun slipped lower. Two horsemen came in by the Deep Run

road and passed rapidly eastward through the town. The afternoon was warm, but the foremost wore a great horseman's cloak. It made all outlines indefinite and hid any insignia of rank. There was a hat or cap, too, pulled low. It was dusty; he rode fast and in a cloud, and there came no recognition. Out of the town, on the Nine-Mile road, he showed the officer of the guard who stopped him a pass signed "R. E. Lee" and entered the Confederate lines. "General Lee's headquarters?" They were pointed out, an old house shaded by oaks. He rode hither, gave his horse to the courier with him, and spoke to the aide who appeared. "Tell General Lee, some one from the Valley."

The aide shot a quick glance, then opened a door to the left. "General Lee will be at leisure presently. Will you wait here, sir?"

He from the Valley entered. It was a large, simply furnished room, with steel engravings on the walls, — the 1619 House of Burgesses, Spotswood on the Crest of the Blue Ridge with his Golden Horseshoe Knights, Patrick Henry in Old St. John's, Jefferson writing the Declaration of Independence, Washington receiving the Sword of Cornwallis. The windows were open to the afternoon breeze and the birds were singing in a rosebush outside. There were three men in the room. One having a large frame and a somewhat heavy face kept the chair beside the table with a kind of granite and stubborn air. He rested like a boulder on a mountain slope; marked with old scars, only waiting to be set in motion again to grind matters small. The second man, younger, slender, with a short red beard, leaned against the window, smelled the roses, and listened to the birds. The third, a man of forty, with a gentle manner and very honest and kindly eyes, studied the engravings. All three wore the stars of major-generals.

The man from the Valley, entering, dropped his cloak and showed the same insignia. D. H. Hill, leaving the engravings, came forward and took him by both hands. The two had married sisters; moreover each was possessed of fiery religious convictions; and Hill, though without the genius of the other, was a cool, intelligent, and determined fighter. The two had not met since Jackson's fame had come upon him.

It clothed him now like a mantle. The man sitting by the table got ponderously to his feet; the one by the window left the contemplation of the rosebush. "You know one another by name only, I believe, gentlemen?" said D. H. Hill. "General Jackson — General Longstreet, General Ambrose Powell Hill."

The four sat down, Jackson resting his sabre across his knees. He had upon him the dust of three counties; he was all one neutral hue like a faded leaf, save that his eyes showed through, grey-blue, intense enough, though quiet. He was worn to spareness.

Longstreet spoke in his heavy voice. "Well, general, Fate is making of your Valley the Flanders of this war."

"God made it a highway, sir. We must take it as we find it."

"Well," said A. P. Hill, smiling, "since we have a Marlborough for that Flanders —"

Jackson shifted the sabre a little. "Marlborough is not my *beau ideal*. He had circumstances too much with him."

An inner door opened. "The artillery near Cold Harbour —" said a voice, cadenced and manly. In a moment Lee entered. The four rose. He went straight to Stonewall Jackson, laid one hand on his shoulder, the other on his breast. The two had met, perhaps, in Mexico; not since. Now they looked each other in the eyes. Both were tall men, though Lee was the tallest; both in grey, both thin from the fatigue of the field. Here the resemblance ended. Lee was a model of manly beauty. His form, like his character, was justly proportioned; he had a great head, grandly based, a face of noble sweetness, a step light and dauntless. There breathed about him something knightly, something kingly, an antique glamour, sunny shreds of the Golden Age. "You are welcome, General Jackson," he said; "very welcome! You left Frederickshall — ?"

"Last night, sir."

"The army is there?"

"It is there, sir."

"You have become a name to conjure with, general! I think that your Valley will never forget you." He took a chair beside the table. "Sit down, gentlemen. I have called this council, and now the sun is sinking and General Jackson has far to ride, and we must hasten. Here are the maps."

The major-generals drew about the table. Lee pinned down a map with the small objects upon the board, then leaned back in his chair. "This is our first council with General Jackson. We wait but for the Army of the Valley to precipitate certainly one great battle, perhaps many battles. I think that the fighting about Richmond will be heavier than all that has gone before." An aide entered noiselessly with a paper in his hand. "From the President, sir," he said. Lee rose and took the note to the window. The four at table spoke together in low tones.

"It is the most difficult ground in the world," said A. P. Hill. "You'll have another guess-time of it than in your Valley, general! No broad pike through the marshes of the Chickahominy!"

"Are there good maps?"

"No," said Longstreet; "damned bad."

Jackson stiffened. D. H. Hill came in hastily. "It's rather difficult to draw them accurately with a hundred and ten thousand Yankees lying around loose. They should have been made last year."

Lee returned. "Yes, the next ten days will write a page in blood." He sighed. "I do not like war, gentlemen. Now, to begin again! We are agreed that to defend Richmond is imperative. When Richmond falls the Confederacy falls. It is our capital and seat of government. Here only have we railroad communications with the far South. Here are our arsenals and military manufactories, our depots of supply, our treasury, our hospitals, our refugee women and children. The place is our heart, and arm and brain must guard it. Leave Richmond and we must withdraw from Virginia. Abandon Virginia, and we can on our part no longer threaten the northern capital. Then General Jackson cannot create a panic every other day, nor will Stanton then withdraw on every fresh alarm a division from McClellan."

He leaned his head on his hand, while with the firm fingers of the other he measured the edge of the table. "No! It is the game of the two capitals, and the board is the stretch of country between. To the end they will attempt to reach Richmond. To the end we must prevent that mate. Let us see their possible roads. Last year McDowell tried it by Manassas, and he failed. It is a strategic point,— Manassas. There may well be fighting there again. The road by Fredericksburg . . . they have not tried that yet, and yet it has a value. Now the road that McClellan has taken,— by sea to Fortress Monroe, and so here before us by the York, seeing that the Merrimac kept him from the James. It is the best way yet, though with a modification it would be better! There is a key position which I trust he 'll not discover — "

"He won't," said D. H. Hill succinctly. "The fairies at his cradle did n't give him intuition, and they made him extremely cautious. He 's a good fellow, though!"

Lee nodded. "I have very genuine respect for General McClellan. He is a gentleman, a gallant soldier, and a good general." He pushed the map before him away, and took another. "Of late Richmond's strongest defence has been General Jackson in the Valley. Well! McDowell and Frémont and Banks may be left awhile to guard that capital which is so very certain it is in danger. I propose now to bring General Jackson suddenly upon McClellan's right — "

Jackson, who had been holding himself with the rigidity of a warrior on a tomb, slightly shifted the sabre and drew his chair an inch nearer the commander-in-chief. "His right is on the north bank of the Chickahominy — "

"Yes. General Stuart brought me much information that I desired. Fitz John Porter commands there — the 5th Army Corps — twenty-five thousand men. I propose, general, that you bring your troops as rapidly as possible from Frederickshall to Ashland, that from Ashland you march by the Ashcake road and Merry Oaks Church to the Totopotomoy Creek road and that, moving by this to Beaver Dam Creek, you proceed to turn and dislodge Porter and his twenty-five thousand, crumpling them back upon McClellan's centre — here." He pointed with a quill which he took from the inkwell.

"Good! good! And the frontal attack?"

"General A. P. Hill and his division will make that. The batteries on the Chickahominy will cover his passage of the bridge. General Longstreet will support him. General Magruder with General Huger and the reserve artillery will be left before Richmond. They will so demonstrate as to distract General McClellan's attention from the city and from his right and General Porter. General Stuart will take position on your line of march from Ashland, and General D. H. Hill will support you."

"Good! good! This is the afternoon of the twenty-third."

"Yes. Frederickshall is forty miles from this point — " He touched the map again. "Now, general, when can you be here?"

"Thursday morning, the twenty-sixth, sir."

"That is very soon."

"Time is everything in war, sir."

"That is perfectly true. But the time is short and the manœuvre delicate. You and your troops are at the close of a campaign as arduous as it is amazing. The fatigue and the strain must be great. You and General Hill are far apart and the country between is rough and unmapped. Yet victory depends on the simultaneous blow."

Jackson sat rigid again, his hand stiffly placed upon the sabre. "It is not given to man to say with positiveness what he can do, sir. But it is necessary that this right be turned before McClellan is aware of his danger. Each day makes it more difficult to conceal the absence of my army from the Valley. Between the danger of forced marching and the obvious danger that lies in delay, I should choose the forced marching. Better lose one man in marching than five in a battle not of our selecting. A straw may bring failure as a straw may bring victory. I may fail, but the risk should be taken. Napoleon failed at Eylau, but his plan was correct."

"Very well," said Lee. "Then the morning of the twenty-sixth be it! Final orders shall await you at Ashland."

Jackson rose. "Good! good! By now my horses will have been changed. I will get back. The army was to advance this morning to Beaver Dam Station."

He rode hard through the country all night, it being the second he had spent in the saddle. Beaver Dam Station and the bivouacking Army of the Valley saw him on Tuesday morning the twenty-fourth. "Old Jack's back from wherever he's been!" went the rumour. Headquarters was established in a hut or two near the ruined railroad. Arriving here, he summoned his staff and sent for Ewell. While the former gathered he read a report, forwarded from Munford in the rear. "Scout Gold and Jarrow in from the Valley. Frémont still fortifying at Strasburg — thinks you may be at Front Royal. Shields at Luray considers that you may have gone to Richmond, but that Ewell remains in the Valley with forty thousand men. Banks at Winchester thinks you may have gone against Shields at Luray, or King at Catlett's, or Doubleday at Fredericksburg, or gone to Richmond — but that Ewell is moving west on Moorefield!"

" Good! good!" said Jackson. Staff arrived, and he proceeded to issue rapid and precise orders. All given, staff hurried off, and the general spoke to Jim. "Call me when General Ewell comes." He stretched himself on a bench in the hut. "I am suffering," he said, "from fever and a feeling of debility." He drew his cloak about him and closed his eyes. It was but half an hour, however, that he slept or did not sleep, for Ewell was fiery prompt.

The Army of the Valley entered upon a forced march through country both difficult and strange. It had been of late in the possession of the enemy, and the enemy had stretched felled trees across forest roads and burned the bridges spanning deep and sluggish creeks. Guides were at fault, cross-roads directions most uncertain. The wood grew intolerably thick, and the dust of the roads was atrocious; the air cut away by the tall green walls on either hand; the sun like a furnace seven times heated. Provisions had not come up in time at Beaver Dam Station and the troops marched upon half-rations. Gone were the mountains and the mountain air, present was the languorous breath of the low country. It had an upas quality, dulling the brain, retarding the step. The men were very tired, it was hot, and a low fever hung in the air.

They marched until late of a night without a moon, and the bugles waked them long ere dawn. A mist hung over all the levels, presaging heat. *Column Forward!* Today was a repetition of yesterday, only accented. The sun girded himself with greater strength, the dust grew more stifling, the water was bad, gnats and mosquitoes made a painful cloud, the feet in the ragged shoes were more stiff, more swollen, more abraded. The moisture in the atmosphere weakened like a vapour bath. The entire army, "foot cavalry" and all, marched with a dreadful slowness. *Press Forward — Press Forward — Press Forward — Press Forward!* It grew to be like the humming insects on either hand, a mere noise to be expected. "Going to Richmond — Going to Richmond — Yes, of course we're going to Richmond — unless, indeed, we're going a roundabout way against McDowell at Fredericksburg! Richmond will keep. It has kept a long time — ever since William Byrd founded it. General Lee is there — and so it is all right — and we can't go any faster. War isn't all it's cracked up to be. Oh, hot, hot, hot! and skeetery! and General Humidity lives down this way. *Press Forward — Press Forward — Press For-*

*ward. If that noise don't stop I'll up with my musket butt and beat
somebody's brains out!"*

Ashland was not reached until the late evening of this day. The
men fell upon the earth. Even under the bronze there could be seen
dark circles under their eyes, and their lips were without colour.
Jackson rode along the lines and looked. There were circles beneath
his own eyes, and his lips shut thin and grey. "Let them rest," he
said imperturbably, "until dawn." There rode beside him an officer
from Lee. He had now the latter's General Order, and he was almost
a day behind.

Somewhat later, in the house which he occupied, his chief of
staff, Ewell and the brigadiers gone, the old man, Jim, appeared
before him. "Des you lis'en ter me er minute, gineral! Ob my sar-
tain circumspection I knows you did n't go ter bed las' night — nurr
de night befo' — nurr de night befo' dat — 'n' I don' see no preper-
ation for yo' gwine ter bed dishyer night! Now, dat ain' right.
W'at Miss Anna gwine say w'en she heah erbout hit? She gwine say
you 'stress her too much. She gwine say you'll git dar quicker, 'n'
fight de battle better, ef you lie down erwhile 'n' let Jim bring you
somethin' ter eat —"

"I have eaten. I am going to walk in the garden for awhile."

He went, all in bronze, with a blue gleam in his eye. Jim looked
after him with a troubled countenance. "Gwine talk wif de Lawd —
talk all night long! Hit ain' healthy. Pray an' pray 'n' look up ter de
sky 'twel he gits paralysis! De gineral better le' me tek his boots
off, 'n' go ter bed 'n' dream ob Miss Anna!"

At three the bugles blew. Again there was incalculable delay.
The sun was up ere the Army of the Valley left Ashland. It was
marching now in double column, Jackson by the Ashcake road and
Merry Oaks Church, Ewell striking across country, the rendezvous
Pole Green Church, a little north and east of Mechanicsville and the
Federal right. The distance that each must travel was something
like sixteen miles.

The spell of yesterday persisted and became the spell of to-day.
Sixteen miles would have been nothing in the Valley; in these green
and glamoury lowlands they became like fifty. Stuart's cavalry
began to appear, patrols here, patrols there, vedettes rising stark
from the broom sedge, or looming double, horsemen and shadow,

above and within some piece of water, dark, still, and clear. Time was when the Army of the Valley would have been curious and excited enough over Jeb Stuart's troopers, but now it regarded them indifferently with eyes glazed with fatigue. At nine the army crossed the ruined line of the Virginia Central, Hood's Texans leading. An hour later it turned southward, Stuart on the long column's left flank, screening it from observation, and skirmishing hotly through the hours that ensued. The army crossed Crump's Creek, passed Taliaferro's Mill, crossed other creeks, crept southward through hot, thick woods. Mid-day came and passed. The head of the column turned east, and came shortly to a cross-roads. Here, awaiting it, was Stuart himself, in his fighting jacket. Jackson drew up Little Sorrel beside him. "Good-morning, general."

"Good-morning, general — or rather, good-afternoon. I had hoped to see you many hours ago."

"My men are not superhuman, sir. There have occurred delays. But God is over us still."

He rode on. Stuart, looking after him, raised his brows. "In my opinion A. P. Hill is waiting for a man in a trance!"

The army turned southward again, marching now toward Totopotomoy Creek, the head of the column approaching it at three o'clock. Smoke before the men, thick, pungent, told a tale to which they were used. "Bridge on fire!" It was, and on the far side of the creek appeared a party in blue engaged in obstructing the road. Hood's Texans gave a faint cheer and dashed across, disappearing in flame, emerging from it and falling upon the blue working party. Reilly's battery was brought up; a shell or two fired. The blue left the field, and the grey pioneers somehow fought the flames and rebuilt the bridge. An hour was gone before the advance could cross on a trembling structure. Over at last, the troops went on, southward still, to Hundley Corner. Here Ewell's division joined them, and here to the vague surprise of an exhausted army came the order to halt. The Army of the Valley went into bivouac three miles north of that right which, hours before, it was to have turned. It was near sunset. As the troops stacked arms, to the south of them, on the other side of Beaver Dam Creek, burst out an appalling cannonade. Trimble, a veteran warrior, was near Jackson. "That has the sound of a general engagement, sir! Shall we advance?"

Jackson looked at him with a curious serenity. "It is the batteries on the Chickahominy covering General Hill's passage of the stream. He will bivouac over there, and to-morrow will see the battle — Have you ever given much attention, general, to the subject of growth in grace?"

CHAPTER XXX

AT THE PRESIDENT'S

A LARGE warehouse on Main Street in Richmond had been converted into a hospital. Conveniently situated, it had received many of the more desperately wounded from Williamsburg and Seven Pines and from the skirmishes about the Chickahominy and up and down the Peninsula. Typhoid and malarial cases, sent in from the lines, were also here in abundance. To a great extent, as June wore on, the wounded from Williamsburg and Seven Pines had died and been buried, or recovered and returned to their regiments, or, in case of amputations, been carried away after awhile by their relatives. Typhoid and malaria could hardly be said to decrease, but yet, two days before the battle of Mechanicsville, the warehouse seemed, comparatively speaking, a cool and empty place.

It was being prepared against the battles for which the beleaguered city waited — waited heartsick and aghast or lifted and fevered, as the case might be. On the whole, the tragic mask was not worn; the city determinedly smiled. The three floors of the warehouse, roughly divided into wards, smelled of strong soap and water and home-made disinfectants. The windows were wide; swish, swish! went the mops upon the floors. A soldier, with his bandaged leg stretched on a chair before him, took to scolding: "Women certainly are funny! What's the sense of wiping down walls and letting James River run over the floors? Might be some sense in doing it *after* the battle! Here, Sukey, don't splash that water this a-way! — Won't keep the blood from the floor when they all come piling in here to-morrow, and makes all of us damned uncomfortable to-day! — Beg your pardon, Mrs. Randolph! Did n't see you, ma'am. — Yes, I should like a game of checkers — if we can find an island to play on!"

The day wore on in the hospital. Floors and walls were all scrubbed, window-panes glistening, a Sunday freshness everywhere.

The men agreed that housecleaning was all right — after it was over. The remnant of the wounded occupied the lower floor; typhoid, malaria, and other ills were upstairs. Stores were being brought in, packages of clothing and lint received at the door. A favorite surgeon made his rounds. He was cool and jaunty, his hands in his pockets, a rose in his buttonhole. "What are you malingerers doing here, anyhow? You're eating your white bread, with honey on it — you are! Propped up and walking around — Mrs. McGuire reading to you — Mrs. Randolph smilingly letting you beat her at her own game — Miss Cooper writing beautiful letters for you — Miss Cary leaving really ill people upstairs just because one of you is an Albemarle man and might recognize a home face! Well! eat the whole slice up to-day, honey and all! for most of you are going home to-morrow. Yes, yes! you're well enough — and we want all the room we can get."

He went on, Judith Cary with him. "Whew! we must be going to have a fight!" said the men. "Bigger'n Seven Pines."

"Seven Pines was big enough!"

"That was what I thought — facing Casey's guns! — Your move, Mrs. Randolph."

The surgeon and nurse went on through cool, almost empty spaces. "This is going," said the surgeon crisply, "to be an awful big war. I should n't be surprised if it makes a Napoleonic thunder down the ages — becomes a mighty legend like Greece and Troy! And, do you know, Miss Cary, the keystone of the arch, as far as we are concerned, is a composition of three, — the armies in the field, the women of the South, and the servants."

"You mean —"

"I mean that the conduct of the negroes everywhere is an everlasting refutation of much of the bitter stuff which is said by the other side. This war would crumble like that, if, with all the white men gone, there were on the plantations faithlessness to trust, hatred, violence, outrage — if there were among us, in Virginia alone, half a million incendiaries! There are n't, thank God! Instead we owe a great debt of gratitude to a dark foster-brother. The world knows pretty well what are the armies in the field. But for the women, Miss Cary, I doubt if the world knows that the women keep plantations, servants, armies, and Confederacy going!"

"I think," said Judith, "that the surgeons should have a noble statue."

"Even if we do cut off limbs that might have been saved — hey? God knows, they often might! and that there's haste and waste enough! — Here's Sam, bringing in a visitor. A general, too — looks like a Titian I saw once."

"It is my father," said Judith. "He told me he would come for me."

A little later, father and daughter, moving through the ward, found the man from Albemarle — not one of those who would go away to-morrow. He lay gaunt and shattered, with strained eyes and fingers picking at the sheet. "Don't you know me, Mocket?"

Mocket roused himself for one moment. "Course I know you, general! Crops mighty fine this year! Never saw such wheat!" The light sank in his eyes; his face grew as it was before, and his fingers picked at the sheet. He spoke in a monotone. "We've had such a hard time since we left home — We've had such a hard time since we left home — We've had such a hard time since we left home — We —"

Judith dashed her hand across her eyes. "Come away! He says just that all the time!"

They moved through the ward, Warwick Cary speaking to all. "No, men! I can't tell you just when will be the battle, but we must look for it soon — for one or for many. Almost any day now. No, I cannot tell you if General Jackson is coming. It is not impossible. 'Washington Artillery?' That's a command to be proud of. Let me see your Tiger Head." He looked at the badge with its motto *Try Us*, and gave it back smilingly. "Well, we do try you, do we not? — on every possible occasion! — Fifth North Carolina? Wounded at Williamsburg! — King William Artillery? — Did you hear what General D. H. Hill said at Seven Pines? He said that he would rather be captain of the King William Artillery than President of the Confederate States. — Barksdale's Mississippians? Why, men, you are all by-words!"

The men agreed with him happily. "You've got pretty gallant fellows yourself, general!" The King William man cleared his throat. "He's got a daughter, too, that I'd like to — I'd like to *cheer!*"

"That's so, general!" said the men. "That's so! She's a chip of the old block."

Father and daughter laughed and went on — out of this ward and into another, quite empty. The two stood by the door and looked, and that sadly enough. "All the cots, all the pallets," said Cary, in a low voice. "And out in the lines, they who will lie upon them! And they cannot see them stretching across their path. I do not know which place seems now the most ghostly, here or there."

"It was hard to get mattresses enough. So many hospitals — and every one has given and given — and beds must be kept for those who will be taken to private houses. So, at last, some one thought of pew cushions. They have been taken from every church in town. See! sewed together, they do very well."

They passed into a room where a number of tables were placed, and from this into another where several women were arranging articles on broad wooden shelves. "If you will wait here, I will go slip on my outdoor dress." One of the women turned. "Judith! — Cousin Cary! — come look at these quilts which have been sent from over in Chesterfield!" She was half laughing, half crying. "Rising Suns and Morning Stars and Jonah's Gourds! Oh me! oh me! I can see the poor souls wrapped in them! The worst of it is, they'll all be used, and we'll be thankful for them, and wish for more! Look at this pile, too, from town! Tarletan dresses cut into nets, and these surgeons' aprons made from damask tablecloths! And the last fringed towels that somebody was saving, with the monogram so beautifully done!" She opened a closet door. "Look! I'll scrape lint in my sleep every night for a hundred years! The young girls rolled all these bandages —" Another called her attention. "Will you give me the storeroom key? Mrs. Haxall has just sent thirty loaves of bread, and says she'll bake again to-morrow. There's more wine, too, from Laburnum."

The first came back. "The room seems full of things, and yet we have seen how short a way will go what seems so much! And every home gets barer and barer! The merchants are as good as gold. They send and send, but the stores are getting bare, too! Kent and Paine gave bales and bales of cotton goods. We made them up into these —" She ran her hand over great piles of nightshirts and drawers. "But now we see that we have nothing like enough, and the store has given as much again, and in every lecture room in town we are sewing hard to get more and yet more done in time. The country people are so good! They have sent in quantities of bar soap — and we needed it more than almost anything! — and candles, and coarse towelling, and meal and bacon — and hard enough to spare I don't doubt it all is! And look here, Cousin Cary!" She indicated a pair of crutches, worn smooth with use. To one a slip of paper was tied with a thread. Her kinsman bent forward and read it: "*I kin mannedge with a stick.*"

Judith returned, in her last year's muslin, soft and full, in the shady Eugénie hat which had been sent her from Paris two years ago. It went well with the oval face, the heavy bands of soft dark hair, the mouth of sweetness and strength, the grave and beautiful eyes. Father and daughter, out they stepped into the golden, late afternoon.

Main Street was crowded. A battery, four guns, each with six horses, came up it with a heavy and jarring sound over the cobblestones. Behind rode a squad or two of troopers. The people on the sidewalk called to the cannoneers cheerful greetings and inquiries, and the cannoneers and the troopers returned them in kind. The whole rumbled and clattered by, then turned into Ninth Street. "Ordered out on Mechanicsville pike — that's all they know," said a man.

The two Carys, freeing themselves from the throng, mounted toward the Capitol Square, entered it, and walked slowly through the terraced, green, and leafy place. There was passing and repassing, but on the whole the place was quiet. "I return to the lines to-morrow," said Warwick Cary. "The battle cannot be long postponed. I know that you will not repeat what I say, and so I tell you that I am sure General Jackson is on his way from the Valley. Any moment he may arrive."

"And then there will be terrible fighting?"

"Yes; terrible fighting — Look at the squirrels on the grass!"

As always in the square, there were squirrels in the great old trees, and on the ground below, and as always there were negro nurses, bright turbaned, aproned, ample formed, and capable. With them were their charges, in perambulators, or, if older, flitting like white butterflies over the slopes of grass. A child of three, in her hand a nut for the squirrel, started to cross the path, tripped and fell. General Cary picked her up, and, kneeling, brushed the dust from her frock, wooing her to smiles with a face and voice there was no resisting. She presently fell in love with the stars on his collar, then transferred her affection to his sword hilt. Her mammy came hurrying. "Ef I des' tuhn my haid, sumpin' bound ter happen, 'n' happen dat minute! Dar now! You ain' hut er mite, honey, 'n' you's still got de goober fer de squirl. Come mek yo' manners to de gineral!"

Released, the two went on. "Have you seen Edward?"

"Yes. Three days ago — pagan, insouciant, and happy! The men adore him. Fauquier is here to-day."

"Oh! — I have not seen him for so long —"

"He will be at the President's to-night. I think you had best go with me —"

"If you think so, father —"

"I know, dear child! — That poor brave boy in his cadet grey and white. — But Richard is a brave man — and their mother is heroic. It is of the living we must think, and this cause of ours. We are on the eve of something terrible, Judith. When Jackson comes General Lee will have eighty-five thousand men. Without reinforcements, with McDowell still away, McClellan must number an hundred and ten thousand. North and South, we are going to grapple, in swamp, and poisoned field, and dark forest. We are gladiators stripped, and which will conquer the gods alone can tell! But we ourselves can tell that we are determined — that each side is determined — and that the grapple will be of giants. Well! to-night, I think the officers who chance to be in town will go to the President's House with these thoughts in mind. To-morrow we return to the lines; and a great battle chant will be written before we tread these streets again. For us it may be a pæan or it may be a dirge, and only the gods know which! We salute our flag to-night — the government that may last as lasted Greece or Rome, or the government which may perish, not two years old! I think that General Lee will be there for a short time. It is something like a recognition of the moment — a libation; and whether to life or to death, to an oak that shall live a thousand years or to a dead child among nations, there is not one living soul that knows!"

"I will go, father, of course. Will you come for me?"

"I or Fauquier. I am going to leave you here, at the gates. There is something I wish to see the governor about, at the mansion."

He kissed her and let her go; stood watching her out of the square and across the street, then with a sigh turned away to the mansion. Judith, now on the pavement by St. Paul's, hesitated a moment. There was an afternoon service. Women whom she knew, and women whom she did not know, were going in, silent, or speaking each to each in subdued voices. Men, too, were entering, though not many. A few were in uniform; others as they came from the Capitol or from office or department. Judith, too, mounted the steps. She was very tired, and her religion was an out-of-door one, but there came upon her a craving for the quiet within St. Paul's and for the beautiful, old, sonorous words. She entered, found a shadowy pew beneath the gallery, and knelt a moment. As she rose another, having perhaps marked her as she entered, paused at the door of the pew. She saw who it was, put out a hand and drew her in. Margaret Cleave, in her black dress, smiled, touched the younger woman's forehead with her lips, and sat beside her. The church was not half filled; there were no people very near them, and when presently there was singing, the sweet, old-world lines beat distantly on the shores of their consciousness. They sat hand in hand, each thinking of battlefields; the one with a constant vision of Port Republic, the other of some to-morrow's vast, melancholy, smoke-laden plain.

As was not infrequently the case in the afternoon, an army chaplain read the service. One stood now before the lectern. "Mr. Corbin Wood," whispered Judith. Margaret nodded. "I know. We nursed him last winter in Winchester. He came to see me yesterday. He knew about Will. He told me little things about him — dear things! It seems they were together in an ambulance on the Romney march."

Her whisper died. She sat pale and smiling, her beautiful hands lightly folded in her lap. For all the years between them, she was in many ways no older than Judith herself. Sometimes the latter called her "Cousin Margaret," sometimes simply "Margaret." Corbin Wood read in a mellow voice that made the words a part of the late sunlight, slanting in the windows. He raised his arm in an occasional gesture, and the sunbeams showed the grey uniform beneath the robe, and made the bright buttons brighter. *Thou turnest man to destruction; and sayest, Return, ye children of men. For a thousand years in thy sight are but as yesterday when it is past, and as a watch in the night.*

The hour passed, and men and women left St. Paul's. The two beneath the gallery waited until well-nigh all were gone, then they themselves passed into the sunset street. "I will walk home with you," said Judith. "How is Miriam?"

"She is beginning to learn," answered the other; "just beginning, poor, darling child! It is fearful to be young, and to meet the beginning! But she is rousing herself — she will be brave at last."

Judith softly took the hand beside her and lifted it to her lips. "I don't see how your children could help being brave. You are well cared for where you are?"

"Yes, indeed. Though if my old friend had not taken us in, I do not know what we should have done. The city is fearfully crowded."

"I walked from the hospital with father. He says that the battle will be very soon."

"I know. The cannon grow louder every night. I feel an assurance, too, that the army is coming from the Valley."

"Sometimes," said Judith, "I say to myself, 'This is a dream — all but one thing! Now it is time to wake up — only remembering that the one thing is true.' But the dream goes on, and it gets heavier and more painful."

"Yes," said Margaret. "But there are great flashes of light through it, Judith."

They were walking beneath linden trees, fragrant, and filled with murmurous sound. The street here was quiet; only a few passing people. As the two approached the corner there turned it a slight figure, a girl dressed in homespun with a blue sunbonnet. In her hands was a cheap carpet-bag, covered with roses and pansies. She looked tired and discouraged, and she set the carpet-bag down on the worn brick pavement and waited until the two ladies came near. "Please, could you tell me —" she began in a soft, drawling voice, which broke suddenly. "Oh, it's Mrs. Cleave! it's Mrs. Cleave! — Oh! oh!"

"Christianna Maydew! — Why, Christianna!"

Christianna was crying, though evidently they were joyful tears.

"I — I was so frightened in this lonely place! — an' — an' Thunder Run's so far away — an' — an' Billy an' Pap an' Dave are n't here, after all — an' I never saw so many strange people — an' then I saw *you* — oh! oh!"

So brushed aside in this war city were all unnecessary conventions, that the three sat down quite naturally upon a wide church step. An old and wrinkled nurse, in a turban like a red tulip, made room for them, moving aside a perambulator holding a sleeping babe. "F'om de mountains, ain' she, ma'am? She oughter stayed up dar close ter Hebben!"

Christianna dried her eyes. Her sunbonnet had fallen back. She looked like a wild rose dashed with dew. "I am such a fool to cry!" said Christianna. "I ought to be laughin' an' clappin' my hands. I reckon I'm tired. Streets are so hard an' straight, an' there's such a terrible number of houses."

"How did you come, Christianna, and when, and why?"

"It was this a-way," began Christianna, with the long mountain day before her. "It air so lonesome on Thunder Run, with Pap gone, an' Dave gone, an' Billy gone, an' — an' Billy gone. An' the one next to me, she's grown up quick this year, an' she helps mother a lot. She planted," said Christianna, with soft pride, "she planted the steep hillside with corn this spring — yes, Violetta did that!"

"And so you thought —"

"An' Pap has — had — a cousin in Richmond. Nanny Pine is her name. An' she used to live on Thunder Run, long ago, an' she was n't like the rest of the Maydews, but had lots of sense, an' she up one mahnin', mother says, an' took her foot in her hand, an' the people gave her lifts through the country, an' she came to Richmond an' learned millinery —"

"Millinery!"

"Yes'm. To put roses an' ribbons on bonnets. An' she married here, a man named Oak, an' she wrote back to Thunder Run, to mother, a real pretty letter, an' mother took it to Mr. Cole at the tollgate (it was long ago, before we children went to school) an' Mr. Cole read it to her, an' it said that she had now a shop of her own, an' if ever any Thunder Run people came to Richmond to come right straight to her. An' so —"

"And you could n't find her?"

"An' so, last week, I was spinning. An' I walked up an' down, an' the sun was shining, clear and steady, an' I could see out of the door, an' there wasn't a sound, an' there wa'n't anything moved. An' it was as though God Almighty had made a ball of gold with green trees on it and had thrown it away, away! higher than the moon, an' had left it there with nothin' on it but a dronin', dronin' wheel. An' it was like the world was where the armies are. An' it was like I had to get there somehow, an' see Pap again an' Dave an' Billy an' — an' see Billy. There wa'n't no help for it; it was like I had to go. An' I stopped the wheel, an' I said to mother, 'I am going where the armies are.' An' she says to me, she says, 'You don't know where they are.' An' I says to her, I says, 'I'll find out.' An' I took my sunbonnet, an' I went down the mountain to the tollgate and asked Mr. Cole. An' he had a letter from — from Mr. Gold —"

"Oh!" thought Margaret. "It is Allan Gold!"

"An' he read it to me, an' it said that not a man knew, but that he thought the army was goin' to Richmond an' that there would be terrible fightin' if it did. An' I went back up the mountain, an' I said to mother, 'Violetta can do most as much as I can now, an' I am goin' to Richmond where the army's goin'. I am goin' to see Pap an' Dave an' — an' Billy, an' I am goin' to stay with Cousin Nanny Pine.' An' mother says, says she, 'Her name is Oak now, but I reckon you'll know her house by the bonnets in the window.' Mother was always like that," said Christianna, again, with soft pride. "Always quick-minded! She sees the squirrel in the tree quicker'n any of us — 'ceptin' it's Billy. An' she says, 'How're you goin' to get thar, Christianna — less'n you walk?' An' I says, 'I'll walk.'"

"Oh, poor child!" cried Judith! "Did you?"

"No, ma'am; only a real little part of the way. It's a hundred and fifty miles, an' we ain't trained to march, an' it would have taken me so long. No, ma'am. Mrs. Cole heard about my goin' an' she sent a boy to tell me to come see her, an' I went, an' she gave me a dollar (I surely am goin' to pay it back, with interest) an' a lot of advice, an' she could n't tell me how to find Pap an' Dave an' Billy, but she said a deal of people would know about Allan Gold, for he was a great scout, an' she gave me messages for him; an' anyhow the name of the regiment was the 65th, an' the colonel was your son, ma'am, an' he would find the others for me. An' she got a man to take me in his wagon, twenty miles toward Lynchburg, for nothin'. An' I thanked him, an' asked him to have some of the dinner mother an' Violetta had put in a bundle for me; but he said no, he was n't hungry. An' that night I slept at a farmhouse, an' they would n't take any pay. An' the next day and the next I walked to Lynchburg, an' there I took the train." Her voice gathered firmness. "I had never seen one before, but I took it all right. I asked if it was goin' to Richmond, an' I climbed on. An' a man came along an' asked me for my ticket, an' I said that I did n't have one, but that I wanted to pay if it was n't more than a dollar. An' he asked me if it was a gold dollar or a Confederate dollar. An' there were soldiers on the train, an' one came up an' took off his hat an' asked me where I was goin', an' I told him an' why, an' he said it did n't matter whether it was gold or Confederate, and that the conductor did n't want it anyhow. An' the conductor — that was what the first man was called — said he did n't reckon I'd take up much room, an' that the road was so dog-goned tired that one more could n't make it any tireder, an' the soldier made me sit down on one of the benches, an' the train started." She shut her eyes tightly. "I don't like train travel. I like to go slower —"

"But it brought you to Richmond —"

Christianna opened her eyes. "Yes, ma'am, we ran an' ran all day, making a lot of noise, an' it was so dirty; an' then last night we got here — an' I slept on a bench in the house where we got out — only I did n't sleep much, for soldiers an' men an' women were going in and out all night long — an' then in the mahnin' a coloured woman there gave me a glass of milk an' showed me where I could wash my face — an' then I came out into the street an' began to look for Cousin Nanny Pine —"

"And you could n't find her?"

"She is n't here, ma'am. I walked all mahnin', looking, but I could n't find her, an' nobody that I asked knew. An' they all said that the army from the Valley had n't come yet, an' they did n't even know if it was coming. An' I was tired an' frightened, an' then at last I saw a window with two bonnets in it, and I said, 'Oh, thank the Lord!' an' I went an' knocked. An' it was n't Cousin Nanny Pine. It was another milliner. 'Mrs. Oak?' she says, says she. 'Mrs. Oak's in Williamsburg! Daniel Oak got his leg cut off in the battle, an' she boarded up her windows an' went to Williamsburg to nurse him — an' God knows I might as well board up mine, for there's nothin' doin' in millinery!' An' she gave me my dinner, an' she told me that the army had n't come yet from the Valley, an' she said she would let me stay there with her, only she had three cousins' wives an' their children, refugeein' from Alexandria way an' stayin' with her, an' there was n't a morsel of room. An' so I rested for an hour, an' then I came out to look for some place to stay. An' it's mortal hard to find." Her soft voice died. She wiped her eyes with the cape of her sunbonnet.

"She had best come with me," said Margaret to Judith. "Yes, there is room — we will make room — and it will not be bad for Miriam to have some one. . . . Are we not all looking for that army? And her people are in Richard's regiment." She rose. "Christianna, child, neighbours must help one another out! So come with me, and we shall manage somehow!"

Hospitality rode well forward in the Thunder Run creed. Christianna accepted with simplicity what, had their places been changed, she would as simply have given. She began to look fair and happy, a wild rose in sunshine. She was in Richmond, and she had found a friend, and the army was surely coming! As the three rose from the church step, there passed a knot of mounted soldiers. It chanced to be the President's staff, with several of Stuart's captains, and the plumage of these was yet bright. The Confederate uniform was a handsome one; these who wore it were young and handsome men. From spur to hat and plume they exercised a charm. Somewhere, in the distance, a band was playing, and their noble, mettled horses pranced to the music. As they passed they raised their hats. One, who recognized Judith, swept his aside with a gesture appropriate to a minuet. With sword and spur, with horses stepping to music, by they went. Christianna looked after them with dazzled eyes. She drew a fluttering breath. "I did n't know things like that were in the world!"

A little later the three reached the gate of the house which sheltered Margaret and Miriam. "I won't go in," said Judith. "It is growing late. . . . Margaret, I am going to the President's tonight. Father wishes me to go with him. He says that we are on the eve of a great battle, and that it is right —"

Margaret smiled upon her. "It *is* right. Of course you must go, dear and darling child! Do not think that I shall ever misunderstand you, Judith!"

The other kissed her, clinging for a moment to her. "Oh, mother, mother! . . . I hear the cannon, too, louder and louder!" She broke away. "I must not cry to-night. To-night we must all have large bright eyes — like the women in Brussels when 'There was revelry by night' — Is n't it fortunate that the heart does n't show?"

The town was all soft dusk when she came to the kinsman's house which had opened to her. Crowded though it was with refugee kindred, with soldier sons coming and going, it had managed to give her a small quiet niche, a little room, white-walled, white-curtained, in the very arms of a great old tulip tree. The window opened to the east, and the view was obstructed only by the boughs of the tree. Beyond them, through leafy openings, night by night she watched a red glare on the eastern horizon — McClellan's five-mile-distant camp-fires. Entering presently this room, she lit two candles, placed them on the dressing table, and proceeded to make her toilette for the President's House.

Through the window came the sound of the restless city. It was like the beating of a distant sea, with a ground swell presaging storm. The wind, blowing from the south, brought, too, the voice of the river, passionate over its myriad rocks, around its thousand islets. There were odours of flowers; somewhere there was jasmine. White moths came in at the window, and Judith, rising, put glass candle-shades over the candles. She sat brushing her long hair; fevered with the city's fever, she saw not herself in the glass, but all the stress that had been and the stress that was to be. Cleave's latest letter had rested in the bosom of her dress; now the thin oblong of bluish paper lay before her on the dressing table. The river grew louder, the wind from the south stirred the masses of her hair, the jasmine odour deepened. She bent forward, spreading her white arms over the dark and smooth mahogany, drooped her head upon them, rested lip and cheek against the paper. The sound of the warrior city, the river and the wind, beat out a rhythm in the white-walled room. *Love — Death! Love — Death! Dear Love — Dark Death — Eternal Love —* She rose, laid the letter with others from him in an old sandalwood box, coiled her hair and quickly dressed. A little later, descending, she found awaiting her, in the old, formal, quaint parlour, Fauquier Cary.

The two met with warm affection. Younger by much than was the master of Greenwood, he was to the latter's children like one of their own generation, an elder brother only. He held her from him and looked at her. "You are a lovely woman, Judith! Did it run the blockade?"

Judith laughed: "No! I wear nothing that comes that way. It is an old dress, and it is fortunate that Easter darns so exquisitely!"

"Warwick will meet us at the house. We both ride back before dawn. Why, I have not seen you since last summer!"

"No. Just before Manassas!"

They went out. "I should have brought a carriage for you. But they are hard to get —"

"I would rather walk. It is not far. You look for the battle to-morrow?"

"That depends, I imagine, on Jackson. Perhaps to-morrow, perhaps the next day. It will be bloody fighting when it comes — Heigho!"

"The bricks of the pavement know that," said Judith. "Sometimes, Fauquier, you can see horror on the faces of these houses — just as plain! and at night I hear the river reading the bulletin!"

"Poor child! — Yes, we make all nature a partner. Judith, I was glad to hear of Richard Cleave's happiness — as glad as I was surprised. Why, I hardly know, and yet I had it firmly in mind that it was Maury Stafford —"

Judith spoke in a pained voice. "I cannot imagine why so many people should have thought that. Yes, and Richard himself. It never was; and I know I am no coquette!"

"No. You are not a coquette. Ideas like that arrive, one never knows how — like thistledown in the air— and suddenly they are planted and hard to uproot. Stafford himself breathed it somehow. That offends you, naturally; but I should say there was never a man more horribly in love! It was perhaps a fixed idea with him that he would win you, and others misread it. Well, I am sorry for him! But I like Richard best, and he will make you happier."

He talked on, in his dry, attractive voice, moving beside her slender, wiry, resolute, trained muscle and nerve, from head to foot. "I was at the Officer's Hospital this morning to see Carewe. He was wounded at Port Republic, and his son and an old servant got him here somehow. He was talking about Richard. He knew his father. He says he'll be a brigadier the first vacancy, and that, if the war lasts, he won't stop there. He'll go very high. You know Carewe?— how he talks? 'Yes, by God, sir, Dick Cleave's son's got the stuff in him! Always was a kind of dumb, heroic race. Lot of iron ore in that soil, some gold, too. Only needed the prospector, Big Public Interest, to come along. Shouldn't wonder if he carved his name pretty high on the cliff.' — Now, Judith, I have stopped beneath this lamp just to see you look the transfigured lover — happier at praise of him than at garlands and garlands for yourself! — Hm! Drawn to the life. Now we'll go on to the President's House."

The President's House on Shockoe Hill was all alight, men and women entering between white pillars, from the long windows music floating. Beyond the magnolias and the garden the ground dropped suddenly. Far and wide, a vast horizon, there showed the eastern sky, and far and wide, below the summer stars, there flared along it a reddish light — the camp-fires of two armies, the grey the nearer, the blue beyond. Faint, faint, you could hear the bugles. It was a dark night; no moon, only the flicker of fireflies in magnolias and roses and the gush of light from the tall, white-pillared house. The violins within were playing "Trovatore." Warwick Cary, an aide with him, came from the direction of the Capitol and joined his daughter and brother. The three entered together.

There was little formality in these gatherings at the White House of the Confederacy. The times were too menacing, the city too conversant with alarm bells, sudden shattering bugle notes, thunderclaps of cannon, men and women too close companions of great and stern presences, for the exhibition of much care for the minuter social embroidery. No necessary and fitting tracery was neglected, but life moved now in a very intense white light, so deep and intense that it drowned many things which in other days had had their place in the field of vision. There was an old butler at the President's door, and a coloured maid hovered near to help with scarf or flounce if needed. In the hall were found two volunteer aides, young, handsome, gay, known to all, striking at once the note of welcome. Close within the drawing-room door stood a member of the President's Staff, Colonel Ives, and beside him his wife, a young, graceful, and accomplished woman. These smilingly greeted the coming or said farewell to the parting guest.

The large drawing-room was fitted for conversation. Damask-covered sofas with carved rosewood backs, flanked and faced by claw-foot chairs, were found in corners and along the walls; an adjoining room, not so brightly lit, afforded further harbourage, while without was the pillared portico, with roses and fireflies and a view of the flare upon the horizon. From some hidden nook the violins played Italian opera. On the mantles and on one or two tables, midsummer flowers bloomed in Parian vases.

Scattered in groups, through the large room, were men in uniform and civilians in broadcloth and fine linen. So peculiarly consti-tuted were the Confederate armies that it was usual to find here a goodly number of private soldiers mingling with old schoolmates, friends, kindred wearing the bars and stars of lieutenants, captains, majors, colonels, and brigadiers. But to-night all privates and all company officers were with their regiments; there were not many even of field and staff. It was known to be the eve of a fight, a very great fight; passes into town were not easy to obtain. Those in uniform who were here counted; they were high in rank. Mingling with them were men of the civil government, — cabinet officers, senators, congressmen, judges, heads of bureaus ; and with these, men of other affairs : hardly a man but was formally serving the South. If he were not in the field he was of her legislatures; if not there, then doing his duty in some civil office; if not there, wrestling with the management of worn-out railways; or, cool and keen, con-cerned in blockade running, bringing in arms and ammunition, or in the Engineer Bureau, the Bureau of Ordnance or the Medical Department, or in the service of the Post, or at the Treasury issuing beautiful Promises to Pay, or at the Tredegar moulding cannon, or in the newspaper offices wrestling with the problem of worn-out type and wondering where the next roll of paper was to come from, or in the telegraph service shaking his head over the latest raid, the latest cut wires; or he was experimenting with native medicinal

plants, with balloons, with explosives, torpedoes, submarine batteries; or thinking of probable nitre caves, of the possible gathering
of copper from old distilleries, of the scraping saltpetre from cellars,
of how to get tin, of how to get chlorate of potassium, of how to get
gutta-percha, of how to get paper, of how to get salt for the country
at large; or he was running sawmills, building tanneries, felling oak
and gum for artillery carriages, working old iron furnaces, working
lead mines, busy with foundry and powder mill. . . . If he was old
he was enlisted in the City Guard, a member of the Ambulance
Committee, a giver of his worldly substance. All the South was at
work, and at work with a courage to which were added a certain
colour and *élan* not without value on her page of history. The men,
not in uniform, here to-night were doing their part, and it was recognized that they were doing it. The women, no less; of whom there
were a number at the President's House this evening. With soft,
Southern voices, with flowers banded in their hair, with bare throat
and arms, with wide, filmy, effective all-things-but-new dresses, they
moved through the rooms, or sat on the rosewood sofas, or walking
on the portico above the roses looked out to the flare in the east.
Some had come from the hospitals, — from the Officer's, from Chim-
borazo, Robinson's, Gilland's, the St. Charles, the Soldier's Rest,
the South Carolina, the Alabama, — some from the sewing-rooms,
where they cut and sewed uniforms, shirts, and underclothing,
scraped lint, rolled bandages; several from the Nitre and Mining
Bureau, where they made gunpowder; several from the Arsenal,
where they made cartridges and filled shells. These last would be
refugee women, fleeing from the counties overrun by the enemy,
all their worldly wealth swept away, bent on earning something
for mother or father or child. One and all had come from work, and
they were here now in the lights and flowers, not so much for their
own pleasure as that there might be cheer, music, light, laughter,
flowers, praise, and sweetness for the men who were going to battle.
Men and women, all did not come or go at once; they passed in
and out of the President's House, some tarrying throughout the
evening, others but for a moment. The violins left "Il Trovatore,"
began upon "Les Huguenots."

The President stood between the windows, talking with a little
group of men, — Judge Campbell, R. M. T. Hunter, Randolph the

Secretary of War, General Wade Hampton, General Jeb Stuart. Very straight and tall, thin, with a clear-cut, clean-shaven, distinguished face, with a look half military man, half student, with a demeanour to all of perfect if somewhat chilly courtesy, by temperament a theorist, able with the ability of the field marshal or the scholar in the study, not with that of the reader and master of men, the hardest of workers, devoted, honourable, single-minded, a figure on which a fierce light has beaten, a man not perfect, not always just, nor always wise, bound in the toils of his own personality, but yet an able man who suffered and gave all, believed in himself, and in his cause, and to the height of his power laboured for it day and night — Mr. Davis stood speaking of Indian affairs and of the defences of the Western waters.

Warwick Cary, his daughter on his arm, spoke to the President's wife, a comely, able woman, with a group about her of strangers whom she was putting at their ease, then moved with Judith to the windows. The President stepped a little forward to meet them. "Ah, General Cary, I wish you could bring with you a wind from the Blue Ridge this stifling night! We must make this good news from the Mississippi refresh us instead! I saw your troops on the Nine-Mile road to-day. They cheered me, but I felt like cheering them! Miss Cary, I have overheard six officers ask to-night if Miss Cary had yet come."

Warwick began to talk with Judge Campbell. Judith laughed. "It was not of me they were asking, Mr. President! There is Hetty Cary entering now, and behind her Constance, and there are your six officers! I am but a leaf blown from the Blue Ridge."

"Gold leaf," said Wade Hampton.

The President used toward all women a stately deference. "I hope," he said, "that, having come once to rest in this room, you will often let a good wind blow you here —" Other guests claimed his attention. "Ah, Mrs. Stanard — Mrs. Enders — Ha, Wigfall! I saw your Texans this afternoon —" Judith found General Stuart beside her. "Miss Cary, a man of the Black Troop came back to camp yesterday. Says he, 'They've got an angel in the Stonewall Hospital! She came from Albemarle, and her name is Judith. If I were Holofernes and a Judith like that wanted my head, by George, I'd cut it off myself to please her!' — Yes, yes, my friend! — Miss

Cary, may I present my Chief of Staff, Major the Baron Heros von Borcke? Talk poetry with him, won't you? — Ha, Fauquier! that was a pretty dash you made yesterday! Rather rash, I thought — "

The other withered him with a look. "That was a carefully planned, cautiously executed manœuvre; modelled it after our old reconnoissance at Cerro Gordo. You to talk of rashness! — Here's A. P. Hill."

Judith, with her Prussian soldier of fortune, a man gentle, intelligent, and brave, crossed the room to one of the groups of men and women. Those of the former who were seated rose, and one of the latter put out an arm and claimed her with a caressing touch. "You are late, child! So am I. They brought in a bad case of fever, and I waited for the night nurse. Sit here with us! Mrs. Fitzgerald's harp has been sent for and she is going to sing — "

Judith greeted the circle. A gentleman pushed forward a chair. "Thank you, Mr. Soulé. My father and I stay but a little while, Mrs. Randolph, but it must be long enough to hear Mrs. Fitzgerald sing — Yes, he is here, Colonel Gordon — there, speaking with Judge Campbell and General Hill. — How is the general today, Mrs. Johnston?"

"Better, dear, or I should not be here. I am here but for a moment. He made me come — lying there on Church Hill, staring at that light in the sky! — Here is the harp."

Its entrance, borne by two servants, was noted. The violins were hushed, the groups turned, tended to merge one into another. A voice was heard speaking with a strong French accent — Colonel the Count Camille de Polignac, tall, gaunt, looking like a Knight of Malta — begging that the harp might be placed in the middle of the room. It was put there. Jeb Stuart led to it the lovely Louisianian. Mrs. Fitzgerald drew off her gloves and gave them to General Magruder to hold, relinquished her fan to Mr. Jules de Saint Martin, her bouquet to Mr. Francis Lawley of the London *Times*, and swept her white hand across the strings. She was a mistress of the harp, and she sang to it in a rich, throbbingly sweet voice, song after song as they were demanded. Conversation through the large room did not cease, but voices were lowered, and now and then came a complete lull in which all listened. She sang old Creole ditties and then Scotch and Irish ballads.

Judith found beside her chair the Vice-President. "Ah, Miss Cary, when you are as old as I am, and have read as much, you will notice how emphatic is the testimony to song and dance and gaiety on the eve of events which are to change the world! The flower grows where in an hour the volcano will burst forth; the bird sings in the tree which the earthquake will presently uproot; the pearly shell gleams where will pass the tidal wave —" He looked around the room. "Beauty, zeal, love, devotion — and to-morrow the smoke will roll, the cannon thunder, and the brute emerge all the same — just as he always does — just as he always does — stamping the flower into the mire, wringing the bird's neck, crushing the shell! Well, well, let's stop moralizing. What's she singing now? Hm! 'Kathleen Mavourneen.' Ha, Benjamin! What's the news with you?"

Judith, turning a little aside, dreamily listened now to the singer, now to phrases of the Vice-President and the Secretary of State. "After this, if we beat them now, a treaty surely. . . . Palmerston — The Emperour — The Queen of Spain — Mason says . . . Inefficiency of the blockade — Cotton obligations — Arms and munitions. . . ." Still talking, they moved away. A strident voice reached her from the end of the room — L. Q. C. Lamar, here to-night despite physicians. "The fight had to come. We are men, not women. The quarrel had lasted long enough. We hate each other, so the struggle had to come. Even Homer's heroes, after they had stormed and scolded long enough, fought like brave men, long and well —"

> " Ye banks and braes and streams around
> The castle o' Montgomery — "

sang Mrs. Fitzgerald.

There was in the room that slow movement which imperceptibly changes a well-filled stage, places a figure now here, now there, shifts the grouping and the lights. Now Judith was one of a knot of younger women. In the phraseology of the period, all were "belles"; Hetty and Constance Cary, Mary Triplett, Turner MacFarland, Jenny Pegram, the three Fishers, Evelyn Cabell, and others. About them came the "beaux," — the younger officers who were here to-night, the aides, the unwedded legislators. Judith listened, talked, played her part. She had a personal success in Richmond. Her

name, her beauty, the at times quite divine expression of her face,
made the eye follow, after which a certain greatness of mind was felt
and the attention became riveted. The pictures moved again, Mrs.
Fitzgerald singing "positively, this time, the last!" Some of the
"belles," attended by the "beaux," drifted toward the portico,
several toward the smaller room and its softly lowered lights. A
very young man, an artillerist, tall and fair, lingered beside
Judith. "'Auld lang Syne!' I do not think that she ought to sing
that to-night! I have noticed that when you hear music just before
battle the strain is apt to run persistently in your mind. She ought
to sing us 'Scots wha hae —' "

A gentleman standing near laughed. "That's good, or my name
is n't Ran Tucker! Mrs. Fitzgerald, Captain Pelham does not wish
to be left in such ' a weavin' way.' He says that song is like an April
shower on a bag of powder. The inference is that it will make the
horse artillery chicken-hearted. I move that you give John Pelham
and the assemblage 'Scots wha hae wi Wallace bled' —"

The singing ended, there was a wider movement through the
room. Judith, with Pelham still beside her, walked on the portico,
in the warm, rose-laden air. There was no moon, and the light in
the east was very marked. "If we strike McClellan's right," said
the artillerist, "all this hill and the ground to the north of it will be
the place from which to watch the battle. If it lasts after nightfall,
you will see the exploding shells beautifully." They stood at the
eastern end, Judith leaning against one of the pillars. Here a poet
and editor of the *Southern Literary Messenger* joined them; with
him a young man, a sculptor, Alexander Galt. A third, Washington
the painter, came, too. The violins had begun again — Mozart now
— "The Magic Flute." "Oh, smell the roses!" said the poet. "To-
night the roses, to-morrow the thorns — but roses, too, among the
thorns, deep and sweet! There will still be roses, will there not,
Miss Cary?"

"Yes, still," said Judith. "If I could paint, Mr. Washington, I
would take that gleam on the horizon."

"Yes, is it not fine? It is a subject, however, for a mystic. I have
an idea myself for a picture, if I can get the tent-cloth to paint it
on, and if some brushes and tubes I sent for ever get through the
block."

"If I had a tent I certainly would give it to you," said Pelham. "What would you paint?"

"A thing that happened ten days ago. The burial of Latané. The women buried him, you know. At Summer Hill. — Mrs. Brockenborough, and her daughter-in-law and grandchildren. Somebody read me a letter about it — so simple it wrung your heart! 'By God,' I said, 'what Roman things happen still!' And I thought I'd like to paint the picture."

"I read the letter, too," said the poet. "I am making some verses about it — see if you like them —

> " For woman's voice, in accents soft and low,
>   Trembling with pity, touched with pathos, read
>   O'er his hallowed dust the ritual for the dead:

> " 'T is sown in weakness, it is raised in power' —
>   Softly the promise floated on the air,
>   While the low breathings of the sunset hour
>   Came back responsive to the mourner's prayer.
>   Gently they laid him underneath the sod
>   And left him with his fame, his country and his God! "

"Yes," said Judith, sweetly and gravely. "How can we but like them? And I hope that you will find the tent-cloth, Mr. Washington."

Reëntering, presently, the large room, they found a vague stir, people beginning to say good-night, and yet lingering. "It is growing late," said some one, "and yet I think that he will come." Her father came up to her and drew her hand through his arm. "Here is General Lee now. We will wait a moment longer, then go."

They stood in the shadow of the curtains watching the Commander-in-Chief just pausing to greet such and such an one in his progress toward the President. An aide or two came behind; the grand head and form moved on, simple and kingly. Judith drew quicker breath. "Oh, he looks so great a man!"

"He looks what he is," said Warwick Cary. "Now let us go, too, and say good-night."

CHAPTER XXXI

THE FIRST OF THE SEVEN DAYS

IRIAM and Christianna sat at the window, watching. The day was parching, the sky hot blue steel, the wind that blew the dust through the streets like a breath from the sun himself. People went by, all kinds of people, lacking only soldiers. There seemed no soldiers in town. Miriam, alternately listless and feverishly animated, explained matters to the mountain girl. "When there's to be a battle, every one goes to the colours. — Look at that old, old, old man, hobbling on his stick. You'd think that death was right beside him, would n't you? — ready to tap him on the shoulder and say, 'Fall, fall, old leaf!' But it is n't so; death is on the battlefield looking for young men. Listen to his stick — tap, tap, tap, tap, tap —"

Christianna rose, looked at the clock, which was about to strike noon, left the room and returned with a glass of milk. "Mrs. Cleave said you was to drink this — Yes, Miss Miriam, do! — There now! Don't you want to lie down?"

"No, no!" said Miriam. "I don't want to do anything but sit here and watch. — Look at that old, old woman with the basket on her arm! I know what is in it — Things for her son; bread and a little meat and shirts she has been making him — There's another helping her, as old as she is. I mean to die young."

The people went by like figures on a frieze come to life. The room in which the two girls sat was on the ground floor of a small, old-fashioned house. Outside the window was a tiny balcony, with a graceful ironwork railing, and heavy ropes and twists of wistaria shaded this and the window. The old brick sidewalk was almost immediately below. For the most part the people who passed went by silently, but when there was talking the two behind the wistaria could hear. A nurse girl with her charges came by. "What's a 'cisive battle, honey? Yo'd better ask yo' pa that. Reckon it's where won't neither side let go. Why won't they? Now you tell me an' then I'll tell you! All I knows is, they're gwine have a turrible rumpus pre-sently, an' yo' ma said tek you to yo' gran'ma kaze she gwine out ter git jes' ez near the battle an' yo' pa ez she kin git!" Nurse and children passed, and there came by an elderly man, stout and amiable-looking. His face was pale, his eyes troubled; he took off his straw hat, and wiped his forehead with a large white handker-chief. Appearing from the opposite direction, a young man, a case of surgeon's instruments in his hand, met him, and in passing said good-day. The elder stopped him a moment, on the hot brick pave-ment before the wistaria. "Well, doctor, they're all out Mechanics-ville way! I reckon we may expect to hear the cannon any moment now. I saw you at Gilland's, did n't I, yesterday?"

"Yes, I am there —"

"Well, if by ill luck my boy is wounded and brought there, you'll look out for him, eh? Youngest boy, you know — Blue eyes, brown hair. I'm on the Ambulance Committee. We've got a string of wagons ready on the Nine-Mile road. You look out for him if he's brought in —"

The surgeon promised and each went his way. Three women passed the window. One was knitting as she walked, one was in deep black, and a third, a girl, carried a great silver pitcher filled with iced drink for some near-by convalescent. Two men came next. A negro followed, bearing a spade. One of the two was in broad-cloth, with a high silk hat. "I told them," he was saying, "better bury her this morning, poor little thing, before the fighting begins. *She* won't mind, and it will be hard to arrange it then—" "Yes, yes," said the second, "better so! Leave to-morrow for the Dead March from 'Saul.'"

They passed. A church bell began to ring. Miriam moved rest-lessly. "Is not mother coming back? She ought to have let me go with her. I can't knit any more, — the needles are red hot when I touch them, — but I can sew. I could help her. — If I knew which sewing-room she went to —"

Christianna's hand timidly caressed her. "Better stay here, Miss Miriam. I'm going to give you another glass of milk now, directly — There's a soldier passing now."

It proved but a battered soldier — thin and hollow-eyed, arm in a sling, and a halt in his walk. He came on slowly, and he leaned for rest against a sycamore at the edge of the pavement. Miriam bent out from the frame of wistaria. "Oh, soldier! don't you want a glass of milk?"

"Oh, soldier" looked nothing loath. He came over to the little balcony, and Miriam took the glass from Christianna and, leaning over, gave it to him. "Oh, but that's nectar!" he said, and drank it. "Yes — just out of hospital. Said I might go and snuff the battle from afar. Needed my pallet for some other poor devil. Glad I'm through with it, and sorry he is n't! — Yes, I've got some friends down the street. Going there now and get out of this sun. Reckon the battle'll begin presently. Hope the Accomac Invincibles will give them hell — begging your pardon, I'm sure. That milk certainly was good. Thank you, and good-bye, Hebe — two Hebes." He wavered on down the street. Christianna looked after him critically. "They ought n't to let that thar man out so soon! Clay white, an' thin as a bean pole, an' calling things an' people out of their names —"

Men and women continued to pass, the church bell to ring, the hot wind to blow the dust, the sun to blaze down, the sycamore leaves to rustle. A negro boy brought a note. It was from Margaret Cleave. "*Dearest: There is so much to do. I will not come home to dinner nor will Cousin Harriet neither. She says tell Sarindy to give you two just what you like best. Christianna must look after you. I will come when I can.*"

Sarindy gave them thin crisp toast, and a pitcher of cool milk, and a custard sweetened with brown sugar. Sarindy was excited. "Yaas, Lawd, dar's sho' gwine ter be doin's this day! What you reckon, Miss Miriam? Dar's er lady from South Callina stayin' cross't de street, 'n' she's got er maid what's got de impidence ob sin! What you reckon dat yaller gal say ter me? She say dat South Callina does de most ob de fightin' 'n' de bes' ob it, too! She say Virginia pretty good, but dat South Callina tek de cake. She say South Callina mek 'em run ebery time! Yaas'm! 'n' I gits up 'n' I meks her er curtsy, 'n' I say ter her, 'Dat's er pretty way ter talk when you're visitin' in Virginia, 'n' ef dat's South Callina manners I'se glad I wuz born in Virginia!' Yaas'm. 'N' I curtsy agin, 'n' I say, 'Ain' nobody or nothin' ever lay over Virginia fer fightin' 'n' never will! 'N' ef Virginia don' mek 'em run ebery time, South Callina need n't hope ter!' 'N' I asks her how come she never hear ob Gineral Stonewall Jackson? Yaas'm. 'N' I curtsy ter her ebery time — lak dis! 'N' ain' she never hear ob Gineral Lee? An' I ain' er doubtin' dat Gineral Wade Hampton is a mighty fine man — 'deed I knows he is — but ain' she never heard ob Gineral Johnston? 'N' how erbout Gineral Stuart — Yaas'm! 'n' the Black Troop, 'n' the Crenshaw Battery, 'n' the Purcell Battery. Yaas'm! 'n' the Howitzers, 'n' the Richmon' Blues — Yaas'm! I sho' did mek her shet her mouf! — Braggin' ter er Virginia woman ob South Callina!"

The two went back to the large room. The air was scorching. Miriam undressed, slipped her thin, girlish arms into a muslin sacque, and lay down. Christianna drew the blinds together, took a palm-leaf fan and sat beside her. "I'll fan you, jest as easy," she said, in her sweet, drawling voice. "An' I can't truly sing, but I can croon. Don't you want me to croon you 'Shining River'?"

Miriam lay with closed eyes. A fly buzzed in the darkened room. The fan went monotonously to and fro. Christianna crooned "Shining River" and then "Shady Grove." Outside, on the brick pavement, the sound of feet went by in a slender stream.

> "Shady Grove! Shady Grove —
> Going to Church in Shady Grove —"

The stream without grew wide and deep, then hurrying. Christianna looked over her shoulder, then at Miriam. The latter's long lashes lay on her cheek. Beneath them glistened a tear, but her slight, girlish bosom rose and fell regularly. Christianna crooned on,

> "Shady Grove! Shady Grove —
> Children love my Shady Grove —"

Boom! Boom! — Boom, Boom! Boom, Boom, Boom, Boom!

Miriam started up with a cry. Outside the window a hoarse and loud voice called to some one across the street. "That's beyond Meadow Bridge! D' ye know what I believe? I believe it's Stonewall Jackson!" The name came back like an echo from the opposite pavement. "Stonewall Jackson! Stonewall Jackson! He thinks maybe it's Stonewall Jackson!"

Boom — Boom — Boom — Boom, Boom!

Miriam rose, threw off the muslin sacque and began to dress. Her eyes were narrowed, her fingers rapid and steady. Christianna opened the window-blinds. The sound of the hurrying feet came strongly in, and with it voices. "The top of the Capitol! — see best from there — I think the hills toward the almshouse — Can you get out on the Brook turnpike? — No; it is picketed — The hill by the President's House — try it!" Christianna, turning, found Miriam taking a hat from the closet shelf. "Oh, Miss Miriam, you must n't go —"

Miriam, a changed creature, steady and sure as a fine rapier, turned upon her. "Yes, I am going, Christianna. If you like, you may come with me. Yes, I am well enough. — No, mother would n't keep me back. She would understand. If I lay there and listened, I should go mad. Get your bonnet and come."

The cannon shook the air. Christianna got her sunbonnet and tied the strings with trembling fingers. All the wild rose had fled from her cheeks, her lips looked pinched, her eyes large and startled. Miriam glanced her way, then came and kissed her. "I forgot it was your first battle. I got used to them in Winchester. Don't be afraid."

They went out into the hot sunshine. By now the greater part of the stream had hurried by. They saw that it flowed eastward, and they followed. The sun blazed down, the pavement burned their feet. The mountain girl walked like a piece of thistledown; Miriam, light and quick in all her actions, moved beside her almost as easily. It was as though the hot wind, rushing down the street behind them, carried them on with the dust and loosened leaves. There were other women, with children clinging to their hands. One or two had babes in their arms. There were old men, too, and several cripples. The lighter-limbed and unencumbered were blown ahead. The dull sound rocked the air. This was a residence portion of the city, and the houses looked lifeless. The doors were wide, the inmates gone. Only where there was illness, were there faces at the window, looking out, pale and anxious, asking questions of the hurrying pale and anxious folk below. The cannonading was not yet continuous. It spoke rather in sullen thunders, with spaces between in which the heart began to grow quiet. Then it thundered again, and the heart beat to suffocation.

The wind blew Miriam and Christianna toward the President's

House. Tall, austere, white-pillared, it stood a little coldly in the heat. Before the door were five saddle horses, with a groom or two. The staff came from the house, then the President in grey Confederate cloth and soft hat. He spoke to one of the officers in his clear, incisive voice, then mounted his grey Arab. A child waved to him from an upper window. He waved back, lifted his hat to the two girls as they passed, then, his staff behind him, rode rapidly off toward the sound of the firing.

Miriam and Christianna, turning a little northward, found themselves on a hillside thronged with people. It was like a section of an amphitheatre, and it commanded a great stretch of lowland broken here and there by slight elevations. Much of the plain was in forest, but in some places the waist-deep corn was waving, and in others the wheat stood in shocks. There were marshes and boggy green meadows and old fields of pine and broom sedge. Several roads could be seen. They all ran into a long and low cloud of smoke. It veiled the northern horizon, and out of it came the thunder. First appeared dull orange flashes, then, above the low-lying thickness, the small white expanding cloud made by the bursting shell, then to the ear rushed the thunder. On the plain, from the defences which rimmed the city northward to the battle cloud, numbers of grey troops were visible, some motionless, some marching. They looked like toy soldiers. The sun heightened red splashes that were known to be battle-flags. Horsemen could be seen galloping from point to point. In the intervals between the thunders the hillside heard the tap of drum and the bugles blowing. The moving soldiers were going toward the cloud.

Miriam and Christianna sank down beneath a little tree. They were on a facet of the hill not quite so advantageous as others. The crowded slopes were beyond. However, one could see the smoke cloud and hear the cannon, and that was all that could be done anyhow. There were men and women about them, children, boys. The women were the most silent, — pale and silent; the men uttered low exclamations or soliloquies, or talked together. The boys were all but gleeful — save when they looked at the grown people, and then they tried for solemnity. Some of the children went to sleep. A mother nursed her babe. Near the foot of this hill, through a hollow, there ran a branch, — Bacon Quarter Branch. Here, in the seventeenth century, had occurred an Indian massacre. The heavy, primeval woods had rung to the whoop of the savage, the groan of the settler, the scream of English woman and child. To-day the woods had been long cut, and the red man was gone. War remained — he had only changed his war paint and cry and weapons.

Miriam clasped her thin brown hands about her knee, rested her chin on them, and fastened her great brown eyes on the distant battle cloud. Christianna, her sunbonnet pushed back, looked too, with limpid, awe-struck gaze. Were Pap and Dave and Billy fighting in that cloud? It was thicker than the morning mist in the hollow below Thunder Run Mountain, and it was not fleecy, pure, and white. It was yellowish, fierce, and ugly, and the sound that came from it made her heart beat thick and hard. Was he there — Was Allan Gold there in the cloud? She felt that she could not sit still; she wished to walk toward it. That being impossible, she began to make a little moaning sound. A woman in black, sitting on the grass near her, looked across. "Don't!" she said. "If you do that, all of us will do it. We've got to keep calm. If we let go, it would be like Rachel weeping. Try to be quiet."

Christianna, who had moaned as she crooned, hardly knowing it, at once fell silent. Another woman spoke to her. "Would you mind holding my baby? My head aches so. I must lie down here on the grass, just a minute." Christianna took the baby. She handled it skilfully, and it was presently cooing against her breast. Were Pap and Dave over there, shooting and cutting? And Billy — Billy with a gun now instead of the spear the blacksmith had made him? And Allan Gold was not teaching in the schoolhouse on Thunder Run. . . .

The woman took the baby back. The sun blazed down, there came a louder burst of sound. A man with a field-glass, standing near, uttered a "Tchk!" of despair. "Impenetrable curtain! The ancients managed things better — they did not fight in a fog!"

He seemed a person having authority, and the people immediately about him appealed for information. He looked through the glass and gave it, and was good, too, about lending the glass. "It's A. P. Hill, I'm sure — with Longstreet to support him. It's A. P. Hill's brigades that are moving into the smoke. Most of that firing is from our batteries along the Chickahominy. We are going undoubtedly to cross to the north bank — Yes. McClellan's right wing — Fitz John Porter — A good soldier — Oh, he'll have about twenty-five thousand men."

A boy, breathing excitement from top to toe, sent up a shrill voice. "Isn't Jackson coming, sir? Aren't they looking for Jackson?"

The soldier who had drunk the milk was discovered by Miriam and Christianna, near their tree. He gave his voice. "Surely! He'll have come down from Ashland and A. P. Hill is crossing here. That's an army north, and a big lot of troops south, and Fitz John Porter is between like a nut in a nut cracker. The cracker has only to work all right, and crush goes the filbert!" He raised himself and peered under puckered brows at the smoke-draped horizon. "Yes, he's surely over there — Stonewall. — Going to flank Fitz John Porter — Then we'll hear a hell of a fuss."

"There's a battery galloping to the front," said the man with the glass. "Look, one of you! Wipe the glass; it gets misty. If it's the Purcell, I've got two sons —"

The soldier took the glass, turning it deftly with one hand. "Yes, think it is the Purcell. Don't you worry, sir! They're all right. Artillerymen are hard to kill — That's Pender's brigade going now —"

Christianna clutched Miriam. "Look! look! Oh, what is it?"

It soared into the blue, above the smoke. The sunlight struck it and it became a beautiful iridescent bubble, large as the moon. "Oh, oh!" cried the boy. "Look at the balloon!"

The hillside kept silence for a moment while it gazed, then — "Is it ours? — No; it is theirs! — It is going up from the hill behind Beaver Dam Creek. — Oh, it is lovely! — Lovely! No, no, it is horrible! — Look, look! there is another!"

A young man, a mechanic, with sleeves rolled up, began to expatiate on "ours." "We haven't got but one — it was made in Savannah by Dr. Langon Cheves. Maybe they'll send it up to-day, maybe not. I've seen it. It's like Joseph's coat in the Bible. They say the ladies gave their silk dresses for it. Here'll be a strip of purple and here one of white with roses on it, and here it is black, and here it is yellow as gold. They melted rubber car-springs in naphtha and varnished it with that, and they're going to fill it with city gas at the gas works —"

The bubbles floated in the clear air, above and beyond the zone of smoke. It was now between four and five in the afternoon. The slant rays of the sun struck them and turned them mother-of-pearl. An old man lifted a dry, thin voice like a grasshopper's. "Once I went to Niagara, and there was a balloon ascension. Everybody held their breath when the fellow went up, and he got into some trouble, I don't remember just what it was, and we almost died of anxiety until he came down; and when he landed we almost cried we were so glad, and we patted him on the back and hurrahed — and he was a Yankee, too! And now it's war time, and there's nothing I'd like better than to empty a revolver into that fine windbag!"

The sound in the air became heavier. A man on horseback spurred along the base of the hill. The people nearest stopped him. "Tell you? I can't tell you! Nobody ever knows anything about a battle till it's over, and not much then. Is Jackson over there? I don't know. He ought to be, so I reckon he is! If he isn't, it's A. P. Hill's battle, all alone."

He was gone. "I don't believe it's much more than long-range firing yet," said the soldier. "Our batteries on the Chickahominy — and they are answering from somewhere beyond Beaver Dam Creek. No musketry. Hello! The tune's changing!"

It changed with such violence that after a moment's exclamation the people sat or stood in silence, pale and awed. Speculation ceased. The plunging torrent of sound whelmed the mind and stilled the tongue. The soldier held out a moment. "Close range now. The North's always going to beat us when it comes to metal soldiers. I wonder how many they've got over there, anyhow!" Then he, too, fell silent.

The deep and heavy booming shook air and earth. It came no longer in distinct shocks but with a continuous roar. The smoke screen grew denser and taller, mounting toward the balloons. There was no seeing for that curtain; it could only be noted that bodies of grey troops moved toward it, went behind it. A thin, elderly man, a school-teacher, borrowed the glass, fixed it, but could see nothing. He gave it back with a shake of the head, sat down again on the parched grass, and veiled his eyes with his hand. "'Hell is murky,'" he said.

No lull occurred in the firing. The sun as it sank reddened the battle cloud that by now had blotted out the balloons. "When it is dark," said the soldier, "it will be like fireworks." An hour later the man with the glass discovered a string of wagons on one of the roads. It was coming citywards. "Ambulances!" he said, in a shaking voice.

"Ambulances — ambulances —" The word went through the crowd like a sigh. It broke the spell. Most on the hillside might have an interest there. Parents, wives, brothers, sisters, children, they rose, they went away in the twilight like blown leaves. The air was rocking; orange and red lights began to show as the shells exploded. Christianna put her hand on Miriam's. "Miss Miriam — Miss Miriam! Mrs. Cleave 'll say I did n't take care of you. Let's go — let's go. They're bringing back the wounded. Pap might be there or Dave or Billy or — Miss Miriam, Miss Miriam, your brother might be there."

The long June dusk melted into night, and still the city shook to the furious cannonading. With the dark it saw, as it had not seen in the sunshine. As the soldier said, it was like fireworks.

Beginning at twilight, the wagons with the wounded came all night long. Ambulances, farm wagons, carts, family carriages, heavy-laden, they rumbled over the cobblestones with the sound of the tumbrels in the Terror. It was stated that a number of the wounded were in the field hospitals. In the morning the knowledge was general that very many had lain, crying for water, all night in the slashing before Beaver Dam Creek.

All the houses in Richmond were lighted. Through the streets poured a tide of fevered life. News — News — News! — demanded from chance couriers, from civilian spectators of the battle arriving pale and exhausted, from the drivers of wagon, cart, and carriage, from the less badly wounded — "Ours the victory — is it not? is it not? — Who led? — who fought? — who is fighting now? Jackson came? Jackson certainly came? We are winning — are we not? are we not?" Suspense hung palpable in the hot summer night, suspense, exaltation, fever. It breathed in the hot wind, it flickered in the lights, it sounded in the voice of the river. For many there sounded woe as well — woe and wailing for the dead. For others, for many, many others, there was a misery of searching, a heart-breaking going from hospital to hospital. "Is he here? — Are they here?" The cannon stopped at nine o'clock.

The Stonewall Hospital was poorly lighted. In ward number 23 the oil lamps, stuck in brackets along the walls, smoked. At one end, where two pine tables were placed, the air from the open window blew the flames distractingly. A surgeon, half dead with fatigue, strained well-nigh to the point of tears, exclaimed upon it. "That damned wind! Shut the window, Miss Cary. Yes, tight! It's hell anyhow, and that's what you do in hell — burn up!"

Judith closed the window. As she did so she looked once at the light on the northern horizon. The firing shook the window-pane. The flame of the lamp now stood straight. She turned the wick higher, then lifted a pitcher and poured water into a basin, and when the surgeon had washed his hands took away the reddened stuff. Two negroes laid a man on the table — a gaunt North Carolinian, his hand clutching a shirt all stiffened blood. Between his eyelids showed a gleam of white, his breath came with a whistling sound. Judith bent the rigid fingers open, drew the hand aside, and cut away the shirt. The surgeon looked. "Humph! Well, a body can but try. Now, my man, you lie right still, and I won't hurt you much. Come this side, Miss Cary — No, wait a moment! — It's no use. He's dying."

The North Carolinian died. The negroes lifted him from the table and put another in his place. "Amputation," said the surgeon. "Hold it firmly, Miss Cary; just there." He turned to the adjoining table where a younger man was sewing up a forearm, ripped from wrist to elbow by a piece of shell. "Lend me your saw, will you, Martin? — Yes, I know the heat's fearful! but I can't work by a lamp that has Saint Vitus!" He turned back to his table. "Now, my lad, you just clench your teeth. Miss Cary and I are n't going to hurt you any more than we can help. Yes, above the knee." The younger surgeon, having finished the cut, wiped away with a towel the sweat that blinded him. "The next. — Hm! Doctor, will you look here a moment? — Oh, I see you can't! It's no use, Mrs. Opie. Better have him taken back. He'll die in an hour. — The next."

The ward was long, low ceiled, with brown walls and rafters. Between the patches of lamplight the shadows lay wide and heavy.

The cots, the pallets, the pew cushions sewed together, were placed each close by each. A narrow aisle ran between the rows; by each low bed there was just standing room. The beds were all filled, and the wagons bringing more rumbled on the cobblestones without. All the long place was reekingly hot, with a strong smell of human effluvia, of sweat-dampened clothing, of blood and powder grime. There was not much crying aloud; only when a man was brought in raving, or when there came a sharp scream from some form under the surgeon's knife. But the place seemed one groan, a sound that swelled or sank, but never ceased. The shadows on the wall, fantastically dancing, mocked this with nods and becks and waving arms, — mocked the groaning, mocked the heat, mocked the smell, mocked the thirst, mocked nausea, agony, delirium, and the rattle in the throat, mocked the helpers and the helped, mocked the night and the world and the dying and the dead. At dawn the cannon began again.

CHAPTER XXXII

DAWN broke cold and pure, the melancholy ashen seas slowly, slowly turning to chill ethereal meads of violets, the violet more slowly yet giving place to Adonis gardens of rose and daffodil. The forests stood dew-drenched and shadowy, solemn enough, deep and tangled woodlands that they were, under the mysterious light, in the realm of the hour whose finger is at her lips. The dawn made them seem still, and yet they were not still. They and the old fields and the marshes and the wild and tangled banks of sluggish water-courses, and the narrow, hidden roads, and the low pine-covered hilltops, and all the vast, overgrown, and sombre low-land were filled with the breathing of two armies. In the cold glory of the dawn there faced each other one hundred and eighty thousand men bent on mutual destruction.

A body of grey troops, marching toward Cold Harbour, was brought to a halt within a taller, deeper belt than usual. Oak and sycamore, pine and elm, beech, ash, birch and walnut, all towered toward the violet meads. A light mist garlanded their tops, and a graceful, close-set underbrush pressed against their immemorial trunks. It was dank and still, dim and solemn within such a forest cavern. Minutes passed. The men sat down on the wet, black earth. The officers questioned knew only that Fitz John Porter was falling back from Beaver Dam Creek, presumably on his next line of intrenchments, and that, presumably, we were following. "Has Jackson joined?" "Can't tell you that. If he has n't, well, we'll beat them anyhow!"

This body of troops had done hard fighting the evening before and was tired enough to rest. Some of the men lay down, pillowing their heads on their arms, dozing, dozing in the underbrush, in the misty light, beneath the tall treetops where the birds were cheeping. In the mean time a Federal balloon, mounting into the amethyst air, discovered that this stretch of woodland was thronged with grey soldiers, and signalled as much to Fitz John Porter, falling back with steadiness to his second line at Gaines's Mill. He posted several batteries, and ordered them to shell the wood.

In the purple light the guns began. The men in grey had to take the storm; they were in the wood and orders had not come to leave it. They took it in various ways, some sullenly, some contemptuously, some with nervous twitchings of head and body, many with dry humour and a quizzical front. The Confederate soldier was fast developing a characteristic which stayed with him to the end. He joked with death and gave a careless hand to suffering. A few of the more imaginative and æsthetically minded lost themselves in open-mouthed contemplation of the bestormed forest and its behaviour.

The cannonade was furious, and though not many of the grey soldiers suffered, the grey trees did. Great and small branches were lopped off. In the dim light they came tumbling down. They were borne sideways, tearing through the groves and coverts, or, caught by an exploding shell and torn twig from twig, they fell in a shower of slivers, or, chopped clean from the trunk, down they crashed from leafy level to level till they reached the forest floor. Beneath them rose shouts of warning, came a scattering of grey mortals. Younger trees were cut short off. Their woodland race was run; down they rushed with their festoons of vines, crushing the undergrowth of laurel and hazel. Other shells struck the red brown resinous bodies of pines, set loose dangerous mists of bark and splinter. As by a whirlwind the air was filled with torn and flying growth, with the dull crash and leafy fall of the forest non-combatants. The light was no longer pure; it was murky here as elsewhere. The violet fields and the vermeil gardens were blotted out, and in the shrieking of the shells the birds could not have been heard to sing even were they there. They were not there; they were all flown far away. It was dark in the wood, dark and full of sound and of moving bodies charged with danger. The whirlwind swept it, the tree-tops snapped off. "*Attention!*" The grey soldiers were glad to hear the word. "*Forward! March!*" They were blithe to hear the order and to leave the wood.

They moved out into old fields, grown with sedge and sassafras, here and there dwarf pines. Apparently the cannon had lost them;

at any rate for a time the firing ceased. The east was now pink, the air here very pure and cool and still, each feather of broom sedge holding its row of diamond dewdrops. The earth was much cut up. "Batteries been along here," said the men. "Ours, too. Know the wheel marks. Hello! What you got, Carter?"

"Somebody's dropped his photograph album."

The man in front and the man behind and the man on the other side all looked. "One of those folding things! Pretty children! one, two, three, four, and their mother. — Keep it for him, Henry. Think the Crenshaw battery, or Braxton's, or the King William, or the Dixie was over this way."

Beyond the poisoned field were more woods, dipping to one of the innumerable sluggish creeks of the region. There was a bridge — weak and shaken, but still a bridge. This crossed at last, the troops climbed a slippery bank, beneath a wild tangle of shrub and vine, and came suddenly into view of a line of breastworks, three hundred yards away. There was a halt; skirmishers were thrown forward. These returned without a trigger having been pulled. "Deserted, sir. They've fallen back, guns and all. But there's a meadow between us and the earthworks, sir, that — that — that —"

The column began to move across the meadow — not a wide meadow, a little green, boggy place commanded by the breastworks. Apparently grey troops had made a charge here, the evening before. The trees that fringed the small, irregular oval, and the great birds that sat in the trees, and the column whose coming had made the birds to rise, looked upon a meadow set as thick with dead men as it should have been with daisies. They lay thick, thick, two hundred and fifty of them, perhaps, heart pierced, temple pierced by minie balls, or all the body shockingly torn by grape and canister. The wounded had been taken away. Only the dead were here, watched by the great birds, the treetops and the dawn. They lay fantastically, some rounded into a ball, some spread eagle, some with their arms over their eyes, some in the posture of easy sleep. At one side was a swampy place, and on the edge of this a man, sunk to the thigh, kept upright. The living men thought him living, too. More than one started out of line toward him, but then they saw that half his head was blown away.

They left the meadow and took a road that skirted another great piece of forest. The sun came up, drank off the vagrant wreaths of mist and dried the dew from the sedge. There was promise of a hot, fierce, dazzling day. Another halt. "What's the matter this time?" asked the men. "God! I want to march on — into something happening!" Rumour came back. "Woods in front of us full of something. Don't know yet whether it's buzzards or Yankees. Get ready to open fire, anyway." All ready, the men waited until she came again. "It's men, anyhow. Woods just full of bayonets gleaming. Better throw your muskets forward."

The column moved on, but cautiously, with a strong feeling that it, in its turn, was being watched — with muskets thrown forward. Then suddenly came recognition. "Grey — grey! — See the flag! They're ours! See —" Rumour broke into jubilant shouting. "It's the head of Jackson's column! It's the Valley men! Hurrah! Hurrah! Stonewall! Stonewall Jackson! Yaaaih! Yaaaaaihhhh! — 'Hello, boys! You've been doing pretty well up there in the blessed old Valley!' 'Hello, boys! If you don't look out you'll be getting your names in the papers!' 'Hello, boys! come to help us kill mosquitoes? Haven't got any quinine handy, have you?' 'Hello, boys! Hello Kernstown, McDowell, Front Royal, Winchester, Harper's Ferry, Cross Keys, Port Republic! Yaaaih! Yaaaaaihh!' 'Hello, you damned Cohees! Are you the foot cavalry?' — 65th Virginia, Stonewall Brigade? Glad to see you, 65th! Welcome to these here parts. What made you late? We surely did hone for you yesterday evening. Oh, shucks! the best gun'll miss fire once in a lifetime. Who's your colonel? Richard Cleave? Oh, yes, I remember! read his name in the reports. We've got a good one, too, — real proud of him. Well, we surely are glad to see you fellows in the flesh! — Oh, we're going to halt. You halted, too? — Regular love feast, by jiminy! Got any tobacco?"

A particularly ragged private, having gained permission from his officer, came up to the sycamore beneath which his own colonel and the colonel of the 65th were exchanging courtesies. The former glanced his way. "Oh, Cary! Oh, yes, you two are kin — I remember. Well, colonel, I'm waiting for orders, as you are. Morally sure we're in for an awful scrap. Got a real respect for Fitz John Porter. McClellan's got this army trained, too, till it isn't any more like the rabble at Manassas than a grub's like a butterfly! Mighty fine fighting machine now. Fitz John's got our old friend Sykes and the Regulars. That does n't mean what it did at Manassas — eh? We're all Regulars now, ourselves. — Yes, Cold Harbour, I reckon, or maybe a little this way — Gaines's Mill. That's their second line. Wonderful breastworks. Mac's a master engineer! — Now I'll clear out and let you and Cary talk."

The two cousins sat down on the grass beneath the sycamore. For a little they eyed each other in silence. Edward Cary was more beautiful than ever, and apparently happy, though one of his shoes was nothing more than a sandal, and he was innocent of a collar, and his sleeve demanded a patch. He was thin, bright-eyed, and bronzed, and he handled his rifle with lazy expertness, and he looked at his cousin with a genuine respect and liking. "Richard, I heard about Will. I know you were like a father to the boy. I am very sorry."

"I know that you are, Edward. I would rather not talk about it, please. When the country bleeds, one must put away private grief."

He sat in the shade of the tree, thin and bronzed and bright-eyed like his cousin, though not ragged. Dundee grazed at hand, and scattered upon the edge of the wood, beneath the little dogwood trees, lay like acorns his men, fraternizing with the "Tuckahoe" regiment. "Your father and Fauquier —?"

"Both somewhere in this No-man's Land. What a wilderness of creeks and woods it is! I slept last night in a swamp, and at reveille a beautiful moccasin lay on a log and looked at me. I don't think either father or Fauquier were engaged last evening. Pender and Ripley bore the brunt of it. Judith is in Richmond."

"Yes. I had a letter from her before we left the Valley."

"I am glad, Richard, it is you. We were all strangely at sea, somehow — She is a noble woman. When I look at her I always feel reassured as to the meaning and goal of humanity."

" I know — I love her dearly, dearly. If I outlive this battle I will try to get to see her —"

Off somewhere, on the left, a solitary cannon boomed. The grey soldiers turned their heads. "A signal somewhere! We're spread over all creation. Crossing here and crossing there, and every half-hour losing your way! It's like the maze we used to read about — this bottomless, mountainless, creeky, swampy, feverish, damned lowland —"

The two beneath the sycamore smiled. "'Back to our mountains,'
eh?" said Edward. Cleave regarded the forest somewhat frowningly.
"We are not," he said, "in a very good humour this morning. Yesterday was a day in which things went wrong."

"It was a sickening disappointment," acknowledged Edward.
"We listened and listened. He's got a tremendous reputation, you
know — Jackson. Foreordained and predestined to be at the crucial point at the critical moment! Backed alike by Calvin and God!
So we looked for a comet to strike Fitz John Porter, and instead we
were treated to an eclipse. It was a frightful slaughter. I saw General Lee afterwards — magnanimous, calm, and grand! What was
really the reason?"

Cleave moved restlessly. "I cannot say. Perhaps I might hazard
a guess, but it's no use talking of guesswork. To-day I hope for a
change."

"You consider him a great general?"

"A very great one. But he's sprung from earth — ascended like
the rest of us. For him, as for you and me, there's the heel undipped
and the unlucky day."

The officers of the first grey regiment began to bestir themselves.
Fall in — Fall in — Fall in! Edward rose. "Well, we shall see what
we shall see. Good-bye, Richard!" The two shook hands warmly;
Cary ran to his place in the line; the "Tuckahoe" regiment, cheered
by the 65th, swung from the forest road into a track leading across
an expanse of broom sedge. It went rapidly. The dew was dried,
the mist lifted, the sun blazing with all his might. During the night
the withdrawing Federals had also travelled this road. It was cut
by gun-wheels, it was strewn with abandoned wagons, ambulances,
accoutrements of all kinds. There were a number of dead horses.
They lay across the road, or to either hand in the melancholy fields
of sedge. From some dead trees the buzzards watched. One horse,
far out in the yellow sedge, lifted his head and piteously neighed.

The troops came into the neighbourhood of Gaines's Mill. Through
grille after grille of woven twig and bamboo vine they descended to
another creek, sleeping and shadowed, crossed it somehow, and came
up into forest again. Before them, through the trees, was visible
a great open space, hundreds of acres. Here and there it rose into
knolls, and on these were planted grey batteries. Beyond the open

there showed a horseshoe of a creek, fringed with swamp growth, a wild and tangled woodland; beyond this again a precipitous slope, almost a cliff, mounting to a wide plateau. All the side of the ascent was occupied by admirable breastworks, triple lines, one above the other, while at the base between hill and creek, within the enshadowing forest, was planted a great abattis of logs and felled trees. Behind the breastwork and on the plateau rested Fitz John Porter, reinforced during the night by Slocum, and now commanding thirty-five thousand disciplined and courageous troops. Twenty-two batteries frowned upon the plain below. The Federal drums were beating — beating — beating. The grey soldiers lay down in the woods and awaited orders. They felt, rather than saw, that other troops were all about them, — A. P. Hill — Longstreet — couched in the wide woods, strung in the brush that bordered creek and swamp, massed in the shelter of the few low knolls.

They waited long. The sun blazed high and higher. Then a grey battery, just in front of this strip of woods, opened with a howitzer. The shell went singing on its errand, exploded before one of the triple tiers. The plateau answered with a hundred-pounder. The missile came toward the battery, overpassed it, and exploded above the wood. It looked as large as a beehive; it came with an awful sound, and when it burst the atmosphere seemed to rock. The men lying on the earth beneath jerked back their heads, threw an arm over their eyes, made a dry, clicking sound with their tongue against their teeth. The howitzer and this shell opened the battle — again A. P. Hill's battle.

Over in the forest on the left, near Cold Harbour, where Stonewall Jackson had his four divisions, his own, D. H. Hill's, Ewell's, and Whiting's, there was long, long waiting. The men had all the rest they wanted, and more besides. They fretted, they grew querulous. "Oh, good God, why don't we move? There's firing — heavy firing — on the right. Are we going to lie here in these swamps and fight mosquitoes all day? Thought we were brought here to fight Yankees! The general walking in the forest and saying his prayers? — Oh, go to hell!"

A battery, far over on the edge of a swamp, broke loose, tearing the sultry air with shell after shell tossed against a Federal breastwork on the other side of the marsh. The Stonewall Brigade grew vividly interested. "That's D. H. Hill over there! D. H. Hill is a fighter from way back! O Lord, why don't we fight too? Holy Moses, what a racket!" The blazing noon filled with crash and roar. Ten of Fitz John Porter's guns opened, full-mouthed, on the adventurous battery.

It had nerve, *élan*, sheer grit enough for a dozen, but it was out-metalled. One by one its guns were silenced, — most of the horses down, most of the cannoneers. Hill recalled it. A little later he received an order from Jackson. "General Hill will withdraw his troops to the left of the road, in rear of his present position, where he will await further orders." Hill went, with shut lips. One o'clock — two o'clock — half-past two. "O God, have mercy! *Is* this the Army of the Valley?"

Allan Gold, detached at dawn on scout duty, found himself about this time nearer to the Confederate centre than to his own base of operations at the left. He had been marking the windings of creeks, observing where there were bridges and where there were none, the depth of channels and the infirmness of marshes. He had noted the Federal positions and the amount of stores abandoned, set on fire, good rice and meat, good shoes, blankets, harness, tents, smoulder-ing and smoking in glade and thicket. He had come upon dead men and horses and upon wounded men and horses. He had given the wounded drink. He had killed with the butt of his rifle a hissing and coiled snake. He had turned his eyes away from the black and winged covering of a dead horse and rider. Kneeling at last to drink at a narrow, hidden creek, slumbering between vine-laden trees, he had raised his eyes, and on the other side marked a blue scout look-ing, startled, out of a hazel bush. There was a click from two mus-kets; then Allan said, "Don't fire! I won't. Why should we? Drink and forget." The blue scout signified acquiescence. "All right, Reb. I'm tired fighting, anyway! Was brought up a Quaker, and would n't mind if I had stayed one! Got anything to mix with the water?"

"No."

"Well, let's take it just dry so." Both drank, then settled back on their heels for a moment's conversation. "Awful weather," said the blue scout. "Did n't know there could be such withering heat! And malaria — lying out of nights in swamps, with owls hooting and jack-o'-lanterns round your bed! Ain't you folks most beat yet?"

"No," said the grey scout. "Don't you think you've about worn your welcome out and had better go home? — Look out there! Your gun's slipping into the water."

The blue recovered it. "It's give out this morning that Stonewall Jackson's arrived on the scene."

"Yes, he has."

"Well, he's a one-er! Good many of you we wish would desert. — No; we ain't going home till we go through Richmond."

"Well," said Allan politely, "first and last, a good many folk have settled hereabouts since Captain John Smith traded on the Chickahominy with the Indians. There's family graveyards all through these woods. I hope you'll like the country."

The other drank again of the brown water. "It wasn't so bad in the spring time. We thought it was awful lovely at first, all spangled with flowers and birds. — Are you married?"

"No."

"Neither am I. But I'm going to be, when I get back to where I belong. Her name's Flora."

"That's a pretty name."

"Yes, and she's pretty, too —" He half closed his eyes and smiled blissfully, then rose from the laurels. "Well, I must be trotting along, away from Cold Harbour. Funniest names! What does it mean?"

"It was an inn, long ago, where you got only cold fare. Shouldn't wonder if history isn't going to repeat itself —" He rose, also, tall and blonde. "Well, I must be travelling, too —"

"Rations getting pretty low, aren't they? How about coffee?"

"Oh, one day," said Allan, "we're going to drink a lot of it! No, I don't know that they are especially low."

The blue scout dipped a hand into his pocket. "Well, I've got a packet of it, and there's plenty more where that came from. —. Catch, Reb!"

Allan caught it. "You're very good, Yank. Thank you."

"Have you got any quinine?"

"No."

The blue scout tossed across a small box. "There's for you! No, I don't want it. We've got plenty. — Well, good-bye."

"I hope you'll get back safe," said Allan, "and have a beautiful wedding."

The blue vanished in the underbrush, the grey went on his way through the heavy forest. He was moving now toward sound, heavy, increasing, presaging a realm of jarred air and ringing ear-drums. Ahead, he saw a column of swiftly moving troops. Half running, he overtook the rear file. "Scout?" — "Yes — Stonewall Brigade —" "All right! all right! This is A. P. Hill's division. — Going into battle. Come on, if you want to."

Through the thinning woods showed a great open plain, with knolls where batteries were planted. The regiment to which Allan had attached himself lay down on the edge of the wood, near one of the cannon-crowned eminences. Allan stretched himself beneath a black gum at the side of the road. Everywhere was a rolling smoke, everywhere terrific sound. A battery thundered by at a gallop, six horses to each gun, straining, red-nostrilled, fiery-eyed. It struck across a corner of the plain. Over it burst the shells, twelve-pounders — twenty-pounders. A horse went down — the drivers cut the traces. A caisson was struck, exploded with frightful glare and sound. About it, when the smoke cleared, writhed men and horses, but the gun was dragged off. Through the rain of shells the battery gained a lift of ground, toiled up it, placed the guns, unlimbered and began to fire. A South Carolina brigade started with a yell from the woods to the right, tore in a dust cloud across the old fields, furrowed with gullies, and was swallowed in the forest about the creek which laved the base of the Federal position. This rose from the level like a Gibraltar, and about it now beat a wild shouting and rattle of musketry. Allan rose to his knees, then to his feet, then, drawn as by a magnet, crept through a finger of sumach and sassafras, outstretched from the wood, to a better vantage point just in rear of the battery.

Behind him, through the woods, came a clatter of horses' hoofs. It was met and followed by cheering. Turning his head, he saw a general and his staff, and though he had never seen Lee he knew that this was Lee, and himself began to cheer. The commander-in-chief lifted his grey hat, came down the dim, overarched, aisle-like road, between the cheering troops. With his staff he left the wood for the open, riding beneath the shelter by the finger of sumach and sassafras, toward the battery. He saw Allan, and reined up iron-grey Traveller. "You do not belong to this regiment. — A scout? General Jackson's? — Ah, well, I expect General Jackson to strike those people on the right any moment now!" He rode up to the battery. The shells were raining, bursting above, around. In the shelter of the hill the battery horses had at first, veteran, undisturbed, cropped the parched grass, but now one was wounded and now another. An arm was torn from a gunner. A second, stooping over a limber chest, was struck between the shoulders, crushed, flesh and bone, into pulp. The artillery captain came up to the general-in-chief. "General Lee, won't you go away? Gentlemen, won't you tell him that there's danger?"

The staff reinforced the statement, but without avail. General Lee shook his head, and with his field-glasses continued to gaze toward the left, whence should arise the dust, the smoke, the sound of Jackson's flanking movement. There was no sign on the left, but here, in the centre, the noise from the woods beyond the creek was growing infernal. He lowered the glass. "Captain Chamberlayne, will you go tell General Longstreet —"

Out of the thunder-filled woods, back from creek and swamp and briar and slashing, from abattis of bough and log, from the shadow of that bluff head with its earthworks one above the other, from the scorching flame of twenty batteries and the wild singing of the minies, rushed the South Carolina troops. The brigadier — Maxey Gregg — the regimental, the company officers, with shouts, with appeals, with waved swords, strove to stop the rout. The command rallied, then broke again. Hell was in the wood, and the men's faces were grey and drawn. "We must rally those troops!" said Lee, and galloped forward. He came into the midst of the disordered throng. "Men, men! Remember your State — Do your duty!" They recognized him, rallied, formed on the colours, swept past him with a cheer and reëntered the deep and fatal wood.

The battery in front of Allan began to suffer dreadfully. The horses grew infected with the terror of the plain. They jerked their heads back; they neighed mournfully; some left the grass and began to gallop aimlessly across the field. The shells came in a stream, great, hurtling missiles. Where they struck flesh or ploughed into the earth, it was with a deadened sound; when they burst in air, it

was like crackling thunder. The blue sky was gone. A battle pall
wrapped the thousands and thousands of men, the guns, the horses,
forest, swamp, creeks, old fields; the great strength of the Federal
position, the grey brigades dashing against it, hurled back like
Atlantic combers. It should be about three o'clock, Allan
thought, but he did not know. Every nerve was tingling, the blood
pounding in his veins. Time and space behaved like waves charged
with strange driftwood. He felt a mad excitement, was sure that if
he stood upright or tried to walk he would stagger. An order ran
down the line of the brigade he had adopted. *Attention!*

He found himself on his feet and in line, steady, clear of head as
though he trod the path by Thunder Run. *Forward! March!* The
brigade cleared the wood, and in line of battle passed the exhausted
battery. Allan noted a soldier beneath a horse, a contorted, purple,
frozen face held between the brute's fore-legs. The air was filled with
whistling shells; the broom sedge was on fire. *Right shoulder. Shift
Arms! Charge!*

Somewhere, about halfway over the plain, he became convinced
that his right leg from the hip down was gone to sleep. He had an
idea that he was not keeping up. A line passed him — another; he
must n't let the others get ahead! and for a minute he ran quite rapidly. There was a yellow, rain-washed gulley before him; the charge
swept down one side and up the other. This crack in the earth was
two thirds of the way across the open; beyond were the wood, the
creek, the abattis, the climbing lines of breastworks, the thirty-five
thousand in blue, and the tremendous guns. The grey charge was
yelling high and clear, preparing to deliver its first fire; the air a
roar of sound and a glaring light. Allan went down one side of the
gulley with some ease, but it was another thing to climb the other.
However, up he got, almost to the top — and then pitched forward,
clutching at the growth of sedge along the crest. It held him steady,
and he settled into a rut of yellow earth and tried to think it over.
Endeavouring to draw himself a little higher, a minie ball went
through his shoulder. The grey charge passed him, roaring on to
the shadowy wood.

He helped himself as best he could, staunched some blood, drew
his own conclusions as to his wounds. He was not suffering much;
not over much. By nature he matched increasing danger with

increasing coolness. All that he especially wanted was for that charge to succeed — for the grey to succeed. His position here, on the rim of the gully, was an admirable one for witnessing all that the shifting smoke might allow to be witnessed. It was true that a keening minie or one of the monstrous shells might in an instant shear his thread of life, probably would do so; all the probabilities lay that way. But he was cool and courageous, and had kept himself ready to go. An absorbing interest in the field of Gaines's Mill, a passionate desire that Victory should wear grey, dominated all other feeling. Half in the seam of the gully, half in the sedge at the top, he made himself as easy as he could and rested a spectator.

The battle smoke, now heavily settling, now drifting like clouds before a wind, now torn asunder and lifting from the scene, made the great field to come and go in flashes, or like visions of the night. He saw that A. P. Hill was sending in his brigades, brigade after brigade. He looked to the left whence should come Jackson, but over there, just seen through the smoke, the forest stood sultry and still. Behind him, however, in the wood at the base of the armed hill, there rose a clamour and deep thunder as of Armageddon. Like a grey wave broken against an iron shore, the troops with whom he had charged streamed back disordered, out of the shadowy wood into the open, where in the gold sedge lay many a dead man and many a wounded. Allan saw the crimson flag with the blue cross shaken, held on high, heard the officers crying, "Back, men, back! Virginians, do your duty!" The wave formed again. He tried to rise so that he might go with it, but could not. It returned into the wood. Before him, racing toward the gully, came another wave — Branch's brigade, yelling as it charged. He saw it a moment like a grey wall, with the colours tossing, then it poured down into the gully and up and past him. He put up his arms to shield his face, but the men swerved a little and did not trample him. The worn shoes, digging into the loose earth covered him with dust. The moving grey cloth, the smell of sweat-drenched bodies, of powder, of leather, of hot metal, the panting breath, the creak and swing, the sudden darkening, heat and pressure — the passage of that wave took his own breath from him, left him white and sick. Branch went on. He looked across the gully and saw another wave coming — Pender, this time. Pender came without yelling, grim and grey and close-mouthed. Pender had suffered before Beaver Dam Creek; to-day there was not much more than half a brigade. It, too, passed, a determined wave. Allan saw Field in the distance coming up. He was tormented with thirst. Three yards from the gully lay stretched the trunk of a man, the legs blown away. He was almost sure he caught the glint of a canteen. He lay flat in the sedge and dragged himself to the corpse. There was the canteen, indeed; marked with a great U. S., spoil taken perhaps at Williamsburg or at Seven Pines. It was empty, drained dry as a bone. There was another man near. Allan dragged himself on. He thought this one dead, too, but when he reached him he opened large blue eyes and breathed, "Water!" Allan sorrowfully shook his head. The blue eyes did not wink nor close, they glazed and stayed open. The scout dropped beside the body, exhausted. Field's charge passed over him. When he opened his eyes, this portion of the plain was like a sea between cross winds. All the broken waves were wildly tossing. Here they recoiled, fled, even across the gully; here they seethed, inchoate; there, regathering form and might, they readvanced to the echoing hill, with its three breastworks and its eighty cannon. Death gorged himself in the tangled slashing, on the treacherous banks of the slow-moving creek. A. P. Hill was a superb fighter. He sent in his brigades. They returned, broken; he sent them in again. They went. The 16th and 22d North Carolina passed the three lines of blazing rifles, got to the head of the cliff, found themselves among the guns. In vain. Morrell's artillerymen, Morrell's infantry, pushed them back and down, down the hillside, back into the slashing. The 35th Georgia launched itself like a thunderbolt and pierced the lines, but it, too, was hurled down. Gregg's South Carolinians and Sykes Regulars locked and swayed. Archer and Pender, Field and Branch, charged and were repelled, to charge again. Save in marksmanship, the Confederate batteries could not match the Federal; strength was with the great, blue rifled guns, and yet the grey cannoneers wrought havoc on the plateau and amid the breastworks. The sound was enormous, a complex tumult that crashed and echoed in the head. The whole of the field existed in the throbbing, expanded brain — all battlefields, all life, all the world and other worlds, all problems solved and insoluble. The wide-flung grey battlefront was now sickle-shaped, convex to the foe. The rolling dense smoke flushed momently with a lurid glare. In places the forest was afire, in others the stubble of the field. From horn to horn of the sickle galloped the riderless horses. Now and again a wounded one among them screamed fearfully.

Allan dragged himself back to the gully. It was safer there, because the charging lines must lessen speed, break ranks a little; they would not be so resistlessly borne on and over him. He was not light-headed, or he thought he was not. He lay on the rim of the gully that was now trampled into a mere trough of dust, and he looked at the red light on the rolling vapour. Where it lifted he saw, as in a pageant, war in mid-career. Sound, too, had organized. He could have beaten time to the gigantic rhythm. It rose and sank; it was made up of groaning, shouting, breathing of men, gasping, and the sounds that horses make, with louder and louder the thunder of the inanimate, the congregated sound of the allies man had devised, — the saltpetre he had digged, the powder he had made, the rifles he had manufactured, the cannon he had moulded, the solid shot, grape, canister, shrapnel, minie balls. The shells were fearful, Allan was fain to acknowledge. They passed like whistling winds. They filled the air like great rocks from a blasting. The staunchest troops blanched a little, jerked the head sidewise as the shells burst and showered ruin. There came into Allan's mind a picture in the old geography, — rocks thrown up by Vesuvius. He thought he was speaking to the geography class. "I'll show you how they look. I was lying, you see, at the edge of the crater, and they were all overhead." The picture passed away, and he began to think that the minies' unearthly shriek was much like the winter wind round Thunder Run Mountain — Sairy and Tom — Was Sairy baking gingerbread? — Of course not; they did n't have gingerbread now. Besides, you did n't want gingerbread when you were thirsty. . . . *Oh, water, water, water, water!* . . . Tom might be taking the toll — if there was anybody to pay it, and if they kept the roads up. Roses in bloom, and the bees in them and over the pansies. . . . The wrens sang, and Christianna came down the road. Roses and pansies, with their funny little faces, and Sairy's blue gingham apron and the blue sky. The water-bucket on the porch, with the gourd. He began to mutter a little. "Time to take in, children — did n't you hear the bell? I rang it loudly. I am ringing it now. Listen! Loud, loud

— like church bells — and cannons. The old lesson. . . . Curtius and the gulf."

In the next onrush a man stumbled and came to his knees beside him. Not badly hurt, he was about to rise. Allan caught his arm. "For God's sake — if you've got any water —" The man, a tall Alabamian, looked down, nodded, jerked loose another U. S. canteen, and dropped it into the other's hand. "All right, all right — not at all — not at all —" He ran on, joining the hoar and shouting wave. Allan, the flask set to his lips, found not water, but a little cold and weak coffee. It was nectar — it was happiness — it was life — though he could have drunk ten times the amount!

The cool draught and the strength that was in it revived him, drew his wandering mind back from Thunder Run to Gaines's Mill. Again he wished to know where was the Army of the Valley. It might be over there, in the smoke pall, turning Fitz John Porter's right . . . but he did not believe it. Brigade after brigade had swept past him, had been broken, had reformed, had again swept by into the wood that was so thick with the dead. A. P. Hill continued to hurl them in, standing, magnificent fighter! his eyes on the dark and bristling stronghold. On the hill, behind the climbing breastworks and the iron giants atop, Fitz John Porter, good and skilful soldier, withdrew from the triple lines his decimated regiments, put others in their places, scoured with the hail of his twenty-two batteries the plain of the Confederate centre. All the attack was here — all the attack was here — and the grey brigades were thinning like mist wreaths. The dead and wounded choked field and gully and wood and swamp. Allan struck his hands together. What had happened — what was the matter? How long had he lain here? Two hours, at the least — and always it was A. P. Hill's battle, and always the grey brigades with a master courage dashed themselves against the slope of fire, and always the guns repelled them. It was growing late. The sun could not be seen. Plain and woods were darkening, darkening and filled with groaning. It was about him like a melancholy wind, the groaning. He raised himself on his hands and saw how many indeed were scattered in the sedge, or in the bottom of the yellow gully, or slanted along its sides. He had not before so loudly heard the complaining that they made, and for a moment the brain wondered why. Then he was aware that the air was less filled with missiles, that the long musketry rattle and the baying of the war dogs was a little hushed. Even as he marked this the lull grew more and more perceptible. He heard the moaning of the wounded, because now the ear could take cognizance.

The shadow deepened. A horse, with a blood-stained saddle, unhurt himself, approached him, stood nickering for a moment, then panic-struck again, lashed out with his heels and fled. All the plain, the sedge below, the rolling canopy above, was tinged with reddish umber. The sighing wind continued, but the noise of firing died and died. For all the moaning of the wounded, there seemed to fall a ghastly silence.

Over Allan came a feeling as of a pendulum forever stopped, as of Time but a wreck on the shore of Space, and Space a deserted coast, an experiment of some Power who found it ineffective and tossed it away. The Now and Here, petrified forever, desolate forever, an obscure bubble in the sea of being, a faint tracing on the eternal Mind to be overlaid and forgotten — here it rested, and would rest. The field would stay and the actors would stay, both forever as they were, standing, lying, in motion or at rest, suffering, thirsting, tasting the sulphur and feeling the heat, held here forever in a vise, grey shadows suffering like substance, knowing the lost battle. . . . A deadly weakness and horror came over him. "O God! — Let us die —"

From the rear, to A. P. Hill's right, where was Longstreet, broke a faint yelling. It grew clearer, came nearer. From another direction — from the left — burst a like sound, increasing likewise, high, wild, and clear. Like a breath over the field went the conviction — *Jackson — Jackson at last!* Allan dropped in the broom sedge, his arm beneath his head. The grey sleeve was wet with tears. The pendulum was swinging; he was home in the dear and dread world.

The sound increased; the earth began to shake with the tread of men; the tremendous guns began again their bellowing. Longstreet swung into action, with the brigades of Kemper, Anderson, Pickett, Willcox, Pryor, and Featherstone. On the left, with his own division, with Ewell's, with D. H. Hill's, Jackson struck at last like Jackson. Whiting, with two brigades, should have been with Jackson, but, missing his way in the wood, came instead to Longstreet, and with him entered the battle. The day was descending. All the plain was smoky or luridly lit; a vast Shield of Mars, with War in action. With Longstreet and with Jackson up at last, Lee put forth his full strength. Fifty thousand men in grey, thirty-five thousand men in blue, were at once engaged — in three hundred years there had been in the Western Hemisphere no battle so heavy as this one. The artillery jarred even the distant atmosphere, and the high mounting clouds were tinged with red. Six miles away, Richmond listened aghast.

Allan forgot his wounds, forgot his thirst, forgot the terror, sick and cold, of the minute past. He no longer heard the groaning. The storm of sound swept it away. He was a fighter with the grey; all his soul was in the prayer. "Let them come! Let them conquer!" He thought, *Let the war bleed and the mighty die.* He saw a charge approaching. Willingly would he have been stamped into the earth would it further the feet on their way. The grey line hung an instant, poised on the further rim of the gully, then swept across and onward. Until the men were by him, it was thick night, thick and stifling. They passed. He heard the yelling as they charged the slope, the prolonged tremendous rattle of musketry, the shouts, the foiled assault, and the breaking of the wave. Another came, a wall of darkness in the closing day. Over it hung a long cloud, red-stained. Allan prayed aloud. "O God of Battles — O God of Battles —"

The wave came on. It resolved itself into a moving frieze, a wide battle line of tall men, led by a tall, gaunt general, with blue eyes and flowing, tawny hair. In front was the battle-flag, red ground and blue cross. Beside it dipped and rose a blue flag with a single star. The smoke rolled above, about the line. Bursting overhead, a great shell lit all with a fiery glare. The frieze began to sing.

> " The race is not to them that's got
> The longest legs to run,
> Nor the battle to that people
> That shoots the biggest gun —"

Allan propped himself upon his hands. "Fourth Texas! Fourth Texas! — Fourth —"

The frieze rushed down the slope of the gully, up again, and on. A foot came hard on Allan's hand. He did not care. He had a vision of keen, bronze faces, hands on gun-locks. The long, grey legs went by him with a mighty stride. Gun-barrel and bayonet gleamed like moon on water. The battle-flag with the cross, the flag with the single star, spread red and blue wings. Past him they sped, gigantic, great ensigns of desperate valour, war goddesses, valkyries, . . . rather the great South herself, the eleven States, Rio Grande to Chesapeake, Potomac to the Gulf! All the shells were bursting, all the drums were thundering —

The Texans passed, he sank prone on the earth. Other waves he knew were following — all the waves! Jackson with Ewell, Longstreet, the two Hills. He thought he saw his own brigade — saw the Stonewall. But it was in another quarter of the field, and he could not call to it. All the earth was rocking like a cradle, blindly swinging in some concussion and conflagration as of world systems.

As dusk descended, the Federal lines were pierced and broken. The Texans made the breach, but behind them stormed the other waves, — D. H. Hill, Ewell, the Stonewall Brigade, troops of Longstreet. They blotted out the triple breastworks; from north, west, and south they mounted in thunder upon the plateau. They gathered to themselves here twenty-two guns, ten thousand small arms, twenty-eight hundred prisoners. They took the plateau. Stubbornly fighting, Fitz John Porter drew off his exhausted brigades, plunged downward through the forest, toward the Chickahominy. Across that river, all day long McClellan, with sixty-five thousand men, had rested behind earthworks, bewildered by Magruder, demonstrating in front of Richmond with twenty-eight thousand. Now, at the twelfth hour, he sent two brigades, French and Meagher.

Night fell, black as pitch. The forest sprang dense, from miry soil. The region was one where Nature set traps. In the darkness it was not easy to tell friend from foe. Grey fired on grey, blue on blue. The blue still pressed, here in disorder, here with a steady front, toward the grapevine bridge across the Chickahominy. French and Meagher arrived to form a strong rearguard. Behind, on the plateau, the grey advance paused, uncertain in the darkness and in its mortal fatigue. Here, and about the marshy creek and on the vast dim field beyond, beneath the still hanging battle cloud, lay, of the grey and the blue, fourteen thousand dead and wounded. The sound of their suffering rose like a monotonous wind of the night.

CHAPTER XXXIII

THE HEEL OF ACHILLES

THE Stonewall Brigade, a unit in Jackson's advance, halted on the plateau near the McGehee house. All was dark, all was confused. In the final and general charge, regiments had become separated from brigades, companies from regiments. Fragments of many commands were on the plateau, — Whiting, Ewell, D. H. Hill, Jackson's own division, portions of Longstreet's brigades, even a number of A. P. Hill's broken, exhausted fighters. Many an officer lay silent or moaning, on the scarped slope, in the terrific tangle about the creek, or on the melancholy plain beyond. Captains shouted orders in the colonels' places; lieutenants or sergeants in the captains'. Here, on the plateau, where for hours the blue guns had thundered, the stars were seen but dimly through the smoke. Bodies of men, and men singly or in twos and threes, wandered like ghosts in Hades. "This way, Second Virginia!" "Fall in here, Hood's Texans!" — "Hampton's men, over here!" — "Fifteenth Alabama! Fifteenth Alabama!" — "I'm looking for the Milledgeville Hornets." — "Iverson's men! Iverson's men!" — "Fall in here, Cary's Legion!" — "First Maryland!"— "Fifth Virginia over here!" — "Where in hell is the Eleventh Mississippi!" — "Lawton! Lawton!" — "Sixty-fifth Virginia, fall in here!"

East and south, sloping toward the Chickahominy, ran several miles of heavy forest. It was filled with sound, — the hoofs of horses, the rumbling of wheels, the breaking through undergrowth of masses of men, — sound that was dying in volume, rolling toward the Chickahominy. On the trampled brow of the plateau, beneath shot-riddled trees, General D. H. Hill, coming from the northern face, found General Winder of the First Brigade standing with several of his officers, trying to pierce the murk toward the river. "You rank here, General Winder?" said Hill.

"I think so, general. Such a confusion of troops I have never seen! They have been reporting to me. It is yours now to command."

"Have you seen General Jackson?"

"No. Not lately."

D. H. Hill looked toward the Chickahominy. "I don't deny it's temptatious! And yet. . . . Very dark. Thick woods. Don't know what obstructions. Men exhausted. Our centre and right not come up. Artillery still across the swamp — What's that cheering toward the river?"

"I don't know. McClellan may have sent reinforcements."

"Have you pickets out?"

"Yes. What do you think, Cleave?"

"I think, sir, the rout outweighs the reinforcements. I think we should press on at once."

"If we had cavalry!" said Winder impatiently. "However, General Stuart has swept down toward the Pamunkey. That will be their line of retreat — to the White House."

"There is the chance," said Cleave, "that General McClellan will abandon that line, and make instead for the James and the gunboats at Harrison's Landing."

Hill nodded. "Yes, it's a possibility. General Lee is aware of it. He'll not unmask Richmond and come altogether on this side the Chickahominy until he knows. All that crowd down there may set to and cross to-night —"

"How many bridges?" asked Lawton.

"Alexander's and Grapevine. Woodbury's higher up."

"I do not believe that there are three, sir. There is a report that two are burned. I believe that the Grapevine is their only road —"

"You believe, colonel, but you do not know. What do you think, General Winder?"

"I think, sir, with Colonel Cleave, that we should push down through the woods to the right of the Grapevine Bridge. They, too, are exhausted, their horses jaded, their ammunition spent. We could gather a little artillery — Poague's battery is here. They are crushed together, in great masses. If we could fall upon them, cause a great panic there at the water, much might come of it."

Hill looked with troubled eyes about the plateau. "And two or three thousand men, perhaps, be swallowed up and lost! A grand charge that took this plateau — yes! and a grand charge at Beaver Dam Creek yesterday at dark, and a grand charge when Albert

Sidney Johnston was killed, and a grand charge when Ashby was killed, and on a number of other occasions, and now a grand night-time charge with worn-out troops. All grand — just the kind of grandeur the South cannot afford! . . . An army yet of blue troops and fresh, shouting brigades, and our centre and right on the other side of the creek. . . . I don't dare do it, gentlemen! — not on my own responsibility. What do you think, General Lawton?"

"I think you are right, sir."

"More and more troops are coming upon the plateau," said Winder. "General Hill, if you will order us to go we will see to it that you do not repent —"

"They are defeated and retreating, sir," said Cleave. "If they are crossing the river, it is at least in the realm of probability that they have but the one path. No one knows better than you what resolute pressure might now accomplish. Every moment that we wait they gain in steadiness, and other reserves will come up. Make their junction with their centre, and to-morrow we fight a terrific battle where to-night a lesser struggle might secure a greater victory."

"Speaking largely, that is true," said Hill. "But — I wish General Jackson were here! I think you know, gentlemen, that, personally, I could wish, at this minute, to be down there in the woods, beside the Grapevine Bridge. But with the knowledge that the enemy is bringing up reserves, with the darkness so thick, with no great force, and that exhausted, and with no artillery, I cannot take the responsibility of the advance. If General Jackson were here —"

"May I send in search of him, sir?"

"Yes, General Winder, you may do that. And if he says, 'Go!' there won't one of you be happier than I."

"We know that, general. — Cleave, I am going to send you. You're far the likeliest. We want him to come and lead us to the completest victory. By God, we want Front Royal and Port Republic again!"

Cleave, turning, disappeared into the darkness. "See to your men, General Winder. Get them ready," said Hill. "I'm going a little way into the woods to see what I can see myself." He went, Lawton with him. Before many minutes had passed they were back. "Nearly walked into their lines! Strung across the Grapevine road.

Massed thick between us and the Chickahominy. Scattered like acorns through the woods. Pretty miserable, I gather. Passed party hunting water. Speech bewrayeth the man, so did n't say anything. Heard the pickets talking. 'T was Meagher and French came up. They 're building great fires by the water. Looks as though they meant to cross. Nothing of General Jackson yet?"

"No, sir. Not yet."

"Well, I 'm going into the house for a morsel of food. Send for me the moment you hear anything. I wish the artillery were up. Who 's this? Colonel Fauquier Cary? In the darkness, could n't tell. Yes, General Winder thinks so, too. We 've sent to ask General Jackson. Come with me, Cary, to the house. Faugh! this stifling heat! And that was Sykes we were fighting against — George Sykes! Remember he was my roommate at the Point?"

The short path to McGehee's house was not trodden without difficulty. All the great plateau was cumbered with débris of the struggle. On the cut and furrowed ground one stumbled upon abandoned stores and arms. There were overturned wagons and ambulances with dead horses; there were ruined gun-carriages; there were wrecked litters, fallen tents, dead men and the wounded. Here, and on the plain below, the lanterns of the surgeons and their helpers moved like glowworms. They gathered the wounded, blue and grey. "Treat the whole field alike," had said Lee. Everywhere were troops seeking their commands, hoarsely calling, joining at last their comrades. Fires had been kindled. Dim, dim, in the southwestern sky beyond the yet rolling vapour, showed a gleaming where was Richmond. D. H. Hill and Fauquier Cary went indoors. An aide managed to find some biscuits, and there was water from the well. "I have n't touched food since daybreak," said the general.

"Nor I. Much as I like him, I am loath to let Fitz John Porter strike down the York River line to-night, if that 's his road, or cross the Chickahominy if that 's the road! We have a victory. Press it home and fix it there."

"I believe that you are right. Surely Jackson will see it so."

"Where is General Jackson?"

"God knows! — Thank you, Reid. Poor fare, Cary, but familiar Come, Reid, get your share."

They ate the hard biscuits and drank the well-water. The air was still and sultry; through the windows they heard, afar off, the bugles — their own and those of the foe.

"High over all the melancholy bugle grieves."

Moths came in to the candle. With his hand Cary warned them away. One lit on his sleeve. "I wonder what you think of it," he said, and put him out of window. There was a stir at the door. A sergeant appeared. "We're gathering up the wounded, general — and we found a Yankee officer under the trees just here — and he said you'd know him — but he's fainted dead away —" He moved aside. "Litters gave out long ago, so we're taking U. S. blankets —"

Four men, carrying by the corners a blanket with an unconscious man upon it, came into the room. The Confederate officers looked. "No, I don't know him. Why, wait — Yes, I do! It's Clitz — Clitz that was so young and red-cheeked and our pet at the Point! . . . Yes, and one day in Mexico his regiment filed past, going into a fight, and he looked so like a gallant boy that I prayed to God that Clitz might not be hurt! . . . Reid, have him put in a room here! See that Dr. Mott sees him at once. — O God, Cary, this fratricidal war! Fighting George Sykes all day, and now this boy —"

"Yes," said Cary. "Once to-day I was opposed to Fitz John Porter. He looked at me out of a cloud, and I looked at him out of one, and the battle roared between. I always liked him." He walked across the room, looked out of the window upon the battlefield, and came back. "But," he said grimly, "it is a war of invasion. What do you think is wrong with Jackson?"

The other looked at him with his fine, kindly eyes. "Why, let me tell you, Cary, — since it won't go any further, — I am as good a Presbyterian as he is, but I think he has prayed too much."

"I see!" said Cary. "Well, I would be willing to put up a petition of my own just now. — Delay! Delay! We have set opportunity against a wall and called out the firing party." He rose. "Thanks for the biscuits. I feel another man. I'll go now and look after my wounded. There are enough of them, poor souls!"

Another stir occurred at the door. The aide appeared. "They've taken some prisoners in the wood at the foot of the hill, sir. One of them says he's General Reynolds —"

"Reynolds! Good God, Reynolds! Bring him in —"

General Reynolds came in. "Reynolds!" — "Hill!" — "How are you, Reynolds?" — "Good Lord, it's Fauquier Cary!"

The aide put a chair. The prisoner sank into it and covered his face with his hands. Presently he let them drop. "Hill, we ought not to be enemies! Messmates and tent-mates for a year! . . . It's ghastly."

"I'll agree with you there, Reynolds. It's ghastlier than ghastly. — You aren't hurt?"

Outside, over the great hilltop upon which Richard Cleave was moving, the darkness might be felt. The air smelled strongly of burned powder, was yet thickened by smoke. Where fires had been kindled, the ruddy light went up like pillars to sustain a cloudy roof. There were treetops, burnished, high in air; then all the land fell to the swampy shores of the creek, and beyond to the vast and sombre battle plain, where the shells had rained. The masses of grey troops upon it, resting on their arms, could be divined by the red points of camp-fires. Lanterns, also, were wandering like marsh lights, up and down and to and fro. Here, on the plateau, it was the same. They danced like giant fireflies. He passed a blazing log, about which were gathered a dozen men. Some wag of the mess had said something jocular; to a man they were laughing convulsively. Had they been blamed, they would perhaps have answered that it was better to laugh than to cry. Cleave passed them with no inclination to blame, and came to where, under the trees, the 65th was gathered. Here, too, there were fires; his men were dropped like acorns on the ground, making a little "coosh," frying a little bacon, attending to slight hurts, cognizant of the missing but not referring to them loudly, glad of victory, burying all loss, with a wide swing of courage making the best of it in the darkness. When they saw Cleave they suspended all other operations long enough to cheer him. He smiled, waved his hand, spoke a short word to Hairston Breckinridge, and hurried on. He passed the 2d Virginia, mourning its colonel — Colonel Allen — fallen in the front of the charge. He passed other bivouacs — men of Rodes's, of Garland's, of Trimble's. "Where is General Jackson?" — "Can't tell you, sir —" "Here is General Ewell."

"Old Dick" squatted by a camp-fire, was broiling a bit of bacon, head on one side, as he looked up with bright round eyes at Cleave, whom he liked. "That you, Richard Cleave? By God, sir, if I were as excellent a major-general as I am a cook! — Have a bit? — Well, we wolloped them! They fought like men, and we fought like men, and by God, I can't get the cannon out of my ears! General Jackson? — I thought he was in front with D. H. Hill. Going to do anything more to-night? It's pretty late, but I'm ready."

"Nothing — without General Jackson," said Cleave. "Thank you, general — if I might have a mouthful of coffee? I have n't the least idea when I have eaten."

Ewell handed him the tin cup. He drank hastily and went on. Now it was by a field hospital, ghastly sights and ghastly sounds, pine boughs set for torches. He shut his eyes in a moment's faintness. It looked a demoniac place, a smoke-wreathed platform in some Inferno circle. He met a staff officer coming up from the plain. "General Lee has ridden to the right. He is watching for McClellan's next move. There's a rumour that everything's in motion toward the James. If it's true, there's a chase before us to-morrow, eh? — A. P. Hill suffered dreadfully. 'Prince John' kept McClellan beautifully amused. — General Jackson? On the slope of the hill by the breastworks."

A red light proclaimed the place as Cleave approached it. It seemed a solitary flame, night around it and a sweep of scarped earth. Cleave, coming into the glow, found only the old negro Jim, squat beside it like a gnome, his eyes upon the jewelled hollows, his lips working. Jim rose. "De gineral, sah? De gineral done sont de staff away ter res'. Fo' de Lawd, de gineral bettah follah dat 'zample! Yaas, sah, — ober dar in de big woods."

Cleave descended the embankment and entered a heavy wood. A voice spoke — Jackson's — very curtly. "Who is it, and what is your business?"

"It is the colonel of the 65th Virginia, sir. General Winder sends me, with the approval of General D. H. Hill, from the advance by the McGehee house."

A part of the shadow detached itself and came forward as Jackson. It stalked past Cleave out of the belt of trees and over the bare red earth to the fire. The other man followed, and in the glare faced the general again. The leaping flame showed Jackson's bronzed face, with the brows drawn down, the eyes looking inward, and the lips closed as though no force could part them. Cleave knew the look, and inwardly set his own lips. At last the other spoke. "Well, sir?"

"The enemy is cramped between us and the Chickahominy, sir. Our pickets are almost in touch of theirs. If we are scattered and disorganized, they are more so, — confused — distressed. We are the victors, and the troops still feel the glow of victory."

"Well?"

"There might be a completer victory. We need only you to lead us, sir."

"You are mistaken. The men are wearied. They worked very hard in the Valley. They need not do it all."

"They are not so wearied, sir. There is comment, I think, on what the Army of the Valley has not done in the last two days. We have our chance to refute it all to-night."

"General Lee is the commander-in-chief. General Lee will give orders."

"General Lee has said to himself: 'He did so wonderfully in the Valley, I do not doubt he will do as wonderfully here. I leave him free. He'll strike when it is time.' — It is time now, sir."

"Sir, you are forgetting yourself."

"Sir, I wish to rouse you."

Jackson walked past the fire to a fallen tree, sat himself down and looked across to the other man. The low flame more deeply bronzed his face. His eyes looked preternaturally sunken. He sat, characteristically rigid, a figure in grey stone. There was about him a momentary air of an Indian, he looked so ruthless. If it was not that, thought Cleave, then it was that he looked fanatic. Whichever it might be, he perceived that he himself stood in arctic air. He had been liked, he knew; now he saw the mist of disfavour rise. Jackson's voice came gratingly. "Who sent you?"

"General Winder and General D. H. Hill."

"You will tell General Hill that I shall make no further attack to-night. I have other important duties to perform."

"I know what I risk," said Cleave, "and I do not risk it lightly. Have you thought of how you fell on them at Front Royal and at Winchester? Here, too, they are confused, retreating — a greater force to strike, a greater result to win, a greater service to do for the country, a greater name to make for yourself. To-morrow morning all the world may say, 'So struck Napoleon —' "

"Napoleon's confidence in his star was pagan. Only God rules."

"And the man who accepts opportunity — is he not His servant? May we not, sir, may we not make the attack?"

"No, sir; not to-night. We have marred too many Sundays —"

"It is not Sunday!"

Jackson looked across with an iron countenance. "So little the fighter knows! See, what war does! But I will keep, in part at least, the Sabbath. You may go, sir."

"General Jackson, this is Friday evening."

"Colonel Cleave, did you hear my order? Go, sir! — and think yourself fortunate that you do not go under arrest."

"Sir — Sir —"

Jackson rose. "One other word, and I take your sword. It occurs to me that I have indulged you in a freedom that — Go!"

Cleave turned with sharp precision and obeyed. Three paces took him out of the firelight into the overhanging shadow. He made a gesture of sorrow and anger. "Who says that magic's dead? Now, how long will that potion hold him?" He stumbled in the loose, bare earth, swamp and creek below him. He looked down into that trough of death. "I gained nothing, and I have done for myself! If I know him — Ugh!"

He shook himself, went on through the sultry, smoky night, alternate lantern-slides of glare and darkness, to the eastern face of the plateau. Here he found Winder, reported, and with him encountered D. H. Hill coming with Fauquier Cary from the McGehee house. "What's that?" said Hill. "He won't pursue to-night? Very well, that settles it! Maybe they'll be there in the morning, maybe not. Look here, Winder! Reynolds's taken — you remember Reynolds?"

Cary and Cleave had a moment apart. "All well, Fauquier? The general? — Edward?"

"I think so. I saw Warwick for a moment. A minie had hurt his hand — not serious, he said. Edward I have not seen."

"I had a glimpse of him this morning. — This morning!"

"Yes — long ago, is it not? You'll get your brigade after this."

The other looked at him oddly. "Will I? I strongly doubt it. Well, it seems not a large thing to-night."

Beyond the main battlefield where A. P. Hill's and Longstreet's shattered brigades lay on their arms, beyond the small farmhouse where Lee waked and watched, beyond the Chickahominy and its swamps, beyond forest and farm land, lay Richmond under the stars. Eastwardly, within and without its girdling earthworks, that brilliant and histrionic general, John Bankhead Magruder, El Capitan Colorado, with a lisping tongue, a blade like Bayard's, and a talent for drama and strategy, kept General McClellan under the impression, confirmed by the whole Pinkerton force, that "at least eighty thousand men" had remained to guard Richmond, when Lee with "at least eighty thousand men" had crossed the Chickahominy. Richmond knew better, but Richmond was stoically calm as to the possibility of a storming. What it had been hard to be calm over was the sound, this Friday, of the guns beyond the Chickahominy. Mechanicsville, yesterday, was bad enough, but this was frightful. Heavy, continuous, it took away the breath and held the heart in an iron grip. All the loved ones there — all the loved ones there! — and heavier and heavier toward night grew the fearful sound. . . . Then began the coming of the wounded. In the long dusk of the summer evening, the cannonading ceased. A little after nine arrived couriers, announcing the victory. The church bells of Richmond, not yet melted into cannon, began to ring. "It was a victory — it was a victory," said the people to one another. . . . But the wounded continued to come in, ambulance, cart, and wagon rolling like tumbrels over the stones. To many a mother was brought tidings of the death of her son, and many a wife must say, "I am widowed," and many children cried that night for their father. The heat was frightful. The city tossed and moaned, without sleep, or nursed, or watched, or wandered fevered through the streets. The noise of the James around its rocky islands was like the groaning of the distant battlefield. The odour of the June flowers made the city like a chamber of death. All windows were open wide to the air, most houses lighted. Sometimes from these there came forth a sharp cry; sometimes womens' forms, restless in the night, searching again the hospitals. "He might be here." — "He might be at this one." Sometimes, before such or such a house, cart or carriage or wagon stopped. "Oh, God! wounded or —?" All night long fared the processions from the field of Gaines's Mill to the hospitals. Toward dawn it began to be "No room. Try Robinson's — try the De Sales." — "Impossible here! We can hardly step between the rows. The beds gave out long ago. Take him to Miss Sally Tompkins." — "No room. Oh, the pity of it! Take him to the St. Charles or into the first private house. They are all thrown open."

Judith, kept at the Stonewall all the night before, had gone home, bathed, drawn the shutters of her small room, lain down and resolutely closed her eyes. She must sleep, she knew, — must gather strength for the afternoon and night. The house was quiet. Last night the eldest son had been brought in wounded. The mother, her cousin, had him in her chamber; she and his mammy and the old family doctor. His sister, a young wife, was possessed by the idea that her husband might be in one of the hospitals, delirious, unable to tell where he belonged, calling upon her, and no one understanding. She was gone, in the feverish heat, upon her search. There came no sounds from below. After the thunder which had been in the ear, after the sounds of the hospital, all the world seemed as silent as a cavern or as the depth of the sea. Judith closed her eyes, determinedly stilled her heart, drew regular breath, put herself out of Richmond back in a certain cool and green forest recess which she loved, and there wooed sleep. It came at last, with a not unhappy dream. She thought she was walking on the hills back of Greenwood with her Aunt Lucy. The two said they were tired and would rest, and entered the graveyard and sat down upon the bank of ivy beside Ludwell Cary's grave. That was all natural enough; a thing they had done many times. They were taught at Greenwood that there was nothing mournful there. Shells lay about them, beneath the earth, but the beneficent activities had escaped, and were active still, beneficent still. . . . The word "shells" in the dream turned the page. She was upon a great sea beach and quite alone. She sat and looked at the waves coming rolling in, and presently one laid Richard at her feet. She bandaged the cut upon his forehead, and called him by his name, and he looked at her and smiled. "Out of the ocean, into the ocean," he said. "All of us. A going forth and a returning." She felt herself, in the dream, in his arms, and found it sweet. The waves were beneath them; they lay now on the crests, now in the hollows, and there seemed no port. This endured a long while, until she thought she heard the sea-fairies singing. Then there came a booming sound, and she thought, "This is the port, or perhaps it is an island that we are passing." She asked Richard which it was, but he did not answer, and she turned upon the wave and found that he was not there. . . . It was seaweed about her arms. The booming grew louder, rattled the window-glass. She opened her eyes, pushed her dark loosened hair from her arms and bosom, and sat up. "The cannon again!"

She looked at her watch. It was two o'clock. Rising, she put on her dark, thin muslin, and took her shady hat. The room seemed to throb to the booming guns. All the birds had flown from the tulip tree outside. She went downstairs and tapped at her cousin's door. "How is he?" — "Conscious now, thank God, my dear! The doctor says he will be spared. How the house shakes! And Walter and Ronald out there. You are going back?"

"Yes. Do not look for me to-night. There will be so much to be done —"

"Yes, yes, my dear. Louder and louder! And Ronald is so reckless! You must have something to eat."

"Shirley will give me a glass of milk. Tell Rob to get well. Good-bye."

She kissed her cousin, drank her glass of milk in the dining-room where the silver was jingling on the sideboard, and went out into the hot, sound-filled air. At three she was at her post in the hospital.

The intermittent thunder, heavier than any on the continent before, was stilled at last, — at nine, as had happened the night before. The mazed city shook the mist from before its eyes, and settled to the hot night's work, with the wagons, bringing the dead and the wounded, dull on the cobblestones to the ear, but loud, loud to the heart. All that night the Stonewall Hospital was a grisly place. By the next morning every hospital in town was choked with the wounded, and few houses but had their quota. The surgeons looked like wraiths, the nursing women had dark rings beneath their eyes, set burningly in pale faces, the negroes who valiantly helped had a greyish look. More emotional than the whites, they burst now and then into a half wail, half chant. So heavy was the burden, so inadequate the small, beleaguered city's provision for the weight of help-less anguish, that at first there was a moment of paralysis. As easy to strive with the tornado as with this wind of pain and death! Then the people rallied and somewhat outstripped a people's best.

From the troops immediately about the city came the funeral escorts. All day the Dead March from "Saul" wailed through the streets, out to Hollywood. The churches stayed open; old and young, every man in the city, white or black, did his part, and so did all the women. The need was so great that the very young girls, heretofore spared, found place now in hospital or house, beside the beds, the pallets, the mere blanket, or no blanket, on the floor. They could keep away the tormenting flies, drawn by the heat, the glare, the blood and effluvia, could give the parched lips water, could watch by the less terrifically hurt. All the city laboured; putting aside the personal anguish, the private loss known, suspected, or but fearfully dreaded. Glad of the victory but with only calamity beneath its eyes, the city wrestled with crowding pain, death, and grief.

Margaret Cleave was at one of the great hospitals. An hour later came, too, Miriam and Christianna. "Yes, you can help. Miriam, you are used to it. Hold this bandage so, until the doctor comes. If it grows blood-soaked — like this one — call some one at once. Christianna, you are strong. — Mrs. Preston, let her have the bucket of water. Go up and down, between the rows, and give water to those who want it. If they cannot lift themselves, help them — so!"

Christianna took the wooden bucket and the tin dipper. For all she looked like a wild rose she was strong, and she had a certain mountain skill and light certainty of movement. She went down the long room, giving water to all who moaned for it. They lay very thick, the wounded, side by side in the heat, the glare of the room, where all the light possible must be had. Some lay outstretched and rigid, some much contorted. Some were delirious, others writhed and groaned, some were most pathetically silent and patient. Nearly all were thirsty; clutched the dipper with burning fingers, drank, with their hollow eyes now on the girl who held it, now on mere space. Some could not help themselves. She knelt beside these, raised the head with one hand, put water to the lips with the other. She gained her mountain steadiness and did well, crooning directions in her calm, drawling voice. This bucket emptied, she found where to fill it again, and pursued her task, stepping lightly between the huddled, painful rows, among the hurrying forms of nurses and surgeons and coloured helpers.

At the very end of the long lane, she came upon a blanket spread on the blood-stained floor. On it lay a man, blond and straight, closed eyes with a line between them, hand across his breast touching his shirt where it was stiff with dried blood. "Air you thirsty?" began Christianna, then set the bucket suddenly down.

Allan opened his eyes. "Very thirsty. . . . I reckon I am lightheaded. I'm not on Thunder Run, am I?"

The frightful day wore on to late afternoon. No guns shook the air in these hours. Richmond understood that, out beyond the entrenchments, there was a pause in the storm. McClellan was leaving his own wonderful earthworks. But would he retreat down the Peninsula by the way he had come, or would he strike across and down the James to his gunboats by Westover? The city gathered that General Lee was waiting to find out. In the mean time the day that was set to the Dead March in "Saul" passed somehow, in the June heat and the odour of flowers and blood.

Toward five o'clock Judith left the Stonewall Hospital. She had not quitted it for twenty-four hours, and she came now into the light and air like a form emerging from Hades, very palely smiling, with the grey of the underworld, its breath and its terror still about her. There was hardly yet a consciousness of fatigue. Twelve hours before she had thought, "If I do not rest a little, I shall fall." But she had not been able to rest, and the feeling had died. For the last twelve she had moved like an automaton, swift, sure, without a thought of herself. It was as though her will stood somewhere far above and swayed her body like a wand. Even now she was going home, because the will said she must; must rest two hours, and come back fresher for the night.

As she came out into the golden light, Cleave left the group of young and old about the door and met her. In the plane along which life now moved, nothing was unnatural; certainly Richmond did not find it so, that a lover and his beloved should thus encounter in the street, a moment between battles. Her dark eyes and his grey ones met. To find him there seemed as natural as it had been in her dream; the street was no more to her than the lonely beach.

They crossed it, went up toward the Capitol Square, and, entering, found a green dip of earth with a bench beneath a linden tree. Behind them rose the terraced slope to the pillared Capitol; as always, in this square children's voices were heard with their answering nurses, and the squirrels ran along the grass or upon the boughs above. But the voices were somewhat distant and the squirrels did not disturb; it was a leafy, quiet nook. The few men or women who passed, pale, distrait, hurrying from one quarter of the city to another, heeded as little as they were heeded. Lovers' meetings — lovers' partings — soldiers — women who loved them — faces pale and grave, yet raised, hands in hands, low voices in leafy places — man and woman together in the golden light, in the breathing space before the cannon should begin again — Richmond was growing used to that. All life was now in public. For the most part a clear altruism swayed the place and time, and in the glow smallness of comment or of thought was drowned. Certainly, it mattered not to Cleave and Judith that it was the Capitol Square, and that people went up and down.

"I have but the shortest while," he said. "I came this morning with Allen's body — the colonel of the 2d. I ride back directly. I hope that we will move to-night."

"Following McClellan?"

"To get across his path, if possible."

"There will be another battle?"

"Yes. More than one, perhaps."

"I have believed that you were safe. I do not see that I could have lived else."

"Many have fallen; many are hurt. I found Allan Gold in the hospital. He will not die, however. . . . Judith, how often do I see your face beside the flag!"

"When I was asleep I dreamed of you. We were drifting together, far out at sea — your arm here —" She lifted his hand, drew his arm about her, rested her head on his breast. "I love you — I love you — I love you."

They stayed in the leafy place and the red-gold light for half an hour, speaking little, sitting sometimes with closed eyes, but hand in hand. It was much as though they were drifting together at sea, understanding perfectly, but weary from battling, and with great issues towering to the inner vision. They would have been less nobly minded had their own passion inexorably claimed them. All about them were suffering and death and the peril of their cause. For one half-hour they drew happiness from the darkly gigantic background, but it was a quiet and lofty form, though sweet, sweet! with whom they companioned. When the time was passed the two rose, and Cleave held her in his arms. "Love — Love —"

When he was gone she waited awhile beneath the trees, then slowly crossed the Capitol Square and moved toward the small room behind the tulip tree. The streets were flooded with a sunset glow. Into Franklin from Main came marching feet, then, dull, dull! the muffled drums. Soldiers and furled colours and the coffin, atop it the dead man's cap and gauntlets and sword; behind, pacing slowly, his war horse, stirrups crossed over saddle. Soldiers, soldiers, and the drums beating like breaking hearts. She moved back to a doorstep and let the Dead March from "Saul" go by.

CHAPTER XXXIV

THE RAILROAD GUN

THE troops, moving at dawn to the Chickahominy, over a road and through woods which testified in many ways of the blue retreat, found the Grapevine Bridge a wreck, the sleepers hacked apart, framework and middle structure cast into the water. Fitz John Porter and the 5th Army Corps were across, somewhere between the river and Savage Station, leaving only, in the thick wood above the stream, a party of sharpshooters and a battery. When the grey pioneers advanced to their work, these opened fire. The bridge must be rebuilt, and the grey worked on, but with delays and difficulties. D. H. Hill, leading Jackson's advance, brought up two batteries and shelled the opposite side. The blue guns and riflemen moved to another position and continued, at short intervals, to fire on the pioneers. It was Sunday the twenty-ninth; fearfully hot by the McGehee house, and on Turkey Hill, and in the dense mid-summer woods, and in the mosquito-breeding bogs and swamps through which meandered the Chickahominy. The river spread out as many arms as Briareus; short, stubby creeks, slow waters prone to overflow and creep, between high knotted roots of live-oak and cypress, into thickets of bog myrtle. The soil hereabouts was black and wet, further back light and sandy. The Valley troops drew the most uncomplimentary comparisons. To a man they preferred mountains, firm rolling champaign, clean rivers with rocky bottoms, sound roads, and a different vegetation. They were not in a good humour, anyhow.

Ewell was at Dispatch Station, seven miles below, guarding Bottom's Bridge and tearing up the York River Railroad. Stuart was before him, sweeping down on the White House, burning McClellan's stations and stores, making that line of retreat difficult enough for an encumbered army. But McClellan had definitely abandoned any idea of return upon Yorktown. The head of his column was set for the James, for Harrison's Landing and the gunboats. There were twenty-five difficult miles to go. He had something like a hundred thousand men. He had five thousand wagons, heavy artillery trains, enormous stores, a rabble of camp followers, a vast, melancholy freight of sick and wounded. He left his camps and burned his depots, and plunged into the heavy, still, and torrid forest. This Sunday morning, the twenty-ninth, the entrenchments before Richmond, skilful, elaborate pieces of engineering, were found by Magruder's and Huger's scouts deserted by all but the dead and a few score of sick and wounded, too far gone to be moved. Later, columns of smoke, rising from various quarters of the forest, betrayed other burning camps or depots. This was followed by tidings which served to make his destination certain. He was striking down toward White Oak Swamp. There the defeated right, coming from the Chickahominy, would join him, and the entire great force move toward the James. Lee issued his orders. Magruder with Huger pursued by the Williamsburg road. A. P. Hill and Longstreet, leaving the battlefield of the twenty-seventh, crossed the Chickahominy by the New Bridge, passed behind Magruder, and took the Darbytown road. A courier, dispatched to Ewell, ordered him to rejoin Jackson. The latter was directed to cross the Chickahominy with all his force by the Grapevine Bridge, and to pursue with eagerness. He had the directest, shortest road; immediately before him the corps which had been defeated at Gaines's Mill. With D. H. Hill, with Whiting and Lawton, he had now fourteen brigades — say twenty thousand men.

The hours passed in languid sunshine on the north bank of the Chickahominy. The troops were under arms, but the bridge was not finished. The smoke and sound of the rival batteries, the crack of the hidden rifles on the southern side, concerned only those immediately at issue and the doggedly working pioneers. Mere casual cannonading, amusement of sharpshooters, no longer possessed the slightest tang of novelty. Where the operation was petty, and a man in no extreme personal danger, he could not be expected to be much interested. The troops yawned; some of the men slept; others fretted. "Why can't we swim the damned old trough? They'll get away! Thank the Lord, I was n't born in Tidewater Virginia! Oh, I'd like to see the Shenandoah!"

The 65th Virginia occupied a rise of sandy ground covered with hazel bushes. Company A had the brink of it, looking out toward the enormously tall trees towering erect from the river's margin of swamp. The hazel bushes gave little shade and kept off the air, the blue above was intense, the buzzards sailing. Muskets were stacked, the men sprawling at ease. A private, who at home was a Sunday School superintendent, read his Bible; another, a lawyer, tickled a hop toad with a spear of grass; another, a blacksmith, rebound the injured ankle of a schoolboy. Some slept, snoring in the scanty shade; some compared diaries or related, scrappily enough, battle experiences. "Yes, and Robinson was scouting, and he was close to Garland's line, and, gosh! he said it was short enough! And Garland rode along it, and he said, said he, 'Boys, you are not many, but you are a noble few.'" Some listened to the booming of the sparring batteries; two or three who had lost close friends or kinsmen moped aside. The frank sympathy of all for these made itself apparent. The shadiest hazel bushes unobtrusively came into their possession; there was an evident intention of seeing that they got the best fare when dinner was called; a collection of tobacco had been taken and quietly pushed their way. Some examined knapsack and haversacks, good oilcloths, belts, rolled blankets, canteens, cartridge-boxes and cartridges, picked up upon the road. Others seriously did incline to search for certain intruders along the seams of shirt and trousers; others merely lay on their backs and looked up into Heaven. Billy Maydew was one of these, and Steve Dagg overturned the contents of a knapsack.

It was well filled, but with things Steve did not want. "O Gawd! picters and pincushions and Testaments with United States flags in them — I never did have any luck, anyhow! — in this here war nor on Thunder Run neither!"

Dave Maydew rolled over. "Steve says Thunder Run did n't like him — Gosh! what's a-going to happen ef Steve takes to telling the truth?"

Sergeant Coffin turned from contemplation of a bursting shell above the Grapevine crossing. "If anybody finds any letter-paper and does n't want it —"

A chorus arose. "Sorry we have n't got any!"— " I have got some —lovely! But I've got a girl, too."—"Sorry, sergeant, but it is n't pale blue, scented with forget-me-nots."—"Just *think* her a letter—

think it out loud! Wait, I'll show you how. *Darling Chloe* — Don't get angry! He's most gotten over getting angry and it becomes him beautifully — *Darling Chloe* — What're *you* coming into it for, Billy Maydew? 'Don't tease him!' — My son, he loves to be teased. All lovers love to be teased. *Darling Chloe.* It is Sunday morning. The swans are warbling your name and so are half a dozen pesky Yankee Parrotts. The gentle zephyrs speak of thee, and so does the hot simoom that blows from Chickahominy, bringing an inordinate number of mosquitoes. I behold thy sinuous grace in the curls of smoke from Reilly's battery, and also in the slide and swoop of black buzzards over a multitude of dead horses in the woods. Darling Chloe, we are stranded on an ant heap which down here they call a hill, and why in hell we don't swim the river is more than at the moment I can tell you. It's rumoured that Old Jack's attending church in the neighbourhood, but we are left outside to praise God from whom all blessings flow. Darling Chloe, this company is not so unpopular with me as once it was. War is teaching it a damned lot, good temper and pretty ways and what not — It is teaching it! Who says it is not? — Darling Chloe, if you could see how long and lean and brown we are and how ragged we are and how lousy — Of course, of course, sergeant, you're not! Only the high private in the rear rank is, and even he says he's not — Darling Chloe, if I could rise like one of those damned crows down there and sail over these damned flats and drop at your feet in God's country beyond the mountains, you would n't walk to church to-day with me. You'd turn up your pretty little nose, and accept the arm of some damned bombproof — Look out! What's the matter here? 'The last straw! shan't slander her!' — I'm not slandering her. I don't believe either she'd do it. Need n't all of you look so glum! I'll take it back. We know, God bless every last woman of them, that they don't do it! They have n't got any more use for a bombproof than we have! — I can't retract handsomer than that! — Darling Chloe, the Company's grown amiable, but it don't think much so far of its part in this campaign. Heretofore in tableaux and amateur theatricals it has had a star rôle, and in this damned Richmond play it's nothing but a walking shadow! Darling Chloe, we want somebody to whoop things up. We demand the centre of the stage —"

It was so hot on the little sandy hill that there was much strag-

gling down through the woods to some one of the mesh of water-
courses. The men nearest Steve were all turned toward the dis-
courser to Chloe, who sat on a lift of sand, cross-legged like an Eastern scribe. Mathew Coffin, near him, looked half pleased, half sulky
at the teasing. Since Port Republic he was a better-liked non-commissioned officer. Billy Maydew, again flat on his back, stared at the
blue sky. Steve stole a tin cup and slipped quietly off through the
hazel bushes.

He found a muddy runlet straying off from the river and quenched
his thirst, then, turning, surveyed through the trees the hump of
earth he had left and the company upon it. Beyond it were other
companies, the regiment, the brigade. Out there it was hot and
glaring, in here there was black, cool, miry loam, shade and water.
Steve was a Sybarite born, and he lingered here. He did n't mean
to straggle, for he was afraid of this country and afraid now of his
colonel; he merely lingered and roamed about a little, beneath the
immensely tall trees and in the thick undergrowth. In doing this
he presently came, over quaking soil and between the knees of cy-
presses, flush with the Chickahominy itself. He sat down, took his
own knees in his arms and looked at it. It was not so wide, but it
looked stiller than the sky, and bottomless. The banks were so low
that the least rain lifted it over. It strayed now, here and there,
between tree roots. There was no such word as "sinister" in Steve's
vocabulary. He only said, "Gawd! I would n't live here for choice!"
The country across the stream engaged his attention. Seen from
this bank it appeared all forest clad, but where his own existence
from moment to moment was in question Steve could read the sign-
boards as well as another. Certain distant, southward moving,
yellowish streaks he pronounced dust clouds. There were roads
beneath, and moving troops and wagon trains. He counted four
columns of smoke of varying thickness. The heavier meant a cluster
of buildings, holding stores probably, the thinner some farmhouse
or barn or mill. From other signs he divined that there were clearings over there, and that the blue troops were burning hayricks and
fences as well as buildings. Sound, too — it seemed deathly still
here on the brim of this dead water, and yet there was sound — the
batteries, of course, down the stream where they built the bridge,
but also a dull, low, dreary murmur from across, — from the thick

forest and the lost roads, and the swamps through which guns were dragged; from the clearings, the corn and wheat fields, the burning depots and encampments and houses of the people—the sound of a hostile army rising from the country where two months before it had settled. All was blended; there came simply a whirring murmur out of the forest beyond the Chickahominy.

Steve rose, yawned, and began again to prowl. Every rood of this region had been in possession of that humming army over there. All manner of desirable articles were being picked up. Orders were strict. Weapons, even injured weapons, ammunition, even half-spoiled ammunition, gun-barrels, ramrods, bayonets, cartridge-boxes, belts — all these must be turned in to the field ordnance officer. The South gleaned her battlefields of every ounce of lead or iron, every weapon or part of a weapon, every manufactured article of war. This done, the men might appropriate or themselves distribute apparel, food, or other matters. Steve, wandering now, his eyes on earth, saw nothing. The black wet soil, the gnarled roots, the gloomy meanders of the stream, looked terribly lonely. "Gawd! even the water-rats don't come here!" thought Steve, and on his way back to the hill entered a thicket of low bushes with shiny green leaves. Here he all but stumbled over a dead soldier in a blue uniform. He lay on his face, arms out, hands clutching at some reed-like grass. His rifle was beside him, haversack— all undisturbed. "Picket," said Steve. "O Gawd, ain't war glorious?"

Not at all without imagination, he had no fondness for touching dead men, but there were several things about this one that he wanted. He saw that the shoes would n't fit, and so he left them alone. His own rifle was back there, stacked with the others on the hot hillside, and he had no intention of bothering with this one. If the ordnance officer wanted it, let him come himself and get it! He exchanged cartridge-boxes, and took the other's rolled oilcloth, and then he looked into the haversack.

Rising to his feet, he glanced about him with quick, furtive, squirrel-like motions of his head. Cool shade, stillness, a creepy loneliness. Taking the haversack, he left the thicket and went back to the brink of Chickahominy. Here he sat down between the cypress knees and drew out of the haversack the prize of prizes. It fixed a grin upon his lean, narrow face, the sight and smell of it, the black, squat bottle. He held it up to the light; it was three quarters full. The cork came out easily; he put it to his lips and drank. "Gawd! it ain't so damned lonely, after all!"

The sun climbed to the meridian. The pioneers wrought as best they might on the Grapevine Bridge. The blue battery and the blue sharpshooters persisted in their hindering, and the grey battery continued to interfere with the blue. In the woods and over the low hills back of the Chickahominy the grey brigades of Stonewall Jackson rested, impatiently wondering, staring at the river, staring at the smoke of conflagrations on the other side and the dust streaks moving southward. Down on the swampy bank, squat between the cypress knees, Steve drank again, and then again, — in fact, emptied the squat, black bottle. The stuff filled him with a tremendous courage, and conferred upon him great fluency of thought. He waxed eloquent to the cypress roots upon the conduct of the war. "Gawd! if they'd listen ter me I'd te — tell them how! — I'd bui — build a bridge for the whole rotten army to cross on! Ef it broke I'd bui — build another. Yah! They don't 'pre — 'preciate a man when they see him. Gawd! they're damn slow, and ain't a man over here got anything to drink! It's all over there." He wept a little. "O Gawd, make them hurry up, so's I kin git across." He put the bottle to his lips and jerked his head far back, but there was not a drop left to trickle forth. He flung it savagely far out into the water. "Ef I thought there was another like you over there —" His courage continued to mount as he went further from himself. He stood up and felt a giant; stretched out his arm and admired the muscle, kicked a clod of black earth into the stream and rejoiced in the swing of his leg. Then he smiled, a satyr-like grin wrinkling the cheek to the ear; then he took off his grey jacket, letting it drop upon the cypress roots; then he waded into the Chickahominy and began to swim to the further shore. The stream was deep but not swift; he was lank and lean but strong, and there was on the other side a pied piper piping of bestial sweetnesses. Several times arms and legs refused to coöperate and there was some likelihood of a death by drowning, but each time instinct asserted herself, righted matters, and on he went. She pulled him out at last, on the southern bank, and he lay gasping among the tree roots, somewhat sobered by the drenching, but still on the whole a courageous giant. He triumphed. "Yah! I got across! Goo' — goo-'bye, ye darned fools squattin' on the hillside!"

He left the Chickahominy and moved through the woods. He went quite at random and with a peculiar gait, his eyes on the ground, looking for another haversack. But just hereabouts there showed nothing of the kind; it was a solemn wood of pines and cedars, not overtrampled as yet by war. Steve shivered, found a small opening where the sun streamed in, planted himself in the middle of the warmth, and presently toppled over on the pine needles and went to sleep. He slept an hour or more, when he was waked by a party of officers riding through the wood. They stopped. Steve sat up and blinked. The foremost, a florid, side-whiskered, magnificently soldierly personage, wearing a very fine grey uniform and the stars of a major-general, addressed him. "What are you doing here, thir? Thraggling? — Anther me!"

Steve saluted. "I ain't the straggling kind, sir. Any man that says I straggle is a liar — exceptin' the colonel, and he's mistaken. I'm one of Stonewall's men."

"Thtonewall! Ith Jackthon acwoss?"

"They're building a bridge. I don't know if they air across yet. I swum."

"What did you thwim for? Where'th your jacket? What's your wegiment? — '65th Virginia?' — Well, 65th Virginia, you appear to me a detherter —"

Steve began to whine. "Gawd, general, I ain't no deserter. If you'll jest have patience and listen, I kin explain —"

"Time 'th lacking, thir. You get up behind one of my couriers, and if Jackthon 's crothed I'll return you to your colonel. Take him up, O'Brien."

"General Magruder, sor, can't I make him trot before me face like any other water-spaniel? He's wet and dhirty, sor."

"All wight, all wight, O'Brien. Come on, Gwiffith. Nine-Mile road and Thavage Thation!"

The officers rode on. The courier regarded with disfavour the unlucky Steve. "Forward march, dhirty, desartin', weak-kneed crayture that ye be! Thrott!"

Beyond the pine wood the two came into an area which had been overtrampled. Indescribably dreary under the hot sun looked the smouldering heaps and mounds of foodstuffs, the wrecked wagons, the abandoned picks and spades and shovels, the smashed camp equipage, broken kettles, pots and pans, the blankets, bedding, overcoats, torn and trampled in the mire, or piled together and a dull red fire slow creeping through the mass. Medicine-chests had been split by a blow of the axe, the vials shivered, and a black mire made by the liquids. Ruined weapons glinted in the sun between the furrows of a ruined cornfield; bags of powder, boxes of cartridges, great chests of shot and shell showed, half submerged in a tortuous creek. At the edge of the field, there was a cannon spiked and overturned. Here, too, were dead horses, and here, too, were the black, ill-omened birds. There was a trench as well, a long trench just filled, with two or three little head boards bearing some legend. "Holy Virgin!" said the courier, "if I was a horse, a child, or a woman, I'd hate war with a holy hathred!"

Steve whined at his stirrup. "Look a-here, sir, I can't keep up! My foot's awful sore. Gawd don't look my way, if it ain't! I ain't desertin'. Who'd I desert to? They've all gone. I wanted a bath an' I swum the river. The regiment'll be over directly an' I'll rejoin. Take my oath, I will!"

"You trot along out of this plundering mess," ordered the courier. "I'm thinking I'll drop you soon, but it won't be just here! Step lively now!"

The two went on through the blazing afternoon sunshine, and in a straggling wood came upon a deserted field hospital. It was a ghastly place. The courier whistled reflectively, while the imaginative Steve felt a sudden sinking at the pit of the stomach, together with a cold dizziness and perspiration on the backs of his hands. The mind of the courier, striking out vigorously for some kind of a stimulant, laid hold of anger as the nearest efficient. "Bedad," he cried, "ye desartin', dhirty hound! it's right here I'll be afther lavin' ye, with the naked dead and the piles of arms and legs! Let go of my bridle or I'll strike you with my pistol butt! Ughrrrrr! — Get out of this, Peggy!"

They left, mare and man, in a cloud of pine needles and parched earth. Steve uttered something like a howl and went too, running without regard to an in truth not mythical sore foot. He ran after the disappearing courier, and when presently he reached a vast patch of whitened raspberry bushes giving on a not wide and very dusty road and halted panting, it was settled forever that he could n't go back to the plundering possibilities or to his original station by the Chickahominy, since to do so would be to pass again the abandoned field hospital. He kept his face turned from the river and somewhat to the east, and straggled on. A signpost told him that the dusty ribbon was the Nine-Mile road. Presently, among the berry bushes, he came upon a grey artilleryman sitting winding a strip of cloth around a wound in his leg. The artilleryman gave him further information. "Magruder's moving this way. I was ahead with my battery, — Griffith's brigade, — and some stinking sharpshooters sitting with the buzzards in the trees let fly at us! Result, I've got to hobble in at the end of the parade! — What's the matter with you?"

"Captain," said Steve, "asked for a volunteer to swim the river (we're on the other side) and find out 'bout the currents. I swam it, and Gawd! jest then a Yankee battery opened and I could n't get back! Regiment'll be over after awhile I reckon."

The two sat down among the berry bushes. The road was visible, and upon it a great approaching pillar of dust. "Head of our column," said the artilleryman. "Four roads and four pursuing forces, and if we can only all strike Mac at once there'll be a battle that'll lay over Friday's, and if he gets to his gunboats at all it will be in a damaged condition. Magruder's bearing toward Savage Station, and if Jackson's across the Chickahominy we might do for Fitz John Porter — eh?"

"We might," agreed Steve. "I'll lie a little flatter, because the sun and the wetting has made my head ache. They're fine troops."

The grey regiments went by, long swinging tread and jingling accoutrements. A major-general, riding at the head of the column, had the air of a Roman consul, round, strong, bullet head, which he had bared to the breeze that was springing up, close-cropped black hair, short black beard, high nose, bold eyes, a red in his cheeks. "That's General Lafayette McLaws," volunteered the artilleryman. "That's General Kershaw with him. It's Kershaw's brigade. See the palmetto on the flags."

Kershaw's went by. Behind came another high and thick dust cloud. "Cobb and Toombs and Barksdale and Kemper and

Semmes," said the artilleryman. "Suppose we canter on? I'll break a staff from those little heaven trees there. We might get to see the show, after all. York River Railroad's just over there."

They went on, first to the ailanthus bushes, then, leaving the road to the troops, they struck across a ruined cornfield. Stalk and blade and tassel, and the intertwining small, pale-blue morning-glory, all were down. Gun-wheels, horses' hoofs, feet of men had made of naught the sower's pains. The rail fence all around was burning. In a furrow the two found a knapsack, and in it biscuit and jerked beef. "My Aunt Eliza! I was hungry!" said the artilleryman. "Know how the Israelites felt when they gathered manna off the ground!" Out of the cornfield they passed into a shaggy finger of forest. Suddenly firing broke out ahead. Steve started like a squirrel. "That's close to us!"

"There's the railroad!" said the other. "There's Fair Oaks Station. They had entrenchments there, but the scouts say they evacuated them this morning. If they make a stand, reckon it'll be at Savage Station. That musketry popping's down the line! Come on! I can go pretty fast!"

He plied his staff. They came into another ragged field, narrow and sloping to a stretch of railroad track and the smoking ruins of a wooden station. Around were numerous earthworks, all abandoned. Beyond the station, on either side the road, grey troops were massing. The firing ahead was as yet desultory. "Just skirmishers passing the time of day!" said the artilleryman. "Hello! What're they doing on the railroad track? Well, I should think so!"

Across the track, immediately below them, had been thrown by the retreating army a very considerable barricade. Broken wagons, felled trees, logs and a great mass of earth spanned it like a landslide. Over and about it worked a grey company detailed to clear the way. From the edge of a wood, not many yards up the track, came an impatient chorus. "Hurry up, boys! hurry up! hurry up! We want to get by — want to get by —"

"A railroad gun on a flat car placed — "

The artilleryman began to crow. "It's Lieutenant Barry and the railroad gun! Siege piece run on a car. Iron penthouse over it, muzzle sticking out — engine behind —"

" The Yankees skedaddle as though in haste
But this thirty-two pounder howitzer imp
It makes them halt and it makes them limp,
This railroad gun on a flat car placed."

"Hurry up there! Hurry up! Hurry! Steam's up! Coal's precious! Can't stay here burning diamonds like this all day!"

"Come on!" said the artilleryman. "I can sit down and dig. We've got to clear that thing away in a hurry." A shell from a hidden blue battery burst over the working party. Steve held back. "Gawd, man, we can't do no good! We're both lame men. If we got back a little into the wood we could see fine. That's better than fighting — when you're all used up like us —"

The artilleryman regarded him. "No, it is n't better than fighting. I've been suspicioning you for some time, and I've stopped liking the company I'm in. All the same, I'm not going to drop it. Now you trot along in front. Being artillery I have n't a gun any more than you have, but I've a stick, and there is n't anything in the world the matter with my arm. It's used to handling a sponge staff. Forward! trot!"

On the other side the ruined station, on the edge of an old field, Magruder, with him McLaws, waited for the return of a staff officer whom he had sent to the Grapevine Bridge three miles away. The shell which had burst over the party clearing the railroad track was but the first of many. Concealed by the heavy woods, the guns of the Federal rearguard opened on the grey brigades. Kershaw and Griffith, to the right of the road, suffered most. Stephen D. Lee sent forward Carlton's battery, and Kemper's guns came to its aid. They took position in front of the centre and began to answer the blue guns. A courier arrived from the skirmishers thrown out toward the dense wood. "Enemy in force and advancing, sir. Sumner and Franklin's corps, say the scouts."

"All wight!" said Magruder. "Now if Jackthon's over, we'll cwush them like a filbert."

The staff officer returned. "Well, thir, well, thir? Ith General Jackthon acroth? Will he take them in the rear while I thrike here? — Bryan, you look intolerably thober! What ith it?"

"The bridge will not be finished for two hours, sir. Two or three infantry companies have crossed by hook or crook, but I should say it would be morning before the whole force is over."

"Damn! Well —"

"I left my horse and got across myself, sir, and saw General Jackson —"

"Well, well, well —"

"He says, sir! 'Tell General Magruder that I have other important duties to perform' " —

There was a dead silence. Then McLaws spoke with Roman directness. "In my opinion there are two Jacksons. The one that came down here left the other one in the Valley."

A great shell came with a shriek and exploded, a fragment mortally wounding General Griffith at the head of the Mississippi brigade. The Mississippians uttered a loud cry of anger. Carleton's battery thundered defiantly. Magruder drew a long breath. "Well, gentlemen; philothophy to the rethcue! If we can't bag the whole rearguard, we'll bag what we can. General advanthe and drive them!"

Back on the railroad, in the long shadows of the late afternoon, the working party cleared away the last layer of earth and log and stood back happy. "Come on, you old railroad gun, and stop your blaspheming! Should think the engine'd blush for you!"

The railroad gun puffed up, cannoneers picturesquely draped where there was hold for foot or hand. There was a momentary pause, filled with an interchange of affectionate oaths and criticism. The lame artilleryman laid hold of the flat car. "Take me along, won't you, and shuck me at my battery! Kemper's, you know. Can't I go, lieutenant?"

"Yes, yes, climb on!"

"And can't my friend here go, too? He's infantry, but he means well. He volunteered to swim the Chickahominy, and now he wants to get back so's he can report to Stonewall Jackson. Sh! don't deny it now. You're too modest. Can't he go, too, lieutenant?"

"Yes, yes. Climb on! All right, Brown! Let her go!"

Kershaw, Griffith, and Semmes' brigades, advancing in line through light and shadow, wood and clearing, came presently into touch with the enemy. There followed a running fight, the Federals slowly retreating. Everywhere, through wood and clearing, appeared McClellan's earthworks. Behind these the blue made stand, but at last from line to line the grey pressed them back. A deep cut appeared, over which ran a railroad bridge; then woods, fields, a second ruined railroad station, beside which were burning cars filled with quartermaster's stores; beyond these a farmhouse, a peach orchard, and a field crossed by long rows of hospital tents. Before the farmhouse appeared a strong Federal line of battle, and from every little eminence the blue cannon blazed. Kershaw charged furiously; the two lines clashed and clanged. Semmes' brigade came into action on the right, Kemper's battery supporting. Griffith's, now Barksdale's — joined battle with a yell, the Mississippians bent on avenging Griffith. The air filled with smoke, the roar of guns and the rattle of musketry. There occurred, in the late afternoon, a bloody fight between forces not large, and fairly matched.

The engine pushing the railroad gun alternately puffed and shrieked through dark woodland and sunset-flooded clearing. A courier appeared, signalling with his hat. "General Magruder's there by the bridge over the cut! Says, 'Come on!' Says, 'Cross the bridge and get into battery in the field beyond.' Says, 'Hurry up!'"

The siege-piece and the engine hurried. With a wild rattle and roar, the crew all yelling, black smoke everywhere, and the whistle screaming like a new kind of shell, the whole came out of the wood upon the railroad bridge. Instantly there burst from the blue batteries a tremendous, raking fire. Shot and shell struck the engine, the iron penthouse roof over the siege-piece, the flat car, the bridge itself. From the car and the bridge slivers were torn and hurled through the air. A man was killed, two others wounded, but engine and gun roared across. They passed Magruder standing on the bank. "Here we are, general, here we are! Yaaih! Yaaaih!"

"Th' you are. Don't thop here! Move down the track a little. Other Richmond howitthers coming."

The other howitzers, four pieces, six horses to each, all in a gallop, captain ahead, men following in a mad run, whips crackling, drivers shouting, came all in thunder on the bridge and across. The blue shells flew like harpies, screaming, swooping, scattering ruin. A red gleam from the declining sun bathed the wild train. In a roar of sound the whole cleared the bridge and plunged from the track to the level field. *Forward into battery, left oblique, march!*

McLaws on the right, hard pressed, sent to Magruder for reinforcements. The 13th and 21st Mississippi answered. Kershaw, supported by Semmes and Kemper, advancing under an iron hail by deserted camp and earthwork, ordered the 2d, 3d and 7th South Carolina to charge. They did so, with a high, ringing cry, through the sunset wood into the fields, by the farm and the peach orchard, where they and the blue lines stubbornly engaged. On both sides, the artillery came furiously into action.

The long twilight faded, the stars began to show. The firing slackened, died to occasional sullen outbursts, then to silence. On both sides the loss was heavy; the action remained indecisive. The grey rested on the field; the blue presently took up again their line of retreat toward White Oak Swamp. They left in the hands of the grey their dead, several hundred prisoners, and twenty-five hundred men in hospital. In the hot and sultry night, dark, with presage of a storm, through a ruined country, by the light of their own burning stores, the blue column wound slowly on by the single road toward White Oak Swamp and its single bridge. The grey brigades lit their small camp-fires, gathered up the wounded, grey and blue, dug trenches for the dead, found food where they might and went hungry where there was none, answered to roll call and listened to the silence after many names, then lay down in field and wood beneath the gathering clouds.

Some time between sunset and the first star Steve Dagg found himself, he hardly knew how, crouching in a line of pawpaw bushes bordering a shallow ravine. The clay upon his shirt and trousers made it seem probable that he had rolled down the embankment from the railroad gun to the level below. That he was out of breath, panting in hard painful gasps, might indicate that he had run like a hare across the field. He could not remember; anyhow here he was, a little out of hell, just fringing it as it were. Lying close to earth, between the smooth pawpaw stems, the large leaves making a night-time for him, Steve felt deadly sick. "O Gawd! why'd I volunteer in, seein' I can't volunteer out?" Behind him he heard the roaring of the guns, the singing of the minies. A chance shell went over his head, dug itself into the soil at the bottom of the ravine, and exploded. The earth came pattering upon the pawpaw leaves. Steve curled up like a hedgehog. "O Gawd! I ain't got a friend in the world. Why did n't I stay on Thunder Run and marry Lucinda Heard?"

At dark the guns ceased. In the silence his nausea lessened and the chill sweat dried upon him. He lay quiet for awhile, and then he parted the pawpaw bushes and crept out. He looked over his shoulder at the field of battle. "I ain't going that-a-way and meet that gunner again — damn him to everlasting hell!" He looked across the ravine toward the west, but a vision came to him of the hospital in the wood, and of how the naked dead men and the severed legs and arms might stir at night. He shivered and grew sick again. Southward? There was a glare upon all that horizon and a sound of distant explosions. The Yankees were sweeping through the woods that way, and they might kill him on sight without waiting for him to explain. A grey army was also over there, — Lee and Longstreet and A. P. Hill. He was as afraid of the grey as of the blue; after the railroad gun he was afraid of a shadow. Finally, he turned northward toward the Chickahominy again.

The night, so dark and hot, presently became darker by reason of masses of clouds rising swiftly from the horizon and blotting out the stars. They hung low, they pressed heavily, beneath them a sulphur-tainted and breathless air. Lightnings began to flash, thunder to mutter. "Yah!" whimpered Steve. "I'm going to get wet again! It's true. Everything's agin me."

He came again upon the swampy margin of the Chickahominy. It was wide, threaded by motionless waters, barred and banded with low-growing swamp shrubs, set with enormously tall and solemn trees. Steve, creeping between protruding roots, heard a screech owl in the distance. It cried and cried, but then the thunder rolled more loudly and drowned its hooting. He came flush with the dark stretch of the river. "Gawd, do I want to get across, or do I want to stay here? I wish I was dead — no, I don't!" He faced the lightning. "Gawd, that was jes' a mistake — don't take any notice of it, please. — Yaaah!" He had set his foot on a log, which gave beneath it and sank into deep water. With a screech like the owl's he drew back and squeezed himself, trembling, between the roots of a live-oak. He concluded that he would stay here until the dawn.

The storm drew nearer, with long lightnings and thunder that crashed and rolled through the swamp. A vivid flash, holding a second or more, showed the stretch of the river, and several hundred yards above Steve's nook a part of a high railroad bridge. The gaunt trestle ran out past midstream, then stopped, all the portion toward the northern shore burned away. It stood against the intensely lit sky and stream like the skeleton of some antediluvian monster, then vanished into Stygian darkness. The thunder crashed at once, an ear-splitting clap followed by long reverberations. As these died, in the span of silence before should come the next flash and crash, Steve became conscious of another sound, dull and distant at first, then nearer and rushingly loud. "Train on the track down there! What in hell — It can't cross!" He stood up, held by a sapling, and craned his neck to look up the river. A great flash showed the bridge again. "Must be Yankees still about here — last of the rear-guard we've been fighting. What they doing with the train? They must have burned the bridge themselves! Gawd!"

A wildly vivid orange flash lit water, wood and sky, and the gaunt half of a bridge, stopping dead short in the middle of the Chicka-hominy. The thunder crashed and rolled, then out of that sound grew another — the noise of a rushing train. Something huge and dark roared from the wooded banks out upon the bridge. It belched black smoke mingled with sparks; behind it were cars, and these were burning. The whole came full upon the broken bridge. It swayed beneath the weight; but before it could fall, and before the roaring engine reached the gap, the flames of the kindled cars touched the huge stores of ammunition sent thus to destruction by the retreat-ing column. In the night, over the Chickahominy, occurred a rend-ing and awful explosion. . . . Steve, coming to himself, rose to his knees in the black mire. The lightning flashed, and he stared with a contorted face. The bridge, too, was gone. There was only the churned water, filled with scantlings and torn branches of trees. The rain was falling, a great hissing sweep of rain, and the wind howled beneath the thunder. Steve turned blindly; he did not know where he was going, but he had a conviction that the river was rising and would come after him. A hundred yards from the water, in the mid-night wood, as he hurried over earth that the rain was fast turning into morass, he stumbled over some obstacle and fell. Putting out his hands, they came flat against a dead man's face. He rose and fled with a screech, southwardly now, in the direction of White Oak Swamp.

CHAPTER XXXV

WHITE OAK SWAMP

THE Grapevine Bridge being at last rebuilt, Stonewall Jackson's fourteen brigades crossed the Chickahominy, the movement occupying a great part of the night. Dawn of the thirtieth found the advance at Savage Station.

The storm in the night had swelled the myriad creeks, and extended all morasses. The roads were mud, the wild tangles of underwood held water like a sponge. But the dawn was glorious, with carmine and purple towers and the coolest fresh-washed purity of air and light. Major-General Richard Ewell, riding at the head of his division, opined that it was as clear as the plains. A reconnoitring party brought him news about something or other to the eastward. He jerked his head, swore reflectively, and asked where was "Old Jackson."

"He rode ahead, sir, to speak to General Magruder."

"Well, you go, Nelson, and tell him — No, you go, Major Stafford."

Stafford went, riding through the cool, high glory of the morning. He found Jackson and Magruder at the edge of the peach orchard. All around were Magruder's troops, and every man's head was turned toward the stark and dust-hued figure on the dust-hued nag. The first had come from the Valley with a towering reputation, nor indeed did the last lack bards to sing of him. Whatever tarn cap the one had worn during the past three days, however bewildering had been his inaction, his reputation held. This was Jackson. . . . There must have been some good reason . . . this was Stonewall Jackson. Magruder's brigades cheered him vehemently, and he looked at them unsmiling, with a mere motion of his hand toward the rusty old cadet cap. Magruder, magnificently soldierly, with much of manner and rich colour, magnanimously forgetful this morning of "other important duties" and affably debonair though his eyelids dropped for want of sleep, came gradually to halt in his fluent speech. — "Weally, you can't talk forever to a potht! If thilenthe be golden he ith the heavietht weight of hith time." — Jackson gathered up his reins, nodded and rode off, the troops cheering as he went by.

Stafford, coming up with him, saluted and gave his message. Jackson received it with impassivity and rode on. Conceiving it to be his duty to attend an answer, the staff officer accompanied him, though a little in the rear. Here were an aide and a courier, and the three rode silently behind their silent chief. At the Williamsburg road there came a halt. Jackson checked Little Sorrel, and sat looking toward Richmond. Down the road, in the sunrise light, came at a canter a knot of horsemen handsomely mounted and equipped, the one in front tall and riding an iron-grey. Stafford recognized the commander-in-chief. Jackson sat very still, beneath a honey locust. The night before, in a wood hard by, the 17th Mississippi had run into a Federal brigade. The latter had fired, at point blank, a withering volley. Many a tall Mississippian had fallen. Now in the early light their fellow soldiers had gone seeking them in the wood, drawn them forth, and laid them in a row in the wet sedge beside the road. Nearly every man had been shot through the brain. They lay ghastly, open-eyed, wet with rain, staring at the cool and pure concave of the sky. Two or three soldiers were moving slowly up and down the line, bent on identifications. Presumably Jackson was aware of that company of the dead, but their presence could not be said to disturb him. He sat with his large hands folded over the saddle-bow, with the forage cap cutting all but one blue-grey gleam of his eyes, still as stone wall or mountain or the dead across the way. As the horsemen came nearer his lips parted. "That is General Lee?"

"Yes, general."

"Good!"

Lee's staff halted; Lee himself came on, checked the iron-grey, dismounted, and walked toward the honey locust. Jackson swung himself stiffly out of the saddle and stepped forward. The two met. Lee stretched out his hand, said something in his gracious voice. The piteous row of dead men, with their open eyes, caught his glance. He drew his brows together, pressed his lips hard, parted them in a sigh and went on with his speech. The two men, so different in aspect, talked not long together. The staff could not hear what was said, but Lee spoke the most and very earnestly. Jackson nodded, said, "Good!" several times, and once, "It is in God's hands, General Lee!"

The courier holding Traveller brought him up. Lee mounted, tarried, a great and gallant figure, a moment longer, then rode toward Magruder at the peach orchard. His staff followed, saluting Stonewall Jackson as they passed. He, too, remounted in his stiff and awkward fashion, and turned Little Sorrel's head down the Williamsburg road. Behind him now, in the clear bright morning, could be heard the tramp of his brigades. Stafford pushed his horse level with the sorrel. "Your pardon, general, but may I ask if there's any order for General Ewell —"

"There is none, sir."

"Then shall I return?"

"No, you will wait, sir. From the cross-roads I may send directions."

They rode on by wood and field. Overhead was a clear, high, azure sky; no clouds, but many black sailing specks. Around, on the sandy road, and in the shaggy, bordering growth, were witnesses enough to the Federal retreat — a confused medley of abandoned objects. Broken and half-burned wagons appeared, like wreckage from a storm. There did not lack dead or dying horses, nor, here and there, dead or wounded men. In the thicker woods or wandering through the ruined fields appeared, forlornly, stragglers from the Federal column. D. H. Hill, leading the grey advance, swept up hundreds of these. From every direction spirals of smoke rose into the crystal air,— barns and farmhouses, mills, fences, hayricks, and monster heaps of Federal stores set on fire in that memorable "change of base." For all the sunshine of the June morning, the rain-washed air, the singing birds in the jewelled green of the forest, there was something in the time and place inexpressibly sinister and sad.

Or so thought Maury Stafford, riding silently with the aide and the courier. At Gaines's Mill he had won emphatic praise for a cool and daring ride across the battlefield, and for the quick rallying and leading into action of a command whose officers were all down. With Ewell at Dispatch Station, he had volunteered for duty at the crossing of the Chickahominy, and in a hand-to-hand fight with a retiring Federal regiment he and his detachment had acquitted themselves supremely well. As far as this warfare went, he had reason to be satisfied. But he was not so, and as he rode he thought the morning scene of a twilight dreariness. He had no enthusiasm for war. In every aspect of life, save one, that he dealt with, he carried a cool and level head, and he thought war barbarous and its waste a great tragedy. Martial music and earth-shaking charges moved him for a moment, as they moved others for an hour or a day. The old, instinctive response passed with swiftness, and he settled to the base of a steadfast conclusion that humanity turned aside to the jungle many times too often in a century. That, individually, he had turned into a certain other allied jungle, he was conscious — not sardonically conscious, for here all his judgment was warped, but conscious. His mind ranged in this jungle with an unhappy fury hardly modern.

As he rode he looked toward Richmond. He knew, though he scarcely knew how he knew, that Judith Cary was there. He had himself meant to ride to Richmond that idle twenty-eighth. Then had come the necessity of accompanying Ewell to Dispatch Station, and his chance was gone. The Stonewall Brigade had been idle enough. . . . Perhaps, the colonel of the 65th had gone. . . . It was a thick and bitter jungle, and he gathered every thorn within it to himself and smelled of every poisonous flower.

The small, silent cavalcade came to a cross-roads. Jackson stopped, sitting Little Sorrel beneath a tall, gaunt, lightning-blackened pine. The three with him waited a few feet off. Behind them they heard the on-coming column; D. H. Hill leading, then Jackson's own division. The sun was above the treetops, the sky cloudless, all the forest glistening. The minutes passed. Jackson sat like a stone. At last, from the heavy wood pierced by the cross-road, came a rapid clatter of hoofs. Munford appeared, behind him fifty of his cavalry. The fifty checked their horses; the leader came on and saluted. Jackson spoke in the peculiar voice he used when displeased. "Colonel Munford, I ordered you to be here at sunrise."

Munford explained. "The men were much scattered, sir. They don't know the country, and in the storm last night and the thick wood they couldn't see their horses' ears. They had nothing to eat and —"

He came to a pause. No amount of good reasons ever for long rolled fluently off the tongue before Jackson. He spoke now, still in the concentrated monotony of his voice of displeasure. "Yes, sir. But, colonel, I ordered you to be here at sunrise. Move on with your men. If you meet the enemy drive in his pickets, and if you want artillery Colonel Crutchfield will furnish you."

Munford moved on, his body of horse increasing in size as the lost troopers emerged in twos and threes or singly from the forest and turned down the road to join the command. The proceeding gave an effect of disordered ranks. Jackson beckoned the courier. "Go tell Colonel Munford that his men are straggling badly."

The courier went, and presently returned. Munford was with him. "General, I thought I had best come myself and explain — they are n't straggling. We were all separated in the dark night and —"

"Yes, sir. But I ordered you to be here at sunrise. Move on now, and drive in the enemy's pickets, and if you want artillery Colonel Crutchfield will furnish you."

Munford and the 2d Virginia went on, disappearing around a bend in the road. The sound of the artillery coming up was now loud in the clear air. Jackson listened a moment, then left the shadow of the pine, and with the two attending officers and the courier resumed the way to White Oak Swamp.

Brigade by brigade, twenty-five thousand men in grey passed Savage Station and followed Stonewall Jackson. The air was fresh, the troops in spirits. Nobody was going to let McClellan get to the James, after all! The brigades broke into song. They laughed, they joked, they cheered every popular field officer as he passed, they genially discussed the heretofore difficulties of the campaign and the roseate promise of the day. They knew it was the crucial day; that McClellan must be stopped before sunset or he would reach the shelter of his gunboats. They were in a Fourth of July humour; they meant to make the day remembered. Life seemed bright again and much worth while. They even grudgingly agreed that there was a curious kind of attractiveness about all this flat country, and the still waters, and the very tall trees, and labyrinthine vivid green undergrowth. Intermittent fevers had begun to appear, but, one and all, the invalids declared that this was their good day. "Shucks!

What's a little ague? Anyhow, it'll go away when we get back to
the Valley. Going back to the Valley? Well, we should think so!
This country's got an eerie kind of good looks, and it raises sweet
potatoes all right, but for steady company give us mountains! We'll
drop McClellan in one of these swamps, and we'll have a review at
the fair grounds at Richmond so's all the ladies can see us, and then
we'll go back to the Valley pike and Massanutton and Mr. Commissary Banks! They must be missing us awful. Somebody sing something, —

> "Old Grimes is dead, that good old man,
> Whom we shall see no more!
> He wore a grey Confederate coat
> All buttoned down before —"

"Don't like it that way? All right —"

> "He wore a blue damn-Yankee coat
> All buttoned down before —"

The Stonewall Brigade passed a new-made grave in a small graveyard, from which the fence had been burned. A little further on they
came to a burned smithy; the blacksmith's house beside it also a
ruin, black and charred. On a stone, between two lilac-bushes, sat a
very old man. Beside him stood a girl, a handsome creature, dark
and bright-cheeked. "Send them to hell, boys, send them to hell!"
quavered the old man. The girl raised a sweet and vibrant voice:
"Send them to hell, men, send them to hell!"

"We'll do our best, ma'am, we'll do our best!" answered the
Stonewall.

The sun mounted high. They were moving now through thick
woods, broken by deep creeks and bits of swamp. All about were
evidences enough that an army had travelled before them, and that
that army was exceedingly careless of its belongings. All manner
of impediments lay squandered; waste and ruin were everywhere.
Sometimes the men caught an odour of burning meat, of rice and
breadstuffs. In a marshy meadow a number of wrecked, canvas-
topped wagons showed like a patch of mushrooms, giant and dingy.
In a forest glade rested like a Siegfried smithy an abandoned travelling forge. Camp-kettles hacked in two were met with, and boxes
of sutlers' wares smashed to fragments. The dead horses were

many, and there was disgust with the buzzards, they rose or settled
in such clouds. The troops, stooping to drink from the creeks, complained that the water was foul.

Very deep woods appeared on the horizon. "Guide says that's
White Oak Swamp! — Guide says that's White Oak Swamp!"
Firing broke out ahead. "Cavalry rumpus! — Hello! Artillery
butting in, too! — everybody but us! Well, boys, I always did
think infantry a mighty no-'count, undependable arm — infantry of the Army of the Valley, anyway! God knows the moss has
been growing on us for a week!"

Munford sent back a courier to Jackson, riding well before the
head of the column. "Bridge is burned, sir. They're in strong force
on the other side —"

"Good!" said Jackson. "Tell Colonel Crutchfield to bring up
the guns."

He rode on, the aide, the courier, and Maury Stafford yet with
him. They passed a deserted Federal camp and hospital, and came
between tall trees and through dense swamp undergrowth to a small
stream with many arms. It lay still beneath the blue sky, overhung
by many a graceful, vine-draped tree. The swamp growth stretched
for some distance on either side, and through openings in the foliage
the blue glint of the arms could be seen. To the right there was
some cleared ground. In front the road stopped short. The one
bridge had been burned by the retreating Federal rearguard. Two
blue divisions, three batteries — in all over twenty thousand men —
now waited on the southern bank to dispute the White Oak
Crossing.

Stafford again pushed his horse beside Jackson's. "Well, sir?"

"I hunted once through this swamp, general. There is an old
crossing near the bridge —"

"Passable for cavalry, sir?"

"Passable by cavalry and infantry, sir. Even the guns might
somehow be gotten across."

"I asked, sir, if it was passable for cavalry."

"It is, sir."

Jackson turned to his aide. "Go tell Colonel Crutchfield I want
to see him."

Crutchfield appeared. "Where are your guns, colonel?"

"General, their batteries on the ridge over there command the road, and the thick woods below their guns are filled with sharp-shooters. I want to get the guns behind the crest of the hill on this side, and I am opening a road through the wood over there. They'll be up directly — seven batteries, Carter's, Hardaway's, Nelson's, Rhett's, Reilly's, and Balthis'. We'll open then at a thousand yards, and we'll take them, I think, by surprise."

"Very good, colonel. That is all."

The infantry began to arrive. Brigade by brigade, as it came up, turned to right or to left, standing under arms in the wood above the White Oak Swamp. As the Stonewall Brigade came, under tall trees and over earth that gave beneath the feet, flush with the stream itself, the grey guns, now in place upon the low ridge to the right, opened, thirty-one of them, with simultaneous thunder. Crutch-field's manœuvre had not been observed. The thirty-one guns blazed without warning, and the blue artillery fell into confusion. The Par-rotts blazed in turn, four times, then they limbered up in haste and left the ridge. Crutchfield sent Wooding's battery tearing down the slope to the road immediately in front of the burned bridge. Wood-ing opened fire and drove out the infantry support from the oppo-site forest. Jackson, riding toward the stream, encountered Mun-ford. "Colonel, move your men over the creek and take those guns."

Munford looked. "I don't know that we can cross it, sir."

"Yes, you can cross it, colonel. Try."

Munford and a part of the 2d Virginia dashed in. The stream was in truth narrow enough, and though it was deep here, with a shifting bottom, and though the débris from the ruined bridge made it full of snares, the horsemen got across and pushed up the shore toward the guns. A thick and leafy wood to the right leaped fire — another and unsuspected body of blue infantry. The echoes were yet ringing when, from above, an unseen battery opened on the luck-less cavalry. The blue rifles cracked again, the horses began to rear and plunge, several men were hit. There was nothing to do but to get somehow back to the north bank. Munford and his men pushed out of the rain of iron, through the wood for some distance down the stream, and there recrossed, not without difficulty.

The thirty-one guns shelled the wood which had last spoken, and drove out the skirmishers with whom it was filled. These took refuge in another deep and leafy belt still commanding the stream and the ruined causeway. A party of grey pioneers fell to work to rebuild the bridge. From the crest on the southern side behind the deep foliage two Federal batteries, before unnoted, opened on the grey cannoneers. Wooding, on the road before the bridge, had to fall back. Under cover of the guns the blue infantry swarmed again into the wood. Shell and bullet hissed and pattered into the water by the abutments of the ruined bridge. The working party drew back. "Damnation! They must n't fling them minies round loose like that!"

Wright's brigade of Huger's division came up. Wright made his report. "We tried Brackett's ford a mile up stream, sir. Could n't manage it. Got two companies over by the skin of our teeth. They drove in some pickets on the other side. Road through the swamp over there covered by felled trees. Beyond is a small meadow and beyond that rising ground, almost free of trees. There are Yankee batteries on the crest, and a large force of infantry lying along the side of the ridge. They command the meadow and the swamp."

So tall were the trees, so thick the undergrowth, so full the midsummer foliage that the guns, thundering at each other across the narrow stream, never saw their antagonists. Sharpshooters and skirmishers were as hidden. Except as regarded the pioneers striving with the bridge, neither side could see the damage that was done. The noise was tremendous, echoing loudly from the opposing low ridges and rolling through the swamp. The hollow filled with smoke; above the treetops a dull saffron veil was drawn across the sky. The firing was without intermission, a monotonous thunder, beneath which the working party strove spasmodically at the bridge, the cavalry chafed to and fro, and the infantry, filling all the woods and the little clearings to the rear, began to swear. "Is it the Red Sea down there? Why can't we cross without a bridge? Nobody's going to get drowned! Ain't more'n a hundred men been drowned since this war began! O Great Day in the Morning! I'm tired of doing nothing!"

General Wade Hampton of D. H. Hill's division, leaving his brigade in a pine wood, went with his son and with an aide, Rawlins Lowndes, on a reconnoitring expedition of his own. He was a woodsman and hunter, with experience of swamps and bayous.

Returning, he sought out Jackson, and found him sitting on a fallen pine by the roadside near the slowly, slowly mending bridge. Hampton dismounted and made his report. "We got over, three of us, general, a short way above. It was n't difficult. The stream's clear of obstructions there and has a sandy bottom. We could see through the trees on the other side. There's a bit of level, and a hillside covered with troops — a strong position. But we got across the stream, sir."

"Yes. Can you make a bridge there?"

"I can make one for infantry, sir. Not, I think, for the artillery. Cutting a road would expose our position."

"Very good. Make the bridge, general."

Hampton's men cut saplings and threw a rude foot-bridge across the stream where he had traversed it. He returned and reported. "They are quiet and unsuspecting beyond, sir. The crossing would be slow, and there may be an accident, but cross we certainly can."

Jackson, still seated on the fallen pine, sat as though he had been there through eternity, and would remain through eternity. The gun thundered, the minies sang. One of the latter struck a tree above his head and severed a leafy twig. It came floating down, touched his shoulder like an accolade and rested on the pine needles by his foot. He gave it no attention, sitting like a graven image with clasped hands, listening to the South Carolinian's report. Hampton ceased to speak and waited. It was the height of the afternoon. He stood three minutes in silence, perhaps, then glanced toward the man on the log. Jackson's eyes were closed, his head slightly lifted. "Praying?" thought the South Carolinian. "Well, there's a time for everything —" Jackson opened his eyes, drew the forage cap far down over them, and rose from the pine. The other looked for him to speak, but he said nothing. He walked a little way down the road and stood among the whistling minies, looking at the slowly, slowly building bridge.

Hampton did as Wright and Munford had done before him — went back to his men. D. H. Hill, after an interview of his own, had retired to the artillery. "Yes, yes, Rhett, go ahead! Do something — make a noise — do something! Infantry's kept home from school to-day — measles, I reckon, or maybe it's lockjaw!"

About three o'clock there was caught from the southward, between the loud wrangling of the batteries above White Oak, another sound, — first two or three detonations occurring singly, then a prolonged and continuous roar. The batteries above White Oak Swamp, the sharpshooters and skirmishers, the grey chafing cavalry, the grey masses of unemployed infantry, all held breath and listened. The sound was not three miles away, and it was the sound of the crash of long battle-lines. There was a curious movement among the men nearest the grey general-commanding. With their bodies bent forward, they looked his way, expecting short, quick orders. He rested immobile, his eyes just gleaming beneath the down-drawn cap, Little Sorrel cropping the marsh grass beside him. Munford, coming up, ventured a remark. "General Longstreet or General A. P. Hill has joined with their centre, I suppose, general? The firing is very heavy."

"Yes. The troops that have been lying before Richmond. General Lee will see that they do what is right."

Stafford, near him, spoke again. "The sound comes, I think, sir, from a place called Glendale — Glendale or Frayser's Farm."

"Yes, sir," said Jackson; "very probably."

The thunder never lessened. Artillery and infantry, Franklin's corps on the south bank of White Oak, began again to pour an iron hail against the opposing guns and the working party at the bridge, but in every interval between the explosions from these cannon there rolled louder and louder the thunder from Frayser's Farm. A sound like a grating wind in a winter forest ran through the idle grey brigades. "It's A. P. Hill's battle again! — A. P. Hill or Longstreet! Magruder and Huger and Holmes and A. P. Hill and Longstreet — and we out of it again, on the wrong side of White Oak Swamp! And they're looking for us to help — *Wish I was dead!*"

The 65th Virginia had its place some distance up the stream, in a tangled wood by the water. Facing southward, it held the extreme right; beyond it only morass, tall trees, swaying masses of vine. On the left an arm of the creek, thickly screened by tree and bush, divided it from the remainder of the brigade. It rested in semi-isolation, and its ten companies stared in anger at the narrow stream and the deep woods beyond, listening to the thunder of Longstreet and A. P. Hill's unsupported attack and the answering roar of the

Federal 3d Army Corps. It was a sullen noise, deep and unintermittent. The 65th, waiting for orders, could have wept as the orders did not come. "Get across? Well, if General Jackson would just give us leave to try! — Oh, hell! listen to that! — Colonel, can't you do something for us? — Where's the colonel gone?"

Cleave was beyond their vision. He had rounded a little point of land and now, Dundee's hoofs in water, stood gazing at the darkly wooded opposite shore. He stood a moment thus, then spoke to the horse, and they entered the stream. It was not deep, and though there were obstructions, old stakes and drowned brushwood, Cleave and Dundee crossed. The air was full of booming sound, but there was no motion in the wood into which they rose from the water. All its floor was marshy, water in pools and threads, a slight growth of cane, and above, the tall and solemn trees. Cleave saw that there was open meadow beyond. Dismounting, he went noiselessly to the edge of the swamp. An open space, covered with some low growth; beyond it a hillside. Wood and meadow and hill, all lay quiet and lonely in the late sunlight.

He went back to Dundee, remounted, passed again through the sombre wood, over the boggy earth, entered the water and recrossed. Turning the little point of the swamp, he rode before his regiment on his way to find Winder. His men greeted him. "Colonel, if you could just get us over there we'd do anything in the world for you! This weeping-willow place is getting awful hard to bear! Look at Dundee! Even he's drooping his head. You know we'd follow you through hell, sir; and if you could just manage it so's we could follow you through White Oak Swamp —"

Cleave passed the arm of the creek separating the 65th from the rest of the brigade, and asked of Winder from the first troops beyond the screen of trees. "General Winder has ridden down to the bridge to see General Jackson."

Cleave, following, found his leader indeed before Jackson, just finishing his representations whatever they were, and somewhat perturbed by the commanding general's highly developed silence. This continuing unbroken, Winder, after an awkward minute of waiting, fell a little back, a flush on his cheeks and his lips hard together. The action disclosed Cleave, just come up, his hand checking Dundee, his grey eyes earnestly upon Jackson. When the latter spoke, it was not to the brigadier but to the colonel of the 65th. "Why are you not with your regiment, sir?"

"I left it but a moment ago, sir, to bring information I thought it my duty to bring."

"What information?"

"The 65th is on General Winder's extreme right, sir. The stream before it is fordable."

"How do you know, sir?"

"I forded it. The infantry could cross without much difficulty. The 65th would be happy, sir, to lead the way."

Winder opened his lips. "The whole Stonewall Brigade is ready, sir."

Jackson, without regarding, continued to address himself to Cleave. His tone had been heard before by the latter — in his own case on the night of the twenty-seventh as well as once before, and in the case of others where there had been what was construed as remonstrance or negligence or disobedience. He had heard him speak so to Garnett after Kernstown. The words were simple enough — they always were. "You will return to your duty, sir. It lies where your regiment is, and that is not here. Go!"

Cleave obeyed. The ford was there. His regiment might have crossed, the rest of the Stonewall following. Together they might traverse the swamp and the bit of open, pass the hillside, and strike Franklin upon the flank, while, brigade by brigade, the rest of the division followed by that ford. Rout Franklin, and push forward to help A. P. Hill. It had appeared his duty to give the information he was possessed of. He had given it, and his skirts were cleared. There was anger in him as he turned away; he had a compressed lip, a sparkling eye. Not till he turned did he see Stafford, sitting his horse in the shadow behind Jackson. The two men stared full at each other for a perceptible moment. But Stafford's face was in the shadow, and as for Cleave his mind was full of anger for the tragedy of the inaction. At the moment he gave small attention to his own life, its heights or depths, past or future. He saw Stafford, but he could not be said to consider him at all. He turned from the road into the wood, and pushed the great bay over spongy ground toward the isolated 65th. Stafford saw that he gave him no thought, and it angered him. On the highroad of his life it would not have done so, but he had left the road and was lost in the jungle. There were few things that Richard Cleave might do which would not now work like madness on the mind astray in that place.

The cannonading over White Oak Swamp continued, and the sound of the battle of Frayser's Farm continued. On a difficult and broken ground Longstreet attacked, driving back McCall's division. McCall was reinforced and Longstreet hard pressed. Lee loosed A. P. Hill, and the battle became furious. He looked for Jackson, but Jackson was at White Oak Swamp; for Huger, but a road covered with felled trees delayed Huger; for Magruder, but in the tangle of wood and swamp Magruder, too, went astray; for Holmes, but Fitz John Porter held Holmes in check. Longstreet and A. P. Hill strove unsupported, fifty thousand grey troops in hearing of their guns. The battle swayed to and fro, long, loud, and sanguinary, with much hand-to-hand work, much use of bayonets, and, over all, a shriek of grape and canister.

Back on White Oak Swamp, Franklin on the southern side, Jackson on the northern, blue and grey alike caught the noise of battle. They themselves were cannonading loudly and continuously. One Federal battery used fifteen hundred rounds. The grey were hardly less lavish. Not much damage was done except to the trees. The trough through which crept the sluggish water was filled with smoke. It drifted through the swamp and the woods and along the opposing hillsides. It drifted over and about the idle infantry, until one command was hidden from another.

Stonewall Jackson, seated on the stump of a felled oak, his sabre across his knees, his hands rigid upon it, his great booted feet squarely planted, his cap drawn low, sent the aide beside him with some order to the working party at the bridge. A moment later the courier went, too, to D. H. Hill, with a query about prisoners. The thunders continued, the smoke drifted heavily, veiling all movements. Jackson spoke without turning. "Whoever is there —"

No one was there at the moment but Maury Stafford. He came forward. "You will find the 1st Brigade," said Jackson. "Tell General Winder to move it nearer the stream. Tell him to cross from his right, with caution, a small reconnoitring party. Let it find out the dispositions of the enemy, return and report."

Stafford went, riding westward through the smoke-filled forest, and came presently to the Stonewall Brigade and to Winder, walking up and down disconsolately. "An order from General Jackson, sir. You will move your brigade nearer the stream. Also you will cross, from your right, with caution, a small reconnoitring party. It will discover the dispositions of the enemy, return and report."

"Very good," said Winder. "I'll move at once. The 65th is already on the brink — there to the right, beyond the swamp. Perhaps, you'll take the order on to Colonel Cleave? — Very good! Tell him to send a picked squad quietly across and find out what he can. I hope to God there'll come another order for us all to cross at its heels!"

Stafford, riding on, presently found himself in a strip of bog and thicket and tall trees masking a narrow, sluggish piece of water. The brigade behind him was hidden, the regiment in front not yet visible. Despite the booming of the guns, there was here an effect of stillness. It seemed a lonely place. Stafford, traversing it slowly because the ground gave beneath his horse's feet, became aware of a slight movement in a laurel thicket and of two eyes gleaming behind the leaves. He reined in his horse. "What are you doing in there? Straggling or deserting? Come out!" There was a pause; then Steve Dagg emerged. "Major, I ain't either stragglin' or desertin'. I was just seperated — I got seperated last night. The regiment's jes' down there — I crept down an' saw it jes' now. I'm goin' back an' join right away — send me to hell if I ain't! — though Gawd knows my foot's awful sore —"

Stafford regarded him closely. "I've seen you before. Ah, I remember! On the Valley pike, moving toward Winchester. . . . Poor scoundrel!"

Steve, his back against a swamp magnolia, undertook to show that he, too, remembered, and that gratefully. "Yes, sir. You saved me from markin' time on a barrel-head, major — an' my foot *was* sore — an' I was n't desertin' that time any more 'n this time — an' I was as obleeged to you as I could be. The colonel's awful hard on the men."

"Is he?" said Stafford gratingly. "They seem to like him."

He sat his horse before the laurel thicket and despised himself for holding conference with this poor thief; or, rather, some fibre in his brain told him that, out of this jungle, if ever he came out of it, he

would despise himself. Had he really done so now, he would have
turned away. He did not so; he sat in the heart of the jungle and
compared hatreds with Steve.

The latter glanced upward a moment with his ferret eyes, then
turned his head aside and spat. "If there's any of my way of
thinkin' they don't like him — But they're all fools! Crept down
through the swamp a little ago an' heard it! 'Colonel, get us
across, somehow, won't you? We'll fight like hell!' 'I can't, men.
I have n't any orders.' Yaah! I wish he'd take the regiment over
without them, and then be court-martialled and shot for doing
it!" Steve spat again. "I seed long ago that you did n't like him
either, major. He gets along too fast — all the prizes come his
way."

"Yes," said Stafford, from the heart of the jungle. "They come
his way. . . . And he's standing there at the edge of the water, hoping for orders to cross."

Steve, beneath the swamp magnolia, had a widening of the lips.
"Luck's turned agin him one way, though. He's out of favour with
Old Jack. The regiment don't know why, but it saw it mighty plain
day before yesterday, after the big battle! Gawd knows I'd like to
see him so deep in trouble he'd never get out — and so would you,
major. Prizes would stop coming his way then, and he might lose
those he has —"

"If I entertain a devil," said Stafford, "I'll not be hypocrite
enough to object to his conversation. Nor, if I take his suggestion,
is there any sense in covering him with reprobation. So go your way,
miserable imp! while I go mine!"

But Steve kept up with him, half-running at his stirrup. "I got to
rejoin,'cause it's jest off one battlefield on to another, and there ain't
nowhere else to go! This world's a sickenin' place for men like me.
So I've got to rejoin. Ef there's ever anything I kin do for you,
major —"

At the head of the dividing arm of the creek they heard behind
them a horseman, and waited for a courier to come up. "You are
going on to the 65th?"

"Yes, sir. I belong there. I was kept by General Winder for some
special duty, and I'm just through it —"

"I have an order," said Stafford, "from General Winder to

Colonel Cleave. There are others to carry and time presses. I'll entrust it to you. Listen now, and get it straight."

He gave an order. The courier listened, nodded energetically, repeated it after him, and gathered up the reins . "I am powerfully glad to carry that order, sir! It means 'Cross,' does n't it?"

He rode off, southward to the stream, in which direction Steve had already shambled. Stafford returned, through wood and swamp, to the road by the bridge. Above and around the deep inner jungle his intellect worked. He knew that he had done a villainy; knew it and did not repent. A nature, fine enough in many ways, lay bound hand and foot, deep in miasmas and primal heat, captive to a master and consuming passion. To create a solitude where he alone might reach one woman's figure, he would have set a world afire. He rode back now, through the woods, to a general commanding who never forgave nor listened overmuch to explanations, and he rode with quietude, the very picture of a gallant soldier.

Back on the edge of White Oak Swamp, Richard Cleave considered the order he had received. He found an ambiguity in the wording, a choice of constructions. He half turned to send the courier again to Winder, to make absolutely sure that the construction which he strongly preferred was correct. As he did so, though he could not see the brigade beyond the belt of trees, he heard it in motion, *coming down through the woods to cross the stream in the rear of the 65th.* He looked at the ford and the silent woods beyond. From Frayser's Farm, so short a distance away, came a deeper roll of thunder. It had a solemn and a pleading sound, *How long are we to wait for any help?* Cleave knit his brows; then, with a decisive gesture of his hand, he dismissed the doubt and stepped in front of his colour company. *Attention! Into column. Forward!*

On the road leading down to the bridge Stafford met his own division general, riding Rifle back to his command. "Hello, Major Stafford!" said Old Dick. "I thought I had lost you."

"General Jackson detained me, general."

"Yes, yes, you are n't the only one! But let me tell you, major, he 's coming out of his spell!"

"You think it was a spell, then, sir?"

"Sure of it! Old Jackson simply has n't been here at all. D. H. Hill thinks he 's been broken down and ill — and somebody else is poetical and says his star never shines when another's is above it, which is nonsense — and somebody else thinks he thought we did enough in the Valley, which is damned nonsense — eh?"

"Of course, sir. Damned nonsense."

Ewell jerked his head. "Yes, sir. No man's his real self all the time — whether he's a Presbyterian or not. Old Jackson simply has n't been in this cursed low country at all! But —— ! I've been trying to give advice down there, and, by God, sir, he's approaching! If it was a spell, it's lifting! That bridge'll be built pretty soon, I reckon, and when we cross at last we'll cross with Stonewall Jackson going on before!"

CHAPTER XXXVI

MALVERN HILL

STAR by star the heavens paled. The dawn came faintly and mournfully up from the east. Beneath it the battlefield of Frayser's Farm lay hushed and motionless, like the sad canvas of a painter, the tragic dream of a poet. It was far flung over broken ground and strewn with wrecks of war. Dead men and dying — very many of them, for the fighting had been heavy — lay stretched in the ghostly light, and beside them dead and dying horses. Eighteen Federal guns had been taken. They rested on ridged earth, black against the cold, grey sky. Stark and silent, far and wide, rolled the field beneath the cold, mysterious, changing light. Beside the dead men there were sleeping troops, regiments lying on their arms, fallen last night where they were halted, slumbering heavily through the dew-drenched summer night. As the sky grew purple and the last star went out, the bugles began to blow. The living men rose. If the others heard a reveille, it was in far countries.

Edward Cary, lying down in the darkness near one of the guns, had put out a hand and touched a bedfellow. The soldier seemed asleep, and Edward slept too, weary enough to have slept in Hades. Now, as the bugles called, he sat up and looked at his companion — who did not rise. "I thought you lay very still," said Edward. He sat a moment, on the dank earth, beside the still, grey figure. The gun stood a little above him; through a wheel as through a rose window he saw the flush of dawn. The dead soldier's eyes were open; they, too, stared through the gun-wheel at the dawn. Edward closed them. "I never could take death seriously," he said; "which is fortunate, I suppose."

Two hours later his regiment, moving down the Quaker road, came to a halt before a small, pillared, country church. A group of officers sat their horses near the portico. Lee was in front, quiet and grand. Out of the cluster Warwick Cary pushed his horse across to the halted regiment. Father and son were presently holding converse beneath a dusty roadside cedar. "I am thankful to see you!" said Edward. "We heard of the great charge you made. Please take better care of yourself, father!"

"The past week has been like a dream," answered the other; "one of those dreams in which, over and over, some undertaking, vital to you and tremendous, is about to march. Then, over and over, comes some pettiest obstacle, and the whole vast matter is turned awry."

"Yesterday should have been ours."

"Yes. General Lee had planned as he always plans. We should have crushed McClellan. Instead, we fought alone — and we lost four thousand men; and though we made the enemy lose as many, he has again drawn himself out of our grasp and is before us. I think that to-day we will have a fearful fight."

"Jackson is over at last."

"Yes, close behind us. Whiting is leading; I saw him a moment. There's a report that one of the Stonewall regiments crossed and was cut in pieces late yesterday afternoon —"

"I hope it was n't Richard's!"

"I hope not. I have a curious, boding feeling about it. — There beat your drums! Good-bye, again —"

He leaned from his saddle and kissed his son, then backed his horse across the road to the generals by the pillared church. The regiment marched away, and as it passed it cheered General Lee. He lifted his hat. "Thank you, men. Do your best to-day — do your best."

"We'll mind you, Marse Robert, we'll mind you!" cried the troops, and went by shouting.

Somewhere down the Quaker Road the word "Malvern Hill" seemed to drop from the skies. "Malvern Hill. Malvern Hill. They're all massed on Malvern Hill. Three hundred and forty guns. And on the James the gunboats. Malvern Hill. Malvern Hill. Malvern Hill."

A man in line with Edward described the place. "My last year at William and Mary I spent Christmas at Westover. We hunted over all Malvern Hill. It rises one hundred and fifty feet, and the top's a mile across. About the base there are thick forests and swamps, and Turkey Creek goes winding, winding to the James.

You see the James — the wide, old, yellow river, with the birds going
screaming overhead. There were no gunboats on it that day, no
Monitors, or Galenas, or Maritanzas, and if you'd told us up there
on Malvern Hill that the next time we climbed it —! At Westover,
after supper, they told Indian stories and stories of Tarleton's troopers, and in the night we listened for the tap of Evelyn Byrd's slipper
on the stair. We said we heard it — anyhow, we did n't hear gunboats and three hundred thirty-two pounders!"

> " 'When only Beauty's eyes did rake us fore and aft,
>   When only Beaux used powder, and Cupid's was the shaft —' "

sang Edward,

> " Most fatal was the war and pleasant to be slain —'"

Malvern Hill, beat out the marching feet. *Malvern Hill. Malvern
Hill. Malvern Hill.*

There was a deep wood, out from which ran like spurs shallow ravines, clad with briar and bush and young trees; there was a stretch
of rail fence; and there was a wheat field, where the grain stood in
shocks. Because of the smoke, however, nothing could be seen
plainly; and because of the most awful sound, few orders were distinctly heard. Evidently officers were shouting; in the rents of the
veil one saw waved arms, open mouths, gesticulations with swords.
But the loud-mouthed guns spoke by the score, and the blast bore
the human voice away. The regiment in which was Edward Cary
divined an order and ceased firing, lying flat in sedge and sassafras,
while a brigade from the rear roared by. Edward looked at his
fingers. "Barrel burn them?" asked a neighbour. "Reckon they
use red-hot muskets in hell? Wish you could see your lips, Edward!
Round black O. Biting cartridges for a living — and it used to be
when you read Plutarch that you were all for the peaceful heroes!
You have n't a lady-love that would look at you now!

> " 'Take, oh, take those lips away
>   That so blackly are enshrined —'

Here comes a lamp-post — a lamp-post — a lamp-post!"

The gunboats on the river threw the "lamp-posts." The long and
horrible shells arrived with a noise that was indescribable. A thousand shrieking rockets, perhaps, with at the end an explosion and a

rain of fragments like rocks from Vesuvius. They had a peculiar faculty for getting on the nerves. The men watched their coming with something like shrinking, with raised arms and narrowed eyes. "Look out for the lamp-post — look out for the lamp-post — look out — Aaahhhh!"

Before long the regiment was moved a hundred yards nearer the wheat-field. Here it became entangled in the ebb of a charge — the brigade which had rushed by coming back, piecemeal, broken and driven by an iron flail. It would reform and charge again, but now there was confusion. All the field was confused, dismal and dreadful, beneath the orange-tinted smoke. The smoke rolled and billowed, a curtain of strange texture, now parting, now closing, and when it parted disclosing immemorial Death and Wounds with some attendant martial pageantry. The commands were split as by wedges, the uneven ground driving them asunder, and the belching guns. They went up to hell mouth, brigade by brigade, even regiment by regiment, and in the breaking and reforming and twilight of the smoke, through the falling of officers and the surging to and fro, the troops became interwoven, warp of one division, woof of another. The sound was shocking; when, now and then there fell a briefest interval it was as though the world had stopped, had fallen into a gulf of silence.

Edward Cary found beside him a man from another regiment, a small, slight fellow, young and simple. A shock of wheat gave both a moment's protection. "Hot work!" said Edward, with his fine camaraderie. "You made a beautiful charge. We almost thought you would take them."

The other looked at him vacantly. "I added up figures in the old warehouse," he said, in a high, thin voice. "I added up figures in the old warehouse, and when I went home at night I used to read plays. I added up figures in the old warehouse — Don't you remember Hotspur? I always liked him, and that part —

> 'To pluck bright honour from the pale-faced moon;
> Or dive into the bottom of the deep —'"

He stood up. Edward rose to his knees and put out a hand to draw him down. "It's enough to make you crazy, I'll confess — but you mustn't stand up like that!"

The downward drawing hand was too late. There were blue sharpshooters in a wood in front. A ball entered the clerk's breast and he sank down behind the wheat. "I added up figures in the old warehouse," he again told Cary, "and when I went home at night I read plays —"

The figure stiffened in Edward's grasp. He laid it down, and from behind the wheat shock watched a grey battery in process of being knocked to pieces. It had arrived in this quarter of the field in a wild gallop, and with a happy insouciance had unlimbered and run up the guns back of a little crest topped with sumach, taking pains meanwhile to assure the infantry that now it was safe. The infantry had grinned. "Like you first-rate, artillery! Willing to bet on the gunners, but the guns are a *leetle* small and few. Don't know that we feel so *awful* safe!"

The grey began. Four shells flew up the long slope and burst among the iron rows that made a great triple crown for Malvern Hill. The grey gunners cheered, and the appreciative infantry cheered, and the first began to reload while the second, flat in scrub and behind the wheat, condescended to praise. "Artillery does just about as well as can be expected! Awful old-fashioned arm — but well-meaning. . . . Look out — look . . . Eeehhh!"

The iron crown that had been blazing toward other points of the compass now blazed toward this. Adversity came to the insouciant grey battery, adversity quickening to disaster. The first thunder blast thickened to a howling storm of shrapnel, grape, and canister.

At the first gun gunner No. 1, ramming home a charge, was blown into fragments; at the second the arm holding the sponge staff was severed from gunner No. 3's shoulder. A great shell, bursting directly over the third, killed two men and horribly mangled others; the carriage of the fourth was crushed and set on fire. This in the beginning of the storm; as it swelled, total destruction threatened from the murk. The captain went up and down. "Try it a little longer, men. Try it a little longer, men. We've got to make up in quality, you know. We've got to make up in quality, you know. Marse Robert's looking — I see him over there! Try it a little longer — try it a little longer."

An aide arrived. "For God's sake, take what you've got left

away! Yes, it's an order. Your being massacred won't help. Look out — Look —"

No one in battle ever took account of time or saw any especial reason for being, now here, and now in quite a different place, or ever knew exactly how the places had been exchanged. Edward was practically certain that he had taken part in a charge, that his brigade had driven a body of blue infantry from a piece of woods. At any rate they were no longer in the wheat field, but in a shady wood, where severed twigs and branches floated pleasantly down. Lying flat, chin on hand, he watched a regiment storm and take a thick abattis — felled trees filled with sharpshooters — masking a hastily thrown up earthwork. The regiment was reserving its fire and losing heavily. An elderly man led it, riding a large old steady horse. "That's Ex-Governor Smith," said the regiment in the wood. "That's Extra Billy! He's a corker! Next time he runs he's going to get all the votes —"

The regiment tried twice to pass the abattis, but each time fell back. The brigadier had ordered it not to fire until it was past the trees; it obeyed, but sulkily enough. Men were dropping; the colour-bearer went down. There was an outcry. "Colonel! we can't stand this! We'll all get killed before we fire a shot! The general don't know how we're fixed —" Extra Billy agreed with them. He rose in his stirrups, turned and nodded vigorous assent. "Of course you can't stand it, boys! You ought n't to be expected to. It's all this infernal tactics and West P'int tomfoolery! Damn it, fire! and flush the game!"

Edward laughed. From the fuss it was apparent that the abattis and earthwork had succumbed. At any rate, the old governor and his regiment were gone. He was of the colour-guard, and all the colour-guard were laughing. "Did n't you ever see him go into battle with his old blue umbrella up! Trotting along same as to a caucus — whole constituency following! Fine old political Roman! Look out, Yedward! Whole pine tree coming down."

The scene changed again, and it was the side of a ravine, with a fine view of the river and with Morell and Couch blazing somewhere above. The shells went overhead, bellowing monsters charging a grey battery on a hillock and a distant line of troops. "That's Pegram — that battery," said some one. "He does well." "Has any one any idea of the time?" asked another. "Sun's so hidden there's no guessing. Don't believe we'll ever see his blessed light again."

A fisherman from the Eastern Shore stated that it was nearly five o'clock. "Fogs can't fool me. Day's drawing down, and tide's going out —"

The lieutenant-colonel appeared. "Somebody with an order has been shot, coming through the cornfield toward us. Three volunteers to bring him in!"

Edward and the Eastern Shore man and a lean and dry and middle-aged lawyer from King and Queen bent their heads beneath their shoulders and plunged into the corn. All the field was like a miniature abattis, stalk and blade shot down and crossed and recrossed in the wildest tangle. To make way over it was difficult enough, and before the three had gone ten feet the minies took a hand. The wounded courier lay beneath his horse, and the horse screamed twice, the sound rising above the roar of the guns. A ball pierced Edward's cap, another drew blood from the lawyer's hand. The fisherman was a tall and wiry man; as he ran he swayed like a mast in storm. The three reached the courier, dragged him from beneath the horse, and found both legs crushed. He looked at them with lustreless eyes. "You can't do anything for me, boys. The general says please try to take those three guns up there. He's going to charge the line beyond, and they are in the way."

"All right, we will," said the lawyer. "Now you put one arm round Cary's neck and one round mine —"

But the courier shook his head. "You leave me here. I'm awful tired. You go take the guns instead. Ain't no use, I tell you. I'd like to see the children, but —"

In the act of speaking, as they lifted him, a ball went through his throat. The three laid the body down, and, heads bent between shoulders, ran over and through the corn toward the ravine. Two thirds of the way across, the fisherman was shot. He came to his knees and, in falling, clutched Edward. "Mast's overboard," he cried, in a rattling voice. "Cut her loose, damn you! — I'll take the helm —" He, too, died. Cary and the lawyer got back to the gully and gave the order.

The taking of those guns was no simple matter. It resembled

child's play only in the single-mindedness and close attention which went to its accomplishment. The regiment that reached them at last and took them, and took what was left of the blue gunners, was not much more than half a regiment. The murk up here on this semi-height was thick to choking; the odour and taste of the battle poisoned brass on the tongue, the colour that of a sand storm, the heat like that of a battleship in action, and all the place shook from the thunder and recoil of the tiers of great guns beyond, untaken, not to be taken. A regiment rushed out of the rolling smoke, by the half regiment. "Mississippi! Mississippi! — Well, even Mississippi is n't going to do the impossible!" As the line went by, tall and swinging and yelling itself hoarse, the colonel was wounded and fell. The charge went on while the officer — he was an old man, very stately looking — dragged himself aside, and sitting in the sedge tied a large bright handkerchief above a wound in his leg. The charge dashed itself against the hillside, and the tier of guns flamed a death's sickle and mowed it down. Breathless, broken, the regiment fell back. When it reached the old man with the bright handkerchief, it would have lifted him and carried him with it to the rear. He would not go. He said, "Tell the 21st they can't get me till they take those guns!"

The 21st mended its gaps and charged again. The old man set his hat on his sword, waved it in the air, and cheered his men as they passed. They passed him but to return. To go up against those lines of bellowing guns was mere heroic madness. Bleeding, exhausted, the men put out their hands for the old man. He drew his revolver. "I'll shoot anybody who touches me! Tell the 21st they can't get their colonel till they take those guns!"

The 21st charged a third time, in vain. It came back — a part of it came back. The old man had fainted, and his men lifted and bore him away.

From the platform where he lay in the shadow of the three guns Edward Cary looked out over Malvern Hill, the encompassing lowland, marsh and forest and fields, the winding Turkey Creek and Western Creek, and to the south the James. A wind had sprung up and was blowing the battle smoke hither and yon. Here it hung heavily, and here a long lane was opened. The sun was low and red behind a filmy veil, dark and ragged like torn crape. He saw four gunboats on the river; they were throwing the long, howling shells. The Monitor was there, an old foe — the cheese box on a shingle. Edward shut his eyes and saw again Hampton Roads, and how the Monitor had looked, darting from behind the Minnesota. The old turtle, the old Merrimac . . . and now she lay, a charred hull, far, far beneath the James, by Craney Island.

The private on his right was a learned man. Edward addressed him. "Have you ever thought, doctor, how fearfully dramatic is this world?"

"Yes. It's one of those facts that are too colossal to be seen. Shakespeare says all the world's a stage. That's only a half-truth. The world's a player, like the rest of us."

Below this niche stretched the grey battle-lines; above it, on the hilltop, by the cannon and over half the slope beneath, spread the blue. A forest stood behind the grey; out of it came the troops to the charge, the flags tossing in front. The upward reaching fingers of coppice and brush had their occupants, fragments of commands under cover, bands of sharpshooters. And everywhere over the open, raked by the guns, were dead and dying men. They lay thickly. Now and again the noise of the torment of the wounded made itself heard — a most doleful and ghostly sound coming up like a wail from the Inferno. There were, too, many dead or dying horses. Others, still unhurt, galloped from end to end of the field of death. In the wheatfield there were several of the old, four-footed warriors, who stood and ate of the shocked grain. There arrived a hush over the battlefield, one of those pauses which occur between exhaustion and renewed effort, effort at its height. The guns fell silent, the musketry died away, the gunboats ceased to throw those great shells. By contrast with the clangour that had prevailed, the stillness seemed that of a desert waste, a dead world. Over toward a cross-road there could be made out three figures on horseback. The captain of Edward's company was an old college mate; lying down with his men, he now drew himself over the ground and loaned Cary his field-glass. "It's General Lee and General Jackson and General D. H. Hill."

A body of grey troops came to occupy a finger of woods below the three captured guns. "That's Cary's Legion," said the captain. "Here comes the colonel now!"

The two commands were but a few yards apart. Fauquier Cary, dismounting, walked up the sedgy slope and asked to speak to his nephew. The latter left the ranks, and the two found a trampled space beside one of the great thirty-two pounders. A dead man or two lay in the parched grass, but there was nothing else to disturb. The quiet yet held over North and South and the earth that gave them standing room. "I have but a moment," said the elder man. "This is but the hush before the final storm. We came by Jackson's troops, and one of his officers whom I knew at the Point rode beside me a little way. They all crossed White Oak Swamp by starlight this morning, and apparently Jackson is again the Jackson of the Valley. It was a curious eclipse. The force of the man is such that, while his officers acknowledge the eclipse, it makes no difference to them. He is Stonewall Jackson — and that suffices. But that is not what I have to tell —"

"I saw father a moment this morning. He said there was a rumour about one of the Stonewall regiments —"

"Yes. It was the 65th."

"Cut to pieces?"

"Yes."

"Richard — Richard was not killed?"

"No. But many were. Hairston Breckinridge was killed — and some of the Thunder Run men — and very many others. Almost destroyed, Carlton said. They crossed at sunset. There were a swamp and a wood and a hollow commanded by hills. The enemy was in force behind the hill, and there was beside a considerable command in ambush, concealed in the woods by the swamp. These had a gun or two. All opened on the 65th. It was cut to pieces in the swamp and in a little marshy meadow. Only a remnant got back to the northern side of the creek. Richard is under arrest."

"He was acting under orders!"

"So Carlton says he says. But General Jackson says there was no such order; that he disobeyed the order that was given, and now tries to screen himself. Carlton says Jackson is more steel-like than usual, and we know how it fared with Garnett and with others. There will be a court-martial. I am very anxious."

"I am not," said Edward stoutly. "There will be an honourable acquittal. We must write and tell Judith that she's not to worry! Richard Cleave did nothing that he should not have done."

"Of course, we know that. But Carlton says that, on the face of it, it's an ugly affair. And General Jackson — Well, we can only await developments."

"Poor Judith! — and his sister and mother. . . . Poor women!"

The other made a gesture of assent and sorrow. "Well, I must go back. Take care of yourself, Edward. There will be the devil's own work presently."

He went, and Edward returned to his fellows. The silence yet held over the field; the westering sun glowed dull red behind the smoke; the three figures rested still by the cross-roads; the mass of frowning metal topped Malvern Hill like a giant, smoke-wreathed *chevaux de frise*. Out of the brushwood to the left of the regiment, straight by it, upward towards the guns, and then at a tangent off through the fields to the woods, sped a rabbit. Legs to earth, it hurried with all its might. The regiment was glad of a diversion — the waiting was growing so intolerable. The men cheered the rabbit. "Go it, Molly Cottontail! — Go it, Molly! — Go it, Molly! — Hi! Don't go that-away! Them's Yankees! They'll cut your head off! Go t'other way — that's it! Go it, Molly! Damn! If 't was n't for my character, I'd go with you!"

The rabbit disappeared. The regiment settled back to waiting, a very intolerable employment. The sun dipped lower and lower. The hush grew portentous. The guns looked old, mailed, dead warriors; the gunboats sleeping forms; the grey troops battle-lines in a great war picture, the three horsemen by the cross-roads a significant group in the same; the dead and wounded over all the fields, upon the slope, in the woods, by the marshes, the jetsam, still and heavy, of war at its worst. For a moment longer the wide and dreary stretch rested so, then with a wild suddenness sound and furious motion rushed upon the scene. The gunboats recommenced with their long and horrible shells. A grey battery opened on Berdan's sharp-shooters strung in a line of trees below the great crown of guns. The crown flamed toward the battery, scorched and mangled it. By the cross-roads the three figures separated, going in different directions. Presently galloping horses — aides, couriers — crossed the plane of vision. They went from D. H. Hill in the centre to Jackson's brigades on the left and Magruder's on the right. They had a mile of open to cross, and the iron crown and the sharpshooters flamed against them. Some galloped on and gave the orders. Some threw up their arms and fell, or, crashing to earth with a wounded horse, disentangled themselves and stumbled on through the iron rain. The sun drew close to the vast and melancholy forests across the river. Through a rift in the smoke, there came a long and crimson shaft. It reddened the river, then struck across the shallows to Malvern Hill, suffused with a bloody tinge wood and field and the marshes by the creeks, then splintered against the hilltop and made a hundred guns to gleam. The wind heightened, lifting the smoke and driving it northward. It bared to the last red light the wild and dreary battlefield.

From the centre rose the Confederate yell. Rodes's brigade, led by Gordon, charged. It had half a mile of open to cross, and it was caught at once in the storm that howled from the crest of Malvern Hill. Every regiment suffered great loss; the 3d Alabama saw half its number slain or wounded. The men yelled again, and sprang on in the teeth of the storm. They reached the slope, almost below the guns. Gordon looked behind for the supporting troops which Hill had promised. They were coming, that grim fighter leading them, but they were coming far off, under clanging difficulties, through a hell of shrapnel. Rodes's brigade alone could not wrest that triple crown from the hilltop — no, not if the men had been giants, sons of Anak! They were halted; they lay down, put muskets to shoulder and fired steadily and fired again on the blue infantry.

It grew darker on the plain. Brigades were coming from the left, the right, the centre. There had been orders for a general advance. Perhaps the aides carrying them were among the slain, perhaps this, perhaps that. The event was that brigades charged singly — sometimes even regiments crossed, with a cry, the twilight, groaning plain and charged Malvern Hill unsupported. The place flamed death and destruction. Hill's ten thousand men pressed forward with the order of a review. The shot and shell met them like a tornado. The men fell by hundreds. The lines closed, rushed on. The Federal infantry joined the artillery. Musketry and cannon, the din became a prolonged and fearful roar of battle.

The sun disappeared. There sprang out in the western sky three long red bands of clouds. On the darkening slope and plain Hill was crushed back, before and among his lines a horror of exploding shells. Jackson threw forward Lawton and Whiting, Winder and the Louisiana troops, while on the right, brigade after brigade, Magruder hurled across the plain nine brigades. After Hill, Magruder's troops bore the brunt of the last fearful fighting.

They stormed across the plain in twilight that was lit by the red flashes from the guns. The clouds of smoke were red-bosomed; the red bars stayed in the west. The guns never ceased their thundering, the musketry to roll. Death swung a wide scythe in the twilight of that first day of July. Anderson and Armistead, Barksdale, Semmes and Kershaw, Wright and Toombs and Mahone, rushed along the slope of Malvern Hill, as Ripley and Garland and Gordon and all the brigadiers of D. H. Hill had rushed before them. Death, issuing from that great power of artillery, laid the soldiers in swathes. The ranks closed, again and again the ranks closed; with diminished numbers but no slackening of courage, the grey soldiers again dashed themselves against Malvern Hill. The red bars in the west faded slowly to a deep purple; above them, in a clear space of sky, showed the silver Venus. Upon her cooling globe, in a day to come, intelligent life might rend itself as here — the old horror, the old tragedy, the old stained sublimity over again! All the drifting smoke was now red lit, and beneath it lay in their blood elderly men, and men in their prime, and young men — very many, oh, very many young men! As the night deepened there sprang, beneath the thunder, over all the field a sound like wind in reeds. It was a sighing sound, a low and grievous sound. The blue lost heavily, for the charges were wildly heroic; but the guns were never disabled, and the loss of the grey was the heaviest. Brigade by brigade, the grey faced the storm and were beaten back, only again to reel forward upon the slope where Death stood and swung his scythe. The last light dwelt on their colours, on the deep red of their battle-flags; then the western sky became no warmer than the eastern. The stars were out in troops; the battle stopped.

D. H. Hill, an iron fighter with a mania for personal valour, standing where he had been standing for an hour, in a pleasantly exposed spot, clapped on his hat and beckoned for his horse. The ground about him showed furrowed as for planting, and a neighbouring oak tree was so riddled with bullets that the weight of a man might have sent it crashing down. D. H. Hill, drawing long breath, spoke half to his staff, half to the stars: "Give me Federal artillery and Confederate infantry, and I'd whip the world!"

CHAPTER XXXVII

A WOMAN

ALLAN GOLD, lying in a corner of the Stonewall Hospital, turned his head toward the high window. It showed him little, merely a long strip of blue sky above housetops. The window was open, and the noises of the street came in. He knew them, checked them off in his mind. He was doing well. A body, superbly healthful, might stand out boldly against a minie ball or two, just as calm nerves, courage and serene judgement were of service in a war hospital such as this. If he was restless now, it was because he was wondering about Christianna. It was an hour past her time for coming.

The ward was fearfully crowded. This, however, was the end by the stair, and he had a little cut-off place to himself. Many in the ward yet lay on the floor, on a blanket as he had done that first morning. In the afternoon of that day a wide bench had been brought into his corner, a thin flock mattress laid upon it, and he himself lifted from the floor. He had protested that others needed a bed much more, that he was used to lying on the earth — but Christianna had been firm. He wondered why she did not come.

Chickahominy, Gaines's Mill, Garnett's and Golding's farms, Peach Orchard, Savage Station, White Oak Swamp, Frayser's Farm, Malvern Hill — dire echoes of the Seven Days' fighting had thronged into this hospital as into all others, as into the houses of citizens and the public buildings and the streets! All manner of wounded soldiers told the story — ever so many soldiers and ever so many variants of the story. The dead bore witness, and the wailing of women which was now and then heard in the streets; not often, for the women were mostly silent, with pressed lips. And the ambulances jolting by — and the sound of funerals — and the church bells tolling, tolling — all these bore witness. And day and night there was the thunder of the cannon. From Mechanicsville and Gaines's Mill it had rolled near and loud, from Savage Station somewhat less so; White Oak Swamp and Frayser's Farm had carried the sound yet further off, and from Malvern Hill it came but distantly. But loud or low, near or far, day by day and into each night, Richmond heard the cannon. At first the vibration played on the town's heart, like a giant hand on giant strings. But at last the tune grew old and the town went about its business. There was so much to do! one could not stop to listen to cannon. Richmond was a vast hospital; pain and fever in all places, and, around, the shadow of death. Hardly a house but mourned a kinsman or kinsmen; early and late the dirges wailed through the streets. So breathlessly filled were the days, that often the dead were buried at night. The weather was hot — days and nights hot, close and still. Men and women went swiftly through them, swift and direct as weavers' shuttles. Privation, early comrade of the South, was here; scant room, scant supplies, not too much of wholesome food for the crowded town, few medicines or alleviatives, much to be done and done at once with the inadequatest means. There was little time in which to think in general terms; all effort must go toward getting done the immediate thing. The lift and tension of the time sloughed off the immaterial weak act or thought. There were present a heroic simplicity, a naked verity, a full cup of service, a high and noble altruism. The plane was epic, and the people did well.

The sky within Allan's range of vision was deep blue; the old brick gable-ends of houses, mellow and old, against it. A soldier with a broken leg and a great sabre cut over the head, just brought into the ward, brought with him the latest news. He talked loudly, and all down the long room, crowded to suffocation, the less desperately wounded raised themselves on their elbows to hear. Others, shot through stomach or bowels, or fearfully torn by shells, or with the stumps of amputated limbs not doing well, raved on in delirium or kept up their pitiful moaning. The soldier raised his voice higher, and those leaning on elbows listened with avidity. "Evelington Heights? Where's Evelington Heights?" — "Between Westover and Rawling's millpond, near Malvern Hill!" — "Malvern Hill! That was ghastly!" — "Go on, sergeant-major! We're been pining for a newspaper."

"Were any of you boys at Malvern Hill?"

"Yes, — only those who were there ain't in a fix to tell about it!

That man over there — and that one — and that one — oh, a middling lot! They're pretty badly off — poor boys!"

From a pallet came a hollow voice. "I was at Malvern Hill, and I ain't never going there again — I ain't never going there again — I ain't never. . . . Who's that singing? I kin sing, too —

> 'The years creep slowly by, Lorena;
> The snow is on the grass again;
> The sun's low down the sky, Lorena;
> The frost gleams where the flowers have been —'"

"Don't mind him," said the soldiers on elbows. "Poor fellow! he ain't got any voice anyhow. We know about Malvern Hill. Malvern Hill was pretty bad. And we heard there'd been a cavalry rumpus — Jeb Stuart and Sweeney playing their tricks! We didn't know the name of the place. Evelington Heights! Pretty name."

The sergeant-major would not be cheated of Malvern Hill. "'Pretty bad!' I should say 't was pretty bad! Malvern Hill was *awful*. If anything could induce me to be a damn Yankee 't would be them guns of their'n! Yes, sirree, bob! we fought and fought, and ten o'clock came and there wasn't any moon, and we stopped. And in the night-time the damn Yankees continued to retreat away. There was an awful noise of gun-wheels all the night long — so the sentries said, and the surgeons and the wounded and, I reckon, the generals. The rest of us, we were asleep. I don't reckon there ever was men any more tired. Malvern Hill was — I can't swear because there are ladies nursing us, but Malvern Hill was — Well, dawn blew at reveille — No, doctor, I ain't getting light-headed. I just get my words a little twisted. Reveille blew at dawn, and there were sheets of cold pouring rain, and everywhere there were dead men, dead men, dead men lying there in the wet, and the ambulances were wandering round like ghosts of wagons, and the wood was too dripping to make a fire, and three men out of my mess were killed, and one was a boy that we'd all adopted, and it was awful discouraging. Yes, we were right tired, damn Yankees and all of us. . . . Doctor, if I was you I wouldn't bother about that leg. It's all right as it is, and you might hurt me. . . . Oh, all right! Kin I smoke? . . . Yuugh! Well, boys, the damn Yankees continued their retreat to Harrison's Landing, where their hell-fire gunboats could stand picket for them. . . . Say, ma'am, would you kindly tell me why that four-post bed over there is all hung with wreaths of roses? — 'Is n't any bed there?' But there is! I see it. . . . Evelington Heights — and Stuart dropping shells into the damn Yankees' camp. . . . They *are* roses, the old Giants of Battle by the beehive. . . . Evelington Heights. Eveling— Well, the damn Yankees dragged their guns up there, too. . . . If the beehive's there, then the apple tree's here — Grandma, if you'll ask him not to whip me I'll never take them again, and I'll hold your yarn every time you want me to —"

The ward heard no more about Evelington Heights. It knew, however, that it had been no great affair; it knew that McClellan with his exhausted army, less many thousand dead, wounded, and prisoners, less fifty-two guns and thirty-five thousand small arms, less enormous stores captured or destroyed, less some confidence at Washington, rested down the James by Westover, in the shadow of gunboats. The ward guessed that, for a time at least, Richmond was freed from the Northern embrace. It knew that Lee and his exhausted army, less even more of dead and wounded than had fallen on the other side, rested between that enemy and Richmond. Lee was watching; the enemy would come no nearer for this while. For all its pain, for all the heat, the blood, the fever, thirst and woe, the ward, the hospital, all the hospitals, experienced to-day a sense of triumph. It was so with the whole city. Allan knew this, lying, looking with sea-blue eyes at the blue summer sky and the old and mellow roofs. The city mourned, but also it rejoiced. There stretched the black thread, but twisted with it was the gold. A pæan sounded as well as a dirge. Seven days and nights of smoke and glare upon the horizon, of the heart-shaking cannon roar, of the pouring in of the wounded, of processions to Hollywood, of anguish, ceaseless labour, sick waiting, dizzy hope, descending despair. . . . Now, at last, above it all the bells rang for victory. A young girl, coming through the ward, had an armful of flowers, — white lilies, citron aloes, mignonette, and phlox — She gave her posies to all who stretched out a hand, and went out with her smiling face. Allan held a great stalk of garden phlox, white and sweet. It carried him back to the tollgate and to the log schoolhouse by Thunder Run. . . . Twelve o'clock. Was not Christianna coming at all?

This was not Judith Cary's ward, but now she entered it. Allan, watching the narrow path between the wounded, saw her coming from the far door. He did not know who she was; he only looked from the flower in his hand and had a sense of strength and sweetness, of something noble approaching nearer. She paused to ask a question of one of the women; answered, she came straight on. He saw that she was coming to the cut-off corner by the stair, and instinctively he straightened a little the covering over him. In a moment she was standing beside him, in her cool hospital dress, with her dark hair knotted low, with a flower at her breast. "You are Allan Gold?" she said.

"Yes."

"My name is Judith Cary. Perhaps you have heard of me. I have been to Lauderdale and to Three Oaks."

"Yes," said Allan. "I have heard of you. I —"

There was an empty box beside the wall. Judith drew it nearer to his bed and sat down. "You have been looking for Christianna? I came to tell you about poor little Christianna — and — and other things. Christianna's father has been killed."

Allan uttered an exclamation. "Isham Maydew! I never thought of his going! . . . Poor child!"

"So she thought she ought not to come to-day. Had there been strong reason, many people dependent upon her, she would have come."

"Poor Christianna — poor wild rose! . . . It's ghastly, this war! There is nothing too small and harmless for its grist."

"I agree with you. Nothing too great; nothing too small. Nothing too base, as there is nothing too noble."

"Isham Maydew! He was lean and tough and still, like Death in a picture. Where was he killed?"

"It was at White Oak Swamp. At White Oak Swamp, the day before Malvern Hill."

Allan looked at her. There was more in her voice than the noncoming of Christianna, than the death of Isham Maydew. She had spoken in a clear, low, bell-like tone that held somehow the ache of the world. He was simple and direct, and he spoke at once out of his thought. He knew that all the men of her house were at the front. "You have had a loss of your own? —"

She shook her head. "I? No. I have had no loss."

"Now," thought Allan, "there's something proud in it." He looked at her with his kindly, sea-blue eyes. In some chamber of the brain there flashed out a picture — the day of the Botetourt Resolutions, winter dusk after winter sunset and Cleave and himself going homeward over the long hilltop — with talk, among other things, of visitors at Lauderdale. This was "the beautiful one." He remembered the lift of Cleave's head and his voice. Judith's large dark eyes had been raised; transparent, showing always the soul within as did his own, they now met Allan's. "The 65th," she said, "was cut to pieces."

The words, dragged out as they were, left a shocked silence. Here, in the corner by the stair, the arch of wood partially obscuring the ward, with the still blue sky and the still brick gables, they seemed for the moment cut away from the world, met on desert sands to tell and hear a dreadful thing. "Cut to pieces," breathed Allan. "The 65th cut to pieces!"

The movement which he made displaced the bandage about his shoulder. She left the box, kneeled by him and straightened matters, then went back to her seat. "It was this way," she said, — and told him the story as she had heard it from her father and from Fauquier Cary. She spoke with simplicity, in the low, bell-like tone that held the ache of the world. Allan listened, with his hand over his eyes. His regiment that he loved! . . . all the old, familiar faces.

"Yes, he was killed — Hairston Breckinridge was killed, fighting gallantly. He died, they say, before he knew the trap they were caught in. And Christianna's father was killed, and others of the Thunder Run men, and very many from the county and from other counties. I do not know how many. Fauquier called it slaughter, said no worse thing has happened to any single command. Richard got what was left back across the swamp."

Allan groaned. "The 65th! General Jackson himself called it 'the fighting 65th!' Just a remnant of it left — left of the 65th!"

"Yes. The roll was called, and so many did not answer. They say other Stonewall regiments wept."

Allan raised himself upon the bench. She started forward. "Don't do that!" and with her hand pressed him gently down again. "I knew," she said, "that you were here, and I have heard Richard speak of you and say how good and likable you were. And I have worked hard all the morning, and just now I thought, 'I must speak to some one who knows and loves him or I will die.' And so I came. I knew that the ward might hear of the 65th any moment now and begin to talk of it, so I was not afraid of hurting you. But you must lie quiet."

"Very well, I will. I want to know about Richard Cleave — about my colonel."

Her dark eyes met the sea-blue ones fully. "He is under arrest," she said. "General Jackson has preferred charges against him."

"Charges of what?"

"Of disobedience to orders — of sacrificing the regiment — of — of retreating at last when he should not have done so and leaving his men to perish — of — of —. I have seen a copy of the charge. *Whereas the said colonel of the 65th did shamefully —*"

Her voice broke. "Oh, if I were God —"

There was a moment's silence — silence here in the corner by the stair, though none beyond in the painful, moaning ward. A bird sailed across the strip of blue sky; the stalk of phlox on the soldier's narrow bed lay withering in the light. Allan spoke. "General Jackson is very stern with failure. He may believe that charge. I don't see how he can; but if he made it he believes it. But you — you don't believe it? —"

"Believe it?" she said. "No more than God believes it! The question is now, how to help Richard."

"Have you heard from him?"

She took from her dress a folded leaf torn from a pocket-book. "You are his friend. You may read it. Wait, I will hold it." She laid it before him, holding it in her slight, fine, strong fingers.

He read. *Judith: You will hear of the fate of the 65th. How it happened I do not yet understand. It is like death on my heart. You will hear, too, of my own trouble. As to me, believe only that I could sit beside you and talk to-day as we talked awhile ago, in the sunset. Richard.*

She refolded the paper and put it back. "The evidence will clear him," said Allan. "It must. The very doubt is absurd."

Her face lightened. "General Jackson will see that he was hasty — unjust. I can understand such anger at first, but later, when he reflects — Richard will be declared innocent —"

"Yes. An honourable acquittal. It will surely be so."

"I am glad I came. You have always known him and been his friend."

"Let me tell you the kind of things I know of Richard Cleave. No, it does n't hurt me to talk."

"I can stay a little longer. Yes, tell me."

Allan spoke at some length, in his frank, quiet voice. She sat beside him, with her cheek on her hand, the blue sky and old house roofs above her. When he ceased her eyes were full of tears. She would not let them fall. "If I began to cry I should never stop," she said, and smiled them away. Presently she rose. "I must go now. Christianna will be back to-morrow."

She went away, passing up the narrow path between the wounded and out at the further door. Allan watched her going, then turned a little on the flock bed, and lifting his unbandaged arm laid it across his eyes. *The 65th cut to pieces — The 65th cut to pieces —*

At sunset Judith went home. The small room up in the branches of the tulip tree — she hardly knew how many months or years she had inhabited it. There had passed, of course, only weeks — but Time had widened its measure. To all intents and purposes she had been a long while in Richmond. This high, quiet niche was familiar, familiar! familiar the old, slender, inlaid dressing-table and the long, thin curtains and the engraving of Charlotte Corday; familiar the cool, green tree without the window and the nest upon a bough; familiar the far view and wide horizon, by day smoke-veiled, by night red-lit. The smoke was lifted now; the eye saw further than it had seen for days. The room seemed as quiet as a tomb. For a moment the silence oppressed her, and then she remembered that it was because the cannon had stopped.

She sat beside the window, through the dusk, until the stars came out; then went downstairs and took her part at the table, about which the soldier sons of the house were gathering. They brought comrades with them. The wounded eldest son was doing well, the army was victorious, the siege was lifted, the house must be made gay for "the boys." No house was ever less bright for Judith. Now she smiled and listened, and the young men thought she did not realize the seriousness of the army talk about the 65th. They themselves were careful not to mention the matter. They talked of a thousand heroisms, a thousand incidents of the Seven Days; but they turned the talk — if any one, unwary, drew it that way — from White Oak Swamp. They mistook her feeling; she would rather they had spoken out. Her comfort was when, afterwards, she went for a moment into the "chamber" to see the wounded eldest. He was a warm-hearted, rough diamond, fond of his cousin.

"What's this damned stuff I hear about Richard Cleave and a court-martial? What — nonsense! I beg your pardon, Judith." Judith kissed him, and finding "Le Vicomte de Bragelonne" face down on the counterpane offered to read to him.

"You would rather talk about Richard," he said. "I know you would. So should I. It's all the damnedest nonsense! Such a charge as that! — Tell you what, Judith. D'ye remember 'Woodstock' and Cromwell in it? Well, Stonewall Jackson's like Cromwell — of course, a better man, and a greater general, and a nobler cause, but still he's like him! Don't you fret! Cromwell had to listen to the truth. He did it, and so will Stonewall Jackson. Such damned stuff and nonsense! It hurts me worse than that old bayonet jab ever could! I'd like to hear what Edward says."

"He says, 'Duck your head and let it go by. The grass'll grow as green to-morrow.'"

"You aren't crying, are you, Judith? — I thought not. You aren't the crying kind. Don't do it. War's the stupidest beast."

"Yes, it is."

"Cousin Margaret's with Richard, isn't she?"

"Not with him — that couldn't be, they said. But she and Miriam have gone to Merry Mount. It's in the lines. I have had a note from her."

"What did she say? — You don't mind, Judith?"

"No, Rob, I don't mind. It was just a verse from a psalm. She said, *I had fainted unless I had believed to see the goodness of the Lord in the land of the living. . . . Be of good courage and He shall strengthen thy heart.*"

Later, in her room again, she sat by the window through the greater part of the night. The stars were large and soft, the airs faint, the jasmine in the garden below smelled sweet. The hospital day stretched before her; she must sleep so that she could work. She never thought — in that city and time no woman thought — of ceasing from service because of private grief. Moreover, work was her salvation. She would be betimes at the hospital to-morrow, and she would leave it late. She bent once more a long look upon the east, where were the camp-fires of Lee and Stonewall Jackson. In imagination she passed the sentries; she moved among the sleeping brigades. She found one tent, or perhaps it would be instead a rude cabin. . . . She stretched her arms upon the window-sill, and they and her thick fallen hair were wet at last with her tears.

Three days passed. On the third afternoon she left the hospital early and went to St. Paul's. She chose again the dusk beneath the gallery, and she prayed dumbly, fiercely, "O God. . . . O God —"

The church was fairly filled. The grey army was now but a little way without the city; it had come back to the seven hills after the seven days. It had come back the hero, the darling. Richmond took the cypress from her doors; put off the purple pall and tragic mask. Last July Richmond was to fall, and this July Richmond was to fall, and lo! she sat secure on her seven hills and her sons did her honour, and for them she would have made herself a waste place. She yet toiled and watched, yet mourned for the dead and hung over the beds of the wounded, and more and more she wondered whence were to appear the next day's yard of cloth and measure of flour. But in these days she overlaid her life with gladness and made her house pleasant for her sons. The service at St. Paul's this afternoon was one of thankfulness; the hymns rang triumphantly. There were many soldiers. Two officers came in together. Judith knew General Lee, but the other? . . . in a moment she saw that it was General Jackson. Her heart beat to suffocation. She sank down in the gold dusk of her corner. "O God, let him see the truth. O God, let him see the truth —"

Outside, as she went homeward in the red sunset, she paused for a moment to speak to an old free negro who was begging for alms. She gave him something, and when he had shambled on she stood still a moment here at the corner of the street, with her eyes upon the beautiful rosy west. There was a garden wall behind her and a tall crape myrtle. As she stood, with the light upon her face, Maury Stafford rode by. He saw her as she saw him. His brooding face flushed; he made as if to check his horse, but did not so. He lifted his hat high and rode on, out of the town, back to the encamped army. Judith had made no answering motion; she stood with lifted face and unchanged look, the rosy light flooding her, the rosy tree behind her. When he was gone she shivered a little. "It is not Happiness that hates; it is Misery," she thought. "When I was happy I never felt like this. I hate him. He is *glad* of Richard's peril."

That night she did not sleep at all but sat bowed together in the window, her arms about her knees, her forehead upon them, and her dark hair loose about her. She sat like a sibyl till the dawn, then rose and bathed and dressed, and was at the hospital earliest of all the workers of that day. In the evening again, just at dusk, she reëntered the room, and presently again took her seat by the window. The red light of the camp-fires was beginning to show.

There was a knock at the door. Judith rose and opened to a turbaned coloured girl. "Yes, Dilsey?"

"Miss Judith, de gin'ral air downstairs. He say, ax you kin he come up to yo' room?"

"Yes, yes, Dilsey! Tell him to come."

When her father came he found her standing against the wall, her hands, outstretched behind her, resting on it. The last soft bloom of day was upon her; indefinably, with her hands so, the wall behind her and her lifted head, she looked a soldier facing a firing party. "Tell me quickly," she said, "the exact truth."

Warwick Cary closed the door behind him and came toward her. "The court found him guilty, Judith."

As she still stood, the light from without upon her face, he took her in his arms, drew her from the wall and made her sit in the chair by the window, then placed himself beside her, and leaning over took her hands in his strong clasp. "Many a court has found many a man guilty, Judith, whom his own soul cleared."

"That is true," she answered. "Your own judgment has not changed?"

"No, Judith, no."

She lifted his hand and kissed it. "Just a moment, and then you'll tell me —"

They sat still in the soft summer air. The stars were coming out. Off to the east showed the long red light where was the army. Judith's eyes rested here. He saw it, and saw, presently, courage lift into her face. It came steady, with a deathless look. "Now," she said, and loosed her hands.

"It is very bad," he answered slowly. "The evidence was more adverse than I could have dreamed. Only on the last count was there acquittal."

"The last count? —"

"The charge of personal cowardice."

Her eyelids trembled a little. "I am glad," she said, "that they had a gleam of reason."

The other uttered a short laugh, proud and troubled. "Yes. It would not have occurred to me — just that accusation. . . . Well, he stood cleared of that. But the other charges, Judith, the others —" He rested his hands on his sword hilt and gazed broodingly into the deepening night. "The court could only find as it did. I myself, sitting there, listening to that testimony. . . . It is inexplicable!"

"Tell me all."

"General Jackson's order was plain. A staff officer carried it to General Winder with perfect correctness. Winder repeated it to the court, and word for word Jackson corroborated it. The same officer, carrying it on from Winder to the 65th came up with a courier belonging to the regiment. To this man, an educated, reliable, trusted soldier, he gave the order."

"He should not have done so?"

"It is easy to say that — to blame because this time there's a snarl to unravel! The thing is done often enough. It should not be done, but it is. Staff service with us is far too irregular. The officer stands to receive a severe reprimand — but there is no reason to believe that he did not give the order to the courier with all the accuracy with which he had already delivered it to Winder. He testified that he did so give it, repeated it word for word to the court. He entrusted it to the courier, taking the precaution to make the latter say it over to him, and then he returned to General Jackson, down the stream, before the bridge they were building. That closed his testimony. He received the censure of the court, but what he did has been done before."

"The courier testified —"

"No. That is the link that drops out. The courier was killed.

A Thunder Run man — Steven Dagg — testified that he had been separated from the regiment. Returning to it along the wooded bank of the creek, he arrived just behind the courier. He heard him give the order to the colonel. 'Could he repeat it?' 'Yes.' He did so, and it was, accurately, Jackson's order."

"Richard — what did Richard say?"

"He said the man lied."

"Ah!"

"The courier fell before the first volley from the troops in the woods. He died almost at once, but two men testified as to the only thing he had said. It was, 'We ought never all of us to have crossed. Tell Old Jack I carried the order straight.' "

He rose and with a restless sigh began to pace the little room. "I see a tangle — something not understood — some stumbling-block laid by laws beyond our vision. We cannot even define it, cannot even find its edges. We do not know its nature. Things happen so sometimes in this strange world. I do not think that Richard himself understands how the thing chanced. He testi-fied — "

"Yes, oh, yes —"

"He repeated to the court the order he had received. It was not the order that Jackson had given and that Winder had sent on to him, though it differed in only two points. And neither — and there, Judith, there is a trouble! — neither was it with entire ex-plicitness an order to do that which he did do. He acknowledged that, quite simply. He had found at the time an ambiguity — he had thought of sending again for confirmation to Winder. And then — unfortunate man! something happened to strengthen the inter-pretation which, when all is said, he preferred to receive, and upon which he acted. Time pressed. He took the risk, if there was a risk, and crossed the stream."

"Father, do you blame him?"

"He blames himself, Judith, somewhat cruelly. But I think it is because, just now, of the agony of memory. He loved his regiment. — No. What sense in blaming where, had there followed success, you would have praised? Then it would have been proper daring; now — I could say that he had been wiser to wait, but I do not know that in his place I should have waited. He was rash, perhaps,

but who is there to tell? Had he chosen another interpretation and
delayed, and been mistaken, then, too, commination would have
fallen. No. I blame him less than he blames himself, Judith. But
the fact remains. Even by his own showing there was a doubt. Even
accepting his statement of the order he received, he took it upon
himself to decide."

"They did not accept his statement —"

"No, Judith. They judged that he had received General Jackson's order and had disobeyed it. — I know — I know! To us it is
monstrous. But the court must judge by the evidence — and the
verdict was to be expected. It was his sole word, and where his own
safety was at stake. 'Had not the dead courier a reputation for
reliability, for accuracy?' 'He had, and he would not lay the blame
there, besmirching a brave man's name.' 'Where then?' 'He did not
know. It was so that he had received the order' — Judith, Judith!
I have rarely seen truth so helpless as in this case."

She drew a difficult breath. "No help. And they said —"

"He was pronounced guilty of the first charge. That carried with
it the verdict as to the second — the sacrifice of the regiment. There,
too — guilty. Only the third there was no sustaining. The loss was
fearful, but there were men enough left to clear him from that
charge. He struggled with desperation to retrieve his error, if error
it were; he escaped death himself as by a miracle, and he brought
off a remnant of the command which, in weaker hands, might have
been utterly swallowed up. On that count he is clear. But on the
others — guilty, and without mitigation."

He came back to the woman by the window. "Judith, I would
rather put the sword in my own heart than put it thus in yours.
War is a key, child, that unlocks to all dreadful things, to all mis-
takes, to every sorrow!"

"I want every worst drop of it," she said. "Afterward I'll look
for comfort. Do not be afraid for me; I feel as strong as the hills,
the air, the sea — anything. What is the sentence?"

"Dismissal from the army."

Judith rose and, with her hands on the window-sill, leaned out into
the night. Her gaze went straight to the red light in the eastern sky.
There was an effect as though the force, impalpable, real, which
was herself, had gone too, flown from the window straight toward

that horizon, leaving here but a fair ivory shell. It was but momentary; the chains held and she turned back to the shadowed room.
"You have seen him?"

"Yes."

"How —"

"He has much of his mother in him, Judith. Eventually he will,
I think, take it that way. But now it is his father that shows. He
is very silent — grey and hard and silent."

"Where is he?"

"At present yet under guard. To-morrow it will all be over."

"He will be free, you mean?"

"Yes, he will be free."

She came and put her arm around her father's neck. "Father,
you know what I want to do then? To do just as soon as I shall have
seen him and made him realize that it is for my happiness. I want to
marry him. . . . Ah, don't look at me so, saying nothing!" She
withdrew herself a little, standing with her clasped hands against
his breast. "You expected that, did you not? Why, what else. . . .
Father, I am not afraid of you. You will let me do it."

He regarded her with a grave, compassionate face. "No. You
need not fear me, Judith. It is hardly father and child with you and
me. It is soul and soul, and I trust your soul with its own concerns.
Moreover, if it is pain to consider what you would do, the pang
would be greater to find you not capable. . . . Yes, I would let you
do it. But I do not think that Richard will."

CHAPTER XXXVIII

CEDAR RUN

THE Seven Days brought a sterner temper into this war. The two sides grew to know each other better; each saw how determined was the other, and either foe, to match the other, raised the bronze in himself to iron. The great army, still under McClellan, at Harrison's Landing, became the Army of the Potomac. The great army guarding Richmond under Lee, became the Army of Northern Virginia. President Lincoln called upon the Governors of the Northern States for three hundred thousand men, and offered bounties. President Davis called upon the Governors of the Southern States for conscripts, and obtained no great number, for the mass of the men had volunteered. The world at large looked on, now and henceforth, with an absorbed regard. The struggle promised to be Homeric, memorable. The South was a fortress beleaguered; seven hundred thousand square miles of territory lost and inland as the steppes of Tartary, for all her ports were blocked by Northern men-of-war. Little news from the fortress escaped; the world had a sense of gigantic grey figures moving here and there behind a great battle veil, of a push against the fortress, a push from all sides, with approved battering rams, scaling ladders, hooks, grapples, mines, of blue figures, all known and described in heroic terms by the Northern public prints, a push repelled by the voiceless, printless, dimly-discerned grey figures. Not that the grey, too, were not described to the nations in the prints above. They were. The wonder was that the creatures could fight — even, it appeared, fight to effect. Around and over the wide-flung fortress the battle smoke rolled and eddied. Drums were distantly heard, now rallying, now muffled. A red flag with a blue cross rose and fell and rose again; grey names emerged, floated, wraith-like, over the sea, not to be stopped by blue men-of-war, names and picturesque nicknames, loved of soldiers. It grew to be allowed that there must be courage in the fortress, and a gift of leadership. All was seen confusedly, but with a mounting, mounting interest. The world gaped at the far-borne clang and smoke and roar. Military men in clubs demonstrated to a nicety just how long the fortress might hold out, and just how it must be taken at last. Schoolboys fought over again in the schoolyards the battles with the heathenish names. The Emperor of the French and the King of Prussia and the Queen of Spain and the Queen of England and the Czar and the Sultan and the Pope at Rome asked each morning for the war news, and so did gaunt cotton-spinners staring in mill towns at tall smokeless chimneys.

Early in June Halleck was appointed commander-in-chief of all the armies of the United States. What to do with McClellan, at present summering on the James twenty-five miles below Richmond, came upon the board. McClellan claimed, quite rightly, that here and now, with his army on both sides of the James, he held the key position, and that with sufficient reinforcements he could force the evacuation of Richmond. Only give him reinforcements with which to face Lee's "not less than two hundred thousand!" Recall the Army of the Potomac, and it might be some time before it again saw Richmond! Halleck deliberated. General Pope had come out of the west to take concentrated command of the old forces of Banks, Sigel, Frémont, and McDowell. He had an attitude, had Pope, at the head of his forty thousand men behind the Rappahannock! The armies were too widely separated, McClellan's location notoriously unhealthy. Impossible to furnish reinforcements to the tune asked for, Washington might, at any moment, be in peril. It was understood that Stonewall Jackson had left Richmond on the thirteenth, marching toward Gordonsville.

The James River might be somewhat unhealthy for strangers that summer, and Stonewall Jackson had marched toward Gordonsville. The desire at the moment most at the heart of General Robert Edward Lee was that General McClellan should be recalled. Therefore he guarded Richmond with something less than sixty thousand men, and he made rumours to spread of gunboats building, and he sent Major-General T. J. Jackson northward with twelve thousand men.

In this July month there was an effect of suspense. The fortress was taking muster, telling its strength, soldering its flag to the staff and the staff to the keep. The besiegers were gathering; the world was watching, expectant of the grimmer struggle. There came a roar and clang from the outer walls, from the Mississippi above Vicksburg, from the Georgian coast, from Murfreesboro in Tennessee, from Arkansas, from Morgan's raids in Kentucky. There was fire and sound enough, but the battles that were to tell were looked for on Virginia soil. Hot and still were the July days, hot and still was the air, and charged with a certain sentiment. Thunderbolts were forging; all concerned knew that, and very subtly life and death and the blue sky and the green leaves came freshlier across the senses. Jackson, arriving at Gordonsville the nineteenth of July, found Pope before him with forty-seven thousand men. He asked for reinforcements and Lee, detaching yet another twelve thousand from the army at Richmond, sent him A. P. Hill and the Light Division. Hill arrived on the second of August, splendid fighter, in his hunting shirt, with his red beard! That evening in Jackson's quarters, some one showed him a captured copy of Pope's Orders, numbers 12 and 75. He read, crumpled the papers and tossed them aside, then turned to Jackson sitting sucking a lemon. "Well, general, here's a new candidate for your attention!"

Jackson looked up. "Yes, sir. By God's blessing he shall have it." He sucked on, studying a map of the country between Slaughter Mountain and Manassas which Hotchkiss had made him. In a letter to his wife from Richmond he had spoken of "fever and debility" attending him during his stay in that section of the country. If it were so he had apparently left them in the rear when he came up here. He sat now tranquil as a stone wall, in sight of the mountains, sucking his lemon and studying his maps.

This was the second. On the sixth of August Pope began to cross the Rappahannock. On the afternoon of the seventh the grey army was in motion. All the eighth it was in column, the heat intense, the dust stifling, an entanglement of trains and a misunderstanding of orders on the part of Hill and Ewell resulting in a confused and retarded march. Night fell, hot and breathless. Twenty-three thousand grey soldiers, moving toward Orange Court House, made the dark road vocal with statements as to the reeking heat, the dust, the condition of their shoes and the impertinence of the cavalry. The latter was more irritating than were the flapping soles, the dust in the throat, and the sweat pouring into the eyes. The infantry swore, swerving again and again to one side of the narrow road to let small bodies of horsemen go by. It was dark, the road going through an interminable hot, close wood. Officers and men were liberal in their vituperation. "Thank the Lord, it ain't my arm!" — "Here you fellows — damn you! look where you are going! Trampling innocent bystanders that way! — Why in hell did n't you stay back where you belong?" — "Of course if you 've positively got to get to the front and can't find any other road it's our place to give you this one! — Just wait a moment and we 'll ask the colonel if we can't *lie down*. It 'll be easier to ride over us that way. — Oh, go to hell!"

The parties passed, the ranks of the infantry straightened out again on the dark road, the column wound on through the hot, midnight wood. More hoof-beats — another party of cavalry to be let by! They passed the infantry in the darkness, pushing the broken line into the ditch and scrub. In the pitchy blackness an impatient command lost at this juncture its temper. The men swore, an officer called out to the horsemen a savage "Halt!" The party pressed on. The officer furious, caught a bridle rein. "Halt, damn you! Stop them, men! Now you cavalry have got to learn a thing or two! One is, that the infantry is the important thing in war! It's the aristocracy, damn you! The other is that we were on this road first anyhow! Now you just turn out into the woods yourself, and the next time I tell you to halt, damn you, halt!"

"This, sir," said a voice, "is General Jackson and his staff."

The officer stammered forth apologies. "It is all right, sir," said the voice in the darkness. "The cavalry must be more careful, but colonel, true aristocrats do not curse and swear."

An hour later the column halted in open country. A pleasant farmhouse with a cool, grassy yard surrounded by an ornamental fence, white paling gleaming in the waved lights, flung wide its doors to Stonewall Jackson. The troops bivouacked around, in field and meadow. A rain came up, a chilly downpour. An aide appeared before the brigade encamped immediately about the farmhouse. "The general says, sir, that the men may take the rail fence over there, but the regimental officers are to see that under no circumstances is the fence about Mrs. Wilson's yard to be touched."

The night passed. Officers had had a hard day; they slept perhaps somewhat soundly, wrapped in their oilcloths, in the chilly rain, by the smallest of sputtering camp-fires. The rain stopped at three o'clock; the August dawn came up gloriously with a cool freshness. Reveille sounded. Stonewall Jackson came from the farmhouse, looked about him and then walked across the grassy yard. A little later five colonels of five regiments found themselves ordered to report to the general commanding the brigade.

"Gentlemen, as you came by did you notice the condition of the ornamental fence about the yard?"

"Not especially, sir."

"I did, sir. One panel is gone. I suppose the men were tempted. It was a confounded cold rain."

The brigadier pursed his lips. "Well, colonel, you heard the order. All of you heard the order. I regret to say, so did I. Dog-gone tiredness and profound slumber are no excuse. You ought — we ought — to have heard them at the palings. General Jackson has ordered you all under arrest."

"Five of us, sir?"

"Five of you. Damn it, sir, six of us!"

The five colonels looked at one another and looked at their brigadier. "What would you advise, sir?"

The brigadier was very red. "I have sent one of my staff to Mrs. Wilson, gentlemen, to enquire the cost of the entire ornamental fence! I'd advise that we pay, and — if we've got any — pay in gold."

By eight o'clock the column was in motion — a fair day and a fair country, with all the harvest fields and the deep wooded hills and the August sky. After the rain the roads were just pleasantly wet; dewdrops hung on the corn blades, blackberries were ripening, ox-eye daisies fringed the banks of red earth. The head of the column, coming to a by-road, found awaiting it there an old, plain country woman in a faded sunbonnet and faded check apron. She had a basket on her arm, and she stepped into the middle of the road before Little Sorrel. "Air this General Jackson?"

Stonewall Jackson checked the horse. The staff and a division general or two stopped likewise. Behind them came on the infantry advance, long and jingling. "Yes, madam, I am General Jackson. What can I do for you?"

The old woman put down her basket and wiped her hands on her apron. "General, my son John air in your company. An' I've brought him some socks an' two shirts an' a chicken, an' a pot of apple butter. An' ef you'll call John I'll be obleeged to you, sir."

A young man in the group of horsemen laughed, but stopped abruptly as Jackson looked round. The latter turned to the old woman with the gentlest blue eyes, and the kindliest slow smile. "I've got a great many companies, ma'am. They are all along the road from Gordonsville. I don't believe I know your son."

But the old woman would not have that. "My lan', general! I reckon you all know John! I reckon John wuz the first man to jine the army. He wuz chopping down the big gum by the crick, an' the news come, an' he chopped on twel the gum wuz down, an' he says, says he, 'I'll cut it up for you, Maw, an' then I'm goin'.' An' he went. — He's about your make an' he has light hair an' eyes an' he wuz wearing butternut —"

"What is his last name, ma'am?"

"His middle name's Henry an' his last name's Simpson."

"In whose brigade is he, and in what regiment?"

But the old woman shook her head. She knew only that he was in General Jackson's company. "We never larned to write, John an' me. He wuz powerful good to me — en I reckon he's been in all the battles 'cause he wuz born that way. Some socks, and two shirts an' something to eat — an' he hez a scar over his eye where a setting hen pecked him when he was little — an' won't you please find him for me, sir?" The old voice quavered toward tears.

Stonewall Jackson dismounted, and looked toward the on-coming column. The advance was now but a few hundred yards away; the whole army to the last wagon train had its orders for expedition. He sent for his adjutant. "Companies from Orange County, sir? Yes, there are a number in different regiments and brigades."

"Well, you will go, colonel, and halt the advance. See if there is an Orange company and a private named John Simpson."

There was not. The woman with the basket was old and tired. She sat down on the earth beneath a sign post and threw her apron over her head. Jackson sent an aide back three miles to the main body. "Captain, find the Orange companies and a private named John Simpson. Bring him here. Tall, light-haired, light eyes, with a scar over one eye. If he is not in the main column go on to the rear."

The aide spurred his horse. Jackson explained matters. "You'll have to wait a while, Mrs. Simpson. If your son's in the army he'll be brought to you. I'll leave one of my aides with you!" He spoke to Little Sorrel and put his hand on the saddle bow. Mrs. Simpson's apron came down. "Please, general, don't you go! Please, sir, you stay! They won't know him like you will! They'll just come back an' say they can't find him! — An' I got to see John — I just got to! — Don't go, please, sir! Ef 't was your mother —"

Stonewall Jackson and his army waited for half an hour while John Simpson was looked for. At the end of that time the cross roads saw him coming, riding behind the aide. Tall and lank, in butternut still, and red as a beet, he slipped from the horse, and saluted the general, then, almost crying, gathered up the checked apron and the sunbonnet and the basket and the old woman. "Maw, Maw! jes' look what you have done! Danged ef you have n't stopped the whole army! Everybody cryin' out 'John Simpson'!"

On went the column through the bright August forenoon. The day grew hot and the dust whirled up, and the cavalry skirmished at intervals with detached blue clouds of horsemen. On the horizon appeared at some distance a conical mountain. "What's that sugar loaf over there?" "That's Slaughter's Mountain south of Culpeper. Cedar Run's beyond."

The day wore on. Slaughter Mountain grew larger. The country between was lovely, green and rolling; despite the heat and the dust and the delay the troops were in spirits. They were going against Major-General John Pope and they liked the job. The old Army of the Valley, now a part of the Army of Northern Virginia, rather admired Shields, had no especial objection to McDowell, and felt a real gratitude toward Mr. Commissary Banks, but it was prepared to fight Pope with a vigour born of detestation. A man of the old Army, marching with Ewell, began to sing: —

> " Pope told a flattering tale
> Which proved to be bravado,
> About the streams that spout like ale
> On the Llano Estacado!

"That's the Staked Plains, you know. Awful hot out there! Pretty hot here, too. Look at them lovely roasting ears! Can't touch 'em. Old Jack says so. Pope may live on the country, but we may n't." "That mountain is getting pretty big." "Hello! Just a cavalry scrimmage — Hello! hello! Artillery's more serious!" "Boys, boys! we've struck Headquarters-in-the-saddle! — What's that awful noise? — Old Jack's coming — Old Jack's coming to the front! — Mercy! did n't know even we could cheer like that! — Yaaaih! Yaaaaaaihhh! Stonewall Jackson! Stonewall Jackson! Yaaaaaaii-iihhh!"

As the day declined the battle swelled in smoke and thunder. The blue batteries were well placed, and against them thundered twenty-six grey rifled guns: two Parrotts of Rockbridge with a gun of Carpenter's appeared at the top of the hill, tore down the long slope and came into battery in an open field, skirted by a wood. Behind was the Stonewall Brigade in column of regiments. The guns were placed *en échelon*, the horses taken away, the ball opened with canister. Immediately the Federal guns answered, got the range of the grey, and began to do deadly mischief. All around young trees were cut off short. The shells came, thick, black, and screaming. The place proved fatal to officers. Carpenter was struck in the head by a piece of shell — mortally wounded. The chief of artillery, Major Snowden Andrews fell, desperately injured, then Captain Caskie was hurt, then Lieutenant Graham. The gunners worked like mad. The guns thundered, recoiled, thundered again. The blue shells arrived in a deadly stream. All was smoke, whistling limbs of trees, glare and roar. General Winder came up on foot. Standing by a grey Parrott he tried with his field glass to make out the Federal batteries. Lowering the glass he shouted some direction to the men about the gun below him. The noise was hideous, deafening. Seeing that he was not understood he raised his arm and hollowed his hand above his mouth. A shell passed beneath his arm, through his side. He fell stiffly back, mangled and dying.

There was a thick piece of woods, deep and dark, stretching westward. The left of Jackson's division rested here. Ewell's brigades and batteries were on the mountain slope; the Light Division, A. P. Hill in his red battle shirt at its head, not yet up; Jubal Early forming a line of battle in the rolling fields. An aide came to "Old Jube." "General Jackson's compliments to General Early, and he says you will advance on the enemy, and General Winder's troops will support you." Early had a thin, high, drawling voice. "My compliments to General Jackson, and tell him I will do it."

The Stonewall Brigade, drawn up in the rear of the Artillery, stood waiting its orders from Winder. There came a rumor. "The general is killed! General Winder is killed!" The Stonewall chose to be incredulous. "It is not so! We don't believe it."

The 65th, cut to pieces at White Oak Swamp, had renewed itself. Recruits — boys and elderly men — a few melancholy conscripts, a number of transferals from full commands had closed its ranks. The 65th, smaller now, of diluted quality, but even so, dogged and promising well, — the 65th, waiting on the edge of a wheat field, looked across it to Taliaferro's and Campbell's brigades and the dark wood in front. Billy Maydew was sergeant now and Matthew Coffin was first lieutenant of Company A. The two had some talk under a big walnut tree.

"Artillery's been shouting for two hours," said Coffin. "They've got a hell lot of cavalry, too, but if there's any infantry I can't see it."

"There air a message gone to Campbell and Taliaferro. I heard Old Jack send it. 'Look well to your left,' he says, says he. That thar wood's the left," said Billy. "It looks lonesomer than lonesome, but thar! when lonesome things do blaze out they blaze out the worst!"

The colonel of the 65th — Colonel Erskine — came along the front. "It's too true, men. We've lost General Winder. Well, we'll avenge him! — Look! there is Jubal Early advancing!"

Early's line of battle was a beautiful sight. It moved through the fields and up a gentle hillside, and pushed before it bright clusters of Federal cavalry. When the grey lines came to the hilltop the Federal batteries opened fiercely. Early posted Dement and Brown and loudly answered. To the left rolled great wheat fields, the yellow grain standing in shocks. Here gathered the beautiful blue cavalry, many and gallant. Ewell with Trimble's South Carolinians and Harry Hayes's Louisianians held the slope of the mountain, and from these heights bellowed Latimer's guns. Over hill and vale the Light Division was seen coming, ten thousand men in grey led by A. P. Hill.

"It surely air a sight to see," said Billy. "I never even dreamed it, back thar on Thunder Run."

"There the Yankees come!" cried Coffin. "There! a stream of them — up that narrow valley! — Now — now — now Early has touched them! — Damn you, Billy! What's the matter?"

"It's the wood," answered Billy. "Thar's something coming out of the lonesome wood."

On the left the 1st and 42d Virginia were the advance regiments. Out of the forest, startling, unexpected, burst a long blue battle line. Banks, a brave man if not a wise one, interpreted Pope's orders somewhat to suit himself, and attacked without waiting for Sigel or McDowell. In this instance valor seemed likely to prove the better part of discretion. Of the grey generals, Hill was not up, Early was hotly engaged, the artillery fire, grey and blue alike, sweeping the defile before Ewell kept him on the mountain side. Bayonets fixed, bright colours tossing, skirmishers advanced, on with verve and determination came Banks's attack. As it crossed the yellow stubble field Taliaferro and Campbell, startled by the apparition but steady, poured in a withering fire. But the blue came on, swung its right and partly surrounded the 1st Virginia. Amid a hell of shots, bayonet work, shouts, and cries 1st Virginia broke; fell back upon the 42d, that in its turn was overwhelmed. Down came the blue wave on Taliaferro's flank. The wheat field filled with uproar. Taliaferro broke, Campbell broke.

The Stonewall stirred like leaves in autumn. Ronald, colonel of the 2d, commanding in Winder's place, made with despatch a line of battle. The smoke was everywhere, rolling and thick. Out of it came abruptly a voice. "I have always depended upon this brigade. Forward!"

Billy had an impression of wheat stubble beneath his feet, wheat stubble thick strewn with men, silent or lamentably crying out, and about his ears a whistling storm of minies. There was, too, a whirl of grey forms. There was no alignment — regiments were dashed to pieces — everybody was mixed up. It was like an overturned beehive. Then in the swirling smoke, in the swarm and shouting and grey rout, he saw Little Sorrel, and Stonewall Jackson standing in his stirrups. He had drawn his sabre; it flashed above his head like a gleam from the sinking sun. Billy spoke aloud. "I've been with him from the first, and this air the first time I ever saw him do that." As he spoke he caught hold of a fleeing grey soldier. "Stand still and fight! Thar ain't nothing in the rear but damned safety!"

The grey surge hung poised, the tide one moment between ebb and flow. The noise was hellish; sounds of triumph, sounds of panic, of anger, encouragement, appeal, despair, woe and pain, with the callous roar of musketry and the loud indifference of the guns. Above it all the man on the quaint war horse made himself heard. From the blue line of steel above his head, from the eyes below the forage cap, from the bearded lips, from the whole man there poured a magic control. He shouted and his voice mastered the storm. "Rally, brave men! Rally and follow me! I will lead you. Jackson will lead you. Rally! Rally!"

Billy saw the 21st Virginia, what was left of it, swing suddenly around, give the Confederate yell, and dash itself against the blue. Taliaferro rallied, Campbell rallied, the Stonewall itself under Ronald rallied. The first of the Light Division, Branch's North Carolinians came on with a shout, and Thomas's Georgians and Lane and Archer and Pender. Early was up, Ewell sweeping down from the mountain. Jackson came along the restored front. The soldiers greeted him with a shout that tore the welkin. He touched the forage cap. "Give them the bayonet! Give them the bayonet! *Forward, and drive them!*"

The cavalry with Banks was fine and staunch. At this moment it undertook a charge useless but magnificent. With clarion sound, with tossing colours, with huzzas and waving sabres, a glorious and fearful sight, the cavalry rushed diagonally across the trampled field, its flank exposed to the North Carolinians. These opened a blasting fire while Taliaferro's brigade met it full, and the 13th Virginia, couched behind a grey zigzag of fence, gave volley after volley. Little more than half of those horsemen returned.

Dusk fell and the blue were in full retreat. After them swept the grey — the Light Division, Jubal Early, Ewell, Jackson's own. In the corn fields, in the wheat fields, in the forest thick, thick! lay the dead and wounded, three thousand men, grey and blue, fallen in that fight of an hour and a half. The blue crossed Cedar Run, the grey crossed it after them. The moon, just past the full, rose above the hilltops. On the whole the summer night was light enough. Stonewall Jackson brought up two fresh brigades and with Pegram's battery pressed on by moonlight. That dauntless artillerist, a boy in years, an old wise man in command, found the general on Little Sorrel pounding beside him for some time through the moonlit night. Jackson spoke but once. "Delightful excitement," he said.

CHAPTER XXXIX

THE FIELD OF MANASSAS

THE column, after an extraordinary march attended by skirmishes, most wearily winding through a pitch black night, heard the "Halt!" with rejoicing. "Old Jack be thanked! So we ain't turning on our tail and going back through Thoroughfare Gap after all! See anything of Marse Robert? — Go away! he ain't any nearer than White Plains. He and Longstreet won't get through Thoroughfare until to-morrow — *Break ranks!* Oh Lord, yes! with pleasure."

Under foot there was rough, somewhat rolling ground. In the dark night men dropped down without particularity as to couch or bedchamber. Nature and the time combined to spread for them a long and echoing series of sleeping rooms, carpeted and tapestried according to Nature's whim, vaulted with whistling storm or drift of clouds or pageantry of stars. The troops took the quarters indicated sometimes with, sometimes without remark. To-night there was little speech of any kind before falling into dreamless slumber. "O hell! Hungry as a dog!" — "Me, too!" — "Can't you just *see* Manassas Junction and Stuart's and Trimble's fellows gorging themselves? Biscuit and cake and pickles and 'desecrated' vegetables and canned peaches and sardines and jam and coffee! — freight cars and wagons and storehouses just filled with jam and coffee and canned peaches and cigars and —" "I wish that fool would hush! I was n't hungry before!" — "and nice cozy fires, and rashers of bacon broiling, and plenty of coffee, and all around just like daisies in the field, clean new shirts, and drawers and socks, and handkerchiefs and shoes and writing paper and soap." — "Will you go to hell and stop talking as you go?" — "Seems somehow an awful lonely place, boys! — dark and a wind. Hear that whippoorwill? Just twenty thousand men sloshin' round — and Pope may be right over there by the whippoorwill. Jarrow says that with McCall and Heintzelman and Fitz John Porter, there are seventy thousand of them. Well? They've got Headquarters-in-the-saddle and we've got Stonewall Jackson — That's so! that's so! Good-night."

Dawn came calmly up, dawn of the twenty-eighth of August. The ghostly trumpets blew — the grey soldiers stirred and rose. In the sky were yet a star or two and a pale quarter moon. These slowly faded and the faintest coral tinge overspread that far and cold eastern heaven. The men were busied about breakfast, but now this group and presently that suspended operations. "What's there about this place anyhow? It has an awful, familiar look. The stream and the stone bridge and the woods and the hill — the Henry Hill. Good God! it's the field of Manassas!"

The field of Manassas, in the half light, somehow inspired a faint awe, a creeping horror. "God! how young we were that day! It seems so long ago, and yet it comes back. Do you remember how we crashed together at the Stone Bridge? There's the Mathews Hill where we first met Sykes and Ricketts — seen them often since. The Henry Hill — there's the house — Mrs. Henry was killed. Hampton and Cary came along there and Beauregard with his sword out and Old Joe swinging the colours high, restoring the battle! — and Kirby Smith, just in time — just in time, and the yell his column gave! Next day we thought the war was over." — "I didn't." — "Yes, you did! You said, 'Well, boys, we're going back to every day, but by jiminy! we've got something to tell our grandchildren!' The ravine running up there — that was where Bee was killed! Bee! I can see him now. Then we were over there." "Yes, on the hilltop by the pine wood. 'Jackson standing like a stone wall.' Look, the light's touching it. Boys, I could cry, just as easy —"

The August morning strengthened. "Our guns were over there by the charred trees. There's where we charged, there's where we came down on Griffin and Ricketts! — the 33d, the 65th. The 65th made its fight there. Richard Cleave —" "Don't!" — "Well, that's where we came down on Griffin and Ricketts. Manassas! Reckon Old Jack and Marse Robert want a *second* battle of Manassas?"

The light grew full. "Ewell's over there — A. P. Hill's over there. All together, north of the Warrenton turnpike. Where's Marse Robert and Longstreet?"

Colonel Fauquier Cary, riding by, heard the last remark and answered it. "Marse Robert and Longstreet are marching by the road we've marched before them. To-night, perhaps, we'll be again a united family."

"Colonel, are we going to have a battle?"

"I was n't at the council, friends, but I can tell you what I think."

"Yes, yes! We think that you think pretty straight —"

"McCall and Heintzelman and Fitz John Porter have joined General Pope."

"Yes. So we hear."

"And others of the Army of the Potomac are on the way."

"Yes, undoubtedly."

"But are not here yet."

"No."

"Well, then, I think that the thing above all others that General Lee wants is an immediate battle."

He rode on. The men to whom he had been speaking looked after him approvingly. "He's a fine piece of steel! Always liked that whole family — Is n't he a cousin of ——? Yes. Wonder what he thinks about that matter! Heigho! Look at the stealing light and the grey shadows! Manassas!"

Cary, riding by Ewell's lines, came upon Maury Stafford lying stretched beneath an oak, studying, too, the old battlefield. The sun was up; the morning cool, fresh, and pure. Dismounting, Cary seated himself beside the other. "You were not in the battle here? On the Peninsula, were you not?"

"Yes, with Magruder. Look at that shaft of light."

"Yes. It strikes the crest of the hill — just where was the Stonewall Brigade."

Silence fell. The two sat, brooding over the scene, each with his own thoughts. "This field will be red again," said Stafford at last.

"No doubt. Yes, red again. I look for heavy fighting."

"I saw you when you came in with A. P. Hill on the second. But we have not spoken together, I think, since Richmond."

"No," said Cary. "Not since Richmond."

"One of your men told me that, coming up, you stopped in Albemarle."

"Yes, I went home for a few hours."

"All at Greenwood are well and — happy?"

"All at Greenwood are well. Southern women are not precisely happy. They are, however, extremely courageous."

"May I ask if Miss Cary is at Greenwood?"

"She remained at her work in Richmond through July. Then the need at the hospital lessening, she went home. Yes, she is at Greenwood."

"Thank you. I am going to ask another question. Answer it or not as you see fit. Does she know that — most unfortunately — it was I who carried that order from General Jackson to General Winder?"

"I do not think that she knows it." He rose. "The bugles are sounding. I must get back to Hill. General Lee will be up, I hope, to-night. Until he comes we are rather in the lion's mouth. Happily John Pope is hardly the desert king." He mounted his horse, and went. Stafford laid himself down beneath the oak, looked sideways a moment at Bull Run and the hills and the woods, then flung his arm upward and across his eyes, and went in mind to Greenwood.

The day passed in a certain still and steely watchfulness. In the August afternoon, Jeb Stuart, feather in hat, around his horse's neck a garland of purple ironweed and yarrow, rode into the lines and spoke for ten minutes with General Jackson, then spurred away to the Warrenton turnpike. Almost immediately Ewell's and Taliaferro's divisions were under arms and moving north.

Near Groveton they struck the force they were going against — King's division of McDowell's corps moving tranquilly toward Centreville. The long blue column — Doubleday, Patrick, Gibbon, and Hatch's brigades — showed its flank. It moved steadily, with jingle and creak of accoutrements, with soldier chat and laughter, with a band playing a quickstep, with the rays of the declining sun bright on gun-stock and bayonet, and with the deep rumble of the accompanying batteries. The head of the column came in the gold light to a farmhouse and an apple orchard. Out of the peace and repose of the scene burst a roar of grey artillery.

The fight was fierce and bloody, and marked by a certain savage picturesqueness. Gibbon and Doubleday somehow deployed and seized a portion of the orchard. The grey held the farmhouse and the larger part of the fair, fruit-bearing slopes. The blue brought their artillery into action. The grey batteries, posted high, threw their shot and shell over the heads of the grey skirmishers into the opposing ranks: Wooding, Poague, and Carpenter did well; and then, thundering through the woods, came John Pelham of Stuart's Horse Artillery, and he, too, did well.

As for the infantry, grey and blue, they were seasoned troops. There was no charging this golden afternoon. They merely stood, blue and grey, one hundred yards apart, in the sunset-flooded apple orchard, and then in a twilight apple orchard, and then in an apple orchard with the stars conceivably shining above the roof of smoke, and directed each against the other a great storm of musketry, round shot, and canister.

It lasted two and a half hours, that tornado, and it never relaxed in intensity. It was a bitter fight, and there was bitter loss. Double-day and Gibbon suffered fearfully, and Ewell and Taliaferro suffered. Grey and blue, they stood grimly, and the tornado raged. The ghosts of the quiet husbandmen who had planted the orchard, of the lovers who may have walked there, of the children who must have played beneath the trees — these were scared far, far from the old peaceful haunt. It was a bitter fight.

Stafford was beside Ewell when the latter fell, a shell dreadfully shattering his leg. The younger man caught him, drew him quite from poor old Rifle, and with the help of the men about got him behind the slight, slight shelter of one of the little curtsying trees. Old Dick's face twitched, but he could speak. "Of course I've lost that leg! ——! —— ——! Old Jackson is n't around, is he? Never mind! Occasion must excuse. Go along, gentlemen. Need you all there. Doctors and chaplains and the teamsters, and Dick Ewell will forgather all right ——!——! Damn you, Maury, I don't want you to stay! What's that that man says? Taliaferro badly wounded ——! —— ——! Gentlemen, one and all you are ordered back to your posts. I've lost a leg, but I'm not going to lose this battle!"

Night came with each stark battle line engaged in giving and receiving as deadly a bombardment as might well be conceived. The orchard grew a place tawny and red and roaring with sound. And then at nine o'clock the sound dwindled and the light sank. The blue withdrew in good order, taking with them their wounded.

The battle was drawn, the grey rested on the field, the loss of both was heavy.

Back of the apple orchard, on the long natural terrace where he had posted his six guns, that tall, blond, very youthful officer whom, a little later, Stuart called "the heroic chivalric Pelham," whom Lee called "the gallant Pelham," of whom Stonewall Jackson said, "Every army should have a Pelham on each flank"— Major John Pelham surveyed the havoc among his men and horses. Then like a good and able leader, he brought matters shipshape, and later announced that the Horse Artillery would stay where it was for the night.

The farmhouse in the orchard had been turned into a field hospital. Thither Pelham's wounded were borne. Of the hurt horses those that might be saved were carefully tended, the others shot. The pickets were placed. Fires were kindled, and from a supply wagon somewhere in the rear scanty rations brought. An embassy went to the farmhouse. "Ma'am, the major — Major Pelham — says kin we please have a few roasting ears?" The embassy returned. "She says, sir, just to help ourselves. Corn, apples — anything we want, and she wishes it were more!"

The six guns gleamed red in the light of the kindled fires. The men sat or lay between them, tasting rest after battle. Below this platform, in the orchard and on the turnpike and in the woods beyond, showed also fires and moving lights. The air was yet smoky, the night close and warm. There were no tents nor roofs of any nature. Officers and men rested in the open beneath the August stars. Pelham had a log beneath a Lombardy poplar, with a wide outlook toward the old field of Manassas. Here he talked with one of his captains. "Too many men lost! I feel it through and through that there is going to be heavy fighting. We'll have to fill up somehow."

"Everybody from this region's in already. We might get some fifteen-year-olds or some sixty-five-year-olds, though, or we might ask the department for conscripts —"

"Don't like the latter material. Prefer the first. Well, we'll think about it to-morrow — It's late, late, Haralson! Goodnight."

"Wait," said Haralson. "Here's a man wants to speak to you."

Running up the hillside, from the platform where were the guns to a little line of woods dark against the starlit sky, was a cornfield — between it and the log and the poplar only a little grassy depression. A man had come out of the cornfield. He stood ten feet away — a countryman apparently, poorly dressed.

"Well, who are you?" demanded Pelham, "and how did you get in my lines?"

"I 've been," said the man, "tramping it over from the mountains. And when I got into this county I found it chock full of armies. I did n't want to be taken up by the Yankees, and so I 've been mostly travelling by night. I was in that wood up there while you all were fighting. I had a good view of the battle. When it was over I said to myself, 'After all they 're my folk,' and I came down through the corn. I was lying there between the stalks; I heard you say you needed gunners. I said to myself, 'I might as well join now as later. We 've all got to join one way or another, that 's clear,' and so I thought, sir, I 'd join you —"

"Why have n't you 'joined,' as you call it, before?"

"I 've been right sick for a year or more, sir. I got a blow on the head in a saw mill on Briony Creek and it made me just as useless as a bit of pith. The doctor says I am all right now, sir. I got tired of staying on Briony —"

"Do you know anything about guns?"

"I know all about a shot-gun. I could learn the other."

"What 's your name?"

"Philip Deaderick."

"Well, come into the firelight, Deaderick, so that I can see you."

Deaderick came, showed a powerful figure, and a steady bearded face. "Well," said the Alabamian, "the blow on your head does n't seem to have put you out of the running! I 'll try you, Deaderick."

"I am much obliged to you, sir."

"I have n't any awkward squad into which to put you. You 'll have to learn, and learn quickly, by watching the others. Take him and enroll him, Haralson, and turn him over to Dreux and the Howitzer. Now, Deaderick, the Horse Artillery is heaven to a good man who does his duty, and it 's hell to the other kind. I advise you to try for heaven. That 's all. Good-night."

Day broke over the field of Groveton, over the plains of Manassas.

Stonewall Jackson moved in force westward from the old battle-ground. South of Bull Run, between Young's Branch and Stony Ridge, ran an unfinished railroad. It was bordered by woods and rolling fields. There were alternate embankments and deep railroad cuts. Behind was the long ridge and Catharpin Run, in front, sloping gently to the little stream, green fields broken to the north by one deep wood. Stonewall Jackson laid his hand on the rail-road with those deep cuts and on the rough and rising ground be-yond. In the red dawn there stretched a battle front of nearly two miles. A. P. Hill had the left. Trimble and Lawton of Ewell's had the centre, Jackson's own division the right, Jubal Early and Forno of Ewell's a detached force on this wing. There were forty guns, and they were ranged along the rocky ridge behind the infantry. Jeb Stuart guarded the flanks.

The chill moisture of the morning, the dew-drenched earth, the quiet woods, the rose light in the sky — the troops moving here and there to their assigned positions, exchanged opinions. "Ain't it like the twenty-first of July, 1861?" — "It air and it ain't — mostly ain't!" — "That's true! Hello! they are going to give us the railroad cut! God bless the Manassas Railroad Company! If we'd dug a whole day we could n't have dug such a ditch as that!" — "Look at the boys behind the embankment! Well, if that is n't the jim-dan-diest breastwork! 'N look at the forty guns up there against the sky!" — "Better tear those vines away from the edge. Pretty, are n't they? All the blue morning glories. Regiment's swung off toward Manassas Junction! Now if Longstreet should come up!" — "Maybe he will. Would n't it be exciting? Come up with a yell same as Kirby Smith did last year! Wonder where the Yankees are?" "Somewhere in the woods, the whole hell lot of them." — "Some of them are n't a hell lot. Some of them are right fine. Down on the Chickahominy I acquired a real respect for the Army of the Po-tomac — and a lot of it 'll be here to-day. Yes, sir, I like Fitz John Porter and Sykes and Reynolds and a lot of them first rate! They can't help being commanded by The-Man-without-a-Rear. That's Washington's fault, not theirs." — "Yes, sir, Ricketts and Meade and Kearney and a lot of them are all right." — "Good Lord, what a shout! That's either Old Jack or a rabbit." — "It's Old Jack! It's Old Jack! He's coming along the front. Stonewall Jackson! Stonewall

Jackson! Stonewall Jackson! He's passed. O God! I wish that Bee and Bartow and all that fell here could see him and us now." — "There's Stuart passing through the fields. What guns are those going up Stony Ridge? — Pelham and the Horse Artillery." — "Listen! Bugles! There they come! There they come! Over the Henry Hill." *Attention!*

About the middle of the morning the cannonading ceased. "There's a movement this way," said A. P. Hill on the left. "They mean to turn us. They have ploughed this wood with shells, and now they're coming to sow it. All right, men! General Jackson's looking! — and General Lee will be here to-night to tell the story to. I suppose you'd like Marse Robert to say, 'Well done!' All right, then, do well! — I don't think we're any too rich, Garrett, in ammunition. Better go tell General Jackson so."

The men talked, Hill's men and Ewell's men on Hill's right — not volubly, but with slow appreciation. "Reynolds? Like Reynolds all right. Milroy? Don't care for the gentleman. Sigel — Schurz — Schenck — Steinwehr? *Nein. Nein!* Wonder if they remember Cross Keys?" — "They've got a powerful long line. There is n't but one thing I envy them and that's those beautiful batteries. I don't envy them their good food, and their good, whole clothes or anything but the guns." — "H'm, I don't envy them anything — our batteries are doing all right! We've got a lot of their guns, and to-night we'll have more. Artillery's done fine to-day." — "So it has! so it has!" — "Listen, they're opening again. That's Pelham — now Pegram — now Washington Artillery — now Rockbridge!" — "Yes sir, yes sir! We're all right. We're ready. Music! They always come on with music. Funny! but they've got the bands. What are they playing? Never heard it before. Think it's 'What are the Wild Waves Saying?'" — "I think it's 'When this Cruel War is Over.'" — "Go 'way, you boys were n't in the Valley! We've heard it several times. It's 'Der Wacht am Rhein.'" — "All right, sir! All right. Now!"

Sometime in the middle of the afternoon, after the third great blue charge, Edward Cary, lips blackened from tearing cartridges, lock and barrel of his rifle hot within his hands, his cap shot away, his sleeve torn to ribbons where he had bared and bandaged a flesh wound in the arm, Edward Cary straightened himself and wiped away the sweat and powder grime which blinded him. An officer's voice came out of the murk. "The general asks for volunteers to strip the field of cartridges."

There were four men lying together, killed by the same shell. The head of one was gone, the legs of another; the third was disembowelled, the fourth had his breast crushed in. Their cartridge boxes when opened were found to be half full. Edward emptied them into the haversack he carried and went on to the next. This was a boy of sixteen, not dead yet, moaning like a wounded hound. Edward gave him the little water that was in his canteen, took four cartridges from his box, and crept on. A minie sang by him, struck a yard away, full in the forehead of the dead man toward whom he was making. The dead man had a smile upon his lips; it was as though he mocked the bullet. All the field running back from the railroad cuts and embankment was overstormed by shot and shell, and everywhere from the field rose groans and cries for water. The word "water" never ceased from use. *Water! — Water, Water! — Water! — Water!* On it went, mournfully, like a wind. — *Water! — Water!* Edward gathered cartridges steadily. All manner of things were wont to come into his mind. Just now it was a certain field behind Greenwood covered with blackberry bushes — and the hot August sunshine — and he and Easter's Jim gathering blackberries while Mammy watched from beneath a tree. He heard again the little thud of the berries into the bucket. He took the cartridges from two young men — brothers from the resemblance and from the fact that, falling together, one, the younger, had pillowed his head on the other's breast, while the elder's arm was around him. They lay like children in sleep. The next man was elderly, a lonely, rugged-looking person with a face slightly contorted and a great hole in his breast. The next that Edward came to was badly hurt, but not too badly to take an interest. "Cartridges? — yes, five. I'm awful thirsty! — Well, never mind. Maybe it will rain. Who's charging now? Heintzelman, Kearney, and Reno — Got 'em all? You can draw one from my gun, too. I was just loading when I got hit. Well, sorry you got to go! It's mighty lonely lying here."

Edward returned to the front, gave up his haversack, and got another. As he turned to resume the cartridge quest there arose a cry. "Steady, men! steady! Hooker hasn't had enough!" Edward, too, saw the blue wall coming through the woods on the other side of the railroad. He took a musket from a dead man near by and with all the other grey soldiers lay flat in the grass above the cut. Hooker came within range — within close range. The long grey front sprang to its feet and fired, dropped and loaded, rose and fired. A leaden storm visited the wood across the track. The August grass was long and dry. Sparks set it afire. Flames arose and caught the oak scrub. Through it all and through the storm of bullets the blue line burst. It came down on the unfinished track, it crossed, it leaped up the ten-foot bank of earth, it clanged against the grey line atop. The grey gave back, the colours fell and rose; the air rocked, so loud was the din. Stonewall Jackson appeared. "General Hill, order in your second line." Field's Virginians, Thomas's Georgians charged forward. They yelled, all their rifles flashed at once, they drove Hooker down into the cut, across the track, up into the burning brushwood and the smoke-filled woods. But the blue were staunch and seasoned troops; they re-formed, they cheered. Hooker brought up a fresh brigade. They charged again. Down from the woods plunged the blue wave, through the fire, down the bank, across and up. Again din and smoke and flame, all invading, monstrous. Jackson's voice rose higher. "General Hill, order in General Pender."

North Carolina was, first and last, a stark fighter. Together with Gregg and Field and Thomas, Pender drove Hooker again down the red escarpment, across the railroad, through the burning brush, into the wood; even drove him out of the wood, took a battery and dashed into the open beyond. Then from the hills the blue artillery opened and from the plains below volleyed fresh infantry. Pender was borne back through the wood, across the railroad, up the red side of the cut.

Hooker had a brigade in column behind a tree-clad hill. Screened from sight it now moved forward, swift and silent, then with suddenness broke from the wood in a splendid charge. With a gleam of bayonets, with a flash of colours, with a loud hurrah, with a staggering volley its regiments plunged into the cut, swarmed up the red side and fell upon A. P. Hill's weakened lines. The grey wavered. Stonewall Jackson's voice was heard again. "General Hill, I have ordered up Forno from the right and a regiment of Lawton's." He jerked his hand into the air. "Here they are. Colonel Forno, give them the bayonet!"

Louisiana and Georgia swept forward, Tennessee, Alabama, and Virginia supporting. They swept Grover's brigade down and back. There was bitter fighting, hand-to-hand, horrible work: the dead lay in the railroad cut thick as fallen leaves. The dead lay thick on either bank and thick in the grass that was afire and thick in the smoky wood. The blue gave way, went back; the grey returned to their lines.

Edward went again for cartridges. He was beside Gregg's South Carolinians when a courier came up. "General Jackson wishes to know each brigade's amount of ammunition," and he heard Gregg's answer, "Tell General Jackson that this brigade has one round to the man, but I'll hold the position with the bayonet." Edward gleaned steadily. "Water! water! water!" cried the field. "O God! water!"

It was growing late, the long, hot day declining. There had been nine hours of fighting. "Nine hours — ninety hours — ninety minutes?" thought Edward. "Time's plastic like everything else. Double it, fold it back on itself, stretch it out, do anything with it —" He took the cartridges from a trunk of a man, crept on to a soldier shot through the hip. The latter clutched him with a blackened hand. "Has Marse Robert come? Has General Lee come?"

"They say he has. Over there on Stuart's Hill, holding Reynolds and McDowell and Fitz John Porter in check."

The man fell back. "Oh, then it is all right. Stonewall Jackson and Robert Edward Lee. It's all right —" He spoke drowsily. "It's all right. I'll go to sleep."

Edward looking sideways toward Stony Ridge saw the forty guns black against the sun. As he looked they blazed and thundered. He turned his eyes. Kearney and Reno, five brigades, were coming at a double across the open. As he looked they broke into the charge. With his bag of cartridges he made for the nearest grey line. The blue came on, a formidable wave indeed. Stonewall Jackson rode along the grey front.

"Men, General Early and two regiments of Lawton's are on their way. You must stand it till they come. If you have only one cartridge, save it until they are up from the cut. Then fire, and use your bayonets. Don't cheer! It makes your hand less steady."

The blue wave plunged into the railroad cut. "I think," said a

grey soldier, "that I hear Jubal Early yelling." The blue wave
mounted to the level. "*Yaaaiih! Yaaaaiih!*" came out of the distance. "We know that we do," said the men. "Now, our friend, the
enemy, you go back!" Out of the dun cloud and roar came a deep
"Steady, men! You've got your bayonets yet. Stand it for five
minutes. General Early's coming. This is Manassas — Manassas
— Manassas! God is over us! Stand it for five minutes — for three
minutes. — General Early, drive them with the bayonet."

Late that night on the banks of Bull Run the general "from the
West, where we have always seen the backs of our enemy" sent a
remarkable telegram to Halleck at Washington. "*We fought a terrific
battle here yesterday with the combined forces of the enemy, which lasted
with continuous fury from daylight until dark, by which time the enemy
was driven from the field which we now occupy. The enemy is still in our
front, but badly used up. We lost not less than eight thousand men killed
and wounded, but from the appearance of the field the enemy lost two to
one. The news has just reached me from the front that the enemy is retreating toward the mountains.*"

The delusion holding, he, at noon of the thirtieth, ordered a general advance. "The troops to be immediately thrown forward in
pursuit of the enemy and to press him vigorously." One of his
officers undertook a comment. "By the Lord Harry, it will be the
shortest pursuit that even he ever saw! Why, damn it all! they're
still here! I tell you the place is unlucky!"

Twenty thousand blue soldiers formed the front that came down
from the hills and moved toward the Groveton wood and the railroad
track. Behind them were supporting masses, forty thousand strong.
On every slope gleamed the great blue guns. The guns opened; they
shelled with vehemence the wood, the railroad cut, and embankment, the field immediately beyond. A line of grey pickets was seen
to leave the wood and make across the track and into cover. Pope
at the Stone House saw these with his field glass. "The last of their
rear guard," he said.

One of his generals spoke. "Their guns are undoubtedly yet on
that ridge, sir."

"I am perfectly well aware of that, sir. But they will not be there
long after our line has crossed the track. Either we will gloriously
take them, or they will limber up and scamper after Jackson. He,

I take it, is well on his way to Thoroughfare Gap. All that we need is expedition. Crush him, and then when Longstreet is up, crush *him*."

"And those troops on Stuart Hill?"

"Give you my word they are nothing, general! A rebel regiment, at the most a brigade, thrown out from Jackson's right. I have positive information. Fitz John Porter is mistaken — arrogantly mistaken. — Ah, the rebel guns are going to indulge in a little bravado."

The twenty thousand gleaming bayonets passed the turnpike, passed Dogan's house, moved on toward the wood. It rose torn and thin and black from yesterday's handling. Immediately beyond was the railroad cut. On the other side of the railroad ran a stretch of field and scrub, mounting to Stony Ridge, that rose from the base of the woods. Stony Ridge looked grey itself and formidable, and all about it was the smoke of the forty grey guns. The twenty thousand bayonets pressed on.

There came a blare of bugles. Loud and high they rang — the bugles of the Light Division, of Ewell's, of Jackson's own. They pierced the thunder of the guns, they came from the wood at the base of Stony Ridge. There was a change in the heart-beat below the twenty thousand bayonets. Porter and Ricketts and Hatch stared, and saw start from the wood a downward moving wall. It moved fast; it approached with a certain impetuous steadiness. Behind it were shorter lines, detached masses. Together all came down from Stony Ridge like an avalanche. The avalanche came to and took the field of yesterday, and stood revealed, — Stonewall Jackson holding the railroad cut. "I thought as much," said Fitz John Porter. "Go ask him to give us Reynolds."

After the third charge the 65th and another regiment of the Stonewall Brigade, finding their ammunition exhausted, armed themselves with stones. Those of the Thunder Run men who had not fallen at White Oak Swamp proved themselves expert. Broken rock lay in heaps by the railroad bed. They brought these into the lines, swung and threw them. With stones and bayonets they held the line. Morell and Sykes were great fighters; the grey men recognized worthy foes. The battle grew Titanic. Stonewall Jackson signalled to Lee on the Warrenton turnpike, "Hill hard pressed. Every brigade engaged. Would like more guns."

Lee sent two batteries, and Stephen D. Lee placed them. There arose a terrific noise, and presently a wild yelling. Lee signalled:—
General Jackson. Do you still need reinforcements? Lee.

The signal officer on the knoll behind the Stonewall wigwagged back.

No. The enemy are giving way. Jackson.

They gave way, indeed. The forty guns upon the ridge, the eight that Lee had sent, strewed the green field beyond the Groveton wood with shot and shrapnel. Morell fell back, Hatch fell back; the guns became deadly, mowing down the blue lines. Stonewall Jackson rode along the front.

"General Hill, it is time for the counterstroke. Forward, and drive them!"

The signaller wigwagged to the Warrenton turnpike:—
General Lee. I am driving them. Jackson.

The signaller on the turnpike signalled back:—
General Jackson. General Longstreet is advancing. Look out for and protect his left flank. Lee.

Lee's great battle was over and won. Every division, brigade, regiment, battery, fifty thousand infantry and cavalry brought by the great leader into simultaneous action, the Army of Northern Virginia moved as in a vast parade over plain and hill. Four miles in length, swept the first wave with, in the centre, seven grey waves behind it. It was late. The grey sea moved in the red and purple of a great sunset. From Stony Ridge the forty guns thundered like grey breakers, while the guns of Longstreet galloped toward the front. Horses and men and guns were at the martial height of passion. To the right Jeb Stuart appeared, magnificent. On swept the resistless sea. A master mind sent it over those Manassas hills and plains, here diverting a portion of its waves, here curbing a too rapid onslaught, here harking the great mass forward, surmounting barriers, overwhelming a stubborn opposition, crumbling and breaking to pieces. Wave on wave, rapid, continuous, unremitting, thundered the assault, in the red sunset of the thirtieth of August. Pope's Army fought bravely, but in the dusk it melted away.

CHAPTER XL

A GUNNER OF PELHAM'S

MAJOR JOHN PELHAM looked at the clouds boiling up above Bull Run Mountains.

> "Rain, rain go away,
> Come again another day! — "

he said. "What's the house they've burned over there?"

"Chantilly, sir."

Ruined wall and chimney, fallen roof-tree, gaping holes where windows had been, the old mansion stood against the turmoil of the sky. It looked a desolation, a poignant gloom, an unrelieved sorrow. A courier appeared. "The enemy's rear-guard is near Ox Hill, sir. They've driven in some of our patrols. The main body is moving steady toward Fairfax Court House. General Jackson has sent the Light Division forward. General Stuart's going, too. He says, 'Come on.'"

The clouds mounted high and dark, thunder began to mutter; by the time a part of the Light Division and a brigade of Ewell's came into touch with Reno and Kearney, the afternoon, already advanced, was of the hue of twilight. Presently there set in a violent storm of thunder and lightning, wind and rain. The trees writhed like wounded soldiers, the rain came level against the face, stinging and blinding, the artillery of the skies out-thundered man's inventions. It grew darker and darker, save for the superb, far-showing lightning flashes. Beneath these the blue and the grey plunged into an engagement at short range.

What with the howling of the storm, the wind that took voices and whirled them high and away, the thunder above and the volleying musketry below, to hear an order was about the most difficult feat imaginable. Stafford gathered, however, that Lawton, commanding since Ewell's wound, was sending him to Jackson with a statement as to affairs on this wing. He went, riding hard against the slanting

rain, and found Jackson standing in the middle of the road, a piece
of bronze played round by lightning. One of the brigadiers was
speaking to him. "The cartridges are soaking wet, sir. I do not
know that I can hold my position." Jackson's voice came deep and
curt. "Yes, sir, you can. If your muskets won't go off, neither will
the enemy's. You are to hold it, whether you can or not. Go and
do it."

The brigadier went. Stafford gave his information, and received
an order. "Go back along the road until you find the horse artillery. Tell Major Pelham to bring his guns to the knoll yonder with
the blasted tree."

Stafford turned his horse and started. The rain and wind were
now at his back — a hundred paces, and the road, lonely save for
stragglers, the grey troops, the battle in front, was all sheeted and
shrouded in the darkly drifting storm. The fitful bursts of musketry
were lost beneath the artillery of the clouds. He travelled a mile,
found Pelham and gave his order, then stood aside under the tossing
pines while the horse artillery went by. It went by in the dusk of
the storm, in the long howl of the wind and the dash of the rain, like
the iron chariots of Pluto, the horses galloping, the gunners clinging
wherever they might place hand or foot, the officers and mounted
men spurring alongside. Stafford let them all turn a bend in the
road, then followed.

All this stretch of road and field and wood had been skirmished
over, Stuart and the blue cavalry having been in touch through the
earlier part of the day. The road was level, with the mournful
boggy fields, with the wild bending woods. In the fields and in the
woods there were dark objects, which might be mounds of turf or
huge twisted roots, or which might be dead men and horses. Stafford,
riding through wind and rain, had no sooner thought this than he
saw, indeed, what seemed a mere hummock beneath a clump of
cedars undoubtedly move. He looked as closely as he might for the
war of water, air, and fire, and made out a horse outstretched and
stark, and a man pinned beneath. The man spoke. "Hello, upon
the road there! Come and do a Christian turn!"

Stafford left his horse and, stepping through a quagmire of watery
turf, came into the ring of cedars. The man who had called upon
him, a tall, long-moustached person in blue, one arm and booted leg

painfully caught beneath the dead steed, spoke in a voice curt with suffering. "Grey, are n't you? Don't care. Can't help it. Get this infernal weight off me, won't you?"

The other bent to the task, and at last managed to free the blue soldier. "There! That position must have been no joke! How long —"

The blue cavalryman proceeded to feel bone and flesh, slowly and cautiously to move the imprisoned limbs. He drew a breath of relief. "Nothing broken! — How long? Well, to reckon by one's feeling I should say about a week. Say, however, since about noon. We drove against a party under Stuart. He got the best of us, and poor Caliph got a bullet. I could see the road. Everything grey — grey as the sea."

"Why did n't you call before? Any one would have helped you."

The other continued to rub his arm and leg. "You have n't got a drop of brandy — eh?"

"Yes, I have. I should have thought of that before." He gave the other a small flask. The cavalryman drank. "Ah! in '55, when I was with Walker in Nicaragua, I got pinned like that beneath a falling cottonwood." He gave the flask back. "You are the kind of Samaritan I like to meet. I feel a new man. Thanks awfully."

"It was foolish of you to lie there for hours —"

The other leaned his back against a cedar. "Well, I thought I might hold out, perhaps, until we beat you and I was again in the house of my friends. I don't, however, object to acknowledging that you 're hard to beat. Could n't manage it. Growing cold and faint — head ringing. Waited as long as I could, then called. They say your prisons are very bad."

"They are no worse than yours."

"That may be. Any of them are bad."

"We are a ravaged and blockaded country. It is with some difficulty that we feed and clothe our armies in the field. As for medicines with which to fight disease, you will not let them pass, not for our women and children and sick at home, and not for your own men in prison. And, for all our representations, you will not exchange prisoners. If there is undue suffering, I think you must share the blame."

"Yes, yes, it is all hellish enough! — Well, on one side of the dice, prisoner of war; on the other, death here under poor Caliph. Might escape from prison, no escape from death. By Jove, what a thunder-clap! It's Stonewall Jackson pursuing us, eh?"

"Yes. I hear Pelham's guns — You are an Englishman?"

"Yes. Francis Marchmont, at your service; colonel of the Marchmont" — he laughed — "Invincibles."

"I am Maury Stafford, serving on General Ewell's staff. — Yes, that's Pelham."

He straightened himself. "I must be getting back to the front. It is hard to hear for the wind and rain and thunder, but I think the musketry is recommencing." He looked about him. "We came through these woods this morning. Stuart has patrols everywhere, but I think that dip between the hills may be clear. You are pretty pale yet. You had better keep the brandy flask. Are you sure that you can walk?"

"Walk beside you into your lines, you mean?"

"No. I mean try a way out between the hills."

"I am not your prisoner?"

"No."

Marchmont pulled at his moustaches. "Yes. I think I can walk. I won't deprive you of your flask — but if I might have another mouthful — Thank you." He rose stiffly. "If at any time I can serve you, I trust that you will remember my name — Francis Marchmont, colonel Marchmont Invincibles. Send me a slip of paper, a word, anything. *Ox Hill* will do — and you will find me at your service. Yes, the firing is beginning again — "

Stafford, once more upon the road, travelled northward in an un-abated storm. Tree and bush, weed, flower and grass, writhed and shrank beneath the anger of the air; the rain hissed and beat, the lightning glared, the thunder crashed. Between the flashes all was dusk. Before him the rattle of musketry, the booming of the guns grew louder. He saw to the right, on a bare rise of ground, Pelham's guns.

There came an attempted flanking movement of the blue — a dash of cavalry met by Stuart and followed by a movement of two of Hill's brigades. The action barred the road and fields before Staf-ford. He watched it a moment, then turned aside and mounted the rise of ground to Pelham's guns. A great lightning-flash lit them, ranged above him. All their wet metal gleamed; about them moved the gunners; a man with a lifted sponge staff looked an unearthly figure against the fantastic castles and battlements, the peaks and abysses of the boiling clouds. The light vanished; Stafford came level with the guns in the dusk.

Pelham welcomed him. "'Trust in God and keep your powder dry,' eh, major? It's the kind of storm you read about — Hello! they've brought up another battery — "

Stafford dismounted. One of the guns had the vent so burned and enlarged that it was useless. It rested cold and silent beside its bellowing fellows. Stafford seated himself on the limber, and watched the double storm. It raged above the little hill, with its chain lightnings, with wind, with reverberations of thunder; and it raged below, between some thousands of grey and blue figures, small, small, in the dusk, shadowy manikins sending from metal tubes glow-worm flashes! He sat, with his chin in his hand, pondering the scene.

Pelham came heavily into action. There was a blue battery on the opposite hill. The two spoke in whispers beneath the storm. The gunners, now in darkness, now in the vivid lightning, moved about the guns. Now they bent low, now they stood upright. The officer gestured to them and they to each other. Several were killed or wounded; and as now this section, now that, was more deeply engaged, there was some shifting among the men, occasional changes of place. The dusk increased; it was evident that soon night and the storm would put an end to the battle. Stafford, watching, made out that even now the blue and grey forms in the tossing woods and boggy meadows were showing less and less their glow-worm fires, were beginning to move apart. The guns above them boomed more slowly, with intervals between their speech. The thunder came now, not in ear-splitting cracks but with long rolling peals, with spaces between filled only by the wind and the rain. The human voice might be heard, and the officers shouted, not gestured their orders. The twilight deepened. The men about the gun nearest Stafford looked but shadows, bending, leaning across, rising upright. They talked, however, and the words were now audible. "Yes, if you could handle lightning — take one of them zigzags and turn it loose on blue people!"— "That battery is tired; it's going home! Right tired myself. Reckon we're all tired but Old Jack. He don't never get tired. This is a pretty behaving gun —" "That's so! and she's got good men. They do first-rate." — "That's so! Even the new one's good" — "Good! He learned that gun same as though they *grew* artillery wherever he came from. Briery Creek — No, Briony Creek — hey, Deaderick?"

"Briony Creek."

Stafford dropped his hand. "Who spoke?"

The question had been breathed, not loudly uttered. No one answered. The gunners continued their movements about the guns, stooping, handling, lifting themselves upright. It was all but night, the lightning less and less violent, revealing little beyond mere shape and action. Stafford sank back. "Storm within and storm without. They breed delusions!"

The blue battery opposite limbered up and went away. The musketry fire in the hollows between the hills grew desultory. A slow crackle of shots would be followed by silence; then might come with fierce energy a sudden volley; silence followed it, too, — or what, by comparison, seemed silence. The thunder rolled more and more distantly, the wind lashed the trees, the rain beat upon the guns. Officers and men of the horse artillery were too tired, too wet, and too busy for much conversation, but still human voices came and went in the lessening blast, in the semi-darkness and the streaming rain.

There was a gunner near Stafford who worked in silence and rested from his work in silence. Stafford became conscious of him during one of the latter periods — a silent man, leaning against his gun. He was not ten feet away, but the twilight was now deep, and he rested indistinct, a shadow against a shadow. Once there came a pale lightning flash, but his arm was raised as if to shield his eyes, and there was seen but a strongly made gunner with a sponge staff. Darkness came again at once. The impression that remained with Stafford was that the gunner's face was turned toward him, that he had, indeed, when the flash came, been regarding him somewhat closely. That was nothing — a man not of the battery, a staff officer sitting on a disabled gun, waiting till he could make his way back to his chief — a moment's curiosity on an artilleryman's part, exhibited in a lull between fighting. Stafford had a certain psychic development. A thinker, he was adventurous in that world; to him, the true world of action. The passion that had seized and bound him had come with the force of an invader, of a barbaric horde, from a world that he ordinarily ignored. It held him helpless, an enslaved spirit, but around it vaguely worked the old habits of mind. Now it interested him — though only to a certain degree — that, in some subtle fashion and for some reason which he could not explain, the gunner with the sponge staff could so make himself felt across space. He wondered a little about this man; and then, insensibly, he began to review the past. He had resolution enough, and he did not always choose to review the past. To-night it was perhaps the atmosphere, the commotion of the elements, the harp of the wind, the scourging rain — at any rate, he reviewed it and fully. When the circle was completed and his attention touched again the storm and the twilight hill near Chantilly, and he lifted his eyes from the soaked and trodden ground, it was to find the double shadow still before him. He felt that the eyes of the gunner with the sponge staff were on him, had been on him for some time. Quite involuntarily he moved, with a sudden gesture, as though he evaded a blow. A sergeant's voice came through the twilight, the wind and the rain. "Deaderick!"

The man by the gun moved, took up the sponge staff that had rested beside him, turned in the darkness and went away.

A little later Stafford left the hilltop. The cannon had ceased their booming, except for here and there a fitful burst; the musketry fire had ceased. Pope's rear-guard, Lee's advance, the two drew off and the engagement rested indecisive. Blue and grey, a thousand or two men suffered death or wounding. They lay upon the miry earth, beneath the pelting storm. Among the blue, Kearney and Stevens were killed. Through the darkness that wrapped the scene, Stafford found at last his way to his general. He found him with Stuart, who was reporting to Stonewall Jackson. "They're retreating pretty rapidly, sir. They'll reach Fairfax Court House presently."

"Yes. They won't stop there. We'll bivouac on the field, general."

"And to-morrow, sir?"

"To-morrow, sir, we will follow them out of Virginia."

September the second dawned bright and clear. From Fairfax Court House Pope telegraphed to Halleck. "There is undoubted purpose on the part of the enemy to keep on slowly turning my position so as to come in on the right. The forces under my command are unable to prevent his doing so. Telegraph what to do."

Halleck telegraphed to fall back to the fortifications of Alexandria and Washington.

CHAPTER XLI

THE TOLLGATE

ON Thunder Run Mountain faint reds and yellows were beginning to show in the maple leaves, while the gum trees dwelling in the hollows had a deeper tinge of crimson. But the mass of the forest was yet green. The September sun was like balm, amber days, at once alert and dreamlike. The September nights were chilly. But the war, that pinched and starved and took away on all hands, left the forest and the wood for fires. On Thunder Run the women cut the wood, and the children gathered dead boughs and pine cones.

The road over the mountain was in a bad condition. It had not been worked for a year. That mattered the less perhaps, that it was now so little travelled. All day and every day Tom Cole sat in the sunshine on the toll gate porch, the box for the toll beside him, and listened for wheels or horses' hoofs. It was an event now when he could hobble out to the gate, take the toll and pass the time of day, He grew querulous over the state of the road. "There'd surely be more travel if 't warn't so bad! Oh, yes, I know there aren't many left hereabouts to travel, and what there are, have n't got the means. But there surely would be more going over the mountain if the road wan't so bad!" He had a touch of fever, and he babbled about the road all night, and how hard it was not to see or talk to anybody! He said that he wished that he had died when he fell out of Nofsinger's hayloft. The first day that he was well enough to be left, Sairy went round to the Thunder Run women, beginning with Christianna Maydew's mother. Several days afterward, Tom hobbling out on the porch was most happily welcomed by the noise of wheels. "Thar now!" said Sairy, "ain't it a real picnic feeling to get back to business?" Tom went out to the gate with the tobacco box. A road wagon, and a sulky and a man on horseback! The old man's eyes glistened. "Mornin', gentlemen!" "Mornin', Mr. Cole! County's mended your road fine! Big hole down there filled up and the bridge that was just a mantrap new floored! The news? Well, Stonewall Jackson's after them!"

But despite the filled-up holes travel was slight, slight! To-day from dawn until eleven, no one had passed. Tom sat in the sun on the porch, and the big yellow cat slept beside him, and the china asters bloomed in the tiny yard. Sairy was drying apples. She had them spread on boards in the sun. Now and then she came from the kitchen to look at them, and with a peach bough to drive the bees away. The close of summer found, as ever, Thunder Run shrunken to something like old age; but even so his murmur was always there like a wind in the trees. This morning there was a fleet of clouds in the September sky. Their shadows drove across the great landscape, the ridges and levels of the earth, out upon which Thunder Run Mountain looked so steadily.

A woman, a neighbour living a mile beyond the schoolhouse, came by. Sairy went over to the little picket fence and the two talked. "How is she?" — "She's dead." — "Sho! You don't say so! Poor thing, poor thing! I reckon I thought of her mor'n I slept last night. — 'N the child?"

"Born dead."

Sairy struck her tongue against the roof of her mouth. "Sho! War killin' 'em even thar!"

The mountain woman spoke on in the slow mountain voice. "She had awful dreams. Somebody was fool enough to tell her 'bout how dreadful thirsty wounded folk get, lyin' thar all round the clock an' no one comin'! An' some other fool read her out of an old newspaper 'bout Malvern Hill down thar at Richmond. Mrs. Cole, she thought she was a soldier. An' when she begun to suffer she thought she was wounded. She thought she was all mangled and torn by a cannon ball. Yes'm, it was pitiful. An' she said thar was a high hill. It was five miles high, she said. An' she said thar was water at the top, which was foolish, but she could n't help that, an' God knows women go through enough to make them foolish! An' she said thar was jest one path, an' thar was two children playing on it, an' she could n't make them understand. She begged us all night to tell the children thar was a wounded soldier wantin' to get by. An' at dawn she said the water was cold an' died."

The woman went on up Thunder Run Mountain. Sairy turned

again the drying apples, then brought her patching out upon the porch and sat down in a low split-bottomed chair opposite Tom. The yellow cat at her feet yawned, stretched, and went back to sleep. The china asters bloomed; the sun drew out the odours of thyme and rue and tansy. Tom read a last week's newspaper. *General Lee crosses the Potomac.*

Christianna came down the road and unlatched the gate. "Come in, come in, Christianna!" said Tom. "Come in and take a cheer! Letter came yesterday —"

Christianna sat down on the edge of the porch, her back against the pillar. She took off her sunbonnet. "Violetta learned to do a heap of things while I was down t' Richmond. I took a heap of them back, too, but somehow I've got more time than I used to have. Somehow I jest wander round —"

Tom took a tin box from beside the tobacco box. "'T would be awful if the letter didn't come once't every ten days or two weeks! Reckon I'd go plumb crazy, an' so would Sairy —"

Sairy turned the garment she was patching. "Sho! I would n't go crazy. What's the use when it's happening all the time? I ain't denying that most of the light would go out of things. Stop imaginin' an' read Christianna what he says about furin' parts."

"After Gaines's Mill it was twelve days," said Tom, "an' the twelfth day we did n't say a word, only Sairy read the Bible. An' now he's well and rejoined at Leesburg."

He cleared his throat. "DEAR AUNT SAIRY AND TOM: — It's fine to get back to the Army! It's an Army that you can love. I do love it. But I love Thunder Run and the School House and Tom and Sairy Cole, too, and sometimes I miss them dreadfully! I rejoined at Leesburg. The 65th — I can't speak of the 65th — you know why. It breaks my heart. But it's reorganized. The boys were glad to see me, and I was glad to see them. Tell Christianna that Billy's all right. He's sergeant now, and he does fine. And Dave's all right, too, and the rest of the Thunder Run men. The War's done a heap for Mathew Coffin. It's made a real man of him. Tom, I wish you could have seen us fording the Potomac. It was like a picture book. All a pretty silver morning, with grey plovers wheeling overhead, and the Maryland shore green and sweet, and the water cool to your waist, and the men laughing and calling and singing 'Maryland, my

Maryland!' Fitzhugh Lee was ahead with the cavalry. It was pretty to see the horses go over, and the blessed guns that we know and love, every iron man of them, and all the white covered wagons. Our division crossed last, Old Jack at the head. When we came up from the river into Maryland we turned toward Frederick. The country's much like our own and the people pleasant enough. You know we've got the Maryland Line, and a number besides. They're fine men, a little dashing, but mighty steady, too. They've expressed themselves straight along as positively certain that all Maryland would rise and join us. There's a line of the song, you know: —

> "Huzzah! huzzah!
> She breathes, she burns, she'll come, she'll come,
> Maryland! my Maryland!"

"She hasn't come yet. The people evidently don't dislike us, and as a matter of course we aren't giving them any reason to. But their farms are all nice and green and well tilled, and we haven't seen a burned house or mill, and the children are going to school, and the stock is all sleek and well fed — and if they haven't seen they've heard of the desolation on our side of the river. They've got a pretty good idea of what War is and they're where more people would be if they had that idea beforehand. They are willing to keep out of it. — So they're respectful, and friendly, and they crowd around to try to get a glimpse of General Lee and General Jackson, but they don't volunteer — not in shoals as the Marylanders said they would! The Maryland Line looks disdain at them. Mathew Coffin is dreadfully fretted about the way we're dressed. He says that's the reason Maryland won't come. But the mess laughs at him. It says that if Virginia doesn't mind, Maryland needn't. I wish you could see us, Aunt Sairy. When I think of how I went away from you and Tom with that trunk full of lovely clean things! — Now we are gaunt and ragged and shoeless and dirty —" Tom stopped to wipe his spectacles.

Sairy threaded a needle. "All that's less lasting than some other things, they air. I reckon they'll leave a brighter streak than a deal of folk who aren't gaunt an' ragged an' shoeless an' dirty."

"I don't ever see them so," said Christianna, in her soft drawling voice. "I see them just like a piece we had in a book of reading pieces at school. It was a hard piece but, I learned it.

> "All furnished, all in arms,
> All plumed like estridges that with the wind
> Bated — like eagles having lightly bathed,
> Glittering in golden coats like images."

"No. I reckon if Virginia don't mind, Maryland need n't."

Tom began again. "We've got a lovely camp here, and it's good to lie and rest on the green grass. The Army has had hard fighting and hard marching. Second Manassas was a big battle. It's in the air that we'll have another soon. Don't you worry about me. I'll come out all right. And if I don't, never forget that you did everything in the world for me and that I loved you and thought of you at the very last. Is living getting hard on Thunder Run? I fear so sometimes, for it's getting hard everywhere, and you can't see the end — I wish I had some pay to send you, but we are n't getting any now. This war's going to be fought without food or pay. Tell me, Aunt Sairy, just right honestly how you are getting on. It's getting toward winter. When I say my prayers I pray now that it won't be a hard winter. A lot of us are praying that. It's right pitiful, the men with wives and children at home, and the country growing to look like a desert. — But that's gloomy talk, and if there's one thing more than another we've got to avoid it's being gloomy! — Tell me everything when you write. Write to Winchester — that's our base of supplies and rendezvous now. Tell me about everybody on Thunder Run, but most of all tell me about yourselves. Give my very best regards to Christianna. She surely was good to me in Richmond. I don't know what I would have done without her. At first, before I —"

Sairy put out her hand. "Give it to me, Tom. I'll read the rest. You're tired."

"No, I'm not," said Tom. — "At first, before I came up with the Army, I missed her dreadfully."

Sairy rose, stepped from the porch, and turned the drying apples. Coming back, she touched the girl on the shoulder — very gently. "They're all fools, Christianna. Once I met a woman who did not know her thimble finger. I thought that beat all! But it's hard to match the men."

"You've put me out!" said Tom. "Where was I? Oh — At first, before I came up with the Army, I missed her dreadfully. Billy reminds me of her at times. — It's near roll call, and I must stop. God bless you both. Allan."

Tom folded the letter with trembling hands, laid it carefully atop of the others in the tin box, and took off and wiped his glasses. "Yes, if a letter did n't come every two weeks I'd go plumb crazy! I've got to hear him say 'dear Tom' that often, anyhow —"

Christianna rose, pulling her sunbonnet over her eyes. "Thank you, Mrs. Cole an' Mr. Cole. I thought I'd like to hear. Now I'll be going back up the mountain. Violetta an' Rosalinda are pulling fodder and mother is ploughing for wheat. I do the spinning mostly. You've got lovely china asters, Mrs. Cole. They have a flower they called magnolia down 't Richmond — like a great sweet white cup, an' they had pink crape myrtles. I liked it in Richmond, for all the death an' mourning. Thunder Run's so far away. Good mahnin', Mrs. Cole. Good mahnin', Mr. Cole."

The slight homespun figure disappeared around the bend of the road. Sairy sewed in silence. Tom went back to the newspaper. The yellow cat slept on, the bees buzzed and droned, the sweet mountain air brushed through the trees, a robin sang. Half an hour passed. Tom raised his head. "I hear some one coming!" He reached for the tobacco box.

It proved to be an old well-loved country doctor, on a white horse, with his saddle bags before him. Sairy hurried out, too, to the gate. "Doctor, I want to ask you something about Tom — " "Psha, I 'm all right," said Tom. "Won't you get down and set a little, doctor?"

The doctor would and did, and after he had prescribed for the toll-gate keeper a two hours' nap every day and not to get too excited over war news, Tom read him Allan's letter, and they got into a hot discussion of the next battle. Sairy turned the drying apples, brushed away the bees, and brought fresh water from the well, then sat down again with her mending. "Doctor, how's the girl at Three Oaks?"

The doctor came back from Maryland to his own county and to the fold which he tended without sleep, without rest, and with little pay save in loving hearts. "Miriam Cleave? She's better, Mrs. Cole, she's better!"

"I'm mighty glad to hear it," said Sairy. "'T ain't a decline, then?"

"No, no! Just shock on shock coming to a delicate child. Her mother will bring her through. And there's a great woman."

"That's so, that's so!" assented Tom cordially. "A great woman."

Sairy nodded, drawing her thread across a bit of beeswax. "For once you are both right. He isn't there now, doctor?"

"No. He wasn't there but a week or two."

"You don't — "

"No, Tom. I don't know where he has gone. They have some land in the far south, down somewhere on the Gulf. He may have gone there."

"I reckon," said Tom, "he couldn't stand it in Virginia. All the earth beginnin' to tremble under marchin' feet and everybody askin', 'Where's the army to-day?' I reckon he couldn't stand it. I couldn't. Allan don't believe he did it, an' I don't believe it either."

"Nor I," said Sairy.

"He came up here," said Tom, "just as quiet an' grave an' simple as you or me. An' he sat there in his lawyer's clothes, with his back to that thar pillar, an' he told Sairy an' me all about Allan. He told us how good he was an' how all the men loved him an' how valuable he was to the service. An' he said that the wound he got at Gaines's Mill wasn't so bad after all as it might have been, and that Allan would soon be rejoining. An' he said that being a scout wasn't as glorious, maybe, but it was just as necessary as being a general. An' that he had always loved Allan an' always would. An' he told us about something Allan did at McDowell and then again at Kernstown — an' Sairy cried an' so did I — "

Sairy folded her work. "I wasn't crying so much for Allan — "

"An' then he asked for a drink of water 'n we talked a little about the crops, 'n he went down the mountain. An' Sairy an' I don't believe he did it."

The doctor drew his hand downward over mouth and white beard. "Well, Mrs. Cole, I don't either. The decisions of courts and judges don't always decide. There's always a chance of an important witness called Truth having been absent. I didn't see Richard

Cleave but once while he was at Three Oaks. He looked and acted then just like Richard Cleave, — only older and graver. It was beautiful to see him and his mother together." The doctor rose. "But I reckon it's as Tom says and he could n't stand it, and has gone where he does n't hear 'the army — the army — the army' — all day long. Mrs. Cleave has n't said anything, and I would n't ask. The last time I saw her — and I think he had just gone — she looked like a woman a great artist might have met in a dream."

The doctor gazed out over the autumn sea of mountains and up at the pure serene of the heavens, and then at his old, patient white horse with the saddle bags across the saddle. "Mrs. Cole, all you've got to do is to keep Tom from getting excited. I'll be back this way the first of the week and I'll stop again — "

Tom cleared his throat. "I don't know when Sairy an' me can pay you, doctor. I never realized till it came how war stops business. I'd about as well be keeping toll gate in the desert of Sahary."

"I'm not doing it for pay," said the doctor. "It's just the place to stop and rest and talk, and as for giving you a bit of opinion and advice, Lord! I'm not so poor that I can't do that. If you want to give me something in return I certainly could use three pounds of dried apples."

The doctor rode on down the mountain. Tom and Sairy had a frugal dinner. Then the former lay down to take the prescribed nap, and the latter set her washtub on a box in the yard beneath the peach trees. Tom did n't sleep long; he said every time he was about to drop off he thought he heard wheels. He came back to his split-bottomed chair on the porch, the tobacco box for the toll, the tin box with Allan's letters, and the view across the china asters of the road. The afternoon was past its height, but bright yet, with the undersong of the wind and of Thunder Run. The yellow cat had had his dinner, too, and after sauntering around the yard, and observing the robin on the locust tree again curled himself on the porch and slept.

Sairy straightened herself from the washtub. "Somebody's comin' up the road. It's a man!" She came toward the porch, wiping her hands, white and crinkled, upon her apron. "He's a soldier, Tom! Maybe one of the boys air come back —

Tom rose too, quickly. He staggered and had to catch at the sapling that made the pillar. "Maybe it's —"

"No, no! no, no! Don't you think that, an' have a setback when you find it ain't! It ain't tall enough for Allan, an' it ain't him anyhow. It *could n't* be."

"No, I reckon it could n't," said Tom. "But anyhow it's one of the boys." He was half way to the gate, Sairy after him, and they were the first to welcome Steve Dagg back to Thunder Run.

Tom Cole forgot that he had no opinion of Steve anyway. Sairy pursed her lips, but a soldier was a soldier. Steve came and sat down on the edge of the porch, beside the china asters. "Gawd! don't Thunder Run sound natural! Yass 'm, I walked from Buford's, an' 't was awful hard to do, cause my foot is all sore an' gangrened. I've got a furlough till it gets well. It's awful sore. Gawd! ef Thunder Run had seen what I've seen, an' heard what I've heard, an' done what I've done, an' been through what I've been through —"

CHAPTER XLII

IN Lee's tent, pitched in a grove a mile from Frederick, was held a council of war, — Lee, Stonewall Jackson, Longstreet, Jeb Stuart. Lee sat beside the table, Jackson faced him, sabre across knees, Longstreet had his place a little to one side, and Stuart stood, his shoulder against the tent pole. The last-named had been speaking. He now ended with "I think I may say, sir, that hardly a rabbit has gotten past my pickets. He's a fine fellow, Little Mac is! but he's mighty cautious, and you could n't exactly call him swift as lightning. He's still a score of miles to the east of us, and he knows mighty little what we are about."

Jackson spoke. "General McClellan does not know if the whole army has crossed or only part of it has crossed. He does not know whether we are going to move against Washington, or move against Baltimore, or invade Pennsylvania. Always mystify, mislead, and deceive the enemy as far as possible."

Longstreet spoke. "Well, by the time he makes those twenty miles the troops should be rested and in condition. We'll have another battle and another victory."

Lee spoke, addressing Stuart. "You have done your work most skilfully, general. It is not every army that has a Jeb Stuart!" He paused, then spoke to all. "McClellan will not be up for several days. Across the river, in Virginia, are yet fourteen thousand of the enemy. I had hoped that, scattered as they are, Washington would withdraw them when it heard of our crossing. It has not done so, however. It is not well to have in our rear that entrenched camp at Harper's Ferry. It is my idea, gentlemen, that it might be possible to repeat the manœuvre of Second Manassas."

Stonewall Jackson hitched his chair closer. Stuart chuckled joyously. Longstreet looked dubious. "Do you mean, general, that you would again divide the army?"

Lee rested his crossed hands on the table before him. "Gentlemen, did I have the Northern generals' numbers, I, too, might be cautious. Having only Robert E. Lee's numbers, I advance another policy. It is my idea again to divide the army."

"In the enemy's country? We have not fifty-five thousand fighting strength."

"Yes, in the enemy's country. And I know that we have not fifty-five thousand fighting strength. My plan is this, gentlemen. General Stuart has proved his ability to hold all roads and mask all movements. We will form two columns, and behind the screen which his cavalry provides, one column will move north and one column will move south. By advancing toward Hagerstown the first will create the impression that Pennsylvania is to be invaded. Moreover Catoctin and South Mountain are strong defensive positions. The other column will move with expedition. Recrossing the Potomac, it will invest and capture Harper's Ferry. That done, it will return at once into Maryland, rejoining me before McClellan is up."

Longstreet swore. "By God, that is a bold plan! — What if McClellan should learn it?"

"As against that, we must trust in General Stuart. These people must be driven out of Harper's Ferry. All our communications are threatened."

Longstreet was blunt. "Well, sir, I think it is madness. Pray don't send me on any such errand!"

Lee smiled. "General Jackson, what is your opinion?"

Jackson spoke with brevity. "I might prefer, sir, to attack McClellan first and then turn upon Harper's Ferry. But I see no madness in the other plan — if the movement is rapid. Sometimes to be bold is the sanest thing you can do. It is necessary of course that the enemy should be kept in darkness."

"Then, general, you will undertake the reduction of Harper's Ferry?"

"If you order me to do it, sir, I will do it."

"Very good. You will start at dawn. Besides your own you shall have McLaws's and Anderson's divisions. The remainder of the army will leave Frederick an hour or two later. Colonel Chilton will at once issue the order of march." He drew a piece of paper toward him and with a pencil made a memorandum — SPECIAL ORDERS, No. 191.

The remainder of the ninth of September passed. The tenth of September passed, and the eleventh, mild, balmy and extremely still. The twelfth found the landscape for miles around Frederick still dozing. At noon, however, upon this day things changed. McClellan's strong cavalry advance came into touch with Jeb Stuart a league or two to the east. There ensued a skirmish approaching in dignity to an engagement. Finally the grey drew off, though not, to the Federal surprise, in the direction of Frederick. Instead they galloped north.

The blue advance trotted on, sabre to hand, ready for the dash into Frederick. Pierced at last was the grey, movable screen! Now with the infantry close behind, with the magnificent artillery rumbling up, with McClellan grim from the Seven Days — now for the impact which should wipe out the memory of the defeat of a fortnight ago, of the second Bull Run, an impact that should grind rebellion small! They came to Frederick and found a quiet shell. There was no one there to sabre.

Information abounded. McClellan, riding in with his staff toward evening, found himself in a sandstorm of news, through which nothing could be distinctly observed. Prominent citizens were brought before him. "Yes, general; they undoubtedly went north. Yes, sir, the morning of the tenth. Two columns, but starting one just after the other and on the same road. Yes, sir, some of our younger men did follow on horseback after an hour or two. They could just see the columns still moving north. Then they ran against Stuart's cordon and they had to turn back. Frederick's been just like a desert island — nobody coming and nobody getting away. For all he's as frisky as a puppy, Jeb Stuart's a mighty good watch dog!"

McClellan laughed. "'Beauty' Stuart! — I wish I had him here." He grew grave again. "I am obliged to you, sir. Who's this, Ames?"

"It is a priest, sir, that's much looked up to. He says he has a collection of maps — Father Tierney, will you speak to the general?"

"Faith, and that I will, my son!" said Father Tierney. "Good avenin', general, and the best of fortunes!"

"Good evening, Father. What has your collection to do with it?"

"Faith," said Father Tierney, "and that's for you to judge, general. It was the avenin' of the eighth, and I was sittin' in my

parlour after Judy O'Flaherty's funeral, and having just parted
with Father Lavalle at the Noviciate. And there came a rap, and
an aide of Stonewall Jackson's — But whisht! maybe I am taking
up your time, general, with things you already know?"

"Go on, go on! 'An aide of Stonewall Jackson's —'"

"'Holy powers!' thinks I, 'no rest even afther a funeral!' but
'Come in, come in, my son!' I said, and in he comes. 'My name is
Jarrow, Father,' says he, 'and General Jackson has heard that you
have a foine collection of maps.'

"'And that's thrue enough,' says I, 'and what then, my son?'
Whereupon he lays down his sword and cap and says, 'May I look
at thim?'"

Father Tierney coughed. "There's a number of gentlemen waiting in the entrry. Maybe, general, you'd be afther learning of the
movement of the ribils with more accuracy from thim. And I could
finish about the maps another time. You are n't under any obligation to be listenin' to me."

"Shut the door, Ames," said the general. "Now Father. —
'May I look at them,' he said."

"'Why, av course,' said I, 'far be it from Benedict Tierney to
put a lock on knowledge!' and I got thim down. 'There's one that
was made for Leonard Calvert in 1643' — says I, 'and there's another showing St. Mary's about the time of the Indian massacre, and
there's a very rare one of the Chesapeake —'

"'Extremely interestin',' he says, 'but for General Jackson's purposes 1862 will answer. You have recent maps also?'

"'Yes, I have,' I said, and I got thim down, rather disappointed,
having thought him interested in Colonial Maryland and maybe in
the location of missions. 'What do you wish?' said I, still polite,
though I had lost interest. 'A map of Pennsylvania,' said he —"

"A map of Pennsylvania! — Ames, get your notebook there."

"And I unrolled it and he looked at it hard. 'Good road to
Waynesboro?' he said, and says I, 'Fair, my son, fair!' And says
he, 'I may take this map to General Jackson?' 'Yes,' said I, 'but I
hope you'll soon be so good as to return it.' 'I will,' said he. 'Bedad,'
said I, 'you ribils are right good at returning things! I'll say that
for you!' said I — and he rolled up the map and put it under his
arm."

The general drew a long breath. "Pennsylvania invaded by way of Waynesboro. I am much obliged, Father —"

"Wait, wait, my son, I'm not done, yet! And thin, says he, 'General Jackson wants a map of the country due east from here, one,' says he, 'that shows the roads to Baltimore.'"

"Baltimore! —"

"'Have you got that one?' says he. 'Yis,' says I, and unrolled it, and he looked at it carefully and long. 'I see,' says he, 'that by going north from Frederick to Double Pipe Creek you would strike there the turnpike running east. Thank you, Father! May I take this one, too?' And he rolled it up and put it under his arm —"

"Baltimore," said McClellan, "Baltimore —"

"'And now, Father,' says he, 'have you one of the region between here and Washington?' . . . Don't be afther apologizing, general! There are times when I want a strong word meself. So I got that map, too, and he looked at it steadily. 'I understand,' says he, 'that going west by north you would strike a road that leads you south again?' — 'And that's thrue,' said I. And he looked at the map long and steadily again, and he asked what was the precise distance from Point of Rocks to Washington —"

"Point of Rocks! Good Lord! Ames, get ready to take these telegrams —"

"And thin he said, 'May I have this, too, Father?' and he rolled it up, and said General Jackson would certainly be obliged and would return thim in good order. (Which he did.) And thin he took up his cap and sword and said good avenin' and went. That's all that I know of the matter, general, saving and excepting that the ribil columns certainly *started* next morning with their faces toward the great State of Pennsylvania. Don't mention it, general! — though if you are interested in good works, and I'm not doubting the same, there's an orphan asylum here —"

Having arrived at a crossroads without a signpost McClellan characteristically hesitated. The activity of the next twelve hours was principally electrical and travelled by wire from Frederick to Washington and Washington to Frederick. The cavalry, indeed was pushed forward toward Boonsboro, but for the remainder of the army, as it came up, corps by corps, the night passed in inaction, and morning dawned on inaction. March north toward Pennsyl-

vania, and leave Washington to be bombarded! — turn south and
east toward Washington and hear a cry of protest and anger from
an invaded state! — turn due east to Baltimore and be awakened by
the enemy's cannon thundering against the other sides of the figure!
— leave Baltimore out of the calculation and lose, perhaps, the
whole of Maryland! McClellan was disturbed enough. And then, in
the great drama of real life there occurred an incident.

An aide appeared in the doorway of the room in which were
gathered McClellan and several of his generals. The discussion had
been a heated one; all the men looked haggard, disturbed. "What is
it?" asked McClellan sharply.

The aide held something in his hand. "This has just been found,
sir. It seems to have been dropped at a street corner. Leaves and
rubbish had been blown over it. The soldier who found it brought
it here. He thought it important — and I think it is, sir."

He crossed the floor and gave it to the general. "Three cigars
wrapped in a piece of paper! Why, what — A piece of paper
wrapped around three cigars. Open the shutters more widely,
Ames!"

HEADQUARTERS ARMY OF NORTHERN VIRGINIA,
September 9, 1862.

SPECIAL ORDERS, NO. 191

The army will resume its march to-morrow, taking the Hagerstown road. General Jackson's command will form the advance, and
after passing Middletown with such portion as he may select, take
the route toward Sharpsburg, cross the Potomac at the most convenient point, and by Friday morning take possession of the Baltimore and Ohio Railroad, capture such of the enemy as may be at
Martinsburg, and intercept such as may attempt to escape from
Harper's Ferry.

General Longstreet's command will pursue the main road as far
as Boonsborough, where it will halt with reserve, supply, and baggage trains of the army.

General McLaws, with his own division and that of General R. H.
Anderson, will follow General Longstreet. On reaching Middletown he will take the route to Harper's Ferry, and by Friday morn-

ing possess himself of the Maryland Heights and endeavour to capture the enemy at Harper's Ferry and vicinity.

General Walker with his division, after accomplishing the object in which he is now engaged, will cross the Potomac at Cheek's Ford, ascend its right bank to Lovettesville, take possession of Loudoun Heights, if practicable, by Friday morning, Key's Ford on his left, and the road between the end of the mountain and the Potomac on his right. He will as far as possible coöperate with generals McLaws and Jackson and intercept the retreat of the enemy.

General D. H. Hill's division will form the rear-guard of the Army, pursuing the road taken by the main body. The reserve artillery, ordnance and supply trains, etc., will precede General Hill.

General Stuart will detach a squadron of cavalry to accompany the commands of generals Longstreet, Jackson, and McLaws, and, with the main body of the cavalry, will cover the route of the army, bringing up all stragglers that may have been left behind.

The commands of Generals Jackson, McLaws, and Walker, after accomplishing the objects for which they have been detached, will join the main body of the army at Boonsboro or Hagerstown.

By command of General R. E. Lee,

R. H. CHILTON,
Assistant Adjutant-General.

In the room at Frederick there was a silence that might have been felt. At last McClellan rose, and stepping softly to the window, leaned his hands upon the sill, and looked out at the bright blue sky. He turned presently. "Gentlemen, the longer I live, the more firmly I believe that old saying, 'Truth is stranger than fiction!' — By the Hagerstown Road — General Hooker, General Reno —"

On the morning of the tenth Stonewall Jackson, leaving Frederick, marched west by the Boonsboro Road. Ahead, Stuart's squadrons stopped all traffic. The peaceful Maryland villages were entered without warning and quitted before the inhabitants recovered from their surprise. Cavalry in the rear swept together all stragglers. The detachment, twenty-five thousand men, almost half of Lee's army, drove, a swift, clean-cut body, between the autumn fields and woods that were beginning to turn. In the fields were farmers ploughing, in the orchards gathering apples. They stopped and stared. "Well, ain't that a sight? — And half of them barefoot! — and their clothes fit for nothing but scarecrows. Well, they ain't robbers. No — and their guns are mighty bright!"

South Mountain was crossed at Turner's Gap. It was near sunset when the bugles rang halt. Brigade by brigade Stonewall Jackson's command left the road, stacked arms, broke ranks in fair, rolling autumn fields and woods. A mile or two ahead was the village of Boonsboro. Jackson sent forward to make enquiries Major Kyd Douglas of his staff. That officer took a cavalryman with him and trotted off.

The little place looked like a Sweet Auburn of the vale, so tranquilly innocent did it lie beneath the rosy west. The two officers commented upon it, and the next moment ran into a Federal cavalry company sent to Sweet Auburn from Hancock for forage or recruits or some such matter. The blue troopers set up a huzzah, and charged. The two in grey turned and dug spur, — past ran the fields, past ran the woods! The thundering pursuit fired its revolvers; the grey turned in saddle and emptied theirs, then bent head to horse's neck and plied the spur. Before them the road mounted. "Pass the hill and we are safe! — Pass the hill and we are safe!" thought the grey, and the spur drew blood. Behind came the blue — a dozen troopers. "Stop there, you damned rebels, stop there! If you don't, when we catch you we'll cut you to pieces!" Almost at the hilltop one of the grey uttered a cry. "Good God! the general!"

Stonewall Jackson was coming toward them. He was walking apparently in deep thought, and leading Little Sorrel. He was quite alone. The two officers shouted. They saw him look up, take in the situation, and put his hand on the saddle bow. Then, to give him time, the two turned. "Yaaiih! Yaaaaiiahh!" they yelled, and charged the enemy.

The blue, taken by surprise, misinterpreted the first shout and the ensuing action. There must, of course, be coming over the hill a grey force detached on some reconnoissance or other from the rebel horde known to be reposing at Frederick. Presumably it would be cavalry — and coming at a gallop! To stop to cut down these two yelling grey devils might be to invite destruction. The blue troopers first emptied their revolvers, then wheeled horse, and retired to Sweet Auburn, out of which a little later the grey cavalry did indeed drive them.

In the last of the rosy light the two officers, now again at the hilltop, saw the camp outspread below it and coming at a double quick the regiment which Jackson had sent to the rescue. One checked his horse. "What's that?" asked the other.

"The general's gloves. He dropped them when he mounted."

He stooped from his horse and gathered them up. Later, back in camp, he went to headquarters. Jackson was talking ammunition with his chief of ordnance, an aide of A. P. Hill's standing near, waiting his turn. "Well, Major Douglas?"

"Your gloves, general. You dropped them on the hilltop."

"Good! put them there, major, if you please. — Colonel Crutchfield, the ordnance train will cross first. As the batteries come up from the river see that every caisson is filled. That is all. Now, Captain Scarborough —"

"General Hill very earnestly asks, sir, that he may be permitted to speak to you."

"Where is General Hill? Is he here?"

"Yes, sir, he is outside the tent."

"Tell him to come in. You have a very good fast horse, Major Douglas. There is nothing more, I think, to-night. Good-night."

A. P. Hill entered alone, without his sword. "Good-evening, General Hill," said Jackson.

Hill stood very straight, his red beard just gleaming a little in the dusky tent. "I am come to prefer a request, sir."

"Yes. What is it?"

"A week ago, upon the crossing of the Potomac, you placed me under arrest for what you conceived — for disobedience to orders. Since then General Branch has commanded the Light Division."

"Yes."

"I feel certain, sir, that battle is imminent. General Branch is a good and brave soldier, but — but — I am come to beg, sir, that I may be released from arrest till the battle is over."

Stonewall Jackson, sitting stiffly, looked at the other standing, tense, energetic, before him. Something stole into his face that without being a smile was like a smile. It gave a strange effect of mildness, tenderness. It was gone almost as soon as it had come, but it had been there. "I can understand your feeling, sir," he said. "A battle *is* imminent. Until it is over you are restored to your command."

The detachment of the Army of Northern Virginia going against Harper's Ferry crossed the Chesapeake and Ohio Canal at Williamsport and forded the Potomac a few hundred yards below the ferry. A. P. Hill, McLaws, Walker, Jackson's own, the long column overpassed the silver reaches, from the willows and sycamores of the Maryland shore to the tall and dreamy woods against the Virginia sky. "We know this place," said the old Army of the Valley. "Dam No. 5's just above there!" Regiment by regiment, as it dipped into the water, the column broke into song. "Carry me back to Old Virginny!" sang the soldiers.

At Martinsburg were thirty-five hundred blue troops. Stonewall Jackson sent A. P. Hill down by the turnpike; he himself made a détour and came upon the town from the west. The thirty-five hundred blue troops could retire southward, a thing hardly to their liking, or they could hasten eastward and throw themselves into Harper's Ferry. As was anticipated, they chose the latter course.

Stonewall Jackson entered Martinsburg amid acclaim. Here he rested his troops a few hours, then in the afternoon swung eastward and bivouacked upon the Opequon. "At early dawn," he marched again. Ahead rode his cavalry, and they kept the roads on two sides of Harper's Ferry. A dispatch came from General Lafayette McLaws. *General Jackson: — After some fighting I have got the Maryland Heights. Loudoun Heights in possession of General Walker. Enemy cut off north and east.*

"Good! good!" said Jackson. "North, east, south, and west."

On the Maryland side of the Potomac, some miles to the north of Harper's Ferry, Lee likewise received a report — brought in haste by a courier of Stuart's. *General: — The enemy seems to have waked up. McClellan reported moving toward South Mountain with some rapidity. I am holding Crampton and Turner's Gaps. What are my orders?*

Lee looked eastward toward South Mountain and southward to Harper's Ferry. "General McClellan can only be guessing. We must gain time for General Jackson at Harper's Ferry." He sent word to Stuart. "D. H. Hill's division returning to South Moun-gain. General Longstreet ordered back from Hagerstown. We must gain time for General Jackson. Hold the gaps."

D. H. Hill and Stuart held them. High above the valleys ran the roads — and all the slopes were boulder-strewn, crested moreover by broken stone walls. Hooker and Reno with the First and Ninth corps attacked Turner's Gap, Franklin's corps attacked Crampton's Gap. High above the country side, bloody and determined, eight thousand against thirty thousand, raged the battle.

Stonewall Jackson, closely investing Harper's Ferry, posting his batteries on both sides of the river, on the Maryland Heights and Loudoun Heights, heard the firing to the northward. He knit his brows. He knew that McClellan had occupied Frederick, but he knew nothing of the copy of an order found wrapped around three cigars. "What do you think of it, general?" ventured one of his brigadiers.

"I think, sir, it may be a cavalry engagement. Pleasanton came into touch with General Stuart and the Horse Artillery."

"It could not be McClellan in force?"

"I think not, sir. Not unless to his other high abilities were added energy and a knowledge of our plans. — Captain Page, this order to General McLaws: *General: — You will attack so as to sweep with your artillery the ground occupied by the enemy, take his batteries in reverse, and otherwise operate against him as circumstances may justify.* Lieutenant Byrd, this to General Walker: *General: — You will take in reverse the battery on the turnpike and sweep with your artillery the ground occupied by the enemy, and silence the batteries on the island of the Shenandoah.* Lieutenant Daingerfield, this to General A. P. Hill: *General: — You will move along the left bank of the Shenandoah, and thus turn the enemy's flank and enter Harper's Ferry.*"

This was Sunday. From every hilltop blazed the grey batteries, and down upon the fourteen thousand blue soldiers cooped in Harper's Ferry they sent an iron death. All afternoon they thundered, and the dusk knew no cessation. Harper's Ferry was flame-ringed, there were flames among the stars. The air rocked and rang, the river shivered and hurried by. Deep night came and a half silence. There was a feeling as if the earth were panting for breath. All the air tasted powder.

A. P. Hill, struggling over ground supposed impassable, was in line of battle behind Bolivar Heights. Lawton and Jones were yet further advanced. All the grey guns were ready — at early dawn they opened. Iron death, iron death! — they rained it down on Harper's Ferry and the fourteen thousand in garrison there. They silenced the blue guns. Then the bugles blew loudly, and Hill assaulted. There were lines of breastworks and before them an abattis. The Light Division tore through the latter, struck against the first. From the height behind thundered the grey artillery.

For a day and a night the blue defence had been stubborn. It was over. Out from the eddying smoke, high from the hilltop within the town, there was shaken a white flag. A. P. Hill received the place's surrender, and Stonewall Jackson rode to Bolivar Heights and then into the town. Twelve thousand prisoners, thirteen thousand stands of arms, seventy-three guns, a great prize of stores, horses, and wagons came into his hand with Harper's Ferry.

On the Bolivar turnpike the Federal General White and his staff met the conqueror. The first, general and staff, were handsomely mounted, finely equipped, sparklingly clean and whole. The last was all leaf brown — dust and rain and wear and tear, scarfed and stained huge boots, and shabby forage cap. The surrender was unconditional. Formalities over, there followed some talk, a hint on the side of the grey of generous terms, some expression on the side of the blue of admiration for great fighters, some regret from both for the mortal wound of Miles, the officer in command. Stonewall Jackson rode into the town with the Federal general. The streets were lined with blue soldiers crowding, staring. "That's him, boys! That's Jackson! That's him! *Well!*"

Later A. P. Hill came to the lower room in a stone house where the general commanding sat writing a dispatch to Lee. Jackson finished the thing in hand, then looked up. "General Hill, the Light Division did well. I move almost at once, but I shall leave you here in command until the prisoners and public property are disposed of. You will use expedition."

"I am not, then, sir, to relinquish the command to General Branch?"

"You are not, sir. Battle will follow battle, and you will lead the Light Division. Be more careful hereafter of my orders."

"I will try, sir."

"Good! good! — What is it, colonel?"

"A courier, sir, from General Lee."

The courier entered, saluted, and gave the dispatch. Jackson read it, then read it aloud, figure, mien, and voice as quiet as if he were repeating some every-day communication.

ON THE MARCH, *September* 14th.

GENERAL, — I regret to say that McClellan has, in some unaccountable fashion, discovered the division of the army as well as its objectives. We have had hard fighting to-day on South Mountain, D. H. Hill and Longstreet both suffering heavily. The troops fought with great determination and held the passes until dusk. We are now falling back on Sharpsburg. Use all possible speed in joining me there.

LEE.

Stonewall Jackson rose. "General Hill, arrange your matters as rapidly as possible. Sharpsburg on the Antietam. Seventeen miles."

CHAPTER XLIII

SHARPSBURG

"SHARPSBURG!" said long afterwards Stephen D. Lee. "Sharpsburg was Artillery Hell!"

"Sharpsburg," said the infantry of the Army of Northern Virginia. "Sharpsburg! That was the field where an infantryman knew that he stood on the most dangerous spot on the earth!"

Through the passes of the South Mountain, over Red Hill, out upon the broken ground east of the Antietam poured the blue torrent — McClellan and his eighty-seven thousand. Lee met it with a narrow grey sea — not thirty thousand men, for A. P. Hill was yet upon the road from Harper's Ferry. In Berserker madness, torrent and uproar, clashed the two colours.

There was a small white Dunkard church with a background of dark woods. It was north of Sharpsburg, near the Hagerstown turnpike, and it marked the Confederate left. Stonewall Jackson held the left. Before him was Fighting Joe Hooker with Meade and Doubleday and Ricketts.

From a knoll behind Sharpsburg the commander-in-chief looked from Longstreet on the right to D. H. Hill, and from Hill to Jackson. He looked to the Harper's Ferry Road, but he did not see what he wished to see — A. P. Hill's red battle shirt. "Artillery Hell" had begun. There was enormous thunder, enormous drifting murk. All the country side, all the little Maryland villages and farmhouses blenched beneath that sound. Lee put down his field glass. He stood, calm and grand, the smoke and uproar at his feet. The Rockbridge Guns came by, going to some indicated quarter of the field. In thunder they passed below the knoll, the iron war-beasts, the gunners with them, black with powder and grime! All saluted; but one, a very young, very ragged, very begrimed private at the guns, lingered a moment after his fellows, stood very straight at the salute and with an upward look, then with quickened step caught up with his gun and disappeared into the smoke ahead. Lee answered a glance of his chief of staff. "Yes. It was my youngest son. It was Rob."

The Dunkard church! In this war it was strange how many and how ghastly battles surged about small country churches! The Prince of Peace, if he indwelled here, must have bowed his head and mourned. Sunrise struck upon its white walls; then came a shell and pierced them. The church became the core of the turmoil, the white, still reef against which beat the wild seas in storm.

Fighting Joe Hooker came out of the North Wood. His battle flags were bright and he had drums and brazen horns. Loud and in time, regular as a beat in music, came the Huzzah! Huzzah! of his fourteen thousand men. He crossed the turnpike, he came down on the Dunkard church. "Yaii! Yaaaii! Yaaaaaaaaiihhh!" yelled the grey sea, — no time at all, only fierce determination. Sometimes a grey drum beat, or bugle called, but there was no other music, save the thunder of the guns and the long rattle, never ceasing, of the musketry. There were battle flags, squares of crimson with a starry Andrew's cross. They went forward, they shrank back. Standard-bearers were killed. Gaunt, powder-grimed hands caught at the staves, lifted them; the battle-flags went forward again.

Doubleday struck and Ricketts. They charged against Stonewall Jackson and the narrow grey sea. All the ground was broken; alignment was lost; blue waves and grey went this way and that in a broken, tumultuous fray. But the blue waves were the heavier; in mass alone they outdid the grey. They pushed the grey sea back, back, back toward the dark wood about the Dunkard church! Then Stonewall Jackson came along the front, riding in a pelting, leaden rain. "Steady, men. Steady! God is over us!" His men received him with a cry of greeting and enthusiasm that was like a shriek, it was so wild and high. His power upon them had grown and grown. He was Stonewall Jackson! He was Stonewall Jackson! First, they would die for those battle-flags and the cause they represented; second, they would die for one another, comrades, brethren! third, they would die for Stonewall Jackson! They lifted their voices for him now, gaunt and ragged troops with burning eyes. *Stonewall Jackson! Stonewall Jackson! Virginia! Virginia! Virginia! the South! the South!* He turned his horse, standing in the whistling, leaden rain. "Forward, and drive them!"

Lawton and D. H. Hill leaped against Meade. He was a staunch fighter, but he gave back. The wood about the Dunkard church appeared to writhe like Dante's wood, it was so full of groaning, of maimed men beside the tree trunks. The dead lay where they fell, and the living stepped upon them. Meade gave back, back — and then Mansfield came in thunder to reinforce the blue.

The grey fought as even in this war they had hardly fought before. They were so gaunt, they were so ragged, they were so tired! But something ethnic was coming more and more rapidly to the front. They were near again to savage nature. The Maryland woods might have been thicker, darker, the small church might have been some boulder altar beside some early Old World river. They were a tribe again, and they were fighting another and much larger tribe whom they had reason, reason, reason to hate! Their existence was at stake and the existence of all that their hearts held dear. They fought with fury. About each were his tribesmen — all were brothers! Brother fought for brother, brother saw brother fall, brother sprang to avenge brother. Their lips were blackened from tearing cartridges; their eyes, large in their thin, bronzed faces, burned against the enemy; their fingers were quick, quick at the musket lock; the spirit was the spirit behind hurled stones of old, swung clubs, thrown javelins! They had a loved leader, a great strong head man who ruled them well and led them on to victory. They fought for him too, for his scant and curt praise, for his " Good, Good! " They fought for their own lives, each man for his own life, for their tribe, their possessions, for women at home and children, for their brethren, their leader, their cause. Something else, too, of the past was there in force — hatred of him who opposed. They fought for hate at Sharpsburg, as they fought for love. The great star drew, the iron thong fell. Led and driven, the tribe fought gigantically.

The battle became furious. Within the din of artillery and musketry human voices, loud, imperative, giving orders, shouting, wailing, died like a low murmur in the blast. Out of the wildly drifting smoke, now dark, now flame-lit, forms emerged, singly or in great bodies, then the smoke drew together, hiding the struggle. There was blackness and grime as from the ash of a volcano. The blood pounded behind the temples, the eyeballs started, the tongue was thick in the mouth, battle smell and battle taste, a red light, and time in crashes like an earthquake-toppling city! The inequalities of the ground became exaggerated. Mere hillocks changed into rocky islands. Seize them, fortify them, take them before the blue can! The tall maize grew gigantically taller. Break through these miles of cane as often before we have broken through them, the foemen crashing before us down to their boats! The narrow tongues of woods widened, widened. Take these deep forests, use them for shelter, from them send forth these new arrows of death — fight, fight! in the rolling murk, the red light and crying!

Before the Dunkard church Starke, commanding Jackson's old division, was killed, Jones was wounded, Lawton wounded. Many field officers were down, many, many of lesser rank. Of the blue, Mansfield was killed, Hooker was wounded, and Hartsuff and Crawford. The grey had pressed the blue back, back! Now in turn the blue drove the grey. The walls of the white church were splashed with blood, pocked with bullets. Dead men lay at the door; within were those of the wounded who could get there. But the shells came too, the shells pierced the roof and entered. War came in, ebon, bloodstained, and grinning. The Prince of Peace was crowded out.

The artillery was deafening. In the midst of a tremendous burst of sound D. H. Hill flung in the remainder of his division. Sumner came through the smoke. The grey and blue closed in a death grapple. From toward the centre, beneath the howling storm rose a singing —

> The race is not to them that's got
> The longest legs to run.

"Hood's Texans! Hood's Texans!" cried the Stonewall and all the other brigades on the imperilled left. "Come on, Hood's Texans! Come on! Yaaaii! Yaaaaaiih!"

> Nor the battle to those people,
> That shoots the biggest gun.

The Texans came to the Dunkard church. Stonewall Jackson launched a thunderbolt, grey as steel, all his men moving up as one, against the opposing, roaring sea. The sea gave back. Then Sumner called in Sedgwick's fresh troops.

Allan Gold, fighting with the 65th, took the colours from the last

of the colour guard. He was tall and strong and he swung them high.
The glare from an exploding shell showed him and the battle flag.
Gone was the quiet schoolteacher, gone even the scout and woodsman. He stood a great Viking, with yellow hair, and the battle rage
had come to him. He began to chant, unconscious as a harp through
which strikes a strong wind. "Come on!" he chanted. "Come on!

"Sixty-fifth, come on!
   Come on, the Stonewall!
Remember Manassas,
   The first and the second Manassas!
Remember McDowell,
   Remember Front Royal,
Remember the battle of Winchester,
   Remember Cross Keys,
   Remember Port Republic,
The battle of Kernstown, and all our battles and skirmishes,
Our marches and forced marches, bivouacs, and camp-fires,
Brother's hand in brother's hand, and the battle to-morrow!
Remember the Seven Days, Seven Days, Seven Days!
Remember the Seven Days! Remember Cedar Run.
The Groveton Wood, and the Railroad cut at Manassas
Where you threw stones when your cartridges were gone, where you struck with
   the bayonet,
And the General spoke to you then, 'Steady, men, steady!'
Remember Chantilly, remember Loudoun and Maryland Heights.
Harper's Ferry was yesterday. Remember and strike them again!
Come on, 65th! Come on, the Stonewall!"

Back through the cornfield before the Dunkard church fell the
blue. Dead and dying choked the cornfield as the dead and dying
had choked the cane brake. Blade and stalks were beaten down, the
shells tore up the earth. The blue reformed and came again, a resistless mass. Heavier and heavier, Fighting Joe Hooker, with Meade
and Doubleday and Ricketts and Sumner, struck against Stonewall Jackson! Back came the grey to the little Dunkard church. All
around it, wood and open filled with clangour. The blue pressed in
— the grey were giving way, were giving way! An out-worn company raised a cry, "They're flanking us!" Something like a shiver
passed over the thinning lines, then, grey and haggard, they tore
another cartridge. Stonewall Jackson's voice came from behind a
reef of smoke. "Stand fast, men! Stand fast. There are troops on
the road from Harper's Ferry. It is General McLaws. Stand fast!"

It was McLaws, with his black bullet head, his air of a Roman Consul! In he thundered with his twenty-five hundred men, tawny with the dust of the seventeen miles from Harper's Ferry. He struck Sedgwick full. For five minutes there was brazen clangour and shouting and an agony of effort, then the blue streamed back, past the Dunkard wood and church, back into the dreadful cornfield.

Maury Stafford, sent with a statement to the commander-in-chief, crossed in one prolonged risk of life from the wild left to the only less stormed-against centre. Here a strong blue current, French and Richardson, strove against a staunch grey ledge — a part of D. H. Hill's line, with Anderson to support. Here was a sunken road, that, later, was given a descriptive name. Here was the Bloody Lane. Lee was found standing upon a knoll, calm and grand. "I yet look for A. P. Hill," he said. "He has a talent for appearing at identically the right moment."

Stafford gave his statement. All over the field the staff had suffered heavily. Some were dead, many were wounded. Those who were left did treble duty. Lee sent this officer on to Longstreet, holding the long ridge on the right.

Stafford rode through the withering storm across that withered field. There seemed no light from the sky; the light was the glare from the guns. He marked, through a rift in the smoke, a battery where it stood upon a height, above felled trees. He thought it was Pelham's — the Horse Artillery. It stood for a moment, outlined against the orange-bosomed cloud, then, like an army of wraiths, the smoke came between and hid it. His horse frightened at a dead man in his path. The start and plunging were unusual, and the rider looked to see the reason. The soldier had drawn letters from his breast and had died with them in his hands. The unfolded, fluttering sheets stirred as though they had life. Stafford, riding on, found the right and found Longstreet looking sombrely, like an old eagle from his eyrie. "I told General Lee," he said "that we ought never to have divided. I don't see A. P. Hill. You tell General Lee that I've only got D. R. Jones and the knowledge that we fight like hell, and that Burnside is before me with fourteen thousand men."

Stafford retraced his way. The ground beneath was burned and scarred, the battle cloud rolled dark, the minies sang beside his ear.

Now he was in a barren place, tasting of powder, smelling of smoke, now lit, now darkened, but vacant of human life, and now he was in a press of men, grey forms advancing and retreating, or standing firing, and now he was where fighting had been and there was left a wrack of the dead and dying. He reached the centre and gave his message, then turned toward the left again. A few yards and his horse was killed under him. He disengaged himself and presently caught at the bridle and stayed another. There were many riderless horses on the field of Sharpsburg, but he had hardly mounted before this one, too, was killed. He went on afoot. He entered a sunken road, dropped between rough banks overhung by a few straggling trees. The road was filled with men lying down, all in shadow beneath the rolling battle smoke. Stafford thought it a regiment waiting for orders; then he saw that they were all dead men. He must go back to the Dunkard wood, and this seemed his shortest way. He entered the lane and went up it as quickly as he might for the forms that lay thick in the discoloured light. It looked as though the earth were bleeding, and all the people were fantastic about him. Some lay as straight as on a sculptured tomb, and some were hooped, and some lay like a cross, and some were headless. As he stepped with what care he might, a fierce yelling broke out on the side that was the grey side. There was a charge coming — already he saw the red squares tossing! He moved to the further side of the sunken road and braced himself against the bank, putting his arm about a twisted, protruding cedar. D. H. Hill's North Carolinians hung a moment, tall, gaunt, yelling, then swooped down into the sunken lane, passed over the dead, mounted the other ragged bank and went on. Stafford waited to hear the shock. It came; full against a deep blue wave. Richardson had been killed and Hancock commanded here. The blue wave was strong. The sound of the mêlée was frightful; then out of it burst a loud huzzahing. Stafford straightened himself. The grey were coming back, and after them the blue. Almost before he could unclasp his arm from the cedar, the first spray of gaunt, exhausted, bleeding men came over and down into the sunken lane. All the grey wave followed. At the moment there outburst a renewed and tremendous artillery battle. The smoke drifting across the Bloody Lane was like the fall of night, a night of cloud and storm. Orange flashes momentarily lit the scene, and the sullen thunders rolled. The grey, gaunt and haggard, but their colours with them, overpassed the dead and wounded, now choking the sunken road. Behind them were heard the blue, advancing and huzzahing. The grey wave remounted the bank down which it plunged fifteen minutes before. At the top it stayed a moment, thin and grey, spectral in the smoke pall, the battle flags like hovering, crimson birds. A line of flame leaped, one long crackle of musketry, then it resumed its retreat, falling back on the west wood. The blue, checked a moment by that last volley, now poured down into the sunken road, overpassed the thick ranks of the dead and wounded, mounted, and swept on in a counter charge.

Maury Stafford had left the cedar and started across with the last broken line of the grey. Going down the crumbling bank his spur caught in a gnarled and sprawling root. The check was absolute, and brought him violently to his knees. Before he could free himself the grey had reached the opposite crest, fired its volley, and gone on. He started to follow. He heard the blue coming, and it was expedient to get out of this trap. Before him, from the figures covering the earth like thrown jackstraws, an arm was suddenly lifted. The hand clutched at him, passing. He looked down. It was a boy of nineteen with a ghastly face. The voice came up: "Whoever you are, you 're alive and well, and I 'm dying. You 'll take it and put a stamp on it and mail it, won't you? I 'm dying. People ought to do things when the dying ask them to."

Stafford looked behind him, then down again. "Do what? Quick! They 're coming."

The hand would not relax its clasp, but its fellow fumbled at the grey jacket. "It 's my letter. They won't know if they don't get it. My side hurts, but it don't hurt like knowing they won't know . . . that I was sorry." The face worked. "It 's here but I can't — Please get it — "

"You must let me go," said Stafford, and tried to unclasp the hand. "Stay any longer and I will be killed or taken."

The hand closed desperately, both hands now. "For God's sake! I don't believe you 've got so hard a heart. Take it and stamp it and mail it. If they don't know they 'll never understand and I 'll die knowing they 'll never understand. For God's sake!"

Stafford knelt beside him, opened the grey jacket, and took out the letter. Blood was upon it, but the address was legible. "Die easy. I'll stamp and mail it. I will send a word with it, too, if you like."

A light came into the boy's face. "Tell them that I was like the prodigal son, but that I'm going home — I'm going home — "

The arms fell, the breast ceased to heave, the head drew backward. Death came and stamped the light upon the face. Before Stafford could get to his feet, the blue wave had plunged into the trough. He remembered using his pistol, and he remembered a dizziness of being borne backward. He remembered that a phrase had gone through his mind "the instability of all material things." Then came a blank. He did not assume that he had lost consciousness, but simply he could not remember. He had been wrecked in a turbulent, hostile ocean. It had made him and others captives, and now they were together at a place which he remembered was called the Roulette House. An hour might have passed, two hours; he really could not tell. There were a number of prisoners, most of them badly wounded. They lay in the back yard of the place, on the steps of out-houses, with blue soldiers for guards. A surgeon came through the yard, and helped a little the more agonizedly hurt. He glanced at Stafford's star and sash, came across and offered to bind up the cut across his forehead. "An awful field," he said. "This war is getting horrible. You're a Virginian, are n't you?"

"Yes."

"Used to know a lot of Virginia doctors. Liked them first rate! Now we are enemies, and it seems to me a pity. Guess it's as Shakespeare says, 'What fools these mortals be!' I know war's getting to seem to me an awful foolishness. That cornfield out there is sickening — Now! that bleeding's stopped — "

On the left, around and before the Dunkard church, the very fury of the storm brought about at last a sudden failing, a stillness and cessation that seemed like those of death. Sound enough there was undoubtedly, and in the centre the battle yet roared, but by comparison there seemed a dark and sultry calm. Far and near lay the fallen. It was now noon, and since dawn twelve thousand men had been killed or wounded on this left, attacked by Fighting Joe Hooker, held by Stonewall Jackson. Fifteen general officers were dead or disabled. Hardly a brigade, not many regiments, were officered as they had been when the sun rose. There was an exhaustion. Franklin had entered on the field, and one might have thought that the grey would yet be overpowered. But all the blue forces were broken, disorganized; there came an exhaustion, a lassitude. McClellan sent an order forbidding another attack. Cornfield and wood lay heavy, hot, and dark, and by comparison, still.

Stonewall Jackson sat Little Sorrel near the Dunkard church. They brought him reports of the misery of the wounded and their great numbers. His medical director, of whom he was fond, came to him. "General, it is very bad! The field hospital looks as though all the fields of the world had given tribute. I know that you do not like hospitals — but would you come and look, sir?"

The general shook his head. "What is the use of looking? There have to be wounded. Do the utmost that you can, doctor."

"I have thought, sir, that, seeing the day is not ended, and they are so overwhelmingly in force, and the Potomac is not three miles in our rear — I have thought that we might manage to get the less badly hurt across. If they attack again and the day should end in defeat —"

"What have you got there?" asked Jackson. "Apples?"

"Yes, sir. I passed beneath a tree and gathered half a dozen. Would you like —"

"Yes. I breakfasted very early." He took the rosy fruit and began to eat. His eyes, just glinting under the forage cap, surveyed the scene before him, — trampled wood where the shells had cut through bough and branch, trampled cornfields where it seemed that a whirlwind had passed, his resting, shattered commands, the dead and the dying, the dead horses, the disabled guns, the drifting sulphurous smoke, and, across the turnpike, in the fields and by the east wood, the masses of blue, overcanopied also by sulphurous smoke. He finished the apple, took out a handkerchief, and wiped fingers and lips. "Dr. McGuire, they have done their worst. And never use the word defeat."

He jerked his hand into the air. "Do your best for the wounded, doctor, do all that is humanly possible, but do it *here!* I am going now to the centre to see General Lee."

Behind the wood, in a grassy hollow moderately sheltered from the artillery fire, at the edge of the ghastly field hospital, a young surgeon, sleeves rolled up and blood from head to foot, met the medical director. "Doctor, the Virginia Legion came on with General McLaws. They've just brought their colonel in — Fauquier Cary, you know. I wish you would look at his arm."

The two looked. "There's but one thing, colonel."

"Amputation? Very well, very well. Get it over with." He straightened himself on the boards where the men had laid him. "Sedgwick, too! Sedgwick and I striking at each other like two savages decked with beads and scalps! Fratricidal strife if ever there was fratricidal strife! All right, doctor. I had a great-uncle lost his arm at Yorktown. Can't remember him, — my father and mother loved to talk of him — old Uncle Edward. All right — it's all right."

The two doctors were talking together. "Only a few ounces left. Better use it here?"

"Yes, yes! — One minute longer, colonel. We've got a little chloroform."

The bottle was brought. Cary eyed it. "Is that all you've got?"

"Yes. We took a fair quantity at Manassas, but God only knows the amount we could use! Now."

The man stretched on the boards motioned with the hand that had not been torn by the exploding shell. "No, no! I don't want it. Keep it for some one with a leg to cut off!" He smiled, a charming, twisted smile, shading into a grimace of pain. "No chloroform at Yorktown! I'll be as much of a man as was my great-uncle Edward! Yes, yes, I'm in earnest, doctor. Put it by for the next. All right; I'm ready."

On the knoll by Sharpsburg Lee and Jackson stood and looked toward the right. McClellan had apparently chosen to launch three battles in one day; in the early morning against the Confederate left, at midday against its centre, now against its right. A message came from Longstreet. "Burnside is in motion. I've got D. R. Jones and twenty-five hundred men."

It was evident that Burnside was in motion. With fourteen thousand men he came over the stone bridge across the Antietam. They were fresh troops; their flags were flying, their drums were beating, their bugles braying. The line moved with huzzahs toward the ridge held by Longstreet. From the left came tearing past the knoll the

Confederate batteries. Lee was massing them in the centre, training them against the eastern foot of the ridge. There had been a lull in the storm, now Pelham opened with loud thunders. Other guns followed. The Federal batteries began to blaze; there broke out a madness of sound. In the midst of it D. R. Jones with his twenty-five hundred men clashed with Burnside's leading brigades.

Stonewall Jackson pulled the forage cap lower, jerked his hand into the air. "Good! good! I will go, sir, and send in my freshest troops."

"Look," said Lee. "Look, general! On the Harper's Ferry road."

All upon the knoll turned and gazed. Air and light played with the battle smoke, drove it somewhat to one side and showed for a few seconds a long and sunlit road, the road from Harper's Ferry. One of the staff began a low uncontrollable laughter. "By God! I see his red battle shirt! By God! I see his red battle shirt!"

Lee with a glance checked the sound. He himself looked nobly lifted, grave and thankful. The battle smoke closed, obscuring the road, but the sound of marching men came along it, distinguishable even beneath the artillery fire. "Good, good!" said Jackson. "A. P. Hill is a good soldier."

Tawny with the dust of the seventeen miles, at a double quick and yelling, the crimson battle flags slanting forward, in swung the Light Division! D. R. Jones rallied. Decimated, outworn, but dangerous, the aiding regiments from the left did well. The grey guns worked with a certain swift and steadfast grimness. From all the ridges of the Antietam the blue cannon thundered, thundered. Blue and grey, the musketry rolled. Sound rose into terrific volume, the eddying smoke blotted out the day. Artillery Hell — Infantry Inferno — the field of Sharpsburg roared now upon the right.

The Horse Artillery occupied a low ridge like a headland jutting into a grassy field. Below, above, behind, the smoke rolled; in front the flame leaped from their guns, the shells sped. There was a great background of battle cloud, lit every ten seconds by the glare from an opposing battery. John Pelham stood directing. Six guns were in fierce and continuous action. The men serving them were picked artillery men. To and fro they moved, down they stooped, up they stood, stepped backward from the gun at fire, moved forward at recoil, fell again to the loading with the precision of the drill ground. They were half naked, they were black with powder, glistening with sweat, some were bleeding. In the light from the guns all came boldly into relief; in the intermediate deep murk they sank from sight, became of the clouds, cloudy, mere shapes in the semi-darkness.

Stonewall Jackson, returning to the Dunkard church and passing behind this headland, turned Little Sorrel's head and came upon the plateau. Pelham met him. "Yes, general, we're doing well. Yes, sir, it's holding out. Caissons were partly filled during the lull."

"Good, good!" said Jackson. He dismounted and walked forward to the guns. Pelham followed. "I don't think you should be out here, general. They've got our range very accurately —"

The other apparently did not notice the remark. He stood near one of the guns and turned his eyes upon the battle on the right. "Longstreet strikes a heavy blow. He and Hill will push them back. Colonel Pelham, train two guns upon that body of the enemy at the ford."

Pelham moved toward the further guns. The howitzer nearest Jackson was fired, reloaded, fired again. The men beside it stood back. It blazed, thundered, recoiled. A great, black, cylindrical shell came with a demoniac shriek. At the moment the platform was lit with the battle glare. Its fall was seen. It fell, smoking, immediately beside Stonewall Jackson. Such was the concussion of the air that for a moment he was stunned. Involuntarily his arm went up before his eyes; he made a backward step. Pelham, returning from the further guns and still some yards away, gave a shout of warning and horror; from all the men who had seen the thing there burst a similar cry. With the motion almost of the shell itself, a man of the crew of the howitzer reached the torn earth and the cylinder. His body half naked, blackened, brushed, in passing, the general. He put his hands beneath the heated, smoking bottle of death, lifted it, and rushed on to the edge of the escarpment fifty feet away. Here he swung it with force, threw it from him with burned hands. Halfway to the field below it exploded.

Pelham, very pale, protested with some sternness. "You can't stay here, general! My men can't work with you here. It does n't matter about us, but it does matter about you. Please go, sir."

"I am going, colonel. I have seen what I wished to see. Who is the man who took up the shell?"

Pelham turned to the howitzer. "Which of you was it?"

Half a dozen voices were raised in answer. "Deaderick, sir. But he burned his hands badly and he asked the lieutenant if he could go to the rear —"

"Good, good!" said Stonewall Jackson. "He did well. But there are many brave men in this army." He went back to Little Sorrel, where he stood cropping the dried grass, and stiffly mounted. As he turned from the platform and the guns, all lit again by the orange glare, there came from the right an accession of sound, then high, shrill, and triumphant the Confederate yell. A shout arose from the Horse Artillery. "They're breaking! they're breaking! Burnside, too, is breaking! Yaaaii! Yaaaaiiihh! Yaaaaaiiihhh!"

CHAPTER XLIV

BY THE OPEQUON

THE battle of Sharpsburg was a triumph neither for blue nor grey, for North nor South. With the sinking of the sun ceased the bloody, prolonged, and indecisive struggle. Blue and grey, one hundred and thirty thousand men fought that battle. When the pale moon came up she looked on twenty-one thousand dead and wounded.

The living ranks sank down and slept beside the dead. Lee on Traveller waited by the highroad until late night. Man by man his generals came to him and made their report — their ghastly report. "Very good, general. What is your opinion?" — "I think, sir, that we should cross the Potomac to-night." — "Very well, general. What is your opinion?" — "General Lee, we should cross the Potomac to-night." — "Yes, general, it has been our heaviest field. What is your advice?" — "General Lee, I am here to do what you tell me to do."

Horse and rider, Traveller and Robert Edward Lee, stood in the pale light above the Antietam. "Gentlemen, we will not cross the Potomac to-night. If General McClellan wants to fight in the morning I will give him battle again. — And now we are all very tired. Good-night. Good-night!"

The sun came up, dim behind the mist. The mist rose, the morning advanced. The September sunshine lay like vital warmth upon the height and vale, upon the Dunkard church and the wood about it, upon the cornfields, and Burnside's bridge and the Bloody Lane, and upon all the dead men in the cornfields, in the woods, upon the heights, beside the stream, in the lane. The sunshine lay upon the dead, as the prophet upon the Shunamite's child, but it could not reanimate. Grey and blue, the living armies gazed at each other across the Antietam. Both were exhausted, both shattered, the blue yet double in numbers. The grey waited for McClellan's attack. It did not come. The ranks, lying down, began to talk. "He ain't

going to attack! He's cautious." — "He's had enough." — "So've
I. O God!" — "Never saw such a fight. Wish those buzzards
would go away from that wood over there! They're so dismal." —
"No, McClellan ain't going to attack!" — "Then why don't we attack?" — "Go away, Johnny! We're mighty few and powerfully
tired." — "Well, *I* think so, too. We might just as well attack.
Great big counter stroke! Crumple up Meade and Doubleday and
Ricketts over there! Turn their right!" — "'T ain't impossible!
Marse Robert and Old Jack could manage it." — "No, they could
n't!" — "Yes, they could!" — "You're a fool! Look at that position, stronger 'n Thunder Run Mountain, and Hooker's got troops
he did n't have in yesterday! 'N those things like beehives in a
row are Parrotts 'n Whitworths' 'n Blakeley's. 'N then look at
us. Oh, yes! we've got *spirit*, but spirit's got to have a body to rush
those guns." — "Thar ain't anything Old Jack could n't do if he
tried!" — "Yes, there is!" "Thar ain't! How *dast* you say that?"
— "There is! He could n't be a fool if he tried — and he ain't
agoing to try!"

The artillerist, Stephen D. Lee, came to headquarters on the
knoll by Sharpsburg. "General Lee sent for me. Tell him, please, I
am here." Lee appeared. "Good-morning, Colonel Lee. You are
to go at once to General Jackson. Tell him that I sent you to report to him." The officer found Stonewall Jackson at the Dunkard church. "General, General Lee sent me to report to you."

"Good, good! Colonel, I wish you to take a ride with me. We
will go to the top of the hill yonder."

They went up to the top of the hill, past dead men and horses, and
much wreckage of caissons and gun wheels. "There are probably
sharpshooters in that wood across the stream," said Jackson. "Do
not expose yourself unnecessarily, colonel." Arrived at the level
atop they took post in a little copse, wildly torn and blackened, a
wood in Artillery Hell. "Take your glasses, colonel, and examine
the enemy's line of battle."

The other lifted the field-glass and with it swept the Antietam,
and the fields and ridges beyond it. He looked at the Federal left,
and he looked at the Federal centre, and he looked along the Federal
right, which was opposite, then he lowered the glasses. "General,
they have a very strong position, and they are in great force."

"Good! I wish you to take fifty pieces of artillery and crush that force."

Stephen D. Lee was a brave man. He said nothing now, but he stood a moment in silence, and then he took his field-glass and looked again. He looked now at the many and formidable Federal batteries clustered like dark fruit above the Antietam, and now at the masses of blue infantry, and now at the positions, under artillery and musketry fire, which the Confederate batteries must take. He put the glass down again. "Yes, general. Where shall I get the fifty guns?"

"How many have you?"

"I had thirty. Some were lost, a number disabled. I have twelve."

"Just so. Well, colonel, I could give you a few, and General Lee tells me he can furnish some."

The other fingered a button on his coat for a moment, then, "Yes, general. Shall I go for the guns?"

"No, not yet." Stonewall Jackson laid his large hands in their worn old brown gauntlets, one over the other, upon his saddle bow. He, too, looked at the Federal right and the guns on the heights like dark fruit. His eyes made just a glint of blue light below the forage cap. "Colonel Lee, can you crush the Federal right with fifty guns?"

The artillerist drew a quick breath, let the button alone, and raised his head higher. "I can try, general. I can do it if any one can."

"That is not what I asked you, sir. If I give you fifty guns can you crush the Federal right?"

The other hesitated. "General, I don't know what you want of me. Is it my technical opinion as an artillery officer? or do you want to know if I will make the attempt? If you give me the order of course I will make it!"

"Yes, colonel. But I want your positive opinion, yes or no. Can you crush the Federal right with fifty guns?"

The artillerist looked again, steadying arm and glass against a charred bough. "General, it cannot be done with fifty guns and the troops you have here."

Hilltop and withered wood hung a moment silent in the air, sunny but yet with a taste of all the powder that had been burned. Then said Jackson, "Good! Let us ride back, colonel."

They turned their horses, but Stephen Lee with some emotion began to put the case. "You forced me, general, to say what I did say. If you send the guns, I beg of you not to give them to another! I will fight them to the last extremity — " He looked to the other anxiously. To say to Stonewall Jackson that you must despair and die where he sent you in to conquer!

But Jackson had no grimness of aspect. He looked quietly thoughtful. It was even with a smile of sweetness that he cut short the other's pleading. "It's all right, colonel, it's all right! Every one knows that you are a brave officer and would fight the guns well." At the foot of the hill he checked Little Sorrel. "We'll part here, colonel. You go at once to General Lee. Tell him all that has happened since he sent you to me. Tell him that you examined the Federal position. Tell him that I forced you to give the technical opinion of an artillery officer, and tell him what that opinion is. That is all, colonel."

The September day wore on. Grey and blue armies rested inactive save that they worked at burying the dead. Then, in the afternoon, information came to grey headquarters. Humphrey's division, pouring through the gaps of South Mountain, would in a few hours be at McClellan's service. Couch's division was at hand — there were troops assembling on the Pennsylvania border. At dark Lee issued his orders. During the night of the eighteenth the Army of Northern Virginia left the banks of the Antietam, wound silently down to the Potomac, and crossed to the Virginia shore.

All night there fell a cold, fine, chilling rain. Through it the wagon trains crossed, the artillery with a sombre noise, the wounded who must be carried, the long column of infantry, the advance, the main, the rear. The corps of Stonewall Jackson was the last to ford the river. He sat on Little Sorrel, midway of the stream, and watched his troops go onward in the steady, chilling rain. Daybreak found him there, motionless as a figure in bronze, needing not to care for wind or sun or rain.

The Army of Northern Virginia encamped on the road to Martinsburg. Thirty guns on the heights above Boteler's Ford guarded its rear, and Jeb Stuart and his cavalry watched from the northern bank at Williamsport. McClellan pushed out from Sharpsburg a heavy reconnoissance, and on his side of the river planted guns. Fitz

John Porter, in command, crossed during the night a considerable body of troops. These advanced against Pendleton's guns, took four of them, and drove the others back on the Martinsburg road. Pendleton reported to General Lee; Lee sent an order to Stonewall Jackson. The courier found him upon the bank of the Potomac, gazing at the northern shore. "Good!" he said. "I have ordered up the Light Division." Seventy guns thundered from across the water. A. P. Hill in his red battle shirt advancing in that iron rain, took, front and flank, the Federal infantry. He drove them down from the bluff, he pushed them into the river; they showed black on the current. Those who got across, under the shelter of the guns, did not try again that passage. McClellan looked toward Virginia, but made no further effort, this September, to invade her. The Army of Northern Virginia waited another day above Boteler's Ford, then withdrew a few miles to the banks of the Opequon.

The Opequon, a clear and pleasing stream, meandered through the lower reaches of the great Valley, through a fertile, lovely country, as yet not greatly scored and blackened by war's torch and harrow. An easy ride to the westward and you arrived in Winchester, beloved of Lieutenant-General T. J. Jackson and the 2d Army Corps. As the autumn advanced, the banks of the Opequon, the yet thick forests that stretched toward the Potomac, the great maples, and oaks and gums and hickories that rose, singly or in clusters, from the rolling farm lands, put on a most gorgeous colouring. The air was mellow and sunny. From the camp-fires, far and near, there came always a faint pungent smell of wood smoke. Curls of blue vapour rose from every glade. The land seemed bathed in Indian summer.

Through it in the mellow sunlight, beneath the crimson of the gums, the lighter red of the maples, the yellow of the hickories, the 2d Army Corps found itself for weeks back on the drill ground. The old Army of the Valley crowed and clapped on the back the Light Division and D. H. Hill's troops. "Old times come again! Jest like we used to do at Winchester! Chirk up, you fellows! Your drill's improving every day. Old Jack 'll let up on you after a while. Lord! it used to be *seven* hours a day!"

Not only did the 2d Corps drill, it refitted. Mysteriously there came from Winchester a really fair amount of shoes and clothing.

Only the fewest were now actually barefoot. In every regiment there went on, too, a careful cobbling. If by any means a shoe could be made to do, it was put in that position. Uniforms were patched and cleaned, and every day was washing day. All the hillsides were spread with soldiers' shirts. The red leaves drifting down on them looked like blood-stains, but the leaves could be brushed away. The men, standing in the Opequon, whistled as they rubbed and wrung. Every day the recovered from hospitals, and the footsore stragglers, and the men detached or furloughed, came home to camp. There came in recruits, too — men who last year were too old, boys who last year were not old enough. "Look here, boys! Thar goes Father Time! — No, it's Rip Van Winkle!" — "No, it's Santa Claus! — Anyhow, he's going to fight!" "Look here, boys! here comes another cradle. Good Lord, he's just a toddler! He don't see a razor in his dreams yet! Quartermaster's out of nursing-bottles!" "Shet up! the way those children fight's a caution!"

October drifted on, smooth as the Opequon. Red and yellow leaves drifted down, wood smoke arose, sound was wrapped as in fine wool, dulled everywhere to sweetness. Whirring insects, rippling water, the wood-chopper's axe, the whistling soldiers, the drum-beat, the bugle-call, all were swept into a smooth current, steady, almost droning, somewhat dream-like. The 2d Corps would have said that it was a long time on the Opequon, but that on the whole it found the place a pleasing land of drowsy-head.

Visitors came to the Opequon; parties from Winchester, officers from the 1st Corps commanded by Longstreet and encamped a few miles to the eastward, officers from the headquarters of the commander-in-chief. General Lee came himself on Traveller, and with Stonewall Jackson rode along the Opequon, under the scarlet maples. One day there appeared a cluster of Englishmen, Colonel the Honourable Garnet Wolseley; the Special Correspondent of the *Times*, the Honourable Francis Lawley, and the Special Correspondent of the *Illustrated London News*, Mr. Frank Vizetelly. General Lee had sent them over under the convoy of an officer, with a note to Stonewall Jackson.

My dear General, — These gentlemen very especially wish to make your acquaintance.   Yours,

R. E. Lee.

They made it, beneath a beautiful, tall, crimson gum tree, where on a floor of fallen leaves Lieutenant-General T. J. Jackson's tent was pitched. A camp-stool, a wooden chair, and two boxes were placed. There was a respectful silence while the Opequon murmured by, then Garnet Wolseley spoke of the great interest which England — Virginia's mother country — was taking in this struggle.

"Yes, sir," said Jackson. "It would be natural for a mother to take an even greater interest."

"And the admiration, general, with which we have watched your career — the career of genius, if I may say so! By Jove — "

"Yes, sir. It is not my career. God has the matter in hand."

"Well, He knows how to pick his lieutenants! — You have the most ideal place for a camp, general! But, I suppose, before these coloured leaves all fall you will be moving?"

"It is an open secret, I suppose, sir," said the correspondent of the *Times*, "that when McClellan does see fit to cross you will meet him east of the Blue Ridge?"

"May I ask, sir," said the correspondent of the *Illustrated News*, "what you think of this latest move on the political chess-board — I mean Mr. Lincoln's Proclamation of Emancipation?"

"The leaves are," said Jackson, "a beautiful colour. I was in England one autumn, Colonel Wolseley, but I did not observe our autumn colours in your foliage. Climate, doubtless. But what was my admiration were your cathedrals."

"Yes, general; wonderful, are they not? Music in stone. Should McClellan cross, would the Fredericksburg route — "

"Good! good! Music in stone! Which of your great church structures do you prefer, sir?"

"Why, sir, I might prefer Westminster Abbey. Would — "

"Good! Westminster Abbey. A soldier's answer. I remember that I especially liked Durham. I liked the Galilee chapel and the tomb of the Venerable Bede. St. Cuthbert is buried there, too, is he not?"

"I really don't remember, sir. Is he, Mr. Lawley?"

"I believe so."

"Yes, he is. You haven't got any cathedrals here, General Jackson, but you 've got about the most interesting army on the globe. Will McClellan — "

"I like the solidity of the early Norman. The foundations were laid in 1093, I believe?"

"Very probably, general. Has General Lee —"

"It has a commanding situation — an advantage which all of your cathedrals do not possess. I liked the windows best at York. What do you think, colonel?"

"I think that you are right, general. When your wars are over, I hope that you will visit England again. I suppose that you cannot say how soon that will be, sir?"

"No, sir. Only God can say that. I should like to see Ely and Canterbury." He rose. "Gentlemen, it has been pleasant to meet you. I hear the adjutant's call. If you would like to find out how my men *drill*, Colonel Johnson may take you to the parade-ground."

Later, there arrived beneath the crimson gum four of Jeb Stuart's officers, gallantly mounted and equipped, young and fine. To-day their usual careless dash was tempered by something of important gravity; if their eyes danced, it was beneath half-closed lids; they did not smile outright, but their lips twitched. Behind them an orderly bore a long pasteboard box. The foremost officer was Major Heros von Borcke, of General Stuart's staff. All dismounted. Jackson came out of his tent. The air was golden warm; the earth was level before the tent, and on the carpet of small bright leaves was yet the table, the chair, the camp-stool, and the boxes. It made a fine, out-of-door room of audience. The cavalry saluted. Jackson touched the forage cap, and sat down. The staff officer, simple, big, and genuine, stood forward. "Major Von Borcke, is it not? Well, major, what is General Stuart about just now?"

"General, he is watching his old schoolmate, General McClellan. My general, I come on a graceful errand, a little gift from General Stuart bearing. He has so great an esteem and friendship for you, general; he asks that you accept so slight a token of that esteem and friendship and he would say affection, and he does say reverence. He says that from Richmond he has for this sent — "

Major Heros von Borcke made a signal. The orderly advanced and placed upon the pine table the box. The other cavalry officers stepped a little nearer; two or three of Stonewall Jackson's military family came also respectfully closer; the red gum leaves made a rustling underfoot.

"General Stuart is extremely kind," said Jackson. "I have a high esteem for Jeb Stuart. You will tell him so, major."

Slowly, slowly, came off the lid. Slowly, slowly came away a layer of silver paper. Where on earth they got — in Richmond in 1862 — the gay box, the silver paper, passes comprehension. The staff thought it looked Parisian, and nursed the idea that it had once held a ball gown. Slowly, slowly, out came the gift.

A startled sound, immediately suppressed, was uttered by the military family. Lieutenant-General T. J. Jackson merely looked a stone wall. The old servant Jim was now also upon the scene. "Fo' de Lawd!" said Jim. "Er new nuniform!"

Fine grey cadet cloth, gold lace, silken facings, beautiful bright buttons, sash, belt, gauntlets — the leaves rustled loudly, but a chuckle from Jim in the background and a murmured "Dat are sumpin' like!" was the only audible utterance. With empressement each article was lifted from the box by Major Heros von Borcke and laid upon the pine boards beneath Stonewall Jackson's eyes. The box emptied, Von Borcke, big, simple, manly, gravely beaming, stepped back from the table. "For General Jackson, with General Stuart's esteem and admiration!"

Stonewall Jackson, big, too, and to appearance simple, looked under the forage cap, smiled, and with one lean brown finger touched almost timidly the beautiful, spotless cadet cloth. "Major von Borcke, you will give General Stuart my best thanks. He is, indeed, good. All this," he gravely indicated the loaded table, "is much too fine for the hard work I'd have to give it, and I shall have it put away for the present. But you tell General Stuart, major, that I will take the best care of his beautiful present, and that I will always prize it highly as a souvenir. It is, I think, about one o'clock. You will stay to dinner with me, I hope, major."

But the banks of the Opequon uttered a protest. "Oh, general!" — "My general, you will hurt his feelings." — "General, just try it on, at least!" "Let us have our way, sir, just this once! We have been right good, have n't we? and we do so want to see you in it!"— "General Stuart will certainly want to know how it fits —"

"Please, sir," — "*Gineral, Miss Anna sholy would like ter see you in hit!*"

Ten minutes elapsed while the Opequon rippled by and the crimson gum leaves drifted down, then somewhat bashfully from the tent came forth Stonewall Jackson metamorphosed. Triumph perched upon the helms of the staff and the visiting cavalry. "Oh! — Oh! —" "General Stuart will be so happy!" "General, the review this afternoon! General, won't you review us *that way?*"

He did. At first the men did not know him, then there mounted a wild excitement. Suppressed with difficulty during the actual evolutions, it burst into flower when the ranks were broken. The sun was setting in a flood of gold; there hung a fairy light over the green fields and the Opequon and the vivid woods. The place rang to the frolic shouting. It had the most delighted sound. "Stonewall! Stonewall Jackson! Stonewall! Stonewall! Old Jack! Old Jack! Old Jack!"

Old Jack touched his beautiful hat of a lieutenant-general. Little Sorrel beneath him moved with a jerk of the head and a distended nostril. The men noticed that, too. "He don't know him either! Oh, Lord! Oh, Lord! Ain't life worth while? Ain't it grand? — Stonewall! Stonewall!"

On went the gold October, passing at last in a rain and drift of leaves into a russet November. The curls of wood smoke showed plainer down the glades, the crows were cawing, the migratory birds going south, but the days were yet mild and still, wrapped in a balm of pale sunshine, a faint, purplish, Indian summer haze. The 2d Corps was hale and soberly happy.

It was the chaplain's season. There occurred in the Army of Northern Virginia a religious revival, a far-spread and lasting deepening of feeling. For many nights in many forest glades there were "meetings" with prayer and singing. "Old Hundred" floated through the air. From tents and huts of boughs came the soldiers. They sat upon the earth, thick carpeted now with the faded leaves, or upon gnarled, out-cropping roots of oak and beech. Above shone the moon; there was a touch of frost in the air. The chaplain had some improvised pulpit; a great fire, or perhaps a torch fastened to a bough, gave light whereby to read the Book. The sound of the voice,

the sound of the singing, blended with the voice of the Opequon
rushing — all rushing toward the great Sea.

> " Come, humble sinner, in whose breast
> A thousand thoughts revolve— "

It made a low thunder, so many soldiers' voices. Always, on these
nights, in some glade or meadow, with some regiment or other, there
was found the commander of the 2d Corps. Beneath the cathedral
roof of the forest, or beneath the stars in the open, sat Stonewall
Jackson, worshipping the God of Battles. Undoubtedly he was
really and deeply happy. His place is on the Judean hills, with Joab
and David and Abner. Late in this November there came to him
another joy. In North Carolina, where his wife had gone, a child was
born to him, his only child, a daughter.

In the first half of October had occurred Jeb Stuart's brilliant
Monocacy raid, two days and a half within McClellan's lines. On
the twenty-sixth McClellan began the passage of the Potomac. He
crossed near Berlin, and Lee, assured now that the theatre of war
would be east of the Blue Ridge, dispatched Longstreet with the 1st
Corps to Culpeper. On the seventh of November McClellan was
removed from the command of the Army of the Potomac. It was
given over to Burnside, and he took the Fredericksburg route to
Richmond.

The Army of the Potomac numbered one hundred and twenty-
five thousand men and officers and three hundred and twenty guns.
At Washington were in addition eighty thousand men, and up and
down the Potomac twenty thousand more. The Army of Northern
Virginia in all, 1st and 2d Corps, had seventy-two thousand men
and officers and two hundred and seventy-five guns. Lee called
Stonewall Jackson to join Longstreet at Fredericksburg.

On the twenty-second the 1st Corps quitted, amid smiles and
tears, many a " God keep you!" and much cheering, Winchester the
beloved. Out swung the long column upon the Valley pike. Advance
and main and rear, horse and foot and guns, Stonewall Jackson and
his twenty-five thousand took the old road. The men were happy.
"Old road, old road, old road, howdy do! How's your health, old
lady? Have n't you missed us? Have n't you missed us? We've
missed *you!* "

It was Indian summer, violet, dreamlike. By now there had been burning and harrowing in the Valley; war had laid his mailed hand upon the region. It was not yet the straining clutch of later days, but it was bad enough. The Indian summer wrapped with a soft touch of mourning purple much of desolation, much of untilled earth, and charred roof-tree, and broken walls. The air was soft and gentle, lying balmy and warm on the road and ragged fields, and the haze so hid the distances that the column thought not so much of how the land was scarred as of the memories that thronged on either side of the Valley pike. "Kernstown! The field of Kernstown. There's Fulkerson's wall. About five hundred years ago ! "

Stonewall Jackson, riding in the van, may be supposed to have had his memories, too. He did not express them. He was using expedition, and he sent back orders. "Press forward, men! Press forward." He rode quietly, forage cap pulled low; or, standing with Little Sorrel on some wayside knoll, he watched for a while his thousands passing. Stuart's gay present had taken the air but once. Here was the old familiar, weather-worn array, leaf brown from sun and wind and dust and rain, patched here and patched there, dull of buttons, and with the lace worn off. Here were the old boots, the sabre, the forage cap; here were the blue glint of the eye and the short "Good! good!" as the men passed. The marching men shouted for him. He nodded, and having noted whatever it was he had paused to note, shook Little Sorrel's bridle and stiffly galloped to the van again.

Past Newtown, past Middletown, on to Strasburg — the Massanuttons loomed ahead, all softly coloured yet with reds and golds. "Massanutton ! Massanutton!" said the troops. "We've seen you before, and you've seen us before! Front Royal's at your head and Port Republic's at your feet."

> "In Virginia there's a Valley,
>   Valley, Valley!
> Where all day the war drums beat,
>   Beat, Beat!
> And the soldiers love the Valley
>   Valley, Valley!
> And the Valley loves the soldiers,
>   Soldiers, soldiers!"

Past Strasburg, past Tom's Brook, past Rude's Hill — through the still November days, in the Indian summer weather, the old Army of the Valley, the old Ewell's Division, the Light Division, D. H. Hill's Division, moved up the Valley Pike. All were now the 2d Corps, Stonewall Jackson riding at its head. The people — the people were mostly women and children — flocked to the great highroad to bring the army things, to wave it onward, to say "God bless you!" — "God keep you!" — "God make you to conquer!"

The 2d Corps passed Woodstock, and Edenburg, and Mt. Jackson, and came to New Market, and here it turned eastward. "Going to leave you," chanted the troops. "Going to leave you, old road, old road! Take care of yourself till we come again!"

Up and up and over Massanutton wound the 2d Corps. The air was still, not cold. The gold leaves drifted on the troops, and the red. From the top of the pass the view was magnificent. Down and down wound the column to the cold, swift Shenandoah. The men forded the stream. "Oh, Shenandoah! Oh, Shenandoah! when will we ford you again?"

Up and up the steeps of the Blue Ridge to Fisher's Gap! All the air was dreamy, the sun sloping to the west, the crows cawing in the mountain clearings. The column was leaving the Valley, and a silence fell upon it. Stonewall Jackson rode ahead, on the mountain path, in the last gold light. At the summit of the pass there was a short halt. It went by in a strange quietness. The men turned and gazed. "The Valley of Virginia! The Valley of Virginia! *Which of us will not see you again?*"

The Alleghenies lay faint, faint, beneath the flooding light. The sun sent out great rays of purple and rose. Between the mountain ranges the vast landscape lay in shadow, though here and there a high hilltop, a mountain spur had a coronet of gold. The 2d Corps, twenty-five thousand men, high on the Blue Ridge, looked and looked. "Some of us will not see you again. Some of us will not see you again, O loved Valley of Virginia!" *Column Forward! Column Forward!*

CHAPTER XLV

THE LONE TREE HILL

THE three beautiful Carys walked together from the road gate toward the house. Before them, crowning the low hill, showed the white pillars between oaks where the deep coloured leaves yet clung. The sun was down, the air violet, the negro children burning brush and leaves in the hollow behind the house quarter. Halfway to the pillars, there ran back from the drive a long double row of white chrysanthemums. The three sisters paused to gather some for the vases.

Unity and Molly gathered them. Judith sat down on the bank by the road, thick with dead leaves. She drew her scarf about her. Molly came presently and sat beside her. "Dear Judith, dear Judith!" she said, in her soft little voice, and stroked her sister's dress.

Judith put her arm about her, and drew her close. "Molly, is n't it as though the earth were dying? Just the kind of fading light and hush one thinks of going in — I don't know why, but I don't like chrysanthemums any more."

"I know," said Molly, "there 's a feel of mould in them, and of dead leaves and chilly nights. But the soldiers are so used to lying out of doors! I don't believe they mind it much, or they won't until the snow comes. Judith —"

"Yes, honey."

"The soldiers that I have dreadful dreams about are the soldiers in prison. Judith, I dreamed about Major Stafford the other night! He had blood upon his forehead and he was walking up and down, walking up and down in a place with a grating."

"You must n't dream so, Molly. — Oh, yes, yes, yes! I'm sorry for him. On the land and on the sea and for them that are in prison —"

Unity joined them, with her arm full of white bloom. "Oh, is n't there a dreadful hush? How gay we used to be, even at twilight! Judith, Judith, let us do something!"

Judith looked at her with a twisted smile. "This morning, very early, we went with Aunt Lucy over the storeroom and the smoke-house, and then we went down to the quarter and got them all to-gether, and told them how careful now we would all have to be with meal and bacon. And Susan's baby had died in the night, and we had to comfort Susan, and this afternoon we buried the baby. After breakfast we scraped almost the last of the tablecloths into lint, and Molly made envelopes, and Daddy Ben and I talked about shoes and how we could make them at home. Then Aunt Lucy and I went into town to the hospitals. There is a rumour of smallpox, but I am sure it is only a rumour. It has been a hard day. A number of sick were brought in from Fredericksburg. So much pneumonia! An old man and woman came up from North Carolina looking for their son. I took them through the wards. Oh, it was pitiful! No, he was not there. Probably he was killed. And Unity went to the sewing-rooms, and has been there sewing hard all day. And then we came home, and found Julius almost in tears, and Molly triumphant with the parlour carpet all up and ready to be cut into squares — sol-diers sleeping in the snowy winter under tulips and roses. And then we read father's letter, and that was a comfort, a comfort! And then we took Susan's little baby and buried it, and did what we could for Susan; and then we walked down to the gate and stopped to gather chrysanthemums. And now we are going back to the house, and I dare say there'll be some work to do between now and bed-time. We're doing something pretty nearly all the time, Unity."

Unity lifted with strength the mass of bloom above her head. "I know, I know! But it's in me to want a brass band to do it by! I want to see the flag waving! I want to hear the *sound* of our work. Oh, I know I am talking foolishness!" She took Judith by the hands, and lifted her to her feet. "Anyhow, you're brave enough, Judith, Judith darling! Come, let us race to the house."

The three were country-bred, fleet of foot. They ran, swiftly, lightly, up the long drive. Twilight was around them, the leaves drifting down, the leaves crisp under foot. The tall white pillars gleamed before them; through the curtainless windows showed, jewel-like, the flame of a wood fire. They reached the steps almost together, soberly mounted them, and entered the hall. Miss Lucy called to them from the library. "The papers have come."

The old room, quiet, grave, book-lined, stored with records of old struggles, lent itself with fitness to the papers nowadays. The Greenwood Carys sat about the wood fire, Judith in an old armchair, Unity on an old embroidered stool, Molly in the corner of a great old sofa. Miss Lucy pushed her chair into the ring of the lamplight and read aloud in her quick, low, vibrant voice. The army at Fredericksburg — that was what they thought of now, day and night. She read first of the army at Fredericksburg — of Lee on the southern side of the Rappahannock, and Burnside on the northern, and the cannon all planted, and of the women and children beginning to leave. She read all the official statements, all the rumours, all the guesses, all the prophecies of victory and the record of suffering. Then she read the news of elsewhere in the vast, beleaguered fortress — of the fighting on the Mississippi, in Louisiana, in Arkansas, in the Carolinas; echoes from Cumberland Gap, echoes from Corinth. She read all the Richmond news — hot criticism, hot defence of the President, of the Secretary of War, of the Secretary of State; echoes from the House, from the Senate; determined optimism as to foreign intervention; disdain, as determined, of Burnside's "On to Richmond"; passionate devotion to the grey armies in the field — all the loud war song of the South, clear and defiant! She read everything in the paper. She read the market prices. Coffee $4 per lb. Tea $20 per lb. Wheat $5 per bushel. Corn $15 per barrel. Bacon $2 per lb. Sugar $50 per loaf. Chickens $10. Turkeys $50.

"Oh," cried Molly. "We have chickens yet, beside what we send to the hospitals! And we have eggs and milk and butter, and I was looking at the turkeys to-day. I feel *wicked!*"

"A lot of the turkeys will die," said Unity consolingly. "They always do. I spoke to Sam about the ducks and the guinea-hens the other day. I told him we were going to send them to Fredericksburg. He did n't like it. 'Miss Unity, what fer you gwine ter send all dem critturs away lak dat? You sen' 'em from Greenwood, dey gwine die ob homesickness!' And we don't use many eggs ourselves, honey, and we 've no way to send the milk."

Miss Lucy having read the paper through, the Greenwood ladies went to supper. That frugal meal over, they came back to the library, the parlour looking somewhat desolate with the carpet up and rolled in one corner, waiting for the shears to-morrow. "The shepherds and shepherdesses look," said Unity, "as though they were shivering a little. I don't suppose they ever thought they'd live to see a Wilton carpet cut into blankets for Carys and other soldiers gone to war! It's impossible not to laugh when you think of Edward drawing one of those coverlets over him! Oh, me!"

"If Edward gets a furlough this winter," said Judith suddenly, "we must give him a party. With the two companies in town, and some of the surgeons, there will be men enough. Then Virginia and Nancy and Deb and Maria and Betty and Agatha and all the refugeeing girls — we could have a real party once more — "

"Just leaving out the things to eat," said Unity; "and wearing very old clothes. We'll do it, won't we, Aunt Lucy?"

Aunt Lucy thought it an excellent idea. "We musn't get old before our time! We must keep brightness about the place. I have seen my mother laugh and look all the gayer out of her beautiful black eyes when other folk would have been weeping! — I hear company coming, now! It's Cousin William, I think."

Cousin William it was, not gone to the war because of sixty-eight years and a rich inheritance of gout. He came in, ruddy as an apple, ridden over to cheer up the Greenwood folk and hear and tell news from the front. He had sons there himself, and a letter which he would read for the thirtieth time. When Judith had made him take the great armchair, and Miss Lucy had rung for Julius and a glass of wine, and Unity had trimmed the light, and Molly replenished the fire, he read, and as in these days no one ever read anything perfunctorily, the reading was more telling than an actor could have made it. In places Cousin William himself and his hearers laughed, and in places reader and listener brushed hand across eyes. "Your loving son," he read, and folded the sheets carefully, for they were becoming a little worn. "Now, what's your news, Lucy? Have you heard from Fauquier?"

"Yes, yesterday. He has reached Fredericksburg from Winchester. It is one of his old, dry, charming letters, only — only a little hard to make out in places, because he's not yet used to writing with his left hand." Miss Lucy's face worked for a moment; then she smiled again, with a certain high courage and sweetness, and taking the letter from her work-basket read it to Cousin William. He listened, nodding his head at intervals. "Yes, yes, to be sure, to be sure! You can't remember Uncle Edward Churchill, Lucy, but I can. He used to read Swift to me, though I did n't care for it much, except for Gulliver. Fauquier reminds me of him often, except that Uncle Edward was bitter — though it was n't because of his empty sleeve; it was for other things. — Fredericksburg! There 'll be another terrible battle. And Warwick?"

"We heard from him to-day — a short letter, hurriedly written; but oh! like Warwick — like Warwick!"

She read this, too. It was followed by a silence in the old Greenwood library. Then said Cousin William softly, "It is worth while to get such letters. There are n't many like Warwick Cary. He's the kind that proves the future — shows it is n't just a noble dream. And Edward?"

"A letter three days ago, just after you were here the last time."

The room smiled. "It was what Edward calls a screed," said Molly; "there was n't a thing about war in it."

Unity stirred the fire, making the sparks go up chimney. "Five pages about Massanutton in her autumn robes, and a sonnet to the Shenandoah! I like Edward."

At ten o'clock Cousin William rode away. The Greenwood women had prayers, and then, linked together, they went up the broad, old shallow stairs to the gallery above, and kissed one another good-night.

In her own room Judith laid pine knots upon the brands. Up flared the light, and reddened all the pleasant chamber. She unclad herself, slipped on her dressing-gown, brushed and braided her dusky hair, rippling, long and thick, then fed again the fire, took letters from her rosewood box, and in the light from the hearth read them for the thousandth time. There was none from Richard Cleave after July, none, none! Sitting in a low chair that had been her mother's, she bowed herself over the June-time letters, over the May-time letters. There had been but two months of bliss, two months! She read them again, although she had them all by heart; she held her hand as though it held a pen and traced the words so that she might feel, "Here and so, his hand rested"; she put the paper to her cheek, against her lips; she slipped to her knees, laid her arms along the seat of the chair and her head upon them, and prayed. "O God! my lover hast Thou put far from me. — O God! my lover hast Thou put far from me."

She knelt there long; but at last she rose, laid the letters in the box, and took from another compartment Margaret Cleave's. These were since July, a letter every fortnight. Judith read again the later ones, the ones of the late summer. "Dear child — dearest child, I cannot tell you! Only be forever sure that wherever he is, at Three Oaks or elsewhere, he loves you, loves you! No; I do not know that his is the course that I should take, but then women are different. I do not think I would ever think of pride or of the world and the world's opinion. If you cried to me I would go, and the world should not hold me back. But men have been trained to uphold that kind of pride. I did not think that Richard had it, but I see now all his father in him. Darling child, I do not think that it will last, but just now, oh, just now, you must possess your heart in patience!"

The words blurred before Judith's eyes. She sunk her head upon her knees. "Possess my heart in patience — Possess my heart in patience — Oh, God, I am not old enough yet to do it!"

She read another letter, one of later date. "Judith, I promised. I cannot tell you. But he is well, oh, believe that! and believe, too, that he is doing his work. He is not the kind to rest from work, he must work. And slowly, slowly that brings salvation. You are a noble woman. Be noble still — and wait awhile — and wait awhile! It *will* come right. Miriam is better. The woods about Three Oaks are gorgeous."

She read another. "Child, he is not at Three Oaks. Now you must rest — rest and wait."

Judith put the letters in the rosewood box. She arose, locked her hands behind her head and walked softly up and down the room. "Rest—rest and wait. Patience—quietude—tranquillity—strength — fortitude — endurance.— Rest — patience — calm quietude—"

It worked but partially. Presently, when she lay down it was to lie still enough, but sleepless. Late in the night she slept, but it was to dream again, much as she had dreamed during the Seven Days, great and tragic visions. Dawn waked her. She lay, staring at the white ceiling; then she arose. It was not cold. The earth lay still at this season, yet wrapped and warmed and softened with the memories of summer. Judith looked out of the window. There was a glow in the eastern sky, the trees were motionless, the brown path over the hills showed like a beckoning finger. She dressed, put a cloak about her, went softly downstairs and left the house.

The path across the meadow, through the wood, up the lone tree hill — she would see the sunrise, she would get above the world. She walked quickly, lightly, through the dank stillness. There was mist in the meadow, above the little stream. The wood was shadowy; mist, like ghosts, between the trees. She passed through it and came out on the bare hillside, rising dome-like to the one tree with the bench around it. The eastern sky was burning gold. Judith stood still. There was a man seated upon the bench, on the side that overlooked Greenwood. He sat with his head buried in his hands. She could not yet tell, but she thought he was in uniform.

With the thought she moved onward. She never remembered afterwards, whether she recognized him then, or whether she thought, "A soldier sleeping through the night up here! Why did he not come to the house?" She made no noise on the bare, moist earth of the path. She was within thirty feet of the bench when Cleave lifted his head from his hands, rose, stood still a moment, then with a gesture, weary and determined, turned to descend the hill — on the side away from Greenwood, toward a cross-country road. She called to him. "Richard!"

It was rapture — all beneath the rising sun forgotten save only this gold-lit hilltop, with its tree from Eden garden! But since it was earth, and Paradise not yet real, and there were checks and bars enough in their human lot, they came back from that seraph flight. This was the lone tree hill above Greenwood, and a November day, though gold-touched, and Philip Deaderick must get back to the section of Pelham's artillery refitting at Gordonsville. — "What do you mean? You are a soldier — you are back in the army? — but you have another name? Oh, Richard, I see, I see! Oh, I might have known! A gunner with Pelham. Oh, my gunner with Pelham, why did you not come before?"

Cleave wrung her hands, clasped in his, then bent and kissed them. "Judith, I will speak to you as to a comrade, because you would be the truest comrade ever man had! What would you do — what would you have done — in my place? What would you do now, in my place, but say — but say, 'I love you; let me go'?"

"I?" said Judith. "What would I have done? I would have re-entered the army as you have reëntered it. I would serve again as you are serving again. If it were necessary — Oh, I see that it was necessary! — I would serve disguised as you are disguised. But — but — when it came to Judith Cary — "

"Judith, say that it was not you and I, but some other disgraced soldier and one of your sisters — "

"You are not a disgraced soldier. The innocent cannot be disgraced."

"Who knows that I was innocent? My mother, and you, Judith, know it; my kinspeople and certain friends believe it; but all the rest of the country — the army, the people — they don't believe it. Let my name be known to-morrow, and by evening a rougher dismissal than before! Do you not see, do you not see, Judith?"

"I see partly. I see that you must serve. I see that you walk with dangers. I see that — that you could not even write. I see that I must possess my soul in patience. I see that we must wait — Oh, God, it is all waiting, waiting, waiting! But I do not see — and I *refuse* to see, Richard — anything at the end of it all but love, happiness, union, home for you and me!"

He held her close. "Judith, I do not know the right. I am not sure that I see the right, my soul is so tempest-tossed. That day at White Oak Swamp. If I could cleanse that day, bring it again into line with the other days of my life, poor and halting though they may have been, though they may be, if I could make all men say 'His life was a whole — one life, not two. He had no twin, a disobedient soldier, a liar and betrayer, as it was said he had.' — If I could do that, Judith! I do not see how I will do it, and yet it is my intention to do it. That done, then, darling, darling! I will make true love to you. If it is not done — but I will not think of that. Only — only — how to do it, how to do it! That maddens me at times — "

"Is it that? Then we must think of that. They are not all dead who could tell? — "

"Maury Stafford is not dead."

"Maury Stafford! — What has he to do with it?"

Cleave laughed, a sound sufficiently grim. "What has he not to do with it? — with that order which he carried from General Jackson to General Winder, and from General Winder — not, before

God! to me! Winder is dead, and the courier who could have told is dead, and others whom I might have called are dead — dead, I will avow, because of my choice of action, though still — given that false order — I justify that choice! And now we hear that Major Stafford was among those taken prisoner at Sharpsburg."

Judith stood upright, her hand at her breast, her eyes narrowed. "Until this hour I never knew the name of that officer. I never thought to ask. I never thought of the mistake lying there. The mistake! All these months I have thought of it as a mistake — as one of those misunderstandings, mishappenings, accidental, incomprehensible, that wound and blister human life! I never saw it in a lightning flash for what it was till now!"

She looked about her, still with an intent and narrowed gaze. "The lone tree hill. It is a good place to see it from. There is nothing to be done but to join this day to a day last June — the day of Port Republic." Raising her hands she pressed them to her eyes as though to shut out a veritable lightning glare, then dropped them. She stood very straight, young, slender, finely and strongly fibred. "He said he would do the worst he could, and he has done it. And I said, 'At your peril!' and at his peril it shall be! And the harm that he has done, he shall undo it!" She turned. "Richard! he shall undo it."

Cleave stood beside her. "Love, love! how beautiful the light is over Greenwood! I thought, sitting here, 'I will not wait for the sunshine; I will go while all things are in shadow.' And I turned to go. And then came the sunshine. I must go now — away from the sunshine. I had but an hour, and half of it was gone before the sunshine came."

"How shall I know," she said, "if you are living? There is a battle coming."

"Yes. Judith, I will not write to you. Do not ask me; I will not. But after each battle I have managed somehow to get a line to my mother. She will tell you that I am living, well and living. I do not think that I shall die — no, not till Maury Stafford and I have met again!"

"He is in prison. They say so many die there. . . . Oh, Richard, write to me — "

But Cleave would not. "No! To do that is to say, 'All is as it

was, and I let her take me with this stain!' I will not — I will not.
Circumstance has betrayed us here this hour. We could not help
it, and it has been a glory, a dream. That is it, a dream. I will not
wake till I have said good-bye!"

They said good-bye, still in the dream, as lovers might, when one
goes forth to battle and the other stays behind. He released her,
turned short and sharp, and went down from the lone tree hill, down
the side from Greenwood, to the country road. A piece of woods hid
him from sight.

Judith stood motionless for a time, then she sat down upon the
bench. She sat like a sibyl, elbows on knees, chin in hands, her gaze
narrowed and fixed. She spoke aloud, and her voice was strange in
her own ears. "Maury Stafford in prison. Where, and how long?"

CHAPTER XLVI

FREDERICKSBURG

SNOW lay deep on the banks of the Rappahannock, in the forest, up and down the river, on the plain about the little city, on the bold heights of the northern shore, on the hills of the southern, commanding the plain. The snow was deep, but somewhat milder weather had set in. December the eleventh dawned still and foggy.

General Burnside with a hundred and twenty thousand blue troops appointed this day to pass the Rappahannock, a stream that flowed across the road to Richmond. He had been responsible for choosing this route to the keep of the fortress, and he must make good his reiterated, genial assurances of success. The Rappahannock, Fredericksburg, and a line of hills masked the onward-going road and its sign, *This way to Richmond.* "Well, the Rappahannock can be bridged! A brigade known to be occupying the town? Well, a hundred and forty guns admirably planted on Stafford Heights will drive out the rebel brigade! The line of hills, bleak and desolate with fir woods? — hares and snow birds are all the life over there! General Lee and Stonewall Jackson? Down the Rappahannock below Moss Neck. At least, undoubtedly, Stonewall Jackson's down there. The balloon people say so. General Lee's got an idea that Port Royal's our point of attack. The mass of his army's there. The gunboat people say so. Longstreet may be behind those hills. Well, we'll crush Longstreet! We'll build our bridges under cover of this fortunate fog, and go over and defeat Longstreet and be far down the road to Richmond before a man can say Jack Robinson!"

"Jack Robinson!" said the brigade from McLaws's division — Barksdale's Mississippians — drawn up on the water edge of Fredericksburg. They were tall men — Barksdale's Mississippians — playful bear-hunters from the cane brakes, young and powerfully made, and deadly shots. "Old Barksdale" knew how to handle them, and together they were a handful for any enemy whatsoever.

Sixteen hundred born hunters and fighters, they opened fire on the bridge-builders, trying to build four bridges, three above, one below the town. Barksdale's men were somewhat sheltered by the houses on the river brink; the blue had the favourable fog with which to cover operations. It did not wholly help; the Mississippians had keen eyes; the rifles blazed, blazed, blazed! Burnside's bridge-builders were gallant men; beaten back from the river they came again and again, but again and again the eyes of the swamp hunters ran along the gleaming barrels and a thousand bronzed fingers pulled a thousand triggers. Past the middle of the day the fog lifted. The town lay defined and helpless beneath a pallid sky.

The artillery of the Army of the Potomac opened upon it. One hundred and forty heavy guns, set in tiers upon the heights to the north, fired each into Fredericksburg fifty rounds. Under that terrible cover the blue began to cross on pontoons.

A number of the women and children had been sent from the town during the preceding days. Not all, however, were gone. Many had no place to go to; some were ill and some were nursing the ill; many had husbands, sons, brothers, there at hand in the Army of Northern Virginia and would not go. Now with the beginning of the bombardment they must go. There were grey, imperative orders. "At once! at once! Go *where?* God knows! but go."

They went, almost all, in the snow, beneath the pallid sky, with the shells shrieking behind them. They carried the children, they half carried the sick and the very old. They stumbled on, between the frozen hills by the dark pointed cedars, over the bare white fields. Behind them home was being destroyed; before them lay desolation, and all around was winter. They had perhaps thought it out, and were headed — the various forlorn lines — for this or that country house, but they looked lost, remnant of a world become glacial, whirled with suddenness into the sidereal cold, cold! and the loneliness of cold. The older children were very brave; but there were babes, too, and these wailed and wailed. Their wailing made a strange, futile sound beneath the thundering of the guns.

One of these parties came through the snow to a swollen creek on which the ice cakes were floating. Cross! — yes, but how? The leaders consulted together, then went up the stream to find a possible

ford, and came in sight of a grey battery, waiting among the hills.
"Oh, soldiers! — oh, soldiers! — come and help!"

Down hastened a detachment, eager, respectful, a lieutenant directing, the very battery horses looking anxious, responsible. A soldier in the saddle, a child in front, a child behind, the old steady horses planting their feet carefully in the icy rushing stream, over went the children. Then the women crossed, their hands resting on the grey-clad shoulders. All were over; all thanked the soldiers. The soldiers took off their caps, wished with all their hearts that they had at command fire-lit palaces and a banquet set! Having neither, being themselves without shelter or food and ordered not to build fires, they could only bare their heads and watch the other soldiers out of sight, carrying the children, half carrying the old and sick, stumbling through the snow, by the dark pointed cedars, and presently lost to view among the frozen hills.

The shells rained destruction into Fredericksburg. Houses were battered and broken; houses were set on fire. Through the smoke and uproar, the explosions and detonations and tongues of flame, the Mississippians beat back another attempt at the bridges and opened fire on boat after boat now pushing from the northern shore. But the boats came bravely on, bravely manned; hundreds might be driven from the bridge-building, but other hundreds sprang to take their places — and always from the heights came the rain of iron, smashing, shivering, setting afire, tearing up the streets, bringing down the walls, ruining, wounding, slaying! McLaws sent an order to Barksdale, Barksdale gave it to his brigade. "Evacuate!" said the Mississippians. "We're going to evacuate. What's that in English? 'Quit?' — What in hell should we quit for?"

Orders being orders, the disgust of the bear-hunters did not count. "Old Barksdale" was fairly deprecating. "Men, I can't help it! General McLaws says, 'General Barksdale, withdraw your men to Marye's Hill.' Well, I've got to do it, have n't I? General McLaws knows, now does n't he? — Yes, — just one more round. *Load! Kneel! Commence firing!*"

In the late afternoon the town was evacuated, Barksdale drawing off in good order across the stormed-upon open. He disappeared — the Mississippi brigade disappeared — from the Federal vision. The blue column, the 28th Massachusetts leading,

entered Fredericksburg. "We'll get them all to-morrow — Longstreet certainly! Stonewall Jackson's from twelve to eighteen miles
down the river. Well! this time Lee will find that he's divided his
army once too often!"

By dark there were built six bridges, but the main army rested
all night on the northern bank. December the twelfth dawned, another foggy day. The fog held hour after hour, very slow, still,
muffled weather, through which, corps by corps, all day long, the
army slowly crossed. In the afternoon there was a cavalry skirmish with Stuart, but nothing else happened. Thirty-six hours
had been consumed in crossing and resting. The Rappahannock,
however, *was* crossed, and the road to Richmond stretched plain
between the hills.

But the grey army was not divided. Certain divisions had been
down the river, but they were no longer down the river. The Army
of Northern Virginia, a vibrant unit, intense, concentrated, gaunt,
bronzed, and highly efficient, waited behind the hills south and west
of the town. There was a creek running through a ravine, called
Deep Run. On one side of Deep Run stood Longstreet and the 1st
Corps, on the other, almost at right angles, Stonewall Jackson and
the 2d. Before both the heavily timbered ridge sank to the open
plain. In the woods had been thrown up certain breastworks.

Longstreet's left, Anderson's division, rested on the river. To
Anderson's right were posted McLaws, Pickett, and Hood. He had
his artillery on Marye's Hill and Willis Hill, and he had Ransom's
infantry in line at the base of these hills behind a stone wall. Across
Deep Run, on the wooded hills between the ravine and the Massaponax, was Stonewall Jackson. A. P. Hill's division with the
brigades of Pender, Lane, Archer, Thomas, and Gregg made his
first line of battle, the divisions of Taliaferro and Early his second,
and D. H. Hill's division his reserve. His artillery held all favourable crests and headlands. Stuart's cavalry and Stuart's Horse
Artillery were gathered by the Massaponax. Hills and forest hid
them all, and over the plain and river rolled the fog.

It hid the North as it hid the South. Burnside's great force rested
the night of the twelfth in and immediately about Fredericksburg —
Hooker and Sumner and Franklin, one hundred and thirteen thousand men. "The balloon people" now reported that the hills south

and west were held by a considerable rebel force — Longstreet evidently, Lee probably with him. Burnside repeated the infatuation of Pope and considered that Stonewall Jackson was absent from the field of operations. Undoubtedly he had been, but the shortest of time before, down the river by Port Royal. No one had seen him move. Jackson away, there was then only Longstreet — strongly posted, no doubt. Well! Form a great line of battle, advance in overwhelming strength across the plain, the guns on Stafford Heights supporting, and take the hills, and Longstreet on them! It sounded simple.

The fog, heavy, fleecy, white, persisted. The grey soldiers on the wooded hills, the grey artillery holding the bluff heads, the grey skirmishers holding embankment and cut of the Richmond, Fredericksburg and Potomac Railroad, the grey cavalry by the Massaponax, all stared into the white sea and could discern nothing. The ear was of no avail. Sound came muffled, but still it came. "The long roll — hear the long roll! My Lord! How many drums have they got, anyway?" — "Listen! If you listen right hard you can hear them shouting orders! Hush up, you infantry, down there! We want to hear." — "They're moving guns, too! Wish there'd come a little sympathizing earthquake and help them — 'specially those siege guns on the heights over there!" — "No, no! I want to fight them. Look! it's lifting a little! the fog's lifting a little! Look at the guns up in the air like that! It's closed again." — "Well, if that wasn't fantastic! Ten iron guns in a row, posted in space!" — "Hm! brass bands. My Lord! there must be one to a platoon!" — "Hear them marching! Saw lightning once run along the ground — now it's thunder. How many men has General Ambrose Everett Burnside got, anyhow?" — "Burnside's been to dances before in Fredericksburg! Some of the houses are burning now that he's danced in, and some of the women he has danced with are wandering over the snow. I hope he'll like the reel presently." — "He's a good fellow himself, though not much of a general! He can't help fighting here if he's put here to fight." — "I know that. I was just stating facts. Hear that music, music, music!"

Up from Deep Run, a little in the rear of the grey centre, rose a bold hill. Here in the clinging mist waited Lee on Traveller, his staff behind him, in front an ocean of vapour. Longstreet came from the left, Stonewall Jackson from the right. Lee and his two lieutenants talked together, three mounted figures looming large on the hilltop above Deep Run. With suddennness the fog parted, was up-gathered with swiftness by the great golden sun.

That lifted curtain revealed a very great and martial picture, — War in a moment of vastness and grandeur, epic, sublime. The town was afire; smoke and flame went up to a sky not yet wholly azure, banded and barred with clouds from behind which the light came in rays fierce and bright, with an effect of threatening. There was a ruined house on a high hill. It gave the appearance of a grating in the firmament, a small dungeon grating. Beyond the burning town was the river, crossed now by six pontoon bridges. On each there were troops; one of the long sun rays caught the bayo-nets. From the river, to the north, rose the heights, and they had an iron crown from which already came lightnings and thunders. There were paths leading down to the river and these showed blue, moving streams, bright points which were flags moving with them. That for the far side of the Rappahannock, but on this side, over the plain that stretched south and west of the smoke-wreathed town, there moved a blue sea indeed. Eighty thousand men were on that plain. They moved here, they moved there, into battle formation, and they moved to the crash of music, to the horn and to the drum. The long rays that the sun was sending made a dazzle of bayonet steel, thousands and thousands and thousands of bayonets. The gleaming lines went here, went there, crossed, recrossed, formed angles, made a vast and glittering net. Out of it soared the flags, bright hovering birds, bright giant blossoms in the air. Batteries moved across the plain. Officers, couriers, galloped on fiery horses; some general officer passed from end to end of a forming line and was cheered. The earth shook to marching feet. The great brazen horns blared, the drums beat, the bugles rang. The gleaming net folded back on itself, made three pleats, made three great lines of battle.

The grey leaders on the hill to the south gazed in silence. Then said Lee, "It is well that war is so terrible. Were it not so, we should grow too fond of it." Longstreet, the "old war horse," stared at the tremendous pageant. "This wasn't a little quarrel. It's been brewing for seventy-five years — ever since the Bill-of-Rights day. Things that take so long in brewing can't be cooled by a breath. It's getting to be a huge war." Said Jackson, "Franklin holds their left. He seems to be advancing. I will return to Hamilton's Crossing, sir."

The guns on the Stafford Heights which had been firing slowly and singly now opened mouth together. The tornado, overpassing river and plain, burst on the southern hills. In the midst of the tempest, Burnside ordered Franklin to advance a single division, its mission the seizing the *unoccupied* ridge east of Deep Run. Franklin sent Meade with forty-five hundred Pennsylvania troops.

Meade's brigades advanced in three lines, skirmishers out, a band playing a quickstep, the stormy sunlight deepening the colours, making a gleaming of bayonets. His first line crossed the Richmond road. To the left was a tiny stream, beyond it a ragged bank topped by brushwood. Suddenly, from this coppice, opened two of Pelham's guns.

Beneath that flanking fire the first blue line faltered, gave ground. Meade brought up four batteries and sent for others. All these came fiercely into action. When they got his range, Pelham moved his two guns and began again a raking fire. Again the blue gunners found the range and again he moved with deliberate swiftness, and again he opened with a hot and raking fire. One gun was disabled; he fought with the other. He fought until the limber chests were empty and there came an imperious message from Jeb Stuart, "Get back from destruction, you infernal, gallant fool, John Pelham!"

The guns across the river and the blue field batteries steadily shelled for half an hour the heavily timbered slopes beyond the railroad. Except for the crack and crash of severed boughs the wood gave no sign. At the end of this period Meade resumed his advance.

On came the blue lines, staunch, determined troops, seasoned now as the grey were seasoned. They meant to take that empty line of hills, willy-nilly a few Confederate guns. That done, they would be in a position to flank Longstreet, already attacked in front by Sumner's Grand Division. On they came, with a martial front, steady, swinging. Uninterrupted, they marched to within a few hundred yards of Prospect Hill. Suddenly the woods that loomed before them so dark and quiet blazed and rang. Fifty guns were within that cover, and the fifty cast their thunderbolts full against the dark blue line. From either side the grey artillery burst the grey musketry, and above the crackling thunder rose the rebel yell. Stonewall Jackson was not down the river; Stonewall Jackson was here! Meade's Pennsylvanians were gallant fighters; but they broke beneath that withering fire, — they fell back in strong disorder.

Grey and blue, North and South, there were gathered upon and above the field of Fredericksburg four hundred guns. All came into action. Where earlier, there had been fog over the plain, fog wreathing the hillsides, there was now smoke. Dark and rolling it invaded the ruined town, it mantled the flowing Rappahannock, it surmounted the hills. Red flashes pierced it, and over and under and through roared the enormous sound. There came reinforcements to Meade, division after division. In the meantime Sumner was hurling brigades against Marye's Hill and Longstreet was hurling them back again.

The 2d Corps listened to the terrible musketry from this front. "Old Pete's surely giving them hell! There's a stone wall at the base of Marye's Hill. McLaws and Ransom are holding it — sorry for the Yanks in front." — "Never heard such hullabaloo as the great guns are making!" — "What're them Pennsylvanians down there doing? It's time for them to come on! They've got enough reinforcements — old friends, Gibbon and Doubleday." — "Good fighters." — "Yes, Lord! we're all good fighters now. Glad of it. Like to fight a good fighter. Feel real friendly toward him." — "A thirty-two-pounder Parrott in the battery on the hill over there exploded and raised hell. General Lee standing right by. He just spoke on, calm and imperturbable, and Traveller looked sideways." — "Look! Meade's moving. *Do you know, I think we ought to have occupied that tongue of land?*"

So, in sooth, thought others presently. It was a marshy, dense, and tangled coppice projecting like a sabre tooth between the brigades of Lane and Archer. So thick was the growth, so boggy the earth, that at the last it had been pronounced impenetrable and left unrazed. Now the mistake was paid for — in bloody coin.

Meade's line of battle rushed across the open, brushed the edge of the coppice, discovered that it was empty, and plunging in, found cover. The grey batteries could not reach them. Almost before the situation was realized, forth burst the blue from the thicket. Lane was flanked; in uproar and confusion the grey gave way. Meade sent in another brigade. It left the first to man-handle Lane, hurled itself on, and at the outskirt of the wood, struck Archer's left, taking Archer by surprise and creating a demi-rout. A third brigade entered on the path of the first and second. The latter, leaving Archer to this new strength, hurled itself across the military road and upon a thick and tall wood held by Maxey Gregg and his South Carolinians. Smoke, cloud, and forest growth — it was hard to distinguish colours, hard to tell just what was happening! Gregg thought that the smoke-wrapped line was Archer falling back. He withheld his fire. The line came on and in a moment, amid shouts, struck his right. A bullet brought down Gregg himself, mortally wounded. His troops broke, then rallied. A grey battery near Bernard's Cabin brought its guns to bear upon Gibbon, trying to follow the blue triumphant rush. Archer reformed. Stonewall Jackson, standing on Prospect Hill, sent orders to his third line. "Generals Taliaferro and Early, advance and clear the front with bayonets."

Yaaaiih! Yaaaiiih! Yaaaaihh! yelled Jubal Early's men, and did as they were bid. *Yaaaaiiih! Yaaiiihhh! Yaaaaiiihhhh!* yelled the Stonewall Brigade and the rest of Taliaferro's, and did as they were bid. Back, back were borne Meade's brigades. Darkness of smoke, denseness of forest growth, treachery of swampy soil! — all order was lost, and there came no support. Back went the blue — all who could go back. A. P. Hill's second line was upon them now; Gibbon was attacked. The grey came down the long slopes like a torrent loosed. Walker's guns joined in. The uproar was infernal. The blue fought well and desperately — but there was no support. Back they went, back across the Richmond Road — all who could get back. They left behind in the marshy coppice, and on the wooded slopes and by the embankment, four thousand dead and wounded. The Light Division, Taliaferro and Early, now held the railroad embankment. Before them was the open plain, and the backward surge to the river of the broken foe. It was three o'clock of the afternoon. Burnside sent an order to Franklin to attack again, but Franklin disobeyed.

Upon the left Longstreet's battle now swelled to giant proportions. Marye's Hill, girdled by that stone wall, crowned by the Washington Artillery, loomed impregnable. Against it the North tossed to destruction division after division. They marched across the bare and sullen plain, they charged; the hill flashed into fire, a thunder rolled, the smoke cloud deepened. When it lifted the charge was seen to be broken, retreating, the plain was seen to be strewed with dead. The blue soldiers were staunch and steadfast. They saw that their case was hapless, yet on they came across the shelterless plain. Ordered to charge, they charged; charged very gallantly, receded with a stubborn slowness. They were good fighters, worthy foes, and the grey at Fredericksburg hailed them as such. Forty thousand men charged Marye's Hill — six great assaults — and forty thousand were repulsed. The winter day closed in. Twelve thousand men in blue lay dead or wounded at the foot of the southern hills, before Longstreet on the left and Stonewall Jackson on the right.

Five thousand was the grey loss. The Rockbridge Artillery had fought near the Horse Artillery by Hamilton's Crossing. All day the guns had been doggedly at work; horses and drivers and gunners and guns and caissons; there was death and wounds and wreckage. In the wintry, late afternoon, when the battle thunders were lessening, Major John Pelham came by and looked at Rockbridge. Much of Rockbridge lay on the ground, the rest stood at the guns. "Why, boys," said Pelham, "you stand killing better than any I ever saw!"

They stood it well, both blue and grey. It was stern fighting at Fredericksburg, and grey and blue they fought it sternly and well. The afternoon closed in, cold and still, with a red sun yet veiled by drifts of crape-like smoke. The Army of the Potomac, torn, decimated, rested huddled in Fredericksburg and on the river banks. The Army of Northern Virginia rested with few or no camp-fires on the southern hills. Between the two foes stretched the freezing plain, and on the plain lay thick the Federal dead and wounded. They lay thick, thick, before the stone wall. At hand, full target for the fire of either force, was a small, white house. In the house lived Mrs. Martha Stevens. She would not leave before the battle, though warned and warned again to do so. She said she had an idea that she could help. She stayed, and wounded men dragged themselves or were dragged upon her little porch, and within her doors. General Cobb of Georgia died there; wherever a man could be laid there were stretched the ghastly wounded. Past the house shrieked the shells; bullets imbedded themselves in its walls. To and fro went Martha Stevens, doing what she could, bandaging hurts till the bandages gave out. She tore into strips what cloth there was in the little meagre house — her sheets, her towels, her tablecloths, her poor wardrobe. When all was gone she tore her calico dress. When she saw from the open door a man who could not drag himself that far, she went and helped him, with as little reck as may be conceived of shell or minie.

The sun sank, a red ball, staining the snow with red. The dark came rapidly, a very cold dark night, with myriads of stars. The smoke slowly cleared. The great, opposed forces lay on their arms, the one closely drawn by the river, the other on the southern hills. Between was the plain, and the plain was a place of drear sound — oh, of drear sound! Neither army showed any lights; for all its antagonist knew either might be feverishly, in the darkness, preparing an attack. Grey and blue, the guns yet dominated that wide and mournful level over which, to leap upon the other, either foe must pass. Grey and blue, there was little sleeping. It was too cold, and there was need for watchfulness, and the plain was too unhappy — the plain was too unhappy.

The smoke vanished slowly from the air. The night lay sublimely still, fearfully clear and cold. About ten o'clock Nature provided a spectacle. The grey troops, huddled upon the hillsides, drew a quickened breath. A Florida regiment showed alarm. "What's that? Look at that light in the sky! Great shafts of light streaming up — look! opening like a fan! What's that, chaplain, what's that? — Don't reckon the Lord's tired of fighting, and it's the Judgment Day?"

"No, no, boys! It's an aurora borealis."

"Say it over, please. Oh, northern lights! Well, we've heard of them before, but we never saw them. Having a lot of experiences here in Virginia!" — "Well, it's beautiful, any way, and I think it's terrible. I wish those northern lights would do something for the northern wounded down there. Nothing else that's northern seems likely to do it." — "Look at them — look at them! pale red, and dancing! I've heard them called 'the merry dancers.' There's a shooting star! They say that every time a star shoots some one dies." — "That's not so. If it were, the whole sky would be full of falling stars to-night. Look at that red ray going up to the zenith. O God, make the plain stop groaning!"

The display in the heavens continued, luminous rays, faintly rose-coloured, shifting from east to west, streaming upward until they were lost in the starry vault. Elsewhere the sky was dark, intensely clear, the winter stars like diamonds. There was no wind. The wide, unsheltered plain across which had stormed, across which had receded, the Federal charges, was sown thick with soldiers who had dropped from the ranks. Many and many lay still, dead and cold, their marchings and their tentings and their battles over. They had fought well; they had died; they lay here now stark and pale, but in the vast, pictured web of the whole their threads are strong and their colour holds. But on the plain of Fredericksburg many and many and many were not dead and resting. Hundreds and hundreds they lay, and could not rest for mortal anguish. They writhed and tossed, they dragged themselves a little way and fell again, they idly waved a hat or sword or empty hand for help, they cried for aid, they cried for water. Those who could not lift their voices moaned, moaned. Some had grown delirious, and upon that plain there was even laughter. All the various notes taken together blended into one long, dreary, weird, dull, and awful sound, steady as a wind in miles of frozen reeds. They were all blue soldiers, and they lay where they fell.

There was a long fringe of them near the stone wall and near the railway embankment behind which now rested the Light Division and Taliaferro and Early. The wind here was loud, rattling a thicker growth of reeds. Above, the long, silent, flickering lights mocked with their rosy hue, and the glittering stars mocked, and the empty concave of the night mocked, and the sound of the Rappahannock mocked. A river moving by like the River of Death, and they could not even get to the river to drink, drink, drink. . . .

A figure kneeling by a wounded man, spoke in a guarded voice to an upright, approaching form. "This man could be saved. I have given him water. I went myself to the general, and he said that if we could get any into the hospital behind the hill we might do so. But I'm not strong enough to lift him."

"I air," said Billy. He set down the bucket that he carried. "I jest filled it from the creek. It don't last any time, they air so thirsty! You take it, and I'll take him." He put his arms under the blue figure, lifted it like a child, and moved away, noiseless in the darkness. Corbin Wood took the bucket and dipper. Presently it must be refilled. By the creek he met an officer sent down from the hillside. "You twenty men out there have got to be very careful. If their sentries see or hear you moving you'll be thought a skirmish line with the whole of us behind, and every gun will be opening! Battle's decided on for to-morrow, not for to-night. — Now be careful, or we'll recall every damned life-in-your-hand blessed volunteer of. you! — Oh, it's a fighting chaplain—I beg your pardon, I'm sure, sir! But you'd better all be very quiet. Old Jack would say that mercy's all right, but you mustn't alarm the foe."

All through the night there streamed the boreal lights. The living and the dying, the ruined town, the plain, the hills, the river lay beneath. The blue army slept and waked, the grey army slept and waked. The general officers of both made little or no pretence at sleeping. Plans must be made, plans must be made, plans must be made. Stonewall Jackson, in his tent, laid himself down indeed for two hours and slept, guarded by Jim, like a man who was dead. At the end of that time he rose and asked for his horse.

It was near dawn. He rode beneath the fading streamers, before his lines, before the Light Division and Early and Taliaferro, before his old brigade — the Stonewall. The 65th lay in a pine wood, down-sloping to a little stream. Reveille was yet to sound. The men lay in an uneasy sleep, but some of the officers were astir, and had been so all night. These, as Jackson checked Little Sorrel, came forward and saluted. He spoke to the colonel. "Colonel Erskine, your regiment did well. I saw it at the Crossing."

Erskine, a small, brave, fiery man, coloured with pleasure. "I'm very glad, sir. The regiment's all right, sir. The old stock was n't quite cut down, and it's made the new like it—" He hesitated, then as the general with his "Good! good!" gathered up the reins he took heart of grace. "It's old colonel, sir — it's old colonel—" he stammered, then out it came: "Richard Cleave trained us so, sir, that we could n't go back!"

"See, sir," said Stonewall Jackson, "that you don't emulate him in all things." He looked sternly and he rode away with no other word. He rode from the pine wood, crossed the Mine Road, and presently the narrow Massaponax. The streamers were gone from the sky; there was everywhere the hush of dawn. The courier with him wondered where he was going. They passed John Pelham's guns, iron dark against the pallid sky. Presently they came to the Yerby House, where General Maxey Gregg, a gallant soldier and gentleman, lay dying.

As Jackson dismounted Dr. Hunter McGuire came from the house. "I gave him your message, general. He is dying fast. It seemed to please him."

"Good!" said Jackson. "General Gregg and I have had a disagreement. In life it might have continued, but death lifts us all from under earthly displeasure. Will you ask him, Doctor, if I may pay him a little visit?"

The visit paid, he came gravely forth, mounted and turned back toward headquarters on Prospect Hill. In the east were red streaks, one above another. The day was coming up, clear and cold. Pelham's guns, crowning a little eminence, showed distinct against the colour. Stonewall Jackson rode by, and, with a face that was a study, a gunner named Deaderick watched him pass.

All this day these two armies stood and faced each other. There was sharpshooting, there was skirmishing, but no full attack. Night came and passed, and another morning dawned. This day, forty-eight hours after battle, Burnside sent a flag of truce with a request that he be allowed to collect and bury his dead. There were few now alive upon that plain. The wind in the reeds had died to a ghostly hush.

That night there came up a terrible storm, a howling wind driving a sleety rain. All night long, in cloud and blast and beating wet, the Army of the Potomac, grand division by grand division, recrossed the Rappahannock.

The storm continued, the rain and snow swelled the river. The Army of the Potomac with Acquia creek at hand, Washington in touch, lay inactive, went into winter quarters. The Army of Northern Virginia, couched on the southern hills, followed its example. Between the two foes flowed the dark river. Sentries in blue paced the one bank, sentries in grey the other. A detail of grey soldiers, resting an hour opposite Falmouth, employed their leisure in raising a tall sign-post, with a wide and long board for arms. In bold letters they painted upon it THIS WAY TO RICHMOND. It rested there, month after month, in view of the blue army.

At the end of January Burnside was superseded. The Army of the Potomac came under the command of Fighting Joe Hooker. In February Longstreet, with the divisions of Pickett and Hood, marched away from the Rappahannock to the south bank of the James. In mid-March was fought the cavalry battle of Kelly's Ford — Averell against Fitz Lee. Averell crossed, but when the battle rested, he was back upon the northern shore. At Kelly's Ford fell John Pelham, "the battle-cry on his lips, and the light of victory beaming from his eye."

April came with soft skies and greening trees. North and south and east and west, there were now gathered against the fortress with the stars and bars above it some hundreds of thousands under arms. Likewise a great navy beat against the side which gave upon the sea. The fortress was under arms indeed, but she had no navy to speak of. Arkansas and Louisiana, Tennessee and North Carolina, vast lengths of the Mississippi River, Fortress Monroe in Virginia and Suffolk south of the James — entrance had been made into all these courts of the fortress. Blue forces held them stubbornly; smaller grey forces held as stubbornly the next bastion. On the Rappahannock and the Rapidan, within fifty miles of the imperilled Capital, were gathered by May one hundred and thirty thousand men in blue. Longstreet gone, there opposed them sixty-two thousand in grey.

Late in April Fighting Joe Hooker put in motion "the finest army on the planet." There were various passes and feints. Sedgwick attempted a crossing below Fredericksburg. Stonewall Jackson sent an aide to Lee with the information. Lee received it with a smile. "I thought it was time for one of you lazy young fellows to come and tell me what that firing was about! Tell your good general that he knows what to do with the enemy just as well as I do."

Flourish and passado executed, Hooker, with suddenness, moved up the Rappahannock, crossed at Richard's Ford, moved up the Rapidan, crossed at Ely and Germanna Fords, turned east and south and came into the Wilderness. He meant to pass through and, with three great columns, checkmate Lee at Fredericksburg. Before he could do so Lee shook himself free, left to watch the Rappahannock, and Sedgwick, ten thousand pawns and an able knight, and himself crossed to the Wilderness.

CHAPTER XLVII

THE WILDERNESS

FIFTEEN by twenty miles stretched the Wilderness. Out of a thin soil grew pine trees and pine trees, scrub oak and scrub oak. The growth was of the densest, mile after mile of dense growth. A few slight farms and clearings appeared like islands; all around them was the sea, the sea of tree and bush. It stretched here, it stretched there, it touched all horizons, vanishing beyond them in an amethyst haze.

Several forest tracks traversed it, but they were narrow and worn, and it was hard to guess their presence, or to find it when guessed. There were, however, two fair roads — the old Turnpike and the Plank Road. These also were sunken in the thick, thick growth. A traveller upon them saw little save the fact that he had entered the Wilderness. Near the turnpike stood a small white church, the Tabernacle church. A little south of the heart of the place lay an old, old, abandoned iron furnace — Catherine Furnace. As much to the north rose a large old house — Chancellorsville. To the westward was Dowdall's Tavern. Around all swept the pine and the scrub oak, just varied by other trees and blossoming shrubs. The ground was level, or only slightly rolling. Look where one might there was tree and bush, tree and bush, a sense of illimitable woodland, of far horizons, of a not unhappy sameness, of stillness, of beauty far removed from picturesqueness, of vague, diffused charm, of silence, of sadness not too sad, of mystery not too baffling, of sunshine very still and golden. A man knew he was in the Wilderness.

Mayday here was softly bright enough, pure sunshine and pine odours, sky without clouds, gentle warmth, the wild azalea in bloom, here and there white stars of the dogwood showing, red birds singing, pine martens busy, too, with their courtship, pale butterflies flitting, the bee haunting the honeysuckle, the snake awakening. Beauty was everywhere, and in portions of the great forest, great as a principality, quiet. In these regions, indeed, the stillness might seem doubled, reinforced, for from other stretches of the Wilderness, specifically from those which had for neighbour the roads, quiet had fled.

To right and left of the Tabernacle church were breastworks, Anderson holding them against Hooker's advance. In the early morning, through the dewy Wilderness, came from Fredericksburg way Stonewall Jackson and the 2d Corps, in addition Lafayette McLaws with his able Roman air and troops in hand. At the church they rested until eleven o'clock, then, gathering up Anderson, they plunged more deeply yet into the Wilderness. They moved in two columns, McLaws leading by the turnpike, Anderson in advance on the Plank Road, Jackson himself with the main body following by the latter road.

Oh, bright-eyed, oh, bronzed and gaunt and ragged, oh, full of quips and cranks, of jest and song and courage, oh, endowed with all quaint humour, invested with all pathos, ennobled by vast struggle with vast adversity, oh, sufferers of all things, hero-fibred, grim fighters, oh, Army of Northern Virginia — all men and all women who have battled salute you, going into the Wilderness this May day with the red birds singing!

On swing the two columns, long, easy, bayonets gleaming, accoutrements jingling, colours deep glowing in the sunshine. To either hand swept the Wilderness, great as a desert, green and jew-elled. In the desert to-day were other bands, great and hostile blue-clad bands. Grey and blue, — there came presently a clash that shook the forest and sent Quiet, a fugitive, to those deeper, distant haunts. Three bands of blue, three grey attacks — the air rocked and swung, the pure sunlight changed to murk, the birds and the beasts scampered far, the Wilderness filled with shouting. The blue gave back — gave back somewhat too easily. The grey followed — would have followed at height of speed, keen and shouting, but there rode to the front a leader on a sorrel nag. "General Anderson, halt your men. Throw out skirmishers and flanking parties and advance with caution."

McLaws on the turnpike had like orders. Through the Wilder-ness, through the gold afternoon, all went quietly. Sound of march-ing feet, beat of hoof, creak of leather, rumble of wheel, low-pitched orders were there, but no singing, laughing, talking. Skirmishers and flanking parties were alert, but the men in the main column moved dreamily, the spell of the place upon them. With flowering thorn and dogwood and the purple smear of the Judas tree, with the faint gilt of the sunshine, and with wandering gracious odours, with its tangled endlessness and feel as of old time, its taste of sadness, its hint of patience, it was such a seven-leagues of woodland as might have environed the hundred-years-asleep court, palace, and princess. The great dome of the sky sprung cloudless; there was no wind; all things seemed halted, as if they had been thus forever. The men almost nodded as they marched.

Back, steadily, though slowly, gave the blue skirmishers before the grey skirmishers. So thickly grew the Wilderness that it was somewhat like Indian fighting, and no man saw a hundred yards in front of him. Stonewall Jackson's eyes glinted under the forage cap; perhaps he saw more than a hundred yards ahead of him, but if so he saw with the eyes of the mind. He was moving very slowly, more like a tortoise than a thunderbolt. The men said that Old Jack had spring fever.

Grey columns, grey artillery, grey flanking cavalry, all came under slant sunrays to within a mile or two of that old house called Chancellorsville set north of the pike, upon a low ridge in the Wilderness. "Open ground in front — open ground in front — open ground in front! Let Old Jack by — Let Old Jack by! Going to see — Going to see —" *Halt!*

The beat of feet ceased. The column waited, sunken in the green and gold and misty Wilderness where the shadows were lengthening and the birds were at evensong. In a moment the evensong was hushed and the birds flew away. The same instant brought explanation of that "Don't-care.-On-the-whole-quite-ready-to-retreat.-Merely-following-instructions" attitude for the past two hours of the blue skirmish line. From Chancellorsville, from Hooker's great entrenchments on the high roll of ground, along the road, and on the plateau of Hazel Grove, burst a raking artillery fire. The shells shrieked across the open, plunged into the wood, and exploded before every road-head. Hooker had guns a-many; they commanded the Wilderness rolling on three sides of the formidable position he had seized; they commanded in iron force the clearing along his front. He had breastworks; he had abattis. He had the 12th Corps, the 2d, the 3d, the 5th, the 7th, the 11th; he had in the Wilderness seventy thousand men. His left almost touched the Rappahannock, his right stretched two miles toward Germanna Ford. He was in great strength.

Jeb Stuart with his cavalry, waiting impatiently near Catherine Furnace, found beside him General Jackson on Little Sorrel. "General Stuart, I wish you to ride with me to some point from which those guns can be enfiladed. Order Major Beckham forward with a battery."

This was the heart of the Wilderness. Thick, thick grew the trees and the all-entangling underbrush. Stuart and Stonewall Jackson, staff behind them, pursued a span-wide bridle path, overarched by dogwood and Judas tree. It led at last to a rise of ground, covered by matted growth, towered above by a few pines. Four guns of the Horse Artillery strove, too, to reach the place. They made it at last, over and through the wild tangle, but so narrow was the clearing, made hurriedly to either side of the path, that but one gun at a time could be brought into position. Beckham, commanding now where Pelham had commanded, sent a shell singing against the not distant line of smoke and flame. The muzzle had hardly blazed when two masked batteries opened upon the rise of ground, the four guns, the artillerymen and artillery horses, and upon Stonewall Jackson, Stuart, and the staff.

The great blue guns were firing at short range. A howling storm of shot and shell broke and continued. Through it came a curt order. "Major Beckham, get your guns back. General Stuart, gentlemen of the staff, push out of range through the underwood."

The guns with their maddened horses strove to turn, but the place was narrow. Ere the movement could be made there was bitter loss. Horses reared and fell, dreadfully hurt; men were mown down, falling beside their pieces. It was a moment requiring action decisive, desperately gallant, heroically intelligent. The Horse Artillery drew off their guns, even got their wounded out of the intolerable zone of fire. Stonewall Jackson, with Stuart, watched them do it. He nodded, "Good! good!"

Out of the raking fire, back in the scrub and pine, there came to a halt near him a gun, a Howitzer. He sat Little Sorrel in the last golden light, a light that bathed also the piece and its gunners. The

Federal batteries were lessening fire. There was a sense of pause. The two foes had seen each other; now — Army of Northern Virginia, Army of the Potomac — they must draw breath a little before they struck, before they clenched. The sun was setting; the cannonade ceased.

Jackson sat very still in the gold patch where, between two pines, the west showed clear. The aureate light, streaming on, beat full upon the howitzer and on the living and unwounded of its men. Stonewall Jackson spoke to an aide. "Tell the captain of the battery that I should like to speak to him."

The captain came. "Captain, what is the name of the gunner there? The one by the limber with his head turned away."

The captain looked. "Deaderick, sir. Philip Deaderick."

"*Philip Deaderick.* When did he volunteer?"

The other considered. "I think, general, it was just before Sharpsburg. — It was just after the battle of Groveton, sir."

"Sharpsburg! — I remember now. So he rejoined at Manassas."

"He had n't been in earlier, sir. He had an accident, he said. He's a fine soldier, but he's a silent kind of a man. He keeps to himself. He won't take promotion."

"Tell him to come here."

Deaderick came. The gold in this open place, before the clear west, was very light and fine. It illuminated. Also the place was a little withdrawn, no one very near, and by comparison with the tornado which had raged, the stillness seemed complete. The gunner stood before the general, quiet, steady-eyed, broad-browed. Stonewall Jackson, his gauntleted hands folded over the saddle bow, gazed upon him fully and long. The gold light held, and the hush of the place; in the distance, in the Wilderness, the birds began again their singing. At last Jackson spoke. "The army will rest to-night. Headquarters will be yonder, by the road. Report to me there at ten o'clock. I will listen to what you have to say. That is all now."

Night stole over the Wilderness, a night of large, mild stars, of vagrant airs, of balm and sweetness. Earth lay in a tender dream, all about her her wild flowers and her fresh-clad trees. The grey and the blue soldiers slept, too, and one dreamed of this and one dreamed of that. Alike they dreamed of home and country and cause, of loved women and loved children and of their comrades. Grey and blue, these two armies fought each for an idea, and they fought well, as people fight who fight for an idea. And that it was not a material thing for which they fought, but a concept, lifted from them something of the grossness of physical struggle, carried away as with a strong wind much of the pettiness of war, brought their strife upon the plane of heroes. There is a beauty and a strength in the thought of them, grey and blue, sleeping in the Wilderness, under the gleam of far-away worlds.

The generals did not sleep. In the Chancellor house, north of the pike, Fighting Joe Hooker held council with his commanders of corps, with Meade and Sickles and Slocum and Howard and Couch. Out in the Wilderness, near the Plank Road, with the light from a camp-fire turning to bronze and wine-red the young oak leaves about them, there held council Robert Edward Lee and Stonewall Jackson. Near them a war horse neighed; there came the tramp of the sentry, then quiet stole upon the scene. The staff was near at hand, but to-night staff and couriers held themselves stiller than still. There was something in the air of the Wilderness; they knew not what it was, but it was there.

Lee and Jackson sat opposite each other, the one on a box, the other on a great fallen tree. On the earth between them lay an unrolled map, and now one took it up and pondered it, and now the other, and now they spoke together in quiet, low voices, their eyes on the map at their feet in the red light. Lee spoke. "I went myself and looked upon their left. It is very strong. An assault upon their centre? Well-nigh impossible! I sent Major Talcott and Captain Boswell again to reconnoitre. They report the front fairly impregnable, and I agree with them that it is so. The right— Here is General Stuart, now, to tell us something of that!"

In fighting jacket and plume Jeb Stuart came into the light. He saluted. "General Lee, their right rests on the Brock road, and the Brock road is as clean of defences as if gunpowder had never been invented, nor breastworks thought of!" He knelt and took up the map. "Here, sir, is Hunting Creek, and here Dowdall's Tavern and the Wilderness church, and here, through the deep woods, runs the old Furnace road, intersecting with the Brock road —"

Lee and his great lieutenant looked and nodded, listening to his further report. "Thank you, General Stuart," said at last the commander-in-chief. "You bring news upon which I think we may act. A flanking movement by the Furnace and Brock roads. It must be made with secrecy and in great strength and with rapidity. General Jackson, will you do it?"

"Yes, sir. Turn his right and gain his rear. I shall have my entire command?"

"Yes, general. Generals McLaws and Anderson will remain with me, demonstrate against these people and divert their attention. When can you start?"

"I will start at four, sir."

Lee rose. "Very good! Then we had better try to get a little sleep. I see Tom spreading my blanket now. — The Wilderness! General, do you remember, in Mexico, the *Noche Triste* trees and their great scarlet flowers? They grew all about the Church of our Lady of Remedies. — I don't know why I think of them to-night. — Good-night! good-night!"

A round of barren ground, towered over by pines, hedged in by the all-prevailing oak scrub, made the headquarters of the commander of the 2d Corps. Jim had built a fire, for the night wind was strengthening, blowing cool. He had not spared the pine boughs. The flames leaped and made the place ruddy as a jewel. Jackson entered, an aide behind him. "Find out if a soldier named Deaderick is here."

The soldier named Deaderick appeared. Jackson nodded to the aide who withdrew, then crossing to the fire, he seated himself upon a log. It was late; far and wide the troops lay sleeping. A pale moon looked down; somewhere off in the distance an owl hooted. The Wilderness lay still as the men, then roused itself and whispered a little, then sank again into deathlike quiet.

The two men, general and disgraced soldier, held themselves for a moment quiet as the Wilderness. Cleave knew most aspects of the man sitting on the log, in the gleam of the fire. He saw that to-night there was not the steel-like mood, cold, convinced, and stubborn, the wintry harshness, the granite hardness which Stonewall Jackson chiefly used toward offenders. He did not know what it was, but he thought that his general had softened.

With the perception there came a change in himself. He had entered this ring in the Wilderness with a constriction of the heart, a quick farewell to whatever in life he yet held dear, a farewell certainly to the soldier's life, to the army, to the guns, to the service of the country, an iron bracing of every nerve to meet an iron thrust. And now the thrust had not yet come, and the general looked at him quietly, as one well-meaning man looks at another who also means well. He had suffered much and long. Something rose into his throat, the muscles of his face worked slightly, he turned his head aside. Jackson waited another moment, — then, the other having recovered himself, spoke with quietness.

"You did, at White Oak Swamp, take it upon yourself to act, although there existed in your mind a doubt as to whether your orders — the orders you say you received — would bear that construction?"

"Yes, general."

"And your action proved a wrong action?"

"It proved a mistaken action, sir."

"It is the same thing. It entailed great loss with peril of greater."

"Yes, general."

"Had the brigade followed there might have ensued a general and disastrous engagement. The enemy were in force there — *as I knew*. Your action brought almost the destruction of your regiment. It brought the death of many brave men, and to a certain extent endangered the whole. That is so."

"Yes, general. It is so."

"Good! There was an order delivered to you. The man from whose lips you took it is dead. His reputation was that of a valiant, intelligent, and trustworthy man — hardly one to misrepeat an important order. That is so?"

"It is entirely so, sir."

"Good! You say that he brought to you such and such an order, the order, in effect, which, even so, you improperly construed and improperly acted upon, an order, however, which was never sent by me. A soldier who was by testifies that it was that order. Well?"

"That soldier, sir, was a known liar, with a known hatred to his officers."

"Yes. He repeated the order, word for word, as I sent it. How did that happen?"

"Sir, I do not know."

"The officer to whom I gave the order, and who, wrongly enough, transferred it to another messenger, swears that he gave it thus and so."

"Yes, general. He swears it."

A silence reigned in the firelit ring. The red light showed form and feature clearly. Jackson sitting on the log, his large hands resting on the sabre across his knees, was full within the glow. It beat even more strongly upon Cleave where he stood. "You believe," said Jackson, "that he swore falsely?"

"Yes, general."

"It is a question between your veracity and his?"

"Yes, general."

"There was enmity between you?"

"Yes, general."

"Where is he now?"

"He is somewhere in prison. He was taken at Sharpsburg."

There fell another silence. The sentry's tread was heard, the crackle of the fire seizing upon pine cone and bough, a low, sighing wind in the wilderness. Jackson spoke briefly. "After this campaign, if matters so arrange themselves, if the officer returns, if you think you can provide new evidence or re-present the old, I will forward, approved, your appeal for a court of inquiry."

"I thank you, sir, with all my heart."

Stonewall Jackson slightly changed his position on the log. Jim tiptoed into the ring and fed again the fire. There was a whinnying of some nearby battery horses, the sound of changing guard, then silence again in the Wilderness. Cleave stood, straight and still, beneath the other's pondering, long, and steady gaze. An aide appeared at an opening in the scrub. "General Fitzhugh Lee, sir." Jackson rose. "You will return to your battery, Deaderick. — Bring General Lee here, captain."

The night passed, the dawn came, red bird and wren and robin began a cheeping in the Wilderness. A light mist was over the face of the earth; within it began a vast shadowy movement of shadowy troops. Silence was so strictly ordered that something approaching it was obtained. There was a certain eeriness in the hush in which the column was formed — the grey column in the grey dawn, in the Wilderness where the birds were cheeping, and the mist hung faint and cold. By the roadside, on a little knoll set round with flowering dogwood, sat General Lee on grey Traveller. A swirl of mist below the two detached them from the wide earth and marching troops, made them like a piece of sculpture seen against the morning sky. Below them moved the column, noiseless as might be, enwound with mist. In the van were Fitzhugh Lee and the First Virginia Cavalry. They saluted; the commander-in-chief lifted his hat; they vanished by the Furnace road into the heart of the Wilderness. Rodes's Division came next, Alabama troops. Rodes, a tall and handsome man, saluted; Alabama saluted. Regiment by regiment they passed into the flowering woods. Now came the Light Division beneath skies with a coral tinge. Ambrose Powell Hill saluted, and all his brigades, Virginia and South Carolina. The guns began to pass, quiet as was constitutionally possible. The very battery horses looked as though they understood that people who were going to turn the flank of a gigantic army in a strong position proceed upon the business without noise. Up rose the sun while the iron fighting men were yet going by. The level rays gilded all metal, gilded Traveller's bit and bridle clasps, gilded the spur of Lee and his sword hilt and the stars upon his collar. The sun began to drink up the mist and all the birds sang loudly. The sky was cloudless, the low thick woodland divinely cool and sweet. Violet and bloodroot, dogwood and purple Judas tree were all bespangled, bespangled with dew.

While the guns were yet quietly rumbling by Stonewall Jackson appeared upon the rising ground. He saluted. Lee put out his hand and clasped the other's. "General, I feel every confidence! I am sure that you are going forth to victory."

"Yes, sir. I think that I am. — I will send a courier back every half hour."

"Yes, that is wise. — As soon as your wagons are by I will make disposition of the twelve thousand left with me. I propose a certain display of artillery and a line of battle so formed as to deceive — and deceive greatly — as to its strength. If necessary we will skirmish hotly throughout the day. I will create the impression that we are about to assault. It is imperative that they do not come between us and cut the army in two."

"I will march as rapidly as may be, sir. The Furnace road, the Brock road, then turn eastward on the Plank road and strike their flank. Good!" He jerked his hand into the air. "I will go now, general."

Lee bent across again. The two clasped hands. "God be with you, General Jackson!"

"And with you, General Lee."

Little Sorrel left the hillock. The staff came up. Stonewall Jackson turned in his saddle, and, the staff following his action, raised his hand in salute to the figure on grey Traveller, above them in the sunlight. Lee lifted his hat, held it so. The others filed by, turned sharply southward, and were lost in the jewelled Wilderness.

The sun cleared the tallest pines; there set in a splendid day. The long, long column, cavalry, Rodes's Division, the Light Division, the artillery, ordnance wagons and ambulances, twenty-five thousand grey soldiers with Stonewall Jackson at their head — the long, long column wound through the Wilderness by narrow, hidden roads. Close came the scrub and pine and all the flowering trees of May. The horsemen put aside vine and bough, the pink honeysuckle brushed the gun wheels; long stretches of the road were grass-grown. Through the woods to the right, by paths nearer yet to the far-flung Federal front, paced ten guardian squadrons. All went silently, all went swiftly. In the Confederate service there were no automata. These thousands of lithe, bronzed, bright-eyed, tattered men knew that something, something, something was being done! Something important that they must all help Old Jack with. Forbidden to talk, they speculated inwardly. "South by west. 'T isn't a Thoroughfare Gap march. They're all here in the Wilderness. We're leaving their centre — their right's somewhere over there in the brush. Should n't wonder — Allan Gold, what's the Latin for 'to flank'? — Lieutenant, we were just whispering! Yes, sir. — All right, sir. We won't make no more noise than so many wet cartridges!"

On they swung through the fairy forest, grey, steady, rapidly moving, the steel above their shoulders gleaming bright, the worn, shot-riddled colours like flowers amid the tender, all-enfolding green. The head of the column came to a dip in the Wilderness through which flowed a little creek. It was about nine o'clock in the morning. All the men looked to the right, for they could see the plateau of Hazel Grove and the great Federal intrenchments. "If those fellows look right hard they can see us, too! Can't help it —march fast and get past.—Oh, that's what the officers think, too! *Double quick!*"

The column crossed the tiny vale. Beyond it the narrow road of bends and turns plunged due south. Now, General Birney, stationed on the high level of Hazel Grove, observed, though somewhat faintly, that movement. He sent a courier to Hooker at Chancellorsville. "Rebel column seen to pass across my front. All arms and wagon train. It has turned to the southward."

"To the south!" said Hooker. "Turned southward. Now what does that mean? It might mean that Sedgwick at Fredericksburg has seized and is holding the road to Richmond. It might mean that Lee contemplated an unobstructed retreat through this Wilderness section southward to Gordonsville, which is not far away. From Gordonsville, he would fall back on Richmond. Say that is what he planned. Then, finding me in strength across his path, he would naturally make some demonstration, and behind it inaugurate a forced march, southward out of this wild place. A retreat to Gordonsville. It's the most probable move. I will send General Sickles toward Catherine Furnace to find out exactly."

Birney from Hazel Grove, Sickles from Chancellorsville, advanced. At Catherine Furnace they found the 23d Georgia, and on both sides of the Plank road discovered Anderson's division. Now began hot fighting in the Wilderness. The brigades of Anderson did gloriously. The 23d Georgia, surrounded at the Furnace, saw fall, in that square of the Wilderness, three hundred officers and men ; but those Georgians who yet stood did well, did well! Full in the front of Chancellorsville, McLaws, with his able, Roman air, his high colour, short black beard and crisp speech, handled his troops like a rightly trusted captain of Cæsar's. He kept the enemy's attention strained in his direction. Standing yet upon the little hillock, in the midst of the flowering dogwood, a greater than McLaws overlooked and directed all the grey pieces upon the board before Chancellorsville, played, all day, like a master, a skilfully complicated game.

Far in the Wilderness, miles now to the westward, the rolling musketry came to the ears of Stonewall Jackson. He was riding with Rodes at the head of the column. "Good! good!" he said. "That musketry is at the Furnace. General Hooker will attempt to drive between me and General Lee."

An aide of A. P. Hill's approached at a gallop. He saluted, gained breath and spoke. "They're cutting the 23d Georgia to pieces, sir! General Anderson is coming into action —"

A deeper thunder rolling now through the Wilderness corroborated his words. "Good! good!" said Jackson imperturbably. "My compliments to General Hill, and he will detach Archer's and Thomas's brigades and a battalion of artillery. They are to coöperate with General Anderson and protect our rear. The remainder of the Light Division will continue the march."

On past the noon point swung light and shadow. On through the languorous May warmth travelled westward the long column. It went with marked rapidity, emphatic even for the "foot cavalry," went without swerving, without straggling, went like a long, gleaming thunderbolt firmly held and swung. Behind it, sank in the distance the noise of battle. The Army of Northern Virginia knew itself divided, cut in two. Far back in the flowering woods before Chancellorsville, the man on the grey horse, directing here, directing there his twelve thousand men, played his master game with equanimity, trusting in Stonewall Jackson rushing toward the Federal right. Westward in the Wilderness, swiftly nearing the Brock road, the man on the sorrel nag travelled with no backward look. In his right hand was the thunderbolt, and near at hand the place from which to hurl it. He rode like incarnate Intention. The officer beside him said something as to that enormous peril in the rear, driving like a wedge between this hurrying column and the grey twelve thousand before Chancellorsville. "Yes, sir, yes!" said Jackson. "But I trust first in God, and then in General Lee."

The infantry swung into the Brock road. It ran northward; it lay bare, sunny, sleepy, walled in by emerald leaves and white and purple bloom. The grey thunderbolt travelled fast, fast, and at three o'clock its head reached the Plank road. Far to the east, in the Wilderness, the noise of the battle yet rolled, but it came fainter, with a diminishing sound. Anderson, Thomas, and Archer had driven back Sickles. There was a pause by Chancellorsville and Catherine Furnace. Through it and all the while the man on grey Traveller kept with a skill so exquisite that it shaded into a grave simplicity those thousands and thousands and thousands of hostile eyes turned quite from their real danger, centred only on a finely painted mask of danger.

At the intersection of the Brock and the Plank roads, Stonewall Jackson found massed the 1st Virginia cavalry. Upon the road and to either side in the flowering woods, roan and bay and black tossed their heads and moved their limbs amid silver dogwood and rose azalea. The horses chafed, the horsemen looked at once anxious and exultant. Fitzhugh Lee met the general in command. The latter spoke. "Three o'clock. Proceed at once, general, down the Plank road."

"I beg, sir," said the other, "that you will ride with me to the top of this roll of ground in front of us. I can show you the strangest thing!"

The two went, attended only by a courier. The slight eminence, all clad with scrub-oak, all carpeted with wild flowers, was reached. The horsemen turned and looked eastward, the breast-high scrub, the few tender-foliaged young trees sheltering them from view. They looked eastward, and in the distance they saw Dowdall's Tavern. But it was not Dowdall's Tavern that was the strangest thing. The strangest thing was nearer than Dowdall's; it was at no great distance at all. It was a long abattis, and behind the abattis long, well-builded breastworks. Behind the breastworks, overlooked by the little hill, and occupying an old clearing in the Wilderness, was a large encampment — the encampment, in short, of the 11th Army Corps, Howard commanding, twenty regiments, and six batteries. From the little hill where the violets purpled the ground, Stonewall Jackson and the cavalry leader looked and looked in silence. The blue soldiers lay at ease on the tender sward. It was *dolce far niente* in the Wilderness. The arms were stacked, the arms were stacked. There were cannon planted by the roadside, but where were the cannoneers? Not very near the guns, but asleep on the grass, or propped against trees smoking excellent tobacco, or in the square on the greensward playing cards with laughter! Battery horses were grazing where they would. Far and wide were scattered the infantry, squandered like plums on the grass. They lay or strolled about in the slant sunshine, in the balmy air, in the magic Wilderness — they never even glanced toward the stacked arms.

On the flowery slope across the road, Stonewall Jackson sat Little

Sorrel and gazed upon the pleasant, drowsy scene. His eyes had a glow, his cheek a warm colour beneath the bronze. Staff, and indeed the entire 2d Corps, had remarked from time to time this spring upon Old Jack's evident good health. "Getting younger all the time! This war climate suits him. Time the peace articles are signed he'll be just a boy again! Arrived at — what do you call it? perennial youth." Now he and Little Sorrel stood upon the flowering hilltop, and his lips moved. "Old Jack's praying — Old Jack's praying!" thought the courier.

Fitz Lee said something, but the general did not attend. In another moment, however, he spoke curt, decisive, final. He spoke to the courier. "Tell General Rodes to move *across* the Plank road. He is to halt at the turnpike. I will join him there. Move quietly."

The courier turned and went. Stonewall Jackson regarded again the scene before him — abattis and breastworks and rifle-pits untenanted, guns lonely in the slanting sunlight, lines of stacked arms, tents, fluttering flags, the horses straying at their will, cropping the tender grass, in a corner of a field men butchering beeves — regarded the German regiments, Schimmelpfennig and Krzyzancerski, regarded New York and Wisconsin, camped about the Wilderness church. Up from the clearing, across to the thick forest, floated an indescribable humming sound, a confused droning as from a giant race of bees. The shadows of the trees were growing long, the sun hung just above the pines of the Wilderness. "Good! good!" said Stonewall Jackson. His eyes, beneath the old, old forage cap, had a sapphire depth and gleam. A colour was in his cheek. "Good! good!" he said, and jerked his hand into the air. Suddenly turning Little Sorrel, he left the hill — riding fast, elbows out, and big feet, down into the woods, his sabre leaping as he rode.

CHAPTER XLVIII

THE RIVER

IT yet lacked of six o'clock when the battle lines were finally formed. Only the tree-tops of the Wilderness now were in gold, below, in the thick wood, the brigades stood in shadow. In front were Rodes's skirmishers, and Rodes's brigades formed the first line. The troops of Raleigh Colston made the second line, A. P. Hill's men the third. A battery — four Napoleons — was advanced; the other guns were coming up. The cavalry, the Stonewall Brigade supporting, took the Plank road, masking the actual movement. On the old turnpike Stonewall Jackson sat his horse beside Rodes. At six o'clock he looked at his watch, closed it, and put it in his pocket. "Are you ready, General Rodes?"

"Yes, sir."

"You can go forward, sir."

High over the darkening Wilderness rang a bugle-call. The sound soared, hung a moment poised, then, far and near, thronged the grey echoes, bugles, bugles, calling, calling! The sound passed away; there followed a rush of bodies through the Wilderness; in a moment was heard the crackling fire of the skirmishers. From ahead came a wild beating of Federal drums — the long roll, the long roll! *Boom!* Into action came the grey guns. Rodes's Alabamians passed the abattis, touched the breastworks, Colston two hundred yards behind, A. P. Hill the third line. *Yaaai! Yaaaiiih! Yaaaaaiiihh!* rang the Wilderness.

Several miles to the eastward the large old house of Chancellorsville, set upon rising ground, reflected the sun from its westerly windows. All about it rolled the Wilderness, shadowy beneath the vivid skies. It lay like a sea, touching all the horizon. On the deep porch of the house, tasting the evening coolness, sat Fighting Joe Hooker and several of his officers. Eastward there was firing, as there had been all day, but it, too, was decreased in volume, broken in continuity. The main rebel body, thought the Federal general, must be about ready to draw off, follow the rebel advance in its desperate attempt to get out of the Wilderness, to get off southward to Gordonsville. The 12th Corps was facing the "main body." The interchange of musketry, eastward there, had a desultory, waiting sound. From the south, several miles in the depth of the Wilderness, came a slow, interrupted booming of cannon. Pleasanton and Sickles were down there, somewhere beyond Catherine Furnace. Pleasanton and Sickles were giving chase to the rebel detachment, — whatever it was; Stonewall Jackson and a division probably — that was trying to get out of the Wilderness. At any rate, the rebel force was divided. When morning dawned it should be pounded small, piece by piece, by the blue impact! "We've got the men, and we've got the guns. We've got the finest army on the planet!"

The sun dropped. The Wilderness rolled like a sea, hiding many things. The shaggy pile of the forest turned from green to violet. It swept to the pale northern skies, to the eastern, reflecting light from the opposite quarter, to the southern, to the splendid west. Wave after wave, purple-hued, velvet-soft, it passed into mist beneath the skies. There was a perception of a vastness not comprehended. One of the men upon the Chancellor porch cleared his throat. "There's an awful feeling about this place! It's poetic, I suppose. Anyhow, it makes you feel that anything might happen — the stranger it was, the likelier to happen —"

"I don't feel that way. It's just a great big rolling plain with woods upon it — no mountains or water —"

"Well, I always thought that if I were a great big thing going to happen I wouldn't choose a chopped up, picturesque place to happen in! I'd choose something like this. I —"

"What's that?"

Boom, boom! Boom, boom, boom!

Hooker, at the opposite end of the porch, sprang up and came across. "Due west! — Howard's guns? — What does that mean —"

Boom, boom! Boom, boom, boom! Boom, boom, boom!

Fighting Joe Hooker ran down the steps. "Bring my horse, quick! Colonel, go down to the road and see —"

"My God! Here they come!"

Down the Plank road, through the woods, back to Chancellorsville, rushed the routed 21st Corps. Soldiers and ambulances, wagons and cattle, gunners lacking their guns, companies out of regiments, squads out of companies, panic-struck and flying units, shouting officers brandishing swords, horsemen, colour - bearers without colours, others with colours desperately saved, musicians, sutlers, camp followers, ordnance wagons with tearing, maddened horses, soldiers and soldiers and soldiers — down, back to the centre at Chancellorsville, roared the blue wave, torn, churned to foam, lashed and shattered, broken against a stone wall — back on the centre roared and fell the flanked right! Down the Plank road, out of the dark woods of the Wilderness, out of the rolling musketry, behind it the cannon thunder, burst a sound, a sound, a known sound! *Yaaaai! Yaaaaaiih! Yaaiii! Yaaaaiiihhhhh!* It echoed, it echoed from the east of Chancellorsville! *Yaaih! Yaaaaiih! Yaaaaaaaiihh!* yelled the troops of McLaws and Anderson. "Open fire!" said Lee to his artillery; and to McLaws, "Move up the turn-pike and attack."

The Wilderness of Spottsylvania laid aside her mantle of calm. She became a mænad, intoxicated, furious, shrieking, a giantess in action, a wild handmaid drinking blood, a servant of Ares, a Titanic hostess spreading with lavish hands large ground for armies and battles, a Valkyrie gathering the dead, laying them in the woodland hollows amid bloodroot and violets! She chanted, she swayed, she cried aloud to the stars, and she shook her own madness upon the troops, very impartially, on grey and on blue.

Down the Plank road, in the gathering night, the very fulness of the grey victory brought its difficulties. Brigades were far ahead, separated from their division commanders; regiments astray from their brigadiers, companies struggling in the dusk through the thickets, seeking the thread from which in the onset and uproar the beads had slipped. They lost themselves in the wild place; there came perforce a pause, a quest for organization and alignment, a drawing together, a compressing of the particles of the thunderbolt; then, then would it be hurled again, full against Chancellors-ville!

The moon was coming up. She silvered the Wilderness about Dowdall's Tavern. She made a pallor around the group of staff and field officers gathered beside the road. Her light glinted on

Stonewall Jackson's sabre, and on the worn braid of the old forage cap. A body of cavalry passed on its way to Ely's Ford. Jeb Stuart rode at the head. He was singing. *"Old Joe Hooker, won't you come out of the Wilderness?"* he sang. An officer of Rodes came up. "General Rodes reports, sir, that he has taken a line of their entrenchments. He's less than a mile from Chancellorsville."

"Good! Tell him A. P. Hill will support. As you go, tell the troops that I wish them to get into line and preserve their order."

The officer went. An aide of Colston's appeared, breathless from a struggle through the thickets. "From General Colston, sir. He's immediately behind General Rodes. There was a wide abattis. The troops are re-forming beyond it. We see no Federals between us and Chancellorsville."

"Good! Tell General Colston to use expedition and get his men into line. Those guns are opening without orders!"

Three grey cannon, planted within bowshot of the Chancellor House, opened, indeed, and with vigour, — opened against twenty-two guns in epaulements on the Chancellorsville ridge. The twenty-two answered in a roar of sound, overtowering the cannonade to the east of McLaws and Anderson. The Wilderness resounded; smoke began to rise like the smoke of strange sacrifices; the mood of the place changed to frenzy. She swung herself, she chanted.

> " Grey or blue,
>   I care not, I!
> Blue and grey
>   Are here to die!
> This human brood
>   Is stained with blood.
> The armed man dies,
>   See where he lies
> In my arms asleep!
>   On my breast asleep!
> The babe of Time,
>   A nestling fallen.
> The nest a ruin,
>   The tree storm-snapped.
> Lullaby, lullaby! sleep, sleep, sleep, sleep! "

The smoke drifted toward the moon, the red gun-flashes showed the aisles of pine and oak. Jackson beckoned imperiously to an aide. "Go tell A. P. Hill to press forward."

The thunder of the guns ceased suddenly. There was heard a tramp of feet, A. P. Hill's brigades on the turnpike. "Who leads?" asked a voice. "Lane's North Carolinians," answered another. General Lane came by, young, an old V. M. I. cadet. He drew rein a moment, saluted. "Push right ahead, Lane! right ahead!" said Jackson.

A. P. Hill, in his battle shirt, appeared. his staff behind him. "Your final order, general?"

"Press them, Hill! Cut them off from the fords. Press them!"

A. P. Hill went. From the east, the guns upon his own front now having quieted, rolled the thunder of those with Lee. The clamour about Chancellorsville where, in hot haste, Hooker made dispositions, streamed east and west, meeting and blending with, westward, a like distraction of forming commands, of battle lines made in the darkness, among thickets. The moon was high, but not observed; the Wilderness fiercely chanting. Behind him Captain Wilbourne of the Signal Corps, two aides and several couriers, Jackson rode along the Plank road.

There was a regiment drawn across this way through the Wilderness, on the road and in the woods on either hand. In places in the Wilderness, the scrub that fearfully burned the next day and the next was even now afire, and gave, though uncertainly and dimly, a certain illumination. By it the regiment was perceived. It seemed composed of tall and shadowy men. "What troops are these?" asked the general.

"Lane's North Carolinians, sir, — the 18th."

As he passed, the regiment started to cheer. He shook his head. "Don't, men! We want quiet now."

A very few hundred yards from Chancellorsville he checked Little Sorrel. The horse stood, fore feet planted. Horse and rider, they stood and listened. Hooker's reserves were up. About the Chancellor House, on the Chancellorsville ridge, they were throwing up entrenchments. They were digging the earth with bayonets, they were heaping it up with their hands. There was a ringing of axes. They were cutting down the young spring growth; they were making an abattis. Tones of command could be heard. "Hurry! hurry — hurry! They mean to rush us. Hurry — hurry!" A dead creeper mantling a dead tree, caught by some flying spark, suddenly flared throughout its length, stood a pillar of fire, and showed redly the enemy's guns. Stonewall Jackson sat his horse and looked. "Cut them off from the ford," he said. "Never let them get out of Virginia." He jerked his hand into the air.

Turning Little Sorrel, he rode back along the Plank road toward his own lines. The light of the burning brush had sunken. The cannon smoke floating in the air, the very thick woods, made all things obscure.

"There are troops across the road in front," said an aide.

"Yes. Lane's North Carolinians awaiting their signal."

A little to the east and south broke out in the Wilderness a sudden rattling fire, sinking, rising, sinking again, the blue and grey skirmishers now in touch. All through the vast, dark, tangled beating heart of the place, sprang into being a tension. The grey lines listened for the word *Advance!* The musket rested on the shoulder, the foot quivered, eyes front tried to pierce the darkness. Sound was unceasing; and yet the mind found a stillness, a lake of calm. It was the moment before the moment.

Stonewall Jackson came toward the Carolinians. He rode quickly, past the dark shell of a house sunken among pines. There were with him seven or eight persons. The horses' hoofs made a trampling on the Plank road. The woods were deep, the obscurity great. Suddenly out of the brush rang a shot, an accidentally discharged rifle. Some grey soldier among Lane's tensely waiting ranks, dressed in the woods to the right of the road, spoke from the core of a fearful dream: "Yankee cavalry!"

"*Fire!*" called an officer of the 18th North Carolina.

The volley, striking diagonally across the road, emptied several saddles. Stonewall Jackson, the aides and Wilbourne, wheeled to the left, dug spur, and would have plunged into the wood. "*Fire!*" said the Carolinians, dressed to the left of the road, and fired.

Little Sorrel, maddened, dashed into the wood. An oak bough struck his rider, almost bearing him from the saddle. With his right hand from which the blood was streaming, in which a bullet was imbedded, he caught the bridle, managed to turn the agonized brute into the road again. There seemed a wild sound, a confusion of voices. Some one had stopped the firing. "My God, men! You are firing into *us!*" In the road were the aides. They caught the rein, stopped the horse. Wilbourne put up his arms. "General, general! you are not hurt ? — Hold there! — Morrison — Leigh! — "

They laid him on the ground beneath the pines and they fired the brushwood for a light. One rode off for Dr. McGuire, and another with a penknife cut away the sleeve from the left arm through which had gone two bullets. A mounted man came at a gallop and threw himself from his horse. It was A. P. Hill. "General, general! you are not much hurt?"

"Yes, I think I am," said Stonewall Jackson. "And my wounds are from my own men."

Hill drew off the gauntlets that were all blood soaked, and with his handkerchief tried to bind up the arm, shattered and with the main artery cut. A courier came up. "Sir, sir! a body of the enemy is close at hand —"

The aides lifted the wounded general. "No one," said Hill, "must tell the troops who was wounded." The other opened his eyes. "Tell them simply that you have a wounded officer. General Hill, you are in command now. Press right on."

With a gesture of sorrow Hill went, returning to the front. The others rested at the edge of the road. At that moment the Federal batteries opened, a hissing storm of shot and shell, a tornado meant measurably to retard that anticipated, grey onrush. The range was high. Aides and couriers laid the wounded leader on the earth and made of their bodies a screen. The trees were cut, the earth was torn up; there was a howling as of unchained fiends. There passed what seemed an eternity and was but ten minutes. The great blue guns slightly changed the direction of their fire. The storm howled away from the group by the road, and the men again lifted Jackson. He stood now on his feet; and because troops were heard approaching, and because it must not be known that he was hurt, all moved into the darkness of the scrub. The troops upon the road came on — Pender's brigade. Pender, riding in advance, saw the group and asked who was wounded. "A field officer," answered one, but there came from some direction a glare of light and by it Pender knew. He sprang from his horse. "Don't say anything about it, General Pender," said Jackson. "Press on, sir, press on!"

"General, they are using all their artillery. It is a very deadly fire. In the darkness it may disorganize —"

The forage cap was gone. The blue eyes showed full and deep. "You must hold your ground, General Pender. You must hold out to the last, sir."

"I will, general, I will," said Pender.

A litter was found and brought, and Stonewall Jackson was laid upon it. The little procession moved toward Dowdall's Tavern. A shot pierced the arm of one of the bearers, loosening his hold of the litter. It tilted. The general fell heavily to the ground, injuring afresh the wounded limb, striking and bruising his side. They raised him, pale, now, and silent, and at last they struggled through the wood to a little clearing, where they found an ambulance. Now, too, came the doctor, a man whom he loved, and knelt beside him. "I hope that you are not badly hurt, general?"

"Yes, I am, doctor. I am badly hurt. I fear that I am dying."

In the ambulance lay also his chief of artillery, Colonel Crutchfield, painfully injured. Crutchfield pulled the doctor down to him. "He isn't badly hurt?"

"Yes. Badly hurt."

Crutchfield groaned. "Oh, my God!" Stonewall Jackson heard and made the ambulance stop. "You must do something for Colonel Crutchfield, doctor. Don't let him suffer."

A. P. Hill, riding back to the front, was wounded by a piece of shell. Boswell, the chief engineer, to whom had been entrusted the guidance through the night of the advance upon the roads to the fords, was killed. That was a fatal cannonade from the ridge of Chancellorsville, fatal and fateful! It continued. The Wilderness chanted a battle chant indeed to the moon, the moon that was pale and wan as if wearied with silvering battlefields. Hill, lying in a litter, just back of his advanced line, dispatched couriers for Stuart. Stuart was far toward Ely's Ford, riding through the night in plume and fighting jacket. The straining horses, the recalling order, reached him.

"General Jackson badly wounded! A. P. Hill badly wounded! I in command! My God, man! all changed like that? *Right about face! Forward! March!*"

There was, that night, no grey assault. But the dawn broke clear and found the grey lines waiting. The sky was a glory, the Wilderness rolled in emerald waves, the redbirds sang. Lee and the 2d

Corps were yet two miles apart. Between was Chancellorsville, and all the strong intrenchments and the great blue guns, and Hooker's courageous men.

Now followed Jeb Stuart's fight. In the dawn the 2d Corps, swung from the right by a master hand, struck full against the Federal centre, struck full against Chancellorsville. In the clear May morning broke a thunderstorm of artillery. It raged loudly, peal on peal, crash on crash! The grey shells struck the Chancellor house. They set it on fire. It went up in flames. A fragment of shell struck and stunned Fighting Joe Hooker. He lay senseless for hours and Couch took command. The grey musketry, the blue musketry, rolled, rolled! The Wilderness was on fire. In places it was like a prairie. The flames licked their way through the scrub; the wounded perished. Ammunition began to fail; Stuart ordered the ground to be held with the bayonet. There was a great attack against his left. His three lines came into one and repulsed it. His right and Anderson's left now touched. The Army of Northern Virginia was again a unit.

Stuart swung above his head the hat with the black feather. His beautiful horse danced along the grey lines, the lines that were very grimly determined, the lines that knew now that Stonewall Jackson was badly wounded. They meant, the grey lines, to make this day and the Wilderness remembered. *"Forward. Charge!"* cried Jeb Stuart. *"Remember Jackson!"* He swung his plumed hat. *Yaaaii! Yaaaaaaiihhh! Yaaaaaii! Yaaaiiiihhh!* yelled the grey lines, and charged. Stuart went at their head, and as he went he raised in song his golden, ringing voice. *"Old Joe Hooker, won't you come out of the Wilderness?"*

By ten o'clock the Chancellor ridge was taken, the blue guns silenced, Hooker beaten back toward the Rappahannock. The Wilderness, after all, was Virginian. She broke into a war song of triumph. Her flowers bloomed, her birds sang, and then came Lee to the front. Oh, the Army of Northern Virginia cheered him! "Men, men!" he said, "you have done well, you have done well! Where is General Jackson?"

He was told. Presently he wrote a note and sent it to the field hospital near Dowdall's Tavern. *General:—I cannot express my regret. Could I have directed events I should have chosen for the good*

*of the country to be disabled in your stead. I congratulate you upon
the victory, which is due to your skill and energy. Very respectfully,
your obedient servant, R. E. Lee.*

An aide read it to Stonewall Jackson where he lay, very quiet, in
the deeps of the Wilderness. For a minute he did not speak, then
he said, "General Lee is very kind, but he should give the praise to
God."

For four days yet they fought, in the Wilderness, at Salem church,
at the Fords of the Rappahannock, again at Fredericksburg. Then
they rested, the Army of the Potomac back on the northern side of
the Rappahannock, the Army of Northern Virginia holding the
southern shore and the road to Richmond — Richmond no nearer
for McDowell, no nearer for McClellan, no nearer for Pope, no
nearer for Burnside, no nearer for Hooker, no nearer after two years
of war! In the Wilderness and thereabouts Hooker lost seventeen
thousand men, thirteen guns, and fifteen hundred rounds of cannon ammunition, twenty thousand rifles, three hundred thousand
rounds of infantry ammunition. The Army of Northern Virginia
lost twelve thousand men.

On the fifth of May Stonewall Jackson was carefully moved from
the Wilderness to Guiney's Station. Here was a large old residence
— the Chandler house — within a sweep of grass and trees; about
it one or two small buildings. The great house was filled, crowded to
its doors with wounded soldiers, so they laid Stonewall Jackson in
a rude cabin among the trees. The left arm had been amputated
in the field hospital. He was thought to be doing well, though at
times he complained of the side which, in the fall from the litter,
had been struck and bruised.

At daylight on Thursday he had his physician called. "I am suffering great pain," he said. "See what is the matter with me." And
presently, "Is it pneumonia?"

That afternoon his wife came. He was roused to speak to her,
greeted her with love, then sank into something like stupor. From
time to time he awakened from this, but there were also times when
he was slightly delirious. He gave orders in a shadow of the old
voice. "You must hold out a little longer, men; you must hold out
a little longer! . . . Press forward — press forward — press forward! . . . Give them canister, Major Pelham!"

Friday went by, and Saturday. The afternoon of this day he asked for his chaplain, Mr. Lacy. Later, in the twilight, his wife sang to him, old hymns that he loved. "Sing the fifty-first psalm in verse," he said. She sang, —

"Show pity, Lord! O Lord, forgive — "

The night passed and Sunday the tenth dawned. He lay quiet, his right hand on his breast. One of the staff came for a moment to his bedside. "Who is preaching at headquarters to-day?" He was told, and said, "Good! I wish I might be there."

The officer's voice broke. "General, general! the whole army is praying for you. There's a message from General Lee."

"Yes, yes. Give it."

"He sends you his love. He says that you must recover; that you have lost your left arm, but that he would lose his right arm. He says tell you that he prayed for you last night as he had never prayed for himself. He repeats what he said in his note that for the good of Virginia and the South he could wish that he were lying here in your place — "

The soldier on the bed smiled a little and shook his head. "Better ten Jacksons should lie here than one Lee."

It was sunny weather, fair and sweet with all the bloom of May, the bright trees waving, the long grass rippling, waters flowing, the sky azure, bees about the flowers, the birds singing piercingly sweet, mother earth so beautiful, the sky down-bending, the light of the sun so gracious, warm, and vital!

A little before noon, kneeling beside him, his wife told Stonewall Jackson that he would die. He smiled and laid his hand upon her bowed head. "You are frightened, my child! Death is not so near. I may yet get well."

The doctor came to him. "Doctor, Anna tells me that I am to die to-day. Is it so?"

"Oh, general, general! — It is so."

He lay silent a moment, then he said, "Very good, very good! It is all right."

Throughout the day his mind was now clouded, now clear. In one of the latter times he said there was something he was trying to remember. There followed a half-hour of broken sleep and wandering, in the course of which he twice spoke a name, "Deaderick." Once he said "Horse Artillery," and once "White Oak Swamp."

The alternate clear moments and the lapses into stupour or delirium were like the sinking or rising of a strong swimmer, exhausted at last, the prey at last of a shoreless sea. At times he came head and shoulders out of the sea. In such a moment he opened his grey-blue eyes full on one of his staff. All the staff was gathered in grief about the bed. "When Richard Cleave," he said, "asks for a court of enquiry let him have it. Tell General Lee —" The sea drew him under again.

It hardly let him go any more; moment by moment now, it wore out the strong swimmer. The day drew on to afternoon. He lay straight upon the bed, silent for the most part, but now and then wandering a little. His wife bowed herself beside him; in a corner wept the old man, Jim. Outside the windows there seemed a hush as of death.

"Pass the infantry to the front!" ordered Stonewall Jackson. "Tell A. P. Hill to prepare for action!" The voice sank; there came a long silence; there was only heard the old man crying in the corner. Then, for the last time in this phase of being, the great soldier opened his eyes. In a moment he spoke, in a very sweet and calm voice. "Let us cross over the river, and rest under the shade of the trees." He died.

The bells tolled, the bells tolled in Richmond, tolled from each of her seven hills! Sombre was the sound of the minute guns, shaking the heart of the city! Oh, this capital knew the Dead March in Saul as a child knows his lullaby! To-day it had a depth and a height and was a dirge indeed. To-day it wailed for a Chieftain, wailed through the streets where the rose and magnolia bloomed, wailed as may have wailed the trumpets when Priam brought Hector home. The great throng to either side the streets shivered beneath the wailing, beneath the low thunder of the drums. There was lacking no pomp of War, War who must have gauds with which to hide his naked horror. The guns boomed, the bells tolled, the muffled drums beat, beat! Regiments marched with reversed arms, with colours furled. There was mournful civic pomp, mournful official. There came a great black hearse drawn by four white horses. On it lay the body of Stonewall Jackson, and over it was drawn the deep blue flag with the arms of Virginia, and likewise the starry banner of the eleven Confederate States. Oh, heart-breaking were the minute guns, and the tolling, tolling bells, and the deep, slow, heroic music, and the sobbing of the people! It was a cloudless day and filled with grief. Behind the hearse trod Little Sorrel.

Beneath arching trees, by houses of mellow red brick, houses of pale grey stucco, by old porches and ironwork balconies, by wistaria and climbing roses and magnolias with white chalices, the long procession bore Stonewall Jackson. By St. Paul's they bore him, by Washington and the great bronze men in his company, by Jefferson and Marshall, by Henry and Mason, by Lewis and Nelson. They bore him over the greensward to the Capitol steps, and there the hearse stopped. Six generals lifted the coffin, Longstreet going before. The bells tolled and the Dead March rang, and all the people on the green slopes of the historic place uncovered their heads and wept. The coffin, high-borne, passed upward and between the great, white, Doric columns. It passed into the Capitol and into the Hall of the Lower House. Here it rested before the Speaker's Chair.

All day Stonewall Jackson lay in state. Twenty thousand people, from the President of the Confederacy to the last poor wounded soldier who could creep hither, passed before the bier, looked upon the calm face, the flag-enshrouded form, lying among lilies before the Speaker's Chair, in the Virginia Hall of Delegates, in the Capitol of the Confederacy. All day the bells tolled, all day the minute guns were fired.

A man of the Stonewall Brigade, pausing his moment before the dead leader, first bent, then lifted his head. He was a scout, a blonde soldier, tall and strong, with a quiet, studious face and sea-blue eyes. He looked now at the vaulted roof as though he saw instead the sky. He spoke in a controlled, determined voice. "What Stonewall Jackson always said was just this: '*Press forward!*'" He passed on.

Presently in line came a private soldier of A. P. Hill's, a young man like a beautiful athlete from a frieze, an athlete who was also a philosopher. "Hail, great man of the past!" he said. "If to-day you consort with Cæsar, tell him we still make war." He, too, went on.

Others passed, and then there came an artilleryman, a gunner of the Horse Artillery. Grey-eyed, broad-browed, he stood his moment and gazed upon the dead soldier among the lilies. "Hooker yet upon the Rappahannock," he said. "We must have him across the Potomac, and we must ourselves invade Pennsylvania."

Library of Congress Cataloging-in-Publication Data

Johnston, Mary, 1870–1936.
  The long roll / by Mary Johnston.
    p.   cm.
  ISBN 0-8018-5524-1 (pbk. : alk. paper)
  1. United States—History—Civil War, 1861–1865—Fiction. 2. Jackson,
Stonewall, 1824–1863—Fiction.   I. Title.
PS2141.L66   1996
813'.52—dc20

96-33094
CIP